A STUDY IN Charlotte

A Charlotte Holmes novel

BRITTANY CAVALLARO

KATHERINE TEGEN BOOKS
An Imprint of HarperCollins Publishers

**HarperCollins**
PUBLISHERS
—— *Since 1817* ——

Katherine Tegen Books is an imprint of HarperCollins Publishers.

A Study in Charlotte
Copyright © 2016 by Brittany Cavallaro
Library of Congress Cataloging-in-Publication Data
Cavallaro, Brittany.
  A study in Charlotte / Brittany Cavallaro. — First edition.
   pages cm
  Summary: Sherlock Holmes and Dr. Watson descendants, Charlotte and Jamie, stu-
dents at a Connecticut boarding school, team up to solve a murder mystery.
  ISBN 978-0-06-239891-8
  [1. Mystery and detective stories. 2. Murder—Fiction. 3. Love—Fiction. 4. Boarding
schools—Fiction. 5. Schools—Fiction.] I. Title.
PZ7.1.C42St 2016   2015015669
[Fic]—dc23   CIP
                                                                              AC

20   CG/LSCH   20 19 18 17 16 15 14 13 12 11
❖
First paperback edition, 2017

For Kit and me, at sixteen

I had no idea that such individuals
existed outside of stories.

A STUDY IN SCARLET, SIR ARTHUR CONAN DOYLE

one

THE FIRST TIME I MET HER WAS AT THE TAIL END OF ONE OF those endless weekday nights you could only have at a school like Sherringford. It was midnight, or just after, maybe, and I'd spent the last few hours icing my sprained shoulder in my room, the result of a rugby scrimmage gone horribly wrong just minutes after it'd started. Practices tended to do that here, something I'd learned in the first week of school when the team captain shook my hand so voraciously I thought he was about to pull me in and eat me. Sherringford's rugby team had landed at the bottom of its division at the end of every season for years. But not this year, no; Kline had made a point of reminding me of that, smiling with every one of his strange little teeth. I was their white whale. Their rugger messiah. The reason why the school shelled out not just a tuition scholarship for my junior year but my transportation costs, too—no mean feat when you visit your mother in London every holiday.

The only real problem, then, was how much I hated rugby. I'd made the fatal mistake of surviving a maul on the rugby field last year at my school in London before accidentally sort of bringing our team to victory. I had only tried because, for once, Rose Milton was in the stands, and I had loved her for two passionate, secret, awful years, but as I learned later, the Sherringford athletic director had been in the stands as well. Front row, scouting. You see, we had quite a good rugby team at Highcombe School.

Damn them all.

Especially my cow-eyed, bull-necked new teammates. Honestly, I even hated Sherringford itself, with its rolling green lawns and clear skies and a city center that felt smaller than even the cinder-block room they gave me in Michener Hall. A city center that had no fewer than four cupcake shops and not one decent place to get a curry. A city center just an hour away from where my father lived. He kept threatening to visit. "Threatening" was the only word for it. My mother had wanted us to get to know each other better; they had divorced when I was ten.

But I missed London like an arm, or a leg, even if I had only lived there for a handful of years, because as much as my mother insisted that my coming to Connecticut would be like coming home, it was more like coming to a manicured jail.

All this is just to give you an understanding of how, that

September, I could have struck a match and happily watched Sherringford burn. And even so, before I had ever met Charlotte Holmes, I was sure she was the only friend I would make in that miserable place.

"You're telling me that you're *that* Watson." Tom was delighted. He smashed his round Midwestern accent into the flattest Cockney I'd ever heard. "My dear chap! My dear fellow! Watson, come here, I want you!"

The cell of a room that we shared was so small that when I flipped him off, I almost poked out his eye. "You're a genius, Bradford. Seriously. Where do you get your material?"

"Oh, but dude, this is perfect." My roommate tucked his hands in the pockets of the argyle sweater-vest he always wore under his blazer. Through a moth hole, I watched his right thumb wriggle in excitement. "Because the party tonight is at Lawrence Hall. And Lena is throwing it because her sister always ships her vodka. And you *know* who Lena rooms with." He waggled his eyebrows.

At that, I finally had to close my book. "Don't tell me you're trying to set me up with my—"

"Your soul mate?" I must've looked violent, because Tom put two very serious hands on my shoulders. "I'm not trying," he said, enunciating each word, "to set you up with Charlotte. I'm trying to get you *drunk*."

Charlotte and Lena had set up camp down in the Lawrence Hall basement. As Tom had promised, it wasn't hard to get past the hall mother. Each dorm had one (in addition to our army of RAs), an older woman from town who oversaw her students from the front desk. They sorted mail, arranged for birthday cakes, lent an ear when you were homesick—but they also enforced the hall rules. Lawrence's was famous for sleeping on the job.

The party was in the basement kitchen. Though it was stocked with plates and pots and even a spindly four-burner stove, the pans were all so dented they looked like they'd been worn to war. Tom squeezed against the stove while I shut the door behind us; within seconds, one of the knobs rubbed a half-moon of grease onto his sweater-vest. The girl next to him smiled thinly and turned back to her friends, a tumbler of something dangling from her hand. There had to be at least thirty people in there, packed in shoulder to shoulder.

Grabbing my arm, Tom began shouldering us to the back of the tiny kitchen. I felt like I was being pulled through a dark, dank wardrobe into some boozy Narnia.

"That's the weird townie dealer," he whispered to me. "He's selling drugs. That's Governor Schumer's son. He's *buying* drugs."

"Great," I said, only half-listening.

"And those two girls? They summer in Italy. Like, they use 'summer' as a verb. Their dads run an offshore drilling operation."

I raised an eyebrow.

"What, I'm poor, I notice these things."

"Right." If it was a joke, it was a lame one. Tom might've had a hole in his sweater-vest, but back in our room, he also had the smallest, thinnest laptop I'd ever seen. "You're poor."

"Comparatively speaking." Tom dragged me along behind him. "You and me, we're upper-middle class. We're peasants."

The party was loud and crowded, but Tom was determined to drag me all the way to the far wall. I didn't know why, until a strange voice curled up through the cigarette smoke.

"The game is Texas Hold'em," it said, hoarse, but with a bizarre, wild precision, like a drunk Greek philosopher orating at a bacchanal. "And the buy-in tonight is fifty dollars."

"Or your soul," chirped another voice, a normal one, and the girls in front of us laughed.

Tom turned to grin at me. "That one's Lena. And that one's Charlotte Holmes."

The first I saw of her was her hair, black and glossy and straight down to her shoulders. She was leaning forward over a card table to pull in a handful of chips, and I couldn't see her face. This wasn't important, I told myself. It wasn't a big deal if she didn't like me. So what if somewhere, back a hundred years and change and across the Atlantic Ocean, some other Watson made best friends with some other Holmes. People became best friends all the time. There were, surely, best friends at this school. Dozens. Hundreds.

Even if I didn't have one.

She sat up, all at once, with a wicked smile. Her brows were startling dark lines on her pale face, and they framed her gray eyes, her straight nose. She was altogether colorless and severe, and still she managed to be beautiful. Not the way that girls are generally beautiful, but more like the way a knife catches the light, makes you want to take it in your hands.

"Dealer goes to Lena," she said, turning away from me, and it was only then that I placed her accent. I was forcibly reminded that she was from London, like me. For a moment, I felt so homesick I thought that I'd make an even worse show of myself and throw myself at her feet, beg her to read me the phone book in that extravagant voice that had no business coming out of such a thin, angular girl.

Tom sat down, flung five chips on the table (on closer inspection, they were the brass buttons from his blazer), and rubbed his hands together theatrically.

I should have had something witty to say. Something strange and funny and just a little bit morbid, something I could say under my breath as I dropped down on the seat beside her. Something to make her look up sharply and think, *I want to know him.*

I had nothing.

I turned tail and fled.

TOM ARRIVED HOME HOURS LATER, CHEERFULLY EMPTY-handed. "She cleaned me out," he laughed. "I'll win it back next time." That's when I learned that Holmes's poker game had been running weekly since she showed up the year before. They'd just gotten more popular since Lena started bringing vodka. "And probably more lucrative for Charlotte too," Tom added.

For the next weeks, I hit snooze over and over in some wild hope that the morning would just pack up and leave me alone. The worst of it was first-period French, taught by the autocratic, red-suspendered Monsieur Cann, whose waxed mustache looked like it belonged on a taxidermist's wall. Almost every other Sherringford student had been there since freshman year, and that early in the morning all anyone wanted to do was sit by their oldest friends and catch up on the night before. I was no one's oldest friend. So I took an empty double desk for myself and tried not to fall asleep before the bell rang.

"I heard she made, like, five hundred dollars last night," the girl in front of me said, pulling her red hair into a ponytail. "She probably practices online. It's not fair. It's not like she *needs* money. Her family has to be loaded."

"Close your eyes," her seatmate said, and blew lightly on her friend's face. "Eyelash. Yeah, I've heard that too. Her mom is like, a duchess. But whatever. It's probably just going up her nose."

The redhead perked up at that. "I heard it was going into her arm."

"I wonder if she'd introduce me to her dealer."

The bell rang, and Monsieur Cann shouted, *"Bonjour, mes petites,"* and I realized that, for the first time in weeks, I was completely awake.

I spent the rest of the morning thinking about that conversation and what it meant for her. Charlotte Holmes. Because they couldn't have been talking about anyone else. I was still mulling it all over as I walked across the quad at lunch, dodging people left and right. The green was choked with students, and so in a way, it wasn't a surprise when the girl I was thinking about stepped out from what seemed to be an invisible door and directly into my path.

I didn't run into her; I'm not that clumsy. But we both froze, and began doing that awful left-right-you-go-first shuffle. Finally, I gave up. *Screw all of this,* I thought mulishly, *it's a small campus and I can't hide forever, I might as well go ahead and—*

I stuck out my hand. "Sorry, I don't think we've met. I'm James. I'm new here."

She looked down at it, eyebrows knitted, like I was offering her a fish, or a grenade. It was sunny and hot that day, early October's last gasp of summer, and most everyone had slung their uniform blazer over one shoulder or was carrying it under their arm. Mine was in my bag, and I'd loosened my tie, walking down the path, but Charlotte Holmes was as fastidiously put together as if she were about to give a speech on etiquette. She had on slim navy pants instead of the pleated skirt most of the girls wore. Her white oxford shirt was buttoned up to her neck and her ribbon tie looked as if it'd been steamed. I was close enough to tell that she smelled like soap, not perfume, and that her face was as bare as if she'd just washed it.

I might've just stared at her for hours—this girl that I'd wondered about off and on my whole life—had her colorless eyes not narrowed at me suspiciously. I started, as if I'd done something wrong.

"I'm Holmes," she said finally, in that marvelous, ragged voice. "But you knew that already, didn't you."

She wasn't going to shake my hand, then. I slid both of them into my pockets.

"I did," I admitted. "So you know who I am. Which is awkward, but I figured—"

"Who put you up to this?" There was a flat kind of acceptance in her face. "Was it Dobson?"

"Lee Dobson?" I shook my head, bewildered. "No. Put me up to what? I mean, I knew you'd be here. At Sherringford. My mum told me that the Holmeses had sent you; she keeps in touch with your aunt Araminta. They met at some charity thing. Right? They signed the *His Last Bow* manuscript? It went for leukemia patients or something, and now they write emails back and forth. Are you in my year? I was never clear on that. But you've got a biology textbook there, so you must be a sophomore. A deduction, ha. Maybe best avoid those."

I was babbling like an idiot, I knew I was, but she had been holding herself so straight and still that she looked like a wax figurine. It was so at odds with the commanding, freewheeling girl I'd seen at the party that I couldn't make heads or tails of it, what had happened to her since then. But my talking seemed to calm her down, and though it wasn't funny, or morbid, or witty, I kept on going until her shoulders relaxed and her eyes finally lost some of their sharp sadness.

"I know who you are, of course," she said when I finally stopped to draw breath. "My aunt Araminta did tell me about you, and Lena, though it would have been obvious anyway. Hello, Jamie." She extended a small white hand, and we shook.

"I hate it when people call me Jamie, though," I said, pained, "so you might as well call me Watson instead."

Holmes smiled at me in a closed-mouth kind of way. "All right, then, Watson," she said. "I have to go to lunch."

It was a dismissal if I'd ever heard one.

"Right," I said, tamping down my disappointment. "I was going to meet Tom anyway; I should go."

"Right, see you." She stepped neatly around me.

I couldn't leave it at that, and so I called after her, "What did I do?"

Holmes flung me an unreadable look over her shoulder. "Homecoming's next weekend," she said drily, and went on her way.

By every account—and by that, honestly, I meant my mother's—Charlotte was the epitome of a Holmes. Coming from my mother, that wasn't a compliment. You'd think that after all this time, our families would have drifted apart, and in most ways I suppose we had. But my mother would run into the odd Holmes at Scotland Yard fund-raisers or the Edgar Awards dinners or, as in the case of Holmes's aunt Araminta, an auction of my great-great-great-grandfather's literary agent's—Arthur Conan Doyle's—things. I had always been enthralled with the idea of this girl, the only Holmes who was my age (as a kid, I thought we'd meet and the two of us would go on wild adventures), but my mother always discouraged me without saying why.

I knew nothing about her but that the police had let her assist on her first case when she was ten years old. The diamonds she helped recover were worth three million pounds. My father had told me about it during our weekly phone call, in an attempt to get me to open up to him. It hadn't worked. At least, not in the way that he'd planned.

I dreamed about that diamond theft for months. How I could've been there by her side, her trusted companion. One night, I lowered her down into the Swiss bank from a skylight, my rope the only thing holding her above the booby-trapped floor. The next, we raced through the cars of a runaway train, chased by black-masked bandits shouting in Russian. When I saw a story about a stolen painting on the front page of the newspaper, I told my mother that Charlotte Holmes and I were going to solve the case. My mother cut me off, saying, "Jamie, if you try to do anything like that before you turn eighteen, I will sell every last one of your books in the night, starting with your autographed Neil Gaiman."

(Before they'd divorced, my father was prone to saying, "You know, your mother's only a Watson by marriage," with a pointedly lofted eyebrow.)

The only real conversation my mother and I'd had about the Holmeses happened right before I left. We'd been discussing Sherringford— Well. *She* had been monologuing about how much I'd like it there while I packed up my closet in silence, wondering if I flung myself out the window, would it properly kill me or just break both my legs. Finally, she made me tell her something I was looking forward to, and to spite her (and because it was true), I told her I was excited, and nervous, to finally meet my counterpart in the Holmes family.

Which didn't go over well.

"Lord knows how your great-great-great-grandfather put

up with that man," she said with a roll of her eyes.

"Sherlock?" I asked. At least now we weren't talking about Sherringford.

My mother harrumphed. "I always imagined he'd just been bored. Victorian gentlemen, you know. Didn't have too much going on. But it never seemed to me that their friendship ran both ways. Those Holmeses, they're *strange*. They still drill their children from birth in deductive skills. Discourage them making friends, or so I've heard. I can't say it's healthy to keep a child away like that. Araminta is nice enough, I suppose, but then again I don't live with her. I can't imagine what it was like for the good Dr. Watson. The last thing you need is to take up with someone like her."

"It's not like I'm going to marry this girl," I said, digging in the back of my closet for my rugby kit. "I was just interested to meet her, that's all."

"I've heard that she's one of the stranger ones," she insisted. "It's not as if they've sent her away to America on a lark."

I looked pointedly down at my suitcase. "No, that's usually not a reward."

"Well, I hope for your sake she's lovely," my mum said quickly. "Just do be careful there, love."

It's stupid to admit to it, but my mother isn't usually wrong. I mean, the whole sending me to Sherringford thing was a terrible idea, but I understood it at its core. She had been paying quite a bit—money we didn't really have—for me to attend Highcombe School, and all because I'd insisted that I wanted to be a writer. There were a few famous novelists who taught there . . . not that any of them had really taken to me. Sherringford, despite its obvious drawbacks (Connecticut, my father) had as strong an English program, or better. And they offered to take me for free, as long as I did my best impression of an excited rugger for them now and again.

But at Sherringford, I kept the writer thing to myself. A constant, low-level drone of fear kept me from showing my work to anyone; with someone like Dr. Watson in your family, you didn't want to invite any comparison. I did my best to hide my work away, so I was surprised when it almost came up that day over lunch.

Tom and I had grabbed sandwiches and sat down under an ash tree off the quad with some other guys from Michener Hall. Tom was digging around in my bag for some paper to spit his gum into. Normally it would've annoyed me, having someone shuffle carelessly through my things, but he was acting like any of my old Highcombe friends would, and so I let him.

"Can I tear a sheet out of this?" he asked, holding up my notebook.

It was only through sheer force of will that I kept from grabbing it out of his hands. "Yeah," I said indifferently, fishing chips out of a bag.

He flipped through it, quickly at first but slowing as he went. "Huh," he said, and I shot him a warning look that he didn't see.

"What is it?" someone asked. "Love poems? Erotic stories?"

"Dirty limericks," Dobson, my hallmate, said.

Tom cleared his throat, like he was about to perform a page from what was, to be honest, my journal.

"No, drawings of your mom." I snagged it and tore a page from the back, making sure to tuck it under my knee afterward. "It's just a journal. Notes to myself, that kind of thing."

"I saw you talking to Charlotte Holmes on the quad," Dobson said. "You writing about her?"

"Right." There was a nasty note in his voice I didn't like, and I didn't want to encourage it with a real response.

Randall, his ruddy-faced roommate—he was on the rugby team with me—shot him a look, and leaned in like he was about to tell me a secret.

"We've been trying to crack that nut for a year," he said. "She's hot. Wears those tight little pants. But she doesn't go out, except for that weird poker game, and she doesn't drink. Only likes the hard stuff, and does it alone."

"They're trying PUA," Tom said to me mournfully, and at my blank look, he elaborated. "Pick-up artistry. You neg the girl—like, an insult hidden in a compliment. Dobson keeps telling her he's the only guy who likes her, that everyone else thinks she's ugly and strung out but that he *likes* the junkie look on girls."

Randall laughed. "Doesn't fucking work, at least not for me," he said. "I'm moving on. Have you *seen* those new freshmen? A lot less work for a lot more payoff."

"Not me. I cracked the nut." Dobson smirked at Randall. "And, you know, she might do me some favors again. Since I can be such a charming date."

Liar.

"Stop talking," I said quietly.

"What?"

When I get angry, my English accent thickens until it's clotted and snotty, a full-on cartoon. And I was furious. I probably sounded like the bloody Queen.

"Say it again, and I'll fucking kill you."

There it was, that weightless rush, that floor-bottoming-out exhilaration that comes from saying something you can't take back. Something that would lead to me smashing in some deserving asshole's face.

This was the reason I played rugby in the first place. It was supposed to be a "reasonable outlet" for what the school counselor called my "acts of sudden and unreasonable aggression." Or, as my father put it, snickering like it was some joke, "the way you get a little punchy sometimes." Unlike him, I never looked back on them with anything like pride, the fights I got into at Highcombe and, before that, in my public school in Connecticut. I always felt disgusted with myself afterward, ashamed. Classmates I liked just fine the rest of the time would say something that would set me off, and immediately, my arm would cock back, ready to swing.

But I wasn't going to be ashamed this time, I thought, as Dobson jumped to his feet, swinging wildly. Randall grabbed his shirt to hold him back, his face a mask of shock. *Good, hold him,* I thought, *that way he can't run,* and I applied my fist to Dobson's jaw. His head snapped back, and when he looked at me again, he was smirking.

"You her boyfriend?" he said, panting. "'Cause Charlotte didn't tell me that last night."

In the background, shouting—the voice sounded like Holmes's. A hand pulled at my arm. In the second I was distracted, Dobson broke free of Randall's grip and tackled me to the grass. He was the size of a steam liner, and with his knee on my chest, I couldn't move, couldn't breathe. Leaning into my face, he said, "Who do you think you are, you little prick?" and spat, long and slow, into my eye. Then he hit me in the face, and hit me again.

A voice cut through the blood-roar. "Watson," Holmes shouted, at what sounded like an enormous distance, "what the fuck do you think you're doing?"

I was maybe the only person to ever have his imaginary friend made real. Not entirely real, not yet—she was still dream-blurred to me. But we'd run through London's sewers together, hand in muddy hand. We'd hidden in a cave in Alsace-Lorraine for weeks because the Stasi were after us for stealing government secrets. In my fevered imagination, she hid them in a microchip in one small red barrette. It held back her blond hair; that's what I'd pictured her with, back then.

Truth be told, I liked that blurriness. That line where reality and fiction jutted up against each other. And when Dobson had said those ugly things, I'd lunged at him because he'd dragged Holmes kicking and screaming into *this* world, one where people left litter on the quad and had to leave a conversation to use the toilet, where assholes tormented a girl because she wouldn't sleep with them.

It took four people—including a visibly shaken Tom—to haul him off me. I lay there for a moment, wiping the spit out of my eyes, until something leaned in to darken my view.

"Get up," Holmes said. She didn't offer me a hand.

There was a crowd around us. Of course there was. I swayed a little on my feet, flushed with adrenaline, feeling nothing. "Hi," I said stupidly, wiping at my bleeding nose.

She looked at me for a measured moment, then turned to face Dobson. "Oh baby, I can't believe you fought for me," she drawled at him. There was a smattering of laughter. He was still restrained by his friends, and I could hear him panting from where I stood. "Now that you've *won* me, I guess I'll lay down and spread for you right here. Or do you only like your girls drugged and unconscious?"

Shouts, jeers. Dobson looked more shocked than angry; he went limp against his restrainers. I snickered; I couldn't help it. Holmes spun, and stared me down.

"And you. You are not my boyfriend," she said evenly, the drawl completely vanished. "Though your wall-eyed stare, your ridiculous rambling, and the way your index finger twitches when I talk says you so very much want to be. You think you're defending my 'honor,' but you're just as bad as he is." She jerked a thumb at Dobson. "I don't need someone to fight for me. I can fight for myself."

Someone whistled; someone else began a slow clap. Holmes's expression didn't change. Some teachers showed up, and after that the dean; I was questioned, given a compress, questioned again. The whole time I couldn't stop replaying it.

As I bled onto my shirt in the infirmary, waiting to see if I'd be expelled and shipped back home, it was still the only thing I had banging around in my head. *You're just as bad as he is,* she'd said, and she'd been absolutely right.

But I had never wanted to be her boyfriend. I wanted something smaller than that, and far, far bigger, something I couldn't yet put into words.

The next time I sought out Charlotte Holmes, it was because Lee Dobson had been murdered.

two

It was close to dawn when the shouting started.

At first, it only registered as part of my dream. The shouts were those of an angry mob; someone had armed them with torches and pitchforks, and they chased me into a barn under a sky full of stars. The only hiding place I could find was behind a nonplussed cow, chewing her cud.

You didn't need to be a psychologist to understand what it meant. After my fight with Dobson, I'd gone from being unknown to notorious. People who didn't even know me suddenly had *opinions* about me. Dobson wasn't very popular; he was a meathead, and nasty to girls, but he had a number of thick-necked friends who made their presence known when I walked into the dining hall. Tom, for his part, was secretly thrilled. Gossip was Sherringford's favorite currency, and by his reckoning, he'd found a key to the Royal Treasury.

But for me, not much had really changed. I was still uncomfortable at Sherringford, only more so. My French class began falling silent when I walked in. A freshman girl stammered out an invitation to homecoming one morning outside the sciences building while her friends smothered giggles behind her. She was cute, in a blond, wispy kind of way, but I told her that I wasn't allowed to go. It was almost true. I'd been suspended from all school functions for a month—clubs, days in town, and thank God, the rugby team, though I'd been assured I would keep my scholarship—but they'd forgotten to ban me from the dance. It was a light punishment, I was told by the nurse who examined my broken nose. To me, it didn't seem like a punishment at all.

After the fight, I'd kept an eye out for Holmes, though I didn't know what I could possibly say if I did see her. That week, she canceled her poker game, though I wouldn't have gone anyway—showing up would've made me look like the awful stalker she already thought me to be. It was hard to avoid someone at Sherringford, with its five hundred students and postage-stamp campus, and yet somehow she had managed it. She wasn't in the dining hall; she wasn't on the quad between lessons.

I don't think I would have spent so much time thinking about it—about her—if I wasn't also coming to grips with how poorly I fit in at Sherringford. By the time all the trouble with Dobson started, I'd made friends—mostly through Tom, who seemed to know everyone from the cute girls in my classes to the upperclassmen playing ultimate Frisbee in the quad. Soon, I knew them too. But there was a flimsiness to all of those friendships, like a strong wind might blow them away.

For one thing, people were always talking about money.

Not upfront, not *How much do your parents make?* More like, *What do your parents do?* Was your mom a senator? Did your dad manage a hedge fund? *Oh my God, I'll be in the Hamptons for Christmas, too,* I heard one girl tell another in a voice that carried across the room. More than once, I saw students buying drugs from the creepy blond townie who lurked in the corners of our parties and around our quad at night. When they weren't using their parents' money to fund their coke habits, my classmates were globe-trotting. I overheard the girls in my French class trading notes on who was building orphanages in Africa last summer (never a specific African country, just "Africa"), who was backpacking through Spain.

Sherringford wasn't one of those schools like Andover or St. Paul's, filled with future presidents and baseball stars and astronauts. Sure, we had electives like screenwriting and Swahili, teachers with PhDs and tweed jackets, students sent off to the lesser Ivy League schools—but we were a rank or two below extraordinary, and maybe that was the problem. If we weren't in the fight to be the best, we'd fight instead to be the most privileged.

Or *they* would, anyway. I'd just landed myself a front-row seat to their match. And somewhere out there, in the dark, Charlotte Holmes prowled, playing entirely by her own rules.

The night of Dobson's murder, I'd been up late mulling over how to fix things between us. Holmes and I. I was fairly sure that I'd blown any chance of our ever being friends, and that thought kept me up until half past three. I'd been asleep for what felt like a moment when I was woken by the panic spreading down our hall. Tom had already thrown on clothes and gone to investigate before I'd even dragged myself from my bed. I thought, hazily, that it must be a fire drill and that I had somehow missed the alarm.

But there was a crowd gathered at the end of the hallway: guys from our floor, mostly, but our gray-haired hall mother was there as well, and beyond her was the school nurse and a knot of policemen in caps and uniforms. I pushed through them until I found Tom, staring blank-faced at a door wrapped in police tape. It stood open about an inch, and beyond it, the room was dark.

"What is it?" I asked him.

"Dobson," Tom said. When he finally turned to face me, I saw the frightened look in his eyes. "He's dead."

I was shocked to realize he was frightened of *me*.

The guy behind me said, "That's James Watson, he's the one who punched him," and the buzz around me ratcheted up to a roar.

Mrs. Dunham, our hall mother, put a protective hand on my shoulder. "It's all right, James," she said, "I'll stay here with you." Her glasses were askew, and she'd thrown a ridiculous silk robe over her pajamas; I hadn't known that she stayed nights in the dorm, or that she even knew my name. Still, I was fiercely glad she was there, because a man in a button-down shirt broke away from the policemen and crossed straight over to me. "James, is it?" he asked, flashing a badge. "We'd like to ask you some questions about tonight."

"Oh no, you don't," Mrs. Dunham said. "He's a minor, and you need his parents' permission to question him without a guardian present."

"He's not under arrest," the man insisted.

"All the same," she said. "Sherringford policy."

"Fine." The detective sighed. "Do they live close by, son?" He produced a notepad and pen from his trouser pocket, like this was *Law & Order*.

Well. It kind of was.

"My mother lives in London," I said, and my voice sounded strained even to my ears. Tom's stare was hardening into something like a glare. Behind him, a boy who lived next door to me was quietly crying. "My father lives here in Connecticut, but I haven't seen him in years."

"Can you give me his number?" the detective asked, and I did, pulling out my phone to read out the digits I'd never once called myself. He said some other things about staying put, and getting some sleep, and them coming by to see me in the early afternoon, all of which I agreed to. Did I have a choice? He gave me his card: it read *Detective Ben Shepard* in a businesslike font. He didn't look much like the other policemen I'd seen, on-screen or otherwise. On first glance, he gave an impression of grocery-store averageness, but as I stared at him, holding his card, I saw that his face had an unusually eager cast to it, like a dog eyeing a lofted ball. He didn't look like he had a tragic past, some murdered mother or brother that drove him to become a detective. He looked like someone who played video games with their kids. Who did the dishes without being asked.

That impression of goodness unsettled me more than if he'd been a mustache-twirling villain. Because it was clear that Detective Shepard thought *I* was the bad guy.

He gave me what was meant to be a reassuring smile. Then he left, him and the other policemen, and everyone else milled around for another few minutes until Mrs. Dunham sent them back to their rooms. They shoved past me. All of them did, Harry and Peter and Mason and even Tom, wrapped in his ubiquitous sweater-vest. The looks they gave me were uniform. *Outsider*, their faces said. *Killer, you deserve what's coming to you.*

Mrs. Dunham offered to make me some cocoa, but I had no idea what I'd say to her, or to anyone, so I said thanks but no thanks, I'd just go to sleep. As if sleep was even a remote possibility.

Tom wasn't in our room. He'd probably decided to sleep on someone's floor, I thought. He was afraid of me now. In a flash of rage, I picked up my pillow to chuck it across the room—and stopped cold. If someone heard me on a rampage, it wasn't going to help my case in the slightest. It was this anger that had gotten me into this mess in the first place, I reminded myself, and squashed the pillow against the bed instead.

Anger, and Charlotte Holmes.

When I snuck back down the hallway, the yellow tape over Dobson's door caught the light like a mirror, one I refused to look too closely into. I kept moving.

I made it all the way to Lawrence Hall before I realized I didn't have her number. Her phone number, or her room number—in fact, I was only vaguely sure she lived in this dorm. The rows of darkened windows stared down at me as I struggled to make a decision. Any moment now, the sky would start to brighten. Lights would begin to go on. The girls who lived here would shower and dress and gather their textbooks on the way out the door. How far would they get before they heard that one of their classmates had been murdered? How long would it take for them to start believing I'd done it?

I didn't even know what I'd say when I found her. What possible reason did she have to believe I was innocent? The last time she saw me, I was beating the daylights out of the victim.

My sense of purpose dissipated like a sputtering balloon, and I sat down on Lawrence's front steps to get my head on straight. Campus was silent and dark, except for the lights of the emergency vehicles that crowded around Michener.

"Watson," the voice hissed. "Jamie Watson."

Holmes stepped neatly out of a small stand of trees; I hadn't seen her there at all. In fact, I didn't think that I was meant to, as she was dressed in head-to-toe blacks: trousers, gloves, a pair of dark sneakers, a jacket zipped all the way to her chin, even the backpack slung over her shoulders. Her face was a pale moon against all that darkness, her lips compressed in anger until she opened her mouth to say something that, from her expression, I didn't want to hear.

So I spoke before she did. "Hi," I said, in my usual stupid way. "I was looking for you."

Her eyes widened, then narrowed, and I watched her rapidly recalculate something in her head. "This is about Dobson."

I didn't bother to ask how she knew. She was a Holmes. But I must've looked surprised enough for her to fill in the gaps. "Look, Tom texted Lena, and Lena texted me. Relatively straightforward. Unfortunately, I was wearing this when I heard"—she indicated her outfit with a frustrated hand—"and so I decided to stay away from the dorm so that nobody would see me. It's bad form to be dressed as a burglar on the night of anyone's murder, much less that of someone you hate."

"Oh," I said. "What were you actually burgling?"

A quicksilver smile flitted across her face. "Pipettes," she said. "I went to go work in my lab after night check."

"You absolute *nerd*," I said, laughing, and her smile came back, and stayed. Incredible. "You have a lab? Wait, no. Later. Because Dobson's dead, and we're easily the prime suspects, and we're *laughing*."

"I know." She scrubbed at her eyes with her hands. "Do you know, at first I thought you came here to accuse me of it."

My eyebrows must've shot up into my hair. "Absolutely not—"

"I know," she said, cutting me off with a searching look. I felt as if she were X-raying me. Her eyes flickered from my face, to my fingers, to my beaten-up Chucks. "But I told him I would kill him. I should have been your primary suspect. And I'm not."

There were a lot of answers to that not-question: *I'm a Watson, it's genetically impossible for me to suspect you* or, *In my imagination, you weren't ever a villain, you were always the hero,* but everything I came up with sounded flip or cute or melodramatic. "Like you said, you can take care of yourself," I told her, finally. "If you'd murdered him, I bet there would be twenty witnesses who saw him put the gun to his own head."

Holmes shrugged but she was clearly pleased. We sat there for a minute; in the distance, birds started calling to each other.

"You know," she said, "that bastard has hit on me in every disgusting way since the day I arrived. Shouted at me, left notes under my door. He slapped my ass in the breakfast line the weekend my brother was visiting." She shook her head. "It took some persuasion on my part, but Dobson wasn't immediately napalmed. Or made the target of a drone hit. Actually, Milo quite wanted to play the long game, wait a few years and then just disappear him from his bed, make it look like aliens. Or so he said. He was trying to cheer me up. . . ." She trailed off; it was clear she'd said more than she meant to. "I should still be mad at you."

"But you aren't."

"And we shouldn't be talking about Dobson like this." She got to her feet, and after a second's hesitation, offered me a hand up.

"I didn't think you'd be so respectful of the dead," I told her. "Just a few hours ago, he was alive and kicking, and practically begging to be napalmed."

The sun was rising in the distance, pulled up by its lazy, invisible string, and the sky was shot through with color. Her hair was washed in gold, her cheeks, in gold, and her eyes were as knowing as a psychic's.

In that moment, I would've followed her anywhere.

"We shouldn't be *talking* about Dobson," she said, starting off across the quad, "because we should be examining his room."

I stopped short. "I'm sorry, what?"

IT WAS ALREADY TEN PAST SEVEN, AND OUR HALLWAY IN Michener was on the second floor. I had no idea how we'd sneak by Mrs. Dunham at the front desk, not to mention the hordes of junior boys emerging from their rooms to shower before breakfast. I watched Holmes consider it for a moment, frowning, before she slid around to the side of the ivy-covered building.

She told me to stand back, then flung herself down on the ground, examining it inch by inch. For footprints, I realized. If we'd thought of accessing Dobson's room this way, someone else probably had too. Nervously, I looked around to see if we were being watched, but we were shrouded by a cluster of ash trees. Thank God Sherringford was so damn picturesque.

"Four girls went by here last night in a group," she said finally, getting to her feet. "You can tell by the stampede of Ugg boots. But no solo travelers, not even to smoke. Strange, this seems like a good spot for it." She methodically brushed the dirt and grass from her clothes. "They must have entered through the front doors. Michener isn't connected to the access tunnels, the way Stevenson and Harris are."

"Access tunnels?" I said.

"You really should explore more. We'll remedy that, but not now." Holmes glanced at the first floor's thick stone windowsills, at the windowsills above those, and bent down to untie her shoes. "Stuff these in my bag, will you," she said, putting a socked foot up on the sill. "Yours too. And put your gloves on. We can't leave prints of any kind. Come on, quickly, they might open their blinds at any moment. At least his roommate is away on that rugby tourney."

"Don't you need to find out which room is theirs?" I asked.

She tossed me a look, like I had asked her if the earth went around the sun. "Watson, just give me a lift."

I cradled my hands for her to step into, and in seconds she had climbed up the ivy to Dobson's second-floor window. Clinging to the sill with one hand, she used the other to pull a length of wire from her pocket, and bent one end into a hook with her teeth. I couldn't see what she did next, but I could hear her humming. It sounded like a Sousa march.

"Right," I whispered. "When I found you, you were just going to your *lab*."

"Shut up, Watson." With a slight hiss and crack, the window opened. Holmes eased herself inside, as delicate as a dancer.

Her head reappeared. "Aren't you coming?"

I swore. Loudly.

Thankfully, all that rugby I'd been playing meant I was in passable shape. I had a good six inches on her too, so I didn't need a leg up to reach the hanging ivy. When I scrambled into Dobson's room, she patted me on the shoulder absently; she was already surveying her surroundings.

Dobson's was the sort of room I'd seen all over Michener: he had that black-and-white poster of two girls kissing, and the floor was thick with crumpled clothing. Randall's side wasn't any cleaner, but at least his bed was made. Dobson's sheets were a mess, kicked down to the end of his mattress. The coroner must've already removed the body.

There was a framed photo of him and what looked like his sister on the bedside table. The two of them were squinting into the lens, big smiles on. I felt an unexpected pang of guilt.

Holmes had no such hesitation. "Hold my bag," she said, and immediately fell to her hands and knees. I jumped back about a foot. From what seemed like thin air, she produced a penlight in one hand, a pair of tweezers in the other.

"Did you order some sort of spy kit online?" I asked, irritated. I'd had barely an hour of sleep, and, to be honest, I was trying hard not to give in to a lurking sort of terror. Anyone could come in at any moment and catch us tampering with the crime scene for a murder I'd sort of wanted to commit.

And then there was Holmes. While I stood there, shaking with fear, she was efficient, cool-headed, working swiftly to get us absolved. I thought once more about the two of us racing through a runaway train and smothered a laugh. In reality, she'd make a clean escape while I'd trip over my own feet and get hauled away for waterboarding.

"Be quiet," she whispered back. "And pull one of those specimen jars from my bag, I've found something."

I took a small glass bottle from her backpack and undid the stopper, then crouched so she could tip the tweezers in. Through the glass, the sample looked like a sliver of onion skin; as I examined it, she added another piece, and a third. She pulled up a bit of the carpet and tucked that into another jar, and used her piece of wire to poke around under the bed, dislodging a number of pens, an old toothbrush, some odds and ends. She inspected a glass of milk by his bed and the old-fashioned slide whistle beside it. With one gloved finger, she traced an invisible line from a high vent down the wall to Dobson's pillow. Then she looked up, sharply, at the ceiling, and I heard her counting—why, I wasn't sure. Every small noise sounded to me like our inevitable imprisonment, and my heart hammered in my ears.

She bent to examine Dobson's pillow and gestured me over. The indentation that his head had made was still visible. "Is that spit?" I whispered, pointing.

"Excellent." She scraped at it with the edge of her tweezers. I'd said it just to make her laugh, but I warmed at the compliment anyway. "Jar," she said, and I handed her one.

"I don't see any blood," I said, and she shook her head. There wasn't any to see, not anywhere.

Outside the door, I heard footsteps—more than one

set—and people talking. To my horror, I heard the edges of my name, of Dobson's. Above the din, a grizzled voice said, "Is this the boy's room?"

"We need to go," I told Holmes, and for a second she looked like she was about to protest. "*Now,*" I said, pulling her to the window—I swear I saw the doorknob begin to turn. Without waiting, I lowered myself down the outside of the building, then jumped the rest of the way.

The second my feet hit the ground, my fear broke open into exhilaration.

I heard the window shut with a snap. Holmes landed behind me, and I spun her around by the arm.

"Were you seen?" I asked breathlessly.

"Of course not."

"Holmes," I said, "that was *brilliant.*"

That flicker of a smile again. "It was, wasn't it. Especially for a first effort."

"A first—you hadn't done that before."

She shrugged, but her eyes were gleaming.

"You had us break into a crime scene to steal evidence—something that could make us look even more guilty than we do already—and you've *never done that before*?" If I sounded a bit shrill, it was because I felt a bit shrill.

Holmes had already moved on. "We need to get to my lab," she said, pulling her shoes from her bag, "without arousing any suspicion for why we're together. Do you want to split up and meet there in twenty? Sciences, room 442." She tossed my sneakers to me in an elegant, underhand lob. "And take the long way, will you? I want to get there first."

SCIENCES 442 WAS A SUPPLY CLOSET.

A big one, but still.

When I walked in, Holmes was already bent over her chemistry set. It was the real deal, the kind I'd only seen in movies—tall beakers, and big fat ones, smoke coming off of the strange green substances inside. Bunsen burners all lit like a row of stage lights. This setup had pride of place in the middle of the room, and she'd lashed a pair of desk lamps to a neighboring bookshelf for light. That bookshelf was filled with a collection of battered-looking textbooks, everything from Darwin's *The Origin of Species* and *Gray's Anatomy* to huge tomes with names like *The History of Dirt* and *Baritsu and You*. There was an entire shelf just on poisons. At the bottom, I spied the famous biography of Dr. Watson, the one my mother had told me was too scandalous to read. (Which meant I had read it immediately. Apparently, he was really, really . . . popular with girls.)

Next to it was the only fiction in the entire bookcase: a handsome leather-bound set of Dr. Watson's Sherlock Holmes tales. The whole series, from *A Study in Scarlet* to *His Last Bow*. Their spines were all broken like they'd been read a million times.

If I was harboring any doubts about my part in this investigation—and to be honest, I'd had some *Titanic*-sized ones ever since we broke into Dobson's room—seeing those well-thumbed books made me feel better. I belonged here, I thought, with her, as surely as anyone belonged anywhere.

As weird as *here* was.

Because there was just so much else crammed in that space, and any one part of it would have made her Prime Suspect #1 in Every Murder Ever. One wall was plastered with diagrams of handguns, obscured by a hanging set of giant bird skeletons. (A vulture peered knowingly at me, its eyehole bullet-black.) The tatty love seat against one wall was spattered in what had to be blood, dripped, most likely, from the riding crops hung above it. There were sagging shelves filled with soil samples, blood samples, what looked like a jar of teeth. Beside the jar was a violin case, a lone bastion of sanity.

I fervently hoped that I was the only visitor she'd ever had to this lab. Or else she was most definitely going to jail.

"Watson," she said, gesturing to the love seat with a set of tongs, "sit." I grimaced. "The blood's all dried," she added, as if that helped.

It was a measure of how tired I was that I obeyed her. "How goes—whatever you're doing? What did you find, anyway?"

"Twelve minutes," she said, and busied herself with her chemistry table.

I waited. Impatiently.

"I don't like to hypothesize in advance of the facts," she said finally. "But what I *have* found suggests that our killer wasn't leaving anything to chance. He used at least two methods of poison, maybe three."

"Poison?" I asked, unable to hide the relief in my voice. I knew nothing about poison; there was no way I could be accused of killing Dobson.

But Holmes could.

I swallowed. "I thought you were a sophomore. You haven't had chemistry yet."

"Not here," she said, holding a pipette to the light. "But I was privately tutored when I was younger."

Of course she was. I thought again of what my mother had said, that the Holmeses drilled their children from birth in the deductive arts. I wondered what else Holmes had learned up there in their vast, lonely Sussex manor.

She cleared her throat. "How to defend myself. How to move silently through a room, how to locate every possible exit within seconds of entering a space. Entire city plans, beginning with London, including the names of every business on every street, and the fastest way to get to any of them. How, in short, to be always aware of what everyone is doing and thinking. From there, you can reason to why they do the things they do." For a moment, her eyes went dark, but her face cleared so quickly I decided I had imagined it. "And I was taught all the other subjects one learns in school, of course. Is that enough of an answer?"

I had no idea how to handle these conversations, where the questions were picked right out of my head. "It sounds incredible," I said honestly, "but I don't know if I'd want to always know what other people are thinking. Where they come from, what they want. Where's the mystery in that?"

She shrugged her shoulders with a nonchalance I didn't quite believe. "I suppose few people hold up to the scrutiny. But my family's business was never in maintaining mysteries. It's in unraveling them."

I wanted to ask her more questions, but I was exhausted. I caught myself smothering a yawn. "What time is it?"

"Eight," she said, and eye-dropped a clear substance onto a slide. "Any minute now, there'll be a campus-wide text saying that classes are off because of the murder. We can skip the optional counseling, I'm sure."

"Wake me up in two hours." I had to curl up small to fit on the sofa. As I pulled my jacket up to my chin, I caught Holmes's pale, considering eyes for the briefest moment before she looked away.

I WOKE UP TO A STALE TASTE IN MY MOUTH, SWEAT COOLING on my forehead. In my pocket, my phone let out the three-note sigh that meant that it was dying. For a horrible second I had no idea where I was. I looked up into the pleated ends of Holmes's riding crops, and remembered. It shouldn't have been as comforting as it was.

"That's been going off now for an hour," Holmes said from across the chemistry set. She was more undone than she'd been before: her jacket was rucked up to her elbows, and her hair was a spider web of frizz from the heat in our cramped quarters.

"And you didn't wake me up? What time is it?"

"You're wearing a watch."

"What time is it, Holmes?"

She looked blankly at me. "Seven?"

I swore, fumbling my phone out of my pocket. It was five till noon. I had a text from the school saying that classes were canceled and that grief counseling would be available in the infirmary. I also had thirteen missed calls. Ten of them were from my father, at least two were from England—*Unavailable*, read the caller ID—and one was a local number that I didn't recognize. I played the message on my voicemail.

"This is Detective Shepard, calling for James Watson. . . ."

At her chemistry set, Holmes peered into the bottom of an Erlenmeyer flask. "Yellow precipitate," she announced, more to herself than for my benefit. "Excellent. Absolutely perfect." Humming tunelessly, she poured the solution into a test tube and stoppered it, sliding it into her pocket.

I listened to the end of Shepard's message with a sinking stomach. "Is there a bathroom nearby?" I asked her blearily. "I need to wash my face."

She pointed wordlessly to the laundry sink in the corner, and I splashed myself with cold water. "According to the detective," I said, "they've all spoken to each other, and apparently my father is afraid I've hung myself from a tree branch, and we're all meeting in my room in thirty minutes. What am I going to say to him?"

It was a rhetorical question, and a confused one, at that, but she walked over to perch on the love seat's battered arm. "Your father?" she asked, and I nodded. She twisted her hands

37

in her lap, and I noticed that the soft inside of one elbow was puckered with scars. *I heard it was going into her arm,* the redhead had said.

"I haven't seen him since I was twelve."

"Do you want to tell me why?" she asked. It was clear that she knew that this was what friends did—showed interest in each other's lives, offered a willing ear when the other was upset—and that she was doing her best to mimic it. It was also clear that she'd rather be pouring a gallon of water onto a live wire.

Then again, maybe she did that for fun, anyway. Who the hell knew.

"You could tell me," I said. "I'm sure you've already come to some deductions. Read some invisible bits of my past in my pinky finger."

"It isn't a party trick, you know."

"I know," I told her. "But it might be easier. For both of us."

"Easier?" Holmes sighed, and tossed me my jacket. "Come on, or we'll be late."

A sharp wind cut through the quad, but the sky above was mercilessly clear. Everywhere, students huddled in clusters of two or three against the cold. Quite a few were openly crying, I noticed as we walked past; freshmen who probably didn't even know Dobson were hugging each other.

But when they spotted me and Holmes, everyone just . . . stopped. Stopped talking, stopped weeping, stopped telling tearful stories. One by one, they turned to glare at us, and then the whispering started.

Holmes tucked her small white hand in the crook of my arm and powered me along. "Listen to me," she said rapidly. "Your parents are English, but you were raised in America; I know that from what my family has said about yours. Your accent isn't very strong, but how you stress your sentences is very specifically London. And you love London; I could tell from the look on your face when you first heard me speak, like you'd had a glimpse of home. You must have lived there, and at a particularly impressionable time in your life. Add in the fact that you said 'bathroom,' not 'toilet' earlier—and other times, you've shied away from using any slang at all, rather than make a decision to be English or American about it—and so you must have moved to London around age eleven or twelve. Am I correct?"

I nodded dizzily.

It was hard to hear Holmes talk, to learn that every one of my insignificant words and actions broadcasted my past, if one just knew how to look. But it would have been harder still to walk through the quad in silence while the rest of the school played judge, jury, and executioner. She'd known that, I thought. That's why she'd saved her deductions for this walk: two terrible birds, one stone.

"Your jacket wasn't always yours. It was made in the 1970s, judging from the cut and the particularly awful brown of the leather, and while it fits you well enough, it's a touch too big in the shoulders. I'd say you'd bought it secondhand, vintage, but everything else you're wearing was made in the last two years. So either you inherited it, or it was a gift." She slipped her hand into my coat pocket to pull it inside out. "Magic marker stains," she said with satisfaction. "I saw this earlier, on the couch. I doubt you were carrying Crayolas around last winter. No, more likely that it was around your house while you were growing up, and either you or your younger sister wore it, at one point, while playing at art teacher."

"I didn't tell you I had a younger sister," I said.

She gave me a pitying look. "You didn't have to."

"Fine, so it was my father's." It wasn't pleasant, being dissected. "So what?"

"You're wearing it," she said. "That's enough to tell me you don't hate him. No, it's not as simple as *hate*. This is veering into psychology, and I'm sorry, I *loathe* psychology, but I imagine you wear the jacket because, somewhere, deep down, you miss him. You left for London at twelve, but your father lives here. You call him that, 'my father'; you don't call him your 'dad.' The very mention of him makes you tense up, and since we've established he hasn't been beating you, I can safely say that it's dread built up from a long silence. The last piece of it, of course, is your watch."

We were nearly at Michener Hall, and Holmes paused, holding out her hand. I didn't really see another option: I unfastened the clasp and handed it over.

"It's one of the first things I noticed when I met you," she said, examining it. "Far more expensive than anything else you wear. A ridiculously large watch face. And the inscription on the back—yes, here we are. *To Jamie, On His Sixteenth Birthday, Love JW, AW, MW and RW.*" Her eyes glittered at her

discovery—no, at the confirmation of what she'd deduced—
and I understood then what it would be like to hate her.

"Go on," I said, so it would finally be over.

She ticked it off on her fingers. "Despised childhood nickname, so he doesn't know you anymore. Very expensive gift for
a teenager? Long-standing guilt. But the key is in the *names*.
He didn't just give you a gift from him; he made sure you knew
it was from the whole family. His *new* family. Your mother's
name is Grace, my aunt's mentioned it. So A stands for . . .
Anna, let's say, and MW and RW would be your half siblings,
then. Even his birthday present to you is a clumsy attempt to
get you to love them. You haven't spoken for years because,
most likely, he was cheating on your mother with . . . Anna?
Alice? When your parents divorced, he stayed in America to
start a new family. Abandoning, at least in your eyes, you and
your sister.

"But your mother doesn't resent him: she didn't insist you
box away a frankly ridiculous gift until you're older. This watch
is worth at least three grand. No, she let you wear it. They're
on good terms, even though they're divorced; perhaps she's
relieved that he's moved on, as she'd already accomplished that
feat before the marriage had ended. Either way, she'd be upset
that you aren't on better terms with him—a boy needs his
father, et cetera, et cetera. Your stepmother must be younger,
then, but not so young that your mother disapproves."

"Abigail," I said. "Her name is Abigail."

Holmes shrugged; it was a small point to concede. Every
other detail had been spot-on, gold star, perfect.

The cold wind chapped at my face. It blew her hair about, obscuring her eyes. "I'm sorry, you know," she said, so quietly I could barely hear her. "I don't mean for it to . . . to hurt. It's just what I've observed."

"I know. It was well done," I said, and meant it. I didn't hate her so much as I hated being reminded of what my father had done. How I couldn't seem to get over it. And I hated the dread in my stomach as I looked at Michener Hall's heavy wooden doors and thought about the people waiting for me inside. My father. The detective. *I'm not guilty,* I reminded myself.

I wondered why I felt like I was.

She took my arm again. "You also wear the jacket because you think it makes you look like James Dean," she said as we walked in. "The eyes are right, but the jaw's all wrong, and though you're handsome, you're no tortured artist. More of a wiry librarian." She thought for a moment. "I suppose that's not all bad."

No one else in the world would put up with this girl. "You are *awful,*" I said, and even then I was forgiving her.

"I'm not." Relief was written all over her face. "How am I awful? I want examples. Give me an itemized list."

"Jamie?" a hesitant voice asked behind me. "Is that you?"

I turned to face my father.

three

I'D BEEN TOLD ALL MY LIFE THAT I WAS MY FATHER'S SPITTING image, and after years apart, I could see it more than ever. The dark, unruly hair—though his was beginning to gray at the temples—and dark eyes, a certain stubborn set to the jaw. *Watsons might be stubborn,* he'd told me when I was younger, *but we temper it with a love of adventure.*

Well, here was my adventure: a dead misogynist jerk, me the prime suspect, and my estranged father waiting to sit in on my questioning. Detective Shepard hovered a few steps behind. Someone must've filled him in on my family history, and he'd decided to give the two of us a moment.

In the background, Mrs. Dunham fussed noisily with an electric kettle. A series of mismatched mugs were lined up on the front desk. "I'm making tea," she said unnecessarily. "So many English people. It seemed like the thing to do."

Honestly, she wasn't far off. "Cheers," my father and I said at the same time. Next to me, Holmes smothered a laugh.

My father's eyes lit on her, clearly casting around for something, anything to say. "So, Jamie, aren't you going to introduce me to your girlfriend?"

Her hand tightened on my arm—in horror, I assumed. I didn't dare look over at her.

"This is Charlotte Holmes," I said quietly. "She's not my girlfriend."

I'm not sure what reaction I expected. My mother would have gone thin-lipped and silent, saving up ammunition to barrage me with in private. *Isn't she a bit pale,* and *She seems very unfriendly, don't you think,* and, ultimately, *You know, she'll just bring you to grief in the end.*

My father was delighted.

"Charlotte! Wonderful!" he said, and to my shock and Holmes's, he pulled her into a bone-crushing hug. She actually squeaked. I hadn't thought she could even make that sound. "Do you know, I sent my son all your press clippings. You did such marvelous work with the Jameson diamonds—and so young! You remember the story, right, Jamie? She'd been eavesdropping on Scotland Yard briefing her brother Milo. From behind a sofa in the library, isn't that how it went? And then she wrote them a detailed letter, in crayon, telling them where to find the loot. Marvelous."

At that, he let her go, and she swayed a bit on her feet. "I never owned a set of crayons," she said, but he didn't seem to hear her. Clucking, Mrs. Dunham pressed a cup of tea into Holmes's hands.

"Wait a minute." Detective Shepard cleared his throat. "You mean that you're *that* Holmes? Which makes you—"

"Yes, yes," my father said, waving a hand. "That Watson. Let's go have a sit-down and clear this whole mess up. Where's your room, Jamie? Upstairs, I imagine." He strode off toward the stairwell, the detective at his heels.

"She was *ten*?" Shepard asked, and my father's laugh echoed down the stairs.

Holmes clutched her mug of tea in disbelief. "He hugged me."

"I know," I said, making to follow them.

"I think I might like him," she said miserably.

I went back and ushered her up the stairs. "Don't feel bad," I told her. "Everyone does, except for me."

THE FIRST THING THE DETECTIVE ESTABLISHED WAS THAT Holmes and I both had alibis for the night before, courtesy of our roommates. The second thing he established was that those alibis didn't really matter.

"We're exploring a number of options," he said, perched in my desk chair, "based on the forensic evidence. And we're not confining our scope to last night. I want to hear the full story of what happened between you two and Lee Dobson. After that, I want to hear exactly why, despite all reports to the contrary, the two of you appear to be thick as thieves." He looked at Holmes, then me, with narrowed eyes. "It wasn't my plan to interrogate you two together, and I don't think I can. Miss Holmes, since I don't have a parent present—"

"Check your email," she said smoothly. "You'll find a message from my parents giving permission for Mr. Watson here to stand in as my guardian."

As Shepard took out his phone, my father pulled a notebook and pen from the inner pocket of his blazer.

"I don't need you to take notes," the detective said, bemused.

"Oh, no. These are for me." He smiled. "I have an interest in crime."

Shepard glanced over at me for help, and I shrugged, sitting down on the bed. I wasn't my father's keeper.

It didn't take very long at all for Holmes to tell her side of it. How she had come here as a freshman, and how Dobson had gone after her almost immediately. (Understandably, she left out the bit about him calling her a junkie, but I watched her tug at her sleeves as she detailed what he'd said to her.) She hadn't been to school before this, and so, she told the detective, she wasn't sure how to handle his abuse. Others had witnessed it—Lena, she said, and her brother—if Shepard wanted to corroborate her account.

"It's important to note that I didn't want him dead." There was steel in her voice. "Of course I wanted him to stop. But quite honestly, I was fine. His actions didn't have much bearing on my life here."

I remembered her wariness when I first approached her on the quad. *Who put you up to this? Was it Dobson?* But then it was my turn to tell a few half-truths, so I guessed I couldn't blame her.

Yes, it was true that I'd punched Dobson because he was being disgusting about a girl, a family friend, and because no one was saying anything to stop him. Yes, there were better ways of solving my problems; yes, if I could do it again, I'd use words instead of fists. (A lie.) Holmes and I had fought, and very publicly, but I told the detective that I'd found her the next day to make sure there were no hard feelings. (A lie.)

As I talked, I watched my father struggle to contain his beaming approval. When I described my right hook to Dobson's chin, he took notes with a stifled grin. Really, with role models like him, it was surprising I wasn't already in jail.

For his part, the detective stuck to asking us simple questions and fiddling with the recorder he'd brought along; we'd given permission for him to tape our statements. After I told him that I'd snuck out of the dorm this morning to see if Holmes was okay (a half-lie) and that we'd hidden away in her lab to avoid our classmates (retroactively true), I came to the end.

Shepard made a show of shuffling through his own notes. "I think that's it," he said, and I reached for my jacket.

He held up a hand before I could stand. "Except for the part where, when we found Dobson's body, he was clutching your school library's copy of *The Adventures of Sherlock Holmes*. With one story in particular bookmarked. Or the part where you had sex with him. Dobson." He was facing Holmes, but his eyes were fixed on me. My father stopped writing.

Nothing could have prepared me for that.

I went cold all over, then hot, and I thought I might retch on the carpet. So Dobson had been telling the truth. Thick-necked, grunting Dobson, who I'd once heard brag about jerking off in the communal shower. I'd kill him. I'd hunt him down and strangle him with my bare hands, even if I had to resurrect him to do it.

Next to me, I felt Holmes go very still. "Yes, I did," she said.

Through that all-too-familiar blood-roar, I heard the detective say, "Is there a reason you decided to keep that fact a secret? Not just from me, either. It looks like even your friend here had no idea."

I shoved my fists under my knees. Was I breathing? I couldn't tell. I didn't care.

"Because I was using a rather large amount of oxy at the time," she said coolly, "and had that come to light, I would have been expelled. Your real question should be whether the sexual act was consensual. Which, considering my impaired state, it wasn't." She paused. "Do you have any more questions?"

Her voice broke on the last word.

At that, I had to leave the room.

I STALKED UP AND DOWN THE HALL, SHAKING. IF I DIDN'T already have a reputation for being a violent dickhead, I definitely had one now: Peter opened his door in a bathrobe, shower caddy in hand, but after one glance at me punching the wall, he ducked back into his room. I heard him lock the door behind him.

Good, I thought. The first person to look at me the wrong way would get the pounding that Dobson had deserved.

As for Holmes . . . it hurt too much to think about her. Of course the fact that she'd done hard drugs wasn't a huge surprise; even without the rumors, I knew about the Holmeses' long, storied history with cocaine and rehab. According to my great-great-great-grandfather's stories, Sherlock Holmes had always fallen back on a seven-percent solution when he was without a case. He needed the stimulation, he'd claimed, and Dr. Watson had only made cursory efforts to stop him. Oxy was just Charlotte Holmes's particular poison. Apparently, old habits died hard in this family.

But I kept *imagining* it, Holmes stretched out on that tattered love seat in her lab, one indolent arm over her face, the empty plastic pouch beside her. That image alone was enough to turn my stomach—her eyes sparkling with a false fever, the sweat on her brow. And then Dobson at the door, disgusting words on his lips. How did it unfold? Did he have to hold her down?

I was aware, then, of my breath, as hard and fast as if I'd been running. I thought about it for another half second. Dobson's face. The empty pouch. Then I slammed my fist again into the cinder-block wall.

My father stepped out into the hallway.

"Jamie," he said in a low voice, and it pushed me over the edge into tears.

I don't cry, as a rule. Nothing good comes out of fighting, I'll give you that, but crying? For a moment, you might feel a touch of release, but for me that's always been followed hard by waves of shame, and helplessness. I hate feeling helpless. I'll do anything to avoid it.

I suppose Holmes and I had that in common.

I half-expected my father to try to hug me, the way he did her, but instead he laid a hand on my shoulder. "It's the worst feeling, isn't it?" he asked. "That there's nothing at all you can do to make it better."

"I didn't kill him, Dad," I said, rubbing angrily at my face. "God, I wish I had."

"You mustn't blame her for this, you know," he said. "I imagine she's doing a good enough job of that herself."

I took a step back. "I'd never blame Holmes for this. It isn't her fault."

My father smiled at that, though sadly. "You're a good man, Jamie Watson. Your mother's raised you well." This was territory that I couldn't get into, not then, and he must've seen it on my face. I waited for him to insist that I sign off campus to go home with him—it would be a reasonable suggestion, after everything that'd happened—but he didn't.

"Come by for dinner next Sunday," he said instead. "Bring Charlotte. You still like steak pie, I'm sure." There wasn't a question there to say no to, and before I could find a way to protest anyway, he said, "It'll just be the three of us." No stepfamily, he meant. I found myself nodding.

Detective Shepard came out into the hall, ushering along an ashen Holmes. Her composure was eggshell-thin but intact.

I admired her self-possession, and still, I wanted to be a million miles away.

"Next Sunday, then," my father said, and fixed the detective with a look that said the interview was absolutely over.

Shepard stood there for an awkward moment. "Neither of you leave town without telling me. We'll talk again soon." He followed my father down the stairs.

Holmes and I stared at each other.

"You've been crying," she said, more hoarse than usual. She lifted a tentative hand to touch my face. "Why?"

I wanted to shout at her. I couldn't turn my feelings off like I was a machine, and as much as she pretended to be one— her spotless appearance, the precise way she spoke—I knew she couldn't either. Her emotions had to be roiling somewhere, deep below the surface, and I wanted to demand that she pull them out for my inspection. As if it were my right.

But instead, I covered her cold hand with mine. "I won't make you talk about it," I said.

"Yes," she said, withdrawing. "Don't."

"Okay." I took a deep breath to steady myself. "Did you give him whatever it was that you slipped into your pocket? That vial?"

"I did."

It was like pulling teeth. "Are you going to tell me what it was?"

She considered it for a moment. Considered me. "Watson," she said, "it looks like we're being framed."

Mrs. Dunham wouldn't let us leave without a promise to go first to the infirmary. My knuckles were bleeding after I'd punched that wall, my fingers bruised and swollen. Holmes promised her we would, and she sat patiently as the nurse examined me. "You're becoming quite a regular," she said, tsking, and gave me bandages and an ice pack.

Holmes ducked into the dining hall to make us sandwiches while I waited by the door. I was surprised that she would remember to eat, as I'd been too upset to realize that I was starving. We were both, I think, too overwhelmed by our internal weather to pay much attention to what was happening outside. This time the stares and whispers as we crossed the quad didn't bother me. How could they? I had so much more to worry about. Up at Sciences 442, Holmes produced a ring of keys, and let us in.

"How did you con them into giving you a lab?" I asked, thankful for a neutral subject to discuss.

"My parents made it a stipulation of my acceptance," she said. Around us, the lab was as strange and dark as we'd left it. "Sherringford was quite eager to have me, and so they agreed. On my transcript, the work I do here is listed as an independent study."

I smirked. "In what? Murder?" She wrinkled her nose at me.

For those few minutes, I'd forgotten about Dobson, but the sight of the battered love seat brought it crashing back. I watched her watch me remember, and with a gust of energy, she slammed the door shut.

"It didn't happen here," she said matter-of-factly. "It happened in Stevenson. Yes, I generally do oxy here, when I do downers, so that was an exception. Yes, it was immensely upsetting; yes, I do get upset. No, I'd rather not tell you the details. I don't want you to *know* the details. I didn't kill him, and I didn't hire anyone to kill him. I had nothing to do with his death. As I've told you before, I can fight for myself. So stop looking at me like I'm an object for your pity."

"I don't pity you," I said, stunned. She turned to the wall, but I could still see her close her eyes, count backward silently from ten.

"No," she said, without turning around. "You just choose to feel all the things that I can't, or don't. It's overwhelming. We've been friends for less than a day." She paused. "Though I suppose we're neither of us very normal."

No one had considered me anything *but* normal, before this. Though I was sure that hadn't been the case for her.

After a long minute, I sat down on her disgusting couch. "Here is your lunch," I said, picking up the sandwiches from where she'd dropped them on the floor. "Normal people eat lunch, and so, for these five minutes, we are going to be normal. After that, you're free to tell me who's framing us for murder."

She flopped down beside me. "I don't have the *who* yet," she said. "Not enough data."

"Normal," I warned her. "At least try."

I wolfed my sandwich down, even though it was pastrami and lettuce on white bread, full stop. No condiments. It was the kind of sandwich only a posh girl with a personal chef

53

and the appetite of a hummingbird would have made, and so maybe I shouldn't have been surprised. For her part, she ate a listless bite or two, eyes fixed on the middle distance.

"What do normal people talk about?" she asked me.

"Football?" I hazarded. She rolled her eyes. "Okay. Did you see that new cop movie?"

"Fiction is a waste of time," she said, pulling a shred of lettuce out of her sandwich and nibbling on its end. A snail. She ate like a snail. "I'm far more interested in real events."

"Like?"

"There was a positively fascinating series of murders in Glasgow last week. Three girls, each garroted with her own hair." She smiled to herself. "Clever. Honestly, I didn't even leave the lab as it unfolded, I was so taken with it. I called in some tips to my contact at Scotland Yard, and she wanted to fly me out to investigate. Then this happened."

"How inconvenient," I said.

She, of course, ignored the sarcasm. "It was, wasn't it?"

"Okay, normal lunch is an abject failure," I said, "so just get on with it. Why are we being framed?"

"You're asking the wrong questions," she said, tossing the sandwich on the floor as she stood. I picked it up and put it in the trash. "We're not on *who*, or *why*, Watson, we're still working out *how*. You can't theorize in advance of facts, or you'll waste everyone's time."

"I don't understand," I said, because I didn't.

I swear, she nearly stamped an impatient foot. "Fact one: Lee Dobson tormented me for an entire year before assaulting me on September 26. Fact two: you and Dobson got into an altercation on October 3. Fact three: Dobson was murdered on Tuesday, October 11, close enough to both incidents to link them all together. When his toxicology reports come back, they'll prove that Dobson was a victim of gradual arsenic poisoning, that it began the night you first punched him, and that the doses increased in amount until the night he died. I'm sure that his roommate and the infirmary will testify to the attendant headaches, nausea, and so on."

"Jesus Christ." I stared at her. "Arsenic? Don't tell me you have access to arsenic."

"Watson," she said patiently, "we're in the sciences building, and I have the keys."

I put my head in my hands.

"He was holding a copy of your great-great-great-grandfather's stories. They'll also find that, last night, Dobson was the victim of a rattlesnake bite, perhaps even shortly postmortem while the blood was still warm. Remember the scale that I found on Dobson's floor?" Stooping, she pulled a book from the bottom of her bookshelf and tossed it to me. I was startled to see it was *The Adventures of Sherlock Holmes*. "No? How about the glass of milk on his bedside table? Or the vent above his bed? Come on, Watson, think!"

I blinked down at the book in my hands, not quite believing what she was implying. "You can't be serious."

"Oh, I'm quite serious. They're re-creating 'The Speckled Band.'"

"The Adventure of the Speckled Band" is one of my

great-great-great-grandfather's most well-known stories; it's definitely the most frightening, and also the most riddled with factual errors. As so many of his tales do, "The Speckled Band" opens in 221B Baker Street, with a shaken woman asking for help. Her sister had died two years before in the middle of the night under mysterious circumstances, and now Helen Stoner, Holmes's client, has been moved by her patently evil stepfather into that same bedroom, weeks before her wedding. During their investigation, Sherlock Holmes and Dr. Watson find that the bed in that room is bolted to the floor. Beside it, a bellpull trails down from a vent above that opens into the stepfather's study next door. There, Holmes finds a saucer of milk, a leash, a locked safe, and, during their stakeout, an Indian swamp adder—the speckled band of the title—that Evil Stepfather is using to kill his stepdaughters, controlling the snake with a whistle and tossing it into the safe when he's finished.

John H. Watson might have been many things—a doctor, a storyteller, and by most accounts a kind and decent man— but he clearly wasn't a zoologist. There's no such thing as a swamp adder. And the idea that Sherlock Holmes deduced its existence from a saucer of milk is ridiculous—snakes have zero interest in milk. They also can't hear anything but vibrations, so they wouldn't hear a whistle. But they *do* breathe, so a snake couldn't survive in a locked safe.

When I was younger, my father and I liked to speculate about what actually happened on that case to drive Dr. Watson to that much invention. My pet theory is still that he slept late that day in Baker Street, missed both the client and the investigation entirely, and was only half-listening when Sherlock Holmes broke it down for him later.

At least, that sounds like something I would do.

"Whoever they are, they're taunting us," Holmes was saying, pacing the length of her lab like a caged cat. "The arsenic would have done Dobson in on its own. The snake is just a ridiculous flourish, there to send a message. Of course, our culprit couldn't find a swamp adder, because your great-great-great-grandfather made those up." I rolled my eyes at her clear disdain. "But honestly, Watson, why would Dobson have a glass of milk? There wasn't a mini-fridge in his room; he'd have to carry it back from the dining hall after dinner. And while I suppose it's possible that Lee Dobson had discovered a passion for folk music, having a slide whistle is too strange in the context of everything else. The presence of these items is *just* plausible enough that the police wouldn't see them as significant, and so, in planting them there, the killer must have known we would make our own investigation."

"We're being toyed with," I said. "But why would he want us to know he's after us?"

"*Us*, specifically." She arched an eyebrow. "Dobson was after me all last year, and nothing happened to him. Then you show up, and all this starts. We'll begin by investigating people who arrived in the area since the summer, or those who have a particular stake in bringing the both of us down."

Why would anyone be after me? Holmes, I understood. She was so clearly smarter than, faster than, braver than—there had to be someone on the other side of that equation to make it work. Maybe I was just collateral damage. Maybe there had been some mistake. Because, no matter how badly I wanted my life to be interesting, it wasn't. There was no reason for anyone to target me.

But if Holmes realized how unimportant a role I actually played in all of this, she might send me packing. Back to chemistry homework and Tom's dirty jokes and all the other trappings of my American exile. Back to dreaming about her at night while she went on, unmoved, with her life. But it would be worse this time, because I'd know exactly what I was missing.

I decided to keep my mouth shut.

Holmes stopped pacing to lean against the wall for support. I remembered that she hadn't slept at all last night. I had no idea how she was still on her feet.

"The police aren't going to let us help them, not if Shepard's any indication," she said. "Idiots. I suppose that they don't like that I tampered with their crime scene."

"We're also their prime suspects," I reminded her. "That sort of puts a damper on our working relationship."

She shrugged, as if that were beside the point. "That's it, then."

"What is?"

"That's all I have to tell you. I'll think on our next move."

It was a dismissal. Whatever use she'd had for me had expired, and our investigation was done for the day. I got to my feet, wondering if I'd made a misjudgment in thinking that I was starting to mean something to her.

Because it seemed that Holmes had already forgotten me. She brought down her violin case from its shelf and drew from it an instrument so warm and polished that it nearly looked alive. I remembered listening to a special on BBC 4 in my kitchen that past summer, in such a profound sulk at leaving that my mother had begun a campaign to cheer me up. That day, she was making cinnamon buns by hand, rolling out the dough in long strips that dangled off the edge of our tiny countertop, and I'd crept from my room, drawn by the smell of the sugar. She looked up at me with floured hands, a brown curl stuck to the side of her face, and before either of us could speak the radio presenter announced a feature on the history of the Stradivarius. Underneath his voice played the famous recording of Sherlock Holmes performing a Mendelssohn concerto on his own Stradivarius for King Edward VII. The music was scratchy and still tremendously alive through the static. I'd drawn nearer, and my mother had pursed her lips but didn't change the station, and so we spent the afternoon that way, icing the rolls she'd made as they cooled and listening to the announcer speak of the violin's shape, the density of its wood, how Antonio Stradivari had stored his instruments under Venice's canals.

The brown-sugar color of Holmes's violin brought it all back to me in a rush, and I stood there, transfixed, watching her run through a scale before beginning to play. The bow stood out against her dark hair; her eyes were closed. The song was both familiar and alien, a folk melody punctuated by bursts of gorgeous dissonance. Though I was standing only a few feet away, the distance between us stretched like the hundred years between Sherlock Holmes playing for the king and my hearing it—that remote, that distant.

I must have listened for a long time before she stopped playing, and I realized that I was standing frozen with my hand on the doorknob, like a fool.

"Watson," she said, letting the violin drop to her side. "I'll see you tomorrow." She turned away from me, and began to play again.

four

After I avoided all my calls for another day, Mrs. Dunham came by my room and politely told me that if she had to speak to my panicked mother one more time, she would very publicly set herself on fire. So, that Thursday, I had to endure my mom's histrionics and my sister Shelby's thousand questions ("What happened? Are you okay? Does this mean that you can come home?"), a call that went on for hours. I told neither of them that I'd been invited to my father's house for dinner; I still hadn't decided if I would go.

Things settled down between Tom and me. Or rather, Tom's good nature won out over his suspicions, and after a day of uncomfortable silence, he came over to my desk while I was writing. I'd been scribbling down everything I could remember since Dobson's murder—times and dates, names of poisons, those things of Dobson's that Holmes had cataloged with her hands. I was thinking of making a story of it, and when Tom peered over my shoulder, it was easy enough to try it out on him.

Or to try out the version that wouldn't get either Holmes or me expelled.

Sherringford had released a statement referring to Lee Dobson's death as an accident—an "accident with a snake," which came off much more bizarre than terrifying. It was their attempt to reassure parents that our campus was safe, but students were still being dragged home in droves. Our hall, in particular, had an emptied-out feeling to it—for two days running, there was no line for the shower, no music blaring from behind closed doors.

Into that silence, the reporters appeared.

One day, they weren't there. The next, they were everywhere, crawling all over the quad with their cameras and flashbulbs and strident voices. They lay in wait after our classes, putting sympathetic hands on our shoulders and pointing the lenses into our faces. Most of the students ignored them. Some didn't. One day, during lunch, I watched the redheaded girl from my French class crying delicately into a camera. Her headshots, she sobbed, were on her website if they needed them. I guess I couldn't blame her for using the press; the press were using her, too.

That same reporter took a particular shine to me.

Following me from class to class, murmuring words of

sympathy before launching into questions like *Do you really think Lee Dobson's death was an accident?* and *Is it true you keep a snake in your dorm room?* From the logo on the cameraman's kit, I knew they were from the BBC. I would have known it anyway from the reporter's plummy accent and haughty chin, the very image of some grown-up Oxbridge wanker. He'd been sent across the pond to try to get some dirt on the Holmeses; I was sure by the way he kept turning the conversation back to Charlotte. Somehow, he'd gotten ahold of my class schedule, and for days he waited for me between classes, his cameraman always towering behind him.

The worst was the afternoon I thought I'd gotten away clean. The two of them were talking to a townie on the sciences building steps as I came out the front door. "Yeah, man," he was telling them, "I've heard the stories too. I have a lot of, uh, friends who say Charlotte Holmes is the head of this messed-up cult and James Watson is, like, her angry little henchman—"

I hurried past them, head down, but the reporter charged after me, calling my name, reaching out to pull on my arm.

I whipped around, ready to deck him. The cameraman stepped forward eagerly, training his lens on my face.

"See what I mean!" the townie said. I got a good look at him, this time. He was around thirty years old, with mean little features and thick blond hair. Tom had pointed him out to me as the campus drug dealer—I'd seen him lurking around campus at night.

Apparently these days he had more credibility than I did.

"Back off," I said quietly, and put my collar up. They let me walk on alone, but we all knew they'd be back the next day.

Except they weren't. Evidently, the reporters bothered enough of us that parents had begun to complain. Sherringford officially closed our campus to the public.

When I asked Holmes if she was relieved, she smiled politely. "My brother has an arrangement with the press," she said. "They've never bothered me."

Morale was low, and so it wasn't a surprise that the school decided to go ahead with our homecoming weekend despite all the commotion. Our school's green and white banners streamed from the chapel and the library; the dining hall announced they would be serving steak and salmon for dinner. In the days leading up to the dance, girls walked in droves to town and returned with long dresses in tied-off plastic bags. They had ordered them months before, from New York, and Boston, and one even from Paris. That was according to Cassidy and Ashton, who gossiped relentlessly through every one of our French classes. But it wasn't just girls who were preening in preparation. Tom was taking Lena, and he must have had his parents ship him his suit from Chicago. I had no idea how else he'd get his hands on a powder-blue jacket and vest.

It might have been a waste of time and money, but for once I understood it. Better to focus on pageantry than on death.

When I told Holmes that, she threw her head back in one of her rare laughs. "For a boy, you are massively melodramatic." I couldn't really argue with that. She had plenty of data to draw from, because I spent every spare moment I had in Sciences 442.

We had lunch there, and dinner—or rather, I ate in the ravenous way I always did while she made a series of deductions about my day. *You had Captain Crunch for breakfast,* she'd say, *and you've tried a new shaving cream you don't like,* the whole while pushing her food around her plate to disguise the fact that she wasn't eating. I bothered her about that, the way she picked at her food, and she'd eat a fry or two to appease me; ten minutes later, I'd bother her some more. One night, I mentioned that my favorite song was Nirvana's "Heart-Shaped Box," and an hour later, messing around on her violin, she played the opening measures of "Smells Like Teen Spirit." I don't think she realized she'd been doing it; when she caught my gaze, she jumped about a foot and slid directly into Bach's "Allemanda." (I learned the names of everything she played. She liked when I asked, and I liked to listen.)

The way we were with each other wouldn't have made sense to anyone else if I'd tried to explain it. I had a habit of volleying any ridiculous statement she'd make back over the net with top spin, and we'd ramp ourselves up into fierce arguments that way about beetles and Christmas plays and the color of Dr. Watson's eyes. We bickered over possible suspects: she was sure that our murderer had a Sherringford association, but I couldn't imagine why he or she wouldn't have acted the year before. I still couldn't imagine why I'd be a target. When I found a nest of prescription bottles hidden in her violin case, we had a pitched battle over the fact that she was still using oxy. "It's none of your business," she'd said, furious, and grew even angrier when I insisted that it, in fact, was. How could it not be? I was her friend. Maybe that's why the worst rows we had were about nothing at all. After we had it out one night about the way she always sprawled out on the love seat, leaving me to sit on the floor, I stormed from the lab to find, the next morning, that she'd brought in a folding chair. "For you," she said, with an idle gesture; it was all we really had room for in that small space.

But we didn't always egg each other on like that—more often, it was the opposite. Instead of yelling at her, I'd find myself sucked in by her hypnotic stare and unrelenting train of logical thought until I was letting her do something like pluck out my nose hair for an experiment. (To be fair, she did promise to do my chemistry homework for a month in exchange.) She taught me how to pick a basic lock, and after I'd finally maneuvered my pins into the right position and heard the telltale *click* and fallen back against the love seat in relief, she pulled a blindfold over my eyes and made me do it again. Later, after Holmes said she hadn't been allowed any when she was little, I bought a full-to-bursting bag of bulk candy from the union store and set it before her like an offering to a king. Deep in thought, she'd refused to try any of it, rolling her eyes at the very suggestion. When I returned from stepping out to take a call from my mother, I found her trying, very unsuccessfully, to bite into an everlasting gobstopper.

With all my time spent in Sciences 442, the outside world grew more and more strange. Sometimes, spending a day in Holmes's lab made it feel like a bunker we'd stocked against a nuclear apocalypse and moved into before it happened. When

Tom texted me to ask who I was taking to the dance, I found myself blinking hard in the lab's dim light, trying to remind myself that I could actually emerge into the unirradiated world and go.

But I didn't have a date, and told myself I didn't want one. When I thought about the dance, I kept imagining it taking place at some other Sherringford: one where spending an evening with the most fascinating girl I knew meant disco balls and shitty music, not Bunsen burners and bloodstains. One where going out into a sea of my classmates would be something other than absolute torture. There was no way to forget I was a murder suspect when people I didn't even know still stopped talking every time I walked into a classroom. Dobson's room was still roped off with yellow police tape. His former roommate Randall still tried to trip me in the hallways. My teachers all either handled me like glass or ignored me, except for whispery Mr. Wheatley, my creative writing teacher, who pulled me aside to say he was happy to listen if I ever needed an ear. I thanked him, though I didn't take him up on it. He was just offering because he was a nice guy. Even so, it felt good to have someone acknowledge, sanely, what was happening to me.

Because the truth of it was I was terrified. I kept expecting to wake up dead. Someone out there had it in for Holmes and me, and we had no idea who it was. More accurately, *I* had no idea who it was. I had the sinking feeling that Holmes did, but she sat on her suspicions with the smug languor of a cat on a pillow.

"I refuse to theorize in advance of the facts," was her response.

"So then let's go get some facts," I said. "Where do we start?"

She drew her bow over her violin, thinking. "The infirmary," she said finally.

Her plan was to see if Dobson, in the throes of arsenic poisoning, had tried to get help with his symptoms before his death. At first, I was a bit surprised that this was our next move. She'd done the tests and confirmed the poison's presence herself—why did she need to dig up more evidence that it had killed him? We knew it had.

But the more I thought about it, the more it made sense. Detective Shepard had completely dismissed Holmes's claim that we were being framed. Every time I stepped out of the sciences building, I saw the plainclothes policeman he'd stationed by the front door. I caught him going through the Dumpster outside my dorm. Holmes told me she'd woken one morning to find a team, on a ladder, examining her dorm room's window from the outside. She was more shaken than she seemed, I could tell. From her stories, and from the phone calls she still took regularly from her contact at Scotland Yard, I knew that Holmes wasn't used to working outside the law. Though she didn't say it out loud, I knew that she wanted to maneuver us back into the police's good graces. Having the school nurse corroborate our evidence would be a good first step.

"She likes you," Holmes said dispassionately as we walked toward the infirmary, a small, squat addition to Harris Hall, with a few overnight beds and a dispensary. Every time I'd been there in the past (cut-up hands, busted nose), I'd been taken care of by the same nurse. I'd never thought she was anything but businesslike with me.

"She likes me fine, I guess," I said. "So that's the plan? I fake some kind of injury, get her sympathy and her attention, and while she's busy, you go rooting around through her records?"

Holmes blinked at me. "Yes," she said, and pushed the door open.

The waiting room was empty. The nurse was finishing a game of Sudoku at the front desk. "Can I help you?" she said, without looking up.

"I'm back," I offered apologetically, holding up my hands. "These were hurting again, and I was kind of worried I might've broken something."

"Poor thing." She had a lilt to her voice that was oddly appealing. "And your girlfriend is here for moral support?"

I glanced over at Holmes, who managed a tearful smile. "I don't know if I can watch," she whispered. "I'm just so worried about him. I think I have to wait out here."

The nurse put a reassuring hand on her arm. "I won't do anything horrible to him, I promise. You can't leave him now. Come, come." She steered me and Holmes both back to the consulting room, where she poked at my hands (which did, in fact, hurt), said that they were healing just fine, handed me some Tylenol, and dismissed us. The whole visit took about five minutes.

"Well," Holmes said, scowling at the door behind us. "That usually works a bit better than it did."

I smirked. "You might have to work on your caring girl-friend routine. Is that it, then? No records?"

"No," she said. "I'll break in around midnight and get what I need. It's just tedious having to dismantle the security cameras again."

"Why didn't you just break in in the first place?"

Her smile flickered. "You seemed so eager to do something. I thought I might as well include you."

"Um, thanks?"

"But tonight I'll go alone. You're about as stealthy as a lame elephant. See you later." She patted me on the shoulder and took off down the path, leaving me behind, both charmed and insulted. The side effects of hanging around Charlotte Holmes.

When I arrived at her lab the next day after classes, Detective Shepard was stepping out of the door. I hadn't known that he could interrogate either of us without a parent there, but he must have found a way to talk to Holmes.

"Jamie," he said heavily. "I'll see you and Charlotte on Sunday night at your father's house. We'll talk then." With that, he fixed me with a pitying look and took off down the hall.

"Wait, you're coming to that?" I called after him, but he didn't respond.

Inside, on the love seat, Holmes was wrapped up in an avalanche of blankets. She looked like one of those Russian nesting dolls, like she was the smallest Holmes in a series.

Whatever words she'd exchanged with Shepard, they'd left her in a mood.

"Why did you let him in? What was that about, exactly?"

"Nothing."

"Nothing," I repeated. "I thought you were giving him Dobson's infirmary records."

"He already had them, of course," she said. "He chided me for breaking and entering, and left."

"So Dobson *did* go to have his symptoms treated."

"He went to the infirmary often," she said. "Mostly rugby-related injuries, Shepard said. He said they'd tested his hair for arsenic and found it, and didn't need any of my proof. Then he asked me to identify all the vials on my poisons shelf. And then he left, saying he'd see us soon, in a voice I think he thought was threatening. Amateur."

"Wait, back up. You let the detective in here. You let him look at your poisons shelf."

"Yes."

"Poisons."

"Yes."

"And there's arsenic on that shelf?"

"Yes."

"And he's interrogating us again this Sunday," I said, feeling sick.

"Yes," she said, drawing the word out like I was an idiot.

I stared at her for a long minute. She had to know something she wasn't telling me. "Right. We need to make a list of possible suspects. We need to find something we can give them. Anything to make you—us—look less guilty."

Turning away, I taped a sheet of butcher paper to the side of her bookcase and wrote "suspects" at the top.

"Watson," she said, "you don't have any suspects."

I glared at her. She brought her cigarette to her lips and took a long drag. We'd reached an unspoken agreement: she'd dump the pill bottles, and I'd stop checking for them. That's how I chose to read the new and constant presence of a lit Lucky Strike in her hand—that she was trying out a drug that wouldn't kill her, at least not as quickly.

But all that smoke meant the unventilated lab was starting to resemble some toxic back room of hell, edging me ever closer to my breaking point. And still Holmes sat, and smoked, and told me nothing.

"What about the person who checked out that copy of *The Adventures of Sherlock Holmes* from the library? There have to be records."

"Correction. That particular copy was new and had never once been checked out from the library. Someone stole it off the shelf," Holmes said. "Currently, the library database has it listed as 'missing.' And as the physical copy is in police possession, I have no way of examining it."

"What about enemies? We could list Dobson's enemies."

"Go on, then. Put down every girl at the school." Her eyes went dark. "Though I can tell you that, from the research I did last year, I know I'm the only one who had a . . . run-in with him."

I swallowed. "We could list our enemies, then."

"You haven't got any enemies."

"I've got ex-girlfriends," I countered. "English ones. American ones. Scottish ones. I could so see Fiona with some sort of tartan apothecary box for her poisons . . ." Although it was hard to actually imagine Fiona doing anything but dumping me in front of my entire class.

Holmes raised an eyebrow. "No," she said, and exhaled.

I kept myself from pulling the cigarette from her hand and grinding it out on the floor.

"I haven't been sleeping," I told her, "because I am worried that either you, or I, or some innocent lunch lady will bite it now that we've gotten ourselves a murderous fan club. So give me a hand, will you?"

Her eyes narrowed in concentration. "The Marquess of Abergavenny," she said, finally. "I set fire to his stables when I was nine."

"Fine," I said, and then, in a smaller voice, "Can you spell that?"

She ignored me. "I suppose you could add Kristof Demarchelier, the chemist. The Frenchman, not the Dane. And the Comtesse van Landingham—Tracy never liked me. She didn't like my brother Milo either, for that matter, but then he did break her heart. Oh, and the headmistress of Innsbruck School in Lucerne, for beating her so often in chess, and the champion table tennis player Quentin Wilde. I suppose you might as well add his teammates Basil and Thom. Thom with an 'h,' of course. Though I can't remember their surnames. Strange."

"Is that it? Or are there peers and MPs that you're forgetting? Maybe a crowned head or two?"

She took a puff that sent her into a coughing fit. When

she regained her composure, she said, "Well, there's August Moriarty," as if that shouldn't have been the first name out of her mouth.

"What," I asked her slowly, "were you doing picking fights with a Moriarty?"

Professor James Moriarty was Sherlock Holmes's greatest enemy. In some ways, he was almost as notorious as the Great Detective himself. Moriarty was the first criminal mastermind of London, who famously died after fighting Sherlock Holmes at the Reichenbach Falls in Switzerland. After that fight, Sherlock faked his own death in order to hunt down the rest of Moriarty's agents in disguise. Even Dr. Watson thought Sherlock was gone for good. Though the official story says differently, I have it on good authority that when Holmes waltzed back into his consulting room three years later, my great-great-great-grandfather delivered one hell of a punch to his former partner's jaw.

Like I said before, I haven't had the best role models.

But then neither had Charlotte Holmes.

She dashed her cigarette out in the ashtray with a delicate, vicious hand. "It's irrelevant." There was smothered hurt in her voice, but I couldn't afford to drop the subject.

"Professor Moriarty still has fans, Holmes. Followers. Did you know that some English serial killers still list him as their greatest inspiration? And they've never recovered all the art he stole. Not to mention the rest of his family actively attempting to live up to his legacy." I drew a line under his name. August. I had never heard of an August Moriarty. "I mean, I know it's been more than a hundred years, but—"

"I'd prefer to think," Holmes said, cutting me off, "that we aren't all so mercilessly bound to our pasts." She rose, shedding her blankets. Underneath, she wore a short pleated skirt, rolled at the waist to appear even shorter, and her white oxford was undone to the fourth button.

Had she dressed this way for the detective? Or for something else? What was she playing at?

I cleared my throat awkwardly. In one of her mercurial shifts of mood, she flashed me a smile and hauled a box out from underneath the love seat.

Inside was a collection of wigs. Dozens of them, stored in soft mesh bags and arranged by color. Holmes drew a hand mirror out from the box and peered at herself for half a second before smoothing her hair up into a knot.

"So this conversation is over," I said, but I might as well have been talking to the air. It was no use; I'd been outplayed. She didn't want to talk about August Moriarty, and so she wouldn't, and nothing I could say would change her mind.

Getting to watch her transform herself helped soften the blow. She did it with all the cool efficiency of a violinist tuning her instrument. A stocking cap went over her hair, followed by the wig—long blond hair, curled at the ends—and makeup that she applied with an expert hand, balancing the small mirror between her knees. I didn't know the terms for what she did, but the face that looked up at me was doe-eyed and glimmering, her cheeks pink, her lips smudged with sticky gloss. She spritzed herself with perfume. Then, without a hint of modesty, she pulled a pair of plastic inserts from a bag and slid them, one at a time, into her bra.

I turned away, my cheeks burning.

"Jamie?" asked a bright American voice as she stepped in front of me. "Are you okay?"

She was like textbook jailbait, all curves where there used to be straight lines. I hadn't registered before that Holmes had perfect posture, but I noticed the absence of it now, as she stood indolently in—dear God, knee socks. The blond wig and makeup lit up her gray eyes, imbuing them with a friendliness that I hadn't thought they could have. And the look those eyes were giving me was *criminal*.

"I'm Hailey," she said, her pronunciation lazy and Californian. "I'm a prospective student? For next year? My mom's in town but I wanted to, like, see the campus for myself. Is there a party tonight?" She touched my chest with a finger. "Do you want to take me?"

I'd never been so turned off in my life.

I stepped back into her chemistry table. The beakers rattled against each other; one crashed to the floor and shattered. And then there Holmes was again, underneath all the false wrapping, severe and mysterious and . . . pleased.

"Good," she said, in her usual hoarse voice, rapidly tossing things into a backpack. "If you hate Hailey, she'll do just fine for my purposes."

"Which are?"

"Be patient," she said. "I promise I'll tell you everything later." She glanced at the suspects list, at the name at the bottom. *August Moriarty.* "Everything, Watson. But not now."

"This is completely unfair," I pointed out.

"It is." Holmes smiled to herself. "We can talk more at the poker game tonight. I'll be there as myself."

"No one's going to come. Everyone thinks we're murderers."

"Everyone will come," she said, correctly, "because every-one thinks we're murderers."

"Well, you'll be lucky if I'm there."

"Yes," she said simply. "I will be."

"Fine," I said, throwing up my hands. Because she'd won, check and mate.

She was already at the door, and, having taken those five steps, she wasn't Holmes anymore.

With a coy wave over her shoulder, Hailey said, "Bye, Jamie."

And then I was alone, with nothing to do but sweep up the shards of the beaker from the floor.

I WASN'T SURE IF IT WAS OUR DUBIOUS CELEBRITY, OR JUST brewing excitement for homecoming weekend, but Holmes had been right about the crowd. When I arrived at Stevenson at half past eleven, the basement kitchen was already overflowing with people. Some freshman boys had spun off a satellite game of five-card stud in the common space, and I had to push past a group of giggling girls to get through the kitchen door. Instead of going silent at my presence, the way everyone else did, they giggled louder. Gritting my teeth, I finally got through to the card table at the back.

Holmes wasn't anywhere to be found, but Lena was holding court in an improbable top hat. I'd seen her around, but I hadn't paid much attention to her before. There wasn't any doubt that she was beautiful, in a way I'd heard Tom wax rhapsodic about late at night: long straight hair, inky eyes, brown skin. Tonight, she was flushed with excitement and something else—probably vodka—and she'd stacked her mountain of chips into a neat pyramid. When she spotted me, she waved me over.

The boy sitting next to her wasn't Tom, and he didn't look happy to see me. "Hey, killer," he spat. I ignored him.

"Hi, Jamie," Lena said, ignoring him too. "Do you want to play? We're out of chairs, but I can totally deal you in if you want to stand."

"Actually, he can have my seat. I need another drink." The girl on her other side—Mariella, I think her name was—pushed herself to her feet and tottered over to the counter, where I spotted a handle of Vodka-brand vodka and some dubious-looking pineapple juice. The freshman girl that had asked me to homecoming was playing bartender. I avoided her eyes, too. Was there anyone I wasn't avoiding?

"I'm happy Mariella left," Lena told me conspiratorially. "At least fifty bucks' worth of this haul is hers. Was hers, I guess. Oops."

If she were anything like the other Sherringford students I'd met, Mariella wouldn't miss her money in the slightest. I thought of the thirty-five dollars left in my checking account that I couldn't afford to lose and turned Lena down when she offered to deal me in, telling her I didn't know how to play.

"I'll try to pick it up, though," I lied. Really, I just wanted to keep my seat until Holmes arrived, since I didn't know anyone else here.

"Oh my God," Lena said, putting a hand to her chest. "You're British, too? You two are adorable, I love it."

In England, I was an American. Here, it was the opposite. "Actually, I was born here," I said.

"Are we going to play or not?" the guy next to Lena asked.

"Not," she said, pushing back her chair. "Or whatever, you guys play. I want to talk to Jamie." She stuffed her chips into the pockets of her dress and pulled me aside. I didn't bother to correct her on my name; I'd just about given up on asking people to call me James.

"I just want you to know," she said, over-enunciating each word, "that I don't think you and Charlotte killed Lee. Look at you! You're adorable, and now you're *blushing*, that's even more adorable. It's like you were invented to get her over that whole August thing. I totally refuse to believe you guys have gone all Bonnie and Clyde on Lee." She frowned. "He sucked, anyway."

"August?" My voice caught on his name, and I winced. "Um. I don't know any Augusts. Who's that?"

"Hold on," she said. "Let me take another shot."

I may have been a terrible liar, but Lena was drunk.

"Oh, you know. *August.* The guy back home. She was pretty upset about it when she got here last year. I mean, she didn't say she was upset but I heard her talking on the phone about him. You know, through the door? Then her brother came to visit and they were all like CIA about it the whole time. I kept hearing his name, which is a weird name, so I remembered it. Anyway, Milo left, but before he left, he was all like, *Rrr, I'm going to do something about this,* and she was a lot happier after that." She put a hand to her mouth. "Shit. Oh, shit. I probably shouldn't have told you that. Girl code."

I wanted to ask her what, in fact, she *had* told me, except maybe about one of Milo's drone hits. "It's fine," I said, drawing from the sane, imaginary place in my head, where no one was brutally killed down the hall and my only friend deigned to tell me the barest facts about her life. "I know all about it. Failed love. Tragic, really. And that house fire, with . . . with all the puppies."

"Exactly!" She pressed her hand against my arm. "You guys are going to homecoming, right? I ordered this dress from Paris—you know, we go there every summer, my family does—but then it didn't fit right, and no one does alterations here. Not good ones, anyway. Charlotte has this beautiful black dress that I asked if I could borrow—Tom would totally flip out—but she said no, so I figured that she had a date."

Holmes probably had that dress made specifically for some Norwegian gala where she beat a foreign minister at chess, stole a French-Yugoslavian treaty, and then smuggled herself into the hotel clothes hamper so that she could escape through the laundry chute. I wondered what it looked like; it had to be pretty spectacular if Lena wanted it that badly. A long dress, I imagined. Black and slinky, something a Bond girl would wear.

But Lena was wrong about Holmes having a date. The only boy she'd ever consider taking was—

I cut off that line of thought. Where was she, anyway? It was past midnight.

"Yeah," I said, craning my head to look over the crowd. "Er, no. No. I don't think Holmes does dances. Is it okay if I step outside and look for her? I can throw out your drink if you're finished." Lena was beginning to look a bit sick. As I eased the cup from her hand, a thought occurred to me.

"Um, Lena?" I said. "Why did Holmes start having these poker nights? She doesn't seem to like"—I was about to say *anyone* before I caught myself—"crowds. Isn't it kind of weird for her to host them?"

"Oh," Lena said, surprised. "You know, her parents don't give her any spending money or anything. And Charlotte burns through a lot. I think she does a lot of online shopping, she always has packages at the front desk." I coughed to cover my laughter. I was positive those packages contained something more sinister than designer clothes. Lena really was the perfect roommate for Holmes, I had to give her that. "Anyway, you know. She always knows when people are lying, so I guess it makes sense for her to play poker for cash. I think it's funny."

Tom snuck up behind Lena and put his arms around her. "Baby, you're drunk," he said, leaning in to kiss her on the cheek.

"Baby, stop. I gotta poker. Charlotte's not here, and I'm making a killing. I think I'm going to get a Prada purse."

"Better split it with me before you cash out." Tom kissed

her again, and she wrinkled her nose. "Since I'm your muse and all."

"Her poker muse," I said, as seriously as I could manage.

"I bet you Charlotte's his," Tom stage-whispered.

"Oh my gosh, that's *so cute*." Lena touched my cheek and turned back to the game, depositing her chips on the table in handfuls. When she looked away, Tom filched a few and slipped them in his pocket.

I pitched Lena's drink in the trash and set off in search of Holmes.

Since I was already in Stevenson, I snuck up to check her room first. It wasn't hard at all to get past the hall mother, asleep on her pillowed arms at the front desk. I quickly found Holmes's door on the first floor: Lena had covered it in paper flowers, and there was a notecard bearing her name in curly purple script. Holmes's name was hastily scribbled in black ink below it. The door was unlocked—Lena's fault, I was sure—so I let myself in.

Unlike the room Tom and I shared, which could've won awards for its messiness, theirs was as neat and orderly as only a girls' dorm room could be. Lena's side was a riot of color, big pillows and bright tapestries, the shut laptop on the desk covered in stickers. She had photos of young Cary Grant pinned to her corkboard, nestled between song lyrics that she'd copied out onto sticky notes. She'd left her keys on the desk. More or less what I'd expected.

I was much more interested in Holmes's side, but it seemed that she had scrubbed all traces of herself from her room, saving her brilliant oddness for Sciences 442. Her desk was bare and clean, except for a digital clock, and the corkboard above boasted a single bright-blue Post-it that read *luv u girlie xo Lena* and had curled a bit with age. (That Holmes had left it up that long was surprisingly endearing.) On the shelf above her bed, her textbooks were all in a neat line, and on the bed itself was a navy coverlet—and below that was a sleeping Charlotte Holmes, wig askew, mascara already beginning to rub off below her eyes.

I shut the door softly behind me. "Holmes," I whispered, and before I could say it again, she sat up like a shot had gone off.

"Watson," she croaked, and reached blindly for her clock. "I just meant to lie down for a moment."

"It's fine," I said, sitting at the edge of her bed. "You're probably still catching up on sleep. It's not healthy to go three days without it, you'll start hallucinating."

"Yes, but the hallucinations are always fascinating." She stacked her pillows behind her back. "So?" she asked, in a *Why are you here* voice.

"So," I said, "how did it go? Did you learn anything? Who were you targeting?"

She heaved a sigh, pulling off her wig and stocking cap. "Watson," she said again, "really."

"I'm a murder suspect too," I reminded her, "and I thought we were partners in this. You dress up in this whole ridiculous *thing* and then you don't tell me how it went? Spill."

"I didn't learn anything. Anything at all. I must've spoken

to at least fifteen first-year male students—statistically, murderers are more often men, and anyway Hailey is useless with girls, they generally want to drown her in the nearest river—and none of them showed the slightest sign of being responsible." She said it all in a rush, like she wanted to expel it from her system. "And I'm starving. I'm never starving. I ate *yesterday.*"

"You had to have learned something," I said, choosing to ignore that last part. In my short experience with her, Holmes had treated her body like an inconvenience, at best, and at the worst of times like an appendage she was actively trying to destroy.

"*No,*" she said petulantly. "It was an utter waste of my time, and I used the last of my Forever Ever Cotton Candy perfume to do it. Which means I have to order more, and they only sell it on the Japanese eBay, and it's not cheap for something that smells that foul. And God, the humiliation of getting those boxes in the post." She stuck a hand under her pillow, producing a trio of wallets. "I was mad enough to pick three of their pockets, which should at least cover the cost, if not the emotional damage."

"Holmes," I said slowly, taking one from her. The wallet itself was worth more than my mother's flat, and it was stuffed with cash. "You can't do that. We have to give these back."

She cocked an eyebrow at me. "These were the ones who tried to get me drunk so they could have their sordid way with me."

"Well then." I pulled out five twenty-dollar bills and tossed them on the bed. "That's more than enough for your perfume. Do you know what we're going to do with the rest?"

"Give it all back to appease your sudden fit of conscience?"

"No," I said. "There's a car key on Lena's ring. We're going out for midnight breakfast. And then giving the rest to, like, charity."

"I'LL HAVE TOAST," HOLMES TOLD THE WAITER, HANDING HIM her menu. "Two pieces, whole wheat. No butter, no jam."

"No, she'll have the silver dollar special, with her eggs sunny-side up and . . . bacon, instead of sausage." I fixed her with a scathing look. "Unless there's something else on the menu she'd rather have. That isn't under 'side orders.'"

She snorted. "Right, then. He'll be having the same thing, except he wants sausage, not bacon, and please do keep on giving him decaf instead of regular. It's a mistake on your part, but it works to my advantage. He's quite cranky when he doesn't sleep."

The waiter scribbled down our orders. "Happy fiftieth anniversary," he muttered, and moved on to the next table.

"Ignore him. He hasn't had a girlfriend in three years," Holmes said. "Did you see his shoes? *White* laces. That alone should tell you."

I couldn't help it; I started snickering. Holmes graced me with one of her quicksilver smiles. She'd wiped most of the mascara from under her eyes and taken off her wig, but she was still done up like a Christmas tree. It was disconcerting, being able to see the thin gauze of persona laid over the real thing.

"There are at least fifty people in this restaurant eating breakfast at two in the morning," she said, sipping at her water. "All under the age of twenty. And forty-eight of them didn't have it this morning, including Will Tillman, the freshman across the room who is never at breakfast and who is, in fact, most likely here to buy drugs. Why on earth is this place so popular? I don't understand."

"That's because you're a bit of a robot," I said fondly, and she rolled her eyes. "So, are you the only one who can go incognito, or do I get to wear the disguise next time?"

"Do you have one in mind?" she asked, clearly struggling to take me seriously.

"I don't get to pull a Hailey on the new girl students?"

She snorted. "Even if I wasn't done pursuing innocent fourteen-year-olds, you really are just not pretty enough for knee socks."

"Well, I do a really good impression of a mindless rugger."

"No, you don't," she said. "Thank God. You should tell your therapist that rugby does nothing whatsoever to alleviate your very real anger issues."

"Not my therapist. My school counselor."

She hid a smile. "All the same. You really should take up boxing, or fencing—"

"Fencing? What century are you from?"

"—or solving crimes."

"Are you prescribing me your company, Doctor?"

"Detective, you can read me like a book." She lifted her glass, and I clinked mine against it.

I was suffused with a sense of well-being. The restaurant was warm, and warmly lit. Someone in the kitchen was making us pancakes. And I was sitting across from Charlotte Holmes.

I felt at home enough to ask her something that had been nagging at me for a while. "Right, so I have a question. Tell me if I'm out of line."

She tipped her head.

"My parents . . ." It took me a minute to find the right words. "Well, my grandfather very notoriously sold his inherited rights to the Sherlock Holmes stories to pay off his gambling debts. We're just not important anymore. At least, we're not in the public eye. We might be trotted out for the occasional press op, but my father does transatlantic sales—which is a lot lamer than it sounds—and my mum works in a bank. The Holmes family, though . . . I mean, you guys have been Yard consultants for generations. So why aren't they helping us? Where are they?"

"In London," she said. Before I could protest her flip answer, she held up a hand. "In London, where they'll stay. They won't interfere."

"But why not?" I asked her. "Have you told them not to?"

"No." Holmes slumped against the back of our booth, rubbing the crook of her left arm. "Do you remember when I told you I'd been taught at home until I came to Sherringford? Did you ever find it strange that I came here in the first place?"

"I didn't, actually," I told her. "I assumed your family had tossed your room for drugs, found out about your habit, and sent you to America to do penance. When Lena told me tonight that your parents had cut you off, it more or less confirmed it."

Holmes blinked at me. Then she started laughing, a rare and surprisingly unwelcome sound. The waiter brought our food, and I'm sure we made quite the sight: Holmes giggling into her hands, me glaring at her across the table.

"Tell me the funny part isn't my solving a mystery on my own," I said, stabbing at a sausage.

She managed to compose herself. "No," she said. "I'm laughing because I was a fool to think you wouldn't. You're entirely right, of course."

"And they cut you off because they thought you'd use the money to buy drugs?"

"No," she said again. "They cut me off because I wasn't fit to be their daughter." She dipped a finger into her water, tinkling the ice cubes. "In their eyes, my vices got in the way of my studies."

I looked at her, so thin and angular and sad, so surprised at herself every time that she laughed, and I wondered what it would have actually been like to grow up in the Holmes household. Long velvet curtains, I thought, and libraries filled with rare books. A hushed fight always happening the next room over. Charlotte and her brother made to wander around the house in blindfolds, listening at doors for practice, scolded for any emotional attachments except to each other. It sounded like a movie, but it must've been hell to live it.

"Eat," I said, pushing her plate at her. To appease me, she took a single bite of bacon. "Did you even want to be a detective?"

"That was never the question. I've been solving crimes ever since I was a child. I do it well. I take pride in how well I do it, do you understand?" I nodded quickly. There was a fire in her eyes. "But I was the second child. Milo has always done everything they've ever wanted him to. I can't say it hasn't paid off—he's one of the most powerful men in the world, and he's twenty-four years old. But I . . ." She smiled a secret, pleased sort of smile. "I'm not interested in doing anything I don't want to do."

"And so they sent you to America to cool your heels."

Holmes shrugged. "The *Mail* had a field day with all that. Will you look it up?"

"No," I said, and it was true. I'd always been afraid to shatter my fantasies of her by researching the real thing. "Unless—do you want me to?"

"There's no point. Milo had every word of the scandal scrubbed from the web. And I don't want you to know all about it. Not yet." Her smile faded. "Anyway, it was awful. They printed my middle name."

She was trying to change the subject, so I let her. "Regina? Mildred? Hulga?"

"None of the above. And to answer your original question, I've got to solve this mess myself. I'm sure that if I rang my family up and said, *Look, I'm about to be chucked in jail, will you help,* they would. Because they don't believe I can do it without them, anymore."

"I believe you can," I said. "Though that might just be a necessary delusion. Otherwise, I'm forced to believe that this Sunday, Detective Shepard will say that after a thorough investigation, it's clear that we are the guiltiest guilty murderers in the world."

"That's not what he's going to say." She took another bite. "How did you know I wanted bacon? Did you deduce that as well?"

"I guessed," I said, and watched the smile come back to her face. "Try the pancakes. They're good. My father used to bring me here when I was in grade school."

"I know," she said. "You ordered without looking at your menu."

We sat in companionable silence for a long time. I'd long since finished my own food, so I watched Holmes cut her pancakes into tiny slivers, dropping each one in a bath of maple syrup before putting it in her mouth. It was nice to linger somewhere. I hadn't been comfortable anywhere at Sherringford outside of Holmes's lab. Still, we were closing in on three in the morning by the time she'd finished eating.

"What's our next move?" I asked. "If we've ruled out the new male students, that's at least a start."

"Exotic animal licenses," she said. "Private owners first, then the zoos. You can begin digging in the morning to see who around here keeps deadly snakes. Surely one has to have been stolen. There's no doubt the police have already looked, but then, I'm able to see things they can't. And everyone's falling over themselves to prepare for homecoming tomorrow, so we should be relatively free to move around."

It was good to have a concrete plan. I felt myself relax a little bit further.

Holmes cleared her throat. "Watson," she said in a funny voice, "you weren't going to ask me to the dance, were you?"

"No," I said, maybe a little too quickly. I tried to imagine Holmes under a disco ball, jumping around to some Top 40 song. It was easier to imagine a whale dancing, or Gandhi. Then I imagined some slow song, one that wasn't complete shit, and the lights down low, and what it'd be like to have her in my arms, and I drank down my glass of water in one go. "Did you want me to? Because I had the impression you didn't."

"Watson," she said again. I didn't know if she meant it as a warning or an endearment. But then, I never knew, with her.

This was a subject I didn't want to touch without full body armor and a ten-foot pole. She'd warned me away from it the first time we ever spoke.

"Right," I said, picking up Lena's keys, "we should go before your hall mother wakes from her thousand-year nap."

I held the door open for her. The parking lot was almost empty. I squinted, waiting for my eyes to adjust, and just then, at the far end of the parking lot, a black sedan started up.

It kept its lights off as it peeled out of the parking lot.

"Holmes?" I said, frozen. "Did that just happen because he saw us?"

But she was already running for Lena's car. "Come on," she barked.

I fumbled to unlock the car, to back out of the space, to

maneuver us out of the lot. Holmes was almost cross-eyed with impatience, but to my relief, she didn't say anything. I hadn't exactly done a lot of driving back in London. I mean, I'd driven my mum's car through a parking lot. Once.

But my life dictated that the first night I was on the road, I'd end up in a car chase. It wasn't like the movies, I thought grimly, as we pulled out onto the empty street. The sedan was only a pair of lights in the distance, speeding toward town. It was almost impossible to stay on its tail. The dark was stripped away by a series of streetlights, and ahead of us, the sedan burned through one red light and then another, leading us away from Sherringford and toward the coast.

Holmes had pulled a pair of folding binoculars from God knows where. She leaned forward, peering through the windshield. "The driver's alone. He has a black coat and a black hat down over his ears. Blond hair under it. I can't see his face. There's—there's a case in his front seat, the kind my old dealer used to carry his—"

"Dealer?" I asked tersely.

She shot me a look from behind the binoculars. "Yes."

I thought about the pinched-face man talking to the BBC reporter. *Charlotte Holmes is the head of this messed-up cult and James Watson is, like, her angry little henchman.* "I think I know who it is. But if he's a dealer, why the hell is he running from us?"

"Watson," she said, in a warning tone, as I bore down on him. We cleared seventy miles an hour. Eighty.

"You're not going to tell me to slow down, are you?" I asked, clutching the wheel.

"No." I heard the smile in her voice. "I was going to tell you to go faster."

We blew past dark farmland and stands of trees, past hints of civilization—a bait shop, a crappy motel. My brain was racing as fast as the car. If the police pulled us over and hauled us back to school, we'd be expelled for sneaking out after hours. If the car in front of us braked or even slowed down—

We'd be dead.

My hands tightened on the wheel. I wasn't going to let up, not this close to finally learning something concrete. *Give us a clue,* I thought, *a real one. Let us get just a little bit closer.*

At the next intersection, he jerked into a hard right turn, trying to take us by surprise. Which is when he lost control. Under the bright streetlights, his car spun out down the center of the road, finally beaching itself on a curb outside a shuttered gas station.

I slammed on the brakes, and we fishtailed after him. Holmes's binoculars flew out of her hands and into the windshield with a sharp crack.

We shuddered to a stop two feet from the sedan.

If I didn't know it before this, I knew it now. I wasn't like Charlotte Holmes. I wouldn't ever be. Because while I was still unbuckling my seat belt with shaking fingers, trying to remember how to breathe, she'd freed herself, cleared our car, and was wrenching open the door of the black sedan.

While he was escaping through the passenger side.

"Holmes," I yelled, stumbling outside. *"Holmes!"*

We were in the middle of nowhere. Trees crowded the

two-lane road, dense with underbrush, and I watched her crash after him into the pitch-black wood, shouting for him to stop.

I took off after them.

It was like a nightmare. Branches lashed back at me as I ran, leaving stinging welts across my face, my arms. More than once, my foot caught on a tree root and sent me sprawling, and when I picked myself up, they were that much farther away. I remembered, suddenly, being a kid in a wood like this one, playing a game of ghost tag in the dark. I'd hidden myself in a burned-out tree trunk, and I remembered the hand reaching in to tag me, a white flash in all that darkness. I'd screamed myself hoarse.

Tonight didn't feel all that much different.

Holmes pulled farther and farther ahead of me. She didn't trip. She didn't fall. She moved like a cat through the night.

And then I couldn't see her anymore.

"Come back!" I shouted, finally skidding to a stop. "Give it up!" I could hear him, faintly, still crashing through the bushes. We weren't going to catch him. Besides, what would we do with him if we did? I didn't have any weapons. I didn't know how to threaten someone with anything but my fist.

In the far distance, I heard sirens.

"Holmes!" I shouted again. "Someone called the police!"

"Jesus, Watson," her voice said a little bit ahead of me. "I'm right here."

She'd stopped to catch her breath. In the dim light, she looked as terrible as I felt, scratched and grim, but I saw her eyes gleaming with the thrill of the hunt.

"We have to get back to the car," I said. "Now."

When we got back to the road, the cops were still out of sight, though the sirens were getting louder. We were a long way from anything, out here.

As I started Lena's car, Holmes quickly rummaged through the dealer's sedan, taking pictures with her cell phone, touching everything through the cloth of her shirt. Careful, I knew, not to leave fingerprints.

"Come on," I hissed.

As she climbed back in, she tucked something small into her pocket. "Pull around to the back of the petrol station. Park next to the owner's truck, turn it off, and duck down."

I did as she said, and not a moment too soon. Red-and-blue lights flooded in through the rear window. I held my breath as the cop car circled the gas station, slowing down behind us. A door opened, closed. Footsteps padded up to our back window.

If he shone a flashlight in—if he even glanced in—he'd see us. I thought I might throw up.

And then a sound of something big thunking onto metal, as if he'd dropped his bag onto the trunk of our car.

"I need to get my gloves out," the cop said, his voice muffled. "I know they're in here somewhere."

"Well, hurry up," the other cop replied.

"My hands are ass-cold, man. Give me a second."

"We've got a single-car crash and a drunk wandering somewhere in these woods, Taylor. We better get to it."

Taylor must've found his gloves, because there were

footsteps again. Retreating. The cruiser ambling back out to the road, and the officers getting out to look again at the sedan.

Holmes turned to me with a look of morbid satisfaction. She had been right. We hadn't been found. Crouched below the steering wheel, I rubbed my face with my hands. One way or another, this year was going to kill me.

I could hear the pair of officers talking as they examined the black car, though I couldn't make out their words. An endless hour passed while they dickered about something. Their lights kept flashing; I fought to keep my eyes open. Holmes had folded herself down to the foot of her seat, still alert, somehow. Our wild chase hadn't exactly been subtle, and if someone had called it in to the police, they would know there was another car. What if they came back around again, searching for us? I dug my hands into the seat, trying to steady my nerves.

Then finally, *finally*, we heard it. The unmistakable groan of a tow truck as the sedan was hauled away. The cop car following after.

When I shut my eyes, I could still see the flashing lights pulsing against the darkness.

It was another half hour before Holmes gave the all clear. "We should wait longer," she said, her voice even hoarser than usual, "but the petrol station will be open any minute now, and I don't want us to get caught back here."

Every joint in my body cracked as I climbed back into the driver's seat. I caught a glimpse of my face in the rearview mirror, scored here and there by the sharp fingers of branches.

"Jesus," I said, with feeling. Holmes cracked her neck. "All that for the campus dealer. Some paranoid freak who probably just ran because we were chasing him."

"Not a dealer," she said. "Something worse."

My heart hammered in my chest. "Like what?"

"It doesn't add up. If he's sampling his wares, as it seems from the powder spilled on the driver's side seat, why is he in such terrific shape? Why was he was wearing four-hundred-dollar shoes and running like an Olympic sprinter? If he's a dealer, he's unlike any I've had contact with. I'd be shocked if he was Lucas, the townie who deals on campus."

"Why?"

Holmes's face twisted. "He ran like one of my brother's men."

"Did you see his face?"

She shook her head.

"Then how—no, wait. Your brother has *men*?"

"Several thousand, at last count. It's the most rational explanation. He has a tail or two on me most of the time. I imagine we ran into one, and he panicked."

I let that sink in. "All that was because your brother was trying to check up on you? Your brother. Who's a *good* guy. It doesn't add up."

"It's likely that Milo wanted to assess you. Find out where your loyalties really lie. My friends . . . well, I haven't ever really had one before."

"Oh," I said.

She considered me for a moment, her eyes bloodshot. "I don't want my brother on your tail. You don't deserve that. You haven't done anything wrong."

"And you have," I said softly. *My vices got in the way of my studies.*

We looked at each other. She bit her lip, took a breath—she was on the cusp of saying something—and then she turned away.

"What did you find?" I asked, finally. "What was that thing you put in your pocket?"

She didn't look at me. "Let's get back," she said. I tried not to look at the square outline of the thing in her jacket, and started the car.

We didn't talk. Instead, I turned on the radio as Holmes peered silently out the window. The passing streetlights washed her face blank and bright.

I couldn't tell you what was in her head. I couldn't even guess. But I was beginning to realize I liked that, the not knowing. I could trust her despite it. If she was a place unto herself, I might have been lost, blindfolded, and cursing my bad directions, but I think I saw more of it than anyone else, all the same.

five

I SPENT THE NIGHT OF THE DANCE CATCHING UP ON HOME-work.

After Tom finished telling me how appalled he was at my decision—this took several hours—he got ready. Out of the corner of my eye, I watched him preen in the mirror. He managed to pull off his baby-blue suit from sheer force of will; I think it would have made me look like Buddy Holly's deranged cousin. After asking me one more time if I wanted to go ("Mariella doesn't have a date, and she doesn't even think you're a murderer!"), he finally cleared out to go pick up Lena, leaving me to write a poem for Mr. Wheatley's class. I traded my contacts for my horn-rimmed glasses in an attempt to get myself in the proper mood.

Pen hovering over the page, I wondered, not for the first time, what I was doing.

For one thing, I used to like dances. That is, I liked taking girls to dances. Well. I supposed I just liked *girls*. I liked getting shy looks from them in class, and the way their hair smelled like flowers, and how it felt to walk along the Thames on an overcast afternoon, talking about which teachers they hated and what they were reading and what they'd do after we finished school. But in my head, all those memories had begun to run together. I couldn't tell you if it was me and Kate at the chip shop the night it snowed, or Fiona; if Anna was allergic to strawberries; if Maisie was the one my sister Shelby had adored. Even Rose Milton, the girl of my daydreams, with her softly curling hair and endless string of awful boyfriends . . . I can't say that I would have left my room, that night at Sherringford, even if she'd asked me to be her date.

Even if Holmes had asked me to be her date.

I wondered if her misanthropy was beginning to wear off on me.

I'd left her in Sciences 442, after a long, trying day. The spectacularly bitchy text war she pitched with her brother wasn't even the worst of it. She didn't show me the original message she sent him, but I saw the ones he'd returned. *No, you didn't find my spy,* he insisted. *He's obviously still at large. For instance, I can tell you right now that you're wearing all black, and that Jamie Watson is annoyed with you. I have eyes watching you right now.*

THAT IS NOT SPYING THAT IS SHODDY AMATEUR

DEDUCTION AND IT IS INCORRECT, she replied furiously.

She was, of course, wearing all black.

"Can we do some actual research, please?" I finally asked, trying to keep the irritation out of my voice.

We'd spent an unsuccessful afternoon running down rattlesnake owners in Connecticut. Even after we extended our search to Massachusetts, and then to Rhode Island, we drew a blank. No one was missing their pet snake—at least, no one who would admit it to me, in the guise of a chipper cub reporter researching a book on deadly animals and the owners who, goshdarnit, loved them anyway.

Holmes, still fuming from her conversation with her brother, sat and watched me work.

I scratched the last name off our list. "So maybe we should start calling the zoos—"

"This is unbearably tedious," Holmes snapped. "Do you know, if I had my Yard resources I'd have this case solved. God, in England, even my *name* would be opening us doors. Instead, I'm sitting here while you try to determine down the phone if these small-minded idiots with pet jaguars are *lying* to you, which you're not at all equipped to do." She flung herself down on the love seat, cradling her violin to her chest like a teddy bear.

"Right, then," I said, standing. "What was that thing you pulled out of that car last night? The thing you wouldn't show me?"

She stared at me evenly.

I threw up my hands. "Fine. I'll just go pack my things. You know. For jail."

When she realized I was waiting for her to reply, she picked up her bow and began sawing out a Dvořák concerto so savagely that it quite literally drove me out the door. We had no leads, no real information, and tomorrow we'd have to account for whatever Detective Shepard had dug up to indict us with.

And if I wasn't arrested, I still had homework.

Which left me in my room, with my blank journal page. I tried to push the rest of it from my mind and get to work. Our assignment for Mr. Wheatley's Monday class was to compose a poem that was difficult for us to write. The prompt didn't help me much, since all poems were difficult for me to write. They were like mirrors you held up to a black hole, or surrealist paintings. I liked things that made sense. Stories. Cause and effect. After an hour or two of agonizing cross-outs, I dropped my head down onto my desk.

There was a rap at the door. "Jamie?" I heard Mrs. Dunham say. "I brought you a cup of tea. And some cookies."

I let her in. She looked a bit dotty, as usual, with her crooked glasses and frizzy hair, but the cookies were chocolate chip and still warm.

"You're the only one in the dorm that stayed in tonight," she said, handing me the steaming mug. "I thought I'd come say hi. I know things have been hard for you lately."

"Thanks," I said, embarrassed. "I needed to finish some homework. Writing a poem."

She made a sympathetic noise. "Any luck?"

"Nope." She'd brought me English breakfast, and the steam fogged up my glasses. Right then, I wasn't sure who was more of a cliché, me or her. "Any advice?"

She hummed, thinking. "I've always liked that Galway Kinnell poem. 'Wait, for now. Distrust everything, if you have to. But trust the hours. Haven't they carried you everywhere, up to now?'" She had a fine voice for reciting poetry, deep-timbered and slow. "Doesn't that just make everything better?"

"It does," I said, and wished it were true.

Behind her, in the doorway, a girl appeared.

"Are you ready, Watson?" It was her strange, fantastic voice, even smokier than usual, and Holmes stepped into my room.

I blinked rapidly. She'd done something with her hair. Instead of its usual glossy fall, it was tousled, in unfinished looking ringlets. Her dress looked nothing like I imagined. It looked, in fact, like the night sky. I could see why Lena had coveted it: the cut of it brought my eye to certain places I'd tried to avoid looking at.

"You look very nice," I said. It was true. She also looked disturbingly like a girl. Hailey had been made from plastic and wet dreams, and everyday Holmes was all exact angles, but this . . . whatever this was, it was something else entirely. I wasn't sure if I liked it. From the way she shifted her weight from one heel to the other, it seemed Holmes wasn't sure either. What plot was she brewing?

"Hi, Charlotte," Mrs. Dunham said. "Jamie didn't tell me you were coming."

"Yes, I'm sure he forgot," she said. "We're in a bit of a hurry.

The dance is nearly halfway done."

"We are, and I—ah—" I was wearing my glasses and a pair of Highcombe sweatpants.

With an expressive sigh, Holmes began rifling through my drawers. "Braces," she muttered. "Or as they say here, suspenders. I know you own the ridiculous things. Here." She tossed them to me, and kept looking.

"So you want me to wear them? Or you don't?"

"Oh, do, it's your thing, with the leather jacket and the—yes, here we go, a skinny black tie, and your nice shirt, and the trousers you wore on the fourth day of school but that haven't reappeared since then. Dark wash. There. Socks, and your oxfords." Mrs. Dunham scurried out of the way as Holmes buried me in a pile of my own clothing.

I looked down. "You're trying to make me into a hipster."

"I don't have to try." Holmes tapped her wrist where the watch would go. "Time, Watson."

"You really can't be here while he's changing," Mrs. Dunham said.

Holmes put a hand over her eyes. "I am counting down from one hundred."

"Thanks for the heads-up," I said, sorting through the clothes she'd given me.

"Ninety-nine. Ninety-eight."

We were out the door with three counts to go.

From across the quad, I could see the union all lit up for the dance. Each time the doors opened, I heard a bit of a song I couldn't quite place. On a bench sat a boy and girl holding hands; he was whispering in her ear. Nearby, a cluster of shivering girls admired each other's dresses.

"Are you going to tell me why we're here?" I asked Holmes, holding the door open for her.

She paused on the threshold. "Not yet," she said, and went in.

Sherringford was a small enough school that we could all fit into the union's alumni ballroom. (Apparently, the school went bigger and fancier for prom. Tom was sure that this year's would be on a yacht.) The theme had something to do with Vegas; the first thing I saw as we entered was a string of blackjack tables, manned by real casino dealers in green-and-white livery. Holmes sidled over, only to make an affronted noise when she saw they were playing with Monopoly money. I was more interested in the chocolate fountain that burbled in the corner, crowded by people holding out skewered marshmallows. Otherwise, there were all the usual trappings: a punch table, strobe lights, a DJ. Bored-looking teachers were "chaperoning," which meant they mostly chatted together in pairs. Out on the dance floor, girls swayed in dresses the colors of Christmas ornaments. We'd won the football game earlier, so the mood was victorious. As I took it all in, Cassidy and Ashton from my French class brushed past us. Cassidy looked lovely, and Ashton looked exactly like one of the Thundercats. I'd never seen such a radioactive-looking tan.

What I noticed most of all was how many students had been pulled home. There couldn't have been more than a hundred of us on the dance floor. Still, everyone seemed like they were having fun—no one thinking of the murder, or their safety, or anything except for the ABBA song that had just begun.

It felt, disconcertingly, as though I stood with one foot in a novel and one foot in a shopping mall. I might've belonged here, but Holmes very much didn't. I turned to ask exactly what her plan was, when I caught her mouthing the words to "Dancing Queen."

"Oh my God," I said as she startled. "Oh my *God*. You just wanted to come here to—"

"There are excellent opportunities for observation and deduction here," she said hurriedly. "Look at the specimen pool! Everyone with their guard down, probably a good few drinking—the girl next to you has a flask of peach schnapps in that little bag of hers—and perhaps that dealer is here, somewhere, and—"

"—to dance." I was trying very hard not to laugh. "Would you like to?"

"Yes," she said, and fairly dragged me out onto the floor.

Holmes, for all her strange and myriad skills, proved to be a terrible dancer. But what she lacked in skill she made up for in absolute abandon. Under the kaleidoscope lights, her hair went blue, then red, then blue again, the music so loud that my head throbbed in time, and she flung her arms straight up as the chorus came, throwing her head back to mouth the words. She knew the words to the next one, too, and the song after that, and she sang them all with her eyes shut, shuffling her feet like a grandfather. For a glorious twelve minutes, I orbited her, and when she grabbed my hand and said, "Twirl me," I spun her around as she laughed.

A slow song came on, some treacly number by an English boy band my little sister liked. All around us, people slipped into each other's arms. Across the room, I saw Tom, resplendent in his ridiculous suit, dip Lena while she giggled.

Holmes and I stood there, in the middle of the floor, trying not to look at each other.

I struggled to hide my panic. From the corner of my eye, I could see that Holmes's cheeks were still pinked from dancing.

"Um," I said.

There was a tap on my shoulder. The wispy blond girl that had asked me to the dance stood there, her dress a dramatic red. "Hi," she said shyly. "I thought you weren't allowed to come."

I watched Holmes rapidly catalog my reaction. After a moment, the girl turned to look at her, too.

"Oh my gosh, I'm sorry. I'm in your way." A little line appeared between her eyebrows, and I thought, for a moment, that she was going to cry. I was sure Holmes noted that too. Her brain was like a bear trap: nothing escaped alive.

This had to be a nightmare. I'd look down, and I'd be naked, and the dance floor would become my math classroom, and then I'd wake up.

I didn't.

"We're not— I'm not— I need something to drink," I managed, and darted away like the coward I was.

The thing was, I didn't know if I wanted to slow dance

with her. Holmes. Or maybe I could just imagine it a bit too readily, how it would feel to have my hands on the small of her back, to have her uncertain breath hot on my neck. Her soft laughter as the boy band sang *I wanna kiss you, girl*. How I'd drop my hands to her waist, pull her even closer to me.

But if I squinted, I could see that blond girl in my arms just as easily. Honestly, it wasn't very fair to any of us. I knew myself pretty well; I could be so easily taken in by the now, not thinking much about the after. But with Holmes, all I could think about was the after. Silent drives at dawn, wildfire conversations, sneaking into locked rooms to steal away evidence to our little lab—I wanted those things. I wanted the two of us to be complicated together, to be difficult and engrossing and blindingly brilliant. Sex was a commonplace kind of complicated. And nothing about Charlotte Holmes was commonplace.

Even the way she filled out her dress.

No. I wasn't going to think about that. Our track record proved that we were too volatile to survive that sort of shake-up. Just this morning, she'd chased me from her lab, wielding her violin like a weapon. Tomorrow night we might be sharing a cell. Tonight?

Tonight, I was getting punch.

Mr. Wheatley, my creative writing teacher, was manning the refreshments table with a pretty-ish woman around his age. He looked deathly bored, but brightened a bit when I made it to the front of the line. It wasn't long. Not many of us were too lame to have someone to slow dance with.

"Jamie," Mr. Wheatley said, though I could hardly hear his

voice above the music. "What'll it be?"

"How's the punch?" I asked.

"Horrible." He leaned in to the woman next to him. "This is one of my best students," he said, pointing to me. "Jamie, this is my friend Penelope. She's keeping me company tonight."

I didn't know that Mr. Wheatley had even liked my writing. Everything I'd turned in, my poems especially, came back to me in a mess of green ink. But I'd been working hard to revise them into something better, and it was nice to know my work was paying off.

"It's lovely to meet you." I shook hands with Penelope. She had a sort of standard art teacher look to her, with her curly hair and loose-fitting dress. A nice counterweight for Mr. Wheatley, I thought, who always buttoned his shirts up to his collar.

"She's a writer friend from New Haven," he said. "A poet. She teaches at Yale. Jamie might be someone you'd want in your freshman workshop, in the not-too-distant future."

"Oh, is this the one you were telling me about?" she asked Mr. Wheatley, who went a bit pale. "The murder investigation? Dr. Watson's descendant? So, do you write mysteries too, Jamie?"

"Not really," I lied, as I processed the rest of what she'd said. She'd heard about the police's suspicions about me. "You've been watching the news coverage?"

Mr. Wheatley pulled at his collar.

"Oh, the media's moved on by now," she said. "But Ted's on top of it. He knows details they haven't even released to the press!"

While I was trying to make sense of this, Holmes appeared, proffering a pair of chocolate-covered marshmallows on a fondue stick. An olive branch, I thought. She seemed to have forgiven me my awkwardness, so I took mine with a thank-you smile.

"Hello," she said to the adults. I made a round of introductions.

"Penelope was just saying that Mr. Wheatley's in the know about all that Dobson stuff," I said, a bit obviously. I wished we'd set up hand signals for this kind of situation, or that she was actually telepathic. There was a good chance that she could have deduced my suspicions just by looking at me, but I didn't want to take the chance.

"Oh?" she asked, her face perfectly blank.

"Yes, ah"—Mr. Wheatley cleared his throat—"I should do another walk around the room. Penelope?" She smiled politely at us, her interest already elsewhere, and the two of them glided away.

"Well, you cocked that up rather badly." Holmes drifted back onto the dance floor. So much for an olive branch. I pulled the second marshmallow off the stick and bit into it hatefully.

I WANDERED THE BALLROOM FOR A WHILE, FLOPPING DOWN finally at an empty table. The dance was coming to a close, and the DJ had put together a long set of slow songs to end the night. The floor was thick with couples that would be social-media official by the morning. I was surprised, and then less surprised, to see Cassidy and Ashton swaying together, so close their foreheads touched. Randall, Dobson's roommate, danced the whole set with the little blond freshman. He kept his hands low, grabbing at the fabric of her red dress. In his giant arms, she looked as small and inconsequential as a snack cake.

I felt vaguely sick.

"Okay." Lena plopped down next to me. "Jamie. You look, like, super pathetic."

"Where's Tom?"

"Playing poker." She pursed her lips. "Go talk to her."

"She's dancing with Randall," I said, being difficult on purpose.

"Jesus, come on. Charlotte's sitting outside, alone. You guys are just *sad* without each other. There's like this obvious empty space next to you." It was poetic, for Lena. She stood and offered me a hand.

"Are you asking me to dance?" I asked.

She cocked an eyebrow. I let her haul me to my feet. And she dragged me all the way across the ballroom and out the front door, where she gave me an unceremonious shove into the night air.

"Bye," Lena trilled, and disappeared.

Holmes sat on a bench by the entrance, staring out across the dark quad at a particular copse of trees. It was where I'd faced down Dobson, I realized. It was the last time we'd talked before he died.

She was shivering. I took off my jacket and draped it over her shoulders.

"Thank you," she said, not looking at me.

A little notebook was open on her lap, her fingers splayed across its pages.

"Is that the thing you took from the sedan last night?"

Holmes nodded.

"And you brought it with you?" I sat down next to her cautiously, the way you'd sit next to a bomb. I had questions. I didn't want her to hide the notebook away before I got a chance to ask them.

To my surprise, she didn't. "I didn't think I'd get to it," she said, and went on, her voice strange (was Holmes *nervous*?), "I played a few rounds of poker, but it wasn't sufficiently distracting. It was me and Tom and one of the chaperones—the school nurse. Tom spent the entire game staring at Lena's butt across the room. So obvious. Everyone is so obvious. For example, that school nurse? She wishes she were a doctor. She misses her boyfriend, who has blond hair and an earring, whom she's been with since high school, and who doesn't like her as much as she likes him."

"How could you—"

Holmes smiled a relieved sort of smile. Better to be making deductions, I supposed, then answering my questions. "She couldn't take her eyes off the dance floor. Her eyes teared up when 'I Luv U Girl' came on. Why would anyone react like that? Especially to *that* song? Nostalgia is the only answer. She's attractive enough, but not a knockout—that is to say, not so attractive to have been popular enough in high school that she pines to be back there. And every time a tall blond boy walked by, her eyes trailed after creepily. She's wearing an ugly tennis bracelet on her left wrist that could only have been chosen by a man, but not one who cares enough to pay attention to her actual taste. And she wishes she were a doctor because she tried to diagnose the cause of my shaking hands three separate times over the course of our game."

"Why were your hands shaking?"

"Exhaustion. I haven't slept since that nap you woke me from. She thought it was pneumonia at first, and then she implied it was from mental illness, the cow. And the whole time I had to pretend to *like* her just in case we need to question her again. So I cleaned her out. It was satisfying, even if it was Monopoly money."

I couldn't help it. I laughed. "You're a terrible person."

It derailed her completely.

She stiffened and put her hands up to her mouth. I looked down reflexively at where they'd been, covering the pages of the notebook.

I got it, then. Why she was nervous.

In her lap was a madman's journal. Its pages were thick with handwriting, the same five words scrawled again and again. Each time they were written in a markedly different style, as though a group of schoolboys had each been made to copy down a line from the chalkboard all into the same notebook. Here, the stark black capitals of a military general. Here, the rounded letters of a high school girl. Here, the elegantly dashed scrawl of a Victorian gentleman.

Every line said the same thing.

CHARLOTTE HOLMES IS A MURDERER
CHARLOTTE HOLMES IS A MURDERER
CHARLOTTE HOLMES IS A MURDERER
CHARLOTTE HOLMES IS A MURDERER

I snatched the notebook off her lap. She didn't try to stop me. She watched in aching silence as I turned one page, another, another, every single one striped with those same five words.

As I stared down uncomprehending, the doors burst open with a bang. The dance was over.

"Holmes," I said, my voice almost drowned out by the people streaming by, "what the hell is this?"

"I have the same book at home," she murmured. "Mine is green. It's a forger's notebook. I was made to practice in it until I could imitate nearly anyone's handwriting. Real people's, those of archetypes, characters I'd made up. You're given a phrase to work with, one that represents most of the alphabet. But this . . . this one is terrible." She reached out to touch the words. "It uses many of the same letters."

"It says you're a murderer. A *murderer*. And that dealer had it," I said. "He can't work for your brother. He's something else, some kind of maniac writing crazy things in the dark. He's probably not a dealer at all. He has to be responsible for Dobson—for framing us—God, and we let him get away—"

"How do we know that man wrote this? We don't. He could have picked it up; someone could have given it to him."

"Why did you wait to show me this?" I demanded.

Something snuffed out behind her eyes.

"Holmes—"

"Do you know that I dusted it for prints? I did, it's clean. Do you know that Professor Moriarty carried a little red memoranda book? He did; I've seen it. My father keeps it in a drawer. Did you know you can buy this particular model that I'm holding from seventy-two different online shops, not to mention innumerable bookstores and gift shops? You can. I ran down the license on that black sedan. It doesn't exist. The car itself was stolen from a Brooklyn street corner five years ago. Why does it reappear now? Watson, there's no *pattern* here. I can't figure this out. *I don't know.* Do you know what it's like to not know?"

I did know. She was the one who kept me in the dark.

"You still could have shown it to me," I said, getting to my feet.

Across the quad, a girl let loose a long, laughing scream as a boy grabbed her around the waist and lifted her over his shoulder.

"What if it read 'Jamie Watson is a murderer'? Would you have shown it to me?"

She set her chin, avoiding my eyes. "You wouldn't, for one single moment, worry that I might believe it?"

There was an unnerving quaver in her voice. I stared down at her, at her thin shoulders, the dark lines of her dress under my jacket. Just last night, I was sure I knew her better than anyone else in the world.

What had Charlotte Holmes really done to get herself sent to America?

"You didn't kill Dobson," I said.

"No," she whispered. "I didn't kill Dobson."

"So then—" I swallowed. "Did you—is August Moriarty still alive?"

At that, she stood and fled into the quad.

I picked up the notebook and followed, pushing past the clusters of shrieking girls, the boys surrounding them like black flies in their suits. Some chaperone's voice shouted for us to get back to our dorms, that night check would be in ten minutes, but Holmes plunged through the crowd, not toward Stevenson Hall, but to the sciences building. As if it were her safe house. Her panic room.

The place where she could hide away from me.

I called for her, hoarsely, as she cut through the small stand of trees in the middle of the quad, and though people turned to look, she plowed straight on ahead. I put on a burst of speed and with a lunge caught her by the arm and whirled her around.

She shook my hand off with a snap. "Don't you *ever* touch me without my explicit permission."

"Look," I said, "I am not saying that you killed him. I'm saying that someone wants me to think that. Wants the world to. Why can't you just tell me if he's dead? Is August dead?"

"You thought it," she said. "I watched you think it. That I killed him."

"Why can't you just *tell* me—"

I must've stepped forward; she must have stepped back. I was pressing her farther into the trees as if every step brought me that much closer to the answer. I was so caught up in *finding out* that I missed what was written all over her face. I was so used to her fearlessness that I couldn't recognize her fear.

But she was afraid. Of me.

Dobson had loomed over her too.

Holmes took another step backward, and stumbled over the little freshman girl's body.

SIX

SHE'D BEEN DISCARDED LIKE AN AFTERTHOUGHT THERE IN THE dark grass. Stretched out on her back, her red dress pooled around her like blood.

God, I thought, *it's starting again.*

I was so used to Holmes taking charge that I stopped and waited for her orders. But none came. Her eyes were fixed on a point somewhere over my shoulder, her hands shaking. *Exhaustion,* I remembered her saying, though I thought now that it was something else. Distress, maybe. Uncertainty. Whatever it was, she didn't know how to master it.

It was down to me, then.

Gently, I knelt down beside the freshman. Her eyes were half-closed, as if she were just falling asleep. *She didn't ask for this,* I thought. *None of us did.*

I realized that I didn't even know her name.

Steeling myself for the worst, I pressed my fingers to her throat. There. A pulse.

"She's still alive," I said, leaning down to hear the girl's breath. It came in agonized rasps. "But she's having trouble breathing. We need to get help."

Holmes nodded, but made no sign of moving.

"Hey," I said to her, gently. "I need to keep an eye on her. Can you call an ambulance?"

She shut her eyes for a moment, collecting herself. Too long a moment. Beneath me, a shudder ripped through the girl's body.

I had to get someone else's help, then. "Hey!" I shouted to some girls cutting through the quad on their way back to the dorms. "There's been an accident! Someone's hurt! Call 911!"

They ran over. One girl pulled her phone out of her purse and dialed. The other saw who I was kneeling next to and began to scream.

"Elizabeth," she sobbed. She put herself between me and the girl on the ground as if to protect her. "That's my roommate! Elizabeth! What did you *do* to her?"

"I didn't do anything," I said, shocked. I hadn't realized how this would look: the darkness, the body, the pair of us. "I found her like this. She was dancing with Randall and then . . . we found her here. Charlotte and I. We were . . . we were just walking."

We were beginning to draw a crowd. Behind me, I heard

murmurs. Angry ones. The sound of feet running toward us.

Elizabeth's roommate turned her tear-streaked face to me. "Murderer," she snarled. "*Murderers.*"

Behind us, the murmurs built to an angry roar.

I think it was that word that did it. How it'd been leveled at Holmes—and at me—in the weeks after Lee Dobson had died. How it was written down thousands of times in the notebook I had in my pocket, each stroke of the pen damningly precise. How, somewhere deep down, I knew there was the possibility that it was true. That Holmes had been sent here for killing a Moriarty. And she had read my thoughts from a glance.

No matter what the reason, Holmes reacted as if she'd been hit with an electrical shock.

She knelt down next to Elizabeth. "You need to go get an adult," she said to the roommate, who stiffened. "Look, believe what you will about my motives, but either way, this crowd will make sure I don't hurt your friend. Okay? So go get help and let me work. I've been trained for this kind of situation."

"CPR?" the girl asked unsteadily.

Holmes's smile was mirthless. "Something like that."

"What do you need me to do?" I asked.

"I need you to hold her mouth open." She tilted Elizabeth's head back. "Keep her steady. Do you see it there, in her throat?"

The skin of Elizabeth's neck was raised and ridged, the unmistakable sign of an object lodged there. With gentle hands, I pulled her chin down until her lips fell apart.

This girl had asked me to the dance. Maybe she'd even wanted something like this: the pads of my fingers against her lips, the shallow breathing, the two of us hitched up in the dark. My stomach roiled. All this—all this was so completely wrong.

"Her body's in shock," Holmes said calmly, reaching down into the hollow of Elizabeth's throat with pincer-like fingers. I shut my eyes against it. The girl thrashed and gurgled under my hands.

"Good girl," Holmes murmured, "good girl," and when I opened my eyes again, she was holding a gleaming blue diamond up against the moonlight.

It gleamed because it was covered in Elizabeth's blood.

I swallowed down bile. Behind me, someone threw up into the grass.

"It's 'The Adventure of the Blue Carbuncle,'" Holmes murmured.

"I know," I said as Elizabeth took a jerking breath.

"You." Holmes tossed the diamond to a boy in the crowd. "Take this thing. It's plastic, so don't bother stealing it, but I'm sure the police will want to see it anyway, and as you're all so keen to cast suspicion on me I'd rather not be held responsible for its safekeeping. Where's Randall? You. Fetch him. Can't you see that this girl has been manhandled by a rugby player? Look at those footprints. Look at her *dress*. I saw them dancing. *Find him*. I need to know if this was consensual. The sex, you idiot, not the paste diamond stuffed down her craw—yes, of course she's had sex, or at minimum a very athletic snog. Look at the marks on the ground, are you blind? And where on earth are the chaperones? What about that bloody nurse?"

"Here," a harried voice said. It was the first time I'd seen Nurse Bryony outside the infirmary; her party dress fit her so tightly that it looked painted on. She smiled reassuringly at me, but I looked away. I didn't deserve reassurances.

"Tend to her, will you?" Holmes told the nurse, straightening. "Where *is* that ambulance?" She shaded her eyes against the nonexistent light.

"Holmes."

"Not now, Watson." She plucked another boy's phone out of his hands, dialing 911 as he sputtered at her in protest. "You talk, then," she said to him, handing it back. "Be of some use."

"Holmes," I said, more urgently.

I'd caught a glimpse, at the very edge of the crowd, of the drug dealer's thick blond hair.

She followed my gaze and made a startled noise. "I didn't think we'd see him again."

"Well." I got to my feet. "What now?"

"Don't look at him directly." But it was too late. As she spoke, he turned in a way he must've thought unobtrusive, beginning to melt into the darkness.

"We're going to have to chase him again," I said. God, my legs hurt at the thought.

That quicksilver smile. "On your marks."

The dealer threw a glance behind him, and took off at a run.

We bolted through the crowd. Some ducked out of our way; others tried to pull us back, thinking we were fleeing the crime scene. We were, but not in the way they thought. There:

he was pelting across the flat green expanse, headed straight for Stevenson Hall. Lots of the underclassmen girls lived there—Holmes did, and Elizabeth did too, and I couldn't think of any reason why he'd be heading there except to do more damage. Guilty people ran. He had to be guilty. I pushed myself to run harder, but I was already topped out. Sirens wailed—the soundtrack of my ridiculous life—and Holmes's dress ahead of me caught the red-and-blue light, strangely beautiful. She was faster than me, smaller, leaner. She was just beginning to gain on him when three cruisers and an ambulance pulled off the road and onto the grassy quad beside us.

"Some help here," Holmes yelled as a group of policemen clambered out. The EMTs were already unloading a stretcher from the ambulance.

"Is that Charlotte Holmes?" It sounded like Detective Shepard. I spared a look and spotted a lone man not in uniform. "Stop! What are you doing? James! Jamie Watson!"

Neither of us slowed down in the slightest. So Shepard took off after us.

The policemen gave confused chase behind him, cursing and breathing heavily. Up ahead, the dealer rounded the corner of Stevenson Hall and disappeared from view.

"The access tunnels," Holmes called. "There's an entrance, there—it's that half door; it has a key code—"

I pushed the building's tangled ivy out of the way as she tapped out the code.

"You have about two and a half seconds," I said, "before the police brutality begins."

She gave me a feral look. "I only needed one."

The lock clicked open. She jerked me inside. The door slammed shut behind us.

WHEN HOLMES HAD FIRST MENTIONED THE SCHOOL'S TUNnel system to me, I'd had trouble wrapping my head around it. A network of passages below campus, connecting Sherringford's buildings underground? I'd done some digging to find out more.

By digging, I mean that I'd turned around in my desk chair and asked Tom, my personal font of useless information, what the deal was.

Legend has it the tunnels had been built at the end of the nineteenth century, back when Sherringford was still a convent school. When the grounds were under a few feet of snow, the nuns used these heated passages to get from their quarters to prayers at dawn and vespers. These days, Tom said, the tunnels were used by the maintenance workers who took care of our dorms. There were boilers down there and supply closets. Every entrance to the tunnels was only accessible via key code, and those codes changed every month. I'd told Tom about how disappointed I was that the tunnels weren't used as Cold War bomb shelters or by moonshine smugglers or something equally interesting, and he'd grinned at me. Even better, he'd said. The codes changed so often because students were always bribing janitors for them—the access tunnels were one of the only private places to hook up on campus.

Holmes, I knew, used the tunnels to practice her fencing.

"They're the only space long enough and private enough at this school," she'd said, bright spots of color on her cheeks, "and if you continue to snicker at me, I swear that I will tell your father you want a weekly lunch date with him to talk about your *feelings*."

Tonight, the tunnel in front of us was empty. Our man was nowhere in sight. As I crept down the hall behind her, the lights above us flickered. Holmes's shoes clicked against the floor, sounding like an insect tapping its legs together. The hair on the back of my neck stood up.

"He'll have holed up here somewhere," she said, a breath of sound.

"Should we start trying doors?"

She shook her head, putting up a finger. There were footsteps ahead of us, creeping ones. We were shifting gears from a chase to a slow, deliberate stalk, and I followed her as she slunk along, her eyes fixed on the ground.

She was following a trail he'd left on the linoleum floor, one I couldn't make out through the dirt tracked in by that week's workmen, the ragged lines from carts and trolleys. What was she tracing, I wondered, straining my eyes to see—and then I remembered. *Why was he wearing four-hundred-dollar shoes?* she'd asked the other night. Looking again, I saw the narrow tread of a dress shoe on the floor.

Silently, we followed his trail through the labyrinthine halls. The shouting of the police outside became a dull echo. Soon, I knew, they'd get ahold of the key code, and they'd be hard on our tail. Holmes knew it too. She roved the halls like a hunting dog. We were under the quad, now. The concrete walls were spotted with damp, and there was a smell in the air I knew from rugby practices. Mud. Wet earth. My mind wandered back to Highcombe School and its rugby pitch, to Rose Milton's shining hair in the stands, her hands clasped together, my cleats tearing into the grass, and the sense that just this once, I was doing what everyone wanted me to do and doing it *well*—

Holmes flung a hand across my chest. "There," she mouthed.

The door at the end of the hall, where the footprints ended.

Behind us, the unmistakable sound of a steel door slamming shut. The detective's voice bellowing Holmes's name.

"After you," she said, with the smile of a hunter closing in on its prey.

She couldn't have known what was behind that door.

She couldn't have.

As I walked inside, Holmes followed on my heels. She let the door shut behind her, cutting off what little light we had. I groped for a switch, a cord, anything to help me see better, but all I found were shelves, rows of shelves, and the cool cinder block of the back wall. I pulled out my phone and clicked it on, using its dim light to sweep the room.

We were alone.

Somehow I'd known from the moment I stepped into the room that our man wasn't going to be in here. Maybe I'd been unconsciously listening through the door for his breath, for some movement; maybe I knew enough about the way our luck worked. Maybe, deep down, I was relieved to not have to confront him. Whatever the case, it was only Holmes and me in there, and I was unsurprised to find us that way. Unsurprised, but not relieved. Not exactly.

We were alone in the killer's lair.

Photographs of Dobson, before and after the fight we'd had—someone had taken a shot of him across the quad with one of those paparazzi cameras, so sharp that you could see the bruises I'd given him. A map of the tunnel system, blueprints for Michener Hall and Stevenson Hall. Dobson's class schedule with classes highlighted and others crossed off, little notations written in beside them in Holmes's crabbed, angry handwriting, and—Jesus Christ—pictures of Elizabeth laid out across the floor, a thick file with her name on it. I stooped to pick it up but stopped; Holmes had trained me too well to leave stray prints.

"Holmes," I said. "That's your handwriting."

"I know." Through the cloth of her dress, she lifted a T-shirt from the pile of clothes on the bare mattress on the floor. I realized that I recognized it; she recognized it too.

"That's yours," I said.

She nodded. "It's a duplicate of one I own."

"Is this your . . . your . . ."

"My lair?" She still held the shirt between her pinched fingers. "Someone certainly wants you to think so, don't they."

I had questions for her. Questions I didn't really want an

answer to. Questions I'd have to ask later, because as we stood there, the police were kicking down doors all up and down the hall. In a minute, they'd find us.

All the while, they were shouting Holmes's name.

We were hauled down to the station, with Sherringford's explicit blessing.

"So much for their protecting minors. But I imagine finding a television-styled murder den changes things," Holmes said next to me in the back of the police cruiser. She wore her handcuffs with a kind of elegant disdain, bringing both hands up to tuck her hair behind her ear. "We're going to be fine, Watson. Do you trust me?"

I didn't say anything. I didn't want to lie.

Detective Shepard cleared his throat in the front seat. "I usually don't warn people about this after I've read them their rights, but you're kids, so. You two don't want to say anything that incriminates you." A pause. "Not like either of you listen to me."

When we got to the station, Shepard separated us. I was put into a poorly lit interrogation room, with a mirror that I knew from the movies was actually one-way glass. There was a chair, a glass of water, and a piece of paper and pencil. For my confession, I imagined.

Really, it was all just like the movies, except in the movies, they don't show you the waiting. And there was so much waiting. For almost two hours, I sat in my desperately uncomfortable chair, jerking in and out of sleep, waiting for someone to come in and ask me to talk about what happened.

What would I even tell them? Well, officer. First, this asshole died after I punched him, but not *because* I punched him. He was poisoned, and also a snake got him. A snake that apparently appeared from thin air, because no one on the eastern seaboard is missing a snake. Then a drug dealer followed us to the diner and ran from us in the woods. I went to a dance, and thought about kissing my best friend, but didn't, and another girl wanted me to dance with her and maybe kiss her instead, but someone shoved a plastic diamond down her throat, so nobody kissed anyone, except maybe her and Randall. In a room underneath the school, I found a whole bunch of evidence that my best friend, who I didn't kiss, is a psycho killer. And now I guess you're questioning me about all these crazy crimes that I haven't committed, but someone wants you to think I've committed, and they've done such a good job of it that I almost believe I committed them too.

That's good, I thought blearily, and started writing it down.

Above my head, a speaker crackled to life. I blinked up at the pair holstered high up in the corner. I'd missed them. I couldn't now: they were speaking with Holmes's voice.

"All last year, I bought from a senior named Aaron Davis," she was saying.

"Hey!" I yelled. "There's something wrong with your sound system!"

No reply. Nothing but Holmes's voice droning on.

"He delivered in packages to my dorm, and I'd put the money in his mailbox. It was all very straightforward like that, when it was pills. But last May, I wanted something harder, and he took me down to that room to—to use in front of him. To make sure I wasn't just buying to rat him out."

Shepard's voice, then. "So that dealer, the one you took it on yourself to chase—"

"I've never even seen him before. In fact, I still haven't even seen his face clearly, and for that reason alone, I thought he worked for—" I heard her about to say *Milo*, or *my brother*, or maybe even *Moriarty*. "I don't know. I don't know what I thought." *Not your best save,* I thought with a wince, and then remembered I wasn't on her side. Not tonight.

"We found your prints there, Charlotte."

"Aaron used to *deal* out of that room. Why aren't you listening to me? If you found my prints there, anywhere, I'm sure it was on the inside of the door or on the wall, not actually on any of the fake-serial-killer things pinned to it, and that they're at least several months old."

"So is that why you were down there? Trying to destroy the things you forgot to touch with your gloves on? Innocent people usually don't give as many excuses as you do."

"You're asking why you found me in the room I went directly to, knowing you were following me—the room that only the most wretched Sherringford students have reason to know about. The room that I decided to style like a network television art director. So that I could destroy *paper records* that I left there in my own handwriting." She snorted. "I won't insult your intelligence, Detective Shepard, by reminding you who my family is. Not to trade on my blood, but on my training. I am not an idiot. And I didn't kill Lee Dobson, or attack Elizabeth Hartwell. I'm sure that when she's fit to speak, she will tell you exactly that."

"She's suffered a traumatic brain injury," Shepard said gravely. "We don't know yet how much she remembers. But with all your *training*, I'm sure you knew that would be the result when you clobbered her with that tree branch."

"Fine. Call my parents. Call Scotland Yard. I have contacts there. They'll tell you that I *help* people."

"You should have called us, Charlotte." The sound of a chair scraping back. And then a final blow. "By the way, what was Jamie Watson's part in all this? Your accomplice? He's clearly not the brains of the operation."

"Hey!" I yelled again. I did *not* want to hear this. "Hey! Anybody!"

"Don't cater to my vanity," she snapped. "You'll find I do that well enough on my own."

"Your accomplice," he said again, louder, "until you needed a fall guy. Someone to stay and swing for all of this when your rich mommy and daddy smuggle you out of the country on a private plane."

At that moment, I was in the awful position of thinking something that I desperately didn't want to believe.

Thought: The police set this up, this weird, "accidental" eavesdropping, so that when Holmes admits she's been using me all this time, I'll flip out and confess to her doing everything. I'd seen *Law & Order*. I knew how this worked, how they divided suspects, got them to tell on each other. But they

131

were wrong. There was nothing to tell.

Except.

What if the police were right?

What if she actually did kill Lee fucking Dobson and decided, for a lark, to drag me along, pretending to solve the crime that she committed? What if Holmes was so unnerved by someone calling her a murderer because she was, in fact, a murderer? What if, in the time between stomping away from me and Mr. Wheatley at the punch table and when I found her on the bench, she clobbered Elizabeth Hartwell on the head and stuffed that plastic jewel down her throat? What if she really did elaborately off Dobson in an act of cold-blooded revenge? What if—oh God—what if our friendship was just a sick footnote in her sick reenactment of these stories? Holmes and Watson, together again, playing out "The Blue Carbuncle" on the dark Sherringford quad. Only, instead of hiding the stolen gem in a goose's craw, we stuffed it down a girl's throat to make her choke to death.

"Jamie Watson," Holmes said evenly, "is far smarter than you think. He isn't my accomplice. He's no one's accomplice. And he isn't guilty of anything."

He isn't, she said. Not the both of us.

I didn't feel any better. Not even when the door swung open to let in my haggard father, who took one look at my face and said, "Right, we're going home."

ON THE WAY OUT, MY FATHER TOLD ME THAT NEITHER Holmes nor I were being charged with a crime. The police didn't have enough evidence to hold us; everything they had right now was circumstantial, so the best they could do was question us. "It's good they didn't get around to you," he said, then looked at me hard and told me, like he was imparting great wisdom, to always remember to request a lawyer.

Usually, I hated that my father didn't act like a father. Most days, I would've traded him and his enthusiasms for the most boring authority figure on the block, but tonight, I was just happy to be spared a lecture and tears.

My father is picking me up from the police station in the middle of the night, I thought, *and he mostly just seems kind of excited.*

"I'll pull around the car," he said at the entrance. "Once we get home, you'll need to sleep. I could only get you a day's reprieve. They want you back for more questioning after dinner. Shepard's keeping his Sunday-night appointment."

I swayed a little on my feet, not thinking much of anything. Not until I felt her creep up behind me on cat feet. I refused to turn around.

When my father pulled the car up, Holmes opened the passenger door and climbed in without a word. Fuming, I got into the backseat, pushing aside a small avalanche of toys and snack wrappers that belonged, no doubt, to the half brothers I'd never met. I tried to fight the feeling that I was a guest star in my own life.

As we drove, my father kept up a steady stream of chatter that Holmes replied to in monosyllables. I couldn't manage any response at all. My brain had roared back to furious, nervous life. When he stopped at a Shell station outside town, I tipped my head against the cold window and tried to steady my breathing. In a few hours, I'd be arrested for a crime I hadn't committed. I wished I'd never come back to America. That I *had* killed Dobson, just so I'd have something to confess to. A way to get this all to end. I thought again about my pathetic fantasy, the two of us on that runaway train. Maybe this was the sensation of it crashing.

Without a word, Holmes reached back, fumbling for my hand, and when she found it, she grasped it firmly in hers. I thought about taking it back. I reminded myself that I was maybe holding the hand of a killer, but I decided I was too tired to care. The three of us drove the rest of the way in silence.

Really I'd been so distracted by what had happened at the station that I'd forgotten to dread the rest of it. Then it came into sight, my childhood house in the country, and I remembered all at once learning to ride a bike down this street, my father holding on to the seat even after I told him he could let go. He did, finally, with a great laugh like a shout, and I went a full three feet before I hit a bump and flew head over handlebars.

Today, despite the cold weather, there was a bike fallen on its side in the yard. It wasn't mine. I watched my father notice it, how his eyes flickered to me in the backseat. I noted the worry there, his own dose of dread. It was the first time I ever felt sorry for my father.

"Abbie and the boys are at her mother's for the weekend," he said with false cheer as we pulled into the garage. "So we'll have the place to ourselves. I made a steak pie that I'll put in the oven for dinner. But right now, you two need to get some rest."

Holmes stumbled into the house and over to the living room couch. Without taking off her shoes, without saying a word to either of us, she stretched out in her homecoming dress and went immediately to sleep.

"There's a guest room," my father said as I folded myself up into the armchair beside her.

"I know," I said to him. "I used to live here."

He didn't have anything to say to that.

The truth was that, for many varied, contradictory reasons, I didn't want Holmes out of my sight. Even as I fell into a dreamless sleep, I kept an ear open. Listening in case she ran, and left me there alone.

WHEN I WOKE, IT WAS DARK AGAIN, THAT SORT OF FALL-evening gloom. The clock on the wall said 6:07. I'd slept the whole day, and from the state of the couch, so had Holmes.

There was a rustling in the kitchen. Inside, it was as well lit as I remembered, and the table and chairs were the same. But the dark cabinets had been given a coat of white, the walls painted a farmhouse blue. A ceramic rooster presided over the sink. Abigail's additions, I was sure. When my father offered, I turned down a tour of the rest of the house.

Holmes had hoisted herself up onto one of the stools at the counter, and she sat there, swinging her legs while her eyes roved around the room. I watched her put together the story of this house, of my childhood, the way a soldier assembles a gun in the dark. At least one of us knew how to behave normally—though for the record, this may have been the first time it was her, and not me.

"Hi," I said to her.

"Hi," she said back. "Did you sleep well?"

"I slept fine."

We avoided each other's eyes.

"Well," my father said as the oven heated up. "Let's get down to it. That Shepard fellow arrives in"—he consulted his watch—"an hour. What have you got for him? To clear yourselves?"

"Nothing," Holmes said. "Well. The fact that we didn't kill anyone, for starters."

"You haven't killed anyone," I repeated. It was the first time she'd admitted it.

She lifted an eyebrow. "We haven't attacked a single person at this school. We've never killed anyone."

She was choosing her words carefully, I could tell.

"And that—that serial killer den wasn't yours."

"That serial killer den wasn't mine." Unexpectedly, she grinned at me. "It wasn't yours, was it? It's a bit rude not to share."

I wrinkled my nose at her, and she hit me in the arm. God help me. I couldn't stay mad at her, even if she did turn out to be a cold-blooded killer. I was in way, way too deep.

"Right," my father said, confused. "I had sort of thought all of that was a given. Do you have any actual proof that clears you?"

"Enough witnesses to prove that we weren't the people who attacked Elizabeth. Elizabeth herself, when she wakes up. But that's moot, anyway. In about an hour and fifteen minutes, I'll have the leverage we need to clear our names and get Shepard to involve us in his investigation."

I didn't know anything about this. "What?"

She tucked a lock of hair behind her ear, and said nothing. Across from us, I swear my father's eyes were sparkling.

I stared at him. "Shouldn't you be, you know, worried?"

But he was already pulling a bottle of champagne from the refrigerator. "A toast is in order, I think. A little glass couldn't hurt at this point."

The cork popped, and steam fizzed out. Holmes and I exchanged a startled glance. She hadn't expected him to believe her. Very few people had the ability to surprise her, but apparently my father was one of them. I didn't care. I had a glass of champagne, possibly my last as a free man. I slurped the foam off the top of my glass.

Holmes, being Holmes, looked at my father and decided to investigate. "Oh, this is lovely, thanks much. But tell us why we're celebrating! You can't trust me *that* much. There has to be something more to it." She leaned on one hand, drawing on the vast reserves of charm she kept hidden away for just this purpose. "That pie smells tremendous," she added. "Can't think of the last time I had good comfort food."

If my father noticed the show—and really, how couldn't he?—he didn't mind it. "It's Jamie's grandmother's recipe. I haven't had a chance to make it in a long time." He beamed.

"I'm happy this worked out for you two. I'd worried it wouldn't."

"What worked out?" Wherever this was headed, I was sure it was a bad, bad place. "If you're about to tell me you killed off Dobson to get me some detective practice, I swear to God—"

With a wave, he cut me off. "Jamie, don't be so melodramatic. Of course not."

"Of course not," Holmes said, under her breath. The machinery in her head was whirring to life. "It began before that."

"Yes," my father said, delighted. "Go on."

She looked me over the way you might do a horse. I shifted uncomfortably in my seat. "And sport. It has to do with rugby."

"Excellent." He lifted his glass to her. "I'm sorry, Jamie, but I still can't believe you bought it. A rugby scholarship? Yes, you're a perfectly adequate player, no doubt, and certainly good enough for their team, but you have to admit that the idea was a bit far-fetched." He took a meditative sip. "No, it was all something that we plotted up in our cups, last summer."

"We?"

"You and my uncle," Holmes said to my father, bypassing me entirely.

"What?" I said faintly. I was still trying to process the fact that I wasn't, in fact, a genius rugger, and that no one had told our poor captain. "Wait. You're going to solve *this* mystery. Not the Dobson-Elizabeth-drug dealer mystery. This one. And you're going to solve it now." I stifled a semi-hysterical laugh. "When I didn't even know there was a mystery. God, what could I possibly have done in a past life to get stuck with someone like you?"

"Go on," my father was saying happily. It was good that one of us was enjoying himself. "Tell me how you know."

She ticked the deductions off on her fingers. "You were born in Edinburgh like the rest of your family, but you have an Oxbridge spin on your words. When you opened your cupboard to fetch these flutes, I saw a mug, top shelf, with the Balliol College blazon on. Oxford, then."

My father spread his hands, waiting for her to continue.

"You hugged me with a surprising amount of familiarity when we met, but you didn't hug your son. Even with your difficult relationship"—my father's smile faltered for a moment—"if you were so prone to hugs, you would have made an attempt on him anyway. No, you felt you knew me. You must have heard of me, then, and not in the papers—or there would have been polite pity and no hug—but from someone who spoke highly of me, and with warmth. The first rules out my parents; the second, most of my relatives. My brother, Milo, doesn't believe in friends, and anyway, you'd have no reason to chat to a pudgy, secretive computer genius who leaves his Berlin flat only under extreme duress. My aunt Araminta is nice enough, which means she's glacial by society's standards. Cousin Margaret is twelve, and Great-Aunt Agatha is dead, and that's the *tour de monde* of the effusive members of my family.

"Excepting, of course, my dear old uncle Leander, Balliol College '89, who gave me my violin, and is the first Holmes in known memory to host a party of his own free will. Of course you're friends." She peered at him for a second. "Oh. And flatmates. For at least a year, no more than three."

I poured another glass of champagne and drank it straight down.

My father, smartly, put the bottle away. "You're as clever as he is, Charlotte, and a great deal quicker. Though Leander, bless him, is lazy enough to solve a crime and forget to tell his client for months.

"He came to your seventh birthday party," my father told me. "Don't you remember?" My seventh birthday party had been held at one of those roadside amusement parks with a go-kart track and a half-dozen arcade games. "He brought you a rabbit as a gift. Giant thing. Big floppy ears. Your mother, being your mother, sent it immediately to a nice home in the country."

"Harold," I said, piecing it together. That had been the rabbit's name. I had an impression of a towering man with slicked-back hair and a lazy smile.

"I roomed with him back before I met your mother," he said. "Bachelor days, before I was lured away to London. Leander had set up as a private detective, and I was . . . well, I was very bored. We were introduced at an alumni event at a pub; I'm sure you've noticed how keen everyone is to introduce a Holmes to a Watson. He was chatting up the bartender. I think he brought him home in the end. Could turn on the charm, Leander, when the situation called for it." He raised an eyebrow at Holmes, who didn't blush but looked like she might've liked to.

"And you're still friends?" I asked.

"Yes, of course," my father said. "The two of us, we're the best kind of disaster. Apples and oranges. Well, more like apples and machetes." He studied my face for a moment. "I thought you could use a little shaking up, Jamie. That school in London was too expensive for what a bloody toff factory it was, and even with what I could contribute, we couldn't afford to keep you there. I told Leander about my frustrations, and he mentioned that Charlotte here had just been deposited, friendless and alone, only an hour from my house. Did you really think this was a coincidence—the two of you winding up here, in America, at the same boarding school?"

I was fed up with all these ridiculous bombshells and rhetorical questions. "Yes," I said pointedly. "Also, your pie smells like it's burning."

Holmes sniffed the air. "It smells quite good, actually," she said, and took it out to cool. I scowled at her. She made a helpless gesture.

"The tuition . . . well, Leander offered to pay it. When I said no, he told me that otherwise he'd just buy another Stradivarius. I tried telling him that he'd have to put an entire town through Sherringford to come close to the price of a Strad, but he held firm. I gave in. And so Leander arranged some sleight-of-hand with the board of trustees and offered you a 'scholarship.' You didn't wonder why you didn't lose your scholarship when you were suspended from the rugby team?" He grinned. "That's why. The whole thing was quite fun. I think he enjoyed it immensely."

"Yes," I said, thinking of all my violent resentment at being sent away, of having to leave London, my friends, my kid sister. "Fun."

"Well then." My father clapped his hands together. "You've met! You're friends! You've found yourselves a murder! I couldn't have asked for more. Come, let's eat before the detective arrives."

Holmes's phone buzzed. "I have to take this, excuse me." She stepped out the back door, and I watched her through the glass as she paced in her dress, speaking rapidly to someone.

"Who could possibly be calling her?" I wondered aloud. "It must be her brother."

My father kept slicing the pie. "I hope you're not terribly mad at me."

"I'm not," I said. "I'm furious."

"It seemed to have worked out rather well, though, you have to give me that." He handed me a heaping plate. I wished, badly, that I wasn't starving.

"*Well*? This worked out well?" I choked. "God, I don't have to give you anything."

"Jamie. Please don't be like this." He was avoiding my eyes. "Aren't you happy you met Charlotte? She's lovely, isn't she?"

"Will you please stop side-stepping the point? This isn't about Holmes, it's about the strings you pulled to get me here. God, you don't even know me! I hadn't seen you for years! How can you not understand that being bored isn't an excuse to reach in and fuck with my life for fun?"

"Language," my father warned.

"You don't get to do that." I heard myself getting loud. "You don't get to deflect every response you don't like. I'm in a horrible mess that you, for whatever reason, have decided to find *charming.*"

With shaking hands, he set down the knife. I was shocked to see his eyes glossed in tears. "You're right, Jamie. I don't know you anymore. God help me for wanting that to change."

The doorbell rang.

"He's early," my father said, and hurriedly plated some pie for Holmes. "I'll get it."

When he left the room, I let out a ragged breath I hadn't known I was holding.

Holmes slipped back into the house. "Well, that looked rather brutal," she said, eyeing me. It was an observation, not an attempt at sympathy, and so I didn't have to respond to it.

"Sit," I said instead, pulling out a stool. "Who called you?"

My father walked in, Detective Shepard behind him. Holmes read something in their faces that I didn't, because her posture, always impeccable, went ramrod-straight.

"Jamie. Charlotte." I noticed that Shepard had dark circles under his eyes. "I'd like to get you back down to the station. Now."

"What are you charging us with?" I asked him.

"I'd like to get you back down to the station," he repeated, a patented non-answer.

"You'll need to wait for my lawyer," Holmes said coolly.

"He'll be representing both of us, but as his office is in New York, it could be several hours until he arrives. Do you mind if I phone him?"

The detective nodded, and she placed the call right there.

I felt a rush of relief. The worst possible outcome was happening. I could finally, finally stop dreading it.

My father, being my father, chose that moment to begin to worry.

"Do you mind if they eat in the meantime?" he asked, a plea in his voice. "I don't know how long they'll be down at— at the station, and dinner's on the table. You're welcome to join us, of course."

Shepard hesitated. He took in Holmes's too-thin frame, the steaming plate in front of me, and I watched him give in. "Fine. They can eat, since we'll have to wait for their lawyer anyway. But be quick about it." He set his bag down, and took a seat.

I made an effort with the pie, though I pushed it aside after a few bites. Shepard's scrutiny made me too uncomfortable to eat. For her part, Holmes decided to develop an appetite. Slowly, fastidiously, she picked the carrots from the crust one by one. Once removed, she sliced them into quarters and then halved them again. After spearing each piece with her fork, she dipped it into the mashed potato and transferred it to her mouth. She chewed each morsel seventeen times. And then she repeated the process. Across the table, my father watched her, one hand gripping the table hard.

I wondered if he was still enjoying himself.

Silence reigned. After twenty minutes, Holmes hadn't even

gotten to the steak, and the detective began to shift unhappily in his chair. I took the chance to catalog him, to try to draw some Holmesian deductions. He was in his late thirties, I decided. Clean-shaven, but in rumpled clothes. He clearly hadn't gotten home to change or shower since interrogating Holmes last night. There was a wedding band on his left hand. I couldn't tell if he had kids of his own, but his decision to let us eat dinner made me think he did. What I couldn't account for was the reluctance that radiated off him, the way he projected unease in his posture, in his frown, his furrowed brow. Like my father, he'd lost his eagerness.

"I understand why you did it. To Dobson," he said quietly, watching Holmes eat. She didn't look up. "Every account I get says that kid was a bastard, and he was fixated on you. But what I don't get is why you didn't just tell the school about his abuse and get it to stop. And I don't get why the two of you would attack Elizabeth Hartwell. Bryony Downs, the Sherringford nurse, told me that you, Charlotte, had been behaving erratically at the dance all night—"

"Way to make friends," I said to her.

"—and then the two of you chase some other guy down into these underground tunnels I've never even *heard* of, where we find you in a room straight out of a TV procedural, just *waiting* for us. I found these in there." He dug a pair of trousers and a black shirt out of the bag, and shook them out for her inspection. "Yours?"

The clothes from the mattress.

She looked up uninterestedly. "Yes," she said. "Though if

you've examined them, you'll see that they've never been worn."

Shepard nodded. She wasn't telling him anything he didn't know. "I examined them, Charlotte. I made a lot of calls this morning. One of those was to your mother."

My father leaned forward. "And?"

Shepard rubbed at his temple, thinking, and then he pulled a binder out of his bag, laying it open on the table. "Jamie, do you mind pointing this purported drug dealer out to me?"

I pushed my plate away. The twelve men in front of me were uniformly blond and ugly. They ranged in age from a few years older than me to forty. One sported an eyebrow scar. Another smiled, missing teeth. The third one from the top looked the closest to what I'd remembered. I racked my memory.

"Him," I said, sounding slightly more confident than I felt.

"That man turned himself in this morning," he said, tapping the photo. "Said that Charlotte has been dealing for him for years. Gave me a record, in her handwriting, of transactions he said she'd done for him. Said he was sorry, that he'd seen the error of his ways, that he just wanted the kids to be safe, now, from *her*." Shepard shut his eyes for a pained moment. "The records are immaculate, you know. They perfectly match the sample of your handwriting, Charlotte, that I got from your biology teacher."

"What's his name?" Holmes asked, showing a glimmer of interest.

Shepard raised an eyebrow. "He gave it as John Smith."

Wordlessly, Holmes left the room, returning a second later with the little red notebook. She flipped through it there at the table until she reached a page near the end. CHARLOTTE HOLMES IS A MURDERER, it read, in her own spiky hand. "Believe me or don't," she said, "but we found this in John Smith's car." She went back to her dinner.

"We're going to follow up with the students that Charlotte sold to," the detective told us. "We'll find out the truth of it then."

"He forged those records," I said, looking at her. "All of them. The ones in that room—"

"Look," Shepard said, interrupting. "One of my calls this morning was to Scotland Yard. Everyone there vouches for you, Charlotte. Okay, some of them might not like you much, and they weren't surprised that you were mixed up in a crime, but to a man, they swore up and down you wouldn't hurt anyone. Annoy them to death, maybe."

One corner of Holmes's mouth turned up, but she stayed silent. The detective rubbed his eyes. "I was also reassured that if you *did* do it, I wouldn't have you on my list of suspects at all." He turned to my father. "Apparently she's that good. Then I talked to Philly PD about Aaron Davis, Sherringford's last dealer, and apparently the kid is doing time down there for dealing oxy at UPenn. I have a buddy down there who owes me a favor, asked Aaron some questions. He remembers Charlotte. Confirmed her story, that he sold to her down in that room last year. He also said she didn't have enough friends or enough patience to ever deal on her own. We'll follow up, like I said. Aaron's a con, so his word isn't golden, but . . ." Shepard shrugged expressively. "But a kid's dead. Another is in the hospital. You two just look too good for it. Charlotte has a private chemistry lab where she keeps a whole bunch of poisons. And you"—he pointed at me—"you could easily get into Lee Dobson's room at night. You were flirting with Elizabeth Hartwell. It looks, for all the world, like the two of you are in some kind of lovers' pact gone wrong. Someone might be doing their best to set you up, might be throwing absolutely everything at the wall to try to find something to stick, but the much more *rational* answer is that Charlotte Holmes isn't half as good as everyone thinks she is. I might not like it, but until I have a better answer—"

Holmes looked up, and a beat later, Shepard's phone rang.

"Hold on." He put it to his ear. "Shepard. Slow down. She *what*? No. No, that's fine. Yeah. Is she—good. Yeah, I'll be there as soon as I can." Glancing over at us with something like relief, he said, "I just need to finish up something here."

"This pie is delicious," Holmes said to my father. He looked back at her helplessly. "Is there any more?"

SOMEONE HAD TRIED TO KILL LENA.

That's how Shepard put it to us. Unbothered by Holmes's absence, Lena had spent the day after homecoming holed up in bed, reading magazines and working her way through a care package of cookies from home. She'd been playing music loud enough that when there was a knock at her door, she wasn't sure, at first, if she'd imagined it. But when she finally got up to check, there it was on the threshold: a parcel, and inside the parcel, a sliding ivory jewelry box.

Though she unwrapped the paper, Lena didn't open the box. With the roommate she had, she'd gotten used to seeing some weird things, and in the past, when mysterious packages had arrived, they'd always been for Holmes. ("I do a lot of online shopping," Holmes told Detective Shepard without batting an eye.) So she'd set it on her roommate's desk and taken a nap.

She woke up twenty minutes later to a man in a ski mask looming over her, one hand at her throat, as if he were about to check her pulse or strangle her. Lena screamed. The man ran. And she immediately called the police, surrendering the mysterious box to their custody. As we spoke, they were examining it at the station.

Something about all this was naggingly familiar, but I couldn't put a finger on what.

"When did this happen?" Holmes demanded, hands shaking. I hadn't realized that she'd cared about Lena so much. "Just now? I spoke with her not twenty minutes ago."

The detective took out a notepad and paper. "What about?"

Holmes's mouth twitched. "She'd spilled punch on me at homecoming and wanted to know if I was still angry. I told her I was over it, and we'd get my dress to the cleaners. No harm, no foul."

So it had been Lena on the phone, earlier. I'd never seen Holmes take one of her roommate's calls before. She always sent them, and everyone else's, straight to voicemail to screen at her leisure.

"Does she know that you went down to the station? Did she know where you were today?" he asked.

"No," she said. "The only person I really talk to is Jamie. I doubt anyone at the school knows I'm gone, unless they saw you haul us away in the cruiser. But it was dark."

My father was taking notes in a chair in the corner. "Dark," he muttered to himself.

"But Lena's okay?" Holmes asked. Her lower lip trembled. "I'm sorry, I just—this sounds awful, but I really do think that man was there to hurt me, not Lena. And that weird box . . . Jamie, doesn't it ring a bell for you too?"

She wasn't acting like herself. She was acting *normal*. Like she'd have any reaction other than swift and extreme mobilization at hearing that that she'd missed a crime in her own dorm room. Like she wasn't . . .

I put it together in a flash.

Oh, she was brilliant. Like a hurtling comet you couldn't look at dead on without burning your retinas right off. Like a bioluminescent lake. She was a sixteen-year-old detective-savant who could tell your life story from a look, who retrofitted little carved boxes with surprise poison springs early on a Saturday morning when everyone else, including me, was asleep in their beds.

She'd set herself up to be the target of a fake crime to get us off the hook for the real one. And she'd used Lena, and some mysterious guy, to do it.

"Culverton Smith," I said, piecing it together aloud for Shepard's sake. "It's from a Holmes story. We're being set up. Jesus Christ, tell your policemen to wear gloves when handling that box. Thick ones."

To his credit, he took me seriously. "Making a call. But I want an explanation as soon as I'm back." He stepped outside.

"You," I said to her, "are a genius."

Across the table, Holmes slipped from false concern into very real satisfaction. "It's quite a good story, you know. 'The Adventure of the Dying Detective.' Pity that Dr. Watson smothered what should have been an exercise in logic in all that sentimental garbage about his partner."

"The Adventure of the Dying Detective," for me, has always been the hardest of the Sherlock Holmes stories to read, and not because it isn't brilliantly done. It's 1890. Dr. Watson, who's living with his wife away from Baker Street, is urgently called to Sherlock Holmes's bedside. The detective has caught a rare, highly contagious disease that, as he tells Dr. Watson, can only be cured by Culverton Smith, a specialist in tropical illnesses living nearby. The catch: Smith hates Holmes because he correctly accused Smith of murder. His victim was infected with, and died of, this same disease. But Holmes insists that Watson bring Smith anyway, that Smith is their only hope. While Holmes rattles off a series of ridiculous-sounding orders on how Watson is to go about fetching this specialist, Watson idly picks up a small ivory box that's been resting on the table. Out of nowhere, Holmes insists that Watson put it down and not touch it again.

All the while, Watson thinks his best friend is dying. It's wrenching to read, and even more so as we watch Watson follow Holmes's orders—the clear product of a hallucinating mind—to the letter. From trust, or affection, or old habit, we're not sure, but either way, the last of these insane directions has Watson hiding himself in the closet in preparation for Smith's arrival. Smith comes in. The gaslight is low. Holmes is sweating in feverish agony on the settee. The specialist begins to gloat, thinking he and the detective are alone. That little ivory box? He'd mailed it, fitted with an infected metal spring, hoping to catch Holmes with it unaware. After Smith has confessed everything to Holmes, who he believes to be a dead man, Holmes asks him to turn up the gaslight. It's a signal: in bursts Inspector Morton of Scotland Yard, who's been waiting at the door, and Watson, who's witnessed the whole conversation from the closet. Smith is hauled away to jail.

And Holmes? Not sick at all. He faked his symptoms. Starved himself for three days until he was skin and bone, then applied a convincing coat of stage makeup to make himself appear at death's door. As for the box—well. He wasn't in any danger. He reminds Watson that he always thoroughly examines his mail.

Charlotte Holmes had stripped the "Dying Detective" for details and rearranged them to make her own narrative, pulling Lena in on her scheme to sell the story. I wondered who the man in the ski mask was. Tom? Unlikely. Still, it was just the sort of story that our Sherlock-obsessed murderer would've seized on and used against us.

The part I couldn't get over, that distracted me from even this show of Charlotte Holmes's powers, was remembering how much my great-great-great-grandfather had trusted hers. Oysters, I remembered. Between the instructions he'd given

Dr. Watson, Sherlock Holmes had been ranting, in his "hallucinations," about oysters.

And his partner had still followed his directions exactly.

I thought about the piped-in interrogation in the police station. About the little notebook that still lay open between us on the table. About how my own doubts about Holmes's innocence ran alongside my doubt that she could get us out of this mess.

She *had* just gotten us out of this mess. And no matter what my head wanted to tell me, I knew in my bones that she wasn't a killer.

"I'm sorry I didn't trust you," I said to my Holmes, in a low voice.

She shook her head. "I needed your shock to be genuine for me to sell it."

"I don't mean about the details. I don't need to hear the details." I reached across the table to put my hand on hers. "I meant to say that I won't doubt you again."

I watched her catalog me. The planes of my face, the tilt of my head, how I sat in my chair, my fingers' heat and the ruck of my hair: she took it all in, deduced from what she saw, and came up, in the end, with something she hadn't expected.

"You won't," she said with flat surprise. "You really won't, will you?"

Next to me, my father cleared his throat. I didn't spare him a glance.

When Shepard returned from speaking to his team, we gave him the background on the Culverton Smith story. And he told us what we already knew. They had, in fact, found a spring loaded into the ivory box, poised to strike when it was slid open. That spring was coated in an infectious tropical disease; the police lab weren't sure of its exact origin, but they guessed it to be Asia. Samples of this kind were tightly controlled, and so far, their search into local scientists who had requested access to them had ended in an absolute null.

(I asked Holmes, much later, how she got her hands on the sample. She said something about Milo, an ex-girlfriend at the CDC, and "catching as catch can.")

"This blows my list of suspects wide open," Shepard said. "So we're back to option one. Someone trying their damnedest to frame you two. We'll need to talk about who out there in the world wants to get you. And I'll have to notify the station that I won't be needing a pair of cells. At least not tonight."

So his plan *had* been to arrest us.

"Let us help you," Holmes said. "I'm an official informant for Scotland Yard, and between Watson and me"—I was gratified to be back on a last-name basis—"we're experts on the killer's MO. Sherlock Holmes stories? We're the obvious choice. Not to mention that we can informally question anyone at Sherringford without arousing suspicion, or that you're getting an excellent chemist and a relatively fearless pugilist in the bargain. We're not a bargain. We're luxury goods."

"No," he said. "Absolutely not."

Holmes shrugged; she'd anticipated this response. "Then I'll conduct my own investigation, and deal with the culprit, after I catch him or her, as I see fit."

"You actually think that threatening vigilante justice will make me want to take you two on?" Shepard demanded. "You're a *child*. I don't know how desperate the police are across the pond, but we play it by the book here. Isn't it enough that you're not suspects anymore? I don't see any reason to put you and Jamie in the line of fire."

"Really. Then perhaps call Scotland Yard again and ask them about what transpired after I sat through this exact conversation with DI Green. If she's reluctant to speak to you, tell her you know all about the deep freezer, the meat hook, and how I found her two minutes before the killer returned. Honestly, I might've gotten myself there sooner if she hadn't been such a cow about it. Just the year before I'd recovered three million pounds' worth of jewels and given her all the credit." She yawned. "Do it in the morning, though. I'm knackered."

"But—"

"Mr. Watson, this was a lovely dinner. Would you mind taking us home now?" Without waiting for a response, Holmes disappeared into the garage, her gown trailing after her.

In her flair for the dramatic, she'd left behind my jacket and her phone. I collected them, trying not to feel like her valet.

"That girl is a piece of work," Shepard said, somewhere between admiration and despair.

"Holmeses." My father laughed, and reached for his car keys. "Would you know she's one of the nicer ones?"

seven

IT TOOK SHEPARD LESS THAN A DAY TO AGREE TO HOLMES'S
terms.

"You have until Thanksgiving break," he said to us; I had
him on speakerphone. He'd spent all that morning sleuthing
in Holmes's and Lena's room, and come up empty-handed. I
wasn't surprised. Holmes, of course, had been thorough. "That's
a little less than a month. We'll share information. *Share* it, do
you understand me? DI Green warned me about how you like
to play the magician so you can do the big reveal at the end.
That won't fly here." A long, scratchy pause. "The only reason
I'm allowing this Encyclopedia Brown business is because I
don't want any more hurt kids. You two are included in that.
So, Jamie, I need you to keep an eye out for her. I've heard

you're a brawler. I'm okay with that."

"Do you honestly think I can't take care of myself?" Holmes asked, draped over the love seat like a boneless cat. "I'll have you know I'm an expert at singlestick and baritsu."

"Yes, and sometimes a pair of fists is much more useful," I said, "if less dramatic. I'll keep an eye out, Detective. Will you clear us publicly?"

"Terrible idea," Holmes put in. "It might lead to escalation on the murderer's part if they think they need to reconvince the police of our guilt. No, tell the school privately, but don't let anyone release a statement."

"Fine." More crackling. "I'll send over what we have so far on the snake."

"And a copy of *The Adventures of Sherlock Holmes*," I said.

"Fine. You should know that we found the ski mask the intruder used in a garbage can outside Stevenson Hall, but we weren't able to lift any prints off it."

"These people are too good for that," Holmes said. I coughed. "But yes, send over the bit about the snake. And I want access to the personnel files of all of Sherringford's students and employees, including any EU immigration information."

"I'd lose my job."

"You'd lose your job anyway when they find out you're letting us help."

Static.

"Done," he said finally. "Charlotte, Jamie—just keep your mouths shut."

"Yes, yes," Holmes said, "thank you," and hung up on him.

It was Monday at lunch. I'd hidden away in Holmes's lab in an attempt to finish writing my poem for Mr. Wheatley's class that afternoon. It was already going badly, but then I watched Holmes finish her calculus problem set in the ten minutes between concluding some frothy, smelly experiment and picking up her violin for a spin through Beethoven's Kreutzer Sonata as if it were "Twinkle, Twinkle Little Star."

She threw her bow down. "I have to wait until the school day is over to investigate. Two hours!" she said. "Do you think, if I set fire to the maths building—"

"No."

"But—"

"Still no. Why don't you help me with this poem?" I asked, an attempt to derail her. "It needs to be one that's 'difficult for me to write,' whatever that means."

"What do you have so far?" she asked.

"'The.' Or maybe 'A,' I'm not sure."

"I'm bad with words." She sat down next to me. "Too imprecise. Too many shades of meaning. And people use them to lie. Have you ever heard someone lie to you on the violin? Well. I suppose it can be done, but it would take far more skill."

"Speaking of lying," I said. "Who played your masked man, the other night?"

"One of Lena's on-and-off hookups. I knew I needed a failsafe, and Lena was willing to play along. We'd laid the groundwork up a week ago. All she needed was the go-ahead. She'd been telling him she loved scary movies, and being afraid sort of turned her on, and asking him if he had a ski mask—that sort of thing. All she had to do was mention that I'd be away on Sunday night. He didn't question it at all when she screamed and chased him out, and after, I had her put a fresh mask I'd taken from the athletics shed into the bin outside. Really, it's a good thing she's so completely insane. It means she can get away with anything."

"And how is she holding up, after her 'scare'?"

"Oh, fine," she said airily. "I think she's counting the days until her new handbag comes in the post."

I put my pen down. "I thought you might pay her off. With what money?"

She bit her lip. "She wouldn't take any. Which, to be honest, makes me nervous."

"The fact that she likes you enough to help you for free? *That* makes you nervous?"

"I'd rather deal in quantifiable transactions," she said. "But she said she'd made a killing at poker and reminded me that her allowance is staggering. After that, she sat me down in front of her laptop and made me help her pick out something called a minaudière. It looks like a bejeweled toad."

"Oh," I said, wondering what it meant that Holmes had never once offered to pay me.

"I have a rainy-day fund, you know," she said, not quite looking at me. "Until recently, it was raining . . . rather a lot. But I . . . I've been trying to use an umbrella."

"See, and you say you're bad with words. I'm stealing that." I scrawled it down.

She drifted over to her bookshelf and lit a cigarette. With the toe of her shoe, she tapped her copy of *The Casebook of Sherlock Holmes* before she leaned down to pick it up. I could tell I'd lost her to her thoughts.

It seemed as good a time as any to do the thing I'd been avoiding.

The hospital corridors were empty when I arrived, carrying a bunch of flowers. It wasn't hard to find the right ward. They had it guarded like Fort Knox. Thankfully, Detective Shepard had had the wherewithal to put my name on the visitor list, and after showing my ID to two separate policemen, I was allowed into her room.

I'd been told that she was awake, but her eyes were closed when I came in. She looked terrible. Her blond hair was matted to her head with sweat, her arms wound in tubes and tape. Strangely enough, she was clutching a whiteboard to her chest in the way you would a teddy bear. As quietly as I could, I put the flowers on the table beside her bed and debated writing her a note. Was that what the board was for?

While I stood there, Elizabeth opened one eye, then the other.

"Hi," I said. "I hope you don't mind that I came."

She shook her head no, though I wasn't sure if it was *No, I don't mind,* or *No, actually, leave.*

"May I sit down?"

A nod.

"How long until you get your voice back?" I asked. When Detective Shepard said that Elizabeth had been unable to speak to the police, I hadn't thought he meant it literally.

Slowly, achingly, she pulled a marker out from the folds of her blanket and scrawled something down on the board. I peered over at what she was writing. *Don't know,* it said.

I didn't mean to interrogate her. That wasn't why I'd come. Besides, Shepard had told us that Elizabeth's parents had asked the police for a few days' grace for their daughter. They said that she had been through enough without being forced to relive it all.

"I'm sorry," I told Elizabeth, looking down at my hands. I'd come to apologize. It was why I hadn't brought Holmes. Apologizing was the kind of thing that made her break out in hives.

A scribbling sound. *For what?*

"For what happened to you. You didn't deserve this. Any of it. I'm sorry."

I don't remember all of it. But the detective told me you found me and got help. Thank you. Her exhausted eyes met mine. Exhausted, and gentle. I didn't deserve that gentleness.

"I hope you feel better soon," I said, standing to leave.

Scribbling again. *Detective said "blue carbuncle" to my parents. He thought I was asleep. Explanation?*

I sat back down. "Do you know the story?"

A headshake. She scrubbed her board blank with her hospital gown and wrote *Talk fast. My parents went to get takeout. They won't tell me anything but I need to know.* She furiously underlined the last four words.

I understood what it was like, being kept in the dark.

"It's a Sherlock Holmes story," I began, "about a rare missing diamond. A blue carbuncle. One that a policeman finds in the throat of a dead Christmas goose on the street. Holmes and Watson trace the goose back to its breeder, and from there, to the breeder's brother. He'd stolen the gem from a countess and hidden it in a goose's craw."

It was the quick and dirty version, the boring one—all facts, no flair. It left out all the details that made the story something I loved. But Sherlock Holmes's strategies and Dr. Watson's observations didn't have a place in this guarded hospital room.

Even so, Elizabeth listened avidly. When I'd finished, she held up her whiteboard. *So I guess I'm the goose.*

I hesitated, and she lifted her eyebrows in a challenge. "Guess so," I said.

Fucked up.

"Yeah." It was, impossibly so. "How much do you remember about that night?"

Not much. Seeing you. Making out with Randall. They showed me the thing that was in my throat.

"Did you recognize it?"

No. Her eyes were imploring. *Do you know anything about it?*

"The police are trying to solve this as fast as they can." I took a deep breath. "Did Randall do this to you? Do you remember?"

She shook her head, blushing a little. *I don't remember his face, but I DO remember what the guy said. "Give my regards to Charlotte Holmes." I don't think Randall would say that.*

There was a commotion outside the door. "Who did you

let in to see my daughter? A friend? What's his name?" I didn't hear the police officer's reply. Hastily, Elizabeth rubbed her board clean and then started writing something else.

Elizabeth's mother barged into the room, her arms full of Chinese food. "Don't tell me," she said in a dangerous voice. "You're Jamie Watson. You're the one that found her."

She might have said *found her*, but it was clear what she meant was *attacked her*. Elizabeth's eyes seized on mine.

"No," I said, extending a hand. "I'm Gary. Gary Snyder." He was a poet we were reading in Mr. Wheatley's class, one I vigorously hated.

"And what exactly are you doing here, Gary Snyder?"

Elizabeth tugged on her mother's sleeve. She held up her whiteboard: a half-completed tic-tac-toe game.

Charlotte Holmes would have been proud.

Her mother deflated. "We've just been so worried, sweetie," she said, and burst into tears over her daughter's bed.

I took that as my cue to leave. *I think I have some leads,* I texted Holmes in the elevator.

Somehow, I wasn't surprised to find Detective Shepard waiting for me on the sofa in Sciences 442.

"So, next time, *tell* me when you're planning on pulling something," I said, hanging up my jacket. "Her parents were conveniently gone? Oh, Elizabeth couldn't talk to the detective, but she could easily talk to *me*. What, did you wait until I stepped out the door and then had the hospital cafeteria closed?" The last was directed at Holmes.

Across the room, she poked at her vulture skeleton until

it spun in circles. "For the record, I merely waited until you left and then had Emperor Kitchen offer free takeout to all the families in the ICU. I'll make Milo pay for it. I told you he'd go either today or tomorrow," she said to Shepard. "You should trust me more often, you know. I *am* the world's foremost Jamie Watson scholar."

"Look, I'm happy to question her, but next time, I want to be in the loop. Otherwise I'm just going to build my own chessboard and let you move me around it."

"Stop being dramatic, and tell us what happened," Shepard said, sounding like he wanted to get out of 442 as quickly as possible. I couldn't blame him—Holmes had lit up her jar of teeth from behind, probably in anticipation of the detective's visit. It was, I thought, her version of hanging fairy lights.

I filled them in. Shepard made a low growling noise. "'Give my regards to Charlotte Holmes,'" he repeated, shaking his head. "I need to talk to John Smith again. He won't confess to the attack. Only to dealing drugs, and then he only gives me information he wants me to use against *you*, Charlotte."

Holmes touched a finger to the skeleton's nose, stilling it in its orbit. "Something else is going to happen if our attacker doesn't get what he wants," she said. "Someone else is going to get hurt."

"What does he want?" I said. "Us locked up, no key. I don't see how he's going to get that. Unless Shepard puts us away for show."

"No." She frowned. "I need unfettered access to the campus, not to be rotting away in some cell. We need to figure out the connection between the man you're holding and the man he claims he is. I need to make a plan."

"*We* need to make a plan," Shepard said.

So we did.

Holmes and I began by retracing our steps through the access tunnels, back to the police-cordoned storage room. John Smith's footprints still ended at its door, a literal dead end. But Holmes refused to give up. We covered what felt like miles of territory that night, her coursing ahead, me yawning clandestinely behind my hand.

When we returned to her lab, we stayed up even later examining the school library's copy of *The Adventures of Sherlock Holmes*. It was a brand-new school edition of the stories. The bookmark the killer had placed inside was one of the Sherringford ones they left on the circulation desk, and it was clean of all but the school librarian's fingerprints. But that was to be expected. Besides, Mr. Jones had no conceivable connection to either me or Holmes. The book itself was completely unremarkable: intact spine, intact pages. The only remarkable thing about it was that the killer had tucked it into Dobson's cold hands. At dawn, when Holmes began going through it page by page with an actual magnifying glass, I curled up on the floor to go to sleep.

I spent the next few nights even more tired, wading through all the BBC America footage that had been shot after Dobson's murder and put online. The police had requested everything that wasn't on their website, and there were hours and hours to contend with. I ran through it all frame by frame, looking for a still shot of the dealer's face. I needed to know if the man Shepard had in custody was the same one I'd seen around Sherringford. It took hours. I found a lot of talking-head speculation about boarding school life, about how privileged kids consider murder to be just another game. I found a number of interviews where our classmates slagged off Holmes, slagged off me, cried for show. I ate a lot of jalapeño-flavored cheese puffs. And I didn't see a single hair of the man we were looking for. After I slept through my French class three days in a row, Monsieur Cann cheerfully suggested that I would perhaps prefer to take Spanish, *n'est-ce pas?*, and I decided to give the solo research up as pointless.

While I'd been chained to my laptop, Holmes had done the legwork, pulling up security footage closer to home. Sherringford didn't have any cameras of their own, so she'd done a circuit of the businesses whose storefronts faced campus, getting the lowdown on their security systems. Then, she told me, it was just the simple expedient of hacking into their feeds, using this particular spring-code that her brother had taught her, which, of course, she had modified herself using the blah-blah differential, and then something else that sounded like conversational calculus, and my eyes began to cross.

She poked my shoulder with her shoe, and I trapped it neatly with my hands. "What?" I asked.

"Since you don't care about the more complex workings of tonight"—she shook her foot free—"do you want to be in charge of the snacks?"

"Snacks are complex," I said. "How do you feel about tasty, tasty puffed corn?"

More footage. More cheese doodles eaten in the dark of Sciences 442, one more long, dreary, wasted weekend. Still no sign of the man we were looking for. Could he make himself go invisible? Did he even exist at all? I fell asleep with my head on a bag of Jiffy Pop and woke up nauseous and pissed off to the dim light of the screen against Holmes's face. My watch read 2:21 in the morning, but her eyes were still wide open.

There was nothing else to do but ask Shepard to let me talk to his prisoner. I was sure that I'd remember his reedy, obnoxious voice even if I couldn't exactly place his face. Shepard dragged his heels on it for days, but when it became clear that neither he nor we were making progress, he agreed to let one of us in to see him. Holmes, tight-lipped, agreed that it should be me; I'd had the clearer look at him, after all.

The night before I was to go to the jail, the prisoner hung himself.

It took another three days before we persuaded Shepard to let us into the morgue.

"You're part of the forensics club," the medical examiner said doubtfully.

I shifted my weight from foot to foot. "Detective Shepard is our adviser," I said. It was true. Sort of. You could look at this semester as the weirdest independent study anyone had ever had.

"I thought forensics was the school speech team." She

blinked at us through her glasses. "Not the science club."

"Huh. I haven't heard that," I said, straight-faced.

Though it was a Saturday, Holmes was wearing her school uniform, her ribbon tie pressed and perfect. She'd found a pair of glasses somewhere, black-framed ones that dwarfed her features, and she'd drawn on her eyebrows to make them seem thicker. Holmes usually looked like a weapon. Today she looked like a teen movie's idea of a dork, the one that could take off her glasses, shake out her hair, and instantly be elected prom queen.

She looked, in short, like the kind of girl that adults found themselves confiding in.

"Can I tell you the truth?" she asked the examiner in an American accent. She sounded eager. Bright. "I mostly wanted to come here because I heard you had an amazing microscope. I have some samples from my bio class in my bag. Could I take a look at them? I'm working on a project for the national Intel contest. Cancer research."

The examiner's face softened slightly. "That's fine," she said, and laughed self-consciously. "For a second, I thought that you wanted to look at a *body*."

Holmes laughed too, her pretty-girl laugh. "Oh my God, I don't know if I could handle that. How do you even get used to it? You must be so brave."

"Practice," the examiner said. It was clear that she didn't get this kind of glowing admiration every day. "Practice, and patience."

"Are they . . . are they scary? Do you still feel like they're people? Or does it change for you depending on the body?" Holmes shook her head. "Wow, thinking about this would keep me up at night."

The examiner pursed her lips philosophically. "It should. These are important questions you're asking, Charlotte. I think about them every day."

I nodded to hide the fact that I thought she was full of shit.

As always, Holmes was better at this than I was. "Wow," she said. "Just—wow. And it's like you run this whole place by yourself. That's awesome. How many do you end up dissecting in a day?"

"It depends, really. I only have one intact body right now." The examiner walked over to the wall of morgue drawers. "Are you feeling brave?"

Game, set, match.

Holmes looked over at me with wide eyes. "Oh my God," she said, a perfect imitation of the bright, well-adjusted girl she'd never been. "Maybe? Yes! Okay, yes, I am."

We put on gloves and masks, and the examiner put on her best fortune-teller voice, saying "John Smith!" as she pulled the drawer out of the wall with a flourish.

I won't describe his face. It's enough to say that his death by hanging left him bloated and bruised and unrecognizable, far past the point where I could positively identify him. But his height was about right, his shoulders. I stared for a moment at his throat, wishing that I could hear his voice to be sure.

"Can I?" Holmes asked, reaching for the corpse's forearm.

A small line appeared between the examiner's brows. "I guess," she said.

Swiftly, Holmes turned it over. The man had a tattoo near his wrist in the shape of a compass. Underneath, the word "navigator."

Holmes looked at me. *Do you remember this?* her eyes were asking. I shook my head no, and said aloud, "That's the kind of tattoo you could hide under long sleeves." At the examiner's sharp look, I coughed. "Um, I've been thinking of getting one."

"The navigator," Holmes said to herself, lifting his arm to examine his fingernails. She checked his fingers one at a time, lifted his chin to look at the veins of his neck. Then she ducked her head to look up the man's nostrils. "Moriarty means 'seaworthy.'"

The examiner stared at us furiously.

"Etymology," I said. "It's really popular. With the kids."

Our grace period was up, and Holmes knew it too. "Manual labor," Holmes said, quickly deducing. She pulled out a folded sheet of paper and an inkpad and took down the man's prints while the examiner sputtered. "Look at those finger callouses. Look at the state of his ankles. He's all muscle, but it isn't from the gym. These are a working man's muscles. Do you see the rope burn on his arm?"

"He's not a dealer," I said. "It's not him."

"It's not him," Holmes said, in the voice that was ragged and wild and hers. "Jamie—it's a Moriarty."

"Get out." The examiner jerked her head toward the door. "Now."

On Monday, I'd skipped all my classes—my grades were falling, lower now than they'd ever been—to be alone, to make my half idea into a project without her peering over my shoulder. I pulled from the resources Shepard had given us access to and from the files we'd put together on our own. Flight passenger lists. Family trees. Moriartys with criminal records and lists of their known aliases. I took down the riding crops from the wall and pinned all of this up in their place, then began the long and arduous task of cross-referencing. I needed to know which of the Moriartys had come into this country and when. If John Smith wasn't a member of the family, he was definitely on their payroll. The trick was to find out who hired him.

In the back of my mind, I knew there was a good chance that I was blowing all of this out of proportion. The simplest answer was almost always the right one, and the idea that the entire Moriarty family was out to get me and Holmes was a big, complicated leap from where I was standing. Even if there had been a conflict between Holmes and that family, it was probably small and contained, nothing like the sprawling conspiracy that I was charting up on the wall.

But I kept thinking how the Sherringford killer was insistently re-creating the Sherlock Holmes stories. Those past wrongs that Sherlock and Dr. Watson had made right were being pushed into our present, and the details of the good deeds they'd done were being used to hurt us and the people we knew. Sure, maybe the killer had a personal vendetta against Holmes, but it felt to me like it was something bigger than that, something older, something reaching back more than a century.

Anyway, I couldn't ignore the way the word *Moriarty* made my skin crawl.

I focused on four of them. The four Moriartys whose whereabouts weren't dictated by respectable jobs, who'd been sloppy enough to have their shadier dealings dragged into the public eye. Whoever was doing this to us was sloppy, there wasn't any doubt of that, and I meant to use it to my advantage.

Hadrian and Phillipa were a brother-and-sister pair of art collectors whose fortune, rumor had it, was used to buy favors from dictators in countries they wanted to plunder. Lucien was August's older brother, an adviser for some of the more scandal-ridden members of the British Parliament. I read a profile of him in the *Guardian* that had hinted strongly that Lucien Moriarty knew how to throw his money around to clear just about anyone's name.

And then there was Lucien's younger brother: August.

For this, I didn't have to look through Shepard's records. It was as easy as plugging August's name into Google and clicking a button.

The first article that came up was from his college at Oxford. August had presented some complicated theorem at an academic conference in Dusseldorf. The reporter took special care to mention his age: he'd been doing his doctorate in pure math at twenty. He must've been a genius to be doing that work so young. The article described his dissertation (fractals, imaginary numbers) in layman's terms, and I still couldn't begin to understand it.

But it was dated two years back. I needed newer information, to know if he was still at Oxford, if he'd graduated or been hit by a car or moved to, I don't know . . . Connecticut.

The rest of the search results linked to academic journals and fellowship competitions, all dated that same year. Not a word about his personal life or about him dating Charlotte Holmes. Just a list of his achievements: August, recipient of a prestigious Institut Zalen grant. August, publishing on vector spaces and the cosmos in *Mathematics Today*. August, flown to the Arctic Circle to collaborate with scientists studying something called "ice fractals."

After that, there was nothing. Not a word had been written about August Moriarty in the last two years.

I put it all up on the wall anyway.

At three o'clock precisely, Holmes swung open the door to 442, humming something under her breath. "Hello, Watson," she said before she'd even seen me, "you're here early," and then she stopped in her tracks, staring at the wall.

I realized, too late, that I'd pretty much re-created the murder den we'd found in the access tunnels.

"Oh," she said.

I waited for the explosion.

She sighed, dropping her backpack on the floor. "It's a place to start. I came to tell you that Milo ran down John Smith's prints in some of the more . . . unusual databases. He's worked as a domestic for the last five years."

"A domestic?"

"A servant, Watson. He was Phillipa Moriarty's driver until his disappearance four months ago. There's our link to the family, sorted. The question is if he was doing all this alone, or . . ."

"You don't think he was. So, Phillipa then?"

We looked at the wall, side by side.

"Have you ever heard of a rat-king?" She reached out and touched the corner of Hadrian's photo. "The Moriartys—their disgusting tails are all tied together. Let's not try to separate them just yet. We'll start by finding out which of them came into this country, and when."

On her direction, ship manifests went up onto the wall, freighters that had traveled from England to Boston and the names of the sailors who manned them. ("Seaworthy," she muttered, taping them up.) We went through lists of private airstrips and private jets. Helicopters. Rowboats. We scrolled through records in New England and in England both. Moriarty was a horrifyingly common last name, but things became even worse when we began running known aliases. Our series of papers grew, day by day, until they engulfed the wall.

Phillipa spoke at a gallery opening in Glasgow. Lucien was photographed with the British prime minister. Hadrian showed up on some German talk show to chat about the Sphinx. How could it be any of them? Were they taking care of business in Europe, flying by night to Connecticut to ruin our lives? It seemed absurd, even by our standards. I spent every moment in 442, working like a madman. (I was even growing the beginnings of a madman's scratchy beard, which I secretly thought was kind of awesome.) And she worked right beside me with a fury I hadn't yet seen. Almost everything else went out the window.

Especially for Holmes.

She'd stopped battling me on August Moriarty. Every time I tried to learn something, anything, about what happened between them, she regarded me with a weary tilt of her head, like I was a fly she couldn't quite get rid of. I was relatively sure she wasn't eating or sleeping. But it wasn't just her attitude. Her eyes were somehow both glassy and dry, and as she scratched absently at her scalp, going over her millionth passenger manifest, her hair made a crackling sound that hair really shouldn't make. I kept stifling the urge to ask her if she was okay, to touch her forehead to see if she had a fever. To take care of her.

I brought her food, but it stayed untouched on the plate no matter how I tried to cajole her into eating. When I caught her taking twenty minutes to eat a single almond, I began wondering if there was some kind of Watsonian guide for the care and keeping of Holmeses.

When I sent my father an email to that effect (subject line I Need Your Help, postscript *Still haven't forgiven you and won't*), he responded that, yes, over the years he'd written down an informal series of suggestions in his journal; he'd do his best to adapt and type them up for me.

When the list arrived the next day, it was twelve pages long, single-spaced.

The suggestions ran from the obvious (*8. On the whole, coaxing works rather better than straightforward demands*) to the irrelevant (*39. Under all circumstances, do not allow Holmes to cook your dinner unless you have a taste for cold unseasoned broth*) to the absurd (*87. Hide all firearms before throwing Holmes a surprise birthday party*) to, finally, the useful (*1. Search often for opiates and dispose of as needed; retaliation will not come often, though is swift and exacting when it does—do not grow attached to one's mirrors or drinking glasses; 2. During your search, always begin with the hollowed-out heels of Holmes's boots; 102. Have no compunctions about drugging Holmes's tea if he hasn't slept; 41. Be prepared to receive compliments once every two to three years; 74.* (underlined twice) *Whatever happens, remember it is* not your fault *and likely could not have been prevented, no matter your efforts*). I wondered if I should create some kind of subclause for when the Holmes in question was a girl and her Watson was a guy who liked girls. *It's not your fault if you care too much about her. If you want impossible things. It couldn't have been prevented, no matter your efforts.*

I had to employ rule #9 (*sometimes for your own sake you must leave Holmes to his own devices, even if you return to find he's set himself on fire*) when real life began to creep in. The rugby team had asked for permission for me to rejoin in what should have been the last week of my suspension, and gotten it from the school. Holmes had insisted that I go. A number of Dobson's friends were on the squad, and she'd decided I should ask them, in a roundabout manner, about his last weeks alive. If he was seeing anyone unusual, leaving campus at late hours, taking strange calls. If some blond man had sold him any drugs, and what he'd said. That sort of thing. I'd figured that I could manage well enough.

Holmes disagreed. "You're a terrible liar," she said, perched on her lab table. I stood before her, like a schoolboy about to recite his lessons. "More specifically, I can read your thoughts as if they were printed in block letters on your forehead. Really, sometimes you think so loudly that I can hear you in the next room. There's no way you can approach your teammates in an innocent manner. We need to fix that."

"I'm so sorry to hear about your unfortunate telepathy," I snapped.

"See, just there? You're frustrated, and think I'm being rude."

"Oh, well done," I told her. "Really fine detective work. Why are we doing this now?"

She ran a hand through her hair. "Watson," she said, "we've hit a brick wall. We've come up with nothing new. Just let's get you into shape, okay?"

"Okay." I deflated at the pleading note in her voice.

She smiled. "Let's start with the basics. How to recognize when others are lying to you, so you can begin to police your own habits."

She walked me through it—where someone looks when they're recalling a memory, and when they're fabricating one; how an honest man stands, and a lying one, how they hold their shoulders (slumped), their hands (behind their back, to hide fidgeting), if they'd prefer to stand or sit (to stand, probably with nervous feet). All of it she rattled off as though reading from a book.

"How young did you learn all this?"

"Five," she said. "My mum was cross with Milo for teasing me. He kept telling me Santa Claus was real."

"I'm sorry," I asked, "was? Don't you mean wasn't?"

"No." She ran her finger down the agenda in her lap and sighed. "Right, so it's eight o'clock already and you're tetchy because you have history homework for tomorrow—I can tell by your feet, stop shuffling—so do a practice run or two and then we'll be finished."

I stuffed my hands in my pockets to keep myself from fidgeting. "Do you want me to try to lie to you?"

At that, I watched Holmes fight back a laugh. "God, no, that would be pointless. No, I'll make a series of statements and you can tell me which are true. Thumb up for truth, thumb down for a lie."

"I'm pretty good at reading you, you know," I told her.

"That might be true," she said gamely. "But did you know that my father worked for the M.O.D. for fourteen years before the Kremlin got wind of a scheme of his and tried to have him assassinated? Or that, growing up, I had a cat called Mouse? She's white and black and very fussy, and once the neighbor boy tried to drown her in a bucket. My mother hates her. Milo joined up with MI5 at age seventeen. No, that's false, Milo runs the world's largest private security company. Or no, actually, he's an *enfant terrible* preparing a hostile takeover of Google. He's unemployed. He's a complete tosser. For years he was my favorite person in the world."

I held my hand out rather stupidly between us; my thumb

hadn't moved. I'd spent too much time imagining what her life was like, before me, so I drank in all these facts—even the contrary ones—as if they were water.

"Pay attention to my face, Watson. Not my words. Listen to my tone. How am I sitting? Where am I looking?" She snapped her fingers. "I own three dressing gowns. I dislike guns; they cheapen confrontations. I first took cocaine at age twelve, and sometimes I take oxycodone when I'm miserable. When I met you, my initial thought was that my parents had set it up. No, it was that you were *dreamy.*" Grinning, I put my thumb up; she pushed it back down. "No, I thought, finally what someone wants from me, I can give them. I know how to play to an audience. I liked you. I thought you were another chauvinistic bastard who thought I couldn't take care of myself."

"All true," I said, quietly, before she could continue. "All of it. At one point or another, including the business about your brother. He's done all those things, been all those things. You thought all those things about me."

"Explain your method." Holmes pulled a cigarette out of her pocket and lit it.

"Because, somewhere in that brain of yours, you've decided I should know more about you, but you don't want to do it outright. No, it can't be simple, you're Charlotte Holmes. You have to do it sideways, and this is the most sideways approach you could dream up."

She exhaled in a long stream, head tipped to the side. I suppressed a cough. "Fine," she said, finally, and I chanced a smile. Grudgingly, she returned it. "But none of those deductions were *methodical*, Watson. That was all psychology. I *loathe* psychology."

"It's okay," I told her. "I hate losing at games, too."

The next day, she put me through another session, this time with a new test subject. I shouldn't have been surprised that she brought in Lena.

We met on the quad after classes, shivering and stomping our boots. Lena's hair hung in a braid down her back, and her hat had a knit flower that drooped down over her brow. She had a date with Tom in town that night, she told us, so she couldn't stay too late. It was odd to watch her next to Holmes in her trim black coat, hands stuffed into the fur muff strung from her neck. When the wind nipped at us, Lena huddled against her roommate with a familiarity that was almost shocking. I wondered what they talked about together. I couldn't imagine it.

For two hours, until the tips of my fingers were literally blue from the cold, I practiced reading Lena's tells. (In the process, I learned her down to the ground. I really didn't need to know that much about her sex life.) By the end of it, I was so exhausted from shivering that I wanted nothing more than to go to bed with a cup of something warm. Thankfully, when I went a full ten minutes without mislabeling one of Lena's statements, Holmes let us call it a day. We ducked into the Stevenson Hall lobby for warmth.

"You guys are up to secret things, I can tell. How are your secret things?" Lena asked, unwinding the scarf from her neck.

"They're about to go much better." Holmes discreetly

stuffed a roll of bills into Lena's coat pocket. "Run the poker game as usual tomorrow, will you? I don't want anyone to note a change in my behavior."

Lena pulled the money back out and pressed it into Holmes's hand. "Keep it," she said. "I kind of like being your test subject."

Holmes froze. "But—"

"Ugh, don't be weird about it. We're friends. And I don't, like, need the money." Standing on her tiptoes, she kissed me on the cheek. "Thanks, Jamie. That was a lot of fun, but I want to get to ask *you* inappropriate questions. Maybe we could have pizza in town sometime."

"You're having pizza in town with Tom tonight," Holmes said.

"Sure," I said, ignoring her. "I'd like that."

Holmes had on the kind of scowl toddlers get when their favorite toy is stolen away. "We're done here," she announced, and dragged me off by my elbow.

When I arrived at practice the next day, Kline was surveying the rugby pitch, fists on hips like a taller, dumber Napoleon. He was mad, and not without cause—their record stood so far at a predictable 0–7.

"We're starting in ten! Look alive!" he shouted. It was true, the team did seem dead. Our fly-half was actually sleeping, on his side, at midfield. Larson, our eight-man, trotted by and kicked him in the small of the back. Without a flicker of interest, Coach Q looked up from his director's chair and then back down at his copy of *Men's Health*.

"We're down to fourteen players, so many students have gone home. I don't think the school would've let you back on if that wasn't the case." Kline looked me over. "So, have you been staying in shape?"

"Running five miles every day," I lied. "But I'll do whatever. I'm happy to be back on the team." Another lie, delivered smoothly. I'd been practicing. "Where's Randall? I haven't talked to him since Elizabeth . . . you know . . . and I wanted to make sure we were on decent terms."

Kline pointed. "He's getting ready to drill with the backs. If you want to talk to him, make it quick." He cupped his hands around his mouth. "We're starting in five!"

When I caught up with him, Randall was even redder-faced than usual. I wasn't sure if it was from exertion or anger.

"Oh hey, the jackass is back," he said, shoving past me on his way to the bench.

A bit of both, then.

"Randall, wait." He slowed down slightly and I pulled up even. "Look. I wanted to say I'm sorry about Dobson. I didn't know him that well, but I know he was your friend."

"You have some issues, dude. That was fucked up. Going after him for saying what's on his mind? He was just messing, and you jumped on him. Then he shows up dead. Fucked up," he repeated, and dug his water bottle out from his bag.

I counted backward from five. "Charlotte Holmes is like my sister. Okay? He said the absolute worst thing he could have said. But I didn't kill him, I promise that."

"Then why do the police keep hauling you in? Why were

you the one who found Elizabeth?"

"Wrong place, wrong time," I said.

"Bullshit," he countered. "I've seen that detective with you like a million times. You got hauled down to the station after Lizzie got hurt. Why does he suspect you, if you're so innocent?"

"Same reason why you would, if you were them." The words came out bitterly. That fear of winding up in an orange jumpsuit hadn't entirely gone away—a bit of it lingered at the edges of everything I did, really—and I pulled from the truth of that feeling, laid it under my words.

Randall eyed me. "I don't know, man."

"Think what you want," I told him. "But you should know I feel like shit about all of it. I've heard all these rumors that Dobson hung himself, and I can't sleep, thinking I somehow drove him to it."

A lie, of course, but I was baiting my trap. Holmes taught me that: people would much rather correct you than answer a straightforward question. Randall wasn't an exception to the rule.

"Dude, you weren't *that* important to him," he said. "No, I heard that he was poisoned. I don't know which one's true."

"Poisoned? From the dining hall food?"

"Maybe." Randall shrugged. "But other people would probably be sick then too. I don't know, he'd been eating these cookies his sister sent him, and they looked nasty. Maybe it was in those. Or that weird protein powder he had. That stuff was the wrong color. He said it was from Germany and expensive, but I didn't buy it. Maybe your little friend slipped something into it."

"Out on the pitch," Kline hollered.

"All right," Randall said, "later." The venom was gone from his voice. I was happy about that, at least.

"You good?" Kline asked.

"Yeah," I said. "Hey, so, he said something about protein powder? Do you . . . do you know a good brand?" I bent to lace a cleat so he couldn't see my face. I wasn't sure I could pull that one off: I wore cable-knit jumpers and read Vonnegut novels and had a girl for a best friend. I was about as likely to build up giant biceps as to build a colony on the moon.

"Talk to Nurse Bryony at the infirmary," he said. "She has some prescription stuff she gets from Europe."

I reached in my bag, ostensibly for my water bottle, and sent Holmes an urgent text. I just hoped her phone was on this time, and not pickled in formaldehyde or in pieces across her chemistry table.

Practice crawled by at a snail's pace, especially once we began running plays. When Kline announced the last of them, I gritted my teeth and waited for my opportunity. Then I threw myself up for a catch in the most insane possible position, sprawling out like a diver going into water. I let myself go limp. My head bounced once, twice, three times against the frozen ground.

No one could say I wasn't dedicated to my game.

I heard Kline holler, "That's it! Watson! Watson!" and the rest of the team roaring.

Things went black.

When I woke, I found myself blinking up into fluorescent lights. Holmes's tear-streaked face was hovering over mine. She seemed genuinely upset, and for a second, I thought there'd been another murder. I struggled to sit up on my elbows.

"Oh, baby," she sniffed, shoving me back down on the bed with a touch more force than was necessary. "I thought you'd never wake up!"

I completely failed to catch on, at first. But then again, I *had* hit my head. "Where am I?" I tried to ask, but it came out more like a woof.

Holmes burst into tears, putting a hand to her mouth. Her nails were painted a bright red, and she smelled like Forever Ever Cotton Candy. Then I noticed she was in a polka-dot sweater. With a *bow* in her hair.

Apparently, she'd been working on her caring-girlfriend routine.

I thought I was going to be sick, but then, it might've been the concussion; I was fairly sure I had one. Everything was out of focus, in a doubled sort of way, and the only solution I could think of was to sleep. I shut my eyes, satisfied that I'd fulfilled my end of our makeshift plan. I had an injury that was bound to keep me in the infirmary for at least a day. Enough time for Holmes to poke around.

Somewhere across the room, a voice said, "Oh, you two are too much," and I snapped my eyes open again. From the little supply station, Nurse Bryony beamed at us. "Do you know she hasn't left your side for the past three hours? You blacked out for a bit, and then you were drifting between asleep and awake, and the whole time she just sat and held your hand, fretting. Poor thing."

The accent was American, but the cadences were faintly, unmistakably English. I don't know how I hadn't noticed it before. Or was it in my head? This time, if I ignored the halos I saw around all the lights and the soft little hum in my head, I could almost pay attention.

"How long will he be here?" Holmes asked, laying her hand against my cheek. "We have dinner reservations for tomorrow in town. It's our two-month anniversary."

Her fingers were cool and soft against my face, and I found myself leaning into her touch. Then I froze. "Sorry," I whispered to her, mortified.

"What are you apologizing for?" she asked, her voice surprisingly rough-edged. With her other hand, she brushed my hair back from my face.

The nurse cleared her throat, cutting into my confusion. "I'll keep a close eye on him. It's not bad enough to send him to the hospital, but I still don't want to take chances. You might have to reschedule your plans, just to be safe."

Holmes smiled down at me. She wasn't Hailey. She was something much more insidious. Charlotte Holmes without the edges, all combed and clean, well loved and loving in return. I knew it would be gone tomorrow, all of it—the gentle way she touched me, the glitter of her undivided attention, the bows and the perfume. It would all go back into her costume box, and she would be the real Holmes again.

Because this wasn't real, even if she spoke to me in what sounded like her real voice. "Do you hear that? You should be fine," she said.

I shouldn't have wanted it the way I did.

I was beginning to go, I could tell, and I knew I would wake up back into our old life. The lights winked at me; they liked the secrets I told them. But silently, I reminded myself, secrets are best when kept to oneself. They began blowing out, one by one, like candles. "Good night," I told Holmes, pulling her hand to my chest, and then I was awash in sleep.

"WATSON," SHE HISSED. "WATSON, WAKE UP, I'VE GOT TO GO. Night check's in ten minutes."

The room was dark, but I could see light coming in from under the door, where the nurse's desk was. Thankfully, it seemed my head had cleared enough to form coherent sentences. "Did you find anything?" I asked. Or tried to ask. It came out cotton-mouthed.

Holmes handed me a glass of water with an impatient look. I was right; she was herself again, and I suppressed a flare of disappointed guilt.

After a gulp, I repeated my question.

"She went out for a smoke, and I picked the lock on the medicine cabinet. There's a store of protein powder in with the other prescriptions, for Gabriel Tinker, according to the tag, but the canisters were all empty. I tasted a bit of powder I found in the cabinet, and it seemed innocent enough."

Tinker was the rugby team's fly-half, the one who'd been

sleeping on the field. "You *tasted* it? Why couldn't you take it back to your lab and examine it there?"

She looked affronted that I should even ask. "Efficiency."

"Right, okay, you nut." I pulled myself, slowly, into a sitting position. Holmes tucked a pillow behind my back. "So let's break it down: she's from England. That's why we flagged her file originally, right?"

"She was born there, but she moved here when she was a teenager. Or so she said when I pressed her, after I shed a few homesick tears. My face is still swollen. I forgot how uncomfortable this whole crying business is."

"No powder, no England. Two near misses, then," I said. "Unless you somehow wronged her back when you were a toddler, if I've got her age right. Twenty-two?"

"Twenty-three." Holmes got to her feet. "If she is, in fact, our culprit, she wouldn't be telling the truth to us anyway, so it hardly matters. As it stands, I can tell she's hiding something, but that could just be the sort of reserve you have around students. I'll try to track down an actual sample of that powder tomorrow, because what I tried tasted more like dust than protein."

"Shouldn't we focus on someone who we have a clear lead on? Like, I don't know . . . August Moriarty?"

"No, I don't think so," she said matter-of-factly. "I'm off to write my *Macbeth* paper. Be careful tonight. And maybe shower. You smell awful."

When she left, I realized I was starving. I wolfed down a roll of crackers I found next to the bed and took the small cup of what looked like Tylenol, washing it down with the rest of the water. As I set the glass carefully back down on the table— depth perception was a bit of an issue, post-concussion—I realized what I'd done. The woman taking care of me might be a poisoner. With a fixation on me and Holmes. And I'd put myself into her overnight care, tossing back the pills she gave me without a second thought.

The light in the next room flicked off. I stared at the door, willing it to stay shut, willing the nurse to pack up her things and leave. I willed this feeling to be just paranoia from my head injury, to remember the cluster of Moriartys sharing space on our wall. I willed Bryony to just be an ordinary woman who took a job at Sherringford because of the pay and the beautiful campus and because she didn't mind taking care of teenagers with the flu, not because she'd tracked Holmes and me across an ocean to frame us on Moriarty's orders.

The knob turned. The door swung open.

"I'm headed out," Nurse Bryony said softly. "Can I get you anything?"

"No, thanks." *Leave*, I thought. *Go home*.

But I heard her set down her bag. She padded into the room, smelling faintly of flowers. An ordinary, pretty-girl smell. I swallowed hard. The room was beginning to sway, like a ship, and I wished badly that Holmes was still there.

"You're nearly out of water." Nurse Bryony refilled my glass at the sink and took another roll of crackers from the cabinet above, setting them both by my bed. "There. Go easy on these. I'm surprised you're not more nauseous."

I wondered if Dobson was nauseous, before he died. I'd never had a concussion before. Was nausea a symptom? Was it a symptom of arsenic poisoning?

That's it, I thought. *Holmes can come up with the next plan.*

In the half-light, Bryony was a dark silhouette, all except the shining hair that fell across her face as she leaned down over me. She had a strange, hot electricity to her. I thought, in my confusion, that she might kiss me, or slap me across the face, that she would pick up the pillow and smother me with it.

But she put a cool hand to my forehead instead. "Get some rest, Jamie, so you can see that girl of yours again tomorrow," she whispered, her breath hot on my face. "The other nurse will be in first thing." She gathered her things and left.

I didn't even try to sleep. Instead, I stayed up listening to the quiet clock of my heart, wondering every moment if I was about to stop breathing. I'd been careless with my life, I knew I was, but if I died tonight, I was going to be furious. I debated texting Holmes a thousand times. If I was wrong, I'd look like an idiot.

Around dawn, I threw the water glass to the floor, needing to hear something shatter. It was plastic. It bounced. When the morning nurse came in—an older woman with round Midwestern vowels—I was shivering with the effort to stay awake.

But she washed and filled the same cup, gave me pills that matched the ones I'd taken earlier. She made some crack about how I looked as if I'd been chased through hell, and I was overcome with the sensation that I was missing something, something huge.

W HEN I FINALLY GOT SIGNED OUT OF THE INFIRMARY, IT WAS dinnertime. Mrs. Dunham insisted on escorting me back to my room.

"Now get into bed," she said, waiting with crossed arms until I did. "I've already talked to Tom, and he's going to bring you something back from the dining hall. I want you to call me if you need anything, or if you start feeling terrible, and we'll get you right to the hospital."

"Yes, Mrs. Dunham," I said unhappily. I was horribly ripe—I hadn't showered since before rugby practice—and starving, and ragged at the edges from my all-night vigil, and I just wanted to be left alone.

She bustled around, gathering extra blankets for my bed and picking Tom's clothes up from the floor. "I got special permission for an after-hours visit, if you'd like to see Charlotte."

"Thanks. I don't really need anything else," I said, because she was genuinely sweet, and she wasn't showing any signs of leaving.

"I love that you two are friends," she said. "Those stories were my favorite when I was younger."

I smiled tightly at her. It was terrible, the way my stomach contracted at that sentence. I'd used to love hearing people talk about the Sherlock Holmes stories, and now I couldn't help making anyone who mentioned them to me into a suspect. "They were mine too."

When Tom returned, he was juggling a sandwich, a pair of apples, and a cup of hot cocoa. "There you are," he said, arranging it all on my desk with a flourish. "I heard you ate it pretty hard at practice. Incredible catch, though, according to Randall."

I tore into the sandwich. "How are you? How are things with Lena?"

"She's good. What's Charlotte paying her off for? Lena's, like, rolling right now."

"That's from poker," I said, mouth full. I wanted to leave the investigation behind at least long enough to get through dinner.

"Well, are you and Charlotte still prime suspects?" he asked, pulling over a chair.

I shrugged. It hurt to. "Can we talk about something else? What did I miss in my history class? I got all my other assignments."

His face fell. "Nothing really," he said, and waited, as if he expected me to cave and tell him all about my adventures. I wished he knew how stressful and humiliating those adventures actually were. It wasn't my job to educate him on that, though, so I let the conversation die, crunching into one of the apples he'd brought. Eventually, Tom gave up on me.

Holmes swung by an hour later. Thankfully, I'd had a chance to shower. "How's the patient?" she asked as she perched on the edge of my bed.

I was always suspicious of Holmes in a good mood. "Has someone else been killed?" I asked, only half-joking.

She smiled at me. "Better. Try again."

Without turning around, Tom tugged out one of his ear-buds, then the other. I don't know why it annoyed me so much, his clumsy attempt at spying. Maybe I was done being grist for the gossip mill. I lifted an eyebrow in his direction to tip Holmes off, but she'd already noticed. She whipped out her phone.

"I've got a date," she announced, texting furiously. My phone lit up silently on the bed between us, and I craned my neck to see. *Apparently Wheatley's brother keeps snakes in NJ.*

"Where'd you find the guy? Craigslist? The sewers?" *Any missing?* I texted back.

Shepard's running it down. "Funny. You're funny. Look, I thought tomorrow you could help me write a poem for him. Maybe show it to Mr. Wheatley tomorrow after class, get his opinion?" *Interrogate him.*

Why don't you? "Love poems? It sounds serious."

"Oh, quite. He's dreamy." *Because you're his student. He doesn't know me.* She swung her legs off the bed. Furtively, she fished a chocolate bar out of her coat pocket and slid it onto the desk. It was a Cadbury Flake; she must've ordered it online. I don't know how she knew it was my favorite. "Feel better," she said, smiling crookedly at me, and then slipped out of the room.

Tom stuck his earphones back in with a sigh.

So you didn't find anything on Nurse Bryony? I texted her.

No. Sciences 442 at lunch. I heard her footsteps retreating down the hall. *We'll make a plan for Wheatley then.*

I LINGERED BY MR. WHEATLEY'S DESK AFTER CLASS, WAVING an inquisitive-looking Tom on to his next class. I had a free period at the end of the day, so I wasn't in a rush.

Wheatley was talking to one of our class's better poets, a shy, small girl who wrote exclusively about communing with nature in her native Michigan. As I waited, he gave her a series of book recommendations in his meandering, sleepy voice, and she scribbled them down. Our journals were identical. I tucked mine discreetly back in my bag, feeling a little cliché, and tried to focus on remembering the strategy that Holmes and I had hammered out at lunchtime.

Finally, he turned to me. "Ah, Mr. Watson," he said to me. "What can I do for you?"

I shuffled my feet. "I wanted to talk to you about my poems," I told him. "I'm having some trouble putting them together. They're a lot harder than stories. I was wondering if you had any books I could borrow to do some outside reading."

He nodded thoughtfully. "I have something in my office I could lend you. Follow me."

Wheatley's office was the kind of book-lined cave that, in other circumstances, I would've let myself get lost in. There was a hooded copper lamp on his desk that spotlit a stack of our manuscripts, and I recognized my most recent short story on the top. In the corner, a stand-up globe was turned so that a dusty Europe faced out. I sat gingerly in a chair and took a harder look around.

I didn't have the facility for observation that Holmes had, I knew that. But I'd always liked cataloging the details of a place and its people, using it as grist for my stories. Maybe that interest was more about romanticizing my surroundings than deducing from them, but it still spurred me to look closely at the authors of the books on his shelves (Kafka, Rumi, some Scandinavian mystery writers), the kind of rug on his floor (it had a folksy, hand-woven feel), the kind of coffee he was drinking (he'd brought it from home, in a stainless steel mug). I'd been too muddled and, frankly, scared to look that closely at Nurse Bryony when I was in the infirmary, and I was determined to have more to show for my efforts this time.

Wheatley hummed to himself as he ran his finger along a bookshelf. Though he was a nervous teacher—a pacer, a hand-wringer who started each sentence two or three times—he seemed at ease now, in his office, and I wondered if it was the confidence of a man who knew he had me in his power. Or maybe he just liked me, and was more comfortable speaking one-on-one. It was impossible for me to tell. I wished that Holmes were there.

"Found them," he said, pulling a few books from the shelf to hand to me. "There's a book of poetry prompts, in case you'd like to practice, and a collection of essays by contemporary poets that you might find useful in thinking about the impetus for writing a poem."

"Thanks." I tucked them in my bag.

"Your fiction is good, as I told you at homecoming," he said. "Clean and sharp, and very readable. Some of your plots are a bit far-fetched, but I don't mind the wish-fulfillment aspect of it. I think it runs in your blood, maybe. I read all your great-great-whatever-grandfather's stories when I was a boy. Wonderful. The movie adaptations from the thirties were very good, too."

I'd always hated those films—they'd portrayed Dr. Watson as a bumbling idiot, and Sherlock Holmes as an automaton. But I saw my opening, and took it. "They're great, aren't they? My favorite is the one about the snake. 'The Speckled Band.'"

"I know that story." Mr. Wheatley shuddered. "I hate snakes. My brother keeps them on his farm, and I—well, I make him visit *me*. Can't do it. After I heard what happened to that Dobson boy, I couldn't sleep for days."

His distress seemed genuine, but I couldn't be sure. "He was attacked by a snake?" I asked innocently.

"After he died," Mr. Wheatley said. "I'm surprised you don't know. Didn't the police talk to you about it?"

"They talked to *you* about it?"

He squirmed a little in his chair. It was strange to see an adult act so squirrelly. "I keep a close tab on the news. I have a friend on the force. You know."

I could tell he was lying. But it didn't mean I knew what the truth was.

"That reminds me," I said, trying a different tack. "I wanted to know about how to write from our lives, especially when things get weird and . . . unbelievable. Can you still do it? Write about them? You talk a lot about how we need to write from our own experiences, but when awful things happen—"

"You can talk to me about it, if you need to," he cut in. "It might help you organize your thoughts. You could even write me a story about it. For extra credit. After all, you've skipped almost a week's worth of classes."

I looked at my hands, wondering what he'd try to get out of me. It might be useful to play along.

Also, I could use the extra credit.

"Sure, I could try that," I said.

He pulled a legal pad out from under the stack of papers on his desk and balanced it on his knee. "So," he said, lifting a page or two and sliding a piece of cardboard beneath it. "What are you finding so unbelievable?"

"Well," I said, "it's a little weird that my best friend is a Holmes. I never really expected that to happen."

"Hm," he said, making a note. "Tell me more about your relationship with Charlotte Holmes?"

Even though I'd led him to the topic, I still found his tone obnoxious. I gritted my teeth. "Like I said, she's my best friend."

"And yet you went to the dance together. She could have more complicated feelings. It's important to consider these kinds of things," he said, slipping into teacher mode. "For character development."

If anyone had complicated feelings, it was me. And those were none of his fucking business. "We're talking about Charlotte Holmes here. I think she has complicated relationships even with the skeletons in her lab. Nothing is straightforward to her."

I thought I'd dodged the question, but his eyes lit up.

"She keeps skeletons in her office," he said, scribbling it down. "Interesting."

"Her lab," I corrected him. Too late, I remembered what Holmes had taught me, about how easy it is to get people to correct you.

"Where's her lab?" he asked, not looking at me.

"I can't remember," I lied. "She doesn't let anyone in there."

"Very private," he said. "Good. She has kind of a goth look to her, doesn't she? Is it cultivated, do you think?"

"Holmes wears what she wants to wear. Like I do." I frowned. "She's not some agent of death. Or a cartoon. I always thought she looked very London, that's all. I don't understand how this would help me write this story."

"Character development," he repeated. "Tell me, when she investigates, does she behave much like her famous forebear?"

"Sherlock?" I asked. "I don't know, I haven't exactly met him in the flesh."

Mr. Wheatley laughed, then abruptly stopped. "No. Really. Does she?"

It went on for a long time. I let him draw me out bit by bit, noting carefully to hear where he directed the conversation. I told him that I'd been struggling to write down the story of Dobson's death and the police's investigation into my life, but Mr. Wheatley didn't want to talk about Dobson at all. I took it as a sign that he already knew all there was to know about "that poor boy" and his murder. And though everyone on campus knew now that Holmes and I had found Elizabeth unconscious in the quad, he didn't even ask about her either.

But Holmes? Mr. Wheatley wanted to know everything: about her childhood, about her older brother (whose name he readily knew), about the circumstances of her coming to Sherringford. Thankfully, my own knowledge of her was patchwork enough that I could plead ignorance. But it was all incredibly damning, watching him write down her whole dossier. Why could he possibly want that information except to use it against us?

That is, until he ripped the sheet he'd been writing on from his legal pad and handed it over to me. I stared at it for a minute, not understanding. "There. Sometimes it helps to say it all aloud before you start shaping your piece. But it all sounds very hard to deal with, Jamie, like I'd said before." He leaned over to scribble something at the top of the paper. "If you'd prefer to talk to someone else, here's the name of the school therapist. She's very kind, and you shouldn't be ashamed about making an appointment. Most people eventually do."

I folded the sheet and put it in my pocket, feeling distinctly ashamed. He'd just been trying to help after all, if a little ham-handedly. Mr. Wheatley was a good man, and he was concerned about me, and still I had been imagining him to be out for my blood. Wondering if he had lowered that rattlesnake onto Dobson's convulsing form.

Was this what it was always like, doing detective work? How could you ever let yourself get close to anyone? No wonder Holmes was so determined to keep herself apart.

When I left Wheatley's office, I went straight to Sciences 442. It had only taken an hour alone for Holmes to trash her lab. The carpet was an explosion of open file folders, their pages spread out like snow. Something bright green was frothing over on a Bunsen burner, and the entire room smelled of cilantro. In the midst of all this chaos, Holmes was slumped on the floor in her uniform like a black-and-white bird, smoking a cigarette and reading *The History of Dirt*. It was so gigantic that she had to brace it against her knees. Above her, the vulture skeletons swung lazily on their strings. During one of our marathon research sessions, I'd decided to name them Julian and George, and today, Julian's skull sported a small knife that looked as if it'd been stabbed there. I shuddered.

"Your book looks great," I said, picking a path across the room. "What's the sequel? *Worms and You?*"

"Don't tease, I know nothing about American soils. And the idea of tracing a murder victim by the contents of their shoe soles is hardly far-fetched." She turned a page, and I could see that she was incredibly tense. "You sound disappointed. You don't suspect Wheatley, then."

"I don't," I said. "Or Nurse Bryony. Or maybe I suspect both of them because we have a disappeared dealer, and I want someone concrete to suspect. I'm in some muddled state where I can't tell what I think."

"It's because you care," she said. "About nearly everyone. It's remarkable, really, but in this instance, it clouds your judgment. It's why I try to avoid sentiment."

"That's heartless," I said, stung. All this time, had I been nothing more to her than someone to carry her bag?

"I said, I *try* to avoid it, do keep up." She shut her book and fixed her lantern eyes on me. "Trust me, if Milo were involved in a murder plot, I'd find it very difficult to assist him. It's not *heartlessness* if it saves lives."

She was spoiling for a fight, but I made myself back down. I thought of the Cadbury Flake on my desk, the time she leaned over to straighten my glasses in the middle of a conversation. She was either much better or much worse at this whole caring business than she thought. "Wheatley's getting information about the two of us somewhere, and he's definitely watching you closely."

"That surprises you?" she asked.

I bit back a remark about her being the center of the universe.

"Well, yes. No. I don't know. He also seems genuinely afraid of snakes," I said, wanting to defend him. "And genuinely concerned with what's happening to me."

"I'd suspect him less if he seemed indifferent," Holmes pointed out. "Did he try to dig into your oh-so-compelling trauma?"

"No." I paused. "Well, a little. He referred me to a therapist."

"Psychology." She snorted. "All the same."

I threw up my hands. "What about the other names on the suspects list? You know, the ones who aren't Romanian royalty or pop stars. The Moriartys. What about August? Is he really dead?"

"Nothing to report." Holmes drew on her cigarette, her eyes narrowing. "Honestly, sod all this, none of this is *correct*. We have the data and the access but we've made no progress, and I've smoked at least twenty of these horrible things today and I am developing a wretched dependency, just you watch, we'll be out in the middle of some sodding field watching a perfectly captivating murder take place firsthand, and I'll have to run off in the middle because I need to have a Lucky Strike right then or *I'll* be the one doing the killing." She stabbed out her cigarette against the love seat's arm, and in the same gesture, lit another. I'd heard her run off on tangents before, but none this frustrated or angry.

"Then stop. Smoking."

"Do you really want me to revert to the alternative?" she snapped.

"Maybe we should take the night off," I said. "Go get pancakes, plan for tomorrow."

I could have blamed myself for having wound her up in the first place, but Holmes had been itching for a confrontation from the moment I walked through the door. The look she gave me then was the one you saved for cockroaches, shoe in hand. "This is what I *do*. You want me to stop? You think you can talk about it like it's a *game*?"

The acid in her tone ate away the last of my patience. "I'm saying that you should take a night off, not that you should abandon it completely."

"You can't handle the pace, then."

"No! God, if we're so stuck, why won't we just call in your parents—"

"I refuse to have them involved—"

"Don't you think that getting your head on straight can

take priority, for once, to proving yourself to your family?"

She pulled herself up, as proud and straight as an ancient queen. Her face was a perfect blank. The only glimmer of Holmes I could see was in the anger darkening her eyes.

"Yes," she said in a flat voice. "I hadn't thought of that. I, of course, have no personal stake in this matter. Since this is all an exercise to please my *parents*."

"Holmes—"

"So yes, take the night off. In the meantime, I'll be tracking down the person who murdered my rapist and tried to murder *your* little girlfriend and then almost had us arrested for it. It might even move faster without you, as you've proven yourself so extraordinarily useless."

It was the first time she'd ever said anything that cruel to me. The word *useless* hung between us, like a millstone on a piece of thread.

"How can I help you," I snarled, "when you keep so much information to yourself? There's a Moriarty plastered all over that wall that you refuse to talk about. You've told me nothing about your relationship with him."

"With him? Don't you mean *to* him?" she asked. "Is this about the case, or your jealousy?"

Her hand flew up to her mouth as if to stop the words from coming out. But it was too late.

"Okay, then." There was nothing else to say. I put my coat on, not sure where I was headed but knowing that it was some-where the hell away from here.

"Watson." Holmes got to her feet.

"I'm fine."

"I know I can be perfectly beastly—"

"You can," I said. "And why don't you just call me Jamie, like everyone else, since I'm too *useless* to be your Watson."

Holmes's mouth opened and snapped shut. I slammed the door hard enough that, behind me, I heard the satisfying crash of a beaker shattering on the floor.

eight

I PACED OUTSIDE OF MICHENER HALL, BLOWING ON MY hands to keep them warm. By the time I banged through the front door, I was mostly in control of myself again. Mrs. Dunham was manning the front desk—did she ever go home?—but I walked straight past her without a word, not wanting to test my hard-won composure.

Usually, my room was empty the hour before dinner, but that day Tom was watching a video on his computer, eating a chocolate bar. On the screen, a girl performed a burlesque routine to a song sung in French. I recognized a few of the words: *leave it, leave it all.* Biting her lip, she lowered one strap, the other.

"Are you okay?" Tom asked, hitting Pause. The girl in the video froze obediently.

"Fine," I said. "Bad day."

"You don't seem to have a lot of good ones," he observed. There was a smear of chocolate on his argyle sweater-vest, and I realized the wrapper on his desk was from the Flake bar Holmes had given me. It shouldn't have been a big deal— Tom and I had standing permission to raid each other's food stashes, within reason—but I took it like a blow to the gut.

"I don't see why that's shocking, considering," I said, and willed him to go away.

Ever since I'd come to Sherringford, I'd existed in a state of constant loneliness without ever actually being alone. Privacy was an illusion at boarding school. There was always another body in the room, and if there wasn't, one could enter at any moment. Being Holmes's friend might have taken the edge off that loneliness, but it didn't dissipate entirely. At best, our friendship made me feel as though I was a part of something larger, something grander; that, with her, I'd been given access to a world whose unseen currents ran parallel to ours. But at our friendship's worst, I wasn't sure I was her friend at all. Maybe some human echo chamber or a conductor for her brilliant light.

I hadn't realized I was thinking out loud until Tom cleared his throat.

"I had a friend like that once," he said.

"Oh?" I said, uninterested. But Tom had a thoughtful expression on, and I didn't want to be cruel.

"Andrew," he said. "He was the only person I really kept in touch with after I left for Sherringford, and last summer, we hung out all the time. He's this all-state football star, and he always gets perfect grades, and I swear he could get away with murder because of it. Because ninety percent of the time, he was so good, he could stay out all night downtown, partying, and he'd come in at dawn and his parents would just buy that he was out late studying. I felt . . . invincible when I was around him."

"What happened?" I asked.

"Cops caught us drinking down by the lake, and he pinned the whole thing on me." Tom flashed a self-deprecating smile. "His family is like a big deal—they have all this money, and we don't, not anymore—so they got the charges dropped. But I was in the doghouse for months. The worst part of it was that he stopped talking to me. If anything, I should've been the one who got to tell him to eat shit."

"I'm sorry." It was hard to imagine Tom being on anyone's bad side. He was the guy who could wear a baby-blue suit to homecoming and still have one of the hottest girls in school as his date.

"It's not worth it being the sidekick," he said. "I bet she just uses you to do her dirty work. Andrew used to do that to me."

"Sometimes," I said, hiding how close to the bone that cut.

He gave me a knowing look. "So she doesn't even let you do that."

"No," I snapped. "She trusted me to sniff out Mr. Wheatley. And I went out and got a fucking concussion because no one would investigate the school nurse. I don't call that doing nothing."

Tom looked like I'd hit him. "You *what?*"

"All right, it was stupid, and I couldn't have planned it exactly—maybe I would've broken my arm, or twisted my ankle—but I couldn't exactly fake having to stay in the infirmary all day, could I? How else could Holmes have snuck in there without breaking in? The door's alarmed, they keep everyone's medicine in there."

"No—I—"

He was casting around for words, but none were coming. Did he really think that I was so useless I couldn't help her out at all?

"I didn't know you were that stupid," he said finally.

"Thanks, you twat."

"Don't mention it," he said. "Look, I'm meeting Lena for dinner, so I gotta go. I'm doing some work at the library after that, but we can talk more about your life choices tonight, if you want to."

Tom and Lena. Mine and Holmes's shadow-selves. Or maybe we were the shadows, and they the happy, well-adjusted versions. "Don't worry about it," I said. "I'm fine."

After throwing some books in his bag, he took off. He must've bumped the keyboard as he went, though, because the video he'd been playing unpaused. The girl on the screen began shimmying out of her clothes again. I plunked down in Tom's chair and closed the window, then sat there for a minute, staring at the notes Tom had pinned above his desk, the tiny mirror he'd put there.

That's when I noticed it.

His desk and mine were across from each other, meaning that most nights we did our homework back to back. The only mirror in our room had been clumsily hung to the right of where I sat, its bottom half obscured by my desk. If I sat up in the middle of the night, I'd catch a glimpse of my reflection and panic that we had an intruder. That was, more or less, all that mirror was good for.

I didn't mind that much. I cared a bit about what I wore on the weekend, but our school uniform was exactly that, a uniform, and so the way I looked in it didn't change. Tom, on the other hand, wore all kinds of product in his hair, and rather than lean awkwardly over my desk to apply it, or do it in the bathroom (which he claimed was "embarrassing," as if he'd be dispelling some notion that his boy-band mop grew in that way), he'd tacked up a locker-sized mirror above his desk.

All this is to say that, when I looked up into Tom's mirror, I was at the precise angle to see that there was a gap between my own mirror and the wall. A small gap. A centimeter.

In that centimeter's worth of dark, I could see the glimmer of a reflection.

Something was back there.

I walked over, got down on my knees, made blinkers with my hands to block the overhead light. Still I couldn't make out what was behind it. After straightening a wire hanger from my closet, I rattled it in the gap in an attempt to dislodge whatever was back there. I hit on nothing, even when I ran it from top to bottom. When I looked again, I could still see the glimmer of light reflecting off something.

Was it a lens?

I took a deep breath and tried to gather my thoughts. On the bed, my phone buzzed, and I seized it, thinking it might be Holmes. It would be a relief. We'd both been horrible to each other, we'd both been keyed up, and defeated, and lost—I couldn't imagine what being lost felt like for someone as whip-smart as Charlotte Holmes—and I refused to believe that she'd meant what she'd said. It had to be her. She'd come right over. Everything would be fine.

But the text was from my mother, asking if I'd forgotten our weekly call. She'd try again later tonight, she said, and signed it with kisses.

I looked back into the gap. The light was still shining.

Someone had been in here. Someone had put this thing in my room.

In a sudden, towering wave of rage, I jerked the desk away from the wall, scattering my textbooks in the process. Standing in the space I'd cleared, I braced both my hands against the mirror and pulled. It refused to give. I planted my feet, trying to remember what Coach Q had taught us about taking down a bigger opponent, and pulled, harder. Harder. There was a faint cracking sound—probably its bolts beginning to pull from the plaster—but it still refused to move. Panting, I stared at my reflection. My eyes were all pupil, my face sweaty and red. I looked how I did at the end of a rugby match. Like a Neanderthal.

Fine. I'd be a Neanderthal. With a grunt, I picked up my chemistry text from the desk and slammed it into the mirror.

It didn't give on the first try, or the second. Around the tenth, I stopped counting and instead watched the webbed crack grow from the middle of the mirror to its edges. Outside, in the hall, someone yelled *What the hell is going on,* but I ignored them; it wasn't hard to. The mirror may have been sturdily constructed, but like all things made of glass, it eventually gave. There was a great loud splintering *crack* as it broke, and I spun away, throwing the textbook up to shield my face. It hadn't shattered out so much as down, but some pieces had flown out and stuck into the flesh of my hands. I was in such a fury that I couldn't feel them there.

Because when I turned to look, I saw a small, circular lens, the size of my thumbnail, with a cord that ran into a wireless device. It'd been adhered to the wall with a bit of tape.

But how could the camera capture anything through the mirror? I bent and gingerly picked up one of its larger pieces—I'm not sure why I bothered; my hands were already bleeding—and turned it front to back. Both sides appeared to be glass. A two-way mirror.

What came next I can only describe as a fugue state. I'd understood what it was to lose myself in the past, when I'd been in a rage, but this time the feeling was coupled with crippling fear and violation. Someone had seen me get dressed. Someone had seen me sleep. And though I couldn't find a microphone on the camera, I was sure that this someone had also recorded every word I'd said.

So there had to be an audio recording device, as well.

I tore the books off my shelf, dumped out my desk drawers,

went through every pocket of every pair of trousers hanging in my closet. I took my Swiss Army knife and cut open my mattress, not caring about the fine I'd have to pay, and searched every inch of it with my bleeding fingers. I got on my hands and knees and pulled up the carpet in our room inch by inch, using the knife to help me along. I cut open the curtains, then looked down the hollow rod that held them up. And I adamantly ignored the noise in the hall that had now increased to a fever pitch—a fist was pounding on the door, and a voice that sounded like Mrs. Dunham's shouted *Jamie, Jamie, I know you're in there,* but I'd already shoved Tom's desk chair under the doorknob and thrown the deadbolt. It was easy to turn the volume for the outside world all the way down, what with the screaming panic in my head.

When all was said and done, I'd come up with two electronic bugs, each the size and shape of my thumbnail. One had been affixed to the wall-facing side of my headboard. The other I found on the bottom of my desk chair. I held them in my cupped hands, striping them with blood. Their data must have been sent to the transmitter wirelessly, because they weren't attached to anything with any cords that I could see. I set them down on my desk in a neat line, along with the camera, which I'd yanked the cord from. Then I threw them into a pillowcase. If they were still transmitting, the spy on the other end would be looking into a black screen.

I heard a buzzing sound. Was it from blood loss? Not unlikely. My room looked as if some howling, wounded beast had ripped it up with its claws. Everything I owned was on the floor, a good deal of it tracked red from my hands, and I hadn't even searched through Tom's things yet. I'd been able to control myself that much, to wait until he returned, but there was still the problem of the bugs. What to do with them? I thought, woozily, that I should call the detective. I should call Holmes. Come to think of it, there was still shouting in the hall. Was I imagining it?

My name: *Jamie, Jamie, Jamie.*

"Go away," I hollered, and eased myself down into the chair. I was beginning to feel the cuts on my hands, the glass that I'd pushed still further into the skin with each new thing I'd rifled through or discarded. I should go to the infirmary, I thought, but I didn't want to tip off anyone—anyone who hadn't already heard the commotion, that is—and Nurse Bryony was still sharing space with Mr. Wheatley on my no-fly list.

I hunted through my shaving kit for a pair of tweezers, put a T-shirt between my teeth, and got down to the business of pulling out the glass. It wasn't sanitary, God knows, but it also hadn't been a good day for making decisions. *You don't seem to have a lot of good ones,* Tom had said. He wasn't wrong. I nearly bit through the cloth trying not to scream, but I didn't manage to keep myself from crying. It wasn't so much from sadness or pain as acceptance of the impossible, a great well of *this is wrong* bubbling up all at once. I wondered absently if the transmitters on my desk were picking up the sound. One more shameful thing in with all the rest. I resisted the urge to smash the audio bugs like the insects they were—I'd need them as evidence, after all.

What I didn't understand was why they'd bugged my room. Who was I, anyway? I wasn't the extraordinary one. I was Jamie Watson, would-be writer, subpar rugger, keeper of the most boring journal in at least five states. I couldn't even get people to call me by my full first name. If I was important, it was only as a conduit. Holmes's only access point.

What information had I revealed, unwittingly, in this room? What had I given away?

With a growing sense of horror, I realized that I'd given away plenty, even some that day. Mr. Wheatley; the faked concussion; the search through Bryony's things: I'd said all of it out loud. I'd spent the week after the murder telling Tom about all our suspicions and our findings, what we'd found in Dobson's room. I'd even bitched about August Moriarty. God, how stupid could I have possibly been?

By now, I was sure they knew I'd found their bugs. I needed to get over to Sciences 442 and sweep our lab, see if Holmes could trace the signal. If she couldn't, I knew that Milo could, and I knew he wasn't more than a phone call away.

The shirt I'd been wearing was ruined, smeared with blood and bits of glass. I stripped it off and shook it out before I tore it into makeshift bandages for my hands. The knots I'd made would hold, but not for long. Maybe we could steal Lena's car keys again and go to the hospital. *We*, I kept thinking, *we*. I knew she'd forgive me. She had to. Without each other, we could, quite literally, die.

I put on a clean shirt and flung open the door only to trip over Mrs. Dunham. She'd slouched down against the wall outside my room, legs kicked out before her. It was clear from her face that she was crying.

"Jamie," she said hoarsely. I knelt down beside her. "What have you done to yourself? Look at your hands! And your face—are you hurt? I heard the worst noises coming from your room."

"I didn't mean to scare you," I told her. "I'm fine. Everything's fine."

That phrase was beginning to sound meaningless.

She leaned over to look inside my room and pulled back in shock. "Oh, *Jamie.* What have you done?"

"I've got to go," I said, "but I'll explain later, I promise, I've got to find Holmes."

She grabbed at my hand to keep me from leaving, and I bit back a yell of pain.

"I guess that means you haven't heard," she said, and her eyes misted over with tears. "Oh, Jamie, I didn't want to be the one to tell you. But there's been an accident. A horrible, horrible accident."

Mrs. Dunham said it'd only happened ten minutes before—had it only been ten minutes since I found that camera? It could have been seconds, or years, for all I could tell—and that campus was being evacuated, building by building. Michener Hall was empty except for the two of us. She'd thought I'd destroyed my room on hearing the news. Because she, unlike everyone else, knew where Holmes's main haunt was.

They were blaming it on a gas explosion, she'd said.

I'd pelted across campus at a dead run. It was beginning to snow, a powder-dusting that clung to my bare arms and the bandages on my hands. I'd forgotten my coat, my phone. My heart beat harder as I got to the quad.

From clear across campus, I could see that the sciences building was a smoking ruin.

My phone. Where was my phone? What if Holmes was trying to call me? What if she was trapped in the building somewhere? That was the worst possibility I'd allowed myself to imagine, that Julian and George's flightless bones had collapsed on top of her, but that she was fine underneath—a little sooty from the smoke, perhaps, but fine . . . but then, I wasn't giving her enough credit. Holmes was a magician. She had to be standing outside, whole and hale and intact, smoking a cigarette as she watched it all burn. Most important, she'd be alive. Still furious with me, I'd give the universe that—she could never want to speak to me again for all I cared—so long as she was alive.

All of that went straight from my mind when I saw it. It wasn't possible. The northwest corner of Sciences was blown clear through: the corner where Holmes's supply closet was. Battered pieces of granite had thudded mightily to the ground. Through the smoke, I could see the building's interior walls, tattered and stacked like the pages of an old book lit with a match. Here and there, bits of broken wall were still smoldering.

Somewhere in the distance sirens sounded. Uniformed

police officers were cordoning off the area, pushing the few bystanders back into a huddled mass of winter coats. Over a bullhorn, a voice ordered any remaining students to report to the union for further instructions. An officer had set up a standing light that sharply illuminated the building's entrance. There would be a thorough search, he was saying. The firemen would pull out any survivors.

Survivors.

I pushed past him, and the other officer waving a pair of plastic flares, and then past a yellow-suited fireman—there were fire engines behind me, now, flashing their lights—who snagged me by the arm. The look I turned on him must've been that of a feral dog because he loosened his grip for the half second it took me to shake him off. I took off in a sprint toward the front door, and was instantly tackled to the ground.

They wrestled me back toward the emergency vehicles where they assigned an officer to be my babysitter and made me sit under his watchful eye on the edge of the fire engine. They didn't want to arrest me, they said, but they would if I tried to take off again. So I sat dully while the red lights washed everything with fire. At some point, the officer, in a moment of compassion, pressed a cup of something hot into my bandaged hands. He tried to convince me to put on his jacket, but I wanted his pity even less than I wanted his attention. Possibly I insulted his mother. I couldn't remember. He kept away from me after that.

I wondered what Holmes's funeral would be like. I felt sick for a while, and then I stopped really feeling anything at all.

Someone must have taken my wallet from my pocket, or done some calling around, because suddenly my father was there at my elbow. He led me to his car, where the heater was running full blast, and said something about taking me to the hospital. My hands. I'd forgotten about my hands. They were the first words of his I'd registered.

"*No.*" I felt my body come alive with terror. "No, Dad, someone is after us, and I can't go to the hospital. I have to find Holmes. Don't you see? I can't tell you until I know it's safe but there's something very *wrong* going on and I need her. I need her here, do you understand?"

I can only imagine what I must have looked like, half-mad with terror and grief and covered in my own blood, ranting at him from the passenger seat.

But my father did an amazing thing. He put the car into park. Slowly, as if he might scare me into flight, he reached over to cup the back of my head. "I understand," he said. "For now, let's just go home."

He put it into drive and turned on the headlights. And there she was, standing in their white glow.

Holmes's skin was smoked black from the explosion, her hair flecked with snow. Her violin dangled from her fingers. She opened her mouth, and I saw her say my name.

I was out of the car in a heartbeat, and in the next, she was in my arms.

Holmes was always Holmes, even after a terrible shock. With the utmost care, she reached around me to place her Stradivarius on the sedan's purring hood. Only once it was secure did she allow herself to be held, and even then, she kept her palms on my chest as if to brace herself. She was slight, and freezing cold. Her posture, as always, was perfect.

"You're alive," I murmured, tucking my head over hers. "I'm so sorry."

For once she didn't chide me for stating the obvious. Instead, she let out a long, shuddering breath. "The only thing I saved was my Strad, and I had to go back in for it. Watson, I was in the bathroom, and if I hadn't been—the bomb was planted in our lab."

I laughed hollowly. "They're saying it's a gas explosion."

She shifted to look up into my face. "A homemade bomb, and in our lab. There was shrapnel stuck in the walls. Watson"—she kept returning to my name—"I assume you look such a mess because you've found wiretaps in your room, and not because you've taken up cage fighting."

"The cut hands," I guessed, seizing on this chance to feel normal, "and what else?"

"The fact that you're stuck all over with glass like some porcupine. Camera behind the mirror, and then, of course, you'd look for the audio. Which made you feel both personally wronged and suspicious—if you don't trust someone, your left eye twitches at the corner. Right now, it's happening every three seconds. By looking at the kinds of mud on your shoes, it'd only take moments to trace your route from Michener—"

I pulled her back up against me, and she battered my chest with ineffective fists.

"You are doing this to shut me up," she complained.

"I am," I said, and she began to cry. I backed off. "I'm sorry, I didn't mean to—"

"It's not you. This is horrifying," she said through her tears. "I'm not in the least sad. Why am I crying?"

My father bundled us together in the backseat under a moth-eaten blanket; I insisted that we wrap her Strad in another. I tucked her under my arm, and she wept quietly the whole way.

ABBIE, MY FATHER'S WIFE, HAD MADE UP THE GUEST ROOM, and after we arrived Holmes took a cursory look at the bugs from my dorm room, pronounced them dead, and put herself straight to bed. While my father went to call the school, my stepmother pulled me aside to ask where she should put the inflatable mattress.

"Are you having sex with her?" Abbie asked, and promptly looked mortified. "I'm sorry. I'm not used to teenagers, and I can't believe the first thing I've ever said to James's son is . . . I don't really know how to . . . are you two having sex?"

"We're not," I assured her. Bizarrely, this was proving the perfect way for us to meet—unscheduled, without expectations. I didn't have the energy to hate her. Honestly, I couldn't feel anything except tempered relief. Holmes was safe, if in shock. We were being looked after, if only for a night. And Abbie had an open, charming face, with a spray of freckles across her nose, and I was so tired. I decided to just get it over with and start liking her.

"Then I'm putting you in with Charlotte," she said, "so don't start tonight. Having sex, I mean. And your nose is blue—are you hypothermic? Go run yourself a hot bath."

Upstairs, I peeled off my makeshift bandages in the bathroom sink. I had to soak in the tub with my hands resting over the sides so I wouldn't bleed into the water. Afterward, I put on some of my father's old sweats and let Abbie lead me down to the kitchen table. After giving me some Advil, she cleaned out the wounds in my hands with antiseptic and, with a pair of tweezers she'd sterilized, took out the rest of the glass shards under my skin. Then she got to work on my scalp. I clamped my mouth shut to keep from yelling.

My father came in halfway through the process. He'd been on hold all that time, as Sherringford's lines were jammed with panicked parents calling in. Finally, the school had sent out a mass email. He read it off to us there at the table. There hadn't been any casualties from the "gas leak," thank God, though the physics teacher had been in his lab and suffered "minor injuries." But Sherringford was shut down for the rest of the semester.

It's about time, I thought.

My father kept reading something about rescheduled finals, and incompletes, but I didn't pay much attention because I didn't care. There was too much else to think about. The letter said that, after the explosion, students had been evacuated to a nearby Days Inn under the supervision of the RAs and house mothers until their parents could come retrieve them. Tomorrow, Sherringford was bringing in a specialist team from Boston to sweep the campus for other possible "leaks," and after they gave the all clear, students would be escorted, in roommate pairs, to get their things. They'd give us each ten minutes to pack. The schedule for each dorm had been attached.

My father put his smartphone away and looked me hard in the eye. "Charlotte is here. She's safe. And I've been very patient. But now I need you to either give me an explanation for why you've fifteen vicious cuts and an exploded science building, or I'm taking you to the hospital."

Abbie's hands stilled in my hair.

I tried my best to sketch it out for him: my fight with Holmes, the bugged room and the broken mirror, the home-made bomb, our suspicions about Mr. Wheatley and Nurse Bryony and the Moriartys, what I'd said to Tom in our room.

My father had out his ever-present notebook, and he jotted things down as I spoke. When I came to the part about August Moriarty—how the records on him just stopped, what Milo had scrubbed from the *Daily Mail*, the thing Charlotte wouldn't tell me—my father made a disgruntled sound. "Jamie. Number fifteen: if you wait for full disclosure from a Holmes, it might be years before you learn a damn thing."

I threw up my hands. "Tabloids, Dad. The *Daily Mail*. Have they ever been an accurate source of information? And anyway, I couldn't look it up even if I wanted to."

"You," my father said sadly, "still have rather a lot to learn. Don't you remember the stories I used to tell you about Charlotte?"

222

"Yes," I said. "I'm not stupid."

"Since you're not stupid, you have, of course, reasoned from that information that I've kept tabs on her since she was a little girl. And that I most likely have a file or two up in my study that could fill you in on some of this."

The answers had been there all this time.

All this time. In my childhood home.

I opened my mouth to ask him for the file when he looked at me and said, "You know, if you hadn't been so unfairly angry with me, you might have gotten your hands on it weeks ago."

That settled it. Because I might have had a burning need to know the truth about Charlotte Holmes, might have obsessed over it for an endless string of awful nights—but I still resented my father more.

"I don't want it."

He looked like I'd struck him. "What?"

"You heard me," I told him. "This is between the two of us, and I trust her."

"But—"

"I trust her, Dad." It was true, after all.

"Of course. Of course you do." My father sighed, pinching the bridge of his nose. "Right. Anyway, that detective of yours has been calling me all night. Do you not have your mobile? No? That explains it. I'll call him back and tell him what you told me"—he lifted his notebook—"if you'd like to go to bed."

"Yes, more than anything." I stood unsteadily. "No hospital, then?"

He gave a surprised laugh. "Are you mad? Someone's trying to kill you. No, you're staying right here." Shaking his head, he disappeared into the hallway.

Abbie was putting away her first-aid kit, smiling to herself. Did she think all of this was fun? I subtracted a few of the points I'd given her.

"What exactly is so funny?"

"It's like you're his mini-me," she said. "Oh, it's awful, all of it, but it's like a spy movie! I mean, how cool."

Well, my father had married the right woman. She was just as insensitive as he was.

"My best friend almost died today," I said to her. "It was a really close call. I don't think that's *cool*."

She patted me on the shoulder. "If you hold on a sec, I'll get a fitted sheet for that mattress."

I stomped up the stairs with an armload of linens. In the guest room, Holmes was curled under the floral coverlet, sound asleep in her clothes. She'd scrubbed some of the dirt from her face, but not all of it, and she looked like a Dickensian orphan against the white sheets. I unfolded the blanket from the end of the bed and tucked it over her, standing for a long moment to watch the moon move across her hair. She was alive. She would wake up tomorrow to scheme and argue with me, to bring me terrible sandwiches, to push against me until I made myself a better partner. Her sad eyes and her sharp tongue and the way she touched my shoulder when she thought I wasn't listening. I was always listening.

She was right there, and still I couldn't believe it. I resisted the urge to brush her hair away from her forehead. She stirred, and I pulled my hand back.

"Watson, what is it?"

"Nothing. Go back to sleep."

"I shouldn't," she said, pushing herself up. "We need to work this case. Something terrible is about to happen."

I gently pushed her back down. "Not tonight. Nothing will happen tonight. Go back to sleep." I pulled my mattress up next to the bed and lay down; it sighed out a long breath of air.

"Watson."

"What?"

"I'm sorry I picked a fight with you," Holmes said sleepily. "But you should know that I had a good reason."

"I know, I was being an idiot." I really didn't want to do this now, I didn't, but I would if I had to.

"No. It wasn't your fault." Her voice was fading into a thin whisper. "The note said you'd be killed if you stayed, so I fixed it. I was horrible until you went away."

I sat straight up into the dark, but Holmes was already asleep.

HAD IT BEEN ANY OTHER DAY IN THE HISTORY OF MY LIFE, and I'd been told something like that, I would have stopped sleeping altogether.

But that night, I was out in the space of ten minutes. It wasn't that I felt particularly brave, or that I'd resigned myself to my violent, rapidly approaching death (though that wasn't a bad plan, really). My body had just proved itself physically incapable of handling more terror. Enough, it decided, and shut the whole thing down.

I woke as the first rays of sun crept into the room. More precisely, I woke to a toddler-shaped eclipse.

"Hi," he said, placing a sticky hand square on my mouth.

I removed it carefully, sitting up. "Hello," I said. "How did you get in here?"

Holmes's bed was rumpled and empty, the door wide open.

"I like ducks." He looked disconcertingly like pictures I'd seen of myself as a child. Guileless eyes, wild dark hair. My mother used to say I could get away with murder, and looking at him, I believed it.

For the record, I'd never resented my half brothers for anything that happened between my father and me. They were little kids, and none of it was their fault.

Besides, he was pretty cute.

"I like ducks too," I said, and scooped him up to take him downstairs with me. Thankfully, I wasn't inexperienced at talking to babies—I had a whole mess of little cousins. "What's your name?"

"Malcolm," he said in a shy voice. "Your name is Jamie."

"That's right." I bounced him a little as we walked into the kitchen.

"It snowed!" he yelled, pointing out the back door at the expanse of white lawn.

I wondered what the wreckage of the sciences building looked like this morning. Our destroyed lab open to the air, all shrouded in white. With a strange pang, I wondered if Holmes's collection of teeth survived.

Abbie turned around from the stove where she was making pancakes. "Oh no, Mal attack! Sorry about that. I wanted to let you sleep in."

I shrugged, juggling Malcolm to my other arm. "It's okay, he was just saying hi. Have you seen Holmes? I need to find her, and kill her."

She gave me a dubious look. "In the family room, with your father and Robbie. He's showing her the cat."

"I didn't know you had a cat," I said, trying to make conversation. I did, in fact, know they had a cat. I was really hoping to get one of those pancakes.

Abbie frowned and didn't offer me one. "It's skittish and hates everyone. Robbie spent the last hour trying to find him for her."

"Come along," I singsonged to Malcolm, "we're going to meet Miss Charlotte, who thinks that keeping Mister Jamie in the dark is a fun, fun game."

In the family room, my father and Holmes were examining a piece of paper they'd laid out on the coffee table. The cat—a handsome tabby—was purring on her lap.

"But it hates me," the small boy at her feet was saying plaintively. "Why does he like *you*?"

She looked down at him, considering. "Because I have a bigger lap for him to sit on. Wait ten or so years, and then he might like you better."

Robbie burst into tears.

"Right," my father said. He took Malcolm from me and grabbed Robbie by the hand, leading him from the room as he sobbed. "Let's see if your mother has finished with those pancakes."

Holmes hardly noticed. She whipped out a tiny magnifying glass and leaned over the paper. "Watson, come here and tell me what you can make of this."

"Is it going to explain why you kept direct communications from our stalker a secret from me, choosing instead to inflict some serious psychic damage with the end goal of getting me to leave you to deal with a bomb all by yourself?"

"Yes." She didn't even look up. "Come here."

She'd squared the note in the middle of the table. As I approached, I saw that she'd laid a sandwich bag between it and the wood.

Holmes handed me a pair of latex gloves. "They were in your stepmother's first-aid kit," she said by way of explanation. "Go on. What do you see?"

I read it aloud.

IF YOU KEEP DRAGGING JAMES WATSON
INTO THIS HE WILL DIE TO
TONIGHT
HE DOESN'T DESERVE IT THE WAY YOU DO
THIS WON'T STOP UNTIL YOU HAVE
LEARNT YOUR LESSON

"A grammar error," I said. " 'To,' instead of 'too.' Spellcheck wouldn't catch that. And learned is spelled the English way. 'Learnt.'"

She gestured impatiently. "What else?"

"Well, it's a death threat. Though they seem to like me more than they like you." Gingerly, I lifted the note by its corner. It was square, cut from regular printer paper, thin to the touch. There was a crease down the middle, probably from where Holmes had put it in her pocket. The ink was black. I held it up to the light, but I couldn't see anything special about the rest of it.

I told her my observations, and she nodded, pleased. Maybe I wasn't so useless after all.

"What did you come up with?" I asked her.

"All the things you didn't," she said, and took the page from me. "Our letter-writer is most likely a woman, and she's writing it on her own behalf. Look, she's used one of those specialty sans-serif fonts, the kind that doesn't come standard. You'd have to download it, and you wouldn't put in that sort of effort if you were someone's lackey—you'd just use Times New Roman, whatever the default was. And that would be the smarter move, too. Either she's so up herself she feels she doesn't need to cover her tracks, or she wrote this in an absolute hurry and that was the default font."

I took it back and squinted at the font. "It doesn't look all that weird to me."

Holmes sighed. The cat on her lap turned its baleful eyes toward me.

I scrubbed at my face. I needed coffee. Or a sedative. "But how do you know it's a woman?"

She snatched the page back. "All it took was a few minutes' research for me to find the origin of this font—it's called Hot Chocolate, how twee—along with a few hundred others on one of those design sites. Well and fine, but that was the ninth hit on Google. The *first* was a website that catered to 'sorority life,' and I found our Hot Chocolate on the page about creating invitations for parties."

"So she's a sorority girl," I said.

"She's someone who looks at sorority websites," Holmes corrected me. "But that was only one search term. After working out the algorithms, I tried one hundred and thirty-nine others, beginning, of course, with the most common syntactical search strings and moving, systematically, to the least likely"—here, my eyes began to glaze—"but each time, this website came up first. I doubt that anyone who makes a typo on their death threat looks past the first Google hit. And this website was absolutely covered in glitter."

"How did the note arrive?"

"It was slipped under my door yesterday morning, like so." She folded it back in half. "Look at that crease. It wasn't just casually folded. That was done with a blunt object and a considerable amount of pressure—you can tell from the dimpling at the seam. Someone was upset when they wrote this and took it out on the paper."

Obviously. It was a death threat. The horrible weight of

what Holmes had done yesterday fell back on my shoulders. "So after you received it, you chased me out, and then . . . waited for someone to come by and kill you?"

She regarded me evenly. "It seemed a good chance to meet them, didn't it? But I expected them to come by with a gun. Bombs are a coward's weapon."

"And if you hadn't been in the bathroom on the other side of the building, you would have *died*." I bit down on a knuckle, reining in my flare of temper.

"I know. That's why I made you leave." She popped the note back into the bag. "I'll have your father give this to Detective Shepard, I'm sure he'll want it now that we're finished. You did very well. You just missed one thing."

"What?"

Leaning over, she held the unsealed bag under my nose. "What does that smell like to you?"

Forever Ever Cotton Candy. I coughed, waving a hand in front of my face. "Didn't you say you could only get that off Japanese eBay?"

"Yes."

"So where the hell did you even find out about it?"

"August Moriarty gave me my first bottle for Christmas," she said. "I'd mentioned that I liked cotton candy in passing, and he'd hunted high and low for a perfume that scent. It had only been manufactured in Japan, he told me, and discontinued in the eighties." Her eyes went faraway. "I wore it for a few weeks, even though it's heinous, because . . . well, no matter. It did prove to be useful, in the end."

I stared at her. Mom jeans and an oversized sweater—borrowed from Abbie, I could deduce that much—and her face assiduously clean. The sun dappled her hair. I had no idea what she was thinking.

"Holmes," I said slowly, "how is this not a warning from August Moriarty?"

"It's not. It's a woman's work, Watson, clearly."

"So . . ."

"Nurse Bryony," Holmes said, as if it was obvious. "Do you really think Phillipa is likely to be visiting a Delta Delta Delta website? More so than the woman who spent all of homecoming requesting old R. Kelly songs and telling me about her sorority formal? The profile is an excellent fit."

"But the perfume points right back to August."

"She most likely wears it too." Holmes shrugged. "Stranger things have happened."

"Have you smelled it on her?"

"People don't wear the same perfume every day, Watson. I'm sure I'll find a bottle in Bryony's flat. It's in Sherringford Town, and we can search through it while she's away."

"Holmes. How does this explain anything about the dealer? Or the forger's notebook? Or the guy in the morgue?"

"Do you not trust me to have this worked out?" she said. "Because I do. They employed one agent, and that agent failed. So they hired another. There. It's sorted."

"Holmes—"

"Earlier, when I spoke to Detective Shepard, I asked him

to bring Bryony in for questioning tomorrow at ten a.m. We'll toss her flat then." She gave me a sympathetic look. "I know the feeling. I'm always disappointed at the end of a case. But we'll find another."

I was beginning to believe it, now, what she'd said about the dangers of caring too much. How emotions only got in the way. It sounded to me exactly as though Holmes was ignoring some obvious conclusions in favor of devising any theory that let August Moriarty off the hook. How hard would it be for him to plant a typo, or to use a special font, to write this note the way a woman would? He knew what Holmes would look for, how she'd interpret it: he could feed her exactly what she wanted to see.

The worst part? She'd kept on buying that perfume he'd given her. Even though it was expensive. Even though she hated it. It was foreign, and hard to find, and that letter was doused in it.

I knew what I had to do.

"It's a good plan," I told her. It would be one, too, if there was any chance Bryony Downs was guilty. "But look, I still feel really awful from yesterday—I didn't sleep much, thanks to your sense of timing, ha—and the pancakes smell amazing, but you know, Malcolm got me up so early—I think I need to—"

"Are you all right?" she asked. I was beginning to sweat.

"I feel terrible." The truth. "I need to go lie down." Also the truth.

"Go," she said, waving me away. "I'll wait for the detective. And maybe I'll go through the note with your father again. He can't follow my reasoning."

I ran into my father at the foot of the stairs. "Can I see that file?" I asked him in a whisper.

He looked at me sadly. "In my study, upstairs. In the second drawer." He had a kind face, my father. I'd remembered a lot of things about him when we moved to England: his dorky enthusiasms and plaid ties, the stupid nicknames he had for Shelby, the way my mother used to shout at him as he slumped at the kitchen table, head buried in his hands. But I'd forgotten how kind he was. How much he'd always trusted me.

"I'll give you some space," he said, and after I found his study, I locked the door behind me.

nine

I PUT THE FILE ON THE DESK.

My father had clipped things from newspapers, printed articles off the internet. It went chronologically: the oldest information was at the front. I resisted the urge to flip to the back.

No. I'd ease myself into it. Into betraying my best friend.

It started with the usual sorts of things. Sherlockian societies and book clubs. Fan sites for my great-great-great-grandfather's stories, but far more for the film and television adaptations. Flipping through the pages, I found printouts from some of the fan sites that tracked the movements of the Holmes clan. They were intensely secretive, Holmes's family, and so gathering kernels of information had become something of a sport for the greater world.

I folded out a taped-together family tree, one in my father's own handwriting. Watsons, always the record-keepers. At the top, he'd placed Sherlock. Then came Henry, the son he'd had so late in life, categorically refusing to name the mother. I traced through Henry's sons down to Holmes's father, Alistair, and his siblings: Leander, Araminta, and Julian. A small line connected Alistair to Emma, Holmes's mother; below that was a fork each for Milo and Charlotte Holmes.

I browsed through the articles about Holmes's first case, when she tracked down the Jameson diamonds. In a photograph with her parents at the Met's press conference, she stood pale and solemn-faced between her parents. On one side stood her father, looking at the camera with hooded eyes. Her mother had blond hair and a dark-red smile, one possessive hand on her daughter's shoulder.

Enough of what I already knew. I flipped through to the last page and worked backward. Information on Leander Holmes's charity. The page before it was a clipping from a Yard fund-raiser. And the one before that, like a lump of pyrite nestled into all that gold, was from the *Daily Mail*.

It was a single paragraph, down at the very end of a long stream of gossip, squeezed between a bit on the Royal Family and another about Shelby's favorite band:

*Remember how the oh-so-secretive Holmeses made a big splash last year inviting boy-genius heartthrob (and DPhil student) **August Moriarty, 20**, to be a live-in tutor for* *their daughter **Charlotte, 14**? The two families have had bad blood between them for more than a hundred years now, and daddy **Alistair** wanted to make a very public peace offering. Well, it looks like things at Casa Holmes took a turn this past week. **August** was escorted out by the police, and not for diddling with the children! Our source tells us that he got caught feeding **Charlotte's** dirty little drugs habit. Oxford's already expelled him, the Moriarty family's disowned him: what's next for the former future professor? As for Miss Charlotte Honoria Holmes, we hear it's boarding school or bust.*

So her middle name was Honoria.

I had to read it again. A third time. A fourth. And then I made myself read between the lines. Was I feeling *bad* for August Moriarty? Was that what this was? Anyone else would look at the age disparity there and think, *Oh, that asshole took advantage of an innocent young girl,* but Charlotte Holmes wasn't innocent. She was imperious, and demanding, with a self-destructive streak that ran as wide as the Atlantic. I thought about the way she'd run roughshod over Detective Shepard when she'd wanted in on this case. About how she'd convinced me of my own worthlessness when she'd wanted to be alone with her homemade bomb. Her blackmailing a math tutor into buying her drugs was only a hop, skip, and a jump away.

The worst part? I'd almost known. I'd made an educated guess, that night in the diner, and she'd let me believe it was the whole story—that she was sent to America because of her drug problem. Never mind the Moriarty at the center of it all.

If any of this was true, August would have a million reasons to want to bring Holmes down. I racked my brain to remember what Lena had said that night at poker. If she was right that Holmes was upset about August her freshman year, it was further proof that she did actually have a heart, and a conscience, despite her protests. (Honestly, if I were Holmes, I'd be worried he was living on a street corner somewhere.) Milo had come to visit and said . . . what? That he'd take care of things. But Lena hadn't known *how*, only that Holmes had been happier after Milo left. At the time, I'd thought, oh, drone hit. And now I just wanted to know how much it had set Milo back to pay August off. I hoped August had been given a sizable check, maybe a little house by the sea. A book-lined study where the poor bastard could continue doing his math on his own terms.

It would've been one thing for a Holmes to fall in love with a Moriarty, I thought bitterly. In fact, it'd be sweepingly, crushingly romantic—and on cue, my imagination began to color it in. Charlotte and August, our star-crossed lovers, locked in a constant battle of deductive wills. Missile codes swapped via elaborate games of footsie. Having veal cutlets in the garden while debating whether to annex France. Et cetera, ad nauseam.

The thing was, Charlotte Holmes didn't fall in love.

And even if, somehow, she had (my stomach roiled again), she'd fucked him over in the end. Jesus, Holmes had screwed a *Moriarty*. A whole family of art forgers and philosophers and blue-blooded assassins sitting in their ivory towers, connected to the lowest reaches of the underworld by the gleaming strands of their ambition. Sure, they weren't all bad, but enough of them were, and after this business with August, every last one would have reason to be out for Charlotte's blood.

I tried to yank myself back from the brink. I could be doing that same thing I did in the diner—seeing ninety percent of the story, but missing the ten percent that actually mattered. Maybe I was all wrong. For one thing, the *Daily Mail* wasn't exactly known for their journalistic integrity. And maybe August really had encouraged her habits—maybe she was the innocent one.

Then why was he trying to kill her?

Well, I thought, as long as I was being awful, I might as well go ahead and be petty with it. I opened my father's computer and, half-covering my eyes, put Moriarty's name into an image search. He was a dork, I told myself, a math nerd; he probably had gelled hair and an overbite.

The page loaded slowly. The pictures came up, one by one.

He looked like a Disney prince.

I shut the laptop hard.

For another hour I sat there, paralyzed in my deliberations. When I finally reached a decision, I didn't feel any better. I spent an hour on Google, trying to dig up what I needed—but as I suspected, it was nowhere to be found.

All right, then. This had to get even more personal.

As silently as I could, I unlocked the study door and crept into the hall. All was still. Downstairs, I heard the lonely, spectral sound of Holmes's violin; she was safely occupied. In the guest room, her dirty clothes were gone from the edge of the bed, but her phone was sitting out in plain view.

A few weeks back, she'd decided to give me the passcode—for emergencies, she'd said. Her eyes had glittered as she rattled it off.

"I thought it was supposed to be a random string of numbers," I'd protested. It was a weak protest: I'd been thrilled. Birthday, snow day, Christmas Day thrilled.

Holmes had graced me with her half-second smile. "If someone can get their hands on my mobile, I'm either dead, or close to it. In any case, you're the only other person I'd want to use it. So I thought I should choose a key code you can remember. Surely you can remember this."

I typed it in quickly, hoping it was still the same, hoping it wasn't.

0707. July 7.

My birthday.

With a heavy sigh, I scrolled through her contacts. There were only four of us on the list: home, Lena, me. And Milo.

"One of the most powerful men in the world," she'd told me. And the only person she'd listen to, if she wouldn't listen to me.

I stabbed out the text one letter at a time. *Milo, this is James Watson.*

"I've been solving crimes ever since I was a child. I do it well," she'd said to me. "I take pride in how well I do it. Do you understand?"

Your sister is making a massive mistake, one that might cost her life. I need your family's help

"They don't believe I can do it anymore."

Come if it's convenient. Even if it's not . . . just get here.

I sent it. Then I deleted any evidence that I'd sent it. It was a futile gesture: God knew it would be a moment's work for Holmes to sniff out my betrayal. I debated trying to make good on my original lie, to get some sleep. But I didn't see how I could. We weren't simply being framed anymore. We were being hunted. If we weren't going to be thrown in jail, August and his accomplice would make sure we'd die instead.

And who was to say he wouldn't make an attempt on our lives while we were here? I froze. How hadn't I thought of that before?

Malcolm and Robbie, I panicked, and dashed down the stairs to find my father.

He was at the front entrance, waving to Abbie and his boys as the minivan backed down the driveway.

"Oh," I said.

"They're going back to her mother's for a few days," he told me, shutting the door. "Charlotte made quite the compelling case for it, and now I feel remiss in not already having sent them away myself." He sighed. "Detective Shepard's in the kitchen, if you'd like to speak to him. Did you find what you needed?"

"Is that Jamie?" Shepard called. "Ask him what the hell Forever Ever Laffy Taffy is."

But Holmes's violin was still crooning. I followed the

sound as if in a dream. There, in the family room. Dressed again in her usual clothes, all the way down to her trim black boots. Against the bright window, she was like a shadow gone abstract, the instrument tucked under her chin. She moved the bow with exquisite slowness. A high note, and then a languorous descent.

She paused, midnote, like some beautiful statue. It wrecked me, watching her.

"Watson?" she asked without turning.

I plodded forward as if I'd been summoned to the judge for sentencing.

"I just spent a good hour telling the detective about the explosion. As if I knew anything he didn't. Oh, and your father said that your assigned time to get your things from the dorm is at ten thirty tomorrow. So I might toss Nurse Bryony's place alone." She held the Strad up to examine its strings and plucked one, listening. "Is that all right?"

"I'd rather go with you," I said, in as normal a tone as I could manage.

She whirled to look at me, her eyes gone dark as a storm. Rapidly, she took in my face, my posture, my bare feet on the carpet, and when she reached her conclusion, she reared back as if I'd struck her.

"You said you wouldn't," she whispered.

"I need to hear it from you," I said. There was no use now in pretending. "What happened between you and August Moriarty?"

"You don't—"

"I do, I need to know."

"Watson, please—"

"Tell me," I insisted. God, I was terrified. I hadn't known that *please* was in her vocabulary. "Just—will you tell me."

Tightly, disbelievingly, she shook her head, like I was a man on the street who'd made the mistake of demanding her wallet and PIN number and ten minutes with her in an alley. Like I hadn't seen the knife she'd been carrying in plain view. In that moment, I invented and discarded a hundred things I could have said to her—platitudes, reassurances, accusations—only to have her walk past me and straight out the front door, the tap of her boots the only sound in the silence.

In the kitchen, Shepard said to my father, "Sororities? Hot cocoa? Um. Can you walk me through it again?"

I DIDN'T TELL MY FATHER OR THE DETECTIVE SHE'D LEFT, FOR the simple reason that I didn't want them to stage a search. She had every reason to want to disappear, I thought, even with our bomber on the loose, but the last thing I wanted was for her to come face-to-face with them right now. Even if I didn't have any doubts about who would win.

It did nothing to stop the sinking feeling in my stomach. Because this wasn't a superhero film (swelling music and inevitable triumph, the enemy at her feet in a tasteful amount of his own blood). This wasn't one of my great-great-great-grandfather's stories (her with hat and cane and pocket watch, dashing out to haul the villain in, me waiting by the fire for the great reveal to be brought safely home). This wasn't even an item on my father's endless list, an anecdote to be summed up in some tasteful, mannered way. I didn't even know how that could be done. *128. When you betray Holmes's trust, _____. 129. When you realize she's cared about someone who isn't you, you selfish bastard, _____. 130. When the direct result of emotions she claims she's incapable of feeling is one dead misogynist creep, one innocent girl choked to almost-death, your every private moment filmed, and Holmes nearly blown up into bloody pieces, _____.*

She'll understand, I told myself after a good hour of stewing. She'll understand why I did it. And, for now, I'll respect her need for distance—I can do that much—and when she's back, I'll apologize, and we can get on with the business of not getting ourselves killed.

That was when I remembered rules 1 and 2.

Search often for opiates and dispose of as needed.

Begin with the hollowed-out heels of Holmes's boots.

Maybe we weren't so divorced from the past as I wanted to believe. I thought, *Oh, I am one stupid son of a bitch,* and I hardly remembered to grab my coat as I flew out the door.

Between our house and the road was a flat expanse of grass, dusted lightly with snow. When I was a child, it had been its own continent, unending. But now it seemed the size of a postage stamp. It was unforgivingly white, and open, and showed no sign of her. How had she managed to move without footprints? All I could pick out were those of rabbit and deer.

We were a half mile from the nearest house, and even farther from any sort of civilization. Still, I tromped out to the middle of the road and shadowed my eyes, looking far in both directions. I saw pavement, flat land, our nearest neighbor's weathervane. I didn't see her.

Well, before I took my father's car to go out looking, I'd rule out the rest of our land. I'd be thorough. Holmes would have been thorough, looking for me.

God knows what I'd say when I found her.

I MADE QUICK WORK OF THE TREES ALONG THE SIDES OF THE house. I spent longer in the shed my father had built to store his tools. The lawnmower was there, and his sawhorses, and though it seemed like there was nothing else, I examined the shed from both the inside and out, looking for unaccounted-for space, a hidden room. I felt every inch of wood with my bandaged hands. Nothing. Still nothing.

I stalked out into the backyard and considered the stretch of open, icy land behind the house, wondering if she'd managed to turn herself the same colors as the landscape, if she was somehow standing right next to me. If she'd erased herself altogether.

Through the back window, I glared at Detective Shepard's bent head. My father was opposite him, trying not to watch me, and failing. I glared at him too.

I'd get in the car, then. I'd scour all the countryside between here and Sherringford, and I'd find her, somehow. After I was sure she hadn't OD'd, I'd let her hate me all she wanted. But my hands, beneath their bandages, were beginning to freeze. I had no intention of getting frostbite twice in two days. *Gloves,*

I thought, climbing the porch steps, *and then the car, and then Holmes—*

Below my feet, I heard snickering.

It was an ugly laugh. A laugh you'd hear from a small boy who'd just plucked the wings from a fly. Still, it was hers, and I jumped off the side of the porch, getting to my hands and knees to peer into the foot of darkness underneath.

In the frozen mud beneath the stairs, Holmes had tucked herself into a small dark ball. Her head was tipped to one languid side, considering me. I knelt there, unmoving. She saw me, it was clear; it was also clear she wasn't processing what she saw. Her bare feet were black with dirt, her hair wild.

She'd hidden herself under the porch the way a beaten dog would.

74. Whatever happens, remember it is not your fault *and likely could not have been prevented, no matter your efforts.*

My father, once again, was proving himself an idiot. "Holmes?" I whispered.

"Hello, Watson," she said drowsily. I crawled up next to her, past her socks and shoes all in a pile, past her tucked-up legs. Her eyes flicked over to me, unconcerned. I noticed, with a shock, that her pupils had constricted to tiny black dots. "Hello," she said again, and laughed.

"How much have you taken?" I asked, shaking out her socks and pulling them back over her freezing feet. She didn't resist, but she didn't respond either, even when I put a hand inside one of her boots and came up with an empty plastic bag. "God, have you always kept this stuff with you?"

"Rainy days," she said, shutting her eyes. Her voice wasn't ragged, or hoarse—it wasn't hers at all. "Oh, Watson. Always so disappointed."

"No, stay awake," I said, tapping at her cold face. She batted my hand away halfheartedly. "What have you taken?" I asked.

"Oxy. Slows it all down." She smiled. "Done with coke. Hate coke. Am I disappointing you?"

"No."

"Liar," she said, with sudden venom. "You expect impossible things, and I refuse to deliver. Can't do it. Won't."

"I am not expecting anything from you," I said, "except for you not to freeze to death." Shucking off my coat, I wrapped it around her. "Come on, let's go inside."

"No."

"Holmes, it's freezing, we need to get you into a hot bath." I tugged on her arm. Immediately, she clawed at my injured palm with her nails. I flinched away.

"I said *no*," she said, staring at me with eyes that were all iris and no pupil.

I cradled my hand to my chest, trying to steady my breathing. "How much have you taken?"

"Enough," she said, looking away. She was bored again. "I won't die. Go away."

"I'm not leaving without you."

"Go away. Take your coat, it smells like guilt."

"Actually," I said, "I think I'm fine right here." I couldn't make her go inside. I probably couldn't make her go anywhere with me ever again. What else could I do? After a moment, I tucked myself in beside her, hoping my body heat, at least, would do something to warm her up.

The world slowed to a standstill, as it does when things go so wrong, the bad news closing in like a lowering ceiling. I should have been thinking up a solution. A way out. Deciding if I should grovel for her forgiveness, or if I should tell Detective Shepard that she and I should be pulled from the case. But I didn't. I curled up against her in the cold and listened for her breathing. What were you supposed to do when you were dealing with drugs like this? How long would the effects last? I wished, for the first time, that I'd done something with my years at Highcombe other than read novels and swoon over icy blond princesses who'd never touch anything harder than pot. I could have gained some practical knowledge. She might be dying, I thought, and I had no way to know; the responsible thing would be to call the police, or an ambulance, or at the very least tell my father and let him sort it out.

I didn't. They'd write that on my tombstone, I thought: *Jamie Watson. He didn't.* The snow sifted down through the porch slats, filling in the tracks her knees had made crawling through the mud. I wasn't Catholic, but this had the distinct feel of purgatory: the bitter cold, the unending wait. No idea of what would come after.

After what felt like forever, the back door slid open. I listened to the heavy footfalls over our heads.

"Jamie?" my father called. "Charlotte? Detective Shepard and I are done talking. Jamie?" I held my breath. After a long minute, he swore and trudged back inside.

"Worried," she observed, after we heard the door shut. I stared at the cloud her breath made in the cold. "Good that he worries. I don't. You're nothing to me."

"Liar," I echoed. I tried to put the force of my affection behind it.

"You did once," said Holmes. "Mean something to me. You don't now."

She began to shiver. Was that a good sign? A bad one? Either way I couldn't stand it. Carefully, I pulled her into my arms, and to my great surprise she let me, curling up against my chest as pliantly as if she were my girlfriend. As if I'd held her before. As if I held her every day.

Somehow that scared me far more than the rest of it. Lee Dobson had found her this way, I thought, and my arms tensed, instinctively. Dobson had—

"Stop thinking about him," she said. "It's not yours to think about."

"What am I allowed to think about?" I asked wearily. If I had a rope, this was its end.

"Let's talk about the things you think you know." That horrible snicker. "Let's disappoint Watson some more."

"No," I said, "you don't—"

"August was my maths tutor. Did you know that? You did. Can tell by how your hands seized."

I'd thought I wanted to hear this. But I didn't. I really, really didn't. "You don't have to—"

"It was my parents' idea. For publicity. Had some bad press, and they wanted to change the story in the media. Forgiving Holmeses. Fucking liars. I hated him at first. But after Milo moved to Germany, I got used to him. It was like having an older brother again. And then it wasn't. It was something else."

"What?" I asked, into the silence.

"I loved him. And he wouldn't have me." The words came sharp and hard, sudden in their ferocity. "He was too old, he said, and even if we waited, it would be a catastrophic mess. Our families, you know. He said that I'd grow out of it. My 'crush.' Him saying that was worse than him rejecting me."

I couldn't quite breathe, hearing her speak this way, as if reciting her sins. When she spoke again, she was horribly precise.

"I wanted to punish him. To make him feel what I was feeling. So I got him to use his family connections to buy me cocaine. I knew he'd do it. I'd been taking so much, and he was so scared that, without it, I'd go through withdrawal." She drew a breath. "I wanted to make him hurt me, and then I wanted him to pay for it. The night his brother Lucien drove up with a boot full of coke, I called the police. Lucien ran, and August stayed to take the blame, as I suspected he would. After all, he felt responsible.

"My mother fired him. Then she phoned his don at Oxford to have him expelled. And after all of that was over, she sat me down in the drawing room. She'd drawn all the curtains. And she explained to me, very patiently, that this was a lesson. It wasn't to happen again."

"The drugs?" I asked quietly.

"The drugs." She laughed. "No. I'd started with 'the drugs' at twelve. I was too soft on the inside, you see. No exoskeleton. I felt everything, and still everything bored me. I was like . . . like a radio playing five stations at once, all of them static. At first, the coke made me feel bigger. More together. Like I was one person, at last. And then it stopped working, and I began taking more, and more, and they sent me to rehab. When I came back, I spent a few months going the classical route—morphine, syringes. It made everything quiet and far away. I was wrong inside, you see. I'd always been wrong. But it was too messy, the morphine, and I was found out—more rehab. So I dropped the morphine for oxy. More rehab. Then more oxy. I've never quite managed to shake it, any of it, and my parents stopped expecting me to. It doesn't scare them anymore."

The whole time she spoke, she didn't look up at me once. She was curled up in my arms like she was my girlfriend, but she was talking to me like I was an empty shell.

"What my mother was afraid of was sentiment," she said. "Of my being sentimental. With my particular skill set, it's a liability. With what I felt for August, I became . . . a worse person. I was sent away to think on what I'd done. It was never about keeping me from the drugs. It was about keeping me away from myself."

"Jesus, Holmes, that's horrible." What kind of monster would demand that her daughter not feel?

"Is it really? I think my mother was right. I don't trust myself anymore. No one does." She lifted her head to study me. She'd gone so pale that the veins on her neck stood out like pen marks. "Not even you."

It was awful to see her like this. "Holmes—"

"You thought *I killed him*. And it's almost true. He lost his life because of me. He got a job, finally. Works for my brother in Germany doing data entry. What a waste. But he's forgiven me. He's a sentimental fool. August even demanded his family leave me alone. I was disturbed, he told them, and no good would come of it. They listened. It was their last favor to him. You see, his family disowned him for taking my fall."

"You aren't disturbed," I said, trying to mean it, to make her feel better. "You aren't disturbed at all. You just made a mistake."

"I don't make mistakes," she said, and pulled away from me. "I know exactly what I'm doing."

"Even if you did. You were still forgiven. They *forgave* you. And accepting their forgiveness isn't a sign of weakness." I was desperate to pull her back to me, back out from where she'd gone, deep inside herself. I'd never wanted this. Never. "I wouldn't have thought any different of you, if you'd told me."

"You wouldn't have?" she asked, the last vestiges of the haze gone from her voice. "How interesting."

"Unfair."

"You keep using that word like it has any real-life implications."

"It does," I insisted.

"Fairness, Watson, would see August Moriarty restored to school and family and his fiancée—he really could have told me about her when I first confessed it to him, I wasn't about to stalk and kill her—but no. He's alone, in a foreign country, and friendless. Really, the parallels are striking."

"You're being melodramatic," I said, and her eyes flashed. Good. Any reaction was better than none. "I'm sitting right here, being your *friend*, and I'm not going anywhere."

"I'd be fine if you did," she snapped.

"I don't doubt that. But I'm still not going anywhere, and because I'm not leaving, I need you to listen to me." I took a breath. "I'm sorry for what happened to you. I am. It's awful, and the fallout from it was . . . unreal. And I'm sorry I broke your trust. I never wanted to hurt you. But I only did it because I was desperate. Don't you think that your trust in him and his family might be a touch unfounded? Like, have you had Milo look into their activities? Has August been in Germany all this time, or has he made any trips to America—"

"He *isn't responsible*," she snarled. "I've told you that from the start. He may hate me—he should hate me—but he isn't a killer. And if you can't believe that—Watson, I will not work with someone who refuses to trust me."

"But you refused to trust me in the first place," I said. "Why didn't you just tell me the truth? I know you have personal stakes in the matter, but so do I!"

"What stake could you possibly have in this?" She was inches from my face now. How could she not understand?

"Your life. Your *life*, and mine. Are they really worth you being right in this?"

"I would never let you die," she said, her breath coming fast and shallow.

"But what about you? What's going to happen to you?" I could hear my voice breaking as I pictured it. Her on the concrete, the blood a halo around her dark hair. Her under a slab of granite in her lab. On a slab in the morgue. In a bath of shattered glass, or poisoned in the night. Her curled up under the goddamn porch to die, her stone-blank eyes staring up at me, Jesus . . . it could happen to either of us, but if my being there meant she had any more of a chance of staying alive, then I would be there. Full stop. I was saying it to her out loud, now, pleading. "I know you don't need me, any fool could see that, but we are in this together. I will be here, right here, until it's over. You . . . you're the most important thing to me, and I can't imagine being without you, but if the moment it's over, you want to send me away, I will, I'll go—"

"You should." It tumbled out of her in a rush. "You don't see it—that I'm not a good person. That I spend every minute of every day trying not to be the person I know I *could* be, if I let myself slip. And I'll bring you down with me. I have. Look at us. Look at where we are."

"That's impossible."

"Is it?" she asked dully. I was losing her again. "Are you blind?"

"You can't be a bad person," I told her, "because you're a robot, remember?"

It really was the lamest, most halfhearted joke I think I'd ever made. But there wasn't anything else that I could say. I'd betrayed her trust; she'd kept things from me I'd needed to know. She'd endangered our lives; I'd endangered our friendship. I had no idea what was next. All I wanted was for her to look at me the way she used to, with that wry half-twist of her mouth, and make some deduction about the sandwich I'd had for lunch.

I realized then that Holmes was laughing.

I looked at her askance, in case she was also bleeding from the head. But there it was: her low chuckle, a hand thrown up to hide it. When our eyes met, there was a kind of confused electricity there, like we'd broken up and simultaneously exchanged vows. It brought back that hallucinatory fear I'd had that night in the infirmary, that Nurse Bryony would just as soon kiss me as smother me with a pillow. I didn't understand girls at all.

Bryony.

Bryony.

"Holmes," I said urgently, "what did you say August's fiancée's name was?"

"I didn't." Her eyes went vague. "I didn't know her at all, only that they were engaged, and that he left her in the wake of . . . Jesus *Christ*, Watson," and she shoved past me in her haste to get out from under the porch.

"Where are you going?" I called.

"Milo," she replied. I snatched up her shoes and crawled out after her. The two of us together burst through the door, covered in clumps of mud, shivering from the cold—we must've looked like we'd come up from some arctic hell. In a way, I guessed we had.

My father was standing with his arms crossed in the

middle of the kitchen. "Jamie," he said, a warning in his voice, as the detective stood up from the table. We pushed past them and ran straight up the stairs. "Where the hell did you two go?" he yelled at our backs.

"Five minutes," I said, spinning around, "just give us five more minutes."

In the guest room, Holmes practically fell on her phone. "Milo," she said into it, and I froze. The text I'd sent. If he ratted me out, this could get ugly all over again. "Where are you? A tarmac? I'm only catching every other word." Her voice went dangerous. "You're coming to New York. Tell me why. No, that's a lie. That is too. Fine, tell me the last time you left your apartment. Before this. No, don't give me that, you were the one who had them *put it in your office building*. Yes—no, I'm not on drugs. No. Yes, fine, I am, don't hang up. Of course I want to see you while you're here, you ass."

He was coming. He was coming, and he wasn't going to tell her that I'd asked him to. I said a silent prayer to the saint of deranged best friends' deranged older brothers.

Holmes paced, tracking bits of frozen mud into the carpet. "No, don't hang up, I have a question." She paused. "What was August's fiancée's name? I don't care. It's important—no, it's not what you think—no I'm not—did you just call me a cow, you whale? Milo—*damn it.*"

She whipped around to face me. "He hung up. The idiot thinks I want her name so I can find her and kill her."

"There's some deep irony there," I said, smiling.

Startled, she smiled back. Just for a second. And then her

phone chirped with a message. I peered over her shoulder.

Bryony Davis. Don't eat her. See you soon.

Bryony Downs. Bryony Davis. She'd barely covered her tracks.

Holmes and I stared at each other. My heart was pounding.

Shepard opened the bedroom door. "So?" he said, his brows knit. "I've examined the note. I've spoken to your father. And I appreciate your passing along Bryony Downs to me for a more, ah, official interrogation. But what is all this"—he gestured to Holmes's muddy pants and my damp hair—"about, exactly? Something I should know?"

She threw me a glance. I caught it.

"Um, well, we're dating now," she said, a hand creeping up to touch her hair. "We just made it official, and—oh God, Jamie, this is kind of embarrassing."

I tugged her hand down into mine. "It's not embarrassing," I said. "I mean, it's been such a long time coming. But I guess I was, um, blind to my own feelings."

Holmes beamed at me, and I pulled her to me, tucking her under my arm. The detective made a small, involuntary noise, like he was choking.

"We were outside in the snow—well, okay, I ran out there because I got mad because I thought he didn't like me, but it turned out he *did* like me, he was just shy, so he ran out there to find me, and—" She smiled at him, and it was strange to see how fatigue made that fake expression real. "I mean, do you want to hear what he said? It was so romantic."

Shepard put up his hands. "I have so much to do," he said,

backing out into the hallway. "You know how it is. All back at the station. Where I should go."

"We'll talk more later," Holmes assured him, with what I could tell were the frayed ends of her composure.

He smiled tightly. "Right. Yes," he said, shutting the door, and from the hall, we heard him mutter, "God, I hate teenagers."

THE NEXT MORNING WAS FOREVER IN COMING, AND STILL, when it finally arrived, I wasn't ready. How could I have been? We didn't have a plan. Or if we did, I wasn't in on it.

To top it all off, I was exhausted. I'd spent the night before taking care of Holmes while she came down. It'd happened right after Shepard left, her falling on the bed like her strings had been cut. She'd insisted she didn't want anything—no surprise there—but I'd forced water on her, and crackers one at a time from a package my father had left outside the door. It was just the two of us, silent, in that dark little floral-sheeted island. She stared at the ceiling fan, her arm thrown over her face. She didn't say a word until I stood to go tell my father what we'd figured out about the school nurse.

"No," Holmes said, grabbing my arm without looking at me. "Stay here."

"You've solved it," I told her. "You don't need to haul her in. Let the police do that."

"I still have more work to do. I need to figure out what part she plays in this. How the Moriartys have been using her." She held on tighter. "This isn't some jewel robbery. This is the woman who's killed one person and tried to kill another. Not to mention trying to ruin our lives, if not end those too. So yes, I will bloody well haul her in."

I should have pressed my case. I should have insisted. But I was exhausted, and she was exhausted, and so I didn't try.

Jamie Watson. He didn't.

I sat back down on the floor and put my head against the mattress. The hours passed that way, day slipping into night, until I fell asleep kneeling by her bedside like a pilgrim before some entombed saint.

There wasn't the barest hint of sun coming through the window when Holmes shook me awake, hustled me into my clothes and down to my father's car. I hadn't spoken a word. "Tea," she said, pressing a mug into my hands from the passenger seat. "Now drive, before anyone realizes we've gone."

As I blearily gripped the steering wheel, reminding myself that I needed to be on the right side of the road, not the left, that this wasn't England, Holmes kept up a low unending monologue, sorting the last few months through this lens of Bryony's guilt. Well. Probable guilt. If it turned out that an entirely different English Bryony was our school nurse, I'd be the first to pack it in and just go home.

"She's only gotten more desperate as she's gone along. She's dropped the conceit of hanging us with our own history, which, personally speaking, was the only part of her campaign that I found at all *interesting*. Come on. Explosions, really"—at this point I was parking the car—"there is nothing interesting about explosions. She ruined a perfectly good lab that I had painstakingly assembled, bit by bit, from things I'd taken from Mr. Lamarr's biology room—oh, don't look at me like that, I've seen you toast marshmallows on those burners, you're just as guilty as I am—and really the only thing I'll miss were my copies of your great-great-great-grandfather's stories. Categorically worthless." She led me down Sherringford's main drag to the side street that held Bryony's flat. "Honestly, I think they're being given away for free on Kindle, but I did love them. And she has footage of you *naked*, most likely, which I can't even begin to unravel the child pornography laws on that one—"

I was having trouble understanding Holmes's relentlessly chipper mood. We'd spent the day before in hell. And, okay, we were about to engage in a little breaking and entering (which, honestly, I was pretty excited for too), but we hadn't even acknowledged anything that had happened the day before. No apologies, on either side. No real conclusion to the fight. No acknowledgment of whatever it was that had passed between us under the porch. And here she was, arm tucked in my elbow like the day—it felt like years ago—I first introduced her to my father.

I turned to say something, I don't know what, and I saw her face. Relief. She was relieved. Somewhere, deep, deep down, she had suspected August Moriarty; she'd been too well trained to ignore it. And now she had good reason to pull her focus away from him and put his fiancée in her crosshairs instead.

I quickly debated with myself how I should react to this realization—jealousy? disapproval?—and decided I was tired of feeling like shit. I might as well cheer up too. Maybe she'd let me pick the lock.

"Holmes," I said. We were standing on the corner of Market and Greene, peering down the block at Bryony's flat above the flower store. It was all very picturesque, with its painted window boxes and iron scrollwork. It didn't look like the flat of someone who had killed a boy in cold blood. "Were you going to tell me why we're here so early? Her interview at the station isn't until ten, and it's just eight now."

"Bryony will be out the door by eight thirty, hair all done, looking like a starlet. She'll stop by the Starbucks outside town. She'll maybe go shopping. She thinks this is a routine set of questions, not an all-day event. Anyone who uses a vanity font on a death threat is far too confident to think they're under suspicion." She was almost bouncing on her heels. "I got into the police database this morning and got the make and model of her car. Registered to Bryony Downs, one black 2009 Toyota RAV4, license 223 APK. Or, that car right there." It was parked on the street outside her flat. "In the meantime, we are going to sit very inconspicuously in the café here until she leaves, and if all goes well, we'll have you to your ten-thirty appointment to collect your things, because those jeans are beginning to smell a bit ripe."

I wasn't sure I could survive cheerful Holmes any more than I could her junkie alter ego. All the same, I let her drag me by the arm into the café, where she set us up with two teas by the window.

It all happened as she'd predicted. Bryony emerged, in

red lipstick and sunglasses like an old movie star. Holmes told me not to be so obvious, but I couldn't help but stare at her as she drove past—that shining blond hair, the way she was singing along to the radio. I almost could have believed she wasn't guilty, then, because it was clear the consequences of her actions hadn't made the slightest impression. She'd put an innocent girl in the hospital. She'd taken Dobson's life. Even someone as disgusting as Dobson deserved the chance to grow up and become a better person. Bryony Downs should be lying on her bathroom floor, racked with guilt, and instead she'd decided she was the star of her own romantic comedy.

Holmes held us back another ten minutes. "Patience is a virtue, Watson," she said. "Besides, she might have forgotten something."

When the coast remained clear, it only took us moments to get to the front door, leading up to both Bryony's flat and the one above it. It was unlocked. As we crept up the steps, I said a quiet *thank you* for not having to pick her locked door right there on the street. When we reached it (#2, like the mailbox by her door, printed BRYONY DOWNS) I went down on one knee to inspect the lock. "It's a Yale," I said casually, "like the ones I practiced on with you. Do you think I could—"

With a disgusted sound, Holmes turned the knob.

"I see that you're still scratching your locks," she said to the man sitting there.

ten

I DIDN'T UNDERSTAND WHAT I WAS LOOKING AT.

The room in front of us was almost empty. As in, no tables, no sofas, no rugs, nails where pictures used to hang—empty. From where I stood, I had the clear view through a doorway to where two dark-suited men with Bluetooth earpieces were methodically sorting through boxes of breakfast cereal. One at a time, they opened them, dumped their contents in a bowl, and then tossed it all into a garbage bag. One of them actually whistled while he worked.

It was distinctly possible that I had dreamed myself into a surrealist film, or that Holmes was pulling some elaborate prank. I might have even believed it, too, if it wasn't for the man sitting in front of us.

He, or one of his minions, had dragged a velvet tufted chair into the center of the bare room. But he wasn't sitting on it the way you'd have expected. He didn't cross his legs, or lean lazily into the wing of the chair, stretching out one arm to check the time on his admittedly very nice watch. Those poses wouldn't have worked on him, anyway: the man was too much of a nerd. A handsome nerd, a very sleek, well-dressed nerd, but a nerd nonetheless. Instead, he sat at the edge of his ridiculous chair, tidily smoking a cigarette.

I sized him up: that was what he clearly wanted, presenting himself in the empty room like an art exhibit. Buddy Holly glasses, a sixties ad-man haircut—a hard side part, tapered at the sides—and from what I could tell, his suit was straight off Savile Row, where James Bond would get fitted for a bespoke jacket, if he were real. Holmes had said he was pudgy, but what I saw instead was a sort of softness from hours spent in front of a computer screen.

None of this would have been all that remarkable on its own. But written invisibly all over him, like white ink on white paper, was power. Electric power. The kind that snapped its fingers and brought a government to its knees. What had Holmes said? MI5? Google? Private security? How much of that was true? Drones, I thought uneasily. He controlled drones.

And I was the genius that had brought him here.

"Where are Nurse Bryony's things?" I asked, trying to sound like I knew the answer already and was just asking to confirm.

Milo Holmes ignored me. "I don't scratch locks," he said in

a sonorous voice, smooth where his sister's was rough. "That was my man Peterson. Wanted to have a go, and I thought there wasn't any harm. We weren't in a rush."

He'd had all of ten minutes to clean out the living room. I hadn't even seen him go in the door. No rush. Right.

"You're very kind, sir," one of the men said from the back, and resumed whistling. They were cracking open Bryony's eggs now.

Holmes crossed her arms. "You do scratch. Every time. I do a very pretty one, as you well know. You should've waited for us."

He drew on his cigarette. "You look better than I was expecting. My sources led me to believe that it was very bad, this time."

I swallowed.

"Yes, well, it's much less razor blades and three a.m. phone calls now, isn't it, and much more saving my own neck from the noose." It was easy for me to imagine them as children: Milo, inexorable as a tank, and Holmes, the dervish circling him. She was so restrained, most of the time, but when she wasn't . . . well. Then, she said things like, "Tell me right now what you have done with my evidence or I will tell Mother about you spying on our fencing instructor in the shower."

"You won't. And you know very well what I've done with your evidence."

Holmes cast one hateful look around the room. "New York? Honestly? And you've missed all the important parts. I was handling this. It was handled."

"Handle August Moriarty's ex-fiancée? Lottie, really." (*Lottie*, I thought gleefully, despite myself. *Lottie*.) "You're emotional. You really should have left this to the adults. Now that this idea of Mother's has run its course, let's bring you home. Boarding school? All wrong. We'll put you in the London flat. I'm sure I could convince Professor Demarchelier to tutor you—"

"Milo, he *hates* me, and—"

"No, you aren't thinking. What if they try to throw you in jail? Americans, with their prisons. My men would get you out before that, of course, but such a hassle. You always did like the skiing in Utah. I would want you to be able to come back. I'd want that, for you."

It was becoming abundantly clear why Holmes didn't want her family involved. Emotional? Leaving things to the adults? Sending her away? *Skiing*?

I was an idiot for calling him in. He could go straight to hell.

"I'd like to know what you've done with the evidence," I said. It came out as a growl. "And how you knew to be here, at this flat."

Milo arched an eyebrow. "Is this your bulldog?" he asked Holmes. There wasn't any venom in it, but that didn't make it better.

"This," Holmes said, "is James Watson, my friend and colleague, and you will give him an answer."

I stood up a bit straighter.

"My sister asked me a question yesterday," Milo said. "Do you know the last time that happened? November 2009. Lottie doesn't ask questions. She deduces and decides for herself. That alone would be enough to get me on a plane, particularly when that question has to do with a Moriarty. Thankfully, I was headed to New York already. And as for her things? This—this nurse?" He said *nurse* the way you'd say *gelatinous slug*. "This bank of flats has a very nice little alley behind it, and we sent away her possessions by armored car right as you walked in. My men at Greystone HQ in the city will sort through them, determine the appropriate angle, and return them to your Detective Ben Shepard."

"By the city, he means New York," Holmes said, not taking her eyes off her brother. "And by Greystone, he means the mercenary company currently razing the Middle East. Which he owns—Greystone, that is—and which apparently works as his personal honor guard, if the breakfast knights back there are any indication."

"Glad to be of service," Peterson called. The other one grunted.

"You know, none of this explains the Moriarty agent practicing your handwriting," Milo said conversationally.

"No," Holmes said. "But my ruining August's life does. His fiancée's decided to play avenging angel on his behalf."

"Two separate people out to get you," he mused. "You really are popular. I'm just not sure why you won't come to the obvious conclusion—that the two of them are working together. That this Bryony Downs creature is in August Moriarty's employ."

Holmes set her chin.

"Fine, Lottie," Milo sighed. "We'll focus on the nurse, at least for now."

"How is any of this efficient?" I asked him, changing the subject. "What is this woman going to do when she returns and finds out her things are gone?"

Milo coughed politely to hide his laugh. "We'll have proof enough before her interview with Detective Shepard is over to have him charge her with murder."

"And you know the facts of the case," I said. "You know what you're looking for, in her things."

"Obviously," he said.

"Will you come up with real proof?" I asked. "Or manufacture it?"

Milo spread his hands wordlessly.

"Do you have to ask?" Holmes said to me.

"Well, now that that's settled. Take this," Milo said, handing me his cigarette. "I want to text Uncle Leander the adorable thing you just said about James."

"*Watson*," she and I said together.

"Of course," he said. "Friend and colleague. I love it."

Holmes snatched the phone away.

"So that's it?" I asked, grinding his cigarette out on the floor. "Is this the end? Detective Shepard gets a confession out of Bryony Davis-Downs, and you take her stuff off to be freelance policed, and . . . what, roll credits?"

"It appears so," Holmes said. Already she was beginning to slump into herself, something I identified now with back porches and mud and pain-pill misery.

I put a hand on her shoulder. I couldn't think of anything else to do.

She looked at it, and then up at me. Slowly, the color returned to her face. The corners of her mouth pulled up into a smile, one that stayed.

"Peterson," she called, "won't you tell your colleague there—yes, you, with the Persian cat and the basement flat in Berlin—to call the armored truck and have them turn around. I want everything back in this room just as it was. I suppose you took photographs of the original, or you're a bigger fool than I'd imagined, disrupting the crime scene as you have. Really, why on earth would you have moved it to your head-quarters except to allow this would-be Orson Welles—sorry, Milo, you're not handsome enough to be Olivier—to pose in an empty room? How dull."

I bit my lip against my smile.

"What I could have told you from the dust trails alone would have solved this case," she continued. "As you've utterly ruined that possibility, I want any powders or creams you find brought straight to me. Cosmetics, of course, but do look for jars marked as protein powder. Any wires or tools, anything to suggest a bomb. And I want the receiver for whatever tracker you've affixed to Bryony's car. Give it to me. No. Bring it here." She held out an impatient hand. "I want to make sure that she's actually arriving at her appointment and not, oh, dashing to the airport and then on to Fiji and thereafter, gone. Have I missed anything, Watson?"

As she examined the tracker she'd been handed, I made

a show of surveying the room. "Were you going to tell him about the molted snakeskin under the chair cushion he's sitting on, or should I?"

With an undignified yelp, Milo leapt to his feet.

"Oh, yes," Holmes said blandly. "That. Peterson, do check the walls for a rattlesnake."

THE TWO GREYSTONE GRUNTS BUSILY REARRANGED THE FURNITURE to Holmes's specifications. Milo watched the proceedings, arms crossed, with a faint air of distaste.

That is, he appeared to, if you didn't look closely. I did. I'd learned to do that much. Whenever Milo's hard gaze fell on his sister, it softened the slightest bit. He could've stopped Peterson and Michaels at any point, ordered Bryony's place stripped bare again, frog-marched Holmes onto the nearest London-bound plane.

He didn't. He stood and watched his sister work.

It seemed safe enough for me to take the few minutes to gather my things from the dorm. Holmes had put me in charge of watching the GPS tracker on Bryony's car, and other than two quick stops for coffee and for gas, she'd driven a straight course to the police station. There wasn't really much else I could do, and honestly, I was looking forward to getting a clean set of my own clothes.

"I'll be back," I told her. She nodded and kept on directing traffic.

The day had turned out to be mild, so I left my father's car parked on the street and walked the half mile up to campus. I was suffused with a sense of well-being, the kind I associated with waking up late on a lazy Sunday, no plans, no obligations. I had no doubts that Holmes would find the necessary evidence to implicate Bryony Downs for every terrible thing that had happened. It was over. Over. And Charlotte Holmes and I were still here.

I let myself daydream about spending Christmas break with her in London. Hopefully Holmes would be at her family's flat there for the month, but if not, I'd jailbreak her from Sussex myself. We'd go get a proper curry, first thing, and then I'd take her to my favorite secondhand bookshop, the one where the owner had asked me to sign my great-great-great-grandfather's books. Maybe she'd want to see a violin program at Royal Albert Hall. And after that, I'd ask her to show me her personal London, the one she'd memorized as a child. We'd see how it had changed and grown in our absence, the way cities do. We'd both have to get to know it again as *our* London.

As I crossed the quad to Michener Hall, I couldn't help but notice how bare Sherringford was. The sciences building was in ruins, still smoking faintly, under the black tarp they'd thrown over the roof. That woman had wanted Holmes dead, I thought with a shiver. It hadn't really hit me until then. Bryony Downs had wanted to end Holmes's life. Thank God we were done with it.

I was a few minutes early, but Tom was already waiting on the steps of our dorm, shivering in his thin jacket. We both looked a little threadbare, I thought: me in my father's coat,

Tom in his raggedy sweater-vest. It was surprisingly good to see him, argyle and all.

"Hey," he said brightly. "Where have you guys been? At your dad's house? And Charlotte's okay? I've been trying to call you but it kept going straight to voicemail."

I told him about the cell phone I'd abandoned on my desk. He'd been evacuated straight from the library, he said, and put on a bus to that Days Inn without anyone telling them what had happened. "We'd heard the explosion," he said. "People were crying. It was awful. But we got filled in eventually. For the first day it was like a church in there. And now it's a total shit show, people climbing the walls. Lots of rumors. Like, what really happened in the science building? Do you have any insider info? No, tell me inside, I want—"

I said a silent *thank you* as the front doors opened, cutting him off. A bored-looking policeman consulted a clipboard. "Thomas Bradford? James Watson? Come with me. The building's secure, but they're having us stay with you as a precaution."

In my haste the other night, I'd forgotten to lock our door or even fully close it. The policeman frowned at me when a slight push threw it open. When he saw what was inside it, his hand went for his gun.

It really did look like a crime scene. The slit mattress and the torn-up curtains and the hollowed-out books. The glint of broken glass over everything. "It's fine, Officer," I said. "I had an accident with the mirror right before we were evacuated."

"Doesn't look fine," he grumbled, but stayed outside.

I turned to Tom to apologize, to explain. He'd be shocked,

I thought. Maybe he'd want to make a statement to Detective Shepard; after all, he'd been recorded too.

All the blood had drained from his face except for two bright spots of color, one on each cheek. His eyes had gone all pupil. He blinked rapidly, staring at the floor.

"Tom?" I said, as gently as I could. I hadn't meant to scare him this badly.

He jerked his head up to look at me. "When did this happen?"

The phrasing caught me off guard. Not *what*, but *when*. "The night we were evacuated," I said cautiously.

"Was it Nurse Bryony?"

I startled, then remembered that I'd told him about my concussion and the infirmary. "I don't know." It seemed the safest answer.

He went a shade paler and nodded to himself, as senselessly fast as a bobblehead doll.

"Five minutes," the policeman called.

"Hey," I said to Tom, "I promise I'll explain later, but can we—"

"Where are they?" he asked in a snarl, shoving me into the door of my closet. His cheerful, bright American face looked like an ugly mask. "Where the fuck are they, Jamie?"

It was like the floor fell open below us.

I shoved him off me and kept him there, an arm's length away. Tears welled up in his eyes as he struggled against my grip.

"What the hell are you talking about?" But I knew exactly what he was talking about. I just wanted to hear him say it.

273

Admit that he'd bugged our room. Confess that all this time, his friendly gossip mongering was a cover for collecting information for Bryony Downs.

"Oh my God, he's going to *kill* me." Tom stopped fighting me off. He fell back, gasping, throwing his hands up over his face, and I felt a flare of satisfaction.

That faded as quickly as it came. *He?*

The dealer. The Moriarty dealer.

"Two minutes," the policeman said. "Cut the dramatics and finish packing."

"Talk fast," I said, pulling my suitcase out from under the bed and yanking armfuls of clothes from the dresser.

"I never even got anything good," Tom said, as if to himself. "Nothing conclusive. Charlotte even stopped coming to the room. You two were always hunkered down in her fucked-up little dungeon."

"I just— I can't deal with this right now." I grabbed the novels from above my bed and dropped them on top of my clothes, one, two, three, like grenades. Textbooks, soap. I had to get in my closet but Tom was still slouched in front of it.

"Move," I said to him, but he stared up at me stupidly, and the bovine look on him eroded the last of my temper. "I swear to God I will break your neck if you don't move. I might break your neck anyway. You were spying on me, Tom? On top of all the other awful shit happening—you had to make it worse? I never did anything to you."

"He offered to split his advance with me," he said. "He already sold it, you know, he's in the middle of writing it now.

It's going to be *huge*, and he's going to have all this money, he'll be famous, he'll finally be able to teach somewhere better than this shithole—his friend Penelope is going to get him a job at Yale—"

I stared at him, at his horrible lying mouth. "Wheatley? You're full of shit. The dealer told you to say that."

Tom went to his desk and, opening the bottom drawer, pulled out a battered legal pad. The top page didn't have any writing on it. Not actual writing, no—someone had painstakingly colored in the indentations made by the words written on the page above. *Skeletons in her office he says starrily as if he's in love with death as much as her.* Lines and lines of florid prose. *He wears the glasses of a Beat philosopher from the 1950s but his face is all Cornwall smooth. When they dance they do not touch.*

They were Mr. Wheatley's notes from our meeting, when he'd so impressed me by interrogating me and then handing over what he'd written down. I remembered the piece of cardboard he'd stuck below the top page. The top *two* pages. I'd thought at the time that he was worried his ink would bleed through, but he had just been making himself a copy.

"He was sure you were guilty," Tom said, almost like he was pleading with me. "Back in October, I was waiting for an appointment with him to talk about my story, and I heard him say it to another teacher inside his office. You. Guilty. And I told him, no, you weren't, and it was actually this great story, you and Charlotte Holmes solving crimes, that you two were totally boning like Bonnie and Clyde, the good-guy version.

He had this idea for a book. True crime. With famous kids as the heroes. The public would eat it up. I'm a good writer, he told me that, better than you, anyway, even if my family's not famous, and I'd do a good job helping, and you'd be happy about it in the end, when you saw how much attention it got you—" He cut himself off.

"So you bugged our room."

"He had me do it. Ordered all the stuff online. The mirror was the worst, replacing it. But yeah, I'd get you to talk and then I'd review the files when you were gone, write everything down, pass it along to him. But—look at this. He's never going to pay me now."

"Why?" I asked him again. I'd thought Tom was my friend. He was one of the only constants in my life, his irrepressible grin and his motor mouth and his ridiculous sweater-vest. We watched stupid videos on his computer at night. We ate each other's candy, borrowed each other's shampoo. He was the first person who was nice to me when I came back to America, miserable and alone.

"I was doing you a favor," he repeated, like he was trying to make himself believe it.

"Time, boys," the officer boomed from the doorway. I slammed the door in his face and bolted it. I was going to get an explanation even if it got me arrested.

"Tell me why."

"Lena's family goes to Paris every summer," Tom said quietly, as the policeman hammered on the door. "She invited me. And she . . . she expects things from me. Dinners out. Presents.

You know her dad's a big oil tycoon out in India. They have a housekeeper. She has her own *plane*. And I'm here, from the Midwest, on scholarship. Do you know what that feels like? He was going to give me ten grand!"

I couldn't wring out an ounce of sympathy for him. "Seriously, what do you think Lena will say when she finds out how you got that money? Jesus Christ, everyone at this fucking school acts like they're so rich and half of them aren't, not even close. When are you going to realize that? What do you think all those people are doing at Holmes's poker game every week, wagering all their money? Here's a solution. Get the hell over yourself. Tell Lena the truth. God, she's actually a decent person, do you think she'd really care?"

"I didn't expect you to understand it. You're a show dog with a pedigree. I'm just someone that escaped from the pound." He shook his head. "It's not like I hurt you or anything. You're my friend. I was doing you a *favor*. It was going to make you famous—"

"Open up the door! Open it up!"

I was disgusted with him, disgusted with Sherringford, with the bullshit and the jealousy and the backstabbing. Furious, I grabbed the handles of my closet doors, ready to throw the rest of the stuff in my suitcase and get the fuck out of Dodge.

Something bit into my skin.

I looked down, stupidly. My hands were so cut up and bandaged that I could hardly tell what had happened. There. A pinprick of blood near the knuckle of my index finger.

I didn't think anything of it. Not until I gripped the handle with the bandaged part of my hand and flung open the door.

Clothes and shoes and the rest of my life's detritus all in a jumble on the closet floor. On the back wall were three giant, jagged lines in marker.

YOU HAVE TWENTY-FOUR HOURS TO LIVE
UNLESS SHE GIVES ME WHAT I WANT
XOXO CULVERTON SMITH

Culverton Smith. The man behind Sherlock Holmes's poisoned ivory box.

I stared back down at my bleeding knuckle. Behind me, Tom raised his iPhone with one shaking hand, and took a picture.

I RIPPED THE INFECTED SPRING FROM THE DOOR HANDLE. Took my phone from the desk (dead), and its charger. Picked up my suitcase. The whole time Tom was loudly pleading his ignorance—*this wasn't me, I wouldn't do something like that*—like the swine he was until I grabbed him by the shirt with one hand.

"This is what you can do for me," I snarled at him. "Deal with the cop."

His eyes were focused on the pinprick of infected blood on his shirt. "But what should I say?"

"Make something up. You're good at that."

As I stalked down the hall, I heard Tom's half-assed babbling. "It's my fault," he was saying to the policeman, "it's my fault, let him go."

I made it to the front doors before my legs began to give out under me.

Bryony Downs had won. She'd taken "The Adventure of the Dying Detective" and turned it back on us with deadly earnest, not knowing that Charlotte Holmes had used that same story to clear our names. I had no idea what she'd dabbed that spring with, but my brain was supplying a cavalcade of answers. Spinal meningitis, I thought, or malaria. I used to want to be a doctor; I'd wanted to treat the scariest diseases, and now I couldn't stop running them through my head. Milo was right. She had to be working with the Moriartys; how else could she have access to this sort of thing? She was a puppet, and this was a message directed at the Holmes family.

And the message was going to be my dead body.

I staggered out the front door and down the steps. The next two students were waiting for the officer to fetch them, and one of them stepped forward to help me.

"Don't touch me," I said, holding up a hand. "I might be contagious."

Because that was the worst of it. Nurse Bryony could have made me into some kind of bomb. A patient zero that could take out the whole eastern seaboard. I needed to get inside, away from everyone, and I had to start making a plan. My parents couldn't know. There was nothing they could do. I wondered if my father would still find all this crime-solving *fun* after he identified my corpse at the morgue.

No. I wasn't going to die. I was sixteen years old. I was going to be a writer; I was going to go to college, get a flat in London, or Edinburgh, or Paris. I'd get to know my stepbrothers. Oh, God, I didn't want my little sister to be an only child. I didn't want to leave Charlotte Holmes with a controlling family and a brilliant mind and a dead best friend. I didn't want to imagine her life without me. Maybe it was selfish to think that way, but I couldn't imagine mine without her.

The sky was open and blue, guileless in its beauty. And the snow everywhere, blinding. The light was beginning to prick at my eyes, and I rubbed at them with the back of my hand. This had to be psychosomatic, I told myself; it had to be in my head. The denial working its hand around me. *I can't possibly be dying,* I thought, and tried to believe it.

One foot, then the other. Where was I going? I'd walked, I remembered, up the hill from town. The distance was impossibly far. I'd sit for a minute, catch my breath. If I could just arrange my suitcase—there.

Holmes told me that, when they found me, I'd passed out in a snowbank.

They bundled me into the back of Milo's town car, her and her brother and his Greystone mercenaries. Blankets. Something hot to drink. Holmes rubbing my chilled hands between hers, strangely smooth and firm. "No," I'd managed to say, "the blood, it's contagious," and then I saw that she was wearing latex gloves.

She knew.

I was racked with chills, and still cold sweat beaded on my forehead before trickling down my face. My mouth burned, my teeth tender to the touch. I couldn't swallow. My throat didn't work. Holmes held a bottle of water to my lips and tipped it, gently, into my mouth. I tried to pull off my shirt, thinking, in my delirium, that it was a straightjacket, and she stilled my hands. All the while Milo watched me from behind his glasses, taking copious notes on his phone. On what, I didn't know. I was a specimen, I thought wildly. I would be experimented on until I died.

When we got to our destination, Peterson had to carry me up the stairs over his shoulder, like he'd rescued me from a burning building. And then there was a bed, with sheets still warm from the dryer, a table beside it. Peterson returned to that table again and again with pill bottles, clean rags. Someone brought in an IV drip and put it into my arm.

What was real? I didn't know. Milo came in, in a suit and watch chain; he lit a pipe by the window, staring broodingly out over the rooftops. My dog Maggie was there, too, though she'd died when I was six. But she put her shaggy head on my mattress and looked up at me with big wet eyes, telling me in silent words what my sister Shelby was reading that week (*A Wrinkle in Time*), how much my mother missed me. My hands were made of lead; I couldn't ruffle her ears the way I wanted. *Good dog,* I wanted to say. *Where have you been?*

Bryony came in through an invisible door and put her arm around Milo's waist. They talked as if I wasn't there.

"Lead him up to the mountain and put the dagger to his

throat," Milo said in his sonorous voice.

"I thought we were done with goats. I thought we only made offerings of sheep." Still, Bryony smiled into his face. He kissed her like they were in a movie, dipping her back in his arms.

Stop, I yelled, *stop*, but she was at my bedside, with a pillow pressed down over my face to keep the words inside my mouth. And then she was gone, and Milo was, too, and I was alone.

I didn't trust anything that was happening to me—Where was Holmes? For that matter, where was I?—but I was so overwhelmed by a wave of exhaustion that I let myself be carried away by it, all the way to sea.

When I woke—when I fully woke—night had fallen. As my eyes adjusted to the dark, I noticed things I hadn't before. There was a dim lamp by my bed, its mouth turned away to throw a white circle on the wall. Beside me, a machine counted out my pulse, reading it from a plastic clip attached to my index finger. My hands had been re-bandaged, expertly this time. I felt present in my body, in a way I hadn't since I opened that closet door.

There was a bright blanket at the end of my bed, a door across from me. In the shadowed corner was a chair. Empty, I thought, and as I squinted to make sure, I saw the velvet fabric, the tufted buttons.

I was in Bryony Downs's flat.

Frantically, I pulled myself up in bed, yanking the heart monitor off my finger and going to work on the medical tape over the needles on my arm. She'd taken me—she'd taken me somewhere. Had Holmes and her brother been hallucinations, too? The heart monitor screamed a warning, and the door across from me flew open.

By the time she came in, I was on my feet, panting, the desk lamp ripped out of the wall and brandished like a weapon before me.

"Watson," Holmes cried from the doorway. "*Watson*. God, I thought you were dead."

It took some doing, but I let her coax me back into bed. She called a name I didn't recognize, and a man in scrubs came in and put my IV back in. He took my vitals while Holmes hovered behind him, biting her lip. She'd pulled her hair back roughly from her face; her nose was red, her face white. She looked ascetic and harsh. She looked, in fact, like she'd been crying. I started to reach out to touch her but then drew back my hand.

"Right now, we're managing your symptoms," the doctor murmured. "We've given you medication to control the pain, and to bring your fever down. Don't try to get up. If you need to use the bathroom, let us know."

I nodded. Now that the adrenaline rush was over, my legs were trembling from my attempt at self-defense.

"You shouldn't be here, Charlotte," the doctor said. "He could be contagious, and I don't want you touching him—"

Stepping forward, she took my hand in hers.

"So be it," the doctor said, and left.

"Holmes," I asked her, "what did she give me? How did you know?"

She hoisted herself up on my bedside. I remembered the night I'd woken her this way, when she'd fallen asleep as Hailey and woken up, again, as my best friend. We'd had pancakes. She'd asked me to trust her.

"It's a created virus," she said hoarsely. "Brewed in a lab. That doctor—Dr. Warner—is a specialist on this particular strain." She rattled off a series of Latin words I didn't know. "That's what it's called."

"Can you give me something easier to call it?" I asked, half-joking. "The Watson flu?"

She shrugged. "As you'd like. It was created, originally, as a bioweapon, for the rapidity with which it kills its victims. Dr. Warner works for the German government. Luckily for us, he was presenting at a conference in Washington. Milo more or less had him clubbed over the head and brought up here."

"Oh," I said. "So it can be cured?"

Holmes bit her lip again. I'd never seen her so ragged. "We think so," she said carefully. "He has some theories. Right now, he's in the other room, researching."

"The other room. Here, in Bryony's flat."

"It was my idea," she admitted. "God knows she won't be returning here after pulling a stunt like this. And I didn't want to bring you to your house, not contagious like this. So we took this place over, changed the locks; Milo called in some favors, as you can see. We'll bring in a professional cleaning crew, of course, after this is all over. The next tenant doesn't deserve to get the Watson flu in the bargain."

After this is all over. One way or another, it would be over soon. She caught my gaze, and with that magician's trick of hers, I watched her read my mind.

She shook her head quickly, hugging her arms around herself.

"You can't do that," I said quietly. "You can't fall apart yet."

She nodded, her face turned from me.

"Come here," I said, moving over in the bed. "If you really don't mind my being patient zero."

She swallowed her tears. I pulled back the sheet, and she crawled in beside me, putting her head on my chest. I pressed my lips against the dark crown of her hair. It was like those hours under the porch, the stillness, the waiting; and it was nothing like it at all. My muscles ached. My limbs were heavy. My lungs were raw in my chest. I had to brace myself against the bed as another round of shivers ground their way through me.

"How did you know?" I asked, gritting my teeth. "About the virus? About what happened to me?"

"Bryony sent me a list of her demands," she said, her voice muffled in my shirt. "Via text, of course. She had it timed to your appointment at Michener Hall. Must've gotten the schedule from the all-campus email."

"Via text? Holmes, that can be used as evidence against her."

"That's not what we're going to do."

"But—"

"Don't, Watson."

I didn't have the strength to argue with her. "What were her demands? What does she want?"

"A pony," she said.

I smiled against the pain. "The very prettiest pony in the land, on a golden lead. Only then will the favorite sidekick be cured."

"You're not my sidekick," Holmes said softly. "That's her first mistake."

"What am I, then?"

But I didn't know if I wanted to hear the answer. Not now.

She must have heard the reticence in my voice. "A pony," she said, "and three million dollars, and safe passage to Russia, a country which, given my father's history as well as the current state of US-Russo relations, won't extradite her to either Britain or America to stand trial for what she's done. Which would be moot, anyway, because she wants me to claim full responsibility for Dobson's murder and Elizabeth's attack."

"Jesus Christ." I struggled against the idea.

"She's done the thing very completely," Holmes said. There was a touch of admiration in her voice. "I should have known."

"This is not your fault," I told her, before she could go on. "You claiming it's your fault makes it sound like I'm just a piece of cargo getting hauled next to you. No will of my own. So stop it."

"But—"

"I'm dying," I told her, with a grim sort of glee. "You have to listen to me."

She laughed hollowly. "Milo has the money, and he's arranging the airfare as we speak. I've written out my confession. It's done. The exchange will be made at nine o'clock in the morning. She has the antidote. I don't know how—Dr. Warner doesn't know how it's possible—but she does, and even if she's lying, it's still a chance we have to take. We're meeting her twenty-two hours after your infection, so you should still be—ah. It should be fine."

"Where?"

"She'll text us the location when it's time."

"You're not going to jail for this," I said. "Detective Shepard won't let you. Wait, isn't she in his custody? What the hell happened there?"

"Remember when we thought she stopped for gas? She switched cars at the police station. Left her Toyota in the lot and picked up another car that she'd left there." Again, that note of admiration. "We saw her as a stupid sorority girl, and she ran circles around us."

"And where is he now? Detective Shepard?"

"Her terms were no police involvement, no sending you to the hospital. So I don't know. I've been focused on you." I felt her shrug. "That's the other part. You'll die. One way or another, you'll die if I don't take this fall. I think it's a good idea to listen to her, as she's proven herself handy with a suitcase bomb."

The door cracked open, and Milo stuck his glossy head in. If he was surprised to see his sister tucked in my arms, he didn't show it.

"You're awake. How are you feeling?" he asked.

Like I'd been run down by a truck. "Fine," I said.

"Do you want us to contact your parents?"

"Oh God. My father thought—"

"—thinks you are discussing strategy with myself and Lottie until late tonight. This afternoon, Peterson and Michaels returned his car and gave him my reassurances. As we've decided to broker with Nurse Bryony for your cure, you don't have a real reason to worry him. Though I understand how one's parents could be a comfort, in a time like this." He said the last part academically, like it was a theory he'd never personally tested.

"Right," I said, trying to keep my voice even. "No, that's fine, don't contact them."

"Get some sleep," he advised. "We'll handle this."

If I wasn't included in that *we*—and how could I be; I couldn't handle even standing up—at least his sister was. I nodded at him, and he nodded back, and shut the door.

"You're not going to jail," I said again. My mouth felt dry. "There has to be another way."

"I need to be arrested, and convicted. Or she'll find another way to end you. She was very specific on those terms."

"Holmes."

"Watson," she said roughly, "I remember a very recent conversation where you detailed all the horrible possibilities of my death. Do you remember that? Would you like to, for just a moment, imagine what it would be like to watch one come true? Think about what this is like for me."

"The trade-off shouldn't be spending the rest of your life in a cell for a crime you didn't commit!"

"No." She curled my shirt into her fist. "No, but perhaps I

should serve time for the crime I did."

"I can't talk about your martyr complex right now," I said, swallowing against the sand in my throat. "I can't." I reached blindly for the glass of water by the bed and drank it down.

She drew back to look at me. "You're flushed," she said, scrambling to her feet, "I think your fever's returning—I'll fetch Dr. Warner—"

"Wait," I said.

She was rumpled, undone, her hair coming out of its elastic to curl in tendrils around her face. There was something I had to say to her, I thought, something necessary, something right at the tip of my tongue.

I guess she knew it before I did.

Leaning over, she smoothed my hair back from my forehead. I closed my eyes at her touch. And so it was a surprise when she kissed me on the lips.

She smelled, unexpectedly, like roses.

"That's all I can do," she whispered, resting her forehead to mine.

"That's a lot," I said, and she laughed.

"No. I mean, that's all—it's nearly too much for me to touch anyone, after Dobson, and I—for you, I'm trying."

I could feel her breath on my lips. "I don't know how long I'll be like this," she said, slowly, "or if I've maybe been this way all along. I don't know if it'll ever be enough."

It was confusing, what she said, but I thought I understood it.

"You don't have to try," I said to her. "Whatever this is, already—it's already enough."

"I know," she said, straightening. "It has to be."

We looked at each other for a minute.

"If you get yourself thrown in jail over this," I told her, "I will never, never forgive you. You need to find another way, or I swear to God I will die on you just out of spite."

Her flickering smile. "Okay."

"Okay? It's that simple?"

"Okay," she said again. I had no choice but to believe her. "Your pulse is racing, and you're far too warm. I'm going for Dr. Warner." She smirked. "Don't want you to die before you can use it as a bargaining chip."

"Thanks," I said, pleased, at least, that she chalked my hammering heart up to my fever.

eleven

I WAS MUCH, MUCH WORSE IN THE MORNING.

It shouldn't have come as a surprise. Logic dictates that a deteriorating illness deteriorates. But then, logic is hard to come by when you're dying.

Whatever brief reprieve Dr. Warner's drugs had granted me ended around midnight, when I maxed out on the highest morphine dosage he'd allow me. The hours after that were . . . well, I've been assured it's best that I can't remember them.

As morning broke, I moved in and out of fitful dreams, dark, sodden landscapes that were at once cruelly hot and cut through by the bitterest winds. At the same time, I was conscious of something happening in the room around me. A hand on my forehead. A pair of voices, shouting. It all added to my unrest, since, for the life of me, I couldn't make myself understand what was happening. Burma, I thought, I was in Burma. I was in Afghanistan. No, my mother was baking cinnamon rolls in the kitchen, and if I was very good, if I made my bed and put all my toys away, she'd bring them in to me. Holmes was there too, dressed in all black. Someone had died. We were headed to the funeral.

I woke to the barest hint of sunlight through the curtains.

My room was silent. I could tell that much without opening my eyes. The effort I had to put into even that simple task left me dizzy and sweating. When I managed it, I realized that I was alone. Was this another hallucination? It didn't feel like one. There was the bedside table, there the tufted chair.

And I wasn't in any pain.

I turned my head to look at the morphine drip (that took another eternity), but I didn't understand how to read the dosage on the bag. Whatever I was being given, it was working. In place of the pain, there was a sort of bodily rebellion. I asked my legs to swing off the bed. They didn't. I asked my arm to reach out for my water glass. It wouldn't. I panted with the effort, and the panting took effort. I was about as weak as a newborn child.

"No," a woman insisted in the other room. It was a voice I recognized, but from where?

"No," she said again, angrier this time, and then fell silent.

It was Bryony Downs.

The meeting was taking place in the next room.

It was brazen of her to do it here, to walk into the enemy's stronghold and cut a deal in the place where they had every advantage. She really did think herself invincible.

The antidote could be out there, nestled in her pocket.

No. She wouldn't have brought it with her, not where it could be taken from her by force. She'd have hidden it somewhere nearby, only giving its location over when she'd gotten what she wanted. If Holmes gave her what she wanted.

Which meant, of course, that I would die, and in the next two hours.

I struggled, again, to get my legs to obey me. *Move*, I told them, as laughter pealed in the next room. *Move*. The shirt and soft pants I'd been dressed in were already drenched through with sweat. Sweat. Was that a good thing, sweating? Did that mean the nerves and veins inside me—I imagined them now, crackled black and breaking—were still healthy? Was I somehow beating this?

If I was beating this, I'd probably have working legs, I reminded myself. Grinding my teeth, I focused on my knees. *Move*.

And I did. I rolled right off the bed and onto the carpeted floor, bringing the bedside table down with me.

The crash was tremendous, and I lay in the middle of it, in the spilled pills and scattered tissues and the shards of my drinking glass, helpless.

I'd been in denial until that point, I think. But that was when it really hit me. That I was going to die. That they were going to put me in the ground, not years from now, not surrounded by books I'd written in the little flat on the Rue du

Rivoli at age seventy-three, but today. In a matter of hours. I'd kissed Charlotte Holmes once, and I would die before I'd see a second time.

The door flung open with a bang.

"Watson," Holmes said, going down to her knees beside me.

"Bring the boy in here." The voice rang out like a sweet bell. "I'd like to see him."

"Can you move?" Holmes asked, unnaturally loud. She put her hands under my arms. "If I get you to your feet, can you lean on me?"

"Yes," I managed to say, though I had no idea if it was true.

She heaved me up to my knees. "Listen to me," she said in my ear. Her black hair brushed against my cheek. "When I blink twice, you play your last card."

"Okay," I said, because *I don't know what the hell you're talking about* was seven more words than I could force out.

"Milo," she called, "I could use a hand."

Together, the two of them manhandled me out of the bedroom and into the sitting room that, when I'd last seen it, had been empty. Under Holmes's direction, Milo's mercenaries had reassembled it into what it had been, which was something like a preppy brothel. A pink shag rug. Lucite chairs around a Lucite table. A sofa that looked like it'd been stuffed with marshmallows, and a pair of men's trousers hung over its arm. An iPod dock and speakers, a haphazard setup of slides and beakers and a microscope (those must've been Dr. Warner's).

A gilt mirror spanned the whole length of one wall, gathering the entire room in its reflection—Charlotte Holmes, in her trim black clothes, sitting on a fuzzy ottoman that looked like it escaped from *Fraggle Rock*; Milo, so close to his sister that their knees were touching; and me, slumped like a beached whale on one of those clear plastic chairs. If the beached whale had lost fifteen pounds overnight, coated his face in Vaseline and blacked his eyes, and then crawled up onto a beach to end it all.

Looking at me, Bryony Downs curled her lip in disgust.

She'd come in no further than the front door. Her purple puffer coat was unzipped, but she still wore her pom-pomed hat and gloves. With her porcelain doll face, flushed from the cold, she could have been taking a breather from the slopes. Really, everything about her belonged in a catalog for Fair Isle sweaters, or an advertisement for a ski lodge in Aspen. Everything except the fanatical gleam in her eyes.

"Hi, Jamie," she said brightly. "It's good to see you."

If I hadn't been an hour from death, I would've walked right up to her and snapped her neck.

But I was. That was the point.

"Okay, where was I? Before this one's attempt to prematurely kick the bucket?" She rested against her doorframe, hands in her pockets.

"You were gloating," Milo offered.

"Yes," Holmes said, leaning forward. "Do go on, it's fascinating." She had that cataloging look to her, with her fingertips pressed together and that line at the bridge of her nose. I noticed, then, that there was a briefcase at Holmes's feet, a pair of plane tickets resting on it. Bryony's terms, fulfilled.

Her eyes flicked to the two of them, and then back to me. "I don't want to bore you," she said, clearly thinking about her getaway.

"Tell me," I coughed, in an attempt to stall her. "Dobson. How?"

"Poor thing," she said. "I'd come over to check your vitals, but I think little Charlotte here might react poorly to my hands on you. A shame. You know, this *orthomyxoviridae surrexit nigrum* virus doesn't have a precise countdown clock. It isn't a bomb. Really, you could croak at any time. So I'll honor your last wish." She put a hand to her heart in apparent sincerity. "I'll do that. Isn't that how all those stories always end? The hero explaining everything to his hapless confidant? You are a Watson, after all, so let's stick with tradition."

Holmes wasn't listening, it was clear. Her eyes were fixed on Bryony's boots. Slowly, her hand stole over to her brother's, and she took it. For comfort, or for another reason, I wasn't sure. So I clamped my eyes on Bryony, giving her the captivated audience she obviously wanted.

"Lee Dobson. Nasty thing, wasn't he? One of my first patients back in September, with a mean case of thrush. He had to come in for a follow-up, and I think he thought . . . well, you know. Attractive older woman, lusty young man. He was trying to impress me. Asking all these 'oblique' questions about narcotics, opiates. For a friend. They always say it's for a friend. How does someone react to heroin? As opposed to morphine? To oxycodone? Did they go nonresponsive? At what dosage? How pliable were they? Were they still able to have sex?"

Holmes's shoulders went stiff, her jaw set. Part of her was listening, after all. Beside her, Milo's expression was set in a determined blank.

"Oh, I was happy to oblige him and answer his questions. I had no qualms about it. Because how many other students at this school could be depraved enough to do drugs of that caliber? I knew I wasn't pointing him toward the innocent. Why, yes, I told him, your friend will be euphoric. So happy, so lazy, so unwilling to move. They should be careful, I said. Terrible things can happen to girls when they're that high. He thanked me profusely. Nearly wrung my hand off. And I had the satisfaction of knowing that I was sending our little whore here exactly the man she'd been asking for.

"And after that he kept coming back. It was clear he was infatuated with me. You can see why, of course." A smile crept over her face like a poisonous fog. "I can see you are, too, Jamie, from the way you look at me. I knew it the day that you got into that tussle with my Lee, the starry-eyed look on your face. Don't be ashamed. I did pageants, you know. Won quite a few prizes. But no. No, I was talking about Lee Dobson and that protein powder.

"Because the two of you had more or less marked him for dead. Charlotte had made her disgust for that poor boy so loudly clear, and, you, Jamie, had made an attempt to kill him. No, don't look at me like that—you would've beaten him stupid, and all for him saying things about your Charlotte that were *true*. I got all of it from Dobson in the infirmary. How he'd tried to warn you about what a slut she was. He was doing you a favor! And look at how he repaid it. Poor thing marked himself for death at that point. From my own experience"—here she huffed, like a disappointed grandmother—"I know that Charlotte is utterly ruthless. She would've taken him out eventually, especially with such a besotted baby mastiff like you by her side. I was doing him a favor, really. At least I got rid of him in a humane way.

"It wasn't hard to start dosing him with arsenic in his protein powder. A little bit at a time, building the dosage each day—I made him come to me to take it, of course. And then I had a blank page to write my story on, once he was dead. You know, I loved Dr. Watson's tales when I was young. It was so much fun to get to do a reenactment. I nicked a brand-new copy of *The Adventures of Sherlock Holmes* out of the library and made a dorm visit that night—came up through the back stairs. I'd asked Lee to prop them open for me. Had a surprise for him, I said. He probably thought he was going to get laid. I knew his roommate was on that rugby tour; he'd told me, so eager to get his hands on me. Well. By the time I arrived, he was dead. They called me to help comfort the students, after."

She studied a nail. In a flash, I remembered seeing her there outside Dobson's door, patting my sobbing hallmate on the shoulder. I swallowed the bile that had risen in my throat.

"Of course, I had help with the snake."

Holmes started. "What help?"

Bryony clucked her tongue. "Speaking out of turn," she said, and for the first time, I heard a trace of anger in her voice.

"But I'll play along. Still haven't thought through the consequences of your actions, have you? Well, birds can't change their feathers. Here's a quick education: when you orchestrated my fiancé's downfall—all for the crime of loving *me*—you ruined my life. You ruined. My *life*." She took a step closer to the two of them, almost inadvertently. When she moved, I saw the gun she'd holstered underneath her puffer coat.

"You whore. I'd been with Augie since we were kids. He'd gone to Eton, and then early to Oxford, while I went to the village school, but all the while he'd always loved me. *Me*, do you understand? I went over to the Moriartys' for every Sunday dinner. They came to my flute recitals, when my own mother was too drunk to scrape herself off the sofa. And when I was seventeen and my mother died, and my father couldn't be fucked to take me in, do you know who did? Oh, that's right. Professor Moriarty and his wife. I don't care what they did on the side—they were saints, do you understand? If they asked me to slit my own throat, I would have, for them."

"I thought you came to the States when you were sixteen," Holmes whispered.

Bryony smiled. "Do you think my name was the only part of my employment records I had falsified? No, *I* was never sent away across an ocean. No one wanted to be rid of me that badly. You see, I was to marry Augie as soon as I finished at uni. His parents paid for me to attend the University of London, and his family had already bought a flat for us to live in as husband and wife. I was to be a doctor. I'm very smart, you know. Though you Holmeses all think that there's no one as bloody brilliant as you, Augie could run circles around you with his eyes shut, and I was going to be a *doctor*.

"And then Augie took that horrible job." She ground her teeth so hard that I could hear it, the enamel and bone. "At *your house*.

"His parents warned him against it. His brother Lucien did too. They thought he was mad, going into a den of vipers like that. Your bitch of a mother and your homicidal brother and you, the enfant terrible, as his student? God, the games the Moriartys play are small compared to yours. But Augie believed the best of people. He believed the best from you, baby Charlotte. That was his downfall."

That was when I realized that she was talking about him as if he were dead. Holmes noticed, too—her eyes finally drifted up from Bryony's boots to her cruelly smiling face. But Holmes kept her immaculate poker face. Either this wasn't a surprise, or her composure was even better than I'd thought.

"The last time I saw Augie alive," Bryony said, "was the day before the drugs bust. He'd come up to London for a few days, to visit me. It was beautiful. He took me to this gorgeous restaurant. White tablecloths. We talked about our wedding. It was going to be small, intimate. In his family's backyard, wildflowers, his mother's wedding dress. We were so happy. We didn't need anything but each other." She lost her dreamy look, then. "He went back to your house the next day. I reckon you could smell me all over him. Made you crazy with jealousy. Just a little girl, but with such big-girl appetites. He told me all about your crush, you know. He thought it was *adorable*."

So much for composure. Holmes flinched, as if she'd been hit across the face.

"The day after, you called the law down on him. After the police left, after they found Lucien and dragged him away to jail—oh, you look so *surprised*, what the hell did you think happened to him?—I drove all over creation, looking for him. The police couldn't find him; he'd made his confession and run. Oxford had expelled him. No other school would have him, not with that record. He'd panicked. Gone home. And he'd taken his father's pistol into his childhood bedroom, and he shot himself in the face."

I didn't understand. I didn't understand at all—I'd thought August had been hauled away to jail, and when he'd been paroled, had gotten a job at Greystone working for Milo. I racked my memory as best as I could. What had Holmes said, exactly, when she was telling me the story?

August stayed to take the blame, as I suspected he would . . . he got a job, finally. Works for my brother in Germany.

There wasn't anything about what happened in between.

Even in my feverish haze, I began filling in the blanks.

August Moriarty had faked his death, most likely with his parents' help. I don't know how I hadn't seen it before: he'd confessed to selling hard drugs to a minor, and the sentence for that would have been much longer than the timeline Holmes had laid out for me between his crime and his new life. His parents had given him up, Holmes had said. They would have had to cut off all public contact to maintain the fiction of his death. But they'd buried the news of it, too. I hadn't found any obituaries when I was researching him, any mention of a funeral. It was as if August Moriarty had simply stopped existing. Frozen in time as a wonder boy, working on the intricate mathematical patterns in the Arctic Circle, his thick blond Disney hair blowing in the frigid wind.

And Bryony Downs didn't know.

It would have been difficult for her to accompany him in his new life, but had he really loved her, he would have found a way, I thought. He was a brilliant man. Too brilliant, maybe, not to see the hint of fanatical darkness in his fiancée. The obsession, the wild selfishness. The willingness to do anything to achieve her own ends.

Maybe August Moriarty saw this as his opportunity to escape her. An understandable decision. Despite it leading to where Holmes and I found ourselves now.

"You," Bryony said, edging still closer to Holmes, who regarded her coolly. "You have his death on your hands. So you'll do time for a death. I'm just the middleman."

And Lee Dobson and Elizabeth Hartwell the sacrificial lambs.

Though she hadn't mentioned Elizabeth at all.

"Who were you working with?" Holmes asked.

Bryony flicked her hair. "Who said I was working with anyone?"

Holmes stared her down until, shifting uncomfortably, Bryony spoke.

"The man who convinced the judge that he'd no idea of the contents of his car's boot and served a minimum sentence.

You didn't forget who drove the car to your house to get you your fix, did you? Lucien Moriarty, you stupid child. God, the best part of all of this has been feeding you from my hand. I offered you warnings. Touched them with ungloved hands, in case you'd manage to lift my fingerprints. Printed them in the font that I write all my medical reports in. Made the spellings English, instead of American. It was a paint-by-numbers murder, and you were too dumb to learn to pick up the paintbrush. I did everything but hand myself over to you. Knowing, of course, that the moment you found me out, Lucien would close the bear trap. You do know what Lucien does for a living, yes?"

"He's a fixer," Milo murmured.

"Precisely," Bryony said. "Gold star, you. Except for the part where he's a Moriarty first. They have connections you can only *dream* of. Tell Lucien you want a rattlesnake as window dressing for your little scene, and he'll make an untraceable one appear. Tell him you want a beautiful little suitcase bomb, and he'll hire a professional to make you one. Tell him you want a plastic jewel shoved down a girl's throat, and she'll choke on it. Tell him you want a new identity, a passport, a job at Charlotte Holmes's boarding school, and he'll give it to you wrapped in a bow. God, the very *lack* of evidence should have been a clue. I gave up my dreams of being a doctor for this. Do you hear that? *I gave up my dreams to make you serve the sentence you deserved.* I'd nearly all the credits necessary for a nursing degree, and if that could get me here and to you faster—well. For once, sweetie, you were the hottest ticket in town."

She knelt down before the ottoman, put her hands on

Holmes's knees, leaned right into her face. "This is why I'm a better person than you. Are you ready? I could kill you right now. No"—she held a finger up to Holmes's lips—"that suitcase bomb was never intended to kill you, don't be stupid. I was just *disgusted* by the thought of you and the Watson boy playing house in there. Acting out your roles. Do you want to know why I set up Dobson's murder as a remake of 'The Speckled Band'? It's a reminder. They're stories. They're stories, and this is real life. *You are not Sherlock Holmes*, and you won't ever be."

Holmes stared straight down her nose at Bryony's sneering face. And then she turned her head to me and, slowly, unmistakably, blinked her eyes twice.

Play your last card, she'd said. What card could I possibly play? Only sheer force of will kept my eyes open now. I could barely speak, much less get to my feet and make a stand. If I was supposed to be the muscle in this operation, I was totally out of commission.

But she knew that. So what could she mean?

Last night—a hand on my forehead, a deliberate, closed-mouth kiss. Roses. And her smile as she walked out the door, telling me not to die before I could use it as a bargaining chip.

Oh.

I let my eyes fall closed. I willed my breathing to slow. And I fell, heavily, out of the chair onto the thick pink carpet.

"Watson!" Holmes cried, a perfect parody of the last time she'd thought I was dead.

Stumbling. Footsteps. Bryony saying, "Oh, *damn*," as she

crouched above me. I could smell the Forever Ever Cotton Candy. A man's cold fingers on my cheek, then moving to my neck to take a pulse.

"He's alive," Milo announced. "He's alive, but barely."

"Don't move him," Holmes said. "I'll get the blanket from the bed."

I opened my eyes to slits. Bryony was still crouched over me, an unexpected look of concern on her face. "Jamie," she said. "It'll be okay. This will be over soon, as soon as your girl-friend agrees to let me go."

I was actually beginning to think that wasn't the worst idea.

More footsteps. Milo saying, "Couldn't you take a look at him, Bryony? For his sake?" Bryony's bit lip as she took her eyes off the bedroom door and fixed them on me.

The sound of a handgun being cocked.

"Get up," Holmes snarled. "With your hands behind your head."

Nurse Bryony got to her feet, stiffly.

"You're wearing a wire," Holmes said. "It's wrapped around your handgun holster, which is in and of itself very clever, as most of us would notice the gun and then instantly avert our eyes. I am not most people, as you well know. So yes, hello Lucien, I'm happy to know that you're well and having your crony deal drugs to the Sherringford milieu, and as I've said in the many letters I sent you in prison, I am very sorry for my part in your two months' incarceration, though I'd wager that one of the dozens of other children you sold coke to would've ratted you out eventually. I hope that you've enjoyed being an accessory to murder."

She walked forward, the gun steady in her hands. "I'd suggest that you don't attempt to blow the suitcase bomb that I found in the linen closet, as I've already defused it. I didn't even need to take to Google for that one. But then, thanks to my father, I imagine I've forgotten more about designing explosives than you've ever learned."

She was close enough now that she and Bryony were eye to eye. With wild eyes, Bryony opened her mouth, and Holmes lifted one black boot and stomped the heel of it onto the nurse's foot.

"Now, now. Speaking out of turn. I'm afraid that I'm not as tolerant of that as you. I really should be taking lessons."

Bryony whimpered against the pain, her hands still tucked behind her head. Swiftly, Holmes pulled the pistol from under Bryony's coat and tossed it to Milo, who caught it neatly.

"Bryony Downs," Holmes mused. "What can I say? If I could apologize to August, I would."

I noticed that she was still maintaining the fiction that August Moriarty was dead, even now, when throwing the truth into Nurse Bryony's face would be the ultimate punishment.

But Holmes was still speaking. "I've been through three separate rehabilitation programs. I may, in fact, simply be a terrible person at heart, but the difference between you and me is that I *fight* it. With every single atom of my being I fight against it. I might be an amateur detective but you are a bloody psychopath, and I would rather put this gun in my mouth than let you skip away to St. Petersburg where you can prey on teen-age boys on my brother's blood money. You orchestrated my *rape*, and you call me a whore? No. This is the absolute end of the line."

"And you're just going to leave your friend to die," Nurse Bryony said in a harsh whisper.

It was what I'd asked her to do, after all. To keep herself out of jail at any cost. I tried to breathe through the panic clench-ing my lungs.

Holmes sighed. "No, of course I'm not," she said, and I almost died right there from relief. "My brother's men are retrieving the antidote from Watson's dorm room as we speak. It's a clever place to hide it, isn't it? The same place where you infected him? Wanted us to really be *kicking* ourselves when we found it. But it was easy enough to deduce from the uni-versity keys sticking out of your pocket, and not your handbag, and the glass shards embedded in your boot soles. Those, I confirmed when Watson here so obligingly fainted and you got to your knees to examine him. Shards of one-way glass, specifically. Any second now, Peterson will text me that he's found the antidote."

As if on cue, her phone chirped.

"How could you know that," Bryony said. "How could you know that for sure," and I was surprised to hear an element of jealousy in her voice.

"Because, right now, you look furious," Holmes said. "So thanks for the confirmation."

Nurse Bryony spat on the floor.

Holmes rolled her eyes. "It was a bloody stupid place to hide it anyway, far too close to your flat—which is perfectly awful, by the by. So close, in fact, that we'd have fetched it and injected Watson before you had proper time to make your getaway. Why, really, would we let you abscond with three million dollars' worth of my brother's money when you had no further cards to play?

"Though I suppose you had Lucien as a last resort. Hello again, Lucien."

Milo's phone rang.

He startled. It was like seeing the Sphinx jump. "No one is supposed to have this number," he muttered, picking it up, and then, into the phone, "Yes. Fine. I'll put you on speaker."

Lucien Moriarty's voice crackled into the room.

"Hello again, Charlotte," he drawled.

Bryony's eyes flickered back and forth. "This wasn't part of the plan," she hissed.

"No, no, darling," he said. "Your part in this is done. Hush, now. Dear Charlotte. You had a question? I'll give you one answer. As your consolation prize."

"Consolation prize?" Holmes laughed. "I won. Lucien, I am quite literally standing here, holding the gun."

"So there's nothing you want me to clear up. Nothing at all. No questions about the drug dealer"—and here, his voice changed to a dark snarl—"who stuffed a plastic gem into that little prize turkey? Who was so obliging as to hang himself to break any remaining links between him and his employer? No questions about that employer who is, even now, calling you from Russia?" A laugh. "That's me, by the way. In case you're as slow as you seem."

I tried to swear, but I couldn't force out any words. Holmes's hand shook. It was almost imperceptible, but I saw it. She'd taught me to notice things, after all.

"Fine," she said. "You win. So tell me. Why did you make it so easy for us to catch Bryony?"

"I never wanted you in *jail*," Lucien purred. "That was never the plan. The plan was to torment you, and how can I do that from within a jail cell? Oh, you could lose yourself within weeks in a juvenile penitentiary, but you could also start a riot. Or break yourself out. No, this was a practice round. I wanted to see what was important to you. I wanted to see how much this foolish boy trusted you. I threaten him, and you kiss him. Cue strings. Cue the applause."

Milo whipped around to stare at his sister, but her eyes were fixed on the phone.

"It's good to know what matters to you, Charlotte. So very little does. My brother didn't. Your own family doesn't. But this boy . . ." I could almost hear him licking his lips. "No, I don't want you in jail. I don't want you to have the satisfaction of this being over."

No one in the room was looking directly at anyone else. I wondered, briefly, if anyone remembered that I was quite literally dying on the floor.

"Well. Go on. Take out the trash," he said. "I see that your antidote is waiting at the door."

A click, and he was gone.

"I knew about his plan," Nurse Bryony said into the silence. "I knew this whole time."

"No," Holmes said, pressing the gun to Bryony's temple. "You're a terrible liar. How sad, you've made me resort to *guns*. How incredibly cheap. Milo, tie her hands. I hope you're ready to take her . . . wherever you're going to take her. I don't want to know."

"I promise not to tell you," Milo said, in a tone that suggested he'd said this many times. He bound her hands neatly in a zip-tie, put her own pistol to the base of her neck, and led her out the door.

I'd missed something. But then, I'd missed a lot of things.

"Holmes," I managed, but Peterson chose that minute to charge in. With brutal precision, he pulled a syringe out of his pocket, flipped my arm, found a vein, and stabbed it in.

"Sir," he said respectfully, and left the two of us alone.

"Hi," Holmes said, getting down beside me. "You look terrible. I'm sorry I didn't tell you everything. I just needed—"

"—my reaction to be genuine," I said, coughing through my smile.

"Precisely."

"Holmes," I said again.

"Yes?"

"Hospital?"

She nodded seriously, as if the idea had only now occurred to her too. "I think that would be wise."

twelve

Five days later

"WHEN'S YOUR FLIGHT?" HOLMES ASKED, PLAYING WITH THE ends of my scarf. "You could always fly back with Milo and me tonight. The offer's still open." Her brother had set aside a seat for me in his company jet.

"I'd like to," I said, "but I think I owe a few more days to my father after all this. I'll be back in London next weekend."

He was, understandably, still upset with me for not having told him I was dying. Ever since I'd been brought home to recover, I'd watched him struggle to understand how he should feel. One minute, he was begging me for a description of Nurse Bryony's face that day in her flat—"Was it more like a snake's, or an assassin's?"—his hands clasped in schoolboy glee, and the next minute he was forbidding me to bring in the mail because it was too dangerous with Lucien Moriarty still at large. My father liked reading about adventures, liked talking them through over a glass of whisky. He even liked the thought of his son having them, up to a certain point.

I had, in this past week, plunged off that point and into a very troubling ocean.

"Well," he'd said, cleaning his glasses, "I suppose you're looking forward to getting back to your mother and sister."

"I am," I'd told him honestly.

"And I imagine you won't be wanting to return here in the spring when school reopens." He hadn't looked at me as he spoke.

"Actually, I've heard that someone got me a full scholarship for the year." I'd hidden my smile. "And though the creative writing teacher left something to be desired, I did make one or two good friends. And I found out my stepmom makes really amazing mac and cheese."

His eyes had shone. "Ah."

"Dad," I'd said. "If your methods were a little obnoxious . . . well. I'm still happy to be here."

He'd patted me on the arm. "You're a good man, Jamie Watson."

It might have even been true. At least, I was trying.

We both were.

"Well, if you stay, you can take over my duties as Robbie's *Mario Kart* opponent," Holmes said now with a wry smile.

"That little bugger is very good. I'm used to playing by myself, though, so maybe I'm just easy to beat. Milo was never one for games."

"You had a Wii," I said, disbelieving.

"Of course." She raised her eyebrows. "Why wouldn't I?"

I shook my head at her.

We'd been spending our days in my father's house after my brief stint in the hospital. After I'd been released, Dr. Warner had stayed on in a nearby hotel, coming by each morning to examine me. But other than a lingering veil of fatigue (I was sleeping fourteen hours a night), a sickly sheen to my skin, and a tremor in my hands, I was well and truly cured.

Despite my clean bill of health, Holmes had appointed herself my nursemaid. This meant I was served endless bowls of tasteless soup (rule #39 finally rearing its ugly head) and gallon after gallon of water while confined to the living room couch. She kept the room dark, the boys from pestering me (when they'd actually have been a welcome distraction), and the television firmly off. I couldn't so much as stand without her appearing at my elbow, ready to bully me back into lying down. When I asked, plaintively, for something to do, she'd brought me a biography of Louis Pasteur. I promptly used it as a coaster. ("But he invented vaccinations!" she'd cried, seeing the water marks on its cover.)

That isn't to say that I didn't have visitors. Mrs. Dunham came by, with a present of Galway Kinnell's first book of poems. She took one look at my face—I did look kind of like a ghoul—and burst into tears. Which was strangely okay. It sounds stupid to say, but after several months of being unparented (my father clearly didn't count), it was almost nice to have someone make a fuss.

Detective Shepard came by, too, in a bluster of frayed nerves and exhaustion. After railing at Holmes for her unprofessional behavior—"You confronted a murderer! In her own apartment! Without telling the police, and with your best friend dying at your feet! And now we have *nothing* to show for it!"—for a good half hour, he paused for breath. And Holmes produced a flash drive from her inner pocket.

"You recorded her confession," the detective had said, weakly.

Holmes smiled. "My brother did, but yes, I thought you'd like this. Though I gather you'll have some difficulty finding Bryony Downs, née Davis. Milo has—what's the term? Oh, that's right—disappeared her."

"Holmes," I'd hissed. Wasn't that supposed to be a state secret?

"What?" She was clearly enjoying herself.

The detective was not.

"Oh," I'd said then, remembering. "I guess there's something I should probably tell you about my creative writing teacher."

"Is there anything else?" Shepard had snapped, when I finished speaking. "Missile codes, maybe, that you happened to pick up? No? Good." He'd left in a huff, slamming the door behind him.

"I rather doubt we'll be invited to assist with solving future

314

murders in the sunny state of Connecticut," Holmes had sighed. "More's the shame."

Lena came by, too. In her bright coat, she perched at the end of my father's armchair and caught us up on all the gossip I'd missed. (Tom had come with her, but Holmes had barred him at the door.) She and Tom were still together, she told us. Holmes forced her mouth into a smile that morphed into a real one when Lena asked if she could come visit over the holiday. "For a few days in January," Lena had said carelessly. "I'll be coming through on my way back to school and I thought it'd be fun to tell my pilot I needed a long layover. We could hang out!"

We both agreed. I always did like Lena, after all.

On the quieter afternoons, when no one came by the house, I found myself sorting through my journal from the last few months, looking at the notes I'd made, the crackpot theories I'd had as to Dobson's murderer, the list of possible suspects that seemed so laughable now. To these, I added sketches of scenes. The jar of teeth on Holmes's laboratory shelf. How her eyes dropped closed as she danced. My leather jacket around her shoulders. The way my father stood so nervously as I walked toward him for the first time in years. It all began to form a story, one I wanted to continue, one thread at a time, onward without a visible end.

Maybe Charlotte Holmes was still learning how to pick apart a case; maybe I was still learning how to write. We weren't Sherlock Holmes and John Watson. I was okay with that, I thought. We had things they didn't, too. Like electricity, and refrigerators. And *Mario Kart*.

"Watson," she said, "you don't need to pretend that you've forgiven me."

This came out of nowhere. "For what?"

"For—for what I did to August. For me not telling you the whole truth, again. You know, in the future, stop me when I think I'm being clever. Because I'm shooting myself in the foot. If we'd both had all the facts at the beginning of this mess—"

"If," I said. "That's a big if. Look. I've forgiven you. You have my implicit forgiveness, you know, even when you're driving me crazy."

"You got dragged into this because of me," she said. "Nurse Bryony was making me do my penance. She used you to get to me."

"So the next crime will have nothing to do with either of us. It'll be a very benign car theft. In another country. A warm one. We'll solve it very lazily, lie on the beach between interrogations. Drink margaritas."

"Thank you," she said, very seriously.

"Don't thank me, you're buying the plane tickets." I stretched out on the couch with my head in her lap. "Fiji is expensive."

"I don't want Fiji. I want home." She put her hands in my hair. "Jamie."

"Charlotte."

"Do come home soon. It won't be London without you."

"You never knew me in London," I said, smiling.

"I know." Holmes looked down at me with gleaming eyes. "I intend to fix that."

Epilogue

AFTER READING WATSON'S ACCOUNT OF THE BRYONY DOWNS affair, I feel the need to make a few corrections.

Perhaps more than a few.

First off, his narrative is so utterly romanticized, especially as regards to me, that the most efficient way of breaking down its more metaphorical misconceptions would be in a list.

To wit:

1. When I speak, I don't sound like Winston Churchill. I sound like Charlotte Holmes.
2. Why on earth would he name my vulture skeletons? They aren't deserving of names. They're *artifacts*. And one of them tried to kill Mouse (Californian vacation, very lazy

cat, vultures have no sense of smell), which made me rather upset, and which is why the two idiot things were hanging in my lab until they exploded. Which, for the record, I am fine with.

3. I took Watson to the homecoming dance because Lena's friend Mariella would have certainly asked him if I didn't, and she eats boys like him for breakfast before flossing with their bones. (See entry two, re: California condors.) I told Lena I'd take him and then forgot to tell Watson until very late not because I'm shy about my enjoyment of dancing and/or pop music, but because I was busy. To be precise, I was busy studying how quickly blood congeals within an iPhone. I had to draw rather a lot of my own for my test sample, and then I was forced to sleep due to its loss, and then I had to pay Lena back for her bloody mobile. (She didn't mind. She even let me draw some of her blood, too. Mine is O negative and hers is O positive, which made for a pleasing symmetry.) It was all very interesting, and homecoming is not, and I only went to find him when my test beaker exploded. The blood never quite came out of the ceiling.

4. Tom looked frightful in his powder-blue tuxedo. In this, as in many things, Watson is far too kind. I never corrected him on the subject because at least one of us should be. Kind, that is.

I suppose the rest of his account is more or less bearable, if I ignore the proliferation of adjectives. But it appears that I am willing to put up with many things for the sake of Jamie Watson. He is fond of watching old episodes of *The X-Files*, which is, to the best of my understanding, a show about a rather appallingly dumb man who is nevertheless very attractive, and aliens. It's tolerable if I pretend there isn't any sound. We began when he was still in hospital, and now we're three seasons in and he shows no sign of giving it up. He was the same way about curry shops in London during our first few days home. I heard quite a bit of rot from him about the curative powers of chicken jalfrezi. He is incapable of eating Indian food without getting red sauce on his clothing; I've taken to carrying a bleach pen.

I am doing all kinds of chemical researches on snake venom. I aim to know everything about it by the end of the month. While Watson was ill I learned all there was to know about oysters, because Watson's father gave them to us at a dinner at his house, and they were delicious. At that dinner, Abbie Watson asked me to watch her two young sons while she did the shopping the next day, most likely because I happen to be a girl and she assumes that this is what girls do for spending money. I agreed, and taught them how to make bombs from dung, and where best to hide them. She didn't ask me again. Watson's father thought it very funny, and Watson did too, though he refuses to admit it. I can tell he's hiding a laugh when he curls his mouth in like he's eating a lemon. Sometimes I say terrible things just to see him do it.

There haven't been any more murders, which makes things a bit dull, though I suppose it's only been a week since we wrapped up our last case. There was an official inquiry into Mr. Wheatley's actions that resulted in his termination; for his part, Tom was merely suspended. Watson has insisted on forgiving his old roommate, which I consider rather foolish. He and Tom had an obscenely long and emotional phone call that I heard every word of from the next room. That said, I don't like to see Watson upset, and so I have withheld my opinion on the matter. As the Americans say, we have bigger fish to fry.

I am fairly sure that Bryony Downs is dead, though I allow Watson to go on believing that she is in Milo's custody. I do think that my theory may be the kinder one. For his part, August Moriarty sent me a card on my birthday. *Verbum sap.*

Lucien Moriarty has been spotted in Thailand. I asked my brother to fit him with a microchip, like the kind they have for dogs, and he categorically refused. Ergo, we are relying on Milo's operatives to trace his movements.

We will be back at Sherringford in the spring. Watson's scholarship meant he was paid up through this year, so we have decided to stay. His family hasn't any money and I don't much care where I study, as my most important work is independently accomplished. Milo agreed that it was best to remain here, for now, though naturally my parents were displeased.

I'm rather beginning to enjoy displeasing them.

I am one week clean and don't wish to say any more on the subject.

A final note on Watson. He flagellates himself rather a lot, as this narrative shows. He shouldn't. He is lovely and warm and quite brave and a bit heedless of his own safety and by any measure the best man I've ever known. I've discovered that I am very clever when it comes to caring about him, and so I will continue to do so.

Later today I will ask him to spend the rest of winter break at my family's home in Sussex. (I must remember to tell my parents, though I'm sure they've already deduced my intentions.) My always-amusing uncle Leander is due in for a visit. We will look for a good murder or, at the very least, an interesting heist to solve. Watson will say yes, I'm sure of it. He always says yes to me.

ACKNOWLEDGMENTS

First of all, so many thanks to my wonderful editor, Anica Rissi, for her keen eyes and edits and her belief in this book. I am so indebted to you. Thanks too to Alexandra Arnold and everyone else at Katherine Tegen Books and HarperCollins. I feel so incredibly lucky to be a Katherine Tegen author.

To Lana Popovic, my amazing agent, editor, and friend—you have encouraged me every single step of the way. I know for sure this wouldn't be a book without you. Thank you, from the bottom of my heart, for taking a chance on me.

Many thanks to Terra Chalberg for championing this book abroad and to everyone else at Chalberg and Sussman, wonder agency.

Thank you to my friends Chloe Benjamin, Rebecca Dunham, Rebecca Hazelton, Emily Temple, and Kit Williamson for being amazing, encouraging readers, and to my professors Liam Callanan and Judy Mitchell, who told me I could. And to Ted Martin, for his endless patience for discussing Sherlockiana with me.

I'm deeply indebted to William S. Baring-Gould for his

Sherlock Holmes scholarship—his *Sherlock Holmes of Baker Street* was invaluable, and I've littered this novel with loving reference to his work. Endless thanks to Leslie Klinger; his *New Annotated Sherlock Holmes* has sat dog-eared on my desk for the last two years. I'm greatly indebted, too, to all the other scholars and writers who have played the Game before me.

Thanks to my parents, for being my biggest champions from day one. To my grandfather, for giving us the Holmes stories in the first place. Thanks and love to Chase, for his love and patience while I've filled my hours and covered our walls with this book. I never thought I'd find somebody like you. I am so lucky I did.

And finally, and most importantly, thanks to Sir Arthur Conan Doyle for giving us all Holmes and Watson in the first place. This is, more than anything, a work written for love of them.

In *THE LAST OF AUGUST*, the feud between the Holmeses and Moriartys deepens as the line between right and wrong—and friendship and romance—blurs.

READ ON FOR AN EXCERPT . . .

one

IT WAS LATE DECEMBER IN THE SOUTH OF ENGLAND, AND though it was only three in the afternoon, the sky outside Charlotte Holmes's bedroom window was as black and full as it would've been in the Arctic Circle. I'd forgotten about this, somehow, during my months in Connecticut away at Sherringford School, even though I'd grown up with one leg on either side of the Atlantic. When I thought of winter, I thought of those reasonable New England nights that arrived punctually just after dinner, disappearing into morning blue by the time you'd stretched awake in bed. British winter nights were different. They came on in October with a shotgun and held you hostage for the next six months.

It would have been better, all told, if I'd visited Holmes

1

for the first time in the summer. Her family lived in Sussex, a county that hugged England's southern coast, and from the top floor of the house they'd built you could see the sea. Or you could if you happened to own a pair of night-vision goggles and a vivid imagination. England's December darkness would have put me into a mood all by itself, but Holmes's family manor was stuck up on a hill like a fortress. I kept waiting for lightning to break the sky above it or for some poor, tortured mutant to come stumbling out of its cellar, mad scientist in hot pursuit.

The inside didn't do much to dispel the feeling that I was in a horror movie. But a different kind of horror movie—some art-house Scandinavian deal. Long dark uncomfortable couches that weren't designed to be sat on. White walls hung with white abstract paintings. A baby grand lurking in a corner. In short, the kind of place that vampires lived in. Really well-mannered vampires. And everywhere, silence.

Holmes's rooms in the basement were the messy, living heart of that cold house. Her bedroom had dark walls and industrial shelving and books, books everywhere, organized alphabetically on shelves or tossed on the floor with their pages flung open. In the room beside, a chemistry table crowded with beakers and burners. Succulent plants, twisted and knobbled in their little pots, that she fed a mixture of vinegar and almond milk each morning from an eyedropper. ("It's an experiment," Holmes told me when I protested. "I'm trying to kill them. *Nothing* kills them.") The floors were scattered with papers and coins and busted cigarettes, and still, in all the endless clutter, there wasn't a single speck of dust or dirt. It was what I'd come to expect from her, except for maybe her stash of chocolate biscuits and the entire hardbound *Encyclopedia Britannica*, which she kept in the low bookshelf that served as her nightstand. Apparently Holmes liked to pore over it on her bed, cigarette in hand. Today was volume C, the entry "Czechoslovakia," and for some unknowable reason, she'd insisted on reading the whole of it out loud to me while I paced back and forth in front of her.

Well. There might have been a reason. It was a way to avoid our talking about anything real.

While she spoke, I tried to avoid looking at the Sherlock Holmes novels she'd stacked on top of volumes D and E. They were her father's, filched from his study. We'd lost her own copies in a bomb blast this fall, along with her chemical experiments, my favorite scarf, and a good deal of my trust in the human race. Those Sherlock Holmes stories reminded me of the girl she was when we met, the girl I'd so badly wanted to know.

In the last few days, we'd somehow managed to retreat backwards from our easy friendship, back to that old territory of distrust and unknowability. The thought made me sick, made me want to climb the walls. It made me want to lay it all out at her feet so we could begin to fix it.

I didn't do that. Instead, in the grand tradition of our friendship, I picked a fight about something completely different.

"Where is it?" I asked her. "Why can't you just tell me where it is?"

"It wasn't until 1918 that Czechoslovakia liberated itself from the Russo-Hungarian Empire and became the country as we knew it in the twentieth century." She ashed her Lucky Strike on the coverlet. "Then, a series of events that transpired in the 1940s—"

"Holmes." I waved a hand in front of her face. "Holmes. I asked you about Milo's suit."

She batted me away. "During which the state did not precisely exist as it had before—"

"The suit that definitely won't fit me. That costs more than my father's house. The suit that you're making me wear."

"Until that particular territory was ceded to the then–Soviet Union in 1945." She squinted down at the volume, cigarette dangling from her fingers. "I can't make out the next bit. I must have spilled something on this page the last time I read it."

"So you reread this entry a lot. A little Eastern Europe before bed. Just as good as Nancy Drew."

"As who?"

"No one. Look," I said, growing impatient, "I understand your wanting me to 'dress for dinner,' and that you can say those words with a straight face because you grew up with this level of unbearable suffocating poshness, and I don't know, maybe you *like* that it makes me uncomfortable—"

She blinked at me, a bit stung. Every word out of my mouth today was crueler than I wanted it to be. "Okay, fine," I said, backtracking, "so I'm having a very American panic attack, but your brother's rooms are locked down more tightly than the Pentagon—"

"Please. Milo has better security than that," she said. "Do you need the access code? I can text him for it. He changes it remotely every two days."

"The code to his childhood bedroom. He changes it. From Berlin."

"Well, he's the head of a mercenary company." She reached for her phone. "Can't have anyone finding Mr. Wiggles. Plush bunnies need the same protection as state secrets, you know."

I laughed, and she smiled back at me, and for a moment I forgot we weren't getting along.

"Holmes," I said, the way I'd done so often in the past—out of reflex, as punctuation, with nothing I really planned to say after.

She let the moment hang longer than was usual. When she finally said "Watson," it was with hesitation.

I thought of the questions I wanted to ask her. All the horrible things I could say instead. But all I said was, "Why are you reading to me about Czechoslovakia?"

Her smile tightened. "Because my father is having the Czech ambassador to dinner tonight along with the newest Louvre curator, and I thought we might as well be prepared, because I rather doubt you know anything about Eastern Europe without my guidance, and we want to prove to my mother that you're not an idiot. Oh," she said, as her phone pinged, "Milo's changed the code to 666, just for us. Charming. Go on and fetch your suit, but be quick. We still need to discuss the Velvet Revolution of 1989."

At that moment, I wanted to take up arms myself. Curators?

Ambassadors? Her mother thinking I was stupid? I was, as usual, in over my head.

To be fair, my own father had insinuated that this would be a difficult trip, though I don't think he'd predicted the particulars. When, a few days after the Bryony Downs affair wrapped up, I told him my plans—we'd spend the break at my place first, then hers—he'd begun by saying that my mother would hate the idea, which was ineffective as a warning because it was so obvious. My mother hated the Holmeses, and the Moriartys, and mysteries. I'm sure she hated tweed capes just on principle. But after what had happened this fall, the thing she hated most was Charlotte Holmes herself.

"Well," my father had said, "if you insist on going to stay with them, I'm sure you'll have a very . . . nice time. The house is lovely." He'd paused, clearly searching for something else to say. "And Holmes's parents are . . . ah. Well. You know, I heard they had six bathrooms in that house. Six!"

This was foreboding. "Leander will be there," I'd said, a bit desperate for something to look forward to. Holmes's uncle was my father's former flatmate and longtime best friend.

"Yes! Leander. Very good. Leander will surely act as a buffer between you and . . . anything you need a buffer for. Excellent." Then he'd trotted out something about my stepmother needing him in the kitchen and hung up, leaving me with a whole new host of doubts about Christmas.

As soon as Holmes had brought up the idea of us spending the break together, I'd begun imagining us somewhere like my mother's apartment in London. Sweaters, and cocoa, maybe watching a *Doctor Who* special by the fire. Holmes in some bobbly knit hat, dismembering a chocolate orange. We were, in fact, already sprawled out on my living room couch when Holmes told me to stop avoiding the subject and just ask my mother if I could go down to Sussex. I'd been actively avoiding that conversation. "Be diplomatic," Holmes had said, then paused. "By that I mean, plan out what you want to say, and then don't say it."

It was no use. Holmes and my father had predicted her reaction more or less exactly. When I told her our plans, she began shouting so loudly about Lucien Moriarty that the usually unflappable Holmes backed herself bodily into a corner.

"You almost *died*," my mother concluded. "The Moriartys almost *killed you*. And you want to spend Christmas in their enemy's stronghold?"

"Their stronghold? What do you think this is, Batman?" I started laughing. Across the room, Holmes buried her head in her hands. "Mum. I'll be fine. I'm almost an adult, I can decide what to do with my holiday. You know, I told Dad not to tell you about that whole near-death thing. I said that you'd overreact, and I was right."

There was a long pause, and then the shouting got somewhat louder.

When she capitulated—which she finally did, with extreme prejudice—it came with a price. Our last few days in London were miserable. My mother sniped at me for everything from the cleanliness of the living room to the way my English accent had returned, with a vengeance, on my return to London. *It's like that girl even took away your voice,* she told me. Maybe I had pushed my mother a little too far to begin with; she certainly wasn't happy I'd brought Holmes to visit in the first place. I think it would've been a relief to both of them had she stayed behind, but I had a point I wanted to make—I was tired of my mother's disdain for someone she'd never met. Someone who was important to me. For my sake, my mother should be able to accept my best friend for the brilliant, thrilling girl she was.

That worked out about as well as you'd expect.

Holmes and I spent a lot of time out of the house.

I took her to my favorite bookstore, where I loaded her up with Ian Rankin novels and she bullied me into buying a book on European snails. I took her to the chip shop on the corner, where she distracted me by giving a detailed-and-probably-bullshit account of her brother's sex life (drones, cameras, his rooftop pool) while she ate all my fried fish and left her own plate untouched. I took her for a walk along the Thames, where I showed her how to skip a stone and she nearly punctured a hole in a passing pontoon boat. We went to my favorite curry place. Twice. In one day. She'd gotten this look on her face when she took her first bite of their pakora, this blissful, lids-lowered look, and two hours later I decided I needed to see it again. It was so good to see her happy that it made up for the embarrassment I felt that night, when I found her instructing my sister, Shelby, on the best way to bleach out bloodstains, using the curry dribble on my shirt as a test case.

In short, it was both the best three days I'd ever had, my

mother notwithstanding, and a fairly standard week with Charlotte Holmes. My sister, unused to this phenomenon, was completely overcome. Shelby had taken to trailing Holmes like a shadow, dressing in all black and straightening her hair, dragging her away to show off things in her room. I didn't know exactly what *things* were, but from the lilting, earnest music coming from under the door, I had a feeling that their soundtrack was L.A.D., Shelby's boy band du jour. My guess was that Shelby was showing off her paintings. My mother had told me that my sister had taken up art with a passion while I'd been away, but that so far, she'd been too shy to show anyone what she'd made.

Not that I would have known what to say to her about it. I didn't know a whole lot about art. I knew what I liked, what made me feel something—portraits, usually. I liked things that felt secret. Scenes set in a dark room. Mysterious books and bottles, or a girl with her face turned away. When asked, I trotted out Rembrandt's *Anatomy Lesson* as my favorite work of art, though to be honest, I'd lost the ability to call it up clearly in my head. I tended to spend too much time with my favorite things, loved them too hard until I wore them down. After a while, they became more like a shorthand for who I was and less like things I actually enjoyed.

"Shelby wanted my advice, and I know enough to give her my opinion," Holmes was saying. I'd asked if she'd been talking to my sister about her art. It was our last night in London; we were leaving for Sussex the next afternoon. My mother had turned my bedroom into a study, so we were where we'd been

9

all week—on a pair of hideaway mattresses in the living room, our bags stacked behind us like a barricade. The sky outside was beginning to lighten. One tradeoff of being friends with Holmes was sleep. As in, you never did again.

"Enough?" I asked.

"My father thought it was an important part of my education. I can go on endlessly about color and composition, thanks to him and"—she scowled—"my old tutor, Professor Demarchelier."

I propped myself up on one arm. "Do you . . . make art?" It struck me, then, how little I knew about her, how all the facts of her life before this September had come to me either secondhand or in bits and reluctant pieces. She'd had a cat named Mouse. Her mother was a chemist. But I had no idea what her first bought book had been, or if she'd ever wanted to be a marine biologist, or even what she was like when she wasn't wanted for murder. She played the violin, of course, and so I imagine she'd tried out other kinds of art as well. I tried to imagine what a Holmes painting would look like. *A girl in a dark room,* I thought, *with her face turned away,* but as I watched her, she tilted her face toward me.

"I don't have the skill, and I don't invest my time in things I'm rubbish at. But I *am* a fair critic. Your sister is quite good. A nice sense of composition, an interesting use of color. See? There you go. Art talk. Her range is limited, though. I saw about thirty paintings of your neighbor's dog."

"Woof is usually sleeping in their backyard." I smiled at her. "Makes him an easy subject."

"We could take her to the Tate Modern. Tomorrow morning, before we go. If you wanted." She stretched her arms out above her head. In the darkness, her skin looked like cream in a pitcher. I jerked my eyes back up to her face. It was late, and when it was late, I had these kinds of slippages.

I had them all the time, if I was being honest. At four in the morning, I could admit to that.

"The Tate," I said, pulling myself together. Her offer had sounded genuine. "Sure. If you actually want to. You've been really nice to Shelby already. I think you've heard enough L.A.D. for a lifetime."

"I love L.A.D.," she said, deadpan.

"You like ABBA," I reminded her. "So I don't actually know if that's a joke. Next I'm going to find out that you wear a fanny pack in the summer. Or that you had a poster of Harry Styles in your room when you were eleven."

Holmes hesitated.

"You did *not*."

"It was *Prince* Harry, actually," she said, folding her arms, "and he was a very good dresser. I have an appreciation for fine tailoring. Anyway, I was eleven years old, and lonely, and if you don't stop smirking at me, I will come over there and—"

"Yes, I'm sure it was his *fine tailoring* you appreciated, and not his—"

She hit me with her pillow.

"To think," I said through a mouthful of goose down. "You're a Holmes. Your family's famous. You could have maybe made it happen. *Princess* Charlotte, and the bad-boy spare.

God knows you're pretty enough to pull it off. I can see it now—you in a tiara, doing that screwing-in-a-lightbulb wave in the back of some convertible."

"Watson."

"You would have had to make *speeches*. To orphans, and general assemblies. You'd have to have your photo taken with puppies."

"Watson."

"What? You know I'm teasing. The way you grew up is just beyond me." I was rambling, I knew it, but I was too tired to put the brakes on. "You've seen our flat. It's a glorified closet. You've seen how my mother gets all weird and tight-lipped when you talk about your family. I think she worries that I'm going to go to the Sussex Downs and get sucked in by the decadent, mysterious Holmeses and never come back. And you smile politely and bite back whatever you actually think of her, and my sister, and where we live. Which, let's face it, has probably taken a ton of effort on your part, because you're not particularly nice. You don't have to be. You're fancy, Charlotte Holmes. Repeat after me. *I'm fancy, and Jamie Watson's a peasant.*"

"Sometimes I think you don't give me enough credit," she said instead.

"What?" I sat up. "I just . . . look, okay, maybe I'm feeling a little punchy. It's late. But I don't want you to feel like you have to act a certain way, or impress anyone. We're impressed already. You don't have to act like you like my mum, or my sister, or where I live—"

"I like your flat."

"It's the size of your lab at school—"

"I like your flat because you grew up here," she said, looking at me steadily, "and I like eating your dinner because it's yours, which makes it better than mine. And I like your sister because she's smart, and she worships you, which means she is *very* smart. You talk about her like she's a child, I've noticed, but the fact that she's attempting to explore her nascent sexuality by listening to a lot of droopy-voiced boy sopranos isn't something you should tease her for. It's certainly safer than the alternative."

The conversation had taken a turn I hadn't expected. Though maybe I should have seen it coming from the moment the words "you're pretty" slipped out of my mouth.

She'd pushed herself up to face me. Her sheets were twisted around her legs, her hair rumpled, and she looked like she was in some French film about illicit sex. Which was not something I should be thinking. I ran through a familiar list in my head, the least erotic things I could think of: Grandma, my seventh birthday party, *The Lion King.* . . .

"The alternative?" I repeated.

"It's rather better to dip in a toe before you get dragged underwater."

"We don't need to talk about this—"

"I'm so sorry if I'm making you *uncomfortable.*"

"I was going to say if you don't want to. How did we even get here?"

"You were trashing your upbringing. I was defending it. I

like it here, Jamie. We're going to my parents' house next, and it won't be like this. I won't be like this."

"Like what, exactly?"

"Stop being dense," she snapped. "It doesn't suit you at all."

For the record, I wasn't being dense. I was trying, repeatedly, to give her an out. I knew she was skirting right around the edges of something we didn't ever talk about. She was raped. We were framed for that rapist's murder. Whatever feelings she had for me were caught up in that trauma, and so whatever feelings I had for her were on ice for the time being. While I might, on occasion, spiral into some stupid reverie about how beautiful she was, I'd never voiced those thoughts. While I'd given her openings to talk to me about the two of us, I'd never pushed her. The closest we'd come were these elliptical conversations at dawn, where we circled around the subject until I said something wrong and she shut down completely. For hours after, she wouldn't even look at me.

"I was just trying to say that I won't go there if you don't want me to," I said, and by *there*, I meant *Sussex*, and *Lee Dobson, who I routinely fantasize about digging up and killing again*, and *talking about the two of us, which frankly, I am not equipped to do*, and *even though your hair keeps brushing your collarbone and you lick your lips when you're nervous, I'm not thinking about you like that, I'm not, I swear to God I'm not.*

The best and worst thing about Holmes was that she heard everything I didn't say along with everything I did.

"Jamie." It was a sad whisper, or maybe it was too quiet for me to tell. To my complete shock, she reached out and took my hand, bringing my palm up to her lips.

This? This had never happened before.

I could feel her hot breath, the brush of her mouth. I bit back a sound at the back of my throat and kept myself still, terrified I might scare her away or worse, that this might break apart the both of us.

She ran a finger down my chest. "Is this what you want?" she asked me, and with that, my willpower broke completely.

I couldn't answer, not with words. Instead, I dropped my hands down to her waist, intending to kiss her the way I'd wanted for months—a deep, searching kiss, one hand tangled in her hair, her pressed up against me like I was the only other person in the world.

But when I touched her, she recoiled. A rush of fear went across her face. I watched as that fear turn to rage, and then to something like despair.

We stared at each other for an impossible moment. Without a word, she pulled away and lay down on her mattress, her back to me. Beyond her, the bruised colors of dawn spread out across the window.

"Charlotte," I said quietly, reaching out to touch her shoulder. She shook off my hand. I couldn't blame her for that. But it twisted something in my chest.

For the first time, I realized that maybe my presence was more of a curse than a comfort.

READ THEM ALL!

You've never seen Watson and Holmes like this before!

A Time of Peril

The inquisitor, Carlos Vicente Solitario, charges a young Jewish midwife, Ruth bas Elazar Saul, with heresy. Ruth may be the daughter of the city's chief rabbi, but this is no protection against the Inquisition's accusations.

A Quest for Justice

Detlef von Tennen, nobleman and canon, cousin to the archbishop, suspects that something other than religion drives Solitario to persecute Ruth. Determined to ensure that justice is done, Detlef joins the investigation—and finds his passions fully aroused by Ruth's impressive intelligence and darkly exotic beauty.

Two Hearts' Desires

All her life, Ruth bas Elazar Saul has thirsted for knowledge, despite th price she paid by concealing her gender and being cast out of her father house. Her faith sustained her through all, even the attentions of the In quisition. Then, in the very heart of danger, God blesses her with the grea est love she has ever known.

The Witch of Cologne

"An historical romance that transcends its genre with meticulous attention to detail and wonderful visual sense."

—*Vogue*

"A rich historical novel with a contemporary feel."

—*Marie Claire*

"If you like juicy historical novels with richly drawn Jewish characters living interesting lives, then this is a novel you must read. [The] characters, both Jewish and Christian, are surprising in their depth of personality and by their believability. The story is a real page-turner. Ruth is noble and honest; a modern woman set in a far-off time."

—*Australian Jewish News*

"Like a tapestry, the setting is meticulously detailed [and] carefully woven. Learner has a rich historical palette to play with and uses it to create a plot that gains pace as it progresses. The novel will appeal to readers who delight in the worlds conjured in Anne Rice's dark historical romances. Like Rice, Learner writes with a leaning toward eroticism."

—*Australian Bookseller & Publisher*

ALSO BY TOBSHA LEARNER

Quiver

The
Witch
of
Cologne

TOBSHA LEARNER

A TOM DOHERTY ASSOCIATES BOOK

New York

THE WITCH OF COLOGNE

Copyright © 2003 by Tobsha Learner

Originally published in 2003 by HarperCollins*Publishers*, a member of the HarperCollins*Publishers* Pty Limited Group, in Australia.

Reading Group Guide for *The Witch of Cologne* copyright © 2005 by Tobsha Learner

A Forge Book
Published by Tom Doherty Associates, LLC
175 Fifth Avenue
New York, NY 10010

www.tor.com

Forge® is a registered trademark of Tom Doherty Associates, LLC.

Library of Congress Cataloging-in-Publication Data

Learner, Tobsha.
    The witch of Cologne / Tobsha Learner.
        p.   cm.
    ISBN 0-765-31430-4
    EAN 978-0765-31430-7
        1. Spinoza, Benedictus de, 1632–1677—Fiction.   2. Jewish women—Fiction.   3. Jews—Persecutions—Fiction.   4. Inquisition—Fiction.   5. Midwives—Fiction.   6. Rabbis—Fiction.
7. Cologne (Germany)—Fiction.   I. Title.

PR6062.E335 W8   2005
823'.914—dc22

                                                                        2004066422

Printed in the United States of America

0   9   8   7

For Eva and Esther.

In lebn zeinen wir ale helden.

In life we are all heroines.

Contents

Author's Note

Although I have chosen to include real historical figures within this story, it is a fictional narrative set against a backdrop of both accuracy and exaggeration, written with the utmost respect and affection for my characters and the cities and countries they live in. I ask readers to forgive any short-comings as they are entirely unintentional.

Main Players

*Indicates real historical figures.

DEUTZ

RUTH BAS ELAZAR SAUL — Midwife, 23, only child of Elazar ben Saul.

MIRIAM — Ruth's assistant, 15.

ELAZAR BEN SAUL — Ruth's father, chief rabbi of the Jewish quarter of Deutz.

SARA BEN SAUL NÉE NAVARRO — Ruth's deceased mother.

ROSA — Ruth's old Spanish nursemaid.

TUVIA HOROWITZ — Elazar's assistant, Polish, 21, follower of the self-proclaimed Messiah, Shabbetai Zevi.*

COLOGNE

DETLEF VON TENNEN — Canon to the cathedral, 33, cousin to Archbishop Maximilian Heinrich, a Wittelsbach aristocrat.

GROOT

Priest, Detlef's clerk.

CARLOS VICENTE SOLITARIO

Spanish Dominican, inquisitor under the Inquisitor-General Pascual de Aragon.*

JUAN

Carlos's secretary.

ARCHBISHOP MAXIMILIAN HEINRICH* (b 1622):

Archbishop of Cologne and Bonn, a Wittelsbach prince of the house of Bavaria.

WILHELM EGON VON FÜRSTENBERG*

Minister to the cathedral, spy for the French. (Arrested by Leopold I in 1674.)

BIRGIT TER LAHN VON LENNEP

Detlef's mistress, wife to the merchant Ter Lahn von Lennep.

PETER TER LAHN VON LENNEP*

Birgit's husband, cloth importer, powerful town councillor.

DAS GRÜNTAL (Green Valley)

COUNT GERHARD VON TENNEN

Detlef's elder brother who has inherited the family estate.

HERMAN WOOLF

Count von Tennen's gamekeeper and lover.

PRINCE FERDINAND OF AUSTRIA

Emperor Leopold's errant nephew, 17.

ALPHONSO DE LORENZO

Italian actor, 18, one of a traveling troupe patronized by the Hapsburgs.

DAS WOLKENHAUS (Cloud House)

HANNAH

Detlef's housekeeper at his country residence.

HOLLAND

BENEDICT SPINOZA* (1632–77)

Portuguese/Dutch philosopher who was excommunicated by the Sephardic Jewish community of Amsterdam. A humanist, Spinoza was an important expositor of Descartes' work.

DIRK KERCKRINCK* (b 1639)

Doctor and a close colleague of Spinoza. (Ruth apprentices herself to him in his early years as a medical student.)

FRANCISCUS VAN DEN ENDEN* (1602–74)

Mentor to many. A radical who ran the Latin school where Spinoza taught and where Kerckrinck (and Ruth) studied.

JAN DE WITT* (1625–72)

Councillor pensionary of Holland from 1653–72. Led the Dutch Republic after the end of its war of independence.

VIENNA

LEOPOLD I*

Holy Roman Emperor of the Hapsburg Empire from 1658–1705.

SAMUEL OPPENHEIMER* (d 1703)

Court Jew (Hofjude) and purveyor general to Leopold I.

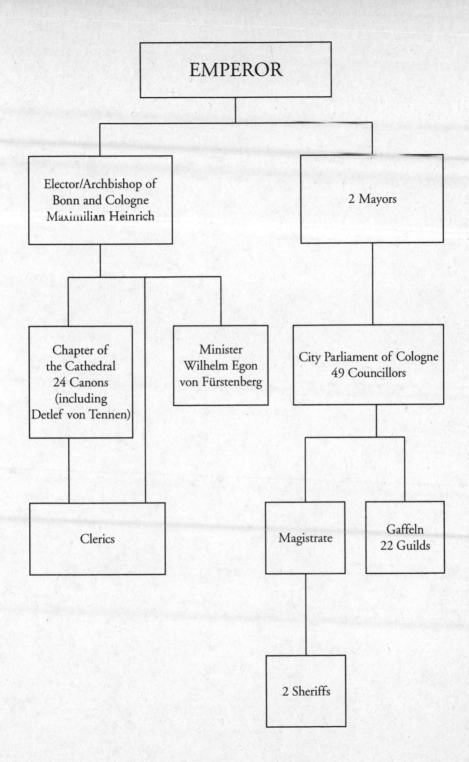

The structure of power in late-seventeenth-century Cologne

KETER

The Infinite

"The end is embedded in the beginning."
Zohar

✶✵✶

DEUTZ, THE JEWISH QUARTER OUTSIDE COLOGNE
JANUARY 1665

*W*rithing in labor, the pregnant woman screams. Sweat beads her brow. In the flickering candlelight her contorted face bears a strong resemblance to the icon which hangs above the curtained bed: Saint Ursula, one of Cologne's many saints, martyred for her virginity.

"Breathe deeply."

The midwife, Ruth bas Elazar Saul, daughter of the chief rabbi of Deutz, runs her fingers over the taut womb, her hands coated with a slippery ointment made of lily oil, birthwort and saffron.

"Breathe, it will help ease the pain," she instructs. A strand of hair falls from under her twin-peaked damask cap, the telltale bonnet of the Jewess. The two points etch a silhouette of horns against the shadowy wall as she bends to examine the position of the baby.

Slipping her fingers into the groaning woman, the midwife feels how much the cervix has dilated. Her assistant, Miriam, a homely fifteen-year-old, wipes the patient's brow and glances anxiously at Ruth. The woman has been laboring for over twenty hours and the baby should have descended by now. Only too aware of the implications for a Jewish midwife should the birthing of a wealthy Catholic patient go wrong, Miriam discreetly nods toward the birthing hooks: three curved steel instruments by the hearth, sinister in the firelight. Used as a last resort, they are for looping around the head of the baby to force its emergence.

"No, Miriam, not yet," Ruth answers the silent query.

The young woman twists suddenly. The purple veins of her huge belly strain as she grasps the bedposts behind her head. Beneath the greasy skin

Ruth traces the geography of the baby, her long fingers searching for the bulge of the head, the tiny knots of the spine and the bones of the feet. Cupping her hands over the vast orb she locates the buttocks, which are pointing toward the cervix. Massaging gently, she tries to manipulate the child so that it will turn, but stubbornly it remains in position.

"Breech," Ruth murmurs softly to Miriam, whose eyes widen in alarm.

The midwife steps away from her patient and opens a leather satchel. Curiously Oriental in design, it has a single letter in Hebrew embossed on the front. With her back turned deliberately away from the bed Ruth lifts out a smoky glass jar filled with a greenish-gray powder.

Crouching, she carefully begins to pour the ashes onto the floor, creating a wide circle which encompasses the writhing woman and the assistant. As she sprinkles with her left hand, she chants the Hebrew names of the three angels—Snwy, Snsnwy and Smnglf—under her breath.

Despite Ruth's concentration, a fluttering panic begins to rise up in her. It is Lilith, she thinks, who is creeping into her fears. Lilith: the demon that strangles newborns and takes the lives of laboring mothers. The secret embodiment of all her uncertainties, all her desires; the nebulous phantom who has haunted her since she was a young girl and witnessed her own mother perish in childbirth. Ruth imagines she feels the air shift above her; she can almost sense the invisible presence of the fiend, almost smell the sulfurous breath drifting over her left shoulder.

This is not good reason, the midwife reminds herself, and summons the cold clarity of her medical training to expel the dread that is squeezing up through her muscles. But the image of the demon persists: the undulating seductress seems to be staring at her from every corner of the dark wood-paneled room, her misty outline hovering at the edge of Ruth's vision.

From outside comes the eerie cry of a screech owl. Looming through the gray dawn its white wide-eyed face is suddenly at the window as it thuds blindly into the glass. It is Lilith's totem, the creature she transforms into to suckle at the breasts of young children or the dugs of goats. Crouching by the bed Miriam gasps in fear, her hand reaching up for the Magen David lying hidden beneath her robe. Ruth, holding down her terror, doggedly continues the hex against the demon.

A second later a long shadow flits suddenly across the ceiling. Shrieking, the laboring woman curls up in agony. Miriam fights to pin down her resistant limbs. Determined, Ruth grits her teeth and completes the circle, her low mantra growing in volume. Soft gray ash meets soft gray ash as the circle of protection is sealed. Sitting back on her haunches, the midwife breathes a sigh of relief. She has taken all possible precautions now, spiritual as well as medical.

She stands and rinses her hands in the washbasin, then steps out to the small chamber that leads off the bedroom.

Meister Franz Brassant rises to his feet. A large man in his early fifties, he is at least twenty-five years older than his wife, nevertheless he wears the fashionable clothes of a younger man: an embroidered velvet waistcoat over a silk undershirt, breeches edged in lace; the uniform of an affluent bürger. Brassant sits on the town council, the Gaffeln, and is connected to the four most powerful merchant families of Cologne.

"How is she?" An odor of stale sweat and fear rises from his clothes, still damp from his earlier rush home through the rain.

Knowing there is no time for protocol Ruth decides to trust in the intelligence of the man standing before her. Fastening her gaze to his she pauses for a moment, reading the intensity of the flickering trepidation in his eyes.

"I will have to cut," she answers bluntly.

Shocked, Meister Brassant breathes in deeply, his hands blindly searching for his wife's coral and silver rosary which he has strung around his thick neck. "It is not my custom to allow a Jewess to touch my wife, or even to be permitted into my abode, but they say you are the best in the province."

"I am a trained midwife not a miracle worker."

"To not believe in miracles is to blaspheme."

"I believe in *scientia nova*, Meister Brassant. Knowledge and nature. To me, these are the proven properties."

"Prayer and faith are the domain of man. All men."

"We are wasting time. If the matrix is not peeled back, the child will suffocate and your wife will perish."

Brassant stares at the small, dark and strangely compelling figure standing before him. This is not a breed of woman he has met before and yet he is expected to surrender the life of his young wife and child to her. His eyes come to rest on a gold crescent pinned at Ruth's neck—the mark of

Spain. She must have Sephardic blood in her. Immediately his demeanor softens: he has traded with the Spanish Jews of Amsterdam and trusts them.

"You have my permission. But if she or the child dies, you die with them."

Ruth hardly pauses, her only concern for the patient she attends. She nods and, with a detachment that implies no servitude, curtsies.

"I will pray anyway," Brassant adds as the midwife steps back through the darkened doorway. Just then the laboring woman cries out. Shuddering, the gold merchant crosses himself and kisses the rosary. He has already lost two wives and four children and he dreads the loss of another.

Sinking to his knees he prepares himself for a desperate bargain with God. After all, wasn't it only last month that he'd paid a hundred Reichstaler for his sins, as much as he hates donating anything to Archbishop Maximilian Heinrich, whom he—like most of his fellow bürgers—regards as an untrustworthy political opponent rather than a spiritual guide. Times are complicated indeed, Brassant thinks, when you have to rely on a Jewish witch to save your wife and a trumped-up French sympathizer in a gilded vestment for redemption.

The copper surgical knife, fashioned by Ruth herself, floats in a cauldron of boiling water slung over the small fire. There is a strong smell of burning cloves. Meister Brassant's personal medic has insisted on smoking the small bedchamber, holding fast to the Christian superstition that the aroma will ward off evil spirits who could steal the soul of the child as it enters the worldly domain. The midwife, having studied medicine in Amsterdam, a city renowned for its innovation in the new science, has her doubts. But her old mentor, Dirk Kerckrinck, has recently sent her a thesis suggesting that disease may be carried by the invisible ether that fills the air. Because of this hypothesis she tolerates the quack's bunches of smoldering herbs that make the air nearly unbreathable. Besides, now that she has called on the old ways as a precaution, it would be a hypocrisy not to allow the medic his quirks.

Stepping into the circle of ashes Ruth again feels between the woman's thighs. The baby has dropped further and the patient's vulva is stretched paper-thin. If she does not cut, the woman will tear. Yet she will never survive the baby emerging buttocks first.

Ruth pauses. She has attended a breech birth like this before, in one of Amsterdam's dockside slums with Dirk Kerckrinck. But then the patient was an unmarried housemaid, not the wife of a wealthy bürger. And while Kerckrinck, son of a nobleman from Hamburg, could afford an accident, for Ruth a mistake now means an instant death sentence.

The midwife recalls how Kerckrinck, having failed to turn the baby from the outside, decided to turn it from within. An audacious move for a student with only two years' training. Ruth, dubious, had argued against it while both of them pored over Galen's definitive anatomy manual, *De usu partium.* Ignoring her qualms, the young medical student had cut the skin of the vulva then slipped enough of his fingers inside to manipulate the unborn child while she assisted from outside the womb. Both the maid and her child lived. In acknowledgment of its miraculous survival, Kerckrinck had christened the baby Moses.

Abigail Brassant groans again, pleading with Ruth to end her agony. Even in extreme pain the young woman radiates a luminosity which reminds Ruth of the Nordic princesses described in Herodotus' *History.* The young girl must have been a prize for the old man waiting anxiously in the next room. Chaucer would have called it the marriage of January and May: a transaction in which romantic love is traded for security. The thought depresses her. For all her fierce practicality and intellectual rigor, she has not been able to exorcise the tantalizing possibility of the existence of a soul mate: a man who would match her in both ideals and vision. Rather than face the inevitable disappointment she believes an arranged marriage would bring, Ruth has secretly wedded herself to a vow of celibacy.

She reaches for a crystal bottle containing an elixir of pure alcohol mixed with thorn apple and tinctured with laburnum, a concoction she has invented herself. She pours a few drops onto a handkerchief and places it over the young woman's nose and mouth. A second later Abigail Brassant calms. With pupils large and dilated she stares up at the fresco painted on the ceiling while Miriam supports her weight. A fresco which depicts the honorable Meister Franz Brassant as a rather overweight and decrepit Perseus slaying the gorgon, the midwife notes wryly.

Remembering the diagram she studied in Soranus' book on midwifery, Ruth takes up the scalpel and carefully makes one diagonal cut at the side of the vagina to open the vulva further. Opiated, her patient barely flinches as blood splashes her white thighs.

Midwife and assistant work together until finally the purple pasty curve of the head appears, pushing the vaginal lips out until they are almost transparent. As the baby begins to emerge Ruth realizes that the pulsating birth cord is wrapped around its neck.

Knowing that the child's death means their own, Miriam stifles a scream with her fist. But Ruth, emotionless, picks up two small copper pegs. She manipulates the slippery head, now half-hanging from the groaning woman, until she can reach the umbilical cord. Clamping it in two places, she deftly cuts the fleshy lifeline and pulls it clear from the neck. Then, carefully, she pushes her fingers inside and eases the child's passage so that one shoulder comes clear of the vagina then the other.

"Push," Ruth urges the young woman who is now delirious. The woman makes one last effort and the rest of the baby shoots out into the midwife's hands.

The baby lies in her grasp, his skin coated in white pungent vernix, his genitals swollen and bulbous, his face blue, lifeless.

Covering the baby's nose and mouth with her mouth, Ruth sucks the viscous fluids clear from the child's airways then spits them into a bowl. Skillfully she swings the baby upside down, slaps it on the bottom.

Silence. Not even a whimper from the small body dangling lifelessly from her clenched hands. Abigail Brassant moans, her eyes half-open. Convinced they are both doomed Miriam falls to her knees.

Ignoring the young woman's hysterics, Ruth slaps the baby again. This time a thin miaow sounds and a rosy hue floods the child, transforming the mauve flesh to pink. Smiling for the first time in hours, the midwife holds up the baby as it coughs then begins bawling.

"It is a boy," she tells Meister Brassant who has appeared in the door-way. "And he is healthy."

The merchant rushes over and gathers the child into his arms, age abruptly etching his face. Then, to Ruth's surprise, he weeps with relief.

Suddenly exhausted, she sinks to the ground.

❋

The town crier, a corpulent Westphalian who lost his left eye in the Thirty
Years' War, steps delicately over the stream of sewage running alongside
the wet cobblestones. Curling his fat fingers firmly around the handle of a
large brass horn he sounds in five o'clock morning tide. Nothing stirs except for a large pig snuffling at a pile of icy turnip peelings and old cabbage
leaves thrown against the wall of a beer hall. The town crier yawns and,
stretching his stiff bones, squints up at Meister Brassant's windows. There
is a light shining in the mistress's bedroom and the maid has hung a gar-
land of winter poppies over the balcony. A child has been born, a male
child. The town crier smiles; with luck he will get a jug of mulled wine
and a kiss if he knocks at the back gate, maybe even a little more.
Whistling, he kicks aside the cabbage leaves and makes his way across the
narrow lane.

While the town crier stands at the wooden shutters waiting for the maid
to respond to his tapping, Ruth, her face concealed by a large hood, steps
out of the servants' quarters further down the lane followed by Miriam
clutching a covered basket full of instruments of midwifery. The gray of
their cloaks blends perfectly with the muted hues of the high rickety
houses, precarious towers of wooden beams and plaster which seem to
reach out to one another across the passageway, almost blotting out the pale
lilac sky overhead. The two women, painfully aware of being trespassers,
fear prickling their scalps, glide across the street toward a waiting cart. Its
outline is barely discernible through the hovering mist which has lingered
on through the night. Both women move silently with the practice of a race
which, over centuries, has learned to survive by making itself invisible.

Ruth takes the basket and hoists it onto the cart, then pulls herself up
to sit shivering on the wooden seat while Miriam climbs in beside her.

The coachman makes a clicking sound and the huge drafthorse rolls its
flanks mournfully into action. As the town crier turns at the sound of
hooves the cart is already disappearing into the fog.

The port master, surly and pockmarked, takes the five Reichstaler bribe
from the coachman and spits into the gutter. For Jews he is prepared to

turn a blind eye, but he is not willing to condemn his soul to eternal damnation. The decree is that no Jew shall stay overnight in the Holy Free Imperial Catholic city of Cologne, but if the rich want the Hebrew doctors to visit them that's their business. Still, if anyone should care to ask the port master, he would care to tell—for a price.

Bleary-eyed with sleep he watches the cart drive through the huge wooden gates. The hooded woman is young and haunting with her chiseled profile and white skin, her green eyes visible below her cowl. The port master knows who she is: the witch from Deutz, the best midwife in the Rhineland. He beckons his son over and picks up a wooden stick. Crouching, he draws the sign of the cross and two wavy lines beneath it in the mud—a hex to ward off the sorceress's evil spirit. Pointing to the cart as it winds down toward the harbor, he tells the boy that he's heard the woman uses Jewish magic, the kabbala, to protect her own and can draw out spirits from the sick as well as create a golem, a slave giant made from the river clay itself.

"They say that on the Passover she sacrifices young boys then drinks their blood. Meister Brassant must have been desperate to employ such a woman," he whispers, checking over his shoulder for spies.

Confused, the pimply-faced adolescent thinks of how he lusted for the woman the moment he saw her. Could that be her magic too? With one hand the boy pushes down his erection, crossing himself with the other in case she has cursed him.

Ruth leans back in the cart. Behind them the hollow thud of the huge wooden gates sounds out; she does not care to turn around.

There are many in Deutz who would consider it an honor to enter the walled bastion; Ruth is not among them. The so-called free city with its churches and holy relics is an irresistible lodestone for the desperate pilgrims who pour through its gates every day seeking redemption, hoping for a miracle as they claw over each other to gaze at the crumbling bones of the three Magi. But Cologne seems quaint to Ruth after five years in Amsterdam, a city bursting with enlightenment. She misses the exhilaration of debate, the fierce intellectual curiosity that had no fear, the celebration

of a Republic, of a democracy which would free all those young spirits after thirty years of war. The energy of revolution. Of change! Here, in this
medieval stronghold, all is backward-looking. Trapped in the Middle
Ages, Cologne still rests on its former glory as a trading power.

If the fifteenth and sixteenth centuries were the glorious mercantile
years of Cologne, the seventeenth century belongs to Holland. The Dutch
religious tolerance, born out of a commercial pragmatism, serves the fledgling Republic well. The Netherlands has become the new axis for philosophy as well as medical and scientific advances. A magnet for all who think
beyond the narrow confines of a world where church and state are one and
the sun still flies around the earth.

The wooden docks and the sailing ships beyond come into view. The
Rhine is broad and majestic in the dawn light. On the right are moored the
great seagoing vessels of Holland, Spain, France, even England. On the left
the smaller German riverboats wait to take the cargo upstream to Münster, Bremen, Hamburg and beyond. This constant exchange of cargo is
how the city has always made its money, exploiting its strategic position on
one of the main trading routes of the Middle Ages. The glorious Rhine.
What must it have been like a hundred years before? A bustling harbor full
of activity and intrigue. Now there is industry but life is harder, the port
quieter. The discovery of the great territory which lies beyond the European horizon—the East Indies, China and the Americas—is destroying
custom. These new trading routes have eclipsed the old paths and
Cologne, starved of commerce, suffers.

Ruth counts ten oceangoing ships and a flotilla of hopeful sailing boats
anchored against the wooden jetties. It is still a magnificent sight. The
crimson light of dawn catches the tips of the small waves rippling across
the river and creeps up across the carved wooden prows of the sleeping
ships, transforming the oiled riggings into snakes of gold and rust. No
matter how familiar the panorama, Ruth can never suppress the excitement which fills her each time she sees a ship with its cargo of mystery,
swooping into the harbor like a swallow.

On the opposite bank lie the small towns of Deutz and Mülheim, located within the Protestant domain belonging to the Hohenzollerns, an
area outside the Catholic territory of Cologne. Looking downriver toward
Mülheim, Ruth can just see the gray tower of the small Calvinist church

which sits at the top of the main street. Its tiny scale forms a stark contrast to the towering half-built spire of the Catholic cathedral on the opposite shore with the wooden crane on top, bent out like a beak.

To the south of Mülheim is Deutz. Ruth grew up in the narrow crowded streets of the small ghetto, among the remnants of what was once the thriving Jewish community of Cologne before the infamous pogrom of St. Bartholomew's night in 1349. That night nearly every Jewish man, woman and child within the city walls was slaughtered. The few who escaped emigrated to more sympathetic cities like Frankfurt or Amsterdam, even as far east as Cracow. But some families struggled on. And, joined by new settlers, re-created a small outpost on the right bank of the Rhine in Protestant territory which was marginally more tolerant.

A cluster of Jewish women are waiting at the riverbank for a barge to take them back across to Deutz. Ruth guesses they have been selling their wares—hot bread, fresh fruit and cheese—to the Dutch and Spanish sailors marooned on their boats due to quarantine. Despite the fact that she is wearing the same uniform, the Orthodox women look archaic to Ruth with their double-peaked caps and long-sleeved robes, the obligatory yellow circle.

The horse whinnies and rears then refuses to go on. The coachman, grumbling, dismounts and trudges through the slush toward a frost-covered mound in the center of the road. He pokes at it with his whip and an arm falls out, the skin mottled blue and muddy against the snow. The coachman lurches back and covers his mouth with his sleeve.

"Plague!"

He stumbles back to the cart. Ruth climbs down to examine the corpse but the driver grabs her arm.

"One touch and we're all doomed!"

"Calm yourself. I will know if it is plague or just poverty—remember I have some training as a medic."

She pulls away from him. Carefully brushing the snow from the wizened face of the man, she finds none of the telltale marks or swellings that speak of the Black Death. The corpse looks about sixty but Ruth guesses he was more likely forty; just another one of the thousands uprooted by the war who spend their lives walking from village to village begging for food, sleeping in ditches and fields. The lost peoples of Middle Europe.

"There is no plague here, just Mother Starvation. Load him up onto the cart, we'll give him a burial back in the village."

"He's a Christian, *you* can't bury him."

"In that case we'll leave him at the church door."

"It's too much trouble. He's just driftwood, he's worth nothing to anyone."

"He still has a soul."

"But is it Lutheran or Catholic?"

"Do you think God cares?"

The coachman stares at her. If she were a man he would hit her. There is something about her authority which intimidates him. Maybe it is true that she has supernatural powers. He once drove her to the house of a possessed man and she had cured the shuddering invalid before his very eyes. The coachman is not prepared to argue with the devil. Still protesting he throws some old sackcloth over the body and hoists it up onto the back of the cart. The corpse weighs as much as a bag of twigs and there isn't even enough flesh on it to sell it to the secret anatomists back in Cologne. Curse the Jewish witch, he thinks, this would be the last time he drives for her if she didn't tip so well.

The cart wheels start up again. Soon the tall pine trees laden with snow give way to small neat fields where the Protestant farmers grow wheat, barley and oats. But now the fields are blanketed in white. Ruth knows some of the families: some, Dutch Calvinists; others, Lutherans from the north. She has delivered their babies. They are hospitable enough but guarded, always cautious.

The cart trundles its way toward Deutz. A hawk circles above, hopeful for carrion. Spiraling up from the cottage roofs are pillars of smoke from the bakeries. Today is Friday and already, even at six in the morning, the wives and daughters of the community are preparing for the sabbath meal.

Ruth is overwhelmed by a sense of homecoming. It is this feeling of belonging which finally drove her back to Deutz and reinforces her desire to reunite with her father. It is stronger even than the soaring emancipation she found in Amsterdam.

*T*he lock of flaxen hair is thick and coarse. It lies entwined in three long fingers that Detlef blearily recognizes as his own. Slowly the crimson coverlet embroidered with the crest of the now-defunct von Dorfel family comes into focus. Birgit . . . the night before . . . the heavy claret still echoing at the back of his furry tongue. Birgit. And sure enough, as his other four senses shake themselves awake, the pungent scent of his lover, the soft hot curve of her buttocks pressed into his hardening groin, the rest of her waist-length hair—some of which now etches an irritating path across his face and up his nose—and finally her light snore, which always reminds him of an indulged cat, confirms his worst fear. That again he has overslept in the illicit bed of his married mistress. The young canon sits up with a jolt and inadvertently pulls the lock of hair with him.

"Detlef!"

Birgit Ter Lahn von Lennep née von Dorfel untangles her hair from Detlef's fingers. Her symmetrically pleasing features are just a little too heavy. Cynicism and good living have already started to thicken the pert nose. Her round cheeks, once concave, are on the verge of burying the ice-blue eyes above them.

"You would render me bald as well as an adulteress?"

Smiling, she slips her hand under the coverlet, reaching for his penis. Detlef allows one caress then scowling pushes her hand away.

"I have a mass to attend."

"Let me be your sacrament."

"You will go to Hell for that."

He swings his legs out of the bed and reaches for his robe, which he notes with some distress lies like an abandoned skin on the checkered tiles of the ornate bedroom.

"Impossible. Are you aware of exactly how many indulgences the good merchant, my husband Meister Ter Lahn von Lennep has purchased on my behalf?"

Birgit smiles at him in the round Italian glass which reflects the sumptuous interior of the bedroom, the rich tapestries and treasures her husband, an importer, has lavished on her in an impotent bid to win her affection. Staring at her reflection, Birgit decides that she looks like Venus herself. Her bountiful white flesh framed by the Moorish silk curtains, one stream of sunlight illuminating her rose-tipped breasts. Arching her back, she shifts slightly to throw her profile into a better light, a minute movement of the consciously beautiful. She doesn't even have to remove her gaze from her lover, the only man who has been able to elicit any emotion from her. The one person she has ever cared for—and, with that terrible realization, fears, for she knows she would not be able to withstand the loss of such a love.

"Four hundred and six indulgences." Detlef's answer is quick and betrays him.

For an instant he looks away, and finds himself confronted by a small portrait of the illustrious couple of the household. Birgit looks so youthful one could almost imagine an innocence, he observes, drawing some satisfaction from the aging evident in a crinkling at the corner of the eyes of the flesh and blood woman sitting before him. Is he capable of discerning between lust and love, or has lassitude stolen even that from him, he wonders. Frightened that she should guess his thoughts, Detlef keeps his gaze averted.

"You should know that as the chief canon under Maximilian Heinrich I have knowledge of all the donations to the cathedral. Your husband is a very generous and a very . . . apprehensive man. He must think you are a compulsive sinner."

Birgit watches him walk across the room. The natural grace of his movements makes her ache for him. His long shapely legs dusted with light blond hair, the line of his narrow hips hearkening back to youth, the high curve of his tight buttocks and finally his heavy sex lolling against his thigh, taunting her with its perfect curved beauty. For a moment she hates him for the power he has over her. A second later she is tempted to confess all. She would like to ask this man of God: is it a sin to love? For surely the magnitude of the affection she feels defines it as a natural act. Instead, generations of aristocratic breeding forces her guard, she dares not be vulnerable. Pulling her robe around her, she finds herself answering, "If I am to be a compulsive sinner, then I am unable to help myself and therefore I am, by definition, an innocent."

Detlef, his robe now slipped securely over his shoulders, laughs. Despite her wantonness Birgit is a wit, a characteristic which draws him back to her bed again and again.

A tap on the bedroom door startles them. Both stop still. Their liaison is tolerated but cannot be openly flaunted. Detlef gestures to Birgit who moves silently toward the door and cautiously opens it. A young housemaid whispers into her ear.

She turns to Detlef. "It's that buffoon, your assistant."

Detlef joins her. Groot, a short stocky man with political ambitions beyond his intellectual capabilities and an unfortunate wall eye, pushes past the maid. Bowing deferentially to Birgit, he keeps his eyes lowered.

"Groot, to have sought me out here in my good lady's chambers is a grave folly for both of us."

"Many apologies, Canon, but you are called suddenly to council this very morn. The inquisitor has arrived."

"Which inquisitor?"

"The Spanish Dominican, Monsignor Carlos Vicente Solitario. Counsel to the Emperor Leopold and member of the Grand Inquisitional Council. They say that the archbishop is in ill humor to receive him, therefore he has bestowed the honor upon your good grace's shoulders."

"A pox on the Spanish."

"A sentiment Heinrich is sure to share, given King Philip's present relations with the French."

"His Highness Maximilian Heinrich to you."

Groot bows low again, muttering apologies as he backs out of the chamber.

"And pray reduce your bulk to a shadow as you leave these premises!"

Detlef slams the door shut on the intrusive cleric. For a moment he leans against the painted wood. Groot's aspirations irritate him; aware that he would trade loyalty for advancement Detlef realizes the cleric knows too much. But there will always be a part of the canon that is exhilarated by the possibility of betrayal.

Danger is an aphrodisiac; Detlef is more decadent than he would care to admit and far more of a free thinker than Groot could ever imagine. He thinks of the revolutionary treatises he has hidden in his chambers: papers from Holland containing the latest philosophical and religious debates which, if discovered, could see him burn as a heretic.

A proverb of his father's floats back into his memory: information is the mortar that both builds and destroys empires. The old viscount, addicted to the battlefield, had drummed the saying into his second son, whom he always regarded as stupidly idealistic. It would be wise to keep a record of the youths Groot favors, the canon reminds himself, should the ambition of his assistant render him untrustworthy.

Birgit moves up behind Detlef and winds her arms around his waist, pressing her breasts against him through the thin calico.

"Who is the inquisitor?"

"Some zealot Emperor Leopold has thrust upon us. Probably another bloodhound for the nervous sovereign who is worried about Maximilian Heinrich's lax French manners. Leopold fears that the archbishop—like a typical Wittelsbach prince—is in bed with King Louis and plans to cuckold him behind his back."

"Is Heinrich such a coquette?"

"Maximilian Heinrich is a politician."

"Is it a contradiction to be both politician and a man of God?"

"Nay. But Heinrich sees no difference between campaigning for God and campaigning for his Parisian friends."

"And yourself? Be politician for me," Birgit murmurs seductively as she runs her fingers across his torso then moves down to bury them into his soft fleece. She loves to reach for him blind like this. Taking him between her fingers, marveling at the way he always blossoms under her touch.

This time he does not move away. Reaching over his shoulder he lifts a strand of her hair.

"You wish for me to usurp Heinrich?"

He curls the lock once around; it tightens but he does not yet pull.

"They say the emperor's nephew, Prince Ferdinand, will be visiting the count your brother this hunting season . . ."

"And you want me to speak to the prince and secure a title for you and your impotent bürger?"

He keeps winding the hair around as she continues to caress him.

"You forget that I was once a von Dorfel, a rank equal to—nay, above—any Wittelsbach."

Her voice detached from her actions only excites him further. He closes his eyes for a second, standing perfectly still as tendrils of pleasure burn up his body.

"Birgit, you are mistaken. Your loyalties are misplaced, they belong to the old world. The future is the new world which belongs to the bürgers and the plain men of Luther."

Instead of answering she frees him from his gown. With his sex between both hands, pressing herself hard against his back, she imagines that his body is an extension of her own, that the throbbing organ between her palms is part of her own flesh. Oh to be a man, to have all fortune's paths laid out before one: what she would have done, could have done, she thinks. Allowing love to delude her, she imagines this is what they are: one being. Irrevocably bound by both ambition and destiny. For a moment she cleaves to him like this.

"Why, Detlef, could you be a heretic?"

"Unfortunately I lack the passion. We differ, Birgit. You are passionately ambitious, whereas I have passion only to forget what I have become."

"Grant my husband and me our title and I promise I will reinstate your faith."

She strokes him faster, sensing his climbing pleasure. He laughs dryly, his voice catching in his throat.

"Do you think that by overthrowing Heinrich and being elected archbishop I should find my vocation?"

"I think we should all be happier . . . and wealthier. You know how fond of you my husband is . . ."

"And all the world loves a rich cuckold. However, for you, and only you, I shall try to speak to the prince."

Smiling, he pulls down sharply on her hair, bringing her to her knees. With a reverent air, she takes him into her mouth.

———

While Detlef walks through the bustling lanes toward the cathedral, Birgit stands before her looking glass as her maid helps her into her lustring petticoats.

The taste of her lover still pervades her senses. His scent lingers on her fingers, a secret reminder she will carry all day. Behind her the maid's chatter is a relentless monotone describing the latest gossip to grip the city: how terrible it is that the archbishop of Münster has sold seven thousand of his citizens as soldiers to the emperor, and how the good merchant Brassant has finally been able to produce a healthy male heir with his child bride. To her surprise Birgit finds her heart contracting as she remembers her own pregnancy. A babe which, had it gone to term, would have been of dubious parentage. Birgit chooses to think that Detlef would have been the father. But as the old merchant forces himself upon her once a month, it was just as likely to have been his, a notion which revolts her.

She looks at the reflected room, at her own visage, a magnificent façade whitened with lead, a flawless artifice unblemished by emotion. And for a moment wishes she was more fallible.

Maximilian Heinrich, prince of Wittelsbach, resident of Bonn and archbishop of the Holy Free Imperial City of Cologne, is squeezed awkwardly into the high-backed throne. In the style of Louis XIV, with baluster turnings adorning its polished walnut legs, it was an expensive gift from the Prince of Burgundy—expensive but unbearably uncomfortable. The archbishop's hose is itching and his gout sends shooting pains across the back of one knee. He is presiding over the ceremonial receiving of the traditional rent the bürgers pay their archbishop on the twelfth day of the year: four hundred florins of gold and one hundred measures of oats, a sack of which sits before him. Heinrich, bending over, thrusts his hand into the sack and lets a handful of the soft grain run between his fingers. It is of poor quality, poorer than last year. An apt metaphor for the dwindling esteem in which the bürgers and the archbishop hold one another. In short, it is nothing less than an insult.

Heinrich, an aristocrat, feels the merchants' distrust keenly. Secretly ambitious to reinstate the old royal families of Cologne who were thrown out of power in 1396, he is at constant loggerheads with the Gaffeln's arti-san policies. It is a delicate balancing act he performs: appeasing them yet privately pursuing his own royalist strategies.

The archbishop tries to comfort himself with the thought that he will be back in his residence in Bonn by the next night. Irritated with the world, and in particular with the divine will which has thrust him reluc-tantly into his current position, Heinrich looks over his court and finds a target for his ill humor.

"Wilhelm! Will you stop being so obsequious!"

The archbishop plucks a truffle from a small silver tray and throws it squarely at the man fawning before him. Deftly Wilhelm Egon von Fürstenberg, minister to the cathedral, catches the truffle, barks once in imitation of the small dachshund lolling at Heinrich's feet, then grinning inanely pops the delicacy into his mouth.

The small entourage of clerics draws a collective gasp and pauses, sus-pended. Each man stares intently at the archbishop, awaiting his cue. Heinrich frowns and the moment stretches out across the wintry beams of sunlight falling upon the gray hessian robes and naked pates of the shiver-ing priests.

"Touché." The archbishop, deciding to be amused, begins to laugh while simultaneously breaking wind.

Relieved by his turn of humor, the entourage bursts into polite ap-plause. Detlef, watching from the stone cloister which leads out into the grass-covered courtyard, smiles wryly then realizes too late that Maximil-ian Heinrich's beady eyes have fastened upon him.

"Detlef is not amused—pay heed to his supercilious smile. He believes such antics are below the dignity of the church."

"Not at all. The clown also is one of God's good creatures," Detlef replies smoothly.

"As is the buffoon," the archbishop retorts, continuing the exchange with relish. As one the waiting clerics turn expectantly to von Fürstenberg, a man not renowned for enduring insult.

"The buffoon implies stupidity whereas Herr von Fürstenberg is far more calculating." Detlef's voice rings out and is joined by the cawing of a crow flying overhead.

The minister's face floods with uncharacteristic confusion, uncertain whether Detlef has insulted him or complimented him. This time Heinrich breaks into a full belly laugh, shaking so vigorously that he further inflames his gout.

"Wilhelm, the lad has the edge on you. He will run rings around this idiot zealot. Why, I am tempted to go myself, just to be witness to the Spanish humiliation."

"Your honor, I am happy to bow to Canon von Tennen's superior wit but I doubt his diplomacy." Von Fürstenberg, unamused, turns his flushed face toward the prelate.

Wilhelm Egon von Fürstenberg's ferocious ambition is legendary, intimidating even the archbishop. The minister has both close allies and enemies within the Gaffeln, but also secret links directly to the French king himself. A portly man in his midforties whose Achilles heel is sensuality, von Fürstenberg's one true ally is his younger brother Franz Egon von Fürstenberg, an individual Heinrich trusts even less since he embroiled him in the siege of Münster four years earlier. Despite Heinrich's initial reservations, Franz Egon von Fürstenberg convinced Cologne to send artillery and troops. It was an expensive exercise that is still dragging on, and has left Heinrich compromised.

Not that Wilhelm is much better, Heinrich muses, with his constant fondling of King Louis' toes. Sometimes Heinrich wonders where the risky courtship will lead him. And whom Wilhelm is actually working for—the archbishop or the ambitious French royal? Distracted, Heinrich twists a large pendant he is wearing—a holy relic, it is a locket containing a desiccated piece of the tongue of Saint Ursula. Suddenly he realizes the court is awaiting his response.

"Even more reason to send Detlef, let him insult the Spanish!"

"Your grace," von Fürstenberg steps forward, "let me remind you that the Inquisition, although now almost toothless, is not entirely without muscle. Remember, this man Carlos Vicente Solitario was too meticulous and enthusiastic a prosecutor even for the Grand Council itself. Of all the inquisitors, Solitario has executed the greatest number of heretics. An achievement the pope himself has recognized by bestowing upon the good friar the title of monsignor. I have heard this from the Inquisitor-General Pascual de Aragon. There must be a reason why the emperor has chosen Solitario as his ambassador. Is it possible that somehow we have fallen out of favor with both Rome and Vienna?"

"If *we* have, I am sure you would be the first to know about it. And

Wilhelm, let me remind *you* that muscle is easily cut by the sword. Detlef will go." Heinrich's reply is frosty with anger.

Von Fürstenberg bows curtly to Detlef, his bulbous eyes full of sarcasm as he assesses his rival.

Heinrich stifles a yawn then dismisses the huddled assembly, who scatter like geese. Detlef waits while the archbishop watches the gray figures scurry across the icy grass, snow beginning to float down with gentle abandonment. Sighing loudly, Heinrich hauls himself to his feet and walks heavily over to Detlef. Inches away from the canon he breathes a heady concoction of cloves and garlic into his face. Then, grabbing his cassock, pulls him closer.

"Cousin, fail me and I will make sure you immediately cease to take confession. I don't care how much money Meisterin Birgit Ter Lahn von Lennep donates."

Detlef, scarcely daring to inhale the malodorous breath, nods imperceptibly. "What would you have me do?"

The archbishop's hand remains gripped around Detlef's robe while he pauses for thought.

"I have heard rumor of whom Solitario is to arrest. Four individuals—two of our own merchants and two denizens of no consequence: one, a Dutchman, the other, a midwife. Curse the Inquisition and their meddling, can't they stay within their own borders! I want you to milk the Spaniard for information and then I shall decide our response: But I promise you: if there is a head they want in Vienna they shall have it, but it will not be my own."

He drops Detlef's cassock and thrusts his left hand imperiously under the canon's nose. The bishop's ring, mark of his holy anointment—a huge ruby set in gold, a stolen trophy from the Crusades—sits upon Heinrich's plump finger. Detlef lowers his head and kisses the glistening jewel, his eyes closed tightly.

*R*uth pours the boiling water into the small tin bath then tests the temperature with a finger. Perfect. She goes over to the wooden shutters and pauses, staring out at the barren field which lies beyond. The plowed broken soil thrown up with the snow; the winter trees like gnarled dwarves against a huge sky. For a moment she watches the gray firmament, the sun a struggling pale disk, the clarity caused by her exhaustion stirring up myriad observations.

Here time moves only with the seasons, as it has always done, even before man, she concludes.

The noisy narrow lanes of Amsterdam appear in her mind: their placement alongside the mephitic canals, the ebullience of the Dutch merchants and their servants as they hurry through the markets, the frenetic shouts of the traders as they call out the latest figures from the East India Company. There man is finally conquering the seasons; he is swept up in the urgency of the future, stopping only for the wild storms on the North Sea and the English war.

In her tiny cottage on the edge of the town Ruth's musings fill her mind, and with that meditation comes memory and questioning.

She had an unusual childhood. Not only had her father married an outsider—a Sephardic woman—but their union was one of the heart and not the customary arranged marriage of Deutz. The young rabbi's choice was unpopular and both his Spanish wife and their young daughter had suffered the brunt of the community's xenophobia. Sara ben Saul died in childbirth when Ruth was six and the small girl wore the solitary air of self-containment that marks bereaved children. She lived alone with her father until his own brother, Samuel, was widowed and with his only son Aaron moved into the large brick house adjacent to the cheder where Elazar ben Saul, as chief rabbi, was entitled to live. The two brothers found solace in their companionship. Elazar, the elder, provided a kernel of stability for Samuel, the more extroverted man, while their children—both motherless—grew to be de facto siblings.

Two years older, wild, defiant and dangerously intelligent, Aaron embodied everything the small girl longed to be. Ruth worshipped the thin boy whose passionate tantrums intimidated even his father. A dreamer, at night Aaron would keep the little girl awake while he whispered how when he grew up he would see countries his father had never seen. How he would travel as a Christian and be free to own land and trade with whomever he liked and employ more than two servants, the maximum allowed to a Jew. Both children knew these blasphemous fantasies could only be murmured in the shadows of the bedroom they shared tucked high into the rafters of the narrow house.

Often, frightened for Aaron and his audacity, the small girl would creep into his bed and fall asleep in his arms. Nevertheless, both children shared an intense intellectual curiosity, which their fathers encouraged, and the small girl became infected by Aaron's passion for free thought. A passion that was fully ignited by an encounter at a fair.

The fairs—huge metropolises of tents and wooden stalls that blossomed like mushrooms beside the medieval walls of the cities—were thriving hubs of bustling commerce where all manner of entrepreneurial denizens, from Jews to gypsies, offered an immense variety of services from moneylending to diamond trading to lacemaking. Here marriages were made, wars declared and secret financial deals brokered.

It was at the Naumburg fair that Ruth, having wandered from her father's side, became transfixed by a Lutheran zealot standing on an old cart covered in straw. The little girl watched and listened, her green eyes dark with amazement as he held forth fearlessly, describing a free society, a place where all—Catholic, Lutheran, woman, Jew and Moor—were equal. The man, painfully thin, his beard pale with dust and a battered cap drawn low over his fiery eyes, spoke with a passion that captivated the young child. Even when pelted by rotten fruit, he continued unperturbed until he was finally hauled off the cart by the city guards.

When Aaron and Elazar eventually found her, Ruth was still standing gazing at the spot where the zealot had preached, her mind saturated with dreams of a universe where she would be allowed to read the Torah, would be free to stand like a man with her father at the holy ark and to choose her own husband—notions that hitherto were unthinkable.

The child was so quiet on the journey home that the rabbi was secretly frightened a dybbuk might have crept into the small girl's soul. In a way it had: the world the zealot described haunted Ruth's imagination. It was a vision that was to shape the course of her adult life.

When Aaron was twelve, Samuel, a small man famous for both his short temper and his sense of humor, was unlucky enough to be caught by the Bund, a marauding band of anti-Semites who had crossed the Rhine seeking amusement.

The young widower was driving back from the kosher slaughterer's with a bag of headless chickens prepared for the Sabbath dinner when the rabble came across him. They made Samuel run like a cockerel himself, then hanged him from a tree. Aaron, hiding in his father's cart, witnessed the whole event. The young boy would never forget the sound of his father's voice cursing the edict which decreed that no Jew could bear arms as he saw the youths with their swords and knives bearing down on him. Nor would he ever forget the terrible powerlessness he felt as he remained hidden under the sackcloth while they strung his father up, legs kicking wildly, from the old linden tree in the center of the town square while everyone else hid behind closed doors.

A year later, just after his bar mitzvah, Aaron secretly joined a gang of Jewish youths dedicated to avenging the tragedies caused by the edict. One night, dressed in dark clothes, their faces smeared with soot, the boys traveled far beyond Deutz. They ambushed and killed a Catholic farmer who had recently slaughtered a Jewish family for squatting on his land.

Ruth was in the small parlor helping Rosa, her nursemaid, to spin when Aaron ran in covered with dust, his hands bloody, a sword strapped defiantly to his waist. While Rosa ran for help, Ruth hid the weapon in her dowry chest and promised her cousin that she would never betray him.

When the soldiers from Cologne finally raided the house they found the thirteen-year-old boy draped in his father's prayer shawl, sitting stiffly in Samuel's place of honor at the dining table. The dignity of the youth momentarily stunned them before they pulled the silent boy from the table and clapped irons on him.

A week later, all six youths were found guilty, some of them aged as young as ten. It was then that Elazar, as chief rabbi, and the community leader, Hirz Uberrhein, donned black hats and made their way across the river to plead with the city mayors for leniency. Despite their supplications, the boys were tried and executed. Their bodies hung on the city gates as a warning to all those who might harbor similar ambitions.

Elazar ben Saul's hair turned white overnight. He covered his windows, blocking out the sight of the Catholic city for a full six months in protest. Ruth's childhood innocence was lost forever, the security of the small world that surrounded her irredeemably destroyed.

While her father buried himself in his grief, Ruth transformed from an outgoing optimistic child to a darkly serious young woman. It was as if some of Aaron's spirit had seeped into her own. She started sleeping with the boy's sword hidden under her pallet and slowly the dangerous dream of revenge began to ferment in her adolescent mind.

A year later, when Ruth was approaching womanhood, Rosa decided that after all this turmoil the child was mature enough to receive her mother's inheritance, hoping to give the girl back some faith after the trauma of Aaron's execution. The Tikkunei Zohar was a collection of mystical texts that specialized in practical magic, both black and white—it would provide the young girl with guidance and, most importantly, personal and cultural self-esteem.

As she lay dying Ruth's mother had asked the nursemaid to become the guardian of the Zohar and to hand it secretly to Ruth when she was of age. The tome was the only heirloom Sara had been able to save from the annihilation of her family. The Navarros' edition of the Zohar was signed by the greatest kabbalistic scholar of them all, Moses de Leon. Priceless, it was a magnificent leatherbound book sealed with an ornate lock encrusted with jewels that dated back to the fourteenth century.

The Zohar was considered the bible for any aspiring kabbalist. But unlike their Sephardic cousins, the Ashkenazi Jews had determined that the only people allowed to study its teachings had to be over forty years of age and male. As a rabbi's daughter Ruth was painfully aware of this strict law. Even Elazar himself, who had secretly taught his daughter how to read the Torah, risking religious condemnation and possible excommunication, was deeply shocked when the precocious young girl demanded that she also be allowed to study the Zohar. What Elazar did not realize was that

Rosa had already begun Ruth's education, narrating its contents to her in allegorical bedtime stories in Spanish, a tongue the rabbi had no knowledge of.

On the occasion of Ruth's first bleeding, Rosa took her into the synagogue in the middle of the night. They stood in the women's section, a sealed-off balcony from which women were allowed to peer down into the main area of worship. From there they could stare at the altar with its brass gates where the scrolls of the Torah were kept beside the everlasting light, the small bronze oil lantern that was kept burning always. There below was the domain of the men, the anointed keepers of the rarefied spiritual world of Judaism. A domain which Ruth wanted desperately to be a part of. Her nursemaid knew this and so, with trembling hands, conscious that she was breaking every religious law, Rosa handed over the ancient Zohar.

In the dim candlelight, in the middle of the night in the silent temple— a venue so outrageous that Rosa knew it was safe—the young girl carefully turned the minute ornate gold key and lifted the ancient embossed leather cover. Immediately the secrets of the kabbala lifted from the open pages, flying dizzily around the closed balcony like a cloud of swarming butterflies, filling the air like a hailstorm of fluttering jewels to settle on the young girl's trembling lips and eyelids: *How to turn water into wine, how to bring a clay man to life, how to ascend to Heaven and consult with the angels, how to bring the dead back to life, how to exorcise a dybbuk, how to ward off the demon Lilith in times of childbirth. . . .*

It was magic rooted in the ethics of living, but more importantly for Ruth, the book was a direct link with her own ancient Sephardic roots, a touchstone for her mother's family and the relatives she had never known.

From then on the girl devoted herself to her studies. She learned that the Zohar contained a description of the essence of God, known in the kabbalistic text as Ein Sof—"without end"—an explanation which deliberately encompassed God's lack of boundaries in both time and space. She read how the kabbalists believed that Ein Sof interacted with the universe through ten emanations from this essence known as the ten Sefirot. The Zohar itself was divided into ten parts, one on each Sefirot, each section opening with a gilded representation of the emanation. The book began with the highest and worked down to the lowest, although the Sefirot themselves were not considered to be separate deities but intimately a part

of God. Their configuration formed an illustration of the Divine connected in an instant with everything in the universe, including humanity.
This idea captivated the young girl and, eager for more knowledge, she
studied the manuscript late into each night, learning how all the good and
all the evil man did resonated through the Sefirot and affected the entire
universe up to and including God himself. She memorized the entire text,
then began to introduce kabbalistic talismans into her own life—to protect her father, to make rain, to end a storm. On each occasion she
recorded the cause and effect in a small diary she kept hidden with the
tome. This journal was the forerunner of her scientific discipline, the
training for later research.

Ruth decided that she would draw on magical powers to avenge her
cousin's execution. If the Jewish elders of Prague could summon up a
golem—a giant made from the river mud of the Moldau—she could do
something similar. Inspired by the lingering heat of her dead cousin's fury,
the bond by which she kept Aaron's memory alive, she started to make a
plan. A witness herself to the terrible power of the she-demon Lilith, she
had hidden behind a curtain and watched her mother bleed to death after
giving birth to a tiny but perfectly formed dead baby boy. If Lilith could
strike down two lives so easily, who knew what else she could do if summoned? The young girl decided to inflict the evil spirit upon the authorities of Cologne.

To prepare, Ruth fasted for several days to ensure her body was pure
enough to evoke the spirits. Feigning an optimistic disposition, she tricked
Rosa into believing that her lack of appetite and strangely pale complexion
were the result of an unnamed, unrequited infatuation. It was a notion the
nursemaid found perfectly acceptable but one which the young girl found
absurd.

Ruth's plan was to wear an amulet for warding off Lilith but to reflect
the lettering backward through a looking glass to cause the reverse effect:
the amulet would summon Lilith instead of repulsing her. She also decided to write the incantation in her own menstrual blood, believing this
to be so profane it could not but attract the female demon.

The night of the waxing moon came. Ruth waited until the rest of the
household was sleeping, then, after lighting four black candles placed at
the points of the compass around her bedroom, she sat naked before a

large curved looking glass and began to chant the kabbalistic incantations she had memorized to put herself into a trance.

At the stroke of midnight Ruth found herself staring at her reflection in the dim looking glass. Her dark hair was loose over her shoulders, the amulet—a handmade card with the three angels, Snwy, Snsnwy and Smnglf, drawn on it—hung between her budding breasts. Closing her eyes she repeated over and over the different names she knew for the demon: Lilith, Karina, Tabi'a, the harlot, the wicked, the false, the grandmother of Satan—until, her head spinning, she began to feel as if her body was lifting from the ground and she had started to float. Her soul streamed out from the top of her head, beyond the ceiling, up into the night sky like light from a thousand candles.

Just at the moment she was terrified that the sensation might be death, a noxious odor swept through the room. It was the smell of sulfur and decay, and under it lay a sickly musk, piercingly sweet, that reminded Ruth of old roses. She opened her eyes.

At first, gazing transfixed into the misty glass, she thought she had imagined the slight movement in the shadows. But as she stared harder, a twitching bluish-white form came suddenly into focus.

It was hideous. The creature, twisted like a crippled thing, lay on its side covered in its own slimy ooze. About seven feet in length, it had the upper form of a woman. A blindingly beautiful maiden with pale blue skin and large silver nipples, she was utterly without hair, her scalp an immaculate shiny dome. But what was most terrifying was her limbs. They ran from her sex into three long tails that Ruth recognized as eels. The writhing, shimmering, marish lengths snaked blindly across the wooden floor.

Paralyzed with horror the young girl could not move, could not utter a sound. Lilith, with a violent convulsion, lashed her whole length about the room so that she could lift her colossal face. Gleaming aquamarine in the candlelight, she glared at her summoner through the looking glass. Her luminous eyes fastened unblinkingly upon Ruth, each pupil shining emerald from lid to lid.

"Daughter! On what premise have you awoken me? I am not pleased. What desire hath called the great Unmaker?" Lilith spoke without moving her vast soft mouth.

The demon's voice filled the young girl's head, its lascivious hiss making her simultaneously shudder with pleasure and retch with fear. All the commands she had learned fled her as the abhorrent reality manifested. Shocked beyond thought she tried to scream but no sound emerged.

Disgust rippled through the demon's body as she gazed at the terrified girl. "You should not have taken my name in vain, girl. From this moment onward I have marked thy soul as mine."

Her body shaking violently, Ruth's voice returned and her cry of anguish filled the room.

A second later she woke in her own bed shivering, with Rosa standing over her.

"'Twas a dream, a nightmare, my child," the woman whispered, rocking the weeping girl to her bosom.

She made her drink a glass of hot milk and cloves and left only when she was convinced Ruth had finally fallen asleep. As she crept across the bedroom floor, the nursemaid slipped on a piece of pungent reed still wet with river water. Puzzling over its origins, Rosa tucked it into her pocket, sensing that somehow it belonged to the phantasm her ward had refused to talk about and, if not disposed of, could be used against her in the future.

For weeks afterward Ruth would not sleep alone and she swore to herself she would never again treat the Zohar or any of its sorcery disrespectfully, especially the magic of the she-demon Lilith. But the idea of harnessing and defeating the evil spirit started to fester within her. She began to plague Rosa with questions about her mother's death. Knowing that Lilith was the slayer of newborns and the stealer of the souls of laboring women, she wanted to find out whether the right precautions had been taken at her mother's second birthing, whether her death could have been prevented.

The old nursemaid, torn between earthly pragmatism and a stoic respect for superstition, evaded the young girl's questioning until, worn down, she blurted out that Elazar, fearing the mysticism of his Spanish wife's *converso* family, had torn away the amulets Rosa herself had hung to ward off Lilith when she realized that Sara was struggling badly. Shocked, Ruth asked whether her father was then to blame for her mother's death? Rosa hastily explained that Sara had been narrow in the hips and birthing was difficult for such women, and that privately she held responsible the quack whom Elazar, desperate to save both mother and child, had rushed in at the last minute. A real butcher who had used birthing hooks, she told Ruth, gesturing graphically with her hands.

The notion that she herself might become the savior of such women started to haunt the young girl. She thought that, somehow, by becoming a midwife she might magically complete her own mother's labor safely over and over, for the reward of seeing her mother live on, flushed with health, and her baby brother pink and fat at the breast.

After months of nagging, Rosa finally allowed Ruth to accompany her to the birthing of a good friend. The young woman was having a difficult labor and the community doctor, Isaac Schlam, had been called in to assist. Rosa, busy helping the frantic doctor, asked Ruth to comfort the terrified mother during the delivery. She had excelled at her task, displaying a precocious gift of authoritative calmness which was of immediate comfort to the patient.

Ruth was captivated by the whole experience; she was astounded that from agony such joy emerged. It was at that moment her ambition was cemented: she would become a midwife. Not a butcher, but one who used herbs and craft.

Slowly her grieving over her cousin's death subsided. But to keep Aaron's memory alive, on the anniversary of his death she would take his sword and talk to it as if it were the boy himself, whispering all the dark adolescent secrets that had begun to crowd her heart, unaware that one day she would wear the weapon openly.

For some time Elazar had been preparing his daughter for an arranged marriage with the son of a scholar who lived in Hamburg. Having covertly indulged Ruth's intellectual curiosity by allowing her access to his vast collection of religious and philosophical works, the bewildered father suddenly found himself confronted with the task of transforming a rebellious spirit—whom he privately thought too masculine—into a traditional Jewish wife. This meant Ruth had to learn to weave, embroider, cook the traditional high holiday dishes, as well as master some accountancy to manage household expenditure. Worst of all, she had to abandon her secret readings of the Torah. It was a rude shock for the strong-willed adolescent who found the tedium of weaving mind-numbing and often got sidetracked by the mystical meaning behind the numbers of her accountancy, forgetting the notion of balancing the books. Frustrated and secretly anxious that his daughter would be discovered to be unmarriageable, Elazar took extreme measures, caning Ruth with rushes and locking her in her bedroom until she finished her tasks.

The date for the marriage drew near. Despite Elazar's praise for the young man and the painted miniature sent from Hamburg which hung over her bed, Ruth felt nothing but dread. She had the overwhelming sense that her life—as she had envisaged it—was about to end.

The harbor and its promise of escape was always visible through her bedroom window, and that was how the fifteen-year-old Ruth saw the Dutch ship with its tricolor of orange, green and white flying from the mast. As a cloud passed over the sun, its shadow fell across her haunted face and her plan of escape suddenly became manifest.

Dressed in Aaron's clothes, the young girl crept out that night with the little money she had saved, her cousin's sword and the kabbalistic word for strength inscribed on an amulet she wore hidden under her shirt.

She bribed the ferryman to take her across to the sleeping port and refusing to give any name other than Aaron, she offered herself as a cabin boy aboard the Dutch ship. The old merchant seaman only agreed to take her when she said she would cook in exchange for a free passage. On board she was befriended by a German chevalier who had fought for both the Dutch and the Spanish and would fight for anyone who would pay him enough. Cynical and bitter, he regaled the young boy with battle stories of famine and rape, of pillage and power.

"Power is a whore and religion her pimp," he proclaimed, wondering why the boy had such smooth skin. "Don't let anyone persuade you otherwise, boy."

On the third night, lying beside her on a narrow wooden bunk, he reached for her and was so shocked to find breasts on the struggling youth that he failed to complete the rape. Ruth, exercising all her wits, managed to hide from him until they docked in Amsterdam the next morning.

Using the little Dutch she had acquired from relatives who had visited from Amsterdam, she made her way to the student quarters attached to the new school of medicine in the Heiligeweg. With rain slanting down behind her, shivering with cold and hunger, she had bashed against the thick wooden doors until a tall lad with a humorous intelligence about the eyes finally lifted the latch. He gazed in amazement as Ruth uttered three words in Latin. *"Knowledge search I."*

Dirk Kerckrinck, only eighteen himself, laughed out loud at the youth's clumsy pronunciation before Ruth dropped like a sack of rags to the pavement in a dead faint. The medical student, recognizing the German insignia embroidered on the breast of the muddy military jacket Ruth wore, carried the insensible young stranger up to his humble quarters. He laid her down by the hearth and as he watched her struggle into consciousness decided that such determination deserved a position. Without even asking, he appointed her his valet.

Later, when Ruth revealed her identity as both female and Jewish, Dirk Kerckrinck was delighted. He risked prosecution by sheltering a Jew, but the young radical's addiction to risk was matched only by his intellectual curiosity. An attribute he soon discovered he shared with his new valet, whom he teasingly reconstructed as Felix van Jos, a shy Calvinist from the city of Utrecht.

In the months following, Dirk Kerckrinck took Ruth to his Latin classes at the house of his teacher, Franciscus van den Enden, on the Singel canal. Van den Enden was a Flemish radical who funded the publication of his own revolutionary ideas by teaching Latin to the children of wealthy and fashionable bürgers. He also had daughters of his own, girls whom he had educated so they were able to hold their side in debate with the outspoken young intellectuals who sought shelter under his roof. If van den Enden suspected the true gender of the awkward youth Kerckrinck insisted on bringing to his tutorials, he never spoke out. The charismatic teacher, mentor to many, could not help noticing that the young man did not shave and his voice was of suspiciously high timbre. But the boy was bright and his enthusiasm for learning phenomenal. Almost as phenomenal as another of van den Enden's prodigies, Benedict Spinoza.

The slight, dark young man with the handsome face was already famous for his very public excommunication from the Sephardic community. Now, bereft of family and friends, Spinoza had not only abandoned his Hebrew name of Baruch for the Latin equivalent, Benedict, but had actively carved out for himself a new family of like-minded intellectuals. The sons of merchants who, like him, sensed there was a greater meaning beyond the commerce and banality of prosperity that was making the

Dutch *nouveau riche* flabby and self-regarding. Suspecting that the youth also had a Hebrew background, Spinoza warmed to Felix van Jos immediately.

Oblivious to Ruth's true sex, Spinoza took to instructing the young valet himself, perceiving the youth's precociousness as a mirror of his own. After the Latin classes when Kerckrinck and Spinoza retired to the beer halls to drink and discuss politics, Spinoza always insisted that the shy youth accompany them. There Spinoza held court, arguing his theory of a God that encompassed all of nature, all of the universe and, even more controversially, that this God's power was not the power of a king, but of nature, of life.

Fascinated, Ruth would watch as Spinoza, holding up an empty beer glass so that the light shone through it like a prism, continued his soliloquy, oblivious to the rowdy revelers around him.

"Everything flows from God, but we are limited by imposing our human perceptions upon him. Man designs God according to his own image and the image man has of himself is flawed. It is not our so-called free will which makes us want or desire something, but the disposition of our mind and body at any given time. Our only freedom lies in exercising reason to such a degree that we transform the passive emotions and the confused ideas which enslave us into a clear awareness of what motivates us. Reason knows exactly and precisely what must be done. Never forget that, young Felix."

As Spinoza spoke, Ruth felt as if the air itself had suddenly congealed then broken into shards of shining clarity. She saw a way she could apply his philosophies to her own life and the choices she had made so far to pursue her intellect.

It was there in the smoky tavern, between the rowdy students and the whores, that Felix van Jos alias Ruth bas Elazar Saul decided that she would consciously rein in her passions and serve God through a vigorous and rational pursuit of knowledge at the expense of all else.

Often when Spinoza looked at the youth with his soft cheek and luminous green eyes, he found himself wondering why the boy always refused to drink beer and fell into an uneasy silence when the subject inevitably turned to women and the latest sexual conquests. The philosopher assumed he must be virgin and was on the brink of suggesting to Kerckrinck that they pool their money to take him to a brothel which, drunk and morose one night, Dirk confessed that his young valet was female and a Jewess. Worse, that he had begun to lust after her.

Deeply shocked, Spinoza—who regarded women as inherently inferior beings—found that he could only accept Ruth as a freak of nature, an abnormal creature with the intellect of a man trapped in the feeble shell of a woman. He told Dirk never to mention the true sex of his apprentice again. Only when Dirk's handsome face collapsed into trembling confusion did the philosopher take pity and, smiling, advised the lovelorn medical student to find a less endangering obsession.

Nevertheless, struggling one night over a translation from the Dutch to the Latin, Ruth leaned over Dirk only to find his lips on her neck. Groaning, the student continued to kiss his way up to her mouth despite her protests.

Amazed by the ripples of pleasure that burst from deep within her body, Ruth was unable to push him off. Tasting his tongue, she searched his face in tender amazement. Months of living together, of knowing each other intimately, flowed over and ran like spilled quicksilver across the bare floorboards, fusing their limbs, their skin, their mouths. Until Dirk, bursting at his hose, hoisted her up onto his hips and was about to carry her across to his bed, at which moment Ruth pleaded with him not to destroy both her ambitions and her maidenhood.

With his whole body trembling, the young man lowered her to the ground. Apologizing profusely he begged her forgiveness, but Ruth, loins aching, silenced him with another kiss then ran.

Confused, she walked for hours through the crowded streets, along the canals, across the bridges. Turning the situation over and over in her mind, dissecting it like the small animals she had watched Dirk meticulously pull apart. It was as if she was searching for an imaginary organ that would somehow render a love between them possible. Rationally she knew there was no future in such an affection, but the overwhelming sensuality of the experience made her realize that she could no longer deny her gender or her sexuality. It was then that she decided to return to Deutz, to reunite with her father and serve her people with the medical knowledge she had acquired.

Three hours later she found herself standing outside Spinoza's door.

They talked until dawn, Ruth watching with relief as the philosopher eventually found within himself the possibility of continuing in his role as her mentor. Although saddened by her decision to leave, Spinoza saw the logic of it and offered to continue their dialogue through correspondence. He confessed that although he regarded her as an aberration, he still respected her intelligence and philosophical ambition. He swore he would send her the latest treatises and pamphlets, thus ensuring she would not be intellectually isolated in Deutz.

They parted with an embrace, a rough gesture any man would give a youth. That night Ruth packed her belongings while Dirk was at a lecture and, after leaving a note, departed without seeing the young medical student again.

"All manner of man and creature are equal in the eyes of nature, and nature is God." The memory of Benedict Spinoza's soft resonant voice comforts Ruth as she stands shivering in the cold Deutz air. Taking moral responsibility for one's actions—isn't that what the philosopher advocates, and before him Descartes? If every man is equal in the eyes of God, and if God is nature and nature is God, then man is not a puppet acting out a preordained fortune but a free agent carving out his own destiny. She is living the life she has chosen and must learn to enjoy it, Ruth reminds herself, and pulls the wooden shutters closed.

In the candlelight she wearily peels off her clothes, damp with the night's efforts and the dew of the morning. As she steps across the room toward the waiting bath, she catches herself in the broken fragment of a looking glass her mother gave her as a child. A pale oval face, pensive, with a mane of long black hair. Large eyes which appear as a streak of green in white, blurred by some distant grief as yet unlived. It is not a face Ruth associates with her own. She has no image of herself: she deliberately stopped looking at her reflection many years before when, as a twelve-year-old, she no longer wanted to be thought of solely as beautiful. It was enough that she could feel with her own hands the health under her skin; nothing else mattered. She would not suffer to be defined by her physicality while she fought to be defined by her intellect.

Should a man ever want her, it must be her nature he embraces, not merely her form, she thinks as she steps into the warm water, one white foot breaking the surface before she submerges the rest of her body.

She lies there, in that unnatural light. In the distance are the faint sounds of the waking town: cockerels crowing; the soft bleating of goats, the growing clatter of their hooves as they are herded past the cottage; the remote peal of the church bells, Protestant bells; the laughter of children; the muted echo of a Hebrew chant; a skipping song she recognizes from her own childhood. And gradually, as the sound expands into a vague medley of activity, an exquisite solitude settles upon her.

The young woman looks down at her body under the water, her breasts that float above the shimmering surface, her narrow hips with the bush of black hair curling up the belly as if it is an independent animal resting momentarily against her thigh, her long legs that are still slim like a girl's. It promises none of the fertile roundness of her patients. A virgin body without the wear and tear of love marked across it. And as she looks it is as if the whole room, even time itself, takes a deep breath and holds it, catching the minute slivers of sunlight, the trembling water and Ruth's pale flesh into one frozen dream. Then, just as suddenly, this second of potency crystalizes and sinks itself like a tiny splinter into her memory.

Ruth, slipping beneath the water, believes the sensation must be happiness.

Dear Benedict,

Thank you for De Court's writings, I have read most of Political Discourses *and have found it most illuminating. How to apply such ambitions to this small town! This place is a thousand years from Franciscus van den Enden's study, where ideas soared like angels with steel wings. Ideas of democracy, of a Republic where all would stand equal in politics as well as mind.*

This morning I was midwife to the young spouse of a bürger within Cologne itself. It seemed barbaric to be so conscious of being a trespasser. I have forgotten the habit of humility and I am loath to adopt it anew.

You would not recognize your little Felix, she has grown her hair and is forced to cover her head. I am a woman. I wear the yellow circle upon my breast like an obscene stigma. All this I tolerate. For I believe that maybe, through my meager practice, I can spawn reform. I am careful, for unlike you I wish to stay within my community, for all that they label me witch. In the dark hours I have often found myself lying in fear—of what? God's reprimand? Only of their God, a jealous God which is not my own. But still I have hung the kabbalistic tree of life with its ten Sefirot over my bed and a pouch of garlic at the back door. And the women still demand that I take these talismans to their birthings to ward off the demon Lilith and other horrors. The practice fortifies them and makes them believe in my skill. Am I a charlatan to exploit such tawdry magic? Faith saves lives and dignifies death; surely that is justification alone. I hear you chastising me already, Benedict. I remember your philosophy on the kabbalists as clearly as if the words were etched on my own skin: "Triflers whose insanity provokes my unceasing astonishment, such arrogance to believe that they alone may be held to possess the secrets of God."

Forgive me, master, but here in Deutz it is still twilight. Enlightenment is yet to reach these battered walls. Let my people dream. It is one of the only things they have left.

Tell Dirk Kerckrinck he is to be congratulated on his promotion to chief medic (pity his poor patients!).

Please write back, there is a Dutch ship nearly every week and your wisdom would be of great encouragement to me.
Always yours,
"Felix van Jos"

"I am sorry to see that his royal highness the archbishop does not grace me with his majestic presence but instead sends a servant."

Carlos Vicente Solitario, inquisitor, Dominican friar and advisor to the great emperor Leopold I, listens intently as Juan, his secretary, translates the sentence from Spanish into bad German. Both parties have refused to speak Latin; it is an unspoken signal that their discourse is of a political not spiritual nature.

Carlos, a short bald man in his sixties whose Mediterranean constitution has begun to suffer the bite of the northern winter, stands in the spartan room the Jesuits have given him and shivers. The confidence and magnetism of the canon Archbishop Maximilian Heinrich has sent makes the inquisitor nervous. There is an arrogance to Detlef's blond beauty, a supercilious intelligence behind the eyes that the Dominican finds untrustworthy.

Solitario has visited Germany before, but in the far north, in Breslau. There he discovered that the phlegmatic nature of the Prussians gave them a strategic advantage over his own Latin emotiveness: in matters of diplomacy they could deceive where he could not. This time the inquisitor is determined not to compromise one degree of his mission. He leans forward and deliberately adopts a grin of utter naivety.

Unperturbed the young canon smiles blandly back. Stalemate.

Gesturing, Detlef gives permission to his assistant to speak for him. Clearing his throat pompously Groot begins.

"Canon Detlef von Tennen is not a servant. He is a Wittelsbach prince, cousin to the archbishop himself. Therefore it is an honor that the archbishop has sent a member of his family to receive Monsignor Solitario."

"Especially as the aristocracy wields such power in Cologne," Carlos replies cynically in perfect German.

Groot is startled by the inquisitor's deliberate insult at choosing not to speak German until now, but also by the Spaniard's knowledge that the local aristocrats, once hugely powerful within Cologne, are now to their great chagrin barely tolerated by the bürgers. Groot swings around to Detlef to determine his reaction, but the canon's cool mien is unaffected.

Behind the inquisitor a hood suddenly falls down from a black robe hanging next to a traveling chest in the corner of the whitewashed cell. Beside it stands a viola da gamba. The unfolded cowl heralds a scent of ambergris which floats through the room.

"I have friends in Breslau. They send their regards and regret that it would be unsafe for them to cross Saxony to welcome you," Detlef replies in good Spanish. They are the first words he has uttered since entering the chamber.

A faint expression of anxiety crosses the inquisitor's face. It is his turn to be worried; the envoy speaks his native tongue fluently and appears to know his background. Detlef has deliberately reminded him of the mortification he faced in that inhospitable northern city and his enforced exodus. He has also reminded him of the fall of Saxony to the Lutherans, a conquest that still chafes Rome.

For a second Carlos wonders what this man would look like under torture, whether his face would retain the same luminous quality. The thought excites him—the execution of power always does—and his sense of inferiority fades.

"As we both speak the same languages, it is safe to assume that we have good grounds for a diplomatic relationship," Carlos offers.

"Sharing the tongue is not the same as sharing the heart."

"Archbishop Maximilian Heinrich can ill afford either tongue or heart."

"I am no judge of my master."

"But there is a master over your master, and he must answer to the Holy Roman Emperor himself—not France."

"Is Leopold unhappy?"

"We are concerned about the archbishop's allegiance, but would be happy to feign ignorance if he were prepared to expedite a request of our own."

"What evidence does the papal council have that the archbishop may have French tendencies?"

"Trust me, Canon von Tennen, our spies are as efficient as your own."

Carlos nods to his young secretary, who pulls a scroll from under his copious scarlet robe. He unfurls it and stretches it across the bare wooden table before them. Detlef does not have to lean toward it to recognize the flowery calligraphy which is the mark of the archbishop. Nor does he have to confirm authorship: the imprint of Maximilian Heinrich's seal pressed next to the stamp of King Louis XIV is evidence enough. Inwardly cursing the archbishop's carelessness he swings back around to the inquisitor.

"What is your request?"

"There are two citizens of Cologne and two of its surrounds whose activities have been brought to the attention of both Leopold and the Grand Inquisitional Council. Activities which are not only unCatholic but speak of devilry."

"Monsignor Solitario, be warned that the bürgers of Cologne are not renowned for their tolerance of outside interference, even from Leopold himself. They are particularly resistant to any meddling which would come in the way of their bartering. A more cynical man might think that commerce was the God in these parts."

"A more cynical man would be wise to value his life over his opinions."

"I value both."

"Good, in that case we might reach a compromise."

"Who are the citizens?"

Detlef can already see the excitement in the inquisitor's eyes, the spittle forming at the corner of his mouth. God pity the accused, the canon thinks, knowing that he himself oscillates between believing in the physical manifestation of evil as opposed to the sheer culpability of human neglect. But how powerful is faith when men imbue it with superstition, he ponders, remembering how he has seen a peasant wished to death and the fields of a hated man suddenly blighted by witchcraft. The terrified face of Katharina Henoth, the daughter of the postmaster who was executed as a witch in 1627, comes to his mind. Detlef's father, determined to strengthen the sensitive five-year-old's moral backbone, took him to the burning. The voyeuristic hysteria that filled the faces of the onlookers engraved itself on the child's memory. As did the horror which shook his whole body as he perceived the agony of the convulsing woman as her skin blackened.

Frustrated fanatics are the most dangerous of men, he observes again now. Here is a man who smells of hate and so the Inquisitional Council of

Aragon will have its way. The canon shifts his gaze from the inquisitor, whose innocently smiling demeanor is betrayed only by a slight twitch beneath one eye, and reluctantly nods to Groot, who lifts his quill ready for dictation.

The inquisitor's cleric steps forward and begins reciting the names from memory.

"Herman Müller, cloth merchant of Cologne. Secret Lutheran and wizard.

"Matthias Voss of Cologne, silversmith. Secret Lutheran and wizard."

The feather's nib scratching against the parchment sounds like a death sentence to Detlef.

"And the individuals outside of the city?" he asks.

"Jan van Dorf of Mülheim, spice merchant. Charges of consorting with the devil to improve his trade. And the Jewess Ruth bas Elazar Saul."

"What is her charge?"

"Witchcraft."

"And the evidence?"

Solitario pushes Juan aside and speaks directly to the canon. "Do you doubt the sources of the Inquisitional Council itself?"

"It is not my place to doubt. I merely wondered whether there were actual witnesses."

"My order has many eyes."

"They say her mother was Spanish, from your own province of Aragon."

"What of it?"

"I have a fascination with coincidence. The woman you accuse is one of the most respected midwives in the Rhineland. There are many who would defend her practice."

"Are you one of them? I have heard rumor that the ranks of the German clergy are rotten with secret Satan-worshippers."

The warning does not go unheeded. Furious, Detlef struggles to maintain a veneer of diplomacy.

"I bow to your greater knowledge of devilry and marvel at the paths of God that have led you to such extraordinary insights. I prefer to find faith in the goodness of man, this inspires me infinitely more than pursuing evil. In the meantime, I suggest you visit the sumptuous chambers of both

Voss and Müller. They are two of the most successful merchants in this fair city."

"Indeed, I suspect that the papal guards and myself will be paying our respects to both men shortly."

"But what of the others? You are aware that Cologne has no jurisdiction over the lands across the Rhine? The domain belongs to the Hohenzollerns, it is Protestant. And the midwife is Jewish."

"I have evidence that she was baptized."

Detlef looks up sharply. The notion that the daughter of the chief rabbi of Deutz could have been baptized seems outrageous, but the forced baptisms of Jewish children was not a completely uncommon phenomenon.

The friar smiles sardonically at the canon's surprise. "Her mother was Spanish and originally a *converso*. It appears that when the Jewess was a babe her mother had a sudden change of heart. The baptism was executed in secrecy; I suspect the rabbi has no idea it ever occurred."

"This evidence is indisputable?"

"I have a sworn affidavit from the priest himself. And as she is baptized, it is within the Inquisition's rights to arrest her. As for the Dutchman, the Hohenzollerns have been informed and are prepared to turn a blind eye; after all, the man is just an itinerant squatter."

Detlef looks thoughtfully at the diminutive man before him. Abandoning all pretense at diplomacy, he switches from the florid Spanish to the plain German that he knows will make his point clearer.

"The archbishop will not fight for the Jewess or the Dutchman, but the two merchants are both on the Gaffeln, the town council, and liked by the bürgers. Believe me, there is one thing the archbishop seeks more than anything: popularity."

"Surely with Vienna as well as Cologne?"

"I will convey your orders to his highness."

"And Canon von Tennen, let us agree that it would be etiquette for the archbishop to act swiftly. Etiquette is a French word, is it not?"

Detlef recognizes the veiled threat but retains his mask-like countenance. Again, Solitario finds himself wondering whether pain, applied correctly, would break the German's impenetrable beauty. Falling into a short reverie he imagines how dark the canon's blood would look against that impossibly fair skin. Then shaking himself out of his lapse of concentration, he gestures to Juan who reaches into a leather sack and pulls out a dark green wine bottle.

"In demonstration of our good faith and knowing that the archbishop has a palate for such things, I have brought this wine from the Benedictine monastery in Najera, center of the Rioja country. It is a sweet red and a vintage I can personally recommend. I hope the archbishop will appreciate the gift."

"The archbishop is a connoisseur of both wine and human nature and as such you can be confident of his appraisal."

The inquisitor, bowing slightly, dismisses the canon and his cleric.

Detlef responds with the smallest of nods and sweeps angrily out of the room. Once outside he swings around to Groot. "Have the wine tasted, I trust that man as I would Lucifer."

Carlos listens to the receding footsteps then sends his secretary away. Once alone his demeanor implodes: the shoulders crumple, the pretense drops from the stoically impassive face to reveal a lacework of anxiety that weighs upon the heavy eyebrows, the sagging cheeks, the globular nose. The distinctive scar that runs down his face from the corner of one eye reddens with anger.

Sighing heavily the priest walks over to the traveling chest and with a grunt swings open the lid. On top of several Bibles and bound manuscripts sits a small black wooden box with two Hebrew characters inscribed on the lid. The scent of cedar, almost overpowering, radiates out from the casket.

Carlos breathes in deeply. It is as if the bouquet is the young Spanish woman herself, the object of his obsession. His Holy Grail that has sent him careering from one corner of the continent to another these past two decades. Reaching for the casket, he lets his hands rest upon its lid for a second, his eyes closed. He is so close, he thinks. It might be too late to destroy the mother, but it is not too late to obliterate the daughter and the whole demonic bloodline of the Navarros.

The priest sits on a low stool—the only seat in the monastic cell—and opens the box with trembling hands. It is the third time in his life that he has unfastened the casket. An intense slow burning, not unlike approaching orgasm, infuses his whole body. With a high sweet note, barely audible, the carved lid falls open and the fragrance of cedar which already fills the room like an invisible cloud is joined by an underscent of something far less discernible, a lemony perfume with an overlay of orange blossom. The scents merge like a filigree of delicate lace flooding with blood. To the quivering friar the bouquet is his youth: the orange blossom still lingering at dusk in the long Aragon summer; the sweet faint sweat of a young woman's armpit; crushed grass beneath soft leather.

Moaning, Carlos throws back his head. This is the aroma that manifests the greatest joy and the greatest tragedy of his life.

He looks back down and traces the empty interior of the box: the ribbed grain of the wood which he imagines to be her silken flesh, the heavy weight of her hair, the dry warm imprint of her hand. Slowly, with a great sense of ritual, he lifts the casket and holds it beneath his flaring nostrils.

Inhaling, the inquisitor conjures up the very odor of the girl's skin, the luminous intelligence of her huge black eyes, the cutting wit which shattered the hopeful soul of a young music tutor, leaving nothing but fixation and bitterness. Sara Navarro of Aragon, later known as Sara bas Elazar Saul, wife of Elazar ben Saul, rabbi of Deutz.

Thirty years before, as a young friar, Carlos had taken to teaching his second great love, the viola da gamba, to supplement his dependency upon the common purse. He applied for a position as a music tutor with the Navarro family. The sumptuousness of their villa combined with their sophistication—all of them traveled regularly across Europe—had intimidated the young country boy. A shy stuttering individual, he was too deeply ashamed to admit that he came from a peasant family in the barren south.

Isaac Navarro was one of the wealthiest diamond merchants in the city of Zaragoza in the province of Aragon. The family were *conversos*, one of the many Jewish families forced into Catholicism by the decree of King Philip and Queen Isabella several generations before. Although they had changed their name from the Jewish de Halevi to the Spanish Navarro, the patriarch Isaac had been shrewd enough to reinforce their assimilation by establishing close relations with the local aristocracy, supplying them with gifts of gemstones and loans of money. When the second wave of persecution hit and the Spanish authorities decided to pursue the *conversos* for being false Christians, Isaac was convinced that his family were untouchable. After all, he had donated a fortune to the Catholic church, his children were educated alongside the sons of princes and invitations to his banquets were the most sought after in all of the city.

It was into this atmosphere that Carlos Vicente Solitario was employed as the music tutor for Sara Navarro. Isaac thought it would benefit his daughter to be seen in the company of an earnest young friar, and that to play the viola da gamba could only increase the chances of a profitable match for the stunning twelve-year-old. Blessed with an intimidating beauty, the young girl spoke four languages, could embroider like an angel and was notorious for dancing her suitors off the dance floor so charged was her energy. The viola da gamba was to be Sara's third instrument as she had already mastered the lute and the clavichord. What Isaac hadn't calculated on was the fanatical nature of the young tutor, a characteristic the diamond merchant had tragically mistaken for diligence.

Still virgin at twenty-seven, Carlos's world was far narrower and darker than that of Sara Navarro, whose attributes were already legendary. The first time the young friar was introduced to his young pupil, she was sitting under a marble arch that led into an interior courtyard filled with bougainvillea and almond trees.

Carlos remembers the tinkling of water. The filtered sunlight across the young girl's elegant hands as they rested on the strings of a lute. Her face lay in shade, her features a shadowy enigma, her head framed by a halo of light which transformed the curls of her thick black hair into something more threatening and animalistic. It was only when Sara Navarro stood up, stepping out into the sun, that the friar realized she was the most glorious being he had ever seen. Gazing at him with smoldering eyes she appeared to intuitively sense his hidden vulnerabilities, his awkwardness as he stuttered through the formalities in his thick rustic accent. As he stared back, it felt to the young friar as if his destiny had suddenly shifted.

Over the months that followed, using his natural intellectual curiosity and stumbling charm, he deliberately cultivated an intimacy with the family in the white marble hacienda in the hills. And as they slowly relaxed their guard he began to notice a trail of tantalizing evidence, fragments of a puzzle. Tiny scrolls he discovered tucked into a music case. Strange Hebrew symbols scratched into stones. The few occasions when he arrived unannounced and interrupted the family in the middle of what looked suspiciously like a sabbat meal. Clues that led him to the conclusion that Sara Navarro was not only a false Christian but a Jew, who, along with the rest of her family, practiced her religion clandestinely.

But by now the young friar was completely besotted. What did it matter that they still observed their faith secretly, he argued with himself every night, alone in his stone cell at the friary. They were still Catholics; in fact the Navarros were the most pious Catholic family he knew. Señor Navarro was the main benefactor of the friar's order, his wife a devout member of the congregation. Besides, the daughter was a miracle, the living embodiment of sainthood, or so the friar thought. Her grace was exceptional, her beauty sublime and her musical ability extraordinary. In twenty lessons she had surpassed Carlos's own craft and had begun to compose sonatas of her own. By the thirtieth lesson they were playing the duets she wrote. Although immature, the work displayed a rare musicality which, Carlos liked to believe, transcended gender.

As the trembling young man guided the soft hands of the girl across the instrument, he imagined that their relationship was a rare discourse, a marriage of emotion and art. A union not besmirched by the sinful fires of lust, but a sacred tie, a consummation of souls. He was positive his love would be reciprocated. Why, had not Sara pressed her thigh against his that time during the recital? More importantly, when he had pressed back she had not pulled away. Surely this was a sign that she loved him also? What about when with sparkling eyes she had untied her shawl during a lesson to reveal her bosom? It was as if she was daring the young friar to respond to the heady perfume that rose up from her perfect cleavage. The vision had nearly crucified Carlos, who, crossing his legs, was thankful for the long weighty cassock concealing his stiffening organ.

He had not slept for a week after that, haunted each night by impossible temptations. To cleanse himself he took to fasting and making endless supplications to Saint Dominic, Saint Anthony and, for good measure, Saint Jude, patron saint of desperate situations. Only after much prayer and several stuttering confessions did the young friar finally convince himself that the rightful action, should his pupil show her affections one more time, would be to declare his love.

The music tutor had arrived at their next lesson trembling with anticipation. Giggling wildly, the twelve-year-old, her lush hair fighting to be released from its demure cowl, presented the blushing friar with a love letter she had written and asked him if he could examine it for grammar. Carlos's heart leaped when she explained that her secret love was a literary man and she wished to make no error.

"It is an affection that dares not declare itself," she told him, her eyes wide and serious.

Abandoning all protocol, convinced now of their mutual adoration, he had flung his arms around her and kissed her passionately. *"Mi corazón, mi tesoro, me llenas el alma.* I knew you would come to me."

Horrified, the girl pushed him away violently then slapped him. The stinging blow shocked Carlos to his very core. Deeply mortified he clutched his reddened cheek while, furious, the young girl stormed up and down in front of him.

"I shall not betray your actions to my father only because you are a great teacher and a great musician, but if you place another finger on me I shall tell of your terrible impudence. What kind of a man of God are you to assume such a thing?"

'Firstly, I *am* a man, despite these robes. Secondly, I had thought that—"

"What? That I should love you? You are a peasant, señor, a peasant wrapped in a cassock. Do not forget your place."

Humiliation scars deeper than the lash.

That night Carlos felt his abasement clawing his back like some hideous hag he could not shake off. Profoundly shamed, he twisted from side to side on the hay pallet in his small cell. When the talons of mortification finally lifted and sleep mercifully descended, a woman visited his dreams. A beautiful creature, seven feet tall, her black hair streaming behind her, her sex a pulsating scented bush that drew his eyes and fingers, her heavy breasts taunting pillows crowned with huge buttonlike nipples that seemed to dance before him as she rode him like a wild bucking mare. The young friar woke in the morning embarrassed to find his thighs stained with his own seed. A demon has visited me, he thought, crossing himself in an attempt to purify what had been made impure. She has stolen my seed and she will steal my sanity.

The next night he had one of the priests bind his wrists together to prevent him inadvertently touching himself during sleep. But the fiend came to him anyway, laughing derisively at the leather bindings, touching his sex with her mouth and hands until the struggling friar surrendered himself to the shuddering pleasures she brought.

After a week of hallucinations, Carlos, now hollow-eyed and thin, borrowed one of the friary donkeys and rode for three hours to visit the seminary at Villanueva de Gállego, famous for its library containing the largest collection of writings on witchcraft in Christendom.

As he turned the pages of an illustrated manuscript in the huge Gothic athenaeum, the vaulted arches above writhing with carved granite forests and imaginary monsters of Satanic proportions, Carlos finally recognized the evil spirit which had been possessing him. Lilith. First wife of Adam, Lilith the seducer, the murderess of newborn children, Lilith who used the nocturnal emissions of innocent men to beget her demon children. Lilith the grandmother of Satan. The discovery sent him running out into the sun-scorched grounds where, trembling, he vomited violently among the gnarled vines.

Shaking with a mysterious ague, the young friar walked for hours in the scrubland of the surrounding countryside until the burning eyes of the evil spirit and her musky fragrance fused with the scent of goats and cacti flowers and the searing heat of the midday sun, and finally he fainted into the soft sand.

He woke hours later in his own cell to the sensation of water dribbling into his mouth from a sponge placed between his burned and peeling lips. He had been discovered by a shepherd who had recognized his order from his robes.

That night, as the shadows lengthened and darkness fell, he feverishly begged his prior to tie him to the bed to prevent him reaching out to the horror he knew would visit. The prior refused, sternly suggesting instead that the young friar should begin a spiritual incantation at the first sight of any visitation. Later, as Carlos tossed in sweaty turmoil, the demon came to him, but this time, as with slippery ease she mounted his writhing body, her face transformed suddenly into that of his young student. Cheeks flushed, her hair twisting away from her, Sara gazed down at him with sickening innocence.

With a great cry the friar woke himself. Determined to catch the witch at her art, he raced through the deserted streets of Zaragoza to the Navarros' hacienda.

Darting past the bubbling fountain in the moonlit courtyard, he climbed a vine to Sara's balcony and entered her bedchamber. He stood there peering around the dim room, looking for evidence that she had flown magically through the sky to reach him. There was nothing except a single feather cast carelessly upon the marble floor. An owl's feather. A screech owl: Lilith's totem. As Carlos bent to pick up the plume he heard the soft breathing of the girl from behind the veiled canopy of the bed.

The young friar walked over to gaze through the fine meshed silk at the girl's white breasts, her black hair running like serpents across the pillow. Suddenly her sleeping face twisted violently into Lilith's visage and Carlos, determined to finish the possession once and for all, threw himself on top of her, tearing off her nightdress to reach down between her legs.

Screaming, Sara woke and struggling wildly cut his face with her ring. The pain held him off long enough for the servants to hear her cries.

The next day Isaac Navarro dismissed the music tutor. The day after that Carlos Vicente Solitario went to the Inquisitional Council and standing before them condemned the Navarro family as false Christians and Satanists.

*R*uth stands outside the narrow house squeezed between the tiny syn-agogue, the mikvah and the small hall which functions as a school for the Jewish boys of the town. She looks up at the window where she knows her father is sitting; she senses his hidden gaze. A boy pushing a hoop runs past, then stops and stares back at her.

"The rabbi is inside but he won't see you."

"I know."

"You are untouchable, they told us at the yeshiva, but you look harmless to me. My mother says you are a good woman."

Ruth recognizes the boy's elfin features, the white skin and jet black hair, the Russian slant of the eyes.

"You are Rebecca's child, Benjamin? I knew your mother when she was your age."

"She has four sons now."

"God grants her a full harvest."

Encouraged, the boy edges closer. He looks at the imposing oak door with the mezuzah fixed above it. The brass lion of Judah which serves as a door knocker glares down at both of them. For a moment Ruth, looking through the child's eyes, sees how the magnificence of the entrance is a symbol of unquestionable authority for the small community.

"Why don't you knock? You have nothing to lose but your pride," the child says with the lucidity of the innocent.

"I have knocked before, therefore I know it will not open."

Instead she presses her cheek against the cool stone and closing her eyes remembers her mother, Sara, with her wild hair. A young Spanish woman with her black eyes smeared with kohl, her head defiantly uncovered, the shining gold in her earlobes that seemed to pull the Mediterranean sun into the gray northern sky. Her winsome grace had intimidated the Ashkenazi women and made them conscious of their own sturdy gaits as they paraded in their best clothes to the synagogue.

"The rabbi's foreign wife," they whispered, drawing their veils across their faces as if her exoticism was contagious. "They say she is like a man, that she knows the secrets of the kabbala as well as the Christian Bible." They were careful not to touch the *anusa* for fear they would catch her mystical ways.

Sara Navarro, who after her escape to Amsterdam had reconverted to Judaism, outraged her Spanish relatives in Holland by marrying an Ashkenazi—a community the Sephardic considered well below their own status. A reaction Sara felt more strongly once she had joined Elazar back in Deutz and was struggling for acceptance from his own people, an acceptance that was never realized.

The image of herself as a six-year-old comes back to Ruth as she stands before the old house, a fierce thin child cowering against her mother's legs as the women passed, refusing to greet them.

"Ruth," Sara would say, in broken Yiddish laced with a mellow Spanish accent, "stand proud, you are the daughter of kings." And a sudden vision of what she might be—if of another sex, another faith—would rock the child's body.

Then Elazar ben Saul would sweep out of the house, young and handsome in his robe and prayer shawl, the deeply serious expression upon his face betrayed only by the wink he gave his young daughter as he marched purposefully toward the temple of worship. He was the great figure of her life, rocking backward and forward in the humble synagogue wrapped in the prayer shawl embroidered by her mother's own hands, a kabbalistic symbol for good health and happiness hidden in the seam.

Only Ruth knew about the amulet. Only she had been there when her mother slipped it in and stitched up the hem. And only Ruth had been there when, hiding under the benches in the women's section, she had heard a mysterious cry. Recognizing her mother's voice, she peered down through the balusters and was shocked to see her parents wrapped around each other, their limbs locked in a strange dance the small child did not recognize at the time. Her mother's hair flung across the temple floor, her cheeks as red as her mouth, while her father, his robe hitched up above his waist, lay on top of her, the pale orbs of his slender buttocks undulating like sleepy sand dunes in the candlelight. There was an ethereal beauty to their movements that held the child in awe and stopped her from calling out. Fascinated, she watched as their dance grew more frantic. The musicality of their sighing and panting reached a crescendo that burst across the rafters like the fireworks Ruth had once seen shooting across the walls of Cologne. Wide-eyed in amazement, the child was convinced that her parents must be praying in the secret manner her father had once alluded to: dancing for God.

Seventeen years later, drawn back to Deutz by such memories, Ruth found herself propelled by the desire to protect her father in his old age.

The shame of Ruth's flight had almost killed Elazar. How to explain to the elders the sudden disappearance of a young girl on the eve of her marriage, the daughter of a rabbi no less? There were rumors of a Christian lover, a secret pregnancy, of abduction. But Elazar ben Saul, refusing to answer the furtive whispers, had grown his beard and smeared ashes on his forehead, wrapping his grief in a leaden silence. "My child is dead," was all he uttered to the leaders of the community when they asked. For him, the child he loved had become a ghost and the woman she had evolved into irrelevant.

A goat bleats and Ruth looks up from her thoughts. Two widows from fields beyond the village are tethering their animals outside the mikvah. Both are shyly excited at the prospect of the ritual bathing and the monthly exchange of local gossip. The midwife turns to the boy but he has gone, running with his hoop between the geese and falling snow.

"Ruth!" A rich alto voice shouts out the banned name defiantly.

Rosa, her old nursemaid, a bustling buxom woman in her fifties with hennaed hair peeping scandalously from under her cowl, stands in the entrance of the mikvah. She wears the uniform of an attendant.

"Don't just stand there gawking at the unbreachable! Come in and sit with me, it's warm in here."

As Ruth steps into the bathhouse Rosa enfolds her in a huge embrace, pressing her against the powdery bosom Ruth remembers from childhood.

"I have news of your father," the Spanish woman whispers conspiratorially as she leads the midwife through a low archway into the waiting area adjacent to the first bathing pool.

Women of all ages and sizes, in various stages of undress, lean against the walls or sit talking to friends in reverent muffled tones occasionally broken by a peal of very unholy laughter. This is a sanctuary for women, their domain from a thousand years before and to a thousand years hence.

Ruth sits down next to Rosa on a low wooden bench and removes her headdress. Her thick black hair falls down her back to hang below her waist. Immediately a window of silence opens up around her.

"Your beauty frightens them," Rosa whispers in Spanish.

"Hush, you know it is not my beauty but my reputation that frightens them. They think I am a female Ba'al Shem, that I can invoke demons."

"Let them think. For me you will always be just a strong-willed little girl," the nursemaid retorts, sentimentality filling her eyes.

"So how is my father?"

"Not wonderful. The reb feels his age, which is good for maybe now he will realize the foolishness of banishing his only child."

"He has sickness?"

"Ruth, your father is near sixty, he has nothing wrong with him except too much religion and not enough soup. He would forgive you if you were to make a marriage."

"A marriage? After my broken engagement who would have me?"

"Rabbi Tuvia."

"Tuvia! He's just a boy."

"A man now and a disciple of your father's."

"I cannot, it would be dishonest."

"Dishonest?"

"I do not love him, nor could I."

"Since when did marriage have anything to do with love? Besides, that much-overrated emotion comes with habit."

"Many things come with habit, like warts. Anyhow, Tuvia would never allow me to continue my study. No, Rosa, it shall not be."

"Be warned: do not make an enemy of Tuvia."

"And this is the man you would have me marry?"

Rosa pulls her closer. "He has your father's ear and that of the whole town."

The other women are murmuring now, whispering in Yiddish, some openly staring, some glancing sideways—the rattle of Spanish makes them suspicious.

Ruth knows what is running through their minds, fed by the rumor-mongers, the web of gossip that links the Jewish communities from as far south as Arles through to Minsk. Has the rabbi's daughter returned a virgin? Is it true she can will a male child upon you by reciting a spell from the Zohar, that she has associated with the heretic Benedict Spinoza and, worse still, Christians? And what about Rachel's baby, the one that was born silent and hasn't made a sound since two summertides ago? What curse did the sorceress lay upon that innocent soul? Is it true that she is a secret worshipper of Lilith, the demon?

The muttering grows louder, swirling around the glistening walls of the bathhouse like a low incantation. Rosa, bristling with indignation, takes Ruth's hand.

"Ignore them, my darling. They are born from a small town and their minds are as small as their bellies are big. Lord knows, I miss Aragon. Now there was sophistication."

A young woman, her face pockmarked, a telltale bruise showing under one eye, emerges out of steamy mist. Ruth recognizes the voluptuous form as Vida, the fourth wife of the baker Schmul. The young girl inherited her husband Schmul's six children as well as having one of her own. The baker is not a cruel man but he has enough money to become irritated when he chooses. Vida's bruised eye is testimony to his short temper but despite this there is a fondness between the two of them: the affection of the protected toward the protector, which Ruth recognizes and respects.

Vida curtsies. Unable to help herself Ruth breaks into a wide grin; the formality seems absurd as the young woman is entirely naked.

"Fräulein Saul, it is an honor to see such a great midwife in the mikvah. May the blessings of the Almighty protect you," Vida says loudly, fully aware of the disapproval rippling through the bathhouse.

"And you, Vida. How is the child?"

"Thanks to you he has lungs like Joshua himself blowing down the walls of Jericho, may I stay so lucky."

The birth had been difficult, further complicated by the size of the baby. But the child had lived and Schmul had been so grateful he supplied Ruth with free challah for a full month afterward.

It was the first of many births Ruth had been called upon to attend. First as a medic then, as her reputation grew, as a midwife. Now even Betsheba, the traditional midwife who delivered Ruth herself twenty-three years before, seeks her advice. And yet they still believe it is witchcraft that makes her good, not her knowledge, she thinks, trying to forgive the women's hostility as, clicking disapproval, they pull Vida away and turn their shimmering wet backs to her.

"Ruth, promise me you will be careful. I had a dream last night that you were a baby again and you were snatched from my arms. The spirit of your mother, God bless her soul, would never forgive me if something happened to you." Rosa distracts her attention away from the women.

"Superstitious nonsense. My work goes well, I am being accepted. Only last night I was called to Cologne to deliver a child."

"Perhaps, but the wind can change, just like that. Here . . ."

Rosa presses a small stone amulet into Ruth's hand. Hiding it from the others, she turns it over. The Shield of David, a six-pointed star surrounded by six circles filled with kabbalistic lettering, is carved into its smooth surface.

"May my love and the love of your forefathers protect you," the old nursemaid mutters, then turns to hand a towel to another customer.

But as Ruth looks back toward the bathing rooms she is convinced she can see the hazy outline of her mother's ghost drifting for a moment between the clouds of steam.

"Outrageous! How dare a trumped-up Spanish rat give orders to the archbishop, protector of the holy bones of the three great Magi themselves! And how dare he intercept my personal correspondence!"

Maximilian Heinrich strides down the center aisle of the great cathedral where sunlight streams in through the half-constructed roof, his green midweek vestments flying behind him. "A pox on Leopold!"

"Sire! Be silent, I beg you, there are spies everywhere!"

Wilhelm Egon von Fürstenberg follows like a hawk at Heinrich's shoulder. The archbishop reaches the altar and stares up at the massive Gothic carving of the crucified Jesus, garish blood oozing from his elongated oak hands and feet. The nobility of the martyr is laudable, he thinks, but regrettably he himself will always err on the cowardly side of human nature. He loves life too much to end it as some forgotten assassinated pawn.

The Hapsburgs' days are numbered, but still Heinrich wrestles with guilt about courting France as a potential ally against the Austrian em-

peror. The future lies with the French king, Louis: he will be the new order. Is he, a Wittelsbach prince, to be silent like a fawning puppy? The
dilemma which has tortured him for years circles again around and around
in his mind. Staring at von Fürstenberg, he is reminded of the wheedling
way the minister has drawn him into this Byzantine maze of information
and intrigue, how he has skillfully manipulated both Heinrich and his in-
formants at the French court. Squeezed between the demands of the bürgers and the expectations of his aristocratic peers, Heinrich sometimes feels
little more than a puppet being jerked by a thousand invisible threads.
Suddenly the complexity of the situation infuriates him.

"No!" he shouts aloud. A flock of roosting pigeons scatter from the rafters. Unruffled, von Fürstenberg gestures to a small page who goes running for a bottle of good wine—the archbishop's favorite tonic.

The minister waits for Heinrich's tantrum to dissipate then tentatively
leans forward, furtiveness arching his corpulent body.

"Your grace, be patient. Emperor Leopold is a young man, he is infected
with the zeal of youth. Soon he will realize that King Louis is a better ally
than enemy."

"In the meantime I am to be sacrificed to these plebeian Dutch-loving
bürgers who will crucify me for these arrests."

"Perhaps there is a way of lessening the blow," von Fürstenberg whispers seductively, like a woman. Heinrich is disgusted at how he virtually
glows with conspiracy—the only blood sport von Fürstenberg enjoys, he
notes bitterly.

"Speak plainly, Wilhelm, my gout has shortened my temper."

"What if Voss and Müller should suddenly be discovered to have been
passing off bad cargo as good, thus endangering the names of their
guilds?"

"This can be arranged?"

"Anything is possible under God's good sky."

"And naturally, as archbishop I can only condone divine intervention."

"Naturally."

The two men laugh, momentarily united in collusion. But Heinrich
stops short with a cough, not wishing to overencourage the minister.

"Wilhelm, you are wasted in the church."

Von Fürstenberg pauses; it is a barbed compliment. "Thank you, my
lord."

He bows, then seizing the opportunity moves closer still to the archbishop. "I just have one request. May I suggest that Detlef von Tennen represent the cathedral during the arrests? It would be prudent for the archbishop to keep a dignified distance."

Before Heinrich has a chance to react, the page arrives and pours out a glass of wine. Heinrich sniffs it, then appalled dashes it to the ground.

"Straight from Saint Pantaleon's cellars! About as aged as a billy goat's balls! Bring me something French!"

A minute later the page returns with a new bottle. The archbishop sips the liquid delicately, then takes a lingering mouthful, swilling it around before swallowing. The rich mellow claret runs through his body like the comforting rush of familial recognition. Heinrich savors the sensation, burps, then rubs his ulcerated stomach under his robe.

Detlef von Tennen. An image of his cousin aged sixteen, the beard barely visible on the cheeks made gaunt by battle, surges up in Heinrich's mind. It is as vivid as if it were yesterday: his childhood companion and cousin, Count Gerhard von Tennen, presenting his young brother, arrogantly pushing Detlef to his knees. "My brother has a vocation that even two years of war could not beat out of him," the young nobleman had sneered.

Both von Tennens had served with the Bavarian army. But while Gerhard had flourished amid the camaraderie and bloodshed, his brother, sensitive to the plight of the soldiers beneath him, had suffered. At fourteen Detlef had entered the Great War convinced that he was fighting for God and the Catholic Church. Two years later he left, revolted by the corruption, the utter waste of human spirit and the incompetence of the aristocratic generals whose outmoded battle maneuvers often caused hundreds of thousands to be unnecessarily slaughtered.

Heinrich recalls the young Detlef, head bowed, trembling, pleading for a position with the ambitious young prelate who, it was rumored, would one day become archbishop. Moved by his enthusiasm and simple belief, Heinrich had nurtured his cousin's career and given him spiritual guidance. Nevertheless, over the years he had watched this ardent young man metamorphose into something entirely different: a creature of politics; a cynic whose faith in the archbishop had been slowly stripped away with every strategic turn Heinrich was forced to make to survive the crippling jurisdiction of the bürgers. Torn between his duties as archbishop and his loyalties as a Wittelsbach prince, Heinrich had tried to prevent the great aristocratic families being further robbed of their powers, in some cases even their land. He had failed. The demise of the old order was unstoppable. It was inevitable but how the archbishop hated to see the adulation in Detlef's eyes dim like the embers of a dying fire. And how he craves to win it back.

Kinship will always be thicker than sworn loyalty, Heinrich thinks, glancing at the eager von Fürstenberg. It is a natural idiocy of man. Detlef is linked to him by both blood and spirit. There is no denying it, he still loves the young canon.

"I will not sacrifice my cousin."

"I promise you, your grace, that no harm will come to the Wittelsbach name."

"Break your promise, Wilhelm, and I will break you."

The horse's velvet nostrils flare in the freezing night air. Pawing impatiently, the bay tosses its head as the young carabinier slips on the bridle. There is no moon and he can see his companions only by the light of the torch held high by a monk, the reflected flames glinting off the steel of the muskets and the gleaming swords that hang from the soldiers' belts.

There are fifteen mounted soldiers—young men recruited from the orphanage of the monastery of Saint Peter, patron saint of the cathedral. The carabinier is twenty years old and lost both father and grandfather to the Thirty Years' War. He smooths down the chainmail vest he wears over his leather jerkin, then adjusts the broad red satin sash which indicates that this morning he rides for the emperor himself. It feels good. Powerful. In this uniform he is a man who belongs, a man who will give his life for the great Holy Roman Empire and Emperor Leopold. A man with purpose, not a terrified boy squatting naked in front of a burning cottage where the raped corpses of his mother and sister swing from the rafters.

The carabinier slips his foot into the silver stirrup and throws his long graceful leg across the stallion.

Detlef, in a scarlet cloak which reaches to his ankles, sits astride his own horse, a beautiful black Hanoverian mare, at the head of the squadron of riders. His expression is stern, hiding the revulsion he feels. He glances back and is privately appalled at the youth of the soldiers waiting behind him in the flickering shadows. Their eager open faces remind him too vividly of the carnage he witnessed himself: death slashing beauty across the throat, bodies ripped open and left bleeding like strange fruits scattered over abandoned fields. The plow still standing buried in mud, poised for a harvest that would never come. An endless war which fragmented his whole world. And for what? To reduce Germania to a motley quilt of princedoms all jostling for power.

Detlef glances at the banner a page carries. It bears the black double-headed eagle with a crown on each head. Clutched in one talon is a scepter, in the other a sword, representing church and state: the symbol of the Hapsburgs. The other side of the banner carries a simple black cross against a white background: the emblem of the city of Cologne.

Often Detlef feels as if he was born into unfortunate times. The noble values of the last century, when Cologne was at the apex of its power, have vanished. All that is left is a dwindling city, an obsolete organ infested with its own petty rivalries and self-importance. And yet the canon senses the promise of a huge transformation; cracks of light in a sky so darkened with confusion it is impossible to see the whole horizon. It is Detlef's great private hope that he will live to see that promised revolution.

The canon glances across at the inquisitor who sits beside the coachman on the prison cart, a vehicle enclosed by iron bars, the dreaded symbol of a finished life.

What was in the mother is in the daughter, Carlos tells himself. It is his duty to eradicate this seam of pure evil. He knows he has the blessing of God, why else would his prayers have been answered? For it was nothing short of miraculous that the German priest should have realized that the raven-haired baby he had baptized so many years before was now the mid-wife of Deutz, accused of practicing kabbalistic rites. The priest, driven by guilt in his dying days, told the Inquisition of the witch's whereabouts and the Navarro investigation was reopened, with Carlos at its head. Yes, such a chain of events could only have been guided by Divine will. After that first blessing God had directed the inquisitor to Vienna, where he presented his case to Leopold. Informed by his spies that the emperor was displeased with Maximilian Heinrich and his whoring for the French king, Carlos offered to act as Leopold's ambassador and sheriff and make his arrests according to the emperor's command. Seeing his opportunity to crush the enemy's spies in Cologne, Leopold agreed to the inquisitor's plans and even provided him with a carriage and finance. So now he is both God's emissary and the emperor's constable, Carlos concludes smugly.

He wonders if the daughter will look like her mother, if he will feel the same rush of exhilaration at those eyes, that hair, those lips. The anticipation makes him tumescent.

Soon he will be absolved of his sins. He will use the sorceress's own powers against her: he will call upon Lilith to fight evil with evil. The prospect of being liberated from an infatuation which has lasted more than thirty years lightens his whole physique. Tapping his foot against the side of the jail cart the friar breaks into a low hum.

Disgusted at his irreverence, Detlef shoots a disapproving glance in his direction. The inquisitor stops and smiles back superciliously.

The canon can be as irritated as he likes, Carlos thinks. I am a Divine soldier, here to perform justice. I will enlighten these provincial German doorstops and show them the work of God's army. I will avenge upon the daughter the humiliation caused by the mother.

With that defiant thought foremost in his mind he clutches the decree closer to his chest.

Silently the horses part as Maximilian Heinrich emerges from the cathedral. In full regalia the archbishop walks down the stone steps and stands before the envoys, oblivious to the stamping hooves, the night chill which drifts across the troops and the shivering animals' flanks, and the aroma of incense floating from the golden thurible an altar boy carries behind him.

Heinrich lifts his hands and blesses the soldiers. Their young faces, some still beardless, lower in reverence.

"My sons, may you go with the power of Jesus Christ pounding in your veins and know that you *are* the Lord in both sword and spirit. Amen."

"Amen," the young men repeat, their soft voices a lingering echo caught in the daybreak.

Believers; may God grant they stay that way, Detlef prays.

Heinrich strides toward him. "Fast and silent, cousin. The Spaniard will want blood. It is your duty to make sure there is none."

Then, his robes swirling behind him, the archbishop is swiftly back in the cathedral. The image of his presence floats suspended over the soldiers and the pawing horses.

It is dawn and the mauve sky hovers between night and day. The colonies of sparrows perched in the plane trees that line the square begin their chorus. The birdsong pierces the sky like a handful of thrown silver.

Detlef jerks his horse's bridle and leads off the procession, across the square and into Komödienstrasse toward the first of the accused. The mare, sensing her rider's reluctance, is slow but then quickens her pace, excited by the scent of a distant ocean brought by a breeze off the Rhine.

❉

Meister Matthias Voss is dreaming of frogs. Dancing frogs dressed in silver hose. They are singing and Meister Voss strains to hear the lyrics. He turns in the bed and pushes his plump buttocks toward his sleeping wife, Gretel. Dimly conscious, she smiles at the bulk of the man she loves and wraps her strong arms around his waist. Meanwhile, Meister Voss is wrestling with the amphibian ballet: he thinks they might be singing about being cooked in a soup, but the lyrics are in French and he is nervous that he has misunderstood the word *consommé*. Suddenly the singing becomes shouting and the frogs are flying everywhere. The dreaming Voss spins around, trying to catch them, then realizes to his great chagrin that he is naked.

He wakes sharply to the sound of loud banging. Gretel clutches him, her long gray plaits falling between her pendulous breasts.

"Matthias! What is it? Maybe Mathilde, maybe she has been taken! Oh, my poor child, to die so young!"

"Don't be ridiculous, woman!" the merchant replies, still struggling with the dull weight of his dreaming. For a second he remains frozen upright in bed, his weeping wife beside him, unable to find a rational meaning for the calamitous pounding below.

"I will go."

"No! Let the servants answer! Please, Matthias."

But the old merchant is already on his feet, the furred nightcap pulled down over his weathered brow, his silk nightdress tumbling over the veined belly, the vulnerable sac of balls and cock, the gnarled feet which have stood on sand, grass, polished wood, marble and straw. Before Meister Voss can pull his old cloak trimmed with mink across his shoulders, his valet bursts into the bedroom followed by three young cathedral guards and a short friar of Mediterranean appearance bristling with self-importance.

For an instant Meister Voss thinks they have come to ravish his wife. Forgetting that she is now old and gray, he throws himself in front of her naked body. A soldier turns away to snicker.

Now visibly quivering with righteousness, the friar steps forward and speaks in German with a heavy Spanish accent. As Voss's senses shake themselves awake and the words slowly penetrate his understanding, he recognizes the man as Inquisitor Carlos Vicente Solitario, the friar he had ridiculed only the night before with his fellow bürgers in the local beer hall.

". . . the Grand Inquisitional Council of Aragon charges you with two indictments of wizardry, one charge of conspiring against the Holy Roman Empire and one charge of consorting with the devil himself," Carlos finishes.

"You pumped-up piece of religious shit! You have no right to do this!"

"Matthias! Please! Don't make them more angry," his wife pleads, but the old man, his fur cloak now over his shoulders, has mustered his full authority. He glares at the friar.

"This is a free city, you have no power over us bürgers! The Gaffeln shall hear of this, they will use your hypocritical shaved pate to wipe their arses!"

Canon von Tennen steps from behind the soldiers and Voss falters. Here is a man he both recognizes and respects. Unable to connect Detlef's presence with the proceedings, confusion muddles the old man for a moment as he ponders the frightening possibility that the canon might be there to give him the last rites.

"My apologies, Meister Voss, for the inconvenience of our visit but the Gaffeln knows about the charges. They also know about the other matter—the passing of bad silver to a certain Portuguese merchant."

"What bad silver? I have never dealt in bad silver in my entire life."

"Nevertheless, the charges must be examined."

"You know these are trumped-up accusations, you know it!" Voss protests, his baritone voice ringing out with false confidence. But Detlef, inwardly mortified by the speciousness of his commission, has already slipped back into the shadows.

Meister Voss looks around wildly. For the first time in his life there is no one to defend him. Instinctively he reaches down for his sword, forgetting that he is still in his nightshirt. The soldiers move forward and grab him roughly by the arms. His wife, screaming, throws herself at him, clinging to his waist.

"Nein! Nein! Nicht mein Mann! No! Not my husband!" she cries out, oblivious to her unclothed state. Several of the soldiers turn their faces away in embarrassment as they drag the merchant out.

Voss, now frail with shock, remembers that in his dream the frogs were not singing but shrieking. As he is pushed down his own ornate wooden stairs, he realizes in a moment of stark clarity that he has always known that time and fear would eventually collide like this and render meaningless all of the life he lived before.

Outside, back on his horse, Detlef presses his hand across his eyes. Shaking with rage he is trying to control an overwhelming desire to strike down the squat Spaniard who watches triumphantly as his first captive is loaded into the jail cart.

The cat lies stretched across a bolt of Indian bombazine that arrived in Cologne on a ship belonging to the East India Company. The first streak of the morning sun falls across the feline's belly. Delighted, it purrs in the warmth.

Suddenly glass fragments scatter over the animal's fur. Terrified, it tears across the shopfront window as the soldiers burst through the entrance. Somewhere above a door slams as Herman Müller's sons run to wake their father.

The younger, fourteen years old, hauls himself up the narrow staircase leading to the attic and his father's bedchamber. His brother, sixteen, is just in front of him. Terror pounds against the back of his throat as both boys throw themselves into the darkened room. But Herman Müller is already on his feet. A widower with only his sons to live for, he pulls both young men to his chest.

"Listen, you must leave, both of you. Go to your uncle in Paris. Tell him to go to the king. Whatever it takes! I have been betrayed . . ."

The hammering of the soldiers' footsteps draws closer. The younger boy begins to weep; the other, conscious of his approaching manhood, moves to protect his father.

"No, Günter, they will take you too. Go now!"

Herr Müller pushes his two sons toward a small window. Thrusting open the shutters he reveals the roofs of Cologne, a gray mountainous range of glistening slate and brick.

"Whatever I have done, forgive me."

Unable to look at their shocked faces fragmenting into grief, Müller grabs the younger one and pushes him through the narrow opening. Following, the elder son turns to kiss his father briefly on the lips then climbs out after his brother.

Herr Müller watches them clamber over the slippery tiles, his heart squeezing with sorrow. His breath catches as the smaller boy slips and his brother reaches out to steady him. Terrified this will be the last time he will ever see his children, the merchant leans against the wall to stop his legs from buckling beneath him.

A moment later, scurrying up the steep slope, the two youths hear the muffled shouts of their father as he struggles with the soldiers.

By the time the prison cart has rumbled off the barge and onto the muddy track that leads to the small Calvinist outpost of Mülheim, the village children are already dancing along behind it.

Hungry for beauty their thin dirty faces stare at the soldiers' crimson sashes, at the golden horn hanging from the trumpeter's neck, at the lush fringed purple of the Hapsburg banner. Turning to the wheeled cage, the ragged urchins begin to mimic the bewildered faces of the two prisoners who shiver in their nightclothes, clutching the bars to stop themselves falling into the foul-smelling straw that covers the rocking floor.

"These are the people from across the river who live in that shiny city which is always out of reach. Now look at them! Dirty as monkeys!" the children chant in Dutch and Flemish as they sprint ahead.

The prison cart lumbers across the small square with its duck pond desolate in the center; past the wooden stocks in front of the town hall, a building as immaculate as a doll's house; the herring stall with its wares already scenting the breeze. It rolls past the Protestant church, its Calvinist severity afire with the sunrise; past the white school with its steep red Dutch roof; past the fishmonger's and the bakery. Finally, wheels squeaking, the cart halts outside the house of Jan van Dorf, the most prosperous merchant of Mülheim.

The children gawk in bewilderment—surely the soldiers must have the wrong address. A God-fearing man such as van Dorf, whose annual donations keep the small school running, clearly such a man is beyond authority. Why, everyone in Mülheim knows that van Dorf is unassailable, the only Dutchman in the village on first-name terms with the Catholic merchants of Cologne. He even travels over to the city and openly trades with the cargo ships; he has an honorary membership of the goldsmiths' guild, verified by the shield with golden urns hanging proudly in his window. But the prison cart has definitely stopped outside the palatial shopfront and the friar is climbing down and walking toward the door. The children, amazed, gather in a cluster behind the steaming flanks of the restless horses.

A second later van Dorf bursts out of the shop. A handsome man in his early thirties, his round Flemish face is florid with agitation. He greets the small priest and the tall elegant blond man courteously but soon he is shouting at them in German. "Witch! Wizard! Inquisition!"

The frightened children understand only every third word, but they know from his face and the scent of terror which fills the morning air with its acrid tang that the world has lurched suddenly like a shipwreck tilting on its side. Stricken with dread they stagger back as the soldiers move forward.

Unexpectedly van Dorf bolts, fleeing down the lane, eyes rolling like those of a terrified hare, his rotund body wobbling violently as his legs pound beneath him. Shocked at the incongruous sight the children fall silent. One small boy breaks into loud weeping as the soldiers languidly turn their horses around as if van Dorf's run for his life is little more than an irritant. The mounted guards transform into beautiful centaurs with tassels flying, hooves stomping and tails lashing through the fine morning air. With nostrils steaming like dragons, heads pointed toward the dashing figure, the horses give chase. In minutes the soldiers catch the Dutchman, drag him facedown through the plowed mud back to the prison cart.

And the watching children think the sky has fallen, for no one is safe if they can take van Dorf. Even the youngest looks up to the heavens, waiting for a vision of the fierce face of God, or lightning, or some other divine sign to show that a terrible mistake has occurred. Instead the church bells start to peal and somewhere a woman begins to wail.

Ruth squats next to her winter herbs, her skirts pulled up while she urinates onto the icy ground. She looks over at the guelder roses and nettles tethered to the long wooden stakes pounded into the hard mud. This is where she grows her medicinal plants—motherwort for breastfeeding, skullcap for pain, rosemary for the inflamed womb.

Spread out before her is the valley beyond her small plot of land. The winter forest winds its way down the gentle slopes, broken only by a stream which turns silver as the sunrise breaks over the horizon. Ruth finishes and shakes herself then pulls her skirts down over her hips. The view before her is without the mark of man. If she were to look closer, she would see new saplings sprouting out of the fallow fields which were once farmland. But she chooses not to. She loves this vista precisely because it is nature untarnished, a deceptive Eden which she likes to think of as spirit personified. She pauses, closes her eyes and listens to the landscape: the rustle of the leaves in the trees, the faint cry of a hawk, the bleating of sheep and, perhaps, the beating of wings.

Suddenly a woman's cries pierce the vision. Miriam bursts screaming from the cottage, followed by two young soldiers who, laughing, catch at her skirts and pull her down. A third soldier comes flying through the cottage door and glancing around sees the midwife. Indignation rises like bile in the back of Ruth's throat but it is laced with a sharp fear which momentarily bolts her to the ground.

Then, without knowing how, she is beside them. She throws herself onto the young soldier's back and hauls him away from Miriam whose face is now as white as the snow she has been flung against. Lucid with horror Ruth barely notices the blow from the soldier's fist. Lying on the ground, her petticoats thrown up, she feels nothing but humiliation and intense frustration that she is not strong enough to attack back. Dizzy, she struggles to her knees, dimly recognizing the warm liquid running down her cheek as blood.

"What do you want of us?" she screams out in German.

She crawls again toward Miriam. Blank with shock her assistant stares back at her. Her white legs are splayed awkwardly like the porcelain peg legs of some grotesque doll as the soldier pounds his body into her over and over. Before Ruth reaches the young girl a leather boot crashes against her shoulder, the pain driving her back down into the muddy snow. This time she rolls herself into a ball, tensing her body for the next blow. It does not come.

"Ruth bas Elazar Saul, you look like your mother."

Ruth, shocked at the Spanish words which float down as if from a great height, tries to peer through the streams of blood which have clouded her eyes.

"Who are you?" she manages to spit out, her mouth now acrid salt.

A face looms above. Olive skin. A face disfigured by a thin red scar, eyes shining with hate. She is struggling to understand whether she knows this man, trying to recall through the dulling pain whether she has slighted him or wronged him, anything to give reason to the violence that is being done to her and her assistant.

The priest smiles, a deceptively benevolent expression.

"I am your savior. I will be your confessor, *bruja*, and you shall surrender all to me."

Again the Spanish words float down like dandelion seeds and Ruth finds it hard to associate the tenderness of his tone with the stabbing pain which shoots through the core of her body.

The Jewess's face has a similarity to her mother's but is different, Carlos observes silently. It has the same narrowness around the jaw and cheeks that widen sharply. The eyes are almond-shaped like her mother's, but instead of deep black, these eyes are green and a different spirit looks out, a psyche which appears more wary and closed. Part of his own soul cannot help but long for some epiphany to link his flesh with that of the dead woman he both loved and persecuted. *Bruja*, witch, how seductive are the echoes of the flesh, he thinks. Sara . . . she feels so close he could almost reach out and crush her with one hand.

Aching with longing the priest stands. With a barely visible nod he gestures to one of the young soldiers. Coarse hands push Ruth back against the frozen ground. Her legs are pulled apart. For a moment she sees herself spreadeagled, a tiny figure of white skin and black and scarlet cotton, as the man above her tears at her clothes.

"Enough!"

Detlef grabs the soldier by his hair and hauls him off the Jewess. The young woman lies still. Broken, like a straw poppet. For a moment he wonders if she is still alive or whether she has died of fright like a caged bird.

"Not the midwife!" he bellows into the flushed face of the uniformed youth.

Outraged, Carlos, his own face red with excitement, pushes forward. "She is the devil's spawn, she must be punished!"

"Nothing has been proved! Besides, she is the rabbi's daughter, it is not politic to defile her!"

Detlef throws Ruth's skirts back over her legs. Standing, he wipes his hands on his breeches, finding it distasteful to be presented with the depravity of man. The vision of the sprawling semiconscious woman is equally repugnant to him. Her dress and manner repulse him, but he knows that her father has some influence among the harbor traders and that it would not behove the archbishop to allow her debasement. Behind him the rape of her serving girl continues.

"I suspect that you have an interest in protecting this creature, Canon."

"I have no interest other than protecting the archbishop's reputation."

"The archbishop is a Jew lover?"

"I will not dignify that question with an answer. May I remind you that we are on Protestant ground here, our presence is perilous. Make the arrest and let us be on our way, Monsignor Solitario, before my patience wears thin."

Detlef steps aside to allow the soldiers to carry the midwife to the prison cart. Miriam is left unconscious, her blood staining the snow.

The three men, each trapped in his own misery, cower against the bars as the soldiers push the young woman toward them. Her face streaked with dirt and blood is barely recognizable. The Dutchman glances at her then looks down in embarrassment, while Herr Müller, disgusted that he should be forced to share the prison cart with a Jewess, spits into the straw. Only Voss, seeing that it is the midwife from Deutz who delivered his own grandchild, reaches over to the bedraggled creature retching with pain and covers her breasts with his own cloak.

"Child, stand proud, we are not at the stake yet," he whispers as he helps Ruth to her feet. Dazed, she grips the bars and stares back at the diminishing view of her cottage.

"When they know who we are, they will release us. There has been a terrible mistake, mark my words, a terrible mistake." The old merchant mutters these words over and over, as if the normalcy of the sentence will reverse what is irreversible.

The prison cart bounces along the cobblestone lane toward the village. As the grim cargo passes each house families come to the windows and stare. Some stand in doorways. Others run inside clutching their children, memories of past pogroms turning their entrails liquid with terror.

Ruth, staring up, wonders why the sun seems to dance. When she looks at the women why do they throw their veils over their faces in shame? And why is the prison cart driving so slowly down the main street?

Carlos glances down the muddy broken road which serves as the central thoroughfare of Deutz. The dark architecture appalls him, as do the yeshiva boys with their outlandish forelocks curling around their exotic narrow faces and their strange long black clothes. The Dominican is convinced that these foreigners are staring at him with hatred; he is certain that if he should step among them, they would tear him to pieces like ravening dogs. Devil worshippers, the killers of our good Lord Jesus, lost souls all, he thinks.

The cart lurches over a pothole, almost pitching the friar out. Clutching the wooden rail he crosses himself vigorously.

When they reach the synagogue, the inquisitor signals for the coachman to halt. The cart pulls to a violent stop, rattling its captives like beans in a box. Carlos glances at the small sanctuary with the brass star of David perched on its dome and he waits.

Behind him, her hands curled around the iron bars, Ruth can see that the street is beginning to fill with the curious. Sanctioned by her arrest, they creep from their houses and out of the back lanes, a silent mob, the voyeurs of disaster, the onlookers who believe that in some mystical way the role of witness will render them immune to the peccadillos of fate. Fascinated, they slide like somnambulists toward the prison cart, staring at the midwife's bare and bruised legs, her exposed shoulders and loose hair.

Ruth, knowing that they are outside her father's house, is so humiliated she can hardly breathe. The silence stretches, then is broken by the startled flight of a loose hen from under the prison cart. The crowd begins to mutter and hiss. Someone throws an old turnip. It hits her, dense as a rock, but she barely flinches. Let them kill her. Better her own people than the Germans.

"Witch!"

"Whore!"

"Shame! You bring shame on us!"

Staring around wildly she searches for familiar faces, and sees Vida watching from the shelter of the bakery door. "Vida! Vida!" she cries hoarsely.

But the baker's young wife, catching Ruth's crazed gaze, turns away to weep in shame.

Detlef, astride his horse, observes from a distance. He does nothing to help the Jewess. Let her people stand in judgment on her, he thinks, but why has the inquisitor halted here in front of the temple? A man who is motivated by a personal vendetta is far more dangerous, he concludes, for such a creature is unpredictable. He watches Carlos's excitement as he waits for a response from the shuttered windows of the synagogue. What history does the Dominican have with the Jewess, the canon wonders, curious as to how such an insignificant woman could move powers as far away as Aragon and Vienna.

Suddenly a frail bearded old man walking heavily with a stick pushes his way through the onlookers.

"Ruth! Ruth!"

The crowd falls silent, parting for the chief rabbi, his white hair sticking up like a feral halo, his embroidered prayer shawl dragging behind him in the dirt. He stops and stares at the prison cart in utter disbelief. He stumbles and in an instant two young men—the same two who were only a second ago yelling insults—are by his side, holding him up. The old man pushes them away and walks up to the bars. He barely recognizes the terrified woman cowering inside.

"Ruth, my child, what have they done to you?"

He pushes his bent arthritic fingers through the iron poles, trying to reach his daughter. He cannot believe that this mute creature who stares at him with bewildered eyes, whose bleeding face retains only a remnant of her beauty, is the proud heretic who ran from the village, who broke the rules she knew he could never trespass himself, even the ones he might secretly have wanted to.

Leaning forward Elazar whispers in Hebrew, "Have they stolen your spirit? Have they taken your strength?"

But Ruth, setting eyes on her father for the first time in three years, is unable to answer, her tongue struggling to find the words between her swollen lips, the mucus and the horror.

"Forgive me, daughter. Forgive me for not forgiving you."

Weeping, the old rabbi reaches in and strokes the long black hair he once combed himself, now matted with blood. And suddenly there are no bars, there is no prison cart, there is nothing between the father and the daughter except clemency.

Many watching lower their eyes, unable to bear the agony of such raw intimacy.

But still the midwife is silent. Through his tears Elazar ben Saul notices a rip in his daughter's dress and under it the scratches welling with blood. A great rage starts to shake his thin frame and it is then, as he spins around to face her captors, that a sudden breeze finally carries back his daughter's answer. "I love you, abba," she whispers in Yiddish, the language of women. But the old man is too furious to hear.

He marches up to the inquisitor. With a great sweep of his bony arm, Elazar smashes his walking stick against the side of the cart.

"What is this outrage? Do you know who you have in your pathetic prison of fear?" the chief rabbi screams.

Every Jew watching flinches, frightened he will bring the wrath of Cologne onto the whole community. The old man in his rage has forgotten who he is shouting at, who has authority. Unmoved the Dominican looks down at him.

"Who are you?" the rabbi demands.

"I was your wife's confessor as I shall be your daughter's. My name is Carlos Vicente Solitario. I am the Inquisitor of Zaragoza, here under orders from both the Grand Inquisitional Council and the Emperor Leopold. Your daughter is charged with witchcraft."

The inquisitor's voice, cool and detached, makes the old rabbi sound hysterical. Surprised, Elazar ben Saul falters, peering up at the man shortsightedly.

"But you have no jurisdiction here, she is a Jew!"

"Rabbi, your daughter was baptized."

Horrified, Elazar stumbles back, then collects himself. "What is your evidence?" His voice cracks with fear.

Carlos reaches into his robe and pulls out the affidavit; leaning over he thrusts it before the old man's eyes. The rabbi reads it then collapses in shock.

Two yeshiva students immediately rush to the old man's aid and lift him to his feet. Held up, Elazar's haggard face stares at the jail cart as it drives off toward the Rhine and Cologne.

חכמה

CHOCHMA

Revelation

DAS GRÜNTAL, THE VON TENNENS' HUNTING LODGE
FEBRUARY 1665

The beautiful young actor, a Grecian robe buckled around his slim waist, rouge circles painted high on his whitened face, dark eyes lined with kohl, stands in front of the seated guests holding a terrified lamb against his fake cleavage and clutching a golden staff. From behind the varnished backdrop painted with an idealized landscape of Mount Olympus but looking suspiciously like the Tuscan hills, the other members of the troupe make bleating sounds. Suddenly a man wearing the massive head of a bull, his muscular torso gleaming with oil, his loins covered only by the briefest of kilts, the added absurdity of a small Ottoman cap pinned precariously between the ears of his bull mask, jumps out from behind the screen. The young shepherdess swoons as the bull advances.

"The rape of Juno!" Count Gerhard von Tennen yells from the front row of the audience. He stands and bows to polite applause. Dressed in scarlet silk hose and pantaloons, his narrow chest squeezed into the tightest of embroidered waistcoats, the count holds the mask of Pan up to his face and addresses the revelers.

"There is of course an added subtlety. Behold the loathsome insignia of the hated Ottoman!"

The actor playing Zeus lowers his head so all can see the Turkish cap pinned between his furry ears.

"And the colors of our poor ravaged Bohemia!"

At this, Juno cheekily throws up his skirts and bending over reveals bloomers adorned with the emperor's double-headed eagle, each head strategically placed over a buttock. Delighted, the onlookers howl with laughter.

Detlef, his face covered with a sinister wolf mask, leans toward his mistress. Birgit, wearing a satin headdress and mask resembling the head of a white peacock, and clothed in a creamy-white ball gown of ducape, its stomacher of matching silk bows embroidered with seed pearls, is the pinnacle of opulent splendor and utterly conscious of it.

"Do we assume that the young royal is amused?" Detlef asks wryly.

Birgit glances across to where Prince Ferdinand, the nephew of Emperor Leopold himself, sits sandwiched between Count Gerhard von Tennen and his gamekeeper, Herman Woolf, a colossal Prussian who is rumored to inhabit the count's bed as well as his hunting lodge.

The prince is an ailing pimply youth who has been sent to the Rhineland to recover his health and, more importantly, to remove him from the corrupting influence of the Viennese court where, at the onset of adolescence, the only precociousness he displayed was a healthy appetite for both sexes.

The seventeen-year-old is an unlikely guest for the older count, but welcomed as a chance to win favor with Leopold. The count's controlled façade is betrayed only slightly by a twitch as he recalls the humiliation he experienced at the hands of the young emperor on his last visit to the Viennese court. Leopold had promised an audience but postponed the meeting four times, then finally failed to show at all, leaving the count mortified before the arrogant Viennese courtiers. So when, months later, the royal messenger arrived at Das Grüntal with the request that Prince Ferdinand be invited to attend the count's winter hunt in an attempt to improve his health—the prince suffered constantly from an old jousting injury—Gerhard was understandably relieved. Here was the golden opportunity to redeem himself in the emperor's eyes and to make it perfectly clear that his alliance lay with the Hapsburgs; unlike Maximilian Heinrich whose attention wavers to the southeast, toward France.

Yawning, the young Austrian nobleman appears bored, but after a tap from his courtier smiles politely and raises both hands to clap. "Droll, very droll, Count von Tennen. What is the name of the delightful Juno?"

"Alphonso, your highness." The count lowers his voice: "And he is most amenable." He taps his fan and on cue the young actor curtsies and smiles brazenly at the prince before skipping off behind the screen.

Birgit returns her attention to Detlef.

"Your brother has mastered the niceties of the Viennese court well. But pray where is the countess?"

"My brother's long-suffering wife resides permanently in Bonn now. She draws comfort from the companionship of her ward, Fräulein Drecker. As you know, the marriage was a convenience, a bloodless and heartless affair."

Detlef wonders whether Merchant Ter Lahn von Lennep realizes that his own marriage could be defined as such.

Birgit nudges her husband who is busy devouring a leg of glazed duck with obscene relish. An obese man in his sixties, afflicted by an acute awareness of his own lack of sophistication, he guiltily wipes the poultry gravy from his chin then pulls down his mask. It is in the unfortunate shape of a rooster—his wife's choice.

"Prince Ferdinand sets an example to the rest of us provincials," Birgit continues, running her hand up Detlef's thigh under the table. "Of course, such manners are in the blood. Such breeding cannot be purchased."

Meister Ter Lahn von Lennep, now scarlet with embarrassment, belches into his napkin. Detlef, feeling sorry for the ridiculous costume the long-suffering merchant has been made to wear, comes to his rescue.

"There are many who would disagree. If absolution is to be bought, why not nobility?"

"The canon is right. It is even rumored that Leopold himself had a chambermaid for a great-grandmother."

"Hush, husband, even tables have ears."

"And legs, I believe," Detlef interjects. Under the table he shifts his swelling erection away from Birgit's deft fingers.

"What is the occasion for the young prince's visit?" the merchant asks, uncomfortably full under his tight waistcoat and velvet breeches. "I have heard whisperings that Leopold has sent him to spy on his henchman, the ambitious inquisitor. Canon, I believe you were witness to the arrests of poor Voss and Müller?"

"Indeed."

"The Gaffeln are most unhappy. Maximilian Heinrich will answer for this latest outrage, that I can assure you."

"The papal powers still have jurisdiction over Cologne. Voss and Müller are accused of wizardry; the archbishop has to bow to the Inquisition."

"And you to the archbishop," the merchant retorts, wondering why the canon has suddenly shifted from his wife's side.

"The prince is here to hunt the wild boar." Birgit, fanning herself to cover her chagrin at Detlef's rejection, deliberately changes the subject. They all glance again at the prince, now fondling Juno who, giggling and preening, is perched on his knee.

"He is a great lover of the hunt," Detlef remarks wryly.

"Evidently, but will he prove to be a great lover of the aspiring bürger?" the merchant continues.

"He has a keen admiration for fine Persian silk, I believe."

Detlef knows full well that the merchant has received a shipment of the cloth only that month.

"In that case we must present him with a length of the best and seek an audience. Are we sure he has influence with his good uncle, the emperor?"

"Influence enough."

The furry ears of the wolf mask sway elegantly as Detlef reaches for another glass of wine. Just then the count gestures to the musicians and they begin to play. Detlef and Birgit stand and, after a tolerant smile from her husband, take their positions on the dance floor for a formal quadrille. The klaviermaster commences his playing and the dancers begin to step backward and forward, their bodies arching stiffly.

Swinging from partner to partner Detlef can't help but notice the recent renovations the count has undertaken.

"I can't believe my brother would allow such sacrilege. This was once a hall radiant in its simplicity," he whispers to Birgit as they dance past an ornate statue of a naked Cupid playing his pipes.

"It was old-fashioned, Gothic. It was time the count invested in the current fashion."

"That Italian artisan . . . what is his name?"

"Philibert Lucchese. He redesigned the Hofburg in the stucco style for Leopold himself and comes at great expense."

"Whatever his reputation, he has ruined Das Grüntal. My dear father would have been scandalized."

As he looks around, discovering one baroque monstrosity after another, Detlef cannot believe how a simple medieval dining hall has been transformed into a ballroom of bacchanalian exaggeration. The hunting lodge was designed in the 1500s, the clumsy marriage of a Renaissance Italian villa and the local Rhenish architecture. Built around a pebbled courtyard, the exterior walls were decorated with a mural depicting a variety of hunts with every kind of prey: the traditional English fox hunt, a stag hunt, a wild boar chase, a falconer sending his hawk after a rabbit, and even Hannibal and his elephants inexplicably chasing tigers. It was a tribute to the idiosyncrasies of the old viscount, who liked to imagine himself as a cosmopolitan huntsman of sophisticated tastes.

Glancing up now, Detlef is confronted by a molded ceiling displaying a painted panorama of the Wittelsbachs' victory in the Crusades. Detlef's great-great-great-grandfather, a famously short, stocky individual, has miraculously become a patriarch of impressive stature; and where there once were crude oak and iron candelabra now hang chandeliers of Venetian crystal and gilt.

As a young boy Detlef spent hours at Das Grüntal, sitting in the courtyard with his tutor who made him count the pebbles in Latin. His brother and his father formed an island of severe masculinity which excluded Detlef completely. As they were often out surveying the local land, it was a lonely childhood and on many occasions Detlef's only companions were the servants and the local peasant children. But this was to prove the seeding of the canon's love for the ordinary man.

The child's favorite refuge was the family chapel. Dedicated to Saint Hubert, the patron saint of all hunters, the small room in the west wing was a place of magical mystery for a young boy. The altar held a beautiful crucifix—melted from gold plate, booty of the Crusades—with a Christ whose crown of thorns contained real rubies and sapphires. Alongside stood an unusually buxom Madonna, a blond Flemish beauty whose obscenely bountiful breasts had crept more than once into Detlef's adolescent fantasies.

His mother, Viscountess Katrina von Tennen, a pious woman driven into religious fervor by marital neglect, was encouraged by her son's fascination with the chapel and convinced of his vocation for the priesthood. After all, the church was the natural destiny for a second son, and knowing that the viscount cared little for the boy, she feared for his welfare after her death.

When Detlef was ten the unhappy woman was taken by the plague and it was at her graveside that the small boy secretly pledged to carry out her wishes. Four years later the Wittelsbach men were called on by the Bavarian court to fight with the Hapsburgs against the Lutherans, and Detlef had no choice but to ride out in the chainmail his father had had fashioned for both his sons.

The first dance draws to an end and Birgit, her hips swaying seductively under the full skirt, bows coquettishly before him, her breasts pushed high above the embroidered stomacher. It excites her to be in the family house of her lover. Looking at him, she imagines she can see the whole lineage of the Wittelbachs in his gray-blue eyes, his patrician nose and high cheekbones, and fantasizes that one day it shall be Detlef and her on the podium, graciously welcoming the costumed guests.

The black ermine against Detlef's blond hair, the short black cape slung rakishly over one shoulder, renders him mysterious and wondrous to her. It arouses her. Gripped by a desire to commit some profanity here on her lover's family estate, under the eyes of her inept husband, Birgit pulls Detlef toward the stone arches that lead out into the courtyard.

The winter moon hangs low in the sky like a huge yellow portal into a better world. The soft light radiates down, lengthening the still shadows. The air is filled with the heavy scent of musk and great swathes of rosemary and lavender are scattered across the cobblestones. Birgit looks like a magical bird of paradise, the feathers of her mask shimmering in the moonlight, her cleavage transformed into the breasts of a ghost. It makes her lover want her; the clandestine nature of their actions excites him too. But it is not only the danger of discovery that intoxicates Detlef, it is also the pagan revelry: the beating music, the clouds of smoldering incense, the rush of the heavy red wine. It makes him want to surrender to the primal, to give himself over to his loins and cock, driven by a violent urge to pound out all the artifice, the machinations, the suffocating stratagems that constantly surround him.

He pushes her behind one of the pillars and takes her mouth into his own. He knows that two steps away on the other side, Peter Ter Lahn von Lennep is discussing the effect of the North Sea war on trading. The thought of discovery makes Detlef harden. Removing his mask, he bites down on one nipple and pushes up her petticoats. Now there is little between them, no history, no familiarity, just the instinctive desire to plunder each other's body. He pulls both breasts over the top of her dress, playing with her as his mouth travels across her flesh. Then kneeling he pulls her gown over his head.

Underneath her scent is mingled with the rosemary and lavender and her own perfume, a musk of civet and myrrh known as Aphrodite's tears. Birgit's silk stockings are rolled up to the top of her thighs. Detlef runs his hands up to her golden bush and, parting her, strums her until she is erect. Pushing his full lips against her, he finds the small hardened organ with his tongue then takes her into his mouth, teasing and sucking gently.

Birgit moans and steadies herself against the pillar. On the other side her husband thinks he has heard a cat. Pushing her breasts back into her bodice, she allows Detlef to propel her toward the open balcony. There she stands, her lower half concealed, fanning herself and smiling mysteriously at her husband through the open portico. Under her skirt her legs are spread wide as Detlef, concealed, pleasures her in the way she has taught him, orchestrating the contractions of pure bliss until they burst into uncontrollable spasms. Birgit concentrates fiercely on the form of her husband, his portly figure absurd in the tight fashionable clothes, his hands waving around with absolutely no grace. At this moment she hates him. She recalls how as a young woman she was forced into the arranged marriage as a means to save her father's estate from ruin. It was easy barter: her nobility for Peter Ter Lahn von Lennep's money. No matter that he was thirty years older, or that Birgit found his openly mercenary manner an affront to the refined discourse into which she had been indoctrinated; no matter that on the wedding night she lay weeping as the old man pounded into her. It is these memories she holds on to, her flesh trembling under her lover's mouth and fingers, until all the unhappiness, futility and tedium is released in a rush of pure pleasure. Overwhelmed, she lifts her mask and rests her hot face a moment against the cool moon-drenched wall.

On the other side of the pillar the merchant finishes his conversation, smug in the knowledge that he has secured yet another patron for his goods. Upon seeing his wife framed in the open window he thinks she looks like Venus herself, so lovely and flushed is she, and for the hundredth time that evening he congratulates himself on his choice of bride.

Detlef wipes his mouth with his fingers then surreptitiously sniffs them before reaching for another goblet of wine. Around him the carousing has become more frenetic. The dancers swirl wildly in the candlelight, their masks transforming them into half-human, half-animal beings. He is reminded of an ancient cave drawing he saw in France, as if the revelers have devolved back to long-buried primordial states of worship. Leaning back in his chair he marvels at the sight.

"Brother, we must have words."

Pan's hairy goat's face suddenly appears before him. Disembodied, it seems to float before a backdrop of glistening naked limbs. The count's muffled laughter jolts Detlef into some semblance of reality and he stands to greet him.

Smiling enigmatically Gerhard slips his perfumed arm through his brother's and Goat and Wolf make their way between the circling dancers whose movements have become drunk with abandonment. Stepping carefully around the flailing arms and legs they move toward Prince Ferdinand and his sycophants, who are conducting a race between two live cockerels among the silver platters piled high with glistening carcasses of fowl, half-picked bones and peeled fruit, the remnants of a feast.

"The inquisitor Solitario is an intriguing individual," the count murmurs. "I have heard rumor he is an extraordinary musician but one with no heart. What heart will he show over the fate of the two merchants, I wonder? What do you make of these arrests?"

"Mere blackmail. As long as the bürgers' anger is contained, Heinrich need not fear."

The two brothers arrive at the table and Detlef is forced into a chair by a jester dressed as a monkey adorned with a huge pair of plaster breasts.

"If only it were that simple; alas, I fear it is not."

The jester holds up two live roosters—one red, one black—and calls out for wagers. The count pledges ten Reichstaler on the red bird while Detlef places five on the black. After throwing the coins down the count leans toward Detlef.

"The three Christian merchants arrested are not as they appear."

"What are you suggesting?"

"Voss has had direct dealings with the French court for years, and Müller . . ."

The count's gamekeeper holds up an ornamental hunting knife for the count's approval, the handle of which is a ram's horn carved in the shape of a penis. Placing his own gloved hand around the man's thick brawny wrist, the count pulls the knife toward him and with deadpan ceremony kisses the tip of the handle for good luck. The prince's entourage roar their approval but Herman waits, his huge handsome face impassive. The count, his gaze locked to his gamekeeper's, gives the thumbs down. With two swift cuts Herman slices the head off each rooster. Amid screams of laughter the headless chickens, blood spurting over the linen cloth, scurry madly down the center of the table in a macabre race while the gamesters shout encouragement.

The count turns back to his brother. "Müller's real name is Metain. He has been acting as a courtier for Heinrich and is a personal favorite of King Louis."

"Next you will tell me that the Dutchman is also a spy."

In lieu of a reply the count shrugs and flicks a feather off his lace sleeve.

The black rooster stumbles and keels over, the last of its blood pumping over the tablecloth. The red cockerel races on, as if trying to outpace death itself. It reaches the edge of the table and for a second flies blindly up, then plummets dead as a stone.

The revelers cheer and whistle as the count calmly sweeps his winnings into the palm of his hand.

"Really, Detlef, I am disappointed in you. Heinrich should keep you better informed; after all, you are his heir apparent. Or has the affable Wilhelm Egon von Fürstenberg now inherited that dubious honor?"

Detlef, noticing the gleam of cynicism in the count's eyes, wonders whether his brother has ever had any real affection for him at all. Or does he regard him merely as an irritating pawn in the endless game of chess he is forced to play between church and state, bishop and prince, in order to maintain his power in the patchwork of different allegiances between which the von Tennen family estate lies?

"Not yet. But pray, illuminate me, why the arrest of the Hebrew woman? Surely she is utterly unknown in Vienna?"

"Naturally. I believe she is a personal obsession of the Dominican, however the oily Spaniard is in bed with both Leopold and the Grand Inquisitional Council. 'Tis a pity—I hear she is a talented medic as well as a midwife."

"So they say."

The young Prince Ferdinand, his face smeared with carmine kisses from the actor Alphonso, leans drunkenly toward the count.

"A good medic? That's exactly what I need."

"The best in the region."

"So why haven't I heard of her?"

"Perhaps because she is a Jew," the count replies smoothly.

Alphonso, removing his tongue from the prince's ear, enters the conversation with a cheeky audacity. "In that case she must be the best."

Intrigued the prince stops running his hands through the actor's long hair. "So where can I find her?"

"Sire, the said medic is currently incarcerated in the cathedral dungeon under the loving care of Monsignor Carlos Vicente Solitario. I believe the unfortunate woman is accused of sorcery."

"Solitario is a sanctimonious oaf who would happily trade lives for promotion. But he has caught my uncle's ear at a particularly pious time. We are all victims of the emperor's sudden virtuousness."

The prince petulantly knocks a bone off the table. One of the hunting dogs lurking beneath lurches up and grabs it.

"The diocese of Cologne is always happy to accommodate the wishes of the Grand Inquisition," Detlef replies diplomatically, sensing a trap.

"Naturally, Canon, everyone accommodates the Inquisition. Come, my lovely Juno, we shall lead the next quadrille."

Ferdinand escorts Alphonso across the marble floor, the actor's Grecian robe trailing behind them. The dancers part and wait for the royal cue as the two young men take their places center stage. The goddess's glistening golden eyelids and scarlet mouth are infused with a raw dignity. The prince, for once looking regal, lifts Juno's hand high and they wait, poised, before the musicians begin.

There is an air of vulnerability about them. It is because of their youth, Detlef finds himself thinking, as if instead of prince and actor they are simply two youths in love at the brink of their lives.

The violinist sounds his first notes, Juno flicks her fan shut and the dance begins.

*D*ear Benedict,

    I write to you in darkness. I am confined in the bowels of the prison of Cologne, a guest of the Inquisition awaiting a reception of horror. They have charged me with witchcraft and heresy. Is it heresy to believe but not in the accepted creeds? Is it sorcery to use one man's herbs and another's faith? If so, I am guilty of both.

    Here it is perpetual night. Here there is but a wisp of candlelight which flickers precariously beyond the bars of my jail. I have stared at it for so long now it has become the sun, God and the embodiment of all my hope. I know from the sliver of light it throws across the wall that there is much damp in here and, amid the filthy sawdust, God's own rodents. They smile at me with long yellow teeth. Strange, but I have no fear of these creatures. There is one in particular, a motley mangy beast, who appears more decrepit than the rest. He is the Solomon of the rat kingdom and will partake of me for hours. In my madness I wonder if he is not the spirit of an ancient ancestor returned. It is such meanderings that have kept me sane. There is no light for me to mark time so I have slipped into a delirium of eternity. The only fellow human I have seen is one prison guard who brings me a thin gruel to eat and who takes out the slops. I have tried to converse with him but the creature appears to be a mute with limited intelligence.

    To further my humiliation they have stripped me not only of my freedom but also of my clothes. I cover my nakedness with a hessian sack; I am reduced to the bare bones of my soul. Despair lurks at every twist of the mind, longing to drag me down into an abyss. My anger saves me. Perhaps it shall be my redemption. It keeps me warm and quiets my starving belly. They shall not see me broken. My physical body shall surrender the spirit before the will. But oh, how I long to hear a friend's voice, anything to remind me that I am not so completely alone . . .

A shifting light which appears behind her shut lids causes her to break concentration. She clears her mind of the letter she is composing and contemplates whether she should open her eyes and let harsh reality annihilate her imagined liberation. Before she has a chance to decide, the reddish glow grows stronger. It is a dancing pinpoint that beckons her seductively: open up, open up . . .

Tentatively she lifts her eyelids and immediately senses that she is in the presence of the unknown.

Oh terror, where are you? she wonders, amazed at the tremendous tranquillity which has placed all of her six senses into suspension, for before her sits a ghost.

He is a tall youth with jet-black hair and black eyes ringed by circles of exhaustion in a narrow face. He sits on the edge of the straw pallet gazing morosely into space. His feet are manacled by heavy chains and his arms and wrists bear the mark of torture. Like her, he is a prisoner in the jail, but unlike her he has no sense of another's presence.

"Aaron?" she whispers but is not surprised when he does not turn, merely exhales deeply, a sigh of complete resignation. He shifts slightly in his chains; to Ruth's astonishment there is no rattle. It is as if the only sounds she can hear are those which emanate from the ghost himself.

"Have they not executed you yet?" she whispers again, her heart leaping with painful love. "Aaron?"

She waits, half-elated half-petrified that the wraith might vanish at the sound of his own name. But absorbed in his own domain he shows no sign of being aware of her existence.

"Ruth, forgive me," he whispers to himself and buries his face in his hands. The fragility of his thin adolescent wrists, the desperation in the narrow shoulders, the lock of unruly black hair falling across his bruised knuckles; release a wave of recognition deep within her. It is as if the memory of him is buried within her very tissue and now this simple gesture has unlocked it, and with it a deluge of grief.

She moves toward him, to touch, to hold, to shelter that unassailable soul.

The rattle of keys breaks the moment. Ruth turns to the sound then swings back. Aaron's ghost has vanished.

Again the jangle of metal startles her. It is the loudest thing she has heard in four days. She cowers against the straw as a shaft of bright light travels across the floor, highlighting the piles of filth, old rags and dank sawdust. It settles on Ruth, who is entirely blinded as she squints to see who waits beyond.

"Midwife, to your feet!"

The voice emerges from the darkness, authoritarian. Ruth, her ankles swollen, her feet bruised and oozing pus, struggles to stand.

A guard steps forward and thrusts a burning torch into the iron holder. The whole cell is illuminated and now she can see that the walls are covered with graffiti carved into the stone. There is a multitude of tongues: Latin, German, Dutch, Arabic, Spanish and even some Hebrew.

> *January 10th 1636. May God speed my demise and Angel wings*
> *carry me up to the skies . . .*
> *I die for Philip, King of Spain, long shall he reign . . .*
> *To all who have borne witness, I have been true to my word . . .*

And finally, in a hand she instantly recognizes:

> *Ruth, forgive your Aaron.*

Suddenly, it is as if her life is already over. As if she is already a sentence hewn into the limestone. The room fills with the whispers of the prosecuted, the forgotten, the executed. Dizzy, she swoons. She lies in the filth, her eyes wide, drinking in the light she has been deprived of for so long. All sensation rushes from her, emptying her completely. She wants to remain here in this great inner silence where it feels safe, in this place of no-being where she is conscious of nothing except the beating of her own blood in her ears.

"I said get up, witch!"

Her fears come tumbling back, inundating her whole being with an appalling cataclysm of dread. Terrified, she pisses herself as she staggers upright.

"Do you know who I am?"

Only vaguely aware of the hot fluid coursing down her thighs she shakes her head dumbly.

Disgusted, Carlos Vicente Solitario, dressed in the dark robe of interrogator, stands over her. Mud streaks the young woman's bare shoulders, her hair is matted and she stinks of her own filth, but still he stands close, breathing in her stench. He regards the proximity as a perverse martyrdom: it is his holy duty to deal with the corrupt, the evil, the unclean. A sense of purity washes through him. He is on a crusade, a just quest which raises him above his fellow humans. Setting his jaw the friar glistens with self-righteousness.

Ruth stares at him. Even with her memory dimmed by pain she recognizes the dark eyes.

Detlef, standing behind Solitario, looks down at the ground ashamed. The midwife, out of her mind with fear, has let the hessian sack slip and stands rawly naked, oblivious. The canon steps forward and pulls the cloth gently over her shoulders. He cannot help but hold his breath as he does so.

"Note how little time it took for the sorceress's true nature to reveal itself. Look at her: she is now more animal than woman. This is why it is so important to enforce the *limpieza de sangre*." The inquisitor addresses Detlef and the guard as if giving a sermon on the methods of exposing the damned.

No doubt he has performed such lectures with more appreciative audiences, Detlef observes, revolted by the obvious intoxication the Dominican displays, his eyes shiny, his scar an ugly throbbing crimson, his mouth wet with saliva.

"For God's sake, she is witless with fear."

"Such a creature knows no terror."

"Such a creature is as human as the rest of us."

"That is for the Inquisition to decide."

They are interrupted by Ruth's voice, cracked and hoarse. "I know you for your cruelty. You are my nemesis, the persecutor of my race."

"I am the persecutor only of those who worship Lucifer, who manipulate simple souls with their sorcery. If you are not one of these, you have nothing to dread."

"You know I am not. You have no evidence other than superstition and fear, the fodder upon which the fat cows of the Inquisition thrive."

Carlos nods and the guard steps forward, delivering a blow to Ruth's head which sends her reeling.

Detlef steps forward. "Enough! At least keep her alive to stand trial. There are many in this city who have benefited at her hands."

"Are you one of them, Canon von Tennen?"

"Don't be ridiculous. I have never met the woman before."

The younger cleric looks vaguely familiar to Ruth. There is an intelligence in his face that makes her instinctively trust him. She turns, blood streaming from her nose. "Please, Canon, tell me: what is the evidence?"

But the inquisitor steps between them. "You will address me and only me during all interrogations, Señorina Navarro."

"My name is Ruth bas Elazar Saul."

"Your status as Jew is not recognized by the Inquisition, therefore I will call you only by your mother's family name. Do you understand?"

At the inquisitor's signal the guard lifts his fist to Ruth again. Flinching, she nods.

"In that case, by what title, sir, do I address you?"

"Monsignor Carlos Vicente Solitario."

The guard pushes her down onto a stool. Displaying no emotion he folds out a small wooden table and places a flask of wine and some freshly baked bread upon it. Ruth can smell the loaf so vividly she can practically taste it. She reaches out only to have her hand knocked away.

"If I allow you to eat, you will answer, understand?"

She nods then begins to stuff the dough into her mouth in handfuls. In a second she is almost choking.

Detlef pours a goblet of wine and holds it out. Tears streaming from her eyes, the midwife gulps the liquid down. Struck by the exquisiteness of her hands, the fingers a chiseled filigree of muscle beneath the grime, Detlef realizes that the bedraggled creature could possibly have some beauty.

The inquisitor's cold voice interrupts.

"We have testimony from two women that you used kabbalistic amulets to assist in the birthings of their children. One child has not spoken since his delivery some two years ago; the other was stillborn, his soul stolen away by the devil himself, a barter you were no doubt responsible for."

"Frau Schmidt," she whispers, remembering the agony of presenting the dead child to his mother, his skin blue and mottled.

"So you confess to the charge?"

"No, I do not. The child had already perished in the womb. Sometimes even God takes without reason."

"Frau Schmidt claims you hung Hebrew symbols over the bed and used devilish instruments upon her body."

"The instruments are from Amsterdam, they are birthing tools designed by the eminent surgeon Doctor Deyman."

"And what qualifications do you, a woman, have that give you the right to use such tools?"

"Those of experience and education."

"I am not aware that a woman—particularly a Jewess—is allowed to attend any university in the whole of Christendom."

The wine has fortified her, it gives her a momentary bravado.

"I did attend, as an assistant and . . . not entirely myself."

"What exactly are you implying: that you transformed yourself?"

Ruth hesitates. Honesty would be as condemning as a lie, but her father has indoctrinated her with utmost respect for the truth, no matter how uncomfortable. *A halber emes iz amol a gantser ligen; a half-truth is a whole lie.* It is her father's favorite proverb. Ruth takes a long shuddering breath and gathers up her courage.

"I was assistant to a student there. My name was Felix van Jos."

"You used magic to transmute your womanly shape to that of a man. Take notice, Canon von Tennen, this is another blasphemy."

"I did not! I merely donned the garments of a youth."

"You expect me to believe that for a number of years you lived as a man, Señorina Navarro?"

The inquisitor reaches over and tears down the coarse sackcloth to reveal her breasts. The guard begins to laugh.

"God has blessed you with the shape of a woman. There is no way to disguise this curse other than resorting to witchcraft."

With trembling hands Ruth covers herself up, her face rigid in an attempt to remain dignified. Her gravity transforms the laughter into an embarrassed silence.

"I have learned that perception is very much in the eye of the beholder, Monsignor Solitario. A man will see what he desires. You see a witch where others simply see a very good midwife."

At another signal the guard whacks her across the face. Ruth barely feels the blow. She has retreated deeper into herself while yet keeping her mind coherent, a scheme of survival she has perfected over the years.

The distance in her eyes infuriates Carlos; he recognizes the detachment as a trait of her mother's. Adrenaline burns at his vitals and he is infused with the desire to finally break the will of the Navarro women.

"I assume this is a philosophy of the heretic of whom you were a disciple, the Jew, Benedict Spinoza, a man who has been excommunicated by his own people."

"I am one of his followers, this I cannot deny."

"This man is evil personified, he does not believe in sin. He does not believe in the notion of Heaven and Hell nor even that a man has a soul. He is godless, señorina, like yourself."

"Liar! I am not godless, and neither is Spinoza. He believes that to understand the knowledge of nature is to know the works of God. And to know the works of God within the creation is to understand God himself, for God dwells in every visible work! Even you, Monsignor."

"I know what I am."

But Detlef notices that the inquisitor hesitates as if, like the canon, he is surprised by the young woman's flawless high German and her urbane articulation of these revolutionary ideas. Concepts Detlef himself has secretly studied in the illegal imported pamphlets Maximilian Heinrich confiscates regularly, heretical treatises by the English Quakers, the Dutch Mennonites, the Tremblers and the Seekers. All pouring across the border from Amsterdam like light radiating out from a submerged city below a dark horizon. The ecstasy he has experienced on reading these writings is tantamount to eroticism. The notions of pantheism, of the marriage of *scientia nova* with religion, the idea that man may shape his destiny through rational conduct, deeply excite the young canon. For the first time in his life he has found himself doubting the indisputable right of the aristocrat—a hierarchy he was born into and has profited by. On occasion he has even feared for his soul.

And now here before him is a creature—a woman, no less—who has studied and had discourse with those revolutionaries of the Enlightenment who challenge not only a faith but a whole worldview. What is she—witch or philosopher?

The inquisitor, refusing to be distracted, holds up a birthing tool. The instrument, a strange curved spoon designed to force open the cervix, glints demonically in the candlelight.

"The human body and all that lies within it is one of the great sacred mysteries," he says. "It is a sin to defile and carve up the embodiment of God."

"I am not an anatomist, Monsignor, nor do I pretend to be, but like my master Spinoza I believe that knowledge is a knowledge of the Divine, for are our minds and our natural curiosity not a manifestation of God also?"

"Benedict Spinoza has no understanding of the true God. He has repudiated the divinity of the Bible and, most blasphemous of all, has denied the existence of the soul. He is also a supporter of de Witt's Republic."

"You are wrong; he believes that the soul is a self-aware being, but that the mind is incapable of imagination or recollection without the existence of the physical body. And that no amount of penance can buy us sanctuary after our death."

"Enough! I refuse to be polluted any further by the ideas of this heretic and antiroyalist." Carlos reaches into his robe and pulls out a small stone. Carefully he holds it before Ruth. "Do you recognize this?"

She peers at it: the stone is rusty with bloodstains but beneath she can make out King David's Shield, the kabbalistic symbol for protection and strength. It is the amulet Rosa gave her in the mikvah.

"This was found sewn into the hem of your gown, Señorina Navarro. Do you deny that it is a spell or some such devilry?"

Ruth looks wildly around the prison, trying to formulate a reply which will not incriminate her further, but her mind has clouded over.

"It is Hebrew."

"I know that."

"Is it not true that Christians wear an image of Saint Christopher to ensure safety on their travels?"

"It has been known," Detlef interjects, encouraging her.

"Hebrews have similar talismen—this one is for protection."

"You lie. This is a mystical number from the kabbala. Only witches and sorcerers carry such a thing upon their bodies."

Carlos turns to the guard who hands him an object wrapped in an oiled cloth. Ceremoniously the inquisitor unrolls the bundle to reveal a sharp metal object with a long pinlike nose and a curious dial at the top inscribed with Latin.

"Do you know what this is?"

"No." But recognizing the tool as the torturer's instrument Ruth is suddenly nauseous with fear.

"It is an instrument designed by another great man, an Englishman called Matthew Hopkins. Have you heard of him?"

Ruth shakes her head; dread has swallowed her tongue.

"He is also known as the Witchfinder General and has done much worthy work beyond the North Sea in this field. His instrument is known as Hopkins' bodkin and is used to discover the secret mark the devil has made upon his womenfolk, the witches. It is not a pleasant *modus operandi* but very effective, let me assure you."

"You would torture me for a confession?"

"Please, this is an investigation driven by the desire to reach the truth, Señorina Navarro. An immediate confession would of course make it unnecessary to resort to such methods."

Ruth remains silent. She is thinking about her mother and father: she cannot betray her lineage or her beliefs. She glances back at the bodkin. She knows they will probe and violate her until her ankles run with blood; that they might place her head in an iron mask to force open her eye sockets, or pull out her tongue; that they will bring her to the point of death over and over and each time revive her. She knows that the rational response would be to confess now and be thankful that burning at the stake will prove a faster death. But she will not confess. Curse them, she thinks, she will die in silence, true to her philosophy and the spirit of the future. *Besser tsu shtarben shtai'endik aider tsu leben oif di k'nien; better to die upright than to live on your knees.* Curse them.

Studying the young woman sitting before him, Carlos watches the icy veneer of willpower closing over her. He has seen it before and as it excited him in the mother, it excites him now in the daughter. He will conquer the midwife's soul even if it destroys him. He will see her annihilated, and with her the last shadow of Sara Navarro will be wiped from his eclipsed heart.

"Your obstinacy is typical of your family and of your race. Very well; we shall take our leave and give you more time to contemplate the evidence I have laid out before you. Unfortunately it seems that even the philosophies of Benedict Spinoza will not be able to save you now."

The guard wraps up the bodkin then roughly pushes Ruth off the stool. She falls into the filthy sawdust. Bowing mockingly, the inquisitor leaves the cell.

Detlef hesitates. He wants to go over and help the midwife up. He wants to wash the filth from her face and rinse the blood from her mouth, then hear her speak. Instead he turns away.

The guard pushes the iron gate shut and Ruth is left alone, the clang of key in lock reverberating in the unequivocal darkness.

On the other side of the heavy door Detlef finds he cannot move. Recognizing his confusion as the onset of a revelation that is holding his body to ransom, he dismisses the guard and waits while the heavy footsteps recede down the corridor.

This woman has spoken the words he himself has longed to speak. She is defending ideas which have secretly possessed him for over two years. What is he to do? Can he let such a mind be destroyed by a petty vendetta?

Nobility of spirit wrestles with the necessity of political survival, but it seems pragmatism has deserted him completely. She cannot be a witch, he tells himself. Witches do not study philosophy; witches do not practice *scientia nova*. She belongs to a new age, a future he longs to be part of.

בינה

BINAH

Reason

♄

Detlef stares at the globe of the world which sits on his desk, a gift from the shipbuilders' guild in gratitude for a piece of diplomacy over taxes he executed on their behalf. It is a decorative sphere painted in sienna yellow and venetian blue, the cities marked in gold leaf, with Rome—as the axis of Christendom—naturally depicted as the center of the world. He spins the orb around to Spain and walking his fingers tries to calculate the distance between Aragon and Cologne. By the time his thumb reaches the Free Imperial City, Ruth's green eyes have fought their way back into his brain. He cannot shake the image of her.

Who is she? And who is she to the inquisitor? The other three arrests are entirely comprehensible now that he knows the two merchants are suspected spies and the Dutchman is an active de Witt sympathizer, but the midwife's arrest is perplexing. The idea that she might be an informant for the Spanish Netherlands has occurred to him, but it is too preposterous—and she would not be demeaning herself in a Jewish ghetto if that were the case. Besides, he believes her story. Even under extreme physical duress she managed to stay articulate.

Detlef has known many educated women, but it was always the kind of learning that showed itself through sophisticated banter at banquets or performance at the musical recitals held by the more affluent bürgers. It never comprised the discussion of ideas as dangerous as a democratic society or a Godless universe. But this Ruth bas Elazar Saul, she has the fire of a man, the intellectual discipline of a scholar and the stamina of a sage. He has never met anyone remotely like her. Strangely moved, he struggles to compartmentalize his feelings. Damn the sorceress! The thought of her permeates his sensibility like a bewitching scent. She cannot be allowed to die at the hands of the Inquisition.

The words of his father come back to him: Intelligence is power; it is the flame behind the spark of intrigue. Find out all the facts and stamp out the fire. Demystify.

Detlef spins the globe again, this time wildly. Then, restless, he throws open the door of his chambers and shouts for Groot.

Beer splashes across the chevalier's purple jacket. Laughing, he grabs the serving wench and pulls her onto his knee. The girl, little more than a child, pales as he thrusts his hand under her skirts. Immediately the madam of the establishment is there. A towering businesswoman with the severity of a chiseled warrior, she yanks the trembling maid away from the soldier and scolds the huge man as if he were a small boy. Then smiling provocatively she ushers into his presence a buxom blonde with ruddy cheeks and a generous cleavage visible above her tight blouse. Placated, the chevalier bows to the prostitute and with a graceful flourish invites her to drink with him. Before he has a chance to sit down a bottle of expensive wine is on the table.

The brothel, known as The Hunter's Sheath, lies just outside the city gates. An ancient building dating back to Roman times, it is located conveniently between the docks and the fish market, its patrons a happy mix of Catholic and Protestant, peppered with sailors and the resident troops from the military base at Mülheim. Inside, the dark oak paneling is decorated with the skulls of hundreds of deer: gifts of hunting trophies that allude to conquest from satisfied clients. Gothic candelabra hang low over tables covered in scarlet cloth, the cheap wax filling the atmosphere with a hazy scent designed to befuddle the senses and separate coin from purse.

The chevalier, a Flemish mercenary who knows no loyalty, glances at three men at a table in the corner. They are dressed in the drab clothes of bondsmen and for an idle moment he wonders if they are spies, then decides that even spies would not clothe themselves so appallingly. Distracted by a hand on his crotch he looks away, but if his curiosity were greater he would notice that the roughly stitched clothes do not fit the dignity of the tall blond man, and that the other two, although obviously underlings, have the distinct air of the church about them.

Detlef nods imperceptibly to the serving wench who immediately fills up the jug sitting before Inquisitor Solitario's secretary. Juan's face is already rosy and flushed but he is not quite drunk enough to lose the veneer of the diplomat.

"What about her?" He elbows Groot in the ribs and points to a tall thin girl whose black hair falls in lanky strands from under her cowl.

"Oh, I'm sure that she would be available, señor."

The young Spaniard stares longingly at the girl then sighs dramatically. Turning back to Detlef he announces in a wheedling tone, "Alas, the stipend the inquisitional court allows me is very meager."

"I think it only fair that the good cleric should sample the finest Cologne has to offer free of charge—do you not agree, Groot?"

"Indeed," Groot replies, sliding his hands around the younger man's shoulders. "They say she has a muscle that can milk a bull dry," he whispers hoarsely into his ear. The secretary practically salivates as he turns back to watch the woman weave her way through the revelers. Already he sees himself being ridden by white thighs, already he can feel her full breasts pressed against his face, taste her salt on his skin. "She could be under you in less than two wags of a dog's tail . . . for just a little information. Your good master, Monsignor Carlos Vicente Solitario . . . ?"

Juan takes his cue. "He is lower than the bastard son of a pox-ridden whore. A puritan bag of hypocrisy. Anything you want to know, it is yours," he replies with a certain relish.

Detlef, privately appalled at the ease with which the secretary betrays his employer, fills the Spaniard's jug again.

"The four arrests—three I understand, but the fourth . . ."

"The Jewess?" Juan bellows, now visibly drunk.

Detlef nods then leans forward. "Young master, it would be wise to keep your voice down. This establishment is patronized by the best and the worst of our esteemed citizens."

"Of course, of course. The first three, as you understand, are politic. The good Inquisitor Solitario dances to only two tunes: that of Pascual de Aragon the Inquisitor-General and of Emperor Leopold. But you must realize that the Inquisition is nervous, it knows it is an aging lion with broken teeth. It shares Leopold's dread that more of the Wittelsbach princes could defect to the Protestants, further reducing the territory of the Holy Roman Empire. This is why they have sanctioned Monsignor Solitario's activities, although he has dismayed even them with his cruelty. The old Catholic guard fears that the dream of a secular Republic could be infectious: the disease is spreading everywhere, even in France."

"But the midwife?"

"A personal vendetta. Her mother was Sara Navarro and the Navarro family were my master's Achilles heel . . . But maybe I divulge too much."

He falls momentarily into a solemn reverie and with a wry smile Detlef realizes that his drunkenness is part artifice. The canon gestures to the tall brunette; within seconds she is at their table.

"The gentleman is a visitor and would like to sample some of our famous Rhineland hospitality."

He addresses the girl using the polite form and the quaint formality coupled with his unnerving beauty actually makes the prostitute blush. With a hesitant smile she sits down beside the grinning cleric and starts unbuttoning Juan's breeches as she prepares to slip under the table.

"But only after the gentleman has shared some invaluable information about his glorious nation," Detlef says, staying her hand. The girl immediately sits back, taunting the plainly tumescent secretary with her high breasts.

"The Navarros were once the wealthiest Marrano family in Aragon," the Spaniard continues, now stammering with excitement, "forced into conversion forty years ago. Solitario was the young friar who pursued them with a vengeance after he had been in their employment as a music tutor. My master's gift for music is surpassed only by his gift for sadism."

He leans forward; the scent of cheap musk mixed with the smell of wine wafts over Detlef, sickening him. "There were rumors of an attempted rape and of a great love scorned. Whatever his motives, our good friar was determined to denounce the Narravos, which he did, and for his troubles was rewarded with the enviable position of inquisitor. The family were charged with being secret Jews, devil worshippers and sorcerers. The father, an eminent diamond merchant, perished denouncing himself on the rack, the mother was burned, the son—a youth of fifteen—died by his own hand before they had a chance to arrest him. Only the daughter, Sara, escaped, but not before Solitario had interrogated her and left his mark upon her body. And what a body. They used to say that the diamond that shone brightest in Señor Navarro's coffers was his daughter. She was as beautiful as the moon and as mysterious as the sea."

"Sir, your sonnet making is as wondrous as a bucket of night soil," Groot interjects impatiently. "How did the daughter escape?"

"They say she bribed the prison guards with a huge diamond of her father's. Smuggled in her undergarments." To emphasize the point he thrusts his hand under the skirt of the girl beside him, who squeals musically but does nothing to resist.

"Where did the good woman flee to?" Detlef asks.

"To Holland where she converted back to Judaism, much to Solitario's chagrin. Fuck him, he's a miserly bastard with about as much love of humanity as a goat turd."

"Now that simile shows true poetic talent."

The two clerics break into full belly laughs of mutual admiration, splattering wine at each other in their drunken mirth. Juan suddenly lurches forward and grabs the collar of Detlef's smock.

"My master struck a deal with the emperor himself. He went to Vienna with the permission of the Grand Inquisitional Council to forge new relations between Austria and Spain. He knew Heinrich was a thorn in Leopold's side so he offered to kill four birds with a single arrow: the French spies, the secret Republican and the witch."

"So our misanthropic friend plans to avenge himself on the daughter because he failed to destroy the mother?" Detlef muses.

"Mark my words, the old bastard will torture her to the brink of her life then torture her some more. And whatever she confesses, I swear on my own mother's life: the Jewess will burn."

"But she remains under the jurisdiction of Cologne?" the canon ventures.

"That won't save her. Besides the witchcraft they say she is an associate of the heretic Benedict Spinoza and the Dutch antiroyalist Franciscus van den Enden. By burning her Monsignor Solitario scores two points with one sorceress. Anyway, what do you care? She is just a Jewish peasant. Let the old bastard have his fun, maybe it'll get him off our backs. And now I believe I am more than ready to sample some Rhenish delight." He pushes back his chair and struggles to his feet.

Detlef tosses several Reichstaler toward the whore who, sensing his authority, scoops them up with a reverent air. Steadying the Spaniard with one arm she guides him to the back stairs which lead to the tiny bedchambers above. Just before they disappear she turns and gives Detlef a cheeky wink.

The canon reaches for the Rheinwein and pours himself a large glass. He drinks it down in one long gulp. Tonight he wants to get drunk, to lose himself. Groot watches, curious; he has never seen his master like this. Excited at the possibility of a new vulnerability to be exploited he immediately fills Detlef's glass again.

"Sire, should I make inquiries about whether the good Merchant Ter Lahn von Lennep is at sea? It could be that his fine lady is in need of spiritual reassurance . . ."

"Why not. Although tonight I believe it is I who is in need of spiritual reassurance."

"Such enlightenment, they say, may be found—although momentarily—in both cunt and flask. Not that I would know," Groot finishes piously.

Depressed, Detlef reaches for the bottle again. There have been many occasions when the complexities and hypocrisies of his church have challenged his faith, but the romantic within him yearns still for the exhilaration of unquestioning belief. To be a priest of a small parish somewhere in the Rhineland, unhindered by the machinations of power, a simple shepherd of souls, this was the life he imagined as a boy; not the convoluted strategies of domination in which men are sacrificed for political gain. Even the plain language of Luther, which dignifies the ordinary man, seems attractive to him at this moment.

Is he suddenly finding his principles again, he wonders, and drains his goblet in an effort to banish any more outrageous notions. His mistress will, at least, provide a distraction.

Two hours later he is with her, the darkened bedchamber heavy with oriental musk and the scent of their bodies. He is between her thighs, pounding with a violence entirely out of character. Birgit, wrapping her legs around his back, arches herself up to embrace him further.

There is a desperation to his lovemaking that estranges her; with each thrust she is taken out of the moment and left pondering.

For the first time her lover is not concerned with her pleasure but rides his own, oblivious. With renewed fury he reaches a climax and shouts out, abandoning their usual protocol of silence. Then he rolls away, turning his back to her. She waits, taking perverse pleasure in observing the emotional gulf that seems to widen between them with each breath. When she can bear it no longer she reaches out and forces him to roll back toward her. Tentatively she nestles on his damp shoulder and listens to his wildly pounding heart.

"I'm sorry," he whispers. "I am no longer worthy of your affections."

For a moment Birgit cannot speak for the fear of loss which grips her. Feeling as if she is falling off the edge of a precipice she hesitates, searching for the right strategy.

"My love, you will always be worthy."

"But where will this lead us, Birgit? There is no longer any redemption in our affection. There is nothing but a mutual indulgence of cynicism, a shared condemnation of the pretensions of our world, and yet we ourselves are the very embodiment of such artifice."

At this she sits upright; never has Detlef spoken so plainly.

"We have joy, wit, humor and immense pleasure," she replies carefully, painfully aware of the risk she takes with every spoken revelation. "Surely this is justification enough?"

"I no longer know."

Birgit, staring into the dark, wonders about her new adversary. Is it a flesh and blood woman or a sudden wave of Puritanism which has possessed her lover like a demon?

Dear Benedict,

I am still incarcerated, although the thin gruel has been supplemented with some aged mutton. I fear this concession is merely to keep me alive long enough to torture a confession out of me. I have been officially charged and know I shall be subjected to the cruelest of interrogations. I can hear the cries of the poor men who were arrested with me, but strangely my isolation is more immediately terrifying. Here in this solitude I begin to forget who I am and what I am. The perimeters of my very existence blur into the damp and the gray light in which nothing is distinct. I keep my sanity through philosophizing, by working your thesis over and over.

If, as you suggest, God does not willfully direct the course of nature then my imprisonment and probable martyrdom occur for no good reason in the greater fabric of destiny. I try to comfort myself with your argument that human beings have a biological need to believe that God acts with purpose, for they themselves are under the illusion that they act with free will.

We are ignorant of the true causes of things, only aware of our own desire to pursue what is useful to us. We delude ourselves by thinking that we are free and that all our actions are guided by what is useful to us. We even have the arrogance to think that God must willfully guide external events for our benefit, since we cannot guide Destiny ourselves . . .

I know you carry this treatise further by suggesting that the Divine does not act with a purpose but that only the most perfect of God's acts are those closest to him. By this argument I deduce that my imprisonment is too removed from God to have any meaning directly to God himself. In that case, why am I? And what meaning has my life and my death?

Such musings keep me teetering on the right side of madness . . .

———

Composing the letter in her mind to comfort herself, Ruth imagines Benedict Spinoza sitting in his small cottage in Rijnsburg, can almost see his narrow handsome face illuminated with passion and hear his low voice with its melodious Portuguese overtones.

"Ruth . . ." A familiar voice sounds softly in the dark.

For a moment she fears that the solitude has finally caused her senses to slip into hallucination. She swings around.

Rosa, her old nursemaid, clutching a candle over her head, squints blindly into the cell. "My child, are you in there? Or have you perished in such filth?"

In her haste to respond the midwife stumbles and falls. Rosa kneels and tries to squeeze her fleshy arms through the bars to reach her.

"What have they done to you?" she whispers in Spanish.

The guard, a massive youth with a shaven head, steps out of the shadows, keys rattling. He pushes the nursemaid away brusquely and opens the gate.

"Speak German otherwise I shall have to imprison you as a spy. And we wouldn't want that, would we?" He guffaws and slaps Rosa good-naturedly on the backside.

"Watch who you are talking to!" she snaps, to Ruth's amazement, then steps into the cell as casually as if she were entering a market stall. Shaking his head the guard locks the gate behind her.

"You have fifteen minutes, Rosa, no more, no less. I'll not lose my head for some old Jewish sow." Placing his lantern on the ground he leaves.

Ruth stands paralyzed, frightened that if she moves the nursemaid might vanish like Aaron's specter.

Rosa barely recognizes the bag of bones crouching before her with its mop of hair and burning eyes. Fearing that Ruth might have lost her sanity the old woman speaks first, pointing in the direction of the departed guard.

"I have broken bread with his mother, she is a good woman."

Then, unable to contain herself, she pulls Ruth into a tight embrace. "Have fortitude," she whispers, this time in Yiddish, hiding the shock she feels at Ruth's shrunken figure and the unbearable stench of her unwashed body.

Ruth, held by those strong arms, the first intimate touch she has had in weeks, bursts into tears. Rosa rocks her until the sobbing has stopped.

"Think of this as a dream and it too shall pass. In the meantime I have something a little more practical . . ."

She pulls a loaf of challah from under her cloak and a small sealed clay bowl of harissa, a savory wheat and meat porridge enriched with melted fat and cinnamon. Ruth falls on the food and Rosa, stroking her matted hair, watches her eat.

"Your father seeks an audience with the archbishop. Herman Hossern, the moneylender, has some outstanding debts to be paid by Heinrich himself—he has agreed to waive them for your release. It is a gamble but better than nothing."

Ruth wipes her mouth with the back of her hand. She is ashamed to be seen like this, so dirty and demeaned.

"Why? Herman Hossern has shown no love of me before." She is suspicious of the moneylender's sudden generosity. Hossern is notorious throughout Deutz for his ruthlessness and misanthropy.

"It is not for you, rather out of respect for your father. Besides, remember that Tuvia is his nephew and the only male heir."

"Is Tuvia pushing his suit?" Ruth asks. The image of the rake-thin young man comes to her mind, his face an acrobatic mask of unfortunate twitches.

Rosa pauses, recognizing an old stubbornness. She realizes that the young woman's huge strength lies in her willpower and spirit, that Ruth is an idealist not a pragmatist. The ramifications of such passion make her fear for both Ruth's safety and her soul. If only there was more of the mother and less of the father in the child. Sara was a survivor, a woman who would adapt and disguise her motives to secure freedom at any cost. But Rosa cannot speak of such things for fear of shattering the young woman's illusions about her mother.

"Child, your father has given his consent and blessing."

"But he cannot!"

"He is an old man, your imprisonment is destroying him. He believes that once you are released you will be safe under the strong guiding hand of a husband. It will be an arranged marriage, like the one you should have made so many years ago."

"It will not!" Ruth cannot hide her anger.

"I see they have not entirely broken your spirit. Maybe there is some meat left on the bone under all that filth."

"Forgive me, I stink, I know it. I cannot bear my own stench. I would kill a man for a river to wash in."

"I would kill a man for a lot less. But my child, listen closely, you must understand that the community is divided. There are many who have spoken out against you: they say you will bring a new pogrom upon us, as bad as St. Bartholomew's night, that all will be driven from their houses and slaughtered. Your father still has influence, but marriage with Tuvia will convince the people that you are no longer a heretic, that you will abide by the laws of the Torah and become a dutiful wife and queen of your own household, God bless."

Rosa, carried away by her own rhetoric, starts to imagine a new era of stability and fecundity in the Saul household, sees herself nursing Ruth's children on her knee. The young woman interrupts her reverie.

"My father must be confident of my release to have arrived at such an arrangement."

"Your father has nothing left but his faith. He is ailing. If you saw how attentive Tuvia is, nursing him day and night, you would not be so quick to judge."

"Perhaps I can postpone the betrothal for as long as possible."

"But not forever."

"I will consider it."

Rosa kisses her. "Now you are using the head on your shoulders."

Ruth smiles to see Rosa's hands weaving patterns in the air as she speaks. The nursemaid is so utterly familiar, it is as if she has swept Ruth's happier past right into the prison cell with her.

"And what of Miriam, is she with the living?" Ruth suddenly asks, guilty that she has forgotten her assistant.

"She lives but has not spoken since the rape. 'Tis a pity, she will not find a husband now. She is living with us until your release. Fear not, she will be taken care of." Rosa lowers her voice. "The charge is of witchcraft, is it not?"

"I am accused of lying with the devil for the promise of a good birthing. I am accused of poisoning cattle, of levitation. I am accused of bewitching two small babes, of consorting with the demon Lilith—"

Rosa breathes in sharply. "Of Lilith you must say nothing," she whispers, as if the evil spirit herself is eavesdropping. Somewhere in the distance a gate clanks shut. The old nurse draws closer. "We haven't very long, child, but listen—I know this man, the inquisitor, from Aragon. He worked as a tutor in your grandfather's house. He was the Judas that destroyed your mother's family, and would have destroyed her if she had not had her wits about her."

"He murdered my mother's family?"

Ruth feels nauseous as she remembers the glint of hatred in the Spaniard's eyes.

"Betrayed them, all of them, after they had extended their friendship to him."

"But Rosa, how is it possible that the Inquisition can ride into Deutz and arrest me? They have no power over the Jewish quarter."

The nursemaid stares into Ruth's eyes, innocent in their confusion, then takes her hand.

"Ruth, you were baptized."

Stunned, Ruth can barely absorb the information. "Baptized? How?"

"It was many years ago when you were a small baby. There was rumor of another pogrom and Sara was petrified. You have to understand that she had seen her own father tortured, her mother burned at the stake. She couldn't bear the idea of you suffering too." Rosa's voice falters. "She just wanted to protect you in case the Christian soldiers came . . ."

"Does my father know?"

"He learned of it at your arrest—the news has devastated him. Sara made me swear on her deathbed never to tell him. I was the only witness. Child, you must find it in your heart to forgive her; it was the desperate act of a terrified woman who wished only for her baby to survive. You see now why you should marry Tuvia—he will have you regardless and it will make the community accept you again."

"If I am freed . . ."

"Understand, you are in extreme peril. When the inquisitor looks at you, he sees your mother. You must placate him as long as you can, for he will push for the pyre. It is the only way your father will have enough time to negotiate for your life. There have already been soldiers at the house, searching for evidence."

"My mother's Zohar?" Ruth barely mouths the word; to be overheard would be immediate verification of the charges and an instant death sentence.

"It is safe," Rosa assures her, "but promise me: whatever Solitario does to you, you must not confess to being a witch or carrying out any heretical practices. A confession will immediately condemn you and then nothing your father can do will save you."

"This I know already."

Footsteps sound in the passageway and the guard shouts for Rosa.

"Believe, my child. Faith is the food of survival."

The nursemaid pulls Ruth to her in one last embrace.

The archbishop of Cologne strides through the narrow dirty streets of his diocese and into the Streitzeuggasse where the silk banner of the armorers' guild hangs proudly overhead and the tiny shops are packed with a huge variety of shields, swords and weaponry. The constant pounding of the blacksmiths' hammers, the shouts of the men trading information about the latest military conflict, the wheezing of the bellows and the pealing of church bells all blend into a medley of impossible noise. Which is precisely why Maximilian Heinrich has chosen the street: the cacophony is exactly what he needs to think.

Behind him, his two assistants struggle to keep up, mincing carefully around the pig shit and the abandoned pieces of twisted metal from the forges, anxiously wondering which latest political drama possesses their master.

Heinrich, a large man, is famous for trebling his pace when riddled with apprehension. The clerics have cause to worry. He has just come from the Church of the Assumption, Saint Rosa Himmelfahrt, the domain of the Jesuits, where he had a reluctant audience with the head of the college, a stiff old priest called Father Hummerlich. A Prussian zealot, proud veteran of the Thirty Years' War and a vehement Luther-hater, Hummerlich has expressed deep concern about the arrests. He wants the trials and the executions to be carried out quickly. Always searching for the political advantage, the Jesuit sees the public condemnation of the three secret Lutherans as an opportunity to galvanize Cologne's lax Catholic community.

"We must show the people that the true and only way to redemption is by confession and atonement. We must pay for our sins: indulgences are a necessary evil. These traitors cannot be allowed to live among us, in the heart of the community, all the while secretly practicing the dreadful blasphemies of that man . . ." The priest, face flushed with vitriol, was unable to complete his sentence.

Heinrich, enjoying the old man's frustration, waited a full minute before putting him out of his misery.

"That man Luther?" The archbishop had rolled his tongue around the name with relish, Jesuit-baiting being one of his favorite pastimes.

"Exactly," Hummerlich had fired back.

"But Father, the two Cologne merchants have been accused of wizardry as well as being secret Protestants. Not forgetting the Jewess . . ."

"The Jewess is irrelevant. You and I both know the sorcery charges are a sham. What I want to know is what you, as the highest anointed official of the Catholic Church in this city, are going to do about it?"

Heinrich's ears are still ringing with the Jesuit's fury and he has come away with a splitting headache. All in all the situation is a catastrophe. On the one hand he has the Jesuits and every other Catholic fanatic bellowing for blood; on the other he has the Gaffeln demanding leniency for the arrested merchants. And that is without taking into consideration the secular politics of the situation. Damn the Dutch, and the French, and damn Leopold and his cronies—especially that oily sadist Solitario, the archbishop thinks.

The Spaniard's latest atrocity is to dust off the cathedral's copy of the infamous *Malleus Maleficarum, The Hammer of the Witches*, a textbook for the identification, prosecution and dispatching of those suspected of sorcery, written by two German Dominicans, Henricus Institor and Jacob Sprenger, in 1487. Solitario actually had the audacity to tell Heinrich that he was honoring Cologne by referring to the tome. Privately the archbishop is appalled. Poor van Dorf and Voss are already half-dead from the rigorous methods of detection pulled from the book.

As a consequence, the entire Voss family, including several bawling babies in arms, have been camped outside Heinrich's chambers for the past week. The young Müller sons are rumored to be in Paris, attempting to gain an audience with King Louis himself; meanwhile Heinrich and von Fürstenberg live in fear that Herr Müller will confess their involvement in his secret activities for the French and condemn them both. In short the whole situation is shaping up to be untenable.

The archbishop kicks out at a mangy kitten which has sidled up to him.

What should he do? Who can he turn to? He trusts no one, least of all von Fürstenberg, who was responsible for planting Müller into the guilds to begin with. Müller—really a Frenchman called Metain—was recruited some fifteen years before and Heinrich had become so accustomed to receiving the clandestine information he had actually forgotten the dangers surrounding his emissary. Without the spy he feels disadvantaged, as if he is missing both his ears and his eyes. After all, the archbishop needs all the information he can get, considering that he is not allowed to remain in the city longer than three days without permission from the bürgers.

What are the guilds actually up to, he wonders. It is impossible to keep track of the machinations of all twenty-two subdivisions of the Gaffeln, damn them. And barely one of them pro-French or supportive of the aristocracy, yet all united in their hatred of the archbishop. And now Müller, a royalist, is paradoxically accused of being a secret Protestant and worse; a supporter of Jan de Witt's Republican party. Understandably Müller is furious and has already demanded an audience with the archbishop and his Machiavellian minister; Heinrich knows it is to demand a pardon they cannot afford to give. Yes, it is a dangerous, ridiculous situation but something will have to be done, and swiftly.

Frustrated, he looks heavenward and is further aggravated to see the town hall tower, a structure built by the triumphant bürgers with confiscated money from the banished patrician families. To Heinrich the sight is a constant and irritating reminder of his own impotence.

Tap-tap, something brushes against his leg. He looks down to see a dirty fleshy stump being held up for his inspection. A cripple, probably a war victim, squats in the gutter begging for alms. Heinrich, feeling anything but charitable, knocks the pewter jug out of the man's hand. Coins go flying as the archbishop continues his excursion.

His two assistants hurriedly collect the scattered money and placate the wheedling beggar with a few Reichstaler of their own, while several onlookers watch disapprovingly.

Heinrich pushes open the wooden door of the chapel of Saint Severin. A simple place of worship, devoid of the baroque trappings of the Church of the Assumption or the Gothic ambition of the cathedral itself, it is Heinrich's personal haven. The small chapel has an asceticism which appeals to his Bavarian sensibility: its white walls, plain wooden pews and unadorned altar speak of humility and an honest spirituality which Heinrich secretly craves.

He nods at one of the nuns and swiftly makes his way toward the altarpiece, a plain wooden carving of the crucifixion. Heinrich particularly likes this depiction of Jesus: the face is the most realistic he has ever seen, carved with the heavy Germanic features he feels his own visage mirrors. This is a man he recognizes, a man who, like himself, has been confronted with the complex and compromising politics of his time, but through spiritual enlightenment has transcended and triumphed. It is a comforting allegory the archbishop returns to often.

He crosses himself then kneels carefully, delicately balancing his goutridden knee on the cold stone. Resting his elbows on a low rail he presses his hands together in prayer. The light streams across his shaved pate and a cloud of incense smoke hangs for an instant above him, suspended.

An hour later he is still there. Awed, his two assistants whisper with the nun at the back of the church. They have never seen their master so observant. In reality the venerable archbishop, lulled by the tranquillity of the chapel and the rare winter sun falling on the back of his neck, has fallen asleep.

He dreams that he is talking with the Lord Jesus, Our Savior. The Galilean, dressed rather confusingly in Parisian court clothes, is advising him to stop worrying about loaves and instead place his faith in blood. Heinrich is moved to tears by the profundity of the statement, which, just a little too late, he realizes he has absolutely no understanding of at all.

Confused, he looks up and is struck by the radiance surrounding the Savior's head. It is not the complex light he had always imagined, but a light he recognizes from his early childhood: the luminosity of his mother's breast as he was feeding there, or perhaps the light shining through the skin of her womb while he lay waiting to be born; whatever the source, it distracts him completely and he forgets to ask Jesus the exact meaning of his parable, despite the twinkle in the Galilean's eyes.

"Your highness?" The wheedling tone of his assistant jolts the archbishop rudely awake.

"What now?"

Heinrich stands, wrestling with the pain which shoots through his body as he shifts his weight.

"The father of the midwife, the chief rabbi, is waiting. He begs for an audience."

The archbishop glances at the chapel door and glimpses Elazar hovering outside, his apprehensive face peering into the shadows. Dressed in traditional robes he looks like the archetypal Jew banned from the Christian temple. Heinrich can only imagine the humiliations the rabbi must have experienced to travel unaccompanied from Deutz into Cologne. Even from this distance Heinrich can see his prayer shawl is muddy and that the old man is fighting exhaustion.

"He won't take no for an answer," the priest adds unnecessarily.

Sighing, Heinrich hobbles to the entrance. He knows the rabbi will not cross the threshold, out of respect and superstition. As the archbishop moves between the pews he tries to compose a rational explanation for the arrest of Ruth bas Elazar Saul.

Over the years he has grown to admire the rabbi's dry wit and gift for strategy. The old man is also a potential ally. His Dutch colleagues are strong supporters of William of Orange—all Jews are royalists, Heinrich reminds himself. This makes the two of them bedfellows, admittedly strange ones. He is unaware that this is an illusion Elazar has been quick to exploit.

"My poor dear man." Heinrich grasps the rabbi's trembling hands. "You must be freezing. Come, come."

With an imperious wave the archbishop dismisses the curious town guards who have followed the old Jew through the icy streets. He ushers Elazar into a small chamber behind the chapel and after helping the old man into a chair sends the nun out for a jug of ale.

Elazar, his long nose purple with cold and the rest of his face shining a ghostly white, cannot quite believe he has made the journey. Anger and desperation have driven him to this place, but now that he is actually here the long supplications he has composed during the dark days since his daughter's arrest abandon him. He is speechless. A huge shudder passes through his frail body.

Heinrich, ever observant and in a particularly benevolent mood since his celestial discourse, again takes the old man's long pale hands between his own.

"Rabbi, we may be of different faiths but we are both spiritual men. I suggest that we pray together—a prayer for clarity and control in a difficult situation over which even I have no jurisdiction."

And with that both men lower their heads and begin two prayers: one in Hebrew, the other in Latin; one an entreaty for leniency, the other for political grace. The two ancient tongues curl around one another in a strange onomatopoeic dance, then float up to the ceiling to settle between the carved rafters like sacred smoke.

The nun returns and, intimidated by their meditations, leaves the two pewter jugs of ale on a side table and glides silently away. The aroma distracts the archbishop and makes his stomach rumble most irreverently.

"Amen," he hurriedly finishes, fearing that the Hebrew litany might drag on. Elazar opens one eye and, taking the archbishop's cue, cuts short his devotion.

"Between you and me, I fear that God is deaf," Heinrich whispers conspiratorially as he hands the rabbi his beer. But Elazar is beyond humor.

"With all due respect, he may not be deaf but from my side of the Rhine he definitely does not understand Hebrew," he replies with barely a smile.

There is a pause. Heinrich, marveling at the renewed sense of faith he is experiencing since his metaphysical encounter, is inspired to extend his benevolence once again.

"Many, many apologies, my friend. The arrest was beyond my control. Even the archbishop of Cologne has a higher power to answer to. I am so sorry."

Elazar, frightened by the unusual warmth and familiarity Heinrich is displaying, begins to shake so violently that he spills ale on his tallith.

"She is my only child, sire, the last light of my life."

"And a good midwife, I hear."

"Too good. If she had kept to her own this would never have happened."

"If the charge were less serious—bribery, theft, perhaps—I could talk to the bürgermeister, but sorcery . . ."

"She is innocent!"

"Do you doubt the wisdom and judgment of the Grand Inquisitional Council as well as that of the Holy Emperor Leopold himself?"

Elazar hesitates, sensing a trap.

"It would not be my place to query such a venerable institution, but my daughter is not a witch."

"Of that I am sure, Herr Saul, but as I indicated before, the matter is out of my hands."

Heinrich stands, signaling that the audience is over, but the rabbi does not move.

"Listen to me, your highness, I have an offer."

"Forgive me, rabbi, but you are in no position to make offers."

"There is money owed." Elazar is unable to keep the desperate tone out of his voice.

Immediately Heinrich sits back down. The loans the archbishop has taken out with Herr Hossern, the Jewish moneylender, are confidential and have gone toward funding his secret efforts to reinstate the Rhineland aristocracy. They are also substantial.

"Go on."

"Herr Hossern is prepared to waive the full five hundred Reichstaler in exchange for my daughter's release."

"All of it?"

"I give you my word of honor. All the debts will be void; more than that, there will be no talk of the debts prior to the exchange or afterward."

Heinrich, tempted, watches Elazar's hands twist in his lap. The cancelation of the monies owed would save him a great deal of potential embarrassment. Although he hates to be accountable to the Jews, an annulled debt would be a straight barter and that notion is very attractive. Swiftly he runs through the possible ramifications: the inquisitor is determined, of that there is no doubt, but perhaps he can override him and make a direct petition to Vienna.

"Please, Archbishop, I appeal to your humanity. My daughter is everything to me."

The rabbi reaches out and grasps a fold of the archbishop's robe, a gesture full of humility. Heinrich is suddenly embarrassed for him.

"Give me a week. In the meantime I promise I shall find every imaginable excuse to prevent the Spaniard beginning his pitiful 'interrogation.'"

Heinrich walks Elazar to the door.

"God bless you in all your endeavors." The old rabbi clasps the archbishop's hand but declines to kiss the proffered ring.

"And may he bless you too, Elazar ben Saul."

Dear Benedict,

You describe yourself as the apostle of Reason, but here it is diffi- cult to see any reason in my fellow men. You have portrayed the fear of Hell as the greatest fallacy of all—a profound lie which cripples the destinies of men and keeps them fearful of taking their lives into their own hands. Here now I see that the life we lead is Gehenna. I exist in it now; there is nothing left to me but the act of grappling with my fears and the incessant inhalation of breath, yet despite all deprivations I keep living.

Remember when you told me that you were expected to reject Reason the very same way the Inquisition forced the rabbis who excommunicated you to reject their Judaism? Now I am expected to reject my beliefs and my heritage and choose a compromised life over a truthful death. I will choose death. Is this rational?

If God is all things—Nature itself—am I not just choosing to dissolve back into nothingness, a nebulous substance that is even less than a soul without a body?

As you see, my doubts have become my demons. My frailty appalls me. It is easy to theorize when one is not confronted with the rack, or worse. My guard has told me that even the Inquisition cannot stomach my persecutor's inhuman appetites. I can but hope that when the torturer begins his hideous art, my mind and conscious body will leave me.

Pray to your reasonable God for me.

In living faith, your good friend,

"Felix van Jos"

The corridor of the dungeon is a hellish jigsaw of long sinister shadows. Above, bats shift uneasily in their baggy leather skins. Like dazed lunatics the nesting creatures squeal as the moving torches beneath illuminate the hidden corners.

It is a somber procession. The dignified priest leads the way, his white robes and solemn face suggesting an office of great importance. A cleric follows, an ancient tome tucked beneath his arm, the quill of the scholar hanging from his neck in a goatskin pouch. A page trails behind, struggling with a viola da gamba, its polished chestnut body glowing in the candlelight. Bringing up the rear is a very different monster, a squat muscular man wearing a rough barras jerkin covered by a barvell. His gnarled forearms are bare and scarred as if he has seen service in the Great War. Could he be a soldier? A blacksmith? Or a bondsman of some exotic guild? The leather apron suggests that he needs to protect himself from something. Fire? Hot oil? Scalding water? And why is he hooded, his eyes barely visible through the neatly stitched slits?

A mysterious procession indeed. One could almost think it funereal, except the corpse is living, a terrified human being, half-dragged, half-stumbling between two guards.

Ruth can barely feel the stones beneath her naked feet. Terror has loosened her bowels and overridden both shame and pride. To stop herself fainting she recites a prayer her father taught her as a child. It flaps around her mind like one of the prison's maddened bats, but the sounding of the words gives her courage and keeps her from collapsing.

The guard on her right glances nervously at his comrade. He fears that the mumbled Hebrew is an incantation and he shall be struck down by a dreadful curse which will render him lame or deaf or, worst of all, blind. But his companion, older and well seasoned in the eccentricities of the condemned, seems oblivious to the Jewess's wild-eyed dread. The lad, pressed into service by dint of poverty, straightens his back and tries to dispel his own qualms by concentrating on the authoritarian stride of the Dominican walking before him. If she has been arrested by the church, then it must be just, he thinks. And so with new confidence he supports Ruth's impossibly narrow shoulders with his own broad frame as they frogmarch her to the torture chamber.

They arrive at a heavy door. Beyond it is a low cellar with a vaulted ceiling. Sawdust is scattered on the floor, some of it rusty with dried blood. Hanging from the ceiling in the center of the room is an iron cage with metal straps to wrap around the torso. A large wooden rack stands in a corner with a vertical wheel, a good nine feet in diameter, next to it.

The guards lower Ruth gently into a large chair in the middle of the room. She stares at the outlandish iron and wooden contraptions: dormant, they look strangely innocent, like huge deviant toys thrown carelessly into a corner by a giant two-year-old.

"The flaying wheel, the torture rack, the iron maiden, the dunking bench," she whispers to herself in Latin, as if by naming each instrument she may strip it of its power.

Although she knows of these tools of horror, she has never seen them before. She recalls the mumbled stories she heard in the past from the broken visitors her father sometimes received in his parlor. He would stroke their maimed hands paternally while, beyond sentiment and in shock, they recounted in emotionless monotones the atrocities that had been inflicted upon their bodies. They came seeking some kind of redemption from the rabbi, in the desperate hope that with his blessing the memories would miraculously vanish from their mutilated minds. Now it is she who is faced with an interrogation that she knows will alter her forever.

Suddenly Ruth notices that her knees are shaking violently. She rolls her fear up into a tight ball and pushes it down into the pit of her stomach, where it is sickening but somehow controllable.

The inquisitor draws up a chair very close to her face. She can feel his breath upon her skin, a revolting mixture of cloves and indigestion. He stares straight into her eyes. His long reddish nose displays the bulbous damage inflicted by syphilis, each pore visible, white hair curling out of the nostrils. His neat goatee beard is streaked with gray and a cut from a shaving blade is visible on one side of his chin. The dark red scar on his cheek is beaded with tissue and his small dark brown eyes have a curious yellow aura around the pupils. They are eyes that speak of absolutely nothing and it is this gaze that makes her feel violated, as if he is trying to penetrate her physically. She realizes that he is utterly convinced of the integrity of his mission and for a reason she cannot fathom this revelation fills her with shame. Finally she turns away.

"Do you know what this is?" The Dominican thrusts an old leather-bound book before her.

"Obviously a manuscript of ancient origin."

Ruth uses sarcasm in a vain attempt to keep fear out of her voice.

"Indeed, a most valuable manuscript: a set of instructions on how to uncover the hidden evil in the *feminine demonitus*. Written by two learned ecclesiastics—fellow Rhinelanders, I believe—the book is called *Malleus Maleficarum . . .*"

"*The Hammer of the Witches,*" Ruth automatically finishes. Her Latin, taught to her by her father and then Franciscus van den Enden, is flawless.

"Exactly, and it has proven most enlightening during the interrogation of your fellow prisoners. We have already extracted a confession from the Dutchman and Meister Voss is on the brink of redemption."

"If he had a tongue to redeem himself with," the hooded man adds with a guttural laugh.

"I believe you have not been formally introduced to Herr Bull?"

The man makes the politest of bows, its grace a striking juxtaposition with his muscular body.

"Herr Bull is a master craftsman. He has worked on both sides of the North Sea and was, I believe, in the employment of Cromwell during the occupation of Ireland. Naturally he has no political or spiritual allegiances. He also has mastered some Spanish—"

"*El potro* and *la garrucha*, the rack and pulley," Herr Bull interrupts proudly, his Spanish a thick-accented abomination. Carlos smiles patronizingly then turns back to Ruth.

"You are a lucky woman to be in the hands of such a cultured professional."

"Fräulein, be assured that I am infamous for bringing a man to the very brink of death then resurrecting him only to take him to further ecstasy. Of course there have been a few mistakes, but in the main I can guarantee a long and arduous journey that will leave your very innards twitching." With another bow Herr Bull steps back into the shadows.

"A poet not of the tongue but of the screw; but let us not dally any further. Juan, please begin."

The secretary removes a small scroll from his sleeve, unrolls it and reads aloud.

"Ruth Navarro, you stand accused of one count of consorting with the devil and the demon Lilith, two counts of murder with the use of witchcraft, and five counts of sorcery. Do you have anything to say in your defense?"

"This is most unorthodox. Am I not to stand trial?"

"An interrogation gives you the benefit of redeeming your soul before you have to go to trial. It is a natural sequence of events."

"I repeat: am I not to stand trial?"

"Not before interrogation."

"In that case, I have nothing to say except that I am innocent."

Her declaration hangs defiantly in the air for a second before being blown away by a hurricane of panic. She is amazed at her courage, but at the same time knows that any confession will condemn both her family and her people.

The inquisitor gestures to the guards who march her over to the dunking bench.

So it is to be the water, she thinks, and bites her tongue in an effort not to scream or betray herself with pleading.

They strap her to the wooden stool attached to the end of the plank. Swinging it out, they hold her precariously above the vat of icy liquid. Ruth stares down and sees her pale oval face reflected back: it is so blank with terror that she does not recognize herself. Instantly she is plunged in.

Breath is knocked out of her and a violent pain like the stabbing of a thousand knives jabs at her skin. The back of her brain is pierced by an ice-cold tongue of steel. She knows this is just the beginning, the glacial water rushing through her body. Blindly she struggles against the ropes, her eyes wide and staring up to the surface at the burning light beyond. Her lungs squeeze out the last remaining air but she dares not open her mouth. It feels as if her chest will explode with the agony of wanting to breathe. Somewhere in her half-conscious mind she knows that if she does she will drown.

Carlos reaches for his viola da gamba. With exquisite slowness he draws the bow across the cat-gut and begins to play a cantata once loved by Sara Navarro.

"You wish to take on the interrogation of the Jewess yourself? What on earth makes you think you have even the remotest qualification to become an inquisitor?"

Maximilian Heinrich leans back in his chair with a certain smugness, enjoying his cousin's uncharacteristic vulnerability.

Detlef has eyes only for the large timepiece behind the archbishop, the hour hand of which stands at just before sext. He is surprised at this compulsion to act. Heinrich is right. What is it about this woman that makes him feel as if he has embarked upon a crusade? As if she is the key that could liberate his world? The clock chimes, jolting him back into the moment. A sympathetic guard has told him that the midwife's interrogation started fifteen minutes earlier and Detlef, painfully aware of passing time, tries to concentrate on the archbishop.

"I am a canon, I can take confession. I am innately capable of recognizing evil just as I am of distinguishing innocence." He finishes his appeal with just the right amount of sincerity.

Heinrich arches one eyebrow, disbelieving. "Indeed, I am told that the pious Meisterin Ter Lahn von Lennep is often seen at your confessions, and I have no doubt that the penance you prescribed her has saved her soul—on more than one occasion."

The archbishop, pleased with his own wit, leans back—a gesture the surrounding entourage takes as permission to laugh. Detlef, ears burning, struggles to remain calm.

"Your excellency, I beg you: I have reason to believe that the inquisitor's motive is personal. The woman is still a German, even if she is a Jew and the daughter of a Spanish *converso*. I cannot believe she poses any threat to the Holy Empire as I truly do not believe she is a sorceress—but she is undeniably an obsession of the good monsignor. Unfortunately it turns out that the woman was baptized, a legality that has allowed the Inquisition to make their arrest."

"Detlef, your logic has become faulty. I have never known you to be politically simplistic. Perhaps the rabbi's daughter *is* a sorceress. Perhaps Monsignor Solitario is not the only man obsessed."

Again Detlef has to suffer the humiliation of ridicule as several of the younger clerics conceal their mirth behind their long sleeves. The hour hand shifts slightly across the clock face. Desperate now, he decides to gamble on how much the archbishop actually knows about Ruth bas Elazar Saul.

"Your highness, both you and I realize that the Sephardic community in Amsterdam is not without royal connections. I have heard that the young woman's mother was persecuted by a younger incarnation of the notorious friar and fled to the safety of the Netherlands. I have also heard rumors that she was held in high esteem within that community. The Jews in Amsterdam will not take kindly to her daughter's martyrdom—and neither will their moneylenders."

Heinrich flinches. Detlef seizes the opportunity and slams a further wedge into the crack.

"It would be impertinent of me to suggest that the cathedral could possibly be beholden to a Jewish moneylender, but if such a rumor should somehow be made public . . ."

There is silence as the archbishop toys with the idea that Detlef has, for once, overstepped his rank. But expediency supersedes pride. Heinrich stands heavily and walks over to the window. The afternoon is drawing to a close and shortly he must make his way by coach to Bonn. All roads seem to be leading to the same path. He wonders if there might be an elegant way of appointing Detlef as prosecutor and appeasing the emperor and the wretched woman's father. Really, all this fuss over a glorified Jewish peasant—it is so exasperating. The gout in his leg suddenly flares and he winces.

What advantage is Detlef seeking through the release of the Jewess? There must be a hidden stratagem he has not perceived. Surely Detlef cannot be acting out of genuine sentiment. Perhaps the rabbi's daughter is more than she appears. If so, what might be the political advantage—or disadvantage—should the archbishop choose to thwart the inquisitor? Heinrich's instinctive wisdom suggests that he play it out and see what happens. He will always be able to reinstate Solitario later if necessary.

Staring at the clock Detlef tries to control his increasing agitation.

Heinrich suddenly remembers his dream in front of the crucifix at Saint Severin. Christ instructed him to have faith in blood and stop worrying about the loaves. Suddenly all becomes clear: as his cousin, Detlef is blood. Could the loaves be Vienna—the inquisitor and all the other "dough" he has to answer to?

"I shall arrange for you to take over the interrogation of Ruth bas Elazar Saul for one month only and I shall challenge the Inquisition on their jurisdiction over her as the daughter of a *conservo* and Spanish citizen, even if she is baptized. My argument shall be that of nationhood: as a denizen of Cologne, the woman has the right to be tried here by Germans. It is a thin justification and will stall the zealot only temporarily but I have a plan to remove him entirely during the trial. Luckily for us, the roads from here to Vienna are still badly war-torn and the good Lord only knows what perils a messenger might face along the way."

Heinrich crosses himself piously. There is a rustle of starched linen and silk as his entourage follows suit.

"In that case, my good lord, I need your testimony immediately. Monsignor Solitario is this very moment at his handiwork and I fear the Jewess may not survive her first ordeal."

Surprised, Heinrich glances across at his assistant who nods. The archbishop claps his hands and a page runs forward with a quill and scroll. Pressing the document against the kneeling boy's back, Heinrich scrawls a hurried note and completes it with the flourish of his distinctive signature. After waving the ink dry and sealing it with a blob of crimson wax, he hands it to Detlef.

"Go, and God speed. I will not have the cathedral soiled by the blood of an innocent," he adds theatrically, relishing the role of moral campaigner.

But Detlef, not quite believing his easy victory, has already tucked the scroll into his cassock and is hurrying to the door. Groot follows, flushed with the exhilaration of his master's triumph.

❊

*B*urning. White splinters of pain.

Somewhere the sound of muffled music.

Ruth is about to surrender. She wants to stop hurting. Her body screams for release. Blinking, she peers up through the pale green light. The tender features of her mother push through the surface of the water, smiling down at her like the carved prow of a drowned ship. Sara is beckoning her: one breath and you are with me . . . come . . . come. Memories of her scent, her soft voice, the warmth of home, dance seductively across Ruth's mind. Just as she is about to breathe in, daggers of glass pierce every inch of her torso. The cold is so severe that she cannot think, her mind squeezing down into the last thread of basic instinct: do not breathe . . . do not breathe . . . For how much longer? Again her mother's face appears, a strand of Sara's hair slips from its cowl and spirals down toward Ruth, a shimmering ebony in the darkness. It is like Jacob's ladder. Ruth knows that if she can only reach out and take hold of it she will climb out of this pain, out of the cold and the darkness, into the safety of her mother's arms. All she need do is surrender, breathe in oblivion. Suddenly a congealing blob appears, floating suspended below her. As Ruth stares at it the mass reveals itself to be a knot of slippery eels writhing around each other in a frenzy. A white hand snakes out from the contorting fish. Lilith. Ruth twists wildly in her ropes but it is too late, the demon's face follows the hand, her huge eyes glowing, her fingers reaching for Ruth, grabbing at her flesh. Her mouth snaps open, teeth glistening; and she lunges for the bound woman.

The viola da gamba clasped between his knees, Carlos watches impassively as a bubble of blood breaks the surface of the dark water. He glances at the hourglass on the walnut table beside him: the sand ran out a full twenty seconds before. His bow trembles in the air before swooping down to begin another stanza.

Juan stares at the floor, watching a cockroach nibble at a clump of human hair with a fragment of skin still attached. It is his way of avoiding witnessing the dunking. A superstitious man who, despite bouts of promiscuity, takes the spiritual aspects of his vocation extremely seriously, the clerk is anxious for his soul. Will he be condemned for partaking even passively in such unholy investigations? He glances up for a second and is relieved to see Carlos finally signal to the torturer.

Herr Bull pushes down on the heavy wooden plank and Ruth's bound form bursts from the vat of freezing water. Rivulets run from the crown of her head and her long black hair is plastered down, her skin is a bluish-white and blood streams from her nostrils and ears. Her violet lips pull down in a grimace of pain as she breathes in a heaving gasp of air then vomits out a clear stream of bile. With the nonchalance of the professional, the torturer throws a bucket of warm water over her which sets her off in a convulsion of shivering.

The inquisitor thrusts a piece of parchment at her. "Confess, Ruth Navarro, and your soul shall be redeemed. Your agony will cease. Do not hide behind the nobility of silence; you are too intelligent to die for some misplaced loyalty. The evidence is indisputable. Why suffer any longer when I promise you not only salvation but sanctuary?"

"Sanct . . . sanct . . ." she stutters. Bowed over, each sound is a gasp between spasms of pain as more bile heaves through her body.

Carlos grabs hold of her wet slippery hair. It feels good to his touch, like cold silk. Her fragility, emphasized by the light weight of her skull, excites him. He yanks her head back.

"You are a witch, girl. Sign your confession."

Ruth merely stares blankly at him. Her pupils dilate as she wills herself away. Far away from this room filled with ugly men, far from the screams which she finally recognizes as her own.

Disgusted, the Dominican lets her hair go. Her head slams forward but she is still conscious.

"Dunk her again."

Herr Bull glances at Ruth's limp figure with a professional eye. "Sire, given the weight and size of the subject it would be advisable to wait five minutes for recuperation—"

"Dunk her!"

Herr Bull shrugs; the little friar's hysterics are beginning to irritate him. If they lose her now it'll serve the weaselly Spaniard right. There is an art to these things and it annoys him when his clients allow their emotions to interfere with his craft. Nevertheless, flexing his massive forearms he pushes down the plank. Ruth, still strapped to the chair at the other end, sails up into the air. The torturer swings the whole contraption back toward the vat and, with a swiftness that belies his control, again immerses the chair in the freezing water.

Carlos watches as Ruth's hair and tunic sink slowly after her, then turns the hourglass over.

The young guard who has been thinking about supper—a mutton stew spiced with caraway and chestnuts waiting for him at the house of his new lover (the wife of his landlord)—watches the water splash over the side of the tarred barrel. If the sorceress dies he will have to stand as witness when they make an official report back to the archbishop, which will take a couple of hours longer. The vision of the steaming stew being handed to him by his mistress, her plump bosom pushed up over her smock, becomes more and more distant. To his amazement he finds himself secretly praying that the witch will survive the interrogation.

The inquisitor takes the hourglass and cradles it in his lap. Through the crystal at the top he can see the granules of sand gathering and shifting as ripples of the moving mass beneath suck them into the vortex. Fascinated, he meditates on the instrument, musing how it is the perfect illustration of life. So many of man's actions appear to have no immediate consequence but, concealed, do their work until finally all catches up and forms a complex web of cause and effect—like this very instant, in which time and events have meshed so that he now holds in his hands the life of the daughter of the woman who almost destroyed his reason. Destiny is a thing of great elegance, he thinks, watching the last of the sand form a shallow pool, which becomes a sharp incline and finally a vacuum as the last grain tumbles through the narrow glass neck. But power is the greater aphrodisiac, he concludes.

"Sire, the girl will perish," Juan ventures nervously.

The inquisitor snaps out of his reverie and realizes that all present, even the guards, are staring at him. The page, his young face blank with shock, is doubled over in a bout of trembling. Carlos ignores him.

"She will not, her blood is stubborn. Trust me, I know her lineage."

"What is she—superhuman?" Herr Bull interjects, abandoning all protocol. "Because If she isn't, and you want me to do my job, we fish her out now else we'll be rolling in the coffin and the priest."

"We wait."

All turn back toward the glistening black water: the young guard worrying about his receding supper; the page trying not to shit himself; Juan, who wonders about Detlef's reaction when he hears of the Jewess's drowning; Herr Bull, appalled at the inquisitor's waste of a good craftsman; and the older guard who knows it will be he who must drag the corpse out of the barrel later and clean the vat.

If the Almighty wills it, she shall live. If he does not, she shall die, Carlos consoles himself. Part of him furtively longs for the spirit of the mother to appear to rescue the daughter. See, Sara, see where your child is now! Carlos, eyes closed, imagines the face of the Spanish woman as she gazes down at the floating black hair, her beauty wiped away by horror.

There is a pounding at the door. Before the inquisitor has a chance to gather his wits, several guards burst in followed by Detlef and Groot. For a moment the intruders stumble to a halt, overpowered by the stench of shit, urine and blood and the underlying smell of fear.

Detlef, peering into the shadows, thinks he must have arrived in a manifestation of Hell. The darkened chamber with its instruments of cruelty, the guilty look stretched across the inquisitor's face as if he has been caught indulging in some covert transgression, combine to disorientate the young canon. He stares frenziedly around the cell, wondering where they have hidden the midwife. It is only when Solitario steps in front of the dunking bench that Detlef, with a sickening lurch, realizes she is completely submerged.

"Release her!"

"On whose orders?"

Detlef knocks the Spaniard to the ground, then with one heave pushes down the dunking lever so the chair lifts up from the vat. Immediately Herr Bull and the guards rush to his aid. Together they untie the prostrate figure and lay her out on the wet stone floor. Her head flops sideways.

"Bring a torch!"

Under the flare Detlef sees that the woman is lifeless, her eyes rolling back into her head. He clasps the slender shoulders, unable to believe she could have perished so easily. Not this spirit, he prays. Desperate, he tears open her tunic. The pallor of her breast is an appallingly poignant sight, a stark reminder of her youth. The nipple a large purple bud on white. Detlef places one hand on her chest and starts massaging her heart. Nothing happens.

Groot, kneeling beside him, picks up her limp wrist to find a sign of life. "Sire, the midwife's spirit has fled us."

But Detlef, refusing to hear him, keeps thumping on her chest, a dull thud which resonates through all of his senses again and again. As if all that matters is made manifest in this one gesture: the absurd scale of his huge hand across her narrow chest; the wet flesh which, like clay, gives with each blow; the mud streaking the skin coating his fingers, linking her degradation with him.

Let her live, he prays to his God. If you are to grant me anything, grant me this.

Groot, frightened by his master's tenacity, tries to pull him away as bruises begin to blossom across Ruth's mottled skin. But the canon, rigid in his determination, continues to pound over and over.

Suddenly, miraculously, her chest heaves and she coughs. Water streams from her purple mouth.

"Sire, she lives!" Groot cries out in amazement.

Detlef rolls her onto her side. Sweat beads on his face despite the freezing air. Only as he watches her shuddering ribs expand does he realize that there is life beneath his hands and for the second time in his existence he is infused with faith.

"So the midwife lives to face another interrogation."

Carlos's voice rings out in the momentary silence and punches Detlef back into the room, to the paper-white faces of his startled audience.

"Perhaps it would have been kinder to let her perish," the friar smirks.

Detlef takes off his cloak and wraps it around Ruth's shaking figure. Again he is amazed at the delicacy of the midwife's frame, how small she is under his hands. "From now on I shall be interrogating the accused myself."

"At whose command?"

Groot hands the sealed scroll to Juan who passes it to Carlos. The inquisitor reads it with pursed lips then crushes it angrily.

"One word to the emperor will obliterate the archbishop's sudden affection for the sorceress."

"Perhaps."

Detlef gestures to one of his guards who gathers up the semiconscious midwife, his face neutral, his eyes only on Detlef.

The canon turns to the inquisitor. "I believe that if you leave now you might just catch the night messenger to Vienna. The coach departs at midnight."

Carlos glances at the soldiers who have accompanied Detlef; several reach for their swords. Acknowledging defeat he turns to Juan who, with an embarrassed air, collects the viola da gamba.

"I shall remember your meteoric promotion to inquisitor, Canon von Tennen. For your sake I pray it shall be temporary." With that comment the Dominican leaves, followed by his clerk.

Herr Bull pulls off his hood to reveal a pockmarked but surprisingly kindly face. "Sire, will you be needing my services? Because if not the missus is waiting."

"You can go." Detlef turns to the guards. "You too."

Empty of the key players the tension in the stone cell dissipates like air out of a balloon.

Detlef kicks at the torture rack. "Wood and iron, Groot—they may break a man's body but never his spirit. That will always remain within the realm of the untouchable."

But Groot experiences a sudden shudder as a half-formed premonition momentarily grips his senses. Repressing his intuition the assistant quickly crosses himself.

The curved ash-wood bow sweeps across the taut strings, drawing a low moan from the viola da gamba. A furious torrent of semiquavers follows, a stanza from a Hungarian rhapsody Carlos stole from a gypsy he accidentally tortured to a premature death. In the spartan cell the Spaniard, naked and annointed with myrrh, plays wildly as the music interlaces with the stillness of the monastery. Clutching the shiny instrument between his bony thighs he throws back his head, eyes closing in ecstasy. A delirium both spiritual and aural in nature.

I held her life in my hands, he rages, and he tore her away. I shall make him pay, I shall break both of them. A crescendo of revenge builds with each screaming note. Now he will use the witch's power against her. He will summon the dark one and bend her to his will. His chair placed in the center of the freezing room, his shivering and exposed flesh beyond sensation, he works himself into a frenzy.

There is only one light source in the darkened chamber: a smoldering pile of incense acquired especially for the secret incantation. The burning fills the chamber with a whitish smoke. On the stone floor lies a single amulet, a marble tablet encrusted with jewels. On one side it is carved with the image of Lilith, her body bound by chains, an emerald adorning her navel. This side is hidden, facedown on the cold floor. The side which is visible carries a depiction of Lilith breaking free from her chains, her wings and hands raised victoriously. The Aramaic words, "Hear me and I shall triumph; worship me and I should serve thee," are inscribed into the marble. Carlos himself had this image and text carved into the tablet twenty years before at a market stall in Istanbul to emulate an amulet confiscated as evidence during the arrest of the Navarro family; evidence that mysteriously disappeared after Isaac Navarro's execution.

The music builds in intensity, swirling arabesques and waterfalls of arpeggios, before sliding into a haunting, teasing love song. It is extraordinarily beautiful, a stark contrast to the grotesquery of the naked old man making love to his instrument.

"Come, my woman, come to me," Carlos murmurs softly in Aramaic, a language he studied in the monastery of Villanueva de Gállego during the desolate years after Sara's flight to Amsterdam. A language which opened him to mystical studies and illustrated texts that existed beyond the kabbala, for he too, in a desperate attempt to draw himself closer to his obsession and nemesis, had become a scholar of the Zohar.

The gleaming haunches of a naked woman appear through the smoke: Lilith. Hips undulating, she dances seductively to the music, long veils trailing from her brow to the ground. Incandescent they float through the air, revealing tantalizing glimpses of the glorious body beneath. Carlos opens his eyes, Transfixed, he paces his rhythm to her movements, his erection hardening with each newly revealed part of her body.

The demon stands tall, some three yards in height; her breasts are high, like those of the Moorish slave girls he has seen dancing in such a fashion, her flesh generous, rounded and luscious, with a bloom like ripe fruit. Her face is ridiculously young and the deceptively innocent eyes, huge and black, are a travesty of shyness above the swaying flesh. It is a paradox he knows he will always succumb to.

"My mistress, my downfall, I appeal to you. Join forces with me and help me destroy the midwife."

The demon swirls, her nude sex glistening for a moment in the dim light of the glowing embers. Her hissing voice fills the friar's head like a maddening perfume he cannot escape. "This I shall do; but know that to dance with Lilith is to surrender more than just your seed." Her reply is not of the voice but of the senses, as if her tone is a blade that cuts through Carlos's very body.

Before he can answer her soft burning hands are reaching for his penis. Trembling with blinding pleasure Carlos lets his bow fall to the ground.

Outside the door of the cell stretches a line of curious Jesuit novices, their young faces flushed with intrigue, their eyes eager for information. They strain to hear more of the Dominican's marvelous music which has been floating down the shadowy passage, drawing them from their monastic cells. In the ensuing silence the Spaniard's loud moan of pleasure is clearly audible, but from their side of the door it sounds like pain.

"The good Spanish friar must be wrestling with Satan himself," whispers one awed novice, scarcely more than fourteen. His companions nod wisely and cross themselves fervently.

חסד

CHESED

Mercy

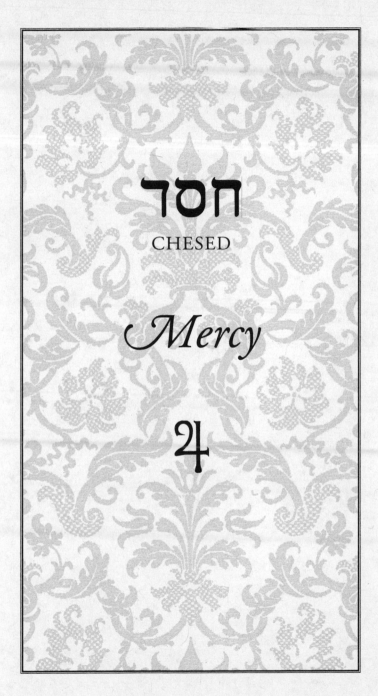

*M*üller lies on his back counting the drops of moisture crawling down the stone wall of his cell. He has made a pledge to himself that when the fiftieth droplet, pregnant with gathered grime, plummets to the granite floor he will call out to the guard again.

They should be here by now, he thinks. Von Fürstenberg promised him; surely twenty years of service means something. He is more than just an employee: he is a confidant; the cathedral minister has trusted him with his very life and now Müller must trust him in return. Von Fürstenberg had explained how his arrest was a mistake, a clumsy attempt by the emperor to frighten the archbishop. He had promised to organize everything—by dawn this day an unlocked cell and a secret passage direct to Paris and his sons. His beautiful boys. So why had no one arrived yet?

Müller's reverie is broken by the rattle of keys. He sits up and tries to brush the straw out of his hair and tidy the torn clothes he has been wearing for over a week.

"Herr von Fürstenberg?" he calls out to the darkened corridor beyond his cell. His words echo back unanswered but still the footsteps approach.

A man, his smiling face lit by the lantern he carries, emerges from the shadows. "We'll have you out of here in no time," he says cheerfully and placing the lantern on the floor unlocks the cell door.

Müller, his gratitude on his lips, steps out. A moment later his head is jerked back and his throat professionally and swiftly slit.

One hand lies in her lap, the other rests on the arm of the plain wooden chair. Eyes half-open, Ruth stares into the fire burning in the small hearth.

Detlef is at the barred window; he looks out at the night sky. It has been four days since he pulled the midwife's broken body from the freezing water, four long days during which he has not been able to banish her image from his mind. Now here he is, standing before her. While his thoughts gather themselves, he returns his focus to the panorama outside: the empty town square through the poplar trees, beyond it the windows flickering yellow and gold with candlelight. It is past evensong and many are preparing for bed: the kitchen table is being cleared, the hearth dampened, the quilts pulled back, each family wrapping itself tight against the frosty winter. A woman with a babe in arms walks across one of the windows. Smiling, she turns back into the room—to whom? A man? Her husband?

Staring out, Detlef wonders what he has sacrificed: this unexamined rhythm of life, the security of being loved without question, the instinctive urge of reproduction—the basic tenets of life which, in this moment, are utterly appealing.

The sound of Ruth coughing makes him swing around. Fully conscious now, she clutches at the robe the canon sent to clothe her. Detlef is gripped by a paroxysm of shyness as he realizes how little he knows about the creature in the chair before him. He moves toward her. But she cringes, fearing some new attack.

Kneeling, he adopts the gentlest tone he can muster. "Have no more terror. You are safe with me."

Awkwardly he waits for her response. Her voice, broken by the torture, comes out in a harsh whisper.

"Why did you save me—only to torment me again?"

"There are more humane methods of interrogation, Fräulein Saul."

Ruth has become so unused to the formal address that for a moment she wonders whom he is talking to. She looks down at the clean shift and wonders whether he has seen her naked. She has no memory of emerging from the water; all she can recall is the icy cold and the terrible pain. Shivering, she wraps the simple nightgown more tightly around herself and looks about the room. Although a prison cell, it is more like a room in a tavern with its small hearth and old rug, two utilitarian chairs and a straw pallet in the corner. There is even a wooden crucifix hanging above the mantelpiece. It is so much more comfortable than her previous quarters that she cannot help speculating on the motives of the man in front of her.

"Where is Monsignor Solitario?"

"His role in your prosecution is suspended."

"But my prosecution is not?"

"No. I have taken on the duty of inquisitor."

There is a knock at the door. Detlef opens it and a serving boy hands him a bowl of steaming soup.

"Here, you must eat."

When Ruth tries to pick up the wooden spoon she realizes her fingers are still too bruised and stiff to function. Grasping the dish clumsily with both hands, she lifts it and drinks directly. It is her first real nourishment for over a week. The heat of the liquid runs through her, sweeping the notion of life back into her numbed flesh.

The canon sits down opposite her. "The inquisitor would have you burned, regardless of the truth. But the archbishop and I are truth seekers. We do not wish to sacrifice innocence for a vendetta, be it religious or political."

Her hunger is so raw it reminds him of other appetites. Fearful that she might read his thoughts he looks down at her naked feet instead: one slim foot curls around the other, the toes long and childlike. Usually unabashed about his carnal desires, he finds himself strangely ashamed and this reticence both amuses and perplexes him. Smiling slightly, he ponders on the wisdom of exorcising this desire with his mistress later that evening.

Ruth misinterprets the source of his amusement. "So I am to be sport for you."

"You doubt my motives?"

"I suspect that you conceal the truth," the midwife replies, a drip of barley soup running down her chin. "You, I do not know, but I have observed the behavior of his highness Maximilian Heinrich. He has sacrificed many souls through his actions or lack of action. Therefore the cathedral must have an ulterior motive. As I am quite convinced I am bound for either the gallows or the pyre, you might as well confess now and then you and I can both die with a clear conscience."

Her audacity takes him by surprise. He cannot remember ever having been addressed so directly by a woman. Disappointed that she should be ungrateful to him for saving her life, he is also deeply intrigued.

"You do my master a disservice, Fräulein. Neither his loyalties nor his ambitions are that simple. Besides, the case against you is as yet unproven. We merely wish to keep you alive for as long as it takes to prove your innocence or your guilt; evidently this was not Monsignor Solitario's intention."

"Tell me, Canon, do you believe in the existence of witches?"

"I believe in the existence of evil."

"But do you believe in the existence of Satan, Hell and eternal damnation?"

"Naturally. I am a Catholic: my faith embraces all of these concepts."

"But where is your evidence?"

"I have seen hellish things inflicted by man upon man on the battlefield. I have seen cattle struck down by curses, and commonplace evils such as envy, jealousy, greed and power corrupt a man's soul. I cannot aspire to a higher existence without believing that our actions are judged both in this life and the next."

"Why can we not live this life and take moral responsibility in this life solely? Why cling to the belief that redemption is possible only in the afterlife? Do you not see that all this belief leads to is the surrender of the dispossessed, the poor and the peasants, who are taught that they should suffer now so they may enter the kingdom of Heaven later?"

"You are truly a heretic to speak so baldly of a Godless universe."

"Not a Godless universe but one in which men strive for equality of spirit and ambition."

"A heretic, a Republican and a witch, Ruth bas Elazar Saul—your discourse only adds weight to the charges against you."

"Would you wish me to lie for my life? The last charge is false. Grant you, there are many things that are unexplained: the magic of nature, what drives a man, how the faith of many can change the life of one. There may even be witches, Canon, but I am not one, I promise you."

Outside, hail suddenly rains down against the slate roof. A coal rolls out of the grate and onto the floor, dangerously close to Ruth's bare feet. Detlef kicks it back into the hearth. He does not know how to answer her; there have been many occasions which have left him marveling at the nature of faith and how it may transform the way men perceive events.

During his childhood the gamekeeper, a surly Italian who had served the von Tennen family for over thirty years, visited the viscountess to complain that all the rabbits had been bewitched and were dying outside their burrows. He charged a local widow with the deaths, claiming she was a sorceress who transformed herself into a fox at night. The woman had lived on the grounds of the manor for as long as Detlef could remember; in truth her meager abode was in the direct path of the seasonal hunt and was considered by the gamekeeper to be an obstruction to the blood sport. Determined to solve the mystery, the viscountess rode out one early morning accompanied by the eight-year-old Detlef. In the hush of that glistening dawn they went from burrow to burrow examining the tiny corpses caught by death in the gentlest of postures: some still wrapped around each other, others with babes still suckling at the teat, but all showing traces of having consumed the same weed. The viscountess ordered the deceptively harmless-looking plant to be pulled from every patch of wild ground and the rabbits stopped dying, but the gamekeeper had never been persuaded that the widow was not a witch. That such circumstantial coincidence can be woven into vindictive accusation is an aspect of life Detlef witnesses every day, and as the spiritual confidant of his community is expected to suspend his disbelief.

"How do you explain your use of the kabbala, Fräulein? I am not ignorant of its associations."

"The kabbala is a system of mystical mathematics, meanings imposed on the Hebrew alphabet by some of our ancient scholars. It is a set of instructions on how to live your life. No more and no less."

"If it has no power, why then do you use it in your midwifery?"

Ruth turns to the window, her aquiline profile a chiseled silhouette against her black hair. "It is a wild, beautiful night. Nature is enchanting, is it not?"

Detlef waits in silence. The stillness deepens then abruptly weaves the air between them into an erotic ambience. He finds himself studying the curve of her slender neck, marveling at the fragility of her bone structure, the narrowness of her skull, her high cheekbones, all tantalizingly exotic to him. To distract himself he averts his gaze; it falls upon a small patch of skin on the inside of her wrist. As he stares, its whiteness becomes translucent and suddenly he can see the blue veins beneath, the blood pumping, in microscopic detail—a vibrant life force he fought to save.

Ruth notices his confusion but is unable to interpret its cause. The intensity of her gaze embarrasses him and he cannot shake the sensation that of the two of them she is the stronger. He coughs and turns away, struggling to maintain his authority.

"The kabbala," he demands.

"Both you and I know the superstition of the uneducated man, his drive to create meaning as a way of refuting the powerlessness of his situation."

"You employ a belief system in which you have no faith?"

"I did not say I had no faith in it. Besides, I am a pragmatist, Canon von Tennen."

Detlef is amazed to find his heart stumbling as he realizes she has remembered his name. He stares at those green eyes, startlingly light against the blackness of her eyelashes and brows.

"If you were such a pragmatist you would not be in the situation you are in now, Fräulein."

"Perhaps, but then again there is a certain pragmatism to martyrdom—even Jesus Christ would agree to that," she replies with a smile.

The smile instantly transforms her naturally pensive features. Again, Detlef sees a radiance which lies not in the classical beauty of his Birgit, but in the gesture, the movement of Ruth's expression.

"Is it true you have studied with Benedict Spinoza?"

"What of it?"

He swallows and wonders whether he can trust her. If he reveals himself to her, will she reciprocate? Surely she must, he tries to reassure himself, for he has saved her life.

"I have an interest in matters west of the border. Some say there is a great change coming," he replies carefully, masking a youthful enthusiasm in his voice.

Ruth pauses. The being before her has unexpectedly transformed from a cleric to a man: he has become an individual she can both recognize and appreciate, his intelligence now glimmering through the arrogance. Thus exposed, his certainty strikes her as a false confidence that covers profound—and far more interesting—vulnerabilities.

She becomes aware of another scent in the air: the faint musk of his masculinity. The awareness is a sudden awakening. There is only one other time she can remember being so affected: in a small attic room near the Kalverstraat. Dirk Kerkrinck. Being held in his arms. It is a perfume that utterly disarms her. A slow blush creeps up her neck and spreads across her cheeks, sending peachy tendrils right to her earlobes. Its heat forces her to adopt a fiercer exterior.

"It would be wise for any enlightened man to look to the Lowlands.

There is to be found the intellectual freedom to soar philosophically; to believe in a God who cannot be bribed, who can exist side by side with knowledge; to dream of other ways of civilizing a nation, to yearn for a democracy in which slave and master no longer exist—"

"Hush, even bricks have ears . . . and wagging tongues."

Detlef leans forward and the brush of his breath on her skin launches Ruth into further excitement.

"In that case I shall whisper also."

"Or speak softly in Latin. It is a tongue you know, I believe?"

"A tongue I know and love," she murmurs in that language.

"Was it to study such ideas that you abandoned your mother country for Holland?"

"It was a natural curiosity."

"Really? I have always been taught that in a woman the desire for knowledge is not natural, that the female role is confined to that of nurturer, and sometimes to commerce—but perhaps my teachers were wrong."

"Evidently. For I am a woman and yet I have complete comprehension of many of the new philosophers."

He laughs, delighted. She smiles with him. Again the flare of desire licks at his groin. Imbued with new confidence he moves closer.

"Tell me of Spinoza, what kind of man is he?"

She breathes in sharply: he has stepped over a boundary. Sensing that his interest is personal, she wonders what he wants from her—a confession that will condemn her or a genuine insight into the reclusive philosopher? Why should a canon of the cathedral take an interest in a Jewish heretic who has been excommunicated from his own people? Unless to entrap her.

"Why do you wish to know, pray? For your own interest or for that of the emperor?"

"I may appear a puppet but from this moment the strings are cut. You may trust me."

"Trust is won not given."

"I saved your life."

"You merely delayed my execution."

"I sincerely hope not. Fräulein, I assure you, you may confide in me. I swear on the Holy Bible itself: I will not betray you."

"A grave pledge indeed. Does this man interest you so much?"

"He fascinates me. I believe he may hold the key to a bridge between two worlds: the old order I belong to and a new one that could be the future."

She shifts her weight and rests her head briefly on her hand.

"*Deus sive natura*: the natural world is God; God is the natural world. All that lies within it makes up an infinite divine substance that possesses infinite forms of phenomena—this is Spinoza's belief. *Amor intellectualis Dei*: the intellectual love of God. If we can achieve this, we will always feel part of the divine substance."

"Your mentor is a hard taskmaster. Are you able to rein in your own passion and drive to surrender to such an arid system of belief? Would it not be easier to draw comfort from the old ways of your own religion?"

"Canon, I am foremost a thinker. I know too much to retreat down the path of ignorance and mysticism. Spinoza's God sits comfortably with what I have experienced through my own observations."

"You are a most unusual woman. I have not met a creature like you."

"Forgive me my eccentricities; do not condemn me to death for them."

Outside, the town crier sounds ten o'clock and the hailstorm stops as quickly as it started. Somewhere a door slams. Detlef has the feeling that he will remember this moment always: the shape of her hands; the way the light from the fire curls around one side of her face; the lilt of her voice, gentle but deep and so musical it is hard for him to focus on her words; the clarity of her very presence which cuts straight to the protector within him. All these impressions culminate to make everything appear infinitely more brilliant.

Secretly overwhelmed, Detlef is at a loss for words. He is content just to be there with her, to drink in her nearness, the light shining off her black hair, as time melts away.

"I saw nothing." Ruth breaks the silence.

Detlef looks up, perplexed by the reference.

"When I was drowning I saw nothing—no angel of death, no Holy Spirit. For a moment I thought I saw my mother, but it was trickery, merely the mind abandoning conscious thought." But her voice sounds uncertain.

"How can you live without faith?"

"You are wrong, Canon, I have faith. I fight to have faith in nature, in knowledge and, despite all, in the goodwill of mankind."

"In that case, Fräulein, you have more than I."

After he has gone, Ruth lies on the narrow bed and stares up at the ceiling. She watches the shadows thrown by the fire dance across the smoke stained expanse. The events of the last few days have been so momentous she feels as if she has lived several lifetimes longer and not a mere week.

An ember flares up and reminds her of the swaying figures of the men praying at temple and her father. Will Elazar be sleeping now? Will he survive her imprisonment? Will she ever see him again?

A sudden nip on the leg makes her flinch. She examines the cover, it is crawling with lice. She tries to pluck one tiny insect off the gray cotton but her fingers, still stiff from the torture, are not nimble enough to crush the minute slippery body. Shrugging, she tugs the thin blanket over her. A faint remnant of her visitor's musk drifts across her face. Maddening. Seductive. Perplexing. Lulled by Detlef's aroma she finally allows exhaustion to consume her and collapses mercifully into a dreamless sleep.

The wind lashes across Detlef's face, whipping up his blood and cleansing his spirit. With a yell he digs his spurs into the mare, goading her on. Behind him the walled city recedes into a thick mist, just the crane of the half-constructed spire, bent like the wooden arm of a huge scarecrow, is visible above the low cloud. Already the fields are giving way to thick dark forest. The broken road is dangerous, notorious for bandits and highway robbers, but exhilarated by the glorious risk of it all Detlef gallops on, the barely discernible low stone walls which run on either side of the narrow lane his only means of navigation. It has been many years since he did anything so rash and the thud of the horse's hooves and the pounding of his own heart and blood roar in his ears like the crash of an angry sea. He is running from the past into a violent future. He is running from caution headlong into uncertainty. But for the first time he feels as if he is truly living in his own skin.

❋

Fifteen miles away, on the other side of the sleeping river, a candle burns at an upstairs window. The glass, misted from the heat inside, frames an ancient face bent over a desk. Rabbi Elazar ben Saul cannot sleep. He has not slept since his audience with the archbishop, his mind and spirit will not allow it. He feels that if he surrenders to rest, his conscious will might relax and stop defending his daughter, as if the ring of protection he has projected around her requires constant vigilance. He is suffering, still caught in the anger of Sara's betrayal. To have baptized their daughter without his knowledge—there could hardly be a greater sin.

A painted miniature lies before him on the small walnut desk. Italian Renaissance in style, the subject seems to stare past the viewer as if her object is far distant—perhaps she is even in a trance. She is beautiful but it is hard to define what makes her beauty. It is not the symmetry of her face, for it proves on close observation asymmetrical: one eye lies slightly lower than the other while the mouth has a subtle but visible downward slant and the nose is strong. It is not the shape of her face, which could be defined as Spanish or even of the Orient, so high are the cheekbones. Nor the eyebrows which are plucked thin in the fashion of twenty years before, nor the groomed hairline set back from the high forehead. Perhaps it is the attentiveness of her gaze which radiates out from deep ebony irises and seems to speak of tragedy yet unrealized, or the air of solemn dignity tinged with pride which makes her appear older than her years, or could it be the intelligence which plays around the mouth in a teasing half-smile? Whatever it is, the woman is undeniably radiant.

The fine varnish of the portrait has begun to crack and the gold leaf that picks out the details of her crimson robe is flaking off. The rosy hue of her cheeks and lips—painted with minuscule brush strokes—has faded. But to the old man it is as if the young woman is sitting there before him, her head tilted, the pensive expression he recalls as the prelude to her mischievous questioning of his gravity playing across her features.

"Elazar, all the prophets had humor so why am I married to such a Jeremiah?"

"Because life is very serious."

"Life is very short, my dear heart, but, like a thing of both beauty and terror, does not bear examination. Laughter allows us for a brief moment to enjoy, but more importantly to forget."

"So is it not enough that I smile occasionally?"

"No. No, it is not."

And then he hears her laugh, a cascade of descant notes shimmering on the air. It is so vivid that the old man actually looks over his shoulder to see whether the ghost might have woken the household. But the rest of the room lies static, untouched by the presence of her iridescent spirit.

He is frightened to look up in case his gaze should drive away the manifestation of his dead wife, for the specter is definitely there, sitting just beyond the desk. The chamber has filled with the scent of lily, the perfume Sara adopted in her new land, determined to exorcise any odor that might sweep her back to the horrors of the past. She wore the musky fragrance especially to please her young scholarly husband, who was so shy they made love under the bedcovers in pitch darkness, until she complained that she might as well be making love to the angel Gabriel or the prophet Elijah so little did she see of her man. The memory makes Elazar smile but still he is afraid to look up. Instead the old man keeps his gaze on the miniature and the string of pearls and coral wound around his fingers, the same necklace highlighted with beads of silvery-white enamel in the tiny portrait.

While he waits an elegant hand—he recognizes the delicacy and length of its fingers with such intensity that he fears that his heart might dam up with tears—reaches forward and gently takes the string of jewels from him.

It is only then that Elazar dares to look at his wife, Sara. He sees that his memory has not imbued her with perfection nor marred her through forgetfulness, but that every detail of her face, from the small scar on the chin to the row of fine black hairs that make up the arch of each brow, is made manifest through love. And as he looks he immediately forgets that the woman before him has been dead for over fifteen years.

"I am here to ask your forgiveness, Elazar." The ghost's voice, instantly recognizable, binds the old man's heart with grief.

"Why, Sara?"

"Fear, my love, the fear of a survivor."

"You committed a sin, a grave sin. She belongs to both of us."

"I wished only to protect her. I wanted her to live, whatever the circumstances. I acted out of love—this you must believe. Forgive me."

Elazar looks into her face, losing himself in the eternity of their history which stretches like a dream beyond her coal-black eyes.

"Have I ever been able to deny you?"

"No." And she smiles, a smile which is both wry and gentle and pulls Elazar like a glistening thread straight back into his youth.

"What now, Sara?"

"Now we wait; our daughter is strong."

"But the inquisitor has her."

"No longer. What will be is already written. Isn't that what you used to tell me?"

The ghost carefully lays the pearl and coral necklace on the polished wooden desktop and stands. She is wearing the same crimson robe he remembers her choosing for the Italian portrait painter, a garment she knew would conceal the swelling of her second pregnancy. Now that the specter is upright he can see the curve of her womb and for a moment he has to shut his eyes to block out the memory of Sara's bloodied thighs and the stillborn baby boy, her pale arms winding around him as he kissed her frightened, dying face.

"Elazar, Elazar." The phantom calls him back as she moves toward the hunched figure still sitting in the carved chair. "Elazar, my love." Her whisper . . . scented chimes. "You must not wander from this life, you are needed yet."

"But I am so weary."

Indeed every cell of his thin body seems to be calling out for the mindless reprieve of oblivion.

"You must be strong just a little longer. Ruth needs you."

Sara laces her fragrant fingers into his mane of silvery hair, sending tremors of forgotten desire through his ancient frame. Forgetting his age the old man grasps the slim wrist and covers it with kisses.

"My love, how I yearn for you. You were my heart's blood, my soul's shadow."

"And you were mine." Her voice now a faint swirl of music.

She allows him to rest his head against her breasts, his hands pressing the taut round womb beneath the velvet. The old man thinks he must have been transported to Heaven, so wonderfully familiar is her perfume, the scent of her skin, her touch. Burying his head deeper into her cool bosom he finds himself missing something undefinable, then with a shock realizes it is the sound of a living heartbeat.

Outside in the corridor, Tuvia, his bladder bursting, rummages around for a chamber pot. Stumbling past Elazar's study he notices the light under the door. Curious, he presses his ear against the wood paneling only to hear the old man burst into loud dry sobs.

DAS GRÜNTAL

Prince Ferdinand lies on the four-poster bed, a quilt embroidered with the royal crest of the Wittelsbachs—an eagle clutching a snake in its talons—slung across him; it is stained with semen and wine. A heavy velvet curtain hangs across the stone alcove to keep out the morning which is already making a furtive attempt to creep beneath the thick fabric. A taper burns in the corner, nearing the end of its life, the flame flickering in a black pond of soft wax. The only sound is the prince's low snore; buried in the back of his throat, it is the snore of a boy. Alphonso, rouge still smeared across both cheeks, lies curled around the sleeping man, his long elegant feet entangled with his, his hands folded up against Ferdinand's blemished back.

The actor is wide awake. He stares up at the painted ceiling where the last of the candlelight illuminates Zeus seducing Adonis. The shadows have transformed Adonis into a beautiful dusky youth with soulful eyes; Zeus, however, still shines with Teutonic robustness. Alphonso imagines that he and the prince could be these two mythical figures, immortalized and, most importantly, sanctified. He is thankful for the count's order the night before for his servants to stay away from the prince's chambers. Understandably the count is forever vigilant with his staff: homosexuality, although tolerated, cannot be flaunted and the count has many enemies who would use information of any indiscretion to their advantage.

The actor turns his attention back to his sleeping lover. He traces with his fingers two recent scars that run across the prince's shoulders. He knows exactly what they are: marks of a whipping. In their lovemaking he has seen the veiled fear in the young man's eyes. Alphonso has not asked, he does not have to: he knows Ferdinand was whipped on the orders of

Emperor Leopold, his uncle, for trespasses far slighter than sleeping with another man, worse still an actor.

At eighteen Alphonso is only a year older than the prince, yet he too has tasted the lash and once narrowly escaped the gallows. He recognizes the youth's lassitude as a thin mask worn as desperate protection from further pain, both physical and emotional. An orphan who learned from the age of six to live by his wits in the crowded Venice ghetto, Alphonso is a master of duplicity. It was a skill noticed by Samuel Oppenheimer, the emperor's court Jew, during the acting troupe's visit to Vienna and Alphonso has been in Oppenheimer's employment ever since. His task is to gather snippets of information as he tours from court to court: trading tips, proposed military strategies, broken marriages and general intrigue; information that provides Oppenheimer with an advantage over his competitors and keeps him the emperor's favorite. But it is a precarious position for the young performer. If his activities should be discovered, Samuel will not be able to rescue him.

As Alphonso lies there beside this youth he knows he is falling in love with, he swears he will defend him whatever the cost, then smiles at the irony and audacity of his sentiment. The prince could have him arrested with one command. The only protection he can offer is that of the actor, the skill of the chameleon to transform a man's face and gender thus enabling him to infiltrate any European court he might desire.

Ferdinand stirs and rolls onto his back, mumbles a broken sentence in Austrian then continues to dream. Alphonso kisses him lightly on the lips and slips out of the bed. Wrapping himself in the great fur stole which lies abandoned on the cold marble, he steps silently across the floor and out into the dew-sodden courtyard. There he steadies himself against a stone arch and after glancing around to ensure no one is watching bares his circumcised penis and begins to urinate. Looking down at the telltale organ he wonders how long he will be able to conceal his religion, as well as his heart, from the suspicious entourage that surrounds his royal lover.

A large raven watches him warily from a wooden rail. As Alphonso finishes and shakes himself dry, the bird takes off. Screeching cynically into the bleak sky, it veers to the left. Alphonso cannot dislodge the sensation that it is a bad omen.

❋

The beast pelts into the muddy hollow, its short thick legs scrabbling desperately at the soft soil as it tries to conceal its shaggy hide with mud. Grunting it pauses, snout twitching in the spring breeze. It can smell the sweat of horses and men and, more horribly, the pungent aroma of the hounds—wet fur, shit and the blood of the last kill dripping from their jaws.

Suddenly the dogs' baying and, below it, the low tone of the hunting horn, join to pervade the air. Squealing in fear the panicked animal wheels around, saliva spraying madly from its hairy mouth, and careers across the open glade beyond the hollow. As it runs it thinks of nothing except how to reach the ray of sunlight just visible in the next ravine.

The hunt rolls nearer until the cacophony of sound, scent and hooves is almost upon the beast. The boar scrambles over a fallen log and leaps toward the tiny valley that has opened up a couple of feet below. Its legs buckle beneath it and it falls heavily. Instantly the mottled back is covered with ravenous dogs. One long-legged yellow and red hound sinks its heavy jaw into the bushy fur at the neck, two others hang from the boar's head. Blood spurts in a scarlet bow across the blue-white snow. The beast, a colossal male of at least three years, shakes its head heavily, its beady reddened eyes rolling in stupefied terror. The hounds hold fast and one ear tears away in a welt of lurid pink. Grunting, the bleeding animal butts blindly against a log in a desperate attempt to free itself of its attackers.

Suddenly a steel arrow soars through the air and pierces the boar as far as its heart. The porcine sovereign stiffens then with a strange grace falls heavily onto its side, its mouth pulling back over the yellowed tusks in a curiously benevolent grimace. Robbed of the final slaughter, the hounds hover over the corpse, disappointed.

The horn is sounded and reluctantly the dogs drop back, sniffing at the oozing blood, pawing the ground impatiently as the huntsmen ride to the ledge above.

"Bravo, your highness, a superb shot."

Count Gerhard von Tennen, wearing a skin-tight leather hunting jerkin and matching breeches, takes off his large feathered hat and salutes Prince Ferdinand who, grinning in amazement, still clutches the crossbow to his breast as if the evidence of his skill might be ripped away from him at any moment.

"Extraordinary" murmurs the prince, astounded at his own marksmanship.

Directly behind him Herman Woolf, the von Tennens' gamekeeper, winks at the count and swiftly lowers his own crossbow, concealing it in a bag hanging from his saddle. The count watches admiringly as the gamekeeper climbs off his stallion and clambers down the hill toward the boar. Herman pauses triumphantly for a moment over the bloodied carcass then thrusts a short spear into the quivering body. The count waves his approval and turns to Ferdinand.

"Your highness, where did you learn such craft? Why, you have the marksmanship of Hercules himself."

The prince's normally petulant face splits into a shy smile.

"I didn't . . . I mean, Uncle forced me to have a few lessons, but I must admit I have never really displayed any skill for it before today."

"Then the Rhineland air must agree with you. And you must tell your uncle of your triumph. He will be proud. Herman! Bring us the prince's trophy," the count calls to the gamekeeper.

Now hopefully the young brat will convey to Leopold how wonderfully invigorating his stay was at Das Grüntal and the von Tennens will at last be reinstated into the emperor's favor, the count thinks smugly, wondering whether it would be possible for Herman to repeat the feat of deception the following day during the pheasant hunt he has planned for his royal guest.

A sedan chair carried by two sweating pages appears over the small hill. Alphonso, dressed extravagantly as the Queen of the Hittites, complete with an ornate feather headdress, pushes his head out of the window.

"Look, Alphonso, your prince has actually killed something!" Ferdinand points triumphantly at the wild boar.

The banner of the Viennese court comes into view and three of the prince's attendants ride up to the young royal. Dropping their reins they clap politely, appropriately awed by the sight of the sprawling corpse.

A shapely foot encased in an outrageously unsuitable crimson kid slipper emerges from the sedan, followed by gold leather leggings and the rest of the actor. "Bravo, my prince! Bravo!" Alphonso blows a kiss in Ferdinand's direction.

One of the attendants purses his lips in disapproval and throws a dead hare at the actor's feet. Immediately the throng of hounds descends on the small furry body and, in a medley of tails, long brindled limbs and bloodied snouts, tear it to shreds within seconds. Alphonso, splattered with blood and fur, falls back overwhelmed.

Several attendants laugh behind their gloves as the prince frantically wheels his horse around to see if Alphonso is injured.

"It is nothing! Just a few drops of blood." The actor, headdress askew and painfully aware of the ridicule, struggles to his feet and brushes madly at his stained costume.

"Do not concern yourself with me. Look to the gamekeeper, he is honoring you."

The prince peers nervously into the ravine where the gamekeeper is kneeling at the side of the boar. With a manly flourish Herr Woolf swiftly slices off its remaining ear with his knife. The mounted spectators break into polite applause which echoes through the dappled forest and causes a flock of sparrows to rise up from the canopy of trees. The gamekeeper strides back through the hounds, his muscular legs clearly delineated by the fine green hose he wears above his spurred boots.

Dismounting clumsily, Ferdinand walks as regally as possible, given the ridiculous amount of padding he is wearing, toward the gamekeeper and the offered organ. With an imperious air he pulls the fleshy purse off the knife and holds it up triumphantly. Prompted by the count the trumpeter sounds his horn.

Ferdinand turns to Alphonso and dropping to one knee presents the ear to him as a gift. The actor, genuinely touched but also reveling in his role, swoons theatrically. Delicately he takes the ear and pretends to nibble the bloody flesh. There is a smattering of appreciative laughter but the prince remains kneeling.

"My love," Alphonso whispers, "you must get up, the ground is freezing."

Ferdinand, face now bent toward the grass, does not move. "I cannot," he groans through clenched teeth.

Alphonso, fearing that his charade has plunged the prince into one of his famous tantrums, leans down toward him. Suddenly Ferdinand rolls over to his side and clutches at his stomach. "Quick! Quick! He is dying!" the actor shrieks.

In seconds the three courtiers are by the prince, opening his clothing to see if there is a hidden injury.

"I'm not wounded, you idiots! It's an old injury, my stomach!" Contorted by cramps the youth can barely gasp.

The count, terrified that he may be landed with the inconvenience of a royal mortality, wheels around on his horse. "A physic! A physic! Where is the damned physic?"

The count's cry is taken up and relayed down the ranks until it reaches the rest of the hunt which is still arriving at the edge of the ravine. The mass of foot servants and mounted courtiers part to allow a gaunt man on a mangy donkey to ride through.

"I am here, sire," he announces in an unhurried tone which exasperates the count further.

"Attend to the prince! Can you not see his highness is stricken?"

The physic, whose long gangly legs drag in the mud even when he is mounted, climbs off his irritable steed and shuffles over to the prince. In his long black cloak and tall crowned hat the doctor looks like Death himself, a fact not lost on Ferdinand as the quack leans over him, blackened teeth exposed in a sneer of concentration.

"Ahh! I am not ready! Sire, please, I am but young," he cries out in his delirium.

Ignoring his pleas, the physic feels beneath the loosened padding. Ferdinand, convinced that the Angel of Death is clawing at his vital organs, struggles madly, his face feverish. But the older man, staring into the distance while his bony fingers read the diseased organs beneath the scarred abdomen, is indifferent.

The hunting party, some standing, some still mounted, form a suspended tableau of scarlet and green against the charcoal of the trees, with only the fluttering of the banners to break the stillness as all hang upon the doctor's verdict. Finally the physic speaks, his gaunt face haggard in the bright sunlight.

"He must be bled, we must get him back to the lodge immediately. I believe it is a case of blood poisoning."

The pages rush the sedan chair over to the prostrate Ferdinand, who cries out as they try to squeeze him into the upright carriage.

"Be careful! You'll kill him, you fools!" Alphonso yells out, forgetting his rank and letting his voice fall three octaves in his terror.

Stumbling in his long skirts, headdress clasped in one hand, he runs through the mud alongside the chair as the prince is raced back to Das Grüntal.

＊

DAS WOLKENHAUS,
SOME MILES FROM THE VON TENNENS' COUNTRY ESTATE

Detlef lies sprawled on a small divan pushed up against the white wall of the simple parlor. There is little furniture in the large high-ceilinged room, a chamber which has faint echoes of a previous grandeur but now, denuded, is humbled in its asceticism. A large fireplace is set into the far wall, an ornate marble mantelpiece arching over it. A portrait of Detlef's aunt depicted as a buxom huntress hangs above, but the painting is dusty and badly in need of restoration.

A virginal, its once glorious gilded frescoes of nymphs and satyrs faded like a beautiful aging spinster, sits mournfully beside the window. Next to the virginal stands a Liebeskabinett, a cabinet of love. Bavarian, the ornate cupboard boasts a kitsch panorama of the bizarre seduction of Hephaestus by Aphrodite; its spindly legs look strangely defenseless in the bleakness of the room. A worn medieval tapestry, threads hanging out, is stretched across the opposite wall giving that end of the chamber a curiously Oriental mood. A leather ball, a childhood toy, lies abandoned at the skirting board, beside it a checkered spinning top.

While Detlef sleeps, his cloak draped over his eyes, a large pink and black sow enters the room followed by several piglets. She trots territorially around the sleeping man, sniffs at the dried manure packed around his riding boots, then wanders toward the leather ball. The piglets follow, squealing.

"Brunehilde!" A matronly woman in a stained smock and sturdy wooden clogs runs into the room waving a straw broom at the pig. "This is a place for people, not for a glorified meat platter on legs!"

The sow, backed into a corner, grins crookedly at her mistress then farts defiantly. The noise and the odor drift across the room to penetrate Detlef's slumber. He stirs and one of his legs slips from the divan.

"Oh!" The housekeeper whirls around and raises the broom ready to defend herself from the intruder. Convinced it must be an impoverished journeyman who has crept in to shelter from the cold, she tiptoes over and sees the royal crest embroidered on the cloak. Confused, she carefully raises the damp wool from the intruder's face. At the same time Detlef opens one eye.

"Master Detlef!"

The cleric, blinking in the bright light, rubs the sleep from his eyes and peers dubiously at the raised broomstick. "Are you going to beat me with that or is it just your latest means of transport?"

"Beg your pardon, Master Detlef, your Hannah's no witch," she says, lowering the broom. "I just thought you was one of those tramps that are forever taking advantage."

To cover her embarrassment she begins to sweep the floor. "If I had known you were coming, I would have made a fire; maybe cooked some broth."

"Well, I'm here now."

"And so you are. There's precious little left of the winter stock in the larder, but I can go borrow some turnips and salted beef from my brother and have you all warm and toasty within the hour."

"How about some bacon?" Detlef glances at the old sow, who glares back with open hostility.

"You might have to wait a couple of months for one of the young ones. It's been a mean winter, most folk are reduced to eating their grain. Brunehilde's fended off several kidnapping attempts, haven't you, darling?" the housekeeper says to the pig with rough affection.

"In that case, reassure Brunehilde. I'll settle for broth."

Yawning, Detlef gets up and shakes his stiff limbs, his body reeking of the damp night. Hannah shoos the sow and her offspring back out to the entrance hall and the serving quarters.

Looking around, Detlef feels a wave of affection for Das Wolkenhaus, the small country retreat where his mother's sister once held her exclusive literary salons far from Cologne. His aunt, an unmarried spinster who had rejected family pressure to enter a convent, had turned the place into an unorthodox sanctuary for the bored wives of wealthy bürgers, and even some of the women merchants. Accompanied only by a few servants they often made the journey by coach or on horseback and stayed several days, gathering in the evening to recite poetry and play music and, more importantly, to exchange valuable information about their men and the webs of power that tenaciously held together the hierarchies of the city.

When his aunt died she left the property to her favorite nephew. The manor has become Detlef's private home, a refuge from the demands of Cologne and from the affairs of his brother, whose own hunting lodge, Das Grüntal, lies several miles up the road. Never close, the gulf between the two brothers has widened over the years. Gerhard regards Detlef's tolerance of Heinrich's vacillating loyalties as weak, while Detlef has long given up hope of discovering anything human beneath his brother's glittering political veneer. While they maintain the semblance of fraternal affection, in reality each lacks respect for the other. It is hard for Detlef to believe now how desperately he craved Gerhard's approval when younger.

The slightly decayed atmosphere of Das Wolkenhaus suits its antiquity. The fields beyond the garden are still fallow after being devastated by the Great War. Detlef, relishing the bleak landscape, has let the ambience spread to the orchard and the garden, deliberately allowing the thick overgrowth to creep across the stone walls and raked gravel paths. Such is the success of his plan that from the outside the manor looks so neglected that no one is ever able to tell whether the canon is in residence or not.

Bathed and dressed in a plain damask shirt and jerkin of paduasoy, Detlef takes a seat at the round wooden table in the long kitchen.

"This should keep the damp from the bones," Hannah says, setting the bowl of watery stew in front of him. She watches anxiously as the canon tentatively picks his way through the pieces of gristle until finally hunger triumphs over his palate and he is compelled to eat.

"Excellent, Hannah," he lies. Relieved, the housekeeper turns back to her salting.

As Detlef spoons the greasy liquid into his mouth he muses on her sturdy figure in its stained skirt and grubby bodice. She seems so content, so unquestioning in her servitude. Is it possible that she might harbor the same ambitions, the same spiritual yearnings as himself? His thoughts are drawn back to Ruth bas Elazar Saul: although no peasant, she is still a woman and of far lower status than a Wittelsbach prince. So where does her intelligence, her constant questioning, stem from? The ether? God? From her lineage?

"Hannah, do you think yourself to be equal to me?" he asks suddenly.

Hannah looks up from her stewing pan, shocked, and spills some of the beef onto the stone floor.

"It isn't a trick question, I'm just curious. Do you think your soul is equal to mine, for example, or to that of my brother the count? Or even to that of the emperor?"

"Sir, are you drunk?"

"No, entirely sober, in fact I've never been more so. But I need to know: under that guise of servility do you, or any of the other peasants you know, believe yourselves to be equal to your masters?"

"Well, we've all got two arms, two legs and a pot, but that's where it stops, if you ask me. I mean, some of them ladies your aunt used to have staying here, it wasn't just that their lives were different, their heads was different too. I'm happy with my lot. I was born to serve, as was my mother and her mother before her. Does that makes us less or more? I don't know. But it doesn't make us equal. Why, that's like comparing Brunehilde with Matti the hunting hound! What next, Master Detlef? Not that man Luther, I hope! You are to the manor born as I am to the pantry. That's how it's always been and that's how it'll end."

"The Dutch Republicans would have it otherwise."

"A pox on the Republic and on the Lutherans. Who's been poisoning your ear, Master Detlef?" she asks impertinently, forgetting that the nobleman before her is no longer the seven-year-old boy who used to chase geese around the orchard.

"Who indeed?"

Detlef swings around. Birgit stands in the doorway framed by the sunlight behind her, dressed in riding clothes, hat and veil. She steps into the pantry with an air of confidence that belies her apprehension.

Hannah drops into a deep curtsy. "Meisterin."

Birgit slaps her riding gloves onto the wooden counter. "No need to stand on ceremony, Hannah, you've known me since I was a child."

"Nevertheless, you are a married woman now and a wealthy one at that, so if you don't mind I will stay with the formal."

An undertone of disapproval taints Hannah's voice; with another genuflection she leaves the room, the hock of salted beef still in her hand.

Detlef studies his mistress. Feigning a casualness, Birgit toys with the plume of her riding bonnet. "I knew you would be here."

"Why was that?"

"It's where you escape to when something has disturbed you profoundly. You came here after we made love for the first time."

She sits, arranging her deep burgundy ferrandine skirt over the hard bench as a means of distracting herself from her growing anxiety.

"You have ridden from Cologne, Birgit?"

Still he does not make one movement toward her. Birgit, distressed by the distant tone in his voice, decides to ignore his coolness. Smiling coquettishly she fills a pewter mug with wine and drinks it thirstily.

"Not from Cologne but from Das Grüntal. I have some bad news. Prince Ferdinand collapsed during the hunt this morning."

"Is his injury serious?"

"It is not an injury but some mysterious ailment. Gerhard's physic attends him now."

"Hah, that humbug. Gerhard must be anxious. If the prince's condition worsens it could become a major political embarrassment and we all know how my brother hates to be embarrassed."

"The prince won't die."

"Is that what you came here to tell me?"

"That and other matters. In town there is talk that the merchant Voss will burn. The bürgermeisters and the Gaffeln are up in arms about it. Is it true? Are the bürgers to be a sacrifice for Maximilian?"

"I fear so."

"But the men are innocent!"

"Don't be naive, Birgit, it doesn't suit you. Now, how *did* you know I was here?"

"A wager with my heart; the instinct of a woman that links her to her lover. Some might call it habit."

Ignoring his detachment she places her hand on his thigh. Surprised by his lack of response and curious to test the depth of his indifference, Detlef does not move.

"I came here to be alone. There is much I have to ponder without the distraction of man or service."

"I will not be a distraction, I promise," she answers lightly and slips her hand further up his leg. He pushes it away gently. Quickly she covers the moment by pulling a handkerchief from her sleeve.

"What of the other three arrests? The Dutchman no one cares about, Müller is not powerful enough for his guild to protest, and as for the witch—"

"Her guilt is yet unproven," Detlef replies, a little too swiftly.

"So it is true? You have secured the role of her inquisitor?"

"It was necessary. The Spaniard is not impartial."

"Of course he isn't. There is no such thing as impartiality, one would be a fool to assume otherwise. But people's tongues have begun to wag, Detlef. It is unnatural for a canon to become the protector of a Jewish woman. You realize that if you continue with this behavior you will endanger my quest for a knighthood for my husband?"

"I have the grace of one month to prove her guilt or her innocence. I intend to carry out my pledge."

Intrigued by his stubbornness, Birgit speculates what the midwife looks like. She cannot believe that an ill-bred heathen from the right bank of the Rhine could hold any fascination for Detlef, so she imagines there must be another dimension to the scenario, something more insidious which will be infinitely harder to battle. Is he suffering a crisis of faith? Has he finally begun to weary of the role of cleric, or even that of politician? Wondering, she caresses his long blond hair. "Are you not pleased to see me, my love?"

"Always."

Kissing her hand, he stands and moves off. Outside it is early afternoon but already he can smell the scent of evening fires on the chilly breeze.

"It is getting late, shouldn't you begin your ride back? Your manservant will be waiting."

She wraps her arms around his waist. "I have an hour."

As he stands passively with the sunlight crossing his face, she reaches into his breeches and finds him soft and pliant. Staring him in the eye she starts to stroke him with hidden fingers. Her long languid caresses cause him to grow hard, but he makes no move. She is careful to keep herself distant except for the delicious strokes of her cool hands which set his thigh muscles quivering. Now her lover is erect, saluting her touch; still he does not reach for her.

"Embrace me," she whispers, but he pushes her away.

"Birgit, I have told you, I am here for solitude. At this time it is a great luxury."

Hurt, she smooths down her skirts.

"I hope it is a profound distraction you suffer, Detlef, one that precludes matters of the heart, for I have ridden far this morning."

"I am not of the disposition for love."

"But your flesh is."

"The flesh is of the man not of the spirit."

"I can make you forget both." Her eyes tease him with her wit.

This time he walks out of the room. Picking up her riding crop she follows.

Detlef strides through the entrance hall out into the wild front garden. An ancient stone border encircles the large lawn at the center of which is an ornamental pond choking with weeds. A lone goose floats sadly upon it. Beyond the wall is the overgrown orchard which even in winter is thick with vines. A northern wind rustles the tall oak and beech trees. Like a row of towers they are guarded by a platoon of ravens. Balancing on the naked slender branches, hunched up against the cold, the birds look like flung splotches of sooty ink.

Detlef takes a deep breath and allows the wind to roar through him like a scythe. "I don't want to forget, not today," he answers finally, eyes shut tight, arms outstretched.

Birgit, steadying herself against a tree trunk, wonders whether his depressed spirit might be a precursor to illness. Comforted by the thought that this might be her only foe she glances to where her page waits patiently.

"I shall be back in the city as of Tuesday morn and shall attend Sunday's confession. I trust you will have returned to Cologne by then?"

"Naturally."

With a formal nod and an air of faint dismay she takes her leave.

Detlef watches her ride down the lane, the trees on either side bowing with the wind, her riding veil a scarlet streak against a panorama of cascading grays, and finally realizes that his affection for her has started to wane.

Carlos's hand sweeps through the air and lands a resounding slap against Juan's cheek. The secretary stumbles slightly then stoically regains his balance. Knowing the inquisitor's penchant for violence, he loathes being the bearer of bad news.

"Illuminate me, Juan: you are trying to tell me that Herr Müller has been murdered before I had a chance to secure a confession and, more importantly, information for the emperor?" the inquisitor murmurs, his soft voice a chilling contrast to his physical outburst.

Juan, trying to control the welling tears of pain, nods dumbly. Carlos, frustrated, kicks at his legs.

"How dangerous of them to thwart the duty of the Inquisition. Do they not know with whom they are toying? First the midwife and now this: it is insulting."

The clerk hobbles to the desk. "Do you wish me to compose a response?"

"Our response shall be with the sword not the quill."

Furious, Carlos bangs the case of his viola da gamba and immediately regrets it.

"You are going to challenge von Fürstenberg to a duel?" the secretary asks incredulously.

Carlos looks at him sharply. "What makes you think it was von Fürstenberg? Do you have information I don't?"

"I . . . I . . ." Realizing he has been caught out, Juan stutters over his reply. Carlos's hand lands a blow on the other cheek.

"I have heard rumors that Müller was working for von Fürstenberg," the clerk manages to squeak.

The inquisitor walks thoughtfully to the window and looks out at the neat orchard beyond the cloisters. He stares at a young peasant boy raking the grass, his mind a million miles away. His meditation is broken by the perilous journey of a small beetle across the inside of the glass window.

"Excellent," he says softly, his whole demeanor shifting into cooler calculation. "So now we know more about our enemies. We shall bide our time, but I swear to you: when the moment comes I shall destroy the arrogance of this archbishop and with it his cousin."

Carlos crushes the beetle with a sharp decisive pinch.

It might as well be a feast day, Maximilian Heinrich notes bitterly, watching the streams of palms and lilies being thrown from the windows of the houses lining the narrow lanes of Cologne. The archbishop, somber in the purple ecclesiastical robe he adopts when in a judicial role, rides behind the open cart which carries the two prisoners. The bright spring sunlight seems to mock their shaven heads and bewildered faces. The white flowers fluttering down land in front of the rolling wheels to create a pathway of broken stems and crushed blooms as the parade of mounted guards and walking priests passes over them.

Heinrich looks up through the cascading petals. Some of the women hanging from the balconies and open windows are dressed in festive clothing. All the world loves an execution, he concludes, disgusted. For an insane moment he wonders whether he should organize an execution for a feast day. At least it would bring out the masses. Demoralized, he straightens his posture and tries to concentrate on the adulation of his congregation who cheer as he rides past.

The auto-da-fé was a sobering procedure, especially after the gruesome business of Müller's murder, an event the archbishop had neither sanctioned nor been a party to. Von Fürstenberg is out of control, Heinrich thinks gloomily as a welling sense of panic stirs in his vitals. He had instructed the minister to eradicate the problem but a mysterious escape to one of the far colonies would have sufficed, not murder. Really, Wilhelm is a brute.

The trial presses heavily on his conscience. It was a mockery of justice with himself as judge. The city's magistrate also sat on the bench, along with his two sheriffs, and finally the jury: a small panel of bürgers, each carefully picked by Solitario himself. The archbishop was loath to admit it but the Dominican had excelled in the task, meticulously recruiting merchants who had a trading relationship with Spain or England and were vehemently anti-Dutch after being affected by the North Sea war. The inquisitor even had the audacity to enlist Voss's archenemy, a rival spice merchant who had everything to gain from the bürger's demise.

Humiliated, Heinrich had sat sweating in the packed courtroom, enduring the confessions which Solitario, acting as prosecutor, had beaten out of his witnesses. The inquisitor had even called the Dutchman's mistress to the stand. A harmless harlot who went by the name of Frau Plum, she had tearfully confessed that one night van Dorf had levitated while lying upon her flesh. The poor woman, whose wrists bore some suspicious bruises, turned scarlet with embarrassment as the court howled with laughter. She could not bear to look her former lover in the eye as he stood tall in the dock, refusing to be humiliated, one bandaged foot missing several toes which had been "misplaced" during his interrogation.

Voss and van Dorf had both pleaded for their cases to be taken to the Hochgericht, the high court, or failing that the Blutgericht, claiming that as taxpayers they came under the jurisdiction of local legislation as well as the broader ordinances of the empire. The prosecution had counterattacked by claiming that because the accuseds' sorcery had affected the local citizens of Cologne, the merchants' trial should remain under the jurisdiction of the Landrecht, the local imperial estate. It was an argument which appealed to the patriotic spirit of the bürgers but also to their antiimperial sentiments: a reaction Monsignor Solitario had been astute enough to count on.

By the time the trial concluded, the screw, the rack and the ducking stool had served to encourage condemning statements by the accused and the inquisitor's prosecution was complete.

The prisoners stand chained together, rocking against the sides of the cart as it trundles over the uneven ground, suffering the howls and mockery of the crowd as they pass by. Six guards from the cathedral follow on foot, behind them rides the archbishop. Flanked by the two von Fürstenberg brothers, the prelate feels hemmed in. Wilhelm, disturbed by the mob's behavior and fearing that his own French sentiments might be exposed by a careless insult, holds his portly form stiffly above his horse. He's shitting himself, the archbishop notes with a certain satisfaction. Serves him right for encouraging me to get involved in the infernal mess to begin with.

Heinrich turns his attention back to the prisoners. Voss is just an old man who, like many others, has made some enemies along the way. This can be the only explanation for his arrest. It is unlikely the emperor would even be aware of Voss's existence, although it was rumored he had once passed poor silk to the empress without realizing. The old merchant clings to the bars of the cart, trying to dodge the rotten tomatoes and turnips being thrown by the crowd. His face, now tongueless, is a decrepit landscape of smashed flesh and livid bruises. Sinking to his knees he clasps his hands above his head in prayer. His wife, her hair a wild gray thatch around a face swollen red with weeping, tears at her clothes as she stumbles after the cart.

Next to Voss, the Dutchman appears strangely resigned to his fate. Van Dorf probably believes this is his preordained destiny, the archbishop thinks, finding the man's pragmatic attitude predictably Calvinist. A living example of their absurd belief that man is born with his destiny etched upon his soul. Heinrich deplores the philosophy. With a certain amount of pleasurable spite he wonders whether the Dutchman will be so dignified when he is hoisted up onto the pyre. A pox on both Luther and Calvin, the archbishop thinks as he waves benevolently to a row of cheering milliners.

Carlos canters up on a white mule.

"God has sent us the blessing of fine weather, your highness," the inquisitor shouts above the mob—students, journeymen and drunken youths—running alongside the procession.

"Indeed, but I fear that heralding in the spring with the burning of souls will not prove auspicious for the future."

"Ahhh, but the cleansing of vermin is always good. It prepares the house for Lent."

The inquisitor is determined to engage Heinrich in conversation for as long as possible, conscious that his presence at the archbishop's side can only improve his status with the populace.

"But where is your cousin?" he continues. "I would have thought it fitting that he attend as a novice inquisitor."

Heinrich, gingerly resting his gout-ridden leg against the bouncing flank of his horse, frowns irritably.

"Canon von Tennen vanished two days ago. I suspect he has retreated to his country residence to ponder the various techniques available to him

as an inquisitor—although, with all due respect, I doubt he will be following in the Spanish tradition. Naturally, if you had not insisted on the executions taking place so soon, he would have been in attendance."

"Pity. He'll miss a good burning," the friar replies with a relish that disgusts the archbishop.

The procession passes the town hall then the cathedral. Turning a corner
it winds alongside the old Roman wall that marks the perimeter of the ancient city toward the armory. Next to the armory stands a tall narrow building, an old warehouse which serves as an annex. Heinrich cannot help
himself: he glances up and sees the midwife at a barred window on the second floor, her face a pale oval topped by a black streak of hair. Despite the
callousness that comes with power Heinrich cannot help but feel pity.

"Isn't that the tavern where you have rehoused the Jewish witch?"
sneers the inquisitor, interrupting his furtive thought.

For a second Heinrich contemplates rearing his horse into the side of
Carlos's diminutive mule, can almost see the Dominican crashing to the
cobbled street. Instead he sets his jaw and silently recites a prayer of redemption for his murderous thoughts, determined to play diplomat for his
own advantage.

"It is not an inn, it is the armory, and I might remind you that my
cousin acts with the blessing of my jurisdiction, Monsignor Solitario."

"I have sent a messenger to Vienna. It will be fascinating to see what the
emperor thinks of *your* intervention."

"I sincerely hope that your messenger finds the roads this side of the
border less treacherous than my own courier. On a more pleasant note, I
have arranged for you and your secretary to accompany me on a trip to the
famous Kloster Eberbach vineyard. It is my thanks to you for presenting
me with that superb bottle from Najera: what it lacked in age it made up
for in character. Kloster Eberbach boasts an outstanding cellar that should
meet with your approval."

And with a swift kick of his stirrups, the archbishop gallops forward.
Carlos watches him go then turns back toward the armory. Gazing up, he
catches Ruth's eye. He bows mockingly to her.

If there is such a thing as manifest evil, then you, Monsignor Solitario, are
it, Ruth thinks. Locking eyes with her persecutor she feels a bolt of pure

fear, as if his mere proximity can cause her body to remember the pain inflicted upon it.

It has been two weeks since Detlef's visit. Since then she has seen only the youth who brings her food and collects her chamber pot. At first she lay on her pallet, allowing her body to mend as much as it could. She had even persuaded the boy to bring her some arnica weed to heal her bruising. But as the flesh revives, so the spirit is resurrected. To Ruth's amazement, her desire to survive burns even brighter than before and with it comes the realization that her fears and desires are as human as those of the women she treats. Now, confronting the prospect of martyrdom, she finds herself yearning to be something she would never have believed her nature could permit: a simple soul with hut, hearth and husband.

The inquisitor rides out of view and Ruth forces herself to look at the prisoners. Voss cowers against the bars. The midwife, remembering his kindness during the arrests, is horrified to see his massive frame now shrunken, the skin falling off him in folds, the blackened hole in his baffled face that was once his mouth. The Dutchman, however, remains stoic, hands locked to the wooden railings, shoulders hunched against the barrage of moldy vegetables.

That will be me in my final hours, she thinks, standing there in the swaying cart, absorbing every image, brain and eyes drinking in the last moments of the world: the horizon, the sun and the cosmos.

Suddenly a rotten apple smashes against the bars, sending pieces of putrid fruit into the room. Ruth ducks then fearfully looks back out. Below a crowd of students and beggars stare up at her.

"Jewish witch, your time will come!" shouts a tall youth in the cheap black garb of a law student, leering at her. Another, a boy with a deformed leg, scrapes up some horse manure and hurls it upward, his face a grimace of hatred.

Overwhelmed, Ruth sinks onto the straw pallet and covers her head with the thin blanket.

The hanging hill outside Mülheim is a desolate place populated by rats and stray dogs who live by day in tiny caves in the bank of the Rhine and feed by night on the putrefying flesh of the executed left to rot on rope or pyre. Above are the ever-present crows, circling in a clamorous medley, vying for a better position to swoop down and pluck a milky-blue eye from a green cheek, a purple sinew from a twisted leg, an intestine from a drawn and quartered torso. It is a graveyard of carnage, lacking the eccentric order of the battlefield, or even the plague yards where child is laid beside mother, grandson next to grandfather. A macabre showground, each gallows, chopping block and smoking pyramid a different sideshow.

Here a murderess dangles, blackened buttocks swaying beneath the decaying skirt, her blond hair a ghoulish remnant of femininity on her sunken skull. There a man who failed to pay his taxes, his headless torso protruding from a shallow grave, half-eaten by dogs, his head, its mouth cavernous, tossed casually a few feet away. Beyond is the burning field with its outlandish crop, each wooden stake bursting out of the ashes like a deathly sapling with its black fruit of charred bones and smoldering flesh.

It is here that the two new pyres have been erected, posts cut from sweet green birch with the flag of the city fluttering in the breeze atop them.

Already the crowd is gathering. Some come from Mülheim, dressed in the somber clothes of the Protestant. Others are from Deutz, the Jewish elders with tumbling forelocks and chest-length beards clutching the hands of their young disciples whose wide black eyes roll nervously beneath the tall hats. Others are families bringing their children to teach them a living lesson in mortality.

The Catholics are there in numbers. Some carry straw baskets with bread and liverwurst poking out; others have brought stools to sit on and are accompanied by servants. Defiantly festive, with the white lily of the Madonna pinned to bosoms or woven through buttonholes, they are determined to enjoy themselves.

Elazar ben Saul leans heavily on his stick as he picks his way across the broken rocks and burned ground through which nothing seems to grow.

"You do not have to witness this barbarity, Reb," says Tuvia, catching the old man's arm as he stumbles.

"I need to see the depth of this Spaniard's hatred," Elazar replies. He pushes through the crowd, trying to ignore the searing pain in his arthritic legs.

Weaving her way behind him, Rosa, panting with the effort, catches up. She is dressed in black, mourning for the imprisonment of her dear child. A flask of mead is strapped to her broad back and she carries a small oak stool, a viewing perch for the rabbi.

"With all due respect, Reb Saul, I can't think why—the man is the devil incarnate. He was an evil bastard when I knew him back in Spain and he has only grown more wicked with age. May the pox strike him down!"

She spits, then rests for a moment, straightening her back. She is able to see the two pyres in the distance, stark against the backdrop of the glistening Rhine.

"If I were a Christian I'd cross myself now," she mutters, but the rabbi overhears her.

"May your God—who is Jewish—forgive you, Rosa." He sits heavily on the stool she has placed beside him.

"God can do what he likes, because frankly, Reb, there's not much he hasn't already done to me—or to you for that matter . . ."

The old nursemaid pauses. In the distance she can hear trumpets heralding the arrival of the accused. The horns sound three times, a haunting cascade from high to low. The crowd turns in the direction of the small docks where the procession is disembarking from its crossing of the Rhine.

Tuvia leans toward the rabbi, his lean face alight with a sudden intensity.

"If your daughter becomes my wife, I swear to you, her father, that next year we shall all be safe in the Holy Land, our people's sanctuary. Shabbatai Zevi is the real Messiah; I have read the signs in the sky myself."

Rosa snorts dismissively but Elazar is silent, contemplating his response to the fervent youth.

God protect us from such fanaticism, he thinks. This Shabbatai Zevi, this young zealot from Asia Minor who claims he is the new Messiah— who is he really and what miracles has he performed? He is just another charlatan exploiting the hysterical delusions of a desperate community. But he has power. His trickery spreads like a disease throughout Poland, Russia, Germany, even as far as Turkey. Too many have already packed food and linen and sent it to Hamburg in preparation for celestial summons to set sail for the Holy Land. May Tuvia see the light before he marries Ruth, Elazar prays silently.

"There have been many Messiahs and all of them false. We are a troubled and oppressed people and such people are always hungry for hope. What makes Zevi different from the others?" the old rabbi says cautiously, knowing that Zevi's followers are quick to condemn those who dare to disbelieve.

"For what have we suffered since 1648, since the Spanish persecuted our people? For what did the Jews of Poland suffer? It is written in the kabbala that the birth pangs of the Messiah will be painful but they will lead to a glorious end: the liberation of the Holy Land. And Shabbatai Zevi is the man who will lead us there. His arrival was prophesied."

Elazar clutches at the young man's sleeve. "Shh! The elders might hear. Listen, Tuvia, I promise Ruth shall be yours, but first we must free her from prison otherwise there will be no redemption, no Holy Land, just this: innocent souls sacrificed and my child sharing in their wretched fate."

The pageant winds its way up the hill. The executioner leads the procession, a masked figure in black and scarlet leather, riding proudly on a drafthorse and flanked by two papal guards holding banners. A squadron of soldiers on horseback follows then comes the prison cart itself with its grim cargo. The condemned, silent and ashen, are beyond prayer. Behind ride the archbishop and his assistants and finally the inquisitor himself.

As the cart rolls past, Elazar mutters a Kaddish for each of the accused, praying that their death will be as swift and painless as possible. Mid-sentence he sees Heinrich, somber and sweating beneath the high hat of his office. Without thinking, the old man stumbles forward, trying to catch the archbishop's attention. He falls inches from the pacing horses. Rosa and Tuvia rush to his side and pull him back before the hooves come crashing down. "Your highness! Your highness!" the rabbi cries out, but his voice is drowned by the horns and the cheering.

Heinrich peers blindly at the wall of spectators, looking for the familiar voice that called out his name. For a second he thinks he sees the chief rabbi, his hat knocked askew, his frail body being supported at either side. But before the archbishop has a chance to reach him, Elazar is swallowed by a sea of people moving forward as the condemned are marched up to the pyres.

"The two accused, Meister Matthias Voss and Herr Jan van Dorf, are charged and found guilty of witchcraft and corruption under the Criminal

Code 410 of the Imperial Estates of the Empire and as such are condemned to burn until declared dead."

The herald, a portly man with a taste for pomposity, pauses to wipe the sweat from his brow with a handkerchief embroidered with the emperor's crest.

The accused are tethered to the stakes atop the piles of faggots. Voss drops his head but the Dutchman stares straight ahead, as if he has somehow transported his conscious being elsewhere. A small redheaded child wriggles his way through the spectators and dives between the legs of the guards.

"*Vader!*" he cries before the guards catch him. "*Vader!* Mama says you are going to Heaven! Tell me it isn't true, *Vader!*"

"Tobias!" Van Dorf tears at his ropes. "Tobias!"

But by now a guard has caught hold of the struggling child who manfully beats against his captor's breastplate. Laughing, the guard carries the boy back to his weeping mother, whose arms reach out of the crowd to take him.

The Dutchman begins to howl, an inhuman sound which stuns the crowd into horrified silence.

Heinrich holds out a limp handkerchief and a young page steps forward, horn in hand. The men at the foot of each pyre stand with burning torches held high, poised for the signal. With bated breath everyone watches as finally, with a weary wave, the archbishop signals his permission and the horn sounds. A great roar rises up from the onlookers as the flames dart up the dry wood like hungry ants.

Elazar, standing on his stool, peers above the heads of those in front of him, determined to witness every moment. He watches aghast as the flames lick the base of Voss's stake. This is a man his own age, the man they said helped his daughter on the terrible day of her arrest.

"May God grant him a speedy death," he whispers and closes his eyes as Voss screams in agony. The fire darkens and the old merchant faints, his body falling limp against the spike. His skin blackens then splits open. The air fills with thick smoke and the sickeningly sweet smell of burning flesh.

Several onlookers burst into laughter as one of Voss's eyes pops out from its socket, dangling for a moment before exploding and shriveling like bacon rind.

Tuvia pulls at Elazar's gown. "Reb Saul, enough. It is not good to watch."

But the rabbi is paralyzed by the multitude of emotions which beat through him. When the setting sun becomes visible on the horizon, he is still there, staring motionless at the piles of twisted flesh that were once men.

"Reb Saul, we must go, before the scavengers get here," Tuvia pleads.

Finally Elazar's concentration is broken. With ten more years burdening his ashen brow, he steps down off his viewing perch and allows Tuvia and Rosa to lead him away.

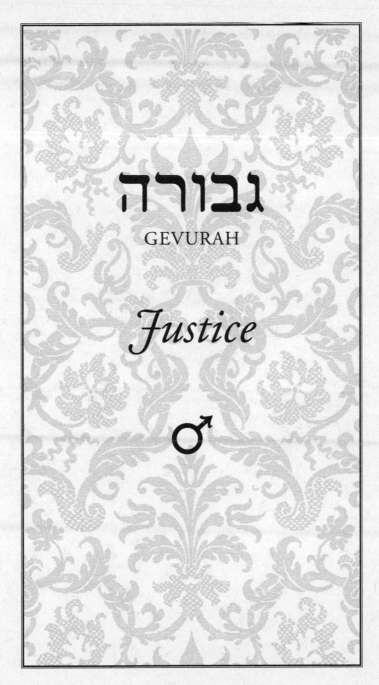

גבורה

GEVURAH

Justice

♂

✠

A hhh!"
Ferdinand arches his body, sending a leech flying through the air. His nightshirt, pushed up to his shoulders, reveals a line of the swollen parasites neatly placed between each rib. His scarred abdomen protrudes like a grotesque fruit from his skinny frame. The air is foul with body gas. The physic, keeping his face averted, presses his patient back down onto the satin-covered bed and swiftly retrieves the leech which has landed in Alphonso's lap.

"He seems dreadfully weak."

The actor anxiously stares at the white face of his lover. It is two days since the prince was first stricken by the mysterious illness; blue rings have appeared around his eyes and he is losing weight at an alarming rate.

"It is natural. When his vitals have replenished themselves he will recover," the physic announces in his painfully slow Swiss-German accent.

The count, who stands beside him, peers with visible distaste at the young royal. Noticing that the prince's mouth is a nasty purple color and his tongue appears yellow he ushers the physic to one side. "Could it be the pox? Or the Black Death? Or perhaps the wasting disease?" he whispers fearfully and, worried about infection, crosses himself.

The physic glances at his patient, whose limp hand is being caressed by Alphonso, then turns back toward the count. Without a word he walks out of the bedroom. The count, steeling himself for the worst news possible, follows. Outside they stand huddled in an alcove containing an icon of Saint Luke which once belonged to Gerhard's mother.

"If it were the pox, sire, there would be dementia and a rash. As for the Black Death, he has no lumps, no weeping sores. And if it were the wasting illness he would be pissing every hour."

"So what in all of Christendom is it, my good physic? You are aware that the prince is fourth in line from the emperor himself—if he should die both our lives are at stake, not to mention those of our families."

The physic winces nervously then, fearing spies, squeezes himself even further into the alcove. "I believe the ailment is intestinal. I suspect it is a blockage."

"The blockage, sir, is in your head. If he is not improved within the day I shall relieve you of your position.

Ferdinand opens his bloodshot eyes, blinks blearily at Alphonso then struggles to sit upright.

"Hush, there is no need for formality, you are much weakened." Alphonso carefully places two pillows behind the prince's bony back.

"Does my uncle know? I fear he will think it the pox."

"Word has been sent. The message merely stated that you are stricken with a fever."

"Still, I think you should make sure the servants light a red candle for Saint Fiacre. He is the patron saint of venereal diseases, is he not?"

"He is, my love. But it has not come to that," Alphonso whispers back.

Distracted, the prince tries to crane his neck to see who else is in the room but finds that he lacks even the energy for this. Frustrated by his frailty he whispers to his lover, "Dismiss the pages."

Alphonso, adopting the persona he uses when playing King Lear, raises his voice and waves his hand regally. "You may all leave now."

Confused about whom to take orders from, the two pages and the prince's personal valet bow then edge backward out of the chamber. Once they have gone, Ferdinand immediately collapses back onto the pillows, his face pallid.

"I fear I am dying."

"But my love, the physic is confident."

"I know myself. I am much weakened since yesterday. What if it is Cupid's itch?"

"I have seen the pox at close quarters, you have none of the markings."

"There is much I wish to achieve. Alphonso, what if I have no time left?"

Surprised by the prince's uncharacteristic intensity, yet honored that he should be privy to such intimacies, Alphonso struggles to find a reply that will encourage recovery.

"You shall have time. You shall have the rest of your life, I swear it. We will find you another physic—perhaps one that has more knowledge of the abdomen."

"I have always wanted to die nobly, on the battlefield, or as an aged reigning monarch or duke. Uncle has promised me a dukedom in Flanders. I will live there and you shall be my queen, my Rebecca of the bedsheets, and we shall love openly. Together we shall breed Arabian stallions and they shall be purple and gold with manes of the finest silver . . ."

As Ferdinand lapses into another fiery delirium, Alphonso, who like his forefathers does not believe in the power of bloodletting, plucks four of the largest leeches from the prince's body. He drops them into a dish of salt beside the bed. The creatures, glutted with blood, writhe atop the white crystals. Watching them die, the actor wonders whether the prince isn't being poisoned slowly. Since Ferdinand fell sick he has been secretly testing his hypothesis by feeding pieces of the prince's food to the count's favorite Kammerhund. So far the animal appears unaffected.

Yesterday Alphonso cornered a Jewish peddler who was in the servants' quarters selling fur pelts and trinkets from Muscovy. After pulling him away from the kitchen servants, the actor almost gave the poor man a heart attack by breaking into fluent Hebrew. Swiftly, before they were discovered, Alphonso questioned him about the Jewish medics who were available in the region.

"There are only two," the man told him, his face weathered leather, creased around the hooked nose and mournful mouth, his Hebrew almost incomprehensible for the heavy Slavic accent. "Both live on the other side of the Rhine. Salomon Moses from Mülheim, Isaac Schlam from Deutz. But the best is not even a man."

"I have heard of her—Ruth bas Elazar Saul, the midwife?"

"They say she has a magic touch, that all she needs to do is hold her hands over you. But you will never get her, the Christians plan to burn her."

"When?"

"Who knows. They burned two of their own last week. I was there, I haven't seen such joviality since Christmas. It really cheered the people up. Man is strange—give me the sky and the open field any day."

Alphonso slipped two Reichstaler into a hand that felt as dry as sand. "My name is Alphonso de Lorenzo, I am a Christian," he whispered.

"For two Reichstaler you can be an Ottoman Mussulman for all I care," the peddler had replied cheerfully, pocketing the money.

Now, looking at the prince's deteriorated condition, Alphonso considers that the midwife might be Ferdinand's only hope of survival. Leaning back with his eyes shut, the actor starts to review the plots' of all the great plays he has performed. Suddenly he remembers a work by a dynamic French playwright that swept through the Viennese court the year before: *Tartuffe* by Molière, a master of convoluted plot and mannered high farce, a genius of exquisite social satire. Drawing a parallel between Emperor Leopold's tolerance of Inquisitor Carlos Vicente Solitario and the disastrous obsession of Molière's fallible nobleman Orgon with the religious hypocrite Tartuffe, Alphonso begins to form a plot of his own. He will appeal to Samuel Oppenheimer, he will ask him to intervene on behalf of the ailing royal.

Inspired he sits down at the prince's desk. Designed in the shape of a medieval castle by Hans Stethaimer, a famous architect of two centuries ago, the desk is one of the few gifts the prince received from his father, now long dead. Treasured by Ferdinand, it travels everywhere with him. With a gesture bordering on the sensual, Alphonso runs his hand along the edge of the lacquered rosewood fringed with tiny bastions, a miniature drawbridge crowning the top shelf. Oh to be an aristocrat surrounded by such artistry, he thinks sadly.

He smooths out a new scroll with a ritualistic flourish, savoring the scent of fresh parchment that wafts up, then reaches for the quill still sitting in the prince's gilded monogrammed inkpot.

To Samuel Oppenheimer, the Great and Honorable Court Jew of Vienna: I, your brother in blood and right hand in stealth, salute you and send you this lyrical stanza upon which the life of another—the nephew of the great Emperor himself, namely the good Prince Ferdinand Hapsburg—and his recovery from a mysterious and sudden ailment depends.

A Rebecca [he chooses the name as homage to Ferdinand's nickname for himself] *of the lower Rhinelands, a deliverer of many, is rumored to have a golden touch—to be a Midas of the Midriff. Deliver her quick I would say, for my Prince suffers mightily, but alas our Rebecca in the armory languishes, for her magic has Christian eyes offended and I fear she will be ashes before my Prince is mended. Can the Lion of Judah save the fledgling of the double-headed Eagle?*

Signed: Alphonso de Lorenzo.

Alphonso smiles proudly then tenderly rolls up the scroll. Very carefully he seals it with a blob of red wax and presses the prince's gold seal into the cooling liquid then his own ring upon that.

Later that day, after making sure the scroll is clearly marked "Samuel Oppenheimer, the Royal Court Jew of Vienna," Alphonso secretly arranges for a loyal nobleman and childhood companion of Ferdinand's, the only one of the prince's chevaliers he trusts, to carry it to Vienna.

Dear Benedict,

It has been two weeks since I last wrote to you and much has come to pass. The conditions of my imprisonment are improved greatly. For this I have to thank one Detlef von Tennen, a canon of the cathedral here and a Wittelsbach aristocrat. An unusual ally indeed and I am yet to discern his motives. Suffice to say that he has expressed an interest in the "heretic" philosophies west of the border and has even confessed to having read your writings. Should I trust such an enthusiast? I fear not. However, he has taken upon himself (with no small risk) the role of my inquisitor, thus preserving me, for a small time only, from the Dominican. Therefore I live longer, in greater comfort, but in greater confusion. I cannot judge the good canon except to say that he disturbs me profoundly so vast are the incongruities that churn within him.

He is a young man—that is to say, older than myself but yet neither elderly nor of middle years. A second son who has followed the custom of these parts by adopting the cloth, he nevertheless has taken the spirituality of his vows to heart, and with it, I believe, a genuine dedication to the betterment of man. It is out of this devotion that he seeks philosophical enlightenment. But Benedict, I sense that firstly he is a man and as much as I look to the somberness of his robes, I fear there is less purity beneath the linen than I would like to believe.

Will he be my savior? I know not. A week ago they burned the two other poor souls who were arrested with me. The third was suspiciously murdered in his own cell. The pageant passed beneath the window of my new prison and was fearful to behold. By evensong the sky was filled with two pillars of smoke and although I prayed for the integration of their souls with the very ether itself, I am ashamed to say that I was paralyzed with fear for my own fate.

Death strips all men of dignity and it is a lie to think otherwise. Execution imposed is one hundredfold a humiliation. When my time comes I would rather die by my own hand by hemlock than wait for the hangman's knock.

"Fräulein?"

Detlef stands at the door, his hand hesitant upon the handle. Under his arm he carries scrolls and a small leather pouch containing several quills and inkpots. Ruth is sitting with her back to him, dressed in a pale blue smock made of serge, her long black hair flowing down to her waist. Upon seeing him she is infused with a secret elation.

"Forgive my absence, I had left for my country retreat. I have taken the time to design a strategy."

"A strategy?"

In lieu of a reply he rolls out the scrolls on the wooden floor.

"I have examined the evidence. Of all the women who have testified to the inquisitor the most promising for our defense is Abigail Brassant."

"Meister Brassant's young wife?"

"She claims that the child was born dead, but then you cast a spell and revived it."

"During the birth I discovered the umbilical cord to be wrapped around the child's neck—I had to cut in such a fashion that would save both babe and mother. After the baby was pulled free its nose and mouth were blocked. I merely sucked the mucus from these passages, thus forcing it to breathe."

"If I am able to prove that it is medical knowledge not witchcraft which makes you a good midwife, we may be able to secure your freedom."

"But how can this be shown without delivering a child in front of the court itself?"

Detlef opens the leather pouch and sets out the quills and ink. "Would you be able to illustrate your methods?"

"I can but try."

"Good. It is the best argument we have. There has been no sighting of levitation, devil worship or the raising of the dead. It is merely the un-orthodoxy of your techniques which has caused superstition."

"Fired by the zeal of the inquisitor. Tell me, Canon, why does he not arrange my murder as he obviously arranged Müller's?" She tries to hide the fear in her voice with anger.

Detlef looks at her sharply. "Who told you about Müller's death?"

"Your serving boy. Do not be angry with him, he is a sweet lad and I have a gift for extracting information."

Indeed, Detlef thinks, wondering whether he can trust her.

"I do not believe the inquisitor was responsible for Müller's murder."

"Who then?"

The canon's silence answers Ruth's worst fear.

"The archbishop? Then why should he not sacrifice me to his politics also? And why should I trust you? You are in his service."

"I give you my word. That is the best I can pledge. Please, Fräulein, I am your only hope."

She stares at him wide-eyed, wondering whether she, like Müller, will receive an unwanted visitor at the dead of night.

"I do not have a choice. But Canon, why should my case be more valuable than the others? And if I am proved innocent, what political purpose will that serve the archbishop, or even yourself?"

What can he say to her? Why has he troubled to take up her cause when there have been so many who have gone before her, many equally innocent? Is he so repelled by the moral compromises, the reduction of his faith, or is it that Ruth bas Elazar Saul embodies a nobler morality toward which he yearns himself? Or is there a more carnal impulse he is struggling to deny?

"Why have I fought to defend you? I cannot answer that myself. But do not deceive yourself. I have enemies also. Monsignor Solitario waited until he knew I had left Cologne to hasten the executions. The two condemned were a warning from Leopold to Maximilian to stop his fraternizing with the French."

"Innocent men sacrificed for petty affairs of state."

"This is the world we live in, Fräulein."

"So enlighten me: what am I, a mere Jew of no consequence, to the inquisitor?"

"Emperor Leopold's gift for being such a good lap dog," he says brutally, then immediately regrets his honesty.

Frightened that he should see her weaken Ruth turns to the wall.

"It is not that your case is entirely without prospect, Fräulein. I can exploit the sentiments of the Gaffeln. Meister Voss was one of their own and highly respected. His execution has been seen as a direct intervention by Leopold, and as you know the Cologners are loath to be dictated to by anyone from outside. Even the Holy Emperor himself. You have delivered many Christian babies safely within these city walls—Jewish or not Jewish, witch or no witch, you are not without your supporters. Meister Brassant himself has told me, in private and with no small risk, that he will anonymously finance any evidence that will prove your innocence."

"There is something else you should know for your argument."

"Pray tell?"

"There is a woman in my town, a mother who has not yet forgiven me for the travesty God fostered upon her and her child. The babe, who I delivered with my own hands, has failed to speak at all for some two years. And the mother, in her grief, has taken it upon herself to speak of sorcery. She is convinced I summoned the she-demon Lilith to the birthing."

"And did you?"

"Canon, it is always my practice to hang amulets against Satan's grandmother, but I swear I did not invoke the demon. In truth, the woman's child does not speak for he cannot hear."

Perplexed by the strange mix of Ruth's practical knowledge of *scientia nova* and her investment in the old ways, Detlef again decides to trust his instincts.

"I believe you. I will search out this woman and make sure that her child and her silence are provided for."

"I am both reassured and sorry to see that you have such a realistic turn of mind, Canon," Ruth replies, a wry twinkle in her eyes. Detlef cannot help but smile back.

"Would you have your inquisitor otherwise?"

"No, I believe I would not."

Again the space between them thickens, empathy catching each like a spiderweb. Awkward in his desire, Detlef steps back.

"There is something else. Your father has made a supplication to the archbishop."

"My father?" Her voice cracks with sudden emotion. "How is he?"

"That I cannot say, but I do know he has offered to waive Maximilian Heinrich's debts in exchange for your freedom."

"They are Herr Hossern's debts, the exchange will include my hand."

"Your hand? But I thought that perhaps you were already . . ."

"Pledged?"

"Forgive me, I know not the customs of your people."

"I am maiden and have vowed to have no congress with man." Then she adds mischievously, "Nor devil."

Surprised, Detlef looks away. What else had he imagined? But then her ways are foreign to him.

"So you are to marry the moneylender?"

"It is his nephew, Tuvia, my father's assistant, who seeks the match."

"In that case we must secure your freedom for then you shall have both husband and father to return to."

"The freedom I desire, the husband not. My father tried to marry me before; it was another reason I fled to Holland."

They both sit and watch each other, she on a small wooden stool, he towering over her on a chair. And for an instant they are neither canon nor heretic but simply man and woman.

"Are a woman's desires ever relevant?" she asks softly, a statement more than a question, a plaintive echo of her own frustrations.

"It is written that a woman needs guidance for her own welfare and that such guidance is best supplied by a husband and the security of the hearth. Most are betrothed by fifteen, Fräulein, you should consider yourself lucky to have a suitor at such an advanced age."

"I am twenty-three."

"Ten years younger than I."

"But you are a man of the cloth, such matters are superfluous to you. If I were a man I should dedicate my life to philosophy and medical knowledge."

"But you are not; you are a woman. And I am a priest."

"You are more than that, I suspect, just as I am more than you know, Canon von Tennen," she adds defiantly, then leans toward him. "You have as much curiosity as I. You seek knowledge."

And upon seeing his ears begin to burn, she realizes she has stumbled upon a hidden truth. "What have you read?"

"Careful, Fräulein, be sure you understand your intentions. After all, if I am to burn too, who will be left to rescue you?"

"See it as a pledge of faith. Confess, as I have confessed to you, and then we shall be equals. I swear on my father's life that I will never betray you."

"Not even under torture?"

"Not even if they rip the bones of my arms from my body."

And as Detlef stares at her, a great exhilaration rises up from the soles of his feet and burns slowly through his body: the thrilling relief of admission, of being released from the burden of secret inspiration, of notions that he had dismissed as flights of wild fancy until he read those incriminating pieces of parchment, one of which alone could condemn a man to death. A colossal excitement, sexual in its intensity, grips him.

"De Witt, Spinoza, John Milton, Everard the Leveler, the mystic John Lilburne among others," he tells her, shaking, then wonders what spell she has cast to make him utter such a damning statement.

"And how does an aristocrat and powerful member of the Catholic church align himself with such radical ideas of humanism and democracy? Could he be a covert supporter of the notion of a republic?"

"Do you wish to damn me further, Fräulein, or are you just toying with my vulnerabilities?"

"Rest assured, sir, I never jest. I just have a fatal curiosity."

"Fatal indeed. If I am defined by my robe and rank, then I grant you there is a growing paradox within me. Sometimes I wonder why I fought in the Great War, why all those young men were slaughtered. To what purpose? How is it that ideology can divide and destroy men? Why is one man worth more than another by dint of his birthright? It is these debates that have driven me to my secret readings. I find that I have more philosophical ambition than I had calculated upon. It leaves me with a restless soul. Another cleric would be more than satisfied with my position."

"The riches toward which your intellect drives you will be far greater and far more rewarding than a bishopric in the Rhineland, that I promise you."

"So the prisoner is making promises to the jailer," he replies, amused by her earnestness. Ruth's intensity is broken by a slight smile before she becomes serious again.

"Tell me, what have you read of Benedict Spinoza?"

"I have read his short treatise on God, man and his well-being, and I subscribe to his notion, *sub specie aeternitatis*, that we should look at our own lives under the aspect of eternity, to try to see our problems in light of the place they actually occupy in a universal perspective. In that idea I find great solace, to know that our short lives are finally and undeniably insignificant in the greater realm of the universe," Detlef replies hesitantly.

"We are of shared sentiment then."

"It appears so. And as such I am desirous of your liberation."

"I am flattered."

"Do not be. Even Catholic canons are able to have an appreciation of a rare intellect."

"So are you a supporter of the republic?" she asks.

"Only at such a time when the common man is educated enough to govern himself. I cannot see it working otherwise."

"But a republic where serf is equal to king, where property belongs to a commonwealth—such a nation would educate its people," Ruth counters.

"Perhaps, but I fear that man is inherently unequal in nature and that all the nurturing in the world will never undo this inequality. It is the cruel law of the forest itself, or of the herd or the gambling pit," he answers, spurred on by her argument.

"But without the social experiment of a republic, we are never to know."

"You speak a somber truth. Tell me, is it true that Benedict Spinoza is a Mennonite?"

"He dwells among them at Rijnsburg. They meet weekly *in collegia* where each is allowed the freedom to voice his hypothesis. Like-minded individuals freely exchanging visions for a new future. Stronger spirits than myself," she adds, unable to keep a note of regret from her voice.

"Fräulein, I will prove your innocence."

Only then, mustering all the courage he has, does he reach across and take her hand, holding it as paternally as he can despite the lust that bolts through him.

"And I your valor," she replies, looking directly at him.

Samuel Oppenheimer, Court Jew and purveyor-general to Leopold I, leans over the table and, with the help of a long brass pole with a carved wooden hand fashioned at one end, pushes the model of the English ship, *The Diamond*, toward the miniature Dutch fleet. Colorfully painted in the orange, white and green of their nation, they sit on a rendition of the North Sea, placed in an arrowhead of advancement. The tall man, in his mid-thirties, his handsome aquiline features denoting an ancient elegance, stands and smooths down the silver curls of his impressive periwig, then flicks back the long lace sleeves which hang past his manicured fingernails.

"Joseph!" Samuel calls out.

His son, barely eight, who is curled up on a low settee, jolts himself out of a light sleep.

Oppenheimer points imperiously at the English fleet which appears to be slamming sideways into the Dutch ships. "Who shall win, Joseph?"

"The English," replies the child in a well-rehearsed response.

Emperor Leopold, watching from a high-backed baroque chair, leans forward on his gold-tipped cane. The rugged features and huge craggy jaw break into a grin that immediately softens the unprepossessing visage. Oppenheimer, exceedingly conscious of Leopold's approval, decides to exploit the young emperor's joviality further.

"And why, my child?" he asks.

"Because we don't like the Dutch," Joseph answers in an uncertain tone.

Leopold's cackle bounces around the small court chamber.

"And . . . ?" the purveyor-general persists. Worried, the boy creases his forehead in imitation of his father. The emperor, recognizing the gesture, laughs again.

"Because we owned some of the East India Company?" the child replies nervously.

"Bravo!" the emperor applauds and turns to Samuel. "You have the child well trained. If only the English were as compliant."

"Protestants are never known for their compliancy, sire, but they do make excellent propagandists."

"Indeed, we have to thank their printing press for that."

Leopold, suddenly sober, falls into a meditation as he gazes uneasily upon the toy battlefield. The Anglo-Dutch war is ravaging the North Sea, and Turkish troops in painted green turbans hover around Austria, while the French, on tiny black horses, line the borders of his own empire and Brandenburg. In short, Europe is a quilt of warring factions.

Samuel, reading his master's disposition and knowing his love of tactics, dramatically pushes half the Dutch fleet up to the east coast of Scotland.

"I have news of the next chess move," he announces mysteriously. "The Smyra fleet is to attack from the north. However . . ." and with the other hand he skillfully maneuvers several of the English Charles II's ships so that they face the Lowlanders, "I am not the only one with spies."

Again Leopold collapses into laughter. "Samuel, you do me more good than any hallowed medic," he gasps, then shakes himself into a semblance of dignity.

"I am undone, exhausted and nearly dethroned. A pox upon the machinations required of today's statesmen. I am exhausted by it all."

The arrival of a page interrupts him. The young servant, caught unaware by the emperor's clandestine presence, blushes and genuflects, stumbling backward in the effort.

"What is it, Fritz?" Samuel says, irritated, wishing the boy would stop bowing like an idiot.

"There is a visitor from the Rhineland; he says he has an important letter to deliver to the Court Jew."

"The Court Jew is there." Leopold points to Samuel with an imperious finger. "However, the emperor is not." And with a wink he steps neatly behind a painted Chinese screen.

"You are not here but you still hear?" Samuel inquires with one of his customary puns, mouth pressed to the thin silk partition. On the other side of the screen the emperor giggles.

A moment later the page ushers in the messenger. With boots still dusty from his ride, the chevalier throws back his cloak and reaches deeply into his breeches. He pulls out the scroll, now grimy with sweat, and hands it to Samuel.

"This comes from one of your people. It is a message of the highest importance and involves a member of the royal family," he announces pompously. "I am to return immediately with a reply."

Samuel, recognizing the royal seal overpressed with Alphonso's ring, looks up at the chevalier. "You may wait outside."

"And then will you have a response? This is an urgent affair, his highness is gravely ill."

"You have my word."

Samuel waits until he is alone before unrolling the scroll. After a quick perusal he pushes back the silk screen, surprising the emperor who has pulled off his long curly wig and is busy scratching his naked scab-covered scalp.

"Sire, I believe this might amuse you."

"Let us hope it is more amusing than the interior of a closet." The emperor throws his wig on again, this time crookedly.

"The writer is a minor actor in my employment. Having some dramatic ambition he writes in the style of Molière, that limp-wristed French copyist of little talent. He is, however, to be trusted," Samuel informs the royal gravely.

"Ferdinand." The emperor looks up mournfully from the letter, his heart sinking at the thought of the latest scandal his errant nephew might have engineered. "I prayed that the Rhenish hunting season might invigorate his manliness, but evidently not. His marriage to the long-suffering Maria of Champagne has served the empire but has done nothing to dampen his temperament."

Leopold sighs heavily as Samuel glances down at Alphonso's florid signature.

"I fear you are right, sire."

The two men pause for a moment as they reflect on the burdens of familial responsibility. The gentle snore of Samuel's young son breaks their musing.

"Is not the inquisitor, Carlos Vicente Solitario, in Cologne in the service of your highness?" Samuel asks.

"Of both myself and the Inquisitor-General—he is acting as prosecutor. Archbishop Maximilian Heinrich has been a bitter disappointment and I am forced to cut off a few of those fluttery fingers he is always waving at brattish King Louis."

"But what of this Rebecca of the lower Rhinelands?"

"A mere nobody, a Jewish witch the inquisitor has some obsession with. I have made her my gift to him for being so obedient."

Oppenheimer strokes his favorite dachshund. If there is one man he loathes at court it is Carlos Vicente Solitario. The Dominican embodies the worst aspects of religious fanaticism and Samuel knows many Sephardic families, some of them *conversos*, some not, who have suffered at the hands of the notorious inquisitor. It isn't just the man's anti-Semitism that rankles; after all, that is commonplace. Every successful Hebrew must learn to live with and work around such ingrained attitudes. It is the palpable ignorance of the man, his belligerent old-world ways which he deliberately cultivates to exploit the emperor's own remorse about his secret lack of Catholic faith. Religious guilt is Leopold's Achilles heel and the Spaniard has been quick to take advantage of it.

Alphonso is right to allude to Molière, Samuel thinks to himself, Solitario is indeed a Tartuffe, but one far more extreme and with infinitely more dangerous political ramifications. He glances back down at the scroll. The Court Jew's ambition is such that he cannot afford enemies. He is able to placate other ambassadors through gifts of jewels or carefully forgotten loans, but Solitario is driven by hatred. And as Samuel knows to his chagrin, hatred is the one emotion impervious to bribery.

The purveyor-general fingers the scarlet cord binding the scroll. This could be an extraordinary opportunity, but only if his next move is the right one.

"Sire, could it be possible that the youth is genuinely ill, maybe even on his deathbed? He is described as suffering mightily."

"The only time I have seen Ferdinand suffer mightily was when he managed to inflict that ridiculous injury upon himself during a jousting competition. He could, of course, be stricken with the pox, in which case 'tis best he suffers in an insignificant hunting lodge in the Rhineland than here under the eyes of the empire. He sets a bad example, Samuel, you know that."

"But his father was a great military hero in the war against the Lutherans."

"For which he was awarded the dubious honor of marrying my sister, God rest his soul. Anyway, what are you getting at?"

"It could be ill-advised to let the son perish when we need heroes to fight against the Hungarians and possibly the Turks."

"Save him for later, in other words?"

"With his father's name he should attract conscripts."

"Possibly. Although Ferdinand on a horse is not an inspiring sight, and he is yet to find his métier with sword, crossbow or arrow despite the best tutors in the empire."

"No one need see him in actual combat. We could use the Lutheran tactic and employ the printing press to proclaim his heroism. Sire, the Hapsburgs could do with another hero."

"An interesting notion. How does the aspiring poet finish his plea?"

"'Can the Lion of Judah save the double-headed Eagle's errant fledgling?' I suspect the witch has some medical training—I have heard she has been in Amsterdam."

"Next they will be allowing women to attend the universities. It is too much for one century."

"Sire, should I send word to secure her release?"

"Is there a way I can disguise my own command?"

"Perhaps if this Alphonso were provided with some secret pledge he could take to the archbishop . . . ?"

"Perhaps."

"And if Maximilian Heinrich were able to muster a defense swiftly and in the utmost confidentiality, the whole business could be over with and the midwife by your nephew's side as quickly as the swallow flies. Speed and discretion are the objectives in this exercise. After all, what is the worth of a Jewess's life next to that of a member of the royal family—unless she is able to save that life?"

"Samuel, yet again your understanding of my nature astounds me."

And with that, the emperor leans across and cheerfully knocks over half the Dutch fleet with his huge thumb.

Maximilian Heinrich, having been called from officiating at Sunday Mass, adjusts his green vestment and throws over his shoulder the short cape made from cloth imported from the Middle East and embroidered with Arabic script heralding the glory of Mohammed, a detail of which the archbishop—German and Latin being his only tongues—is completely oblivious.

Sweating profusely, he indicates to the young cleric assisting him that he wants to be rid of the irritating *cappa* decorated with a lurid depiction of the Resurrection that hangs down his back. As the trembling young novice clumsily unties the cape before tackling the rest of the heavy garments, Heinrich swings his glance to the young Jesuit priest who, with a rather annoying irreverence, slouches before him.

"Young man, last time I cut my Sunday sermon short was for the beheading of the English King Charles. I cannot tell you how much that irritated the bürgers. It almost made it worth it."

The archbishop, abandoning all protocol, glares aggressively at the young visitor. He looks Mediterranean, probably in cahoots with that damnable Dominican, Heinrich speculates grimly. Aggravated, he pulls off the heavy chain with the pectoral cross hanging from it containing the holy relic of the virgin Saint Ursula's tongue.

"A matter of great secrecy and urgency, eh?" He plonks the relic down on the plain wooden table. "Of royal import?" he continues sardonically, his tirade in full swing. Stripped back to his daimatic, which he pulls roughly over his head, he finally stands defiantly in his undergarments, a simple long cotton vest and thin plain breeches. After farting with great satisfaction, the archbishop swipes a handkerchief from the young priest and begins mopping up the patches of sweat staining his undershirt. "What, pray, would a young pipsqueak like yourself, and a Jesuit to boot, have to say to the archbishop of Cologne, eh?"

The Jesuit, his attractive features almost feminine in their beauty, appears bewildered and painfully shy. Breaking into a passionate avalanche of Italian, he somehow manages to stammer and spit at the same time. Appalled, Heinrich wipes the spray from his face.

"For God's sake, at least speak German!" the archbishop exclaims, fearing that the young Jesuit might be deranged.

Suddenly the priest's whole demeanor transforms. His shoulders straighten, he pulls himself up to his full height, his chest puffs out. Miraculously a whole new air of confidence, even humor, seems to split his earnest face.

Now convinced that he is dealing with a dangerously crazed assassin, Heinrich grabs his crosier for protection, while his novice takes shelter behind the archbishop's corpulent near-naked figure. Laughing, the Jesuit pulls off his hood and appears to peel away his scalp: instantly, rich black locks fall to his shoulders.

"What witchery is this!" Heinrich cries.

" 'Tis not witchery at all, merely the craft of a professional trickster, the actor," Alphonso replies, bowing deeply.

Heinrich covers his embarrassment by banging the crosier sharply on the floor. "And whose puppet are you, sir? Do you belong to the French or to our good emperor himself?"

"Neither, your highness. A traveling performer is his own master, but on this particular occasion I merely represent the wishes of our good emperor, Leopold."

Alphonso reaches into his cassock and pulls out a scroll of the finest paper. He presents it to Heinrich who sniffs it suspiciously.

"You will find it authentic."

Still apprehensive, Heinrich examines the seal—the double-headed eagle with its crowns appears genuine enough. Carefully he breaks the missive open with a paper knife and rolls it out. As he studies it, Alphonso winks cheekily at the blushing novice.

Heinrich sits down heavily and without thinking reaches for the bottle of Hattenheimer Engelmannsberg, a riesling made by the Cistercians that is ever-present on his desk. Sighing, he pours himself a glass. His pudgy forehead wrinkles with concentration as he begins to read. Outside, the sounds of the departing congregation drift into the small chamber: snippets of conversation about the local harvests, the trade index of the Dutch

East India Company and the impact of the English war, a complaint about the emperor stealing Cologne's gold to finance his war with the Turks. Somewhere a young woman laughs and is hushed by another.

Finally Heinrich looks up. With an imperious flick of the wrist he dismisses his assistant then turns to Alphonso.

"This is a grave matter indeed and one not easily solved."

"Sir, it has to be. Prince Ferdinand is on his deathbed. A desperate situation requires unorthodox measures."

"You realize that Fräulein Saul has been charged with grave offenses of witchcraft: that she has lain with the devil to ensure a good birthing, that she consorted with the demon Lilith to steal the voice from a poor babe—"

"Serious indeed, but if she is able to save the life of one of the heirs apparent . . ."

"A witch is a witch, my good sir. I assume the emperor realizes the danger to my station and reputation if I act upon his wishes?"

"The emperor is deeply fond of his nephew and will be eternally indebted if his requirements are fulfilled."

Alphonso, calling on the best performance technique he knows for lying, looks the archbishop straight in the eye and maintains a steady gaze. Heinrich, no virgin to deception, smiles smoothly back.

"And as we both know, the emperor's fondness for his nephew is legendary." The archbishop's cynical smile widens. "I shall be happy to contribute to his ongoing affection for the youth. However, there is one small obstacle: the zealot Carlos Vicente Solitario . . ."

At which Alphonso, resorting to another hue from his palette of performances, throws on the guise of Othello. "Leopold will take care of the inquisitor. If you can free the midwife to look after Ferdinand, and swiftly, all shall be rewarded," he announces in a sudden rich baritone.

The deep Moorish tone confuses the archbishop. The actor, with a certain lewdness, picks a grape off the table in front of him, sucks the skin off it, then, leaning forward, looks brazenly into Heinrich's bloodshot eyes.

"I have it on the emperor's word."

After the actor has left, Heinrich sits staring out of the small stained-glass window. Through the azure and gold figure of the archangel Gabriel proclaiming the annunciation to the Virgin Mary—an image the archbishop desperately hopes might be an allegory for his recent visitor—he can see the struggling branches of a grape vine given to him as a gift by a visiting Cistercian abbot a few years earlier. The twisting tendrils remind him of the beauty of the vineyard it originated from. Suddenly he has an idea, a plan which promises to resolve everything.

Cheered, the archbishop laughs then bellows for Detlef.

The low marble table is set among the vines beside an ancient stone bench. A burning lantern sits at one end, casting a crimson glow that makes ruddy the faces of the monks gathered around it. The moon, the slenderest of crescents, still hovers in the dawn sky. Carlos, a fur jacket wrapped around his hooded robe, shivers. Heinrich, who has metamorphosed into the quintessence of conviviality, well lubricated with the best Rheinwein since his arrival, stands with his bare head bowed in prayer, indifferent to the strong wind blowing up from the Rhine below.

"May this season bring bounty to the vines, joy to our parishioners and fecundity to the Rhineland. In the immortal words of our own Saint Hildegard: *Mann macht den Menschen gewund; der Wein macht den Menschen gesund; man hurts men but wine heals them.* Amen," the prelate finishes.

"Amen," murmur the Cistercian monks, pale ghosts in their white cassocks.

The archbishop suddenly yawns, stretching his arms wide against the cosmos. Standing at the top of the mountain of Ruesdesheim, his figure cuts an imposing cross against the vast panorama filled with nothing but the last of the night's stars and the paling moon. It is five o'clock and Heinrich has insisted that the inquisitor accompany him and an entourage of seven local monks, each carrying a stone flask of wine and a glass, to witness the "birth of the day" from the highest point within the ancient walled vineyard.

It is the morning of the third day of their sojourn and, although Carlos distrusts the prelate's motives for inviting him along, he cannot help but be seduced by the gentle rhythm and unspoken camaraderie of the white monks, the result of years of cohabitation and shared labor which has transformed them into a perfectly coordinated colony of superb viticulturists. Their discipline and unquestioning acceptance of his presence, the severity of the terraced slopes descending down to the river, the immaculately groomed ancient vines now bedecked with luminous spring growth, the simple beauty of the white and red wooden monastery with its old press house containing giant wine presses from the Middle Ages, are all balm to his Spanish soul. It is the first time the inquisitor has felt welcome since his arrival in Germania. And, to his surprise, he begins to feel a begrudging gratitude toward his host.

"Ahh, there fades Venus, the first and last of the celestial goddesses." The archbishop points to the planet whose glistening light dims until, all of a sudden, it disappears.

Carlos gazes up; the empyrean hangs over them like a billowing tapestry embroidered with the most delicate of gold and silver threads. Noticing the slight shift in the position of the stars, the Dominican cannot help but long for his own Spanish sky.

"This year has not been well aspected, your grace. You must have seen in January, as we did from Vienna, the inauspicious comet that blazed its fiery way over all of Europa. A bad sign, I fear: the rest of the year will bring much suffering and perhaps more war."

Carlos stares grimly into the brightening firmament where the first glow of buried sunshine is just beginning to bleed into the mauve horizon.

Heinrich glances at the Spaniard. The proximity of the last few days has allowed him the luxury of observation: now he can see the hues and subtleties of the man. There is some buried tragedy which has scarred this man, the archbishop muses, having found that in discussion he always hits the same immovable spot in the inquisitor's soul: a boulder of hate that, like a hostile coastline, defines his character.

"Indeed," Heinrich responds. "However, my personal astrologer is more optimistic than the hacks who make money foretelling doom and disaster. He predicts a hot summer and a good harvest—that's enough future for me. We cannot choose the times we live in. Just as, sometimes, we cannot choose whom we love."

"Of such secular matters I know nothing. My only love is for Jesus Christ, our Good Lord who died on the Cross for our sins," the inquisitor replies with the taint of the prude in his voice.

"Oh, I don't know. I think the nature of faith is love and love of the goodness in man. Hate is not Christian; it is a toxin that can only fester like a canker, do you not think, Monsignor?"

The sun is now a throbbing crimson lip pushing up over the muddy vineyards. The inquisitor turns from the archbishop feeling like a crab which has been stripped of its shell. Torn between the temptation to unburden his heart and the terror of his constructions and beliefs being dismantled, Carlos hesitates and stares directly into the ascending ball of fire. A gray cloud has begun to race across the edge of the orb. It is like Apollo himself, the friar fancies, imagining that the thin wisps of vapor are the fiery steeds, with the beautiful young god, his golden hair streaming behind him, his naked body a muscular arc of honed grace, following the stallions in his chariot of spun gold. Shall I ever be that brave, Carlos thinks; was I ever that rash? Frightened of the answer that is forming deep within him, he turns back to Heinrich.

"I have faith and love for my mission, your grace. It is not an easy task and often requires me to harden my heart. Righteousness is not to be confused with hate," he finishes, his shell now firmly clamped back around him.

Disappointed that he has failed to liberate the man within the inquisitor, Heinrich gestures to the waiting monks. With silent decorum they place the seven bottles of wine—each with two wineglasses beside it—on the table before the two men.

"I have arranged a little tasting for our pleasure, Monsignor Solitario. Seven bottles for the seven stages of Christ's life. It is a beloved allegory of mine that I have been meditating upon for many years. I hope you will appreciate it."

The Dominican cannot help but smile at the gleeful gleam in the prelate's eye. "Indeed, I am honored."

The archbishop takes up the first bottle. He pours out two glasses then lifts one up against the sunrise. The wine shines a pale yellow.

"This is for the baptism of our Lord by John the Baptist. I think of the Galilean, infused with belief but still uncertain of his calling, up to his knees in the clear water of the River Jordan as the fervent words of his black-eyed and wild-haired cousin stir his soul. The wine is a simple innocent white, a youthful Chasselas from Alsace, a favorite once with the English playwright Shakespeare. Still green but dry, soft and gently fruity, laced with tremendous promise—just like our young Lord, and ourselves once upon a time."

He goes to the second bottle, this time pouring out a dark red.

"The temptation of Christ in the wilderness. Satan's manifestation, every sinful seduction whirling before our Lord's eyes."

Heinrich glances wryly at the Spaniard, searching for a glint of recognition, having sensed that the sins of the flesh might be the inquisitor's weakness. Carlos's face remains an expressionless mask.

"Christ's torment is the anguish that strikes every young monk once he resigns himself to his vocation. After all, are we not all men under the robe?"

Heinrich laughs but Carlos remains ominously silent. Shrugging off the inquisitor's sudden frostiness, the prelate turns to the wine, lifts a glass and sniffs it.

"Naturally I have chosen a red wine from the Benedictine vineyards at Savigny-les-Beaune. A vineyard once owned by the Knights Templar, who themselves were guilty of succumbing to all sorts of temptations, accused of buggery and many other profanities by King Philip IV. So this wine has a dangerous history of temptation—satiated and otherwise. Wickedly full-bodied, it lingers on the palate like a lascivious dream."

Carlos lifts the wine to his face. The aroma is rich and pungent and, tickling the back of his nose, reminds him of something. Blushing furiously he realizes it is the smell of the sex of a woman. Heinrich, watching, winks knowingly at him then turns to the next wine.

"On a happier note, the next bottle represents Christ's miracles. After much thought, the wonder I decided upon was the wedding feast in Cana when our Lord turned the water into wine. A difficult decision, but I imagine the wine to have been of a light festive nature, symbolizing the rejoicing by his flock at the recognition of our Savior as the Messiah. So I have chosen a Mosel-Ruwer wine, a Maximin Gruenhaus—this grape would be from the Abtsberg at the center of the slope. A delicate drop, unbelievably fine yet with an aroma and flavor of an intensity I believe would be impossible from such stony ground without God's intervention, and a little help from our Benedictine brothers." As he speaks he pours the light red fluid into the handmade glass goblets, then moves on to the next bottle.

"After that we have the Last Supper. Imagine the atmosphere, a poignant mixture of quiet joy and sadness: joy at what Christ and his disciples had achieved so far and sadness caused by his announcement that one of them is to betray him. For this I chose a sober wine with a poetic background: a red from St. Emillion. The town is a medieval labryinth, it-self a matrix of spiritual complexity. The wine has a limpidity, almost a grief, that undercuts its darkness. You can imagine Christ holding up a glass and speaking those immortal words: *This is my blood.*"

He lifts the glass; a ray of sunlight streaming through the dark liquid casts an ominous burgundy shadow across his eyes. For a moment Carlos has the uncomfortable sensation that he himself might have been Judas at that immortal table. The spell is broken by a shepherd's horn sounding out in the valley below. Heinrich replaces the glass on the cold marble.

"Next we move on to the most pivotal event in the history of Christian-ity: the crucifixion. Our most Holy Father's sacrifice of his son, martyred for his love of mankind. When I imagine the crucifixion I always think of the elation of spiritual enlightenment through intense physical suffering and pain. That moment of utter exhilaration Jesus must have felt when he surrendered both his spirit and his life. In honor of this I have chosen the wine of Madeu near Perpignan in Roussillon. The grapes are so rich and the wine so opulent that I like to think there is some divinity in its sweet-ness."

He pours two glasses of the rich red. The fragrance drifts over and Car-los finds himself salivating. Heinrich smiles at him as if guessing his thoughts.

"Patience, brother, we have two events to go."

"The resurrection and the ascension," Carlos murmurs, now swept up in the corpulent German's narrative.

"Exactly. For the resurrection, what would you have chosen?"

Carlos pauses, imagining Christ's wrapped corpse lying peacefully in the cave covered from head to toe with its shroud, then the slow, magical rippling movement of life as warm blood begins to pump through the stilled heart.

"A white perhaps?"

"My thoughts exactly. The Spirit would be fresh and pure, an embodi-ment that floats above the ground. For this I chose a silky white from the Liebfrauenstift, in commemoration of the joy of Our Lady upon meeting her resurrected son. The vineyard surrounds the Church of Our Lady in Worms and the wine is both gentle and lively. And lastly, for the glory of the ascension?"

"Red?"

"Red, full-bodied and extraordinary. A bold declaration that rings out over cities, bells tolling, angel horns blowing, yet illustrating the simplicity of Jesus' ascension into the arms of his Father. The 1540 Würzburger Stein from Würzburg on the Main—the history of the vintage itself is miraculous. That year the Rhine dried up and wine was cheaper than water; consequently they stored the vintage for over a hundred years in casks in the cellars of the Archbishop of Main, who himself sent me this as a gift."

"I am doubly honored."

"Indeed you are, but not as much as you might like to think—I have several more bottles in storage."

With a smile he pours out the last two glasses of wine in front of the Dominican. Now the sun has risen, a blood-red orb that has turned the clouds above a glorious amaranthine. Carlos, turning back to the table, counts seven glasses of wine poured out for him to taste. The desire to shout out, to laugh, to celebrate the glory of the unknown the new day brings, sweeps through him.

"What next?" he asks, his breath a faint mist in the chill morning air.

"Next we drink," the archbishop replies, grinning hugely.

Carlos leans against the huge winepress, the rich scent of hundreds of vintages ingrained into the oak pores of the ancient machine seeping out into the damp afternoon air.

"She was a creature not of the flesh but of something far more refined, undefinable. Her beauty, in every aspect: musically, the grace of her gestures, the soaring heights of her wit; all of this was not of this world but one far more devious . . ."

He pauses, wondering why it suddenly feels as if the winepress has begun to tilt to one side. Heinrich, noticing the Dominican's hesitation, immediately fills his wineglass again. It is late in the day and the two have been drinking solidly since the dawn toasting. However, Heinrich, blessed with a liver steeled by decades of drinking, is far less intoxicated than the frugal Spaniard—a situation the archbishop foresaw and has every intention of exploiting.

"You really believed she was of the Devil?" He leans forward to steady the swaying Dominican with one strong arm.

"Oh, absolutely. Once during a musical recital I swear I saw her feet hovering at least half an inch from the ground. Not to mention the way she bewitched me with her breasts, her perfume, the fluttering movements of those long pale fingers—all sorcery." Carlos demonstrates, swaying his own hips in imitation.

Just another idiot who thought with his cock, Heinrich muses privately, but adopts an air of genuine sympathy.

"It must have been terrible for you, barely a novice, to have to wrestle with such demonic forces. But Monsignor, I think you won then, for you have managed to cleanse this world of her evil family. Surely it would be Christian of you to forgive the daughter and let her disappear back into the Jewish swamp of Deutz. After all, would the emperor really notice since we have burned the other two accused?"

"I cannot let her go free," Carlos announces loudly from where he has climbed on top of the wooden press.

"Cannot . . . or will not?" the archbishop insists, sensing an opportunity.

The Dominican, the world a giddy collage of spinning parts, peers down. The archbishop appears as a tiny figure at the end of one of those newfangled inventions by the Italian heretic, Galileo: the *telescopio*.

"I will not! I have my duty to God and country!" he cries out then topples off the press in a drunken faint.

Clucking with disapproval, Heinrich walks over. He stares down at the sprawling friar, now snoring loudly, his habit flung about him. What a waste of a good man, he thinks, how obsession can decay and corrupt the heart. Then, just in case the condition could be contagious, reaches for his rosary.

*T*he onlookers are gathered in the small wood-paneled courtroom with its elaborate ceiling divided into carved reliefs, each crowned with one of the shields of the guilds of Cologne.

The two witnesses fidget in the railed witness box. Merchant Brassant, painfully aware of his belly straining against his tight velvet doublet, his high-standing collar stiffened with buckram chafing his chin, and his groin itching beneath the new French breeches his young wife has insisted he wear, is unbearably uncomfortable. Beside him, in a cream dress made of poplin, hair hidden beneath a white cowl, with gold at her waist and neck, stands Abigail Brassant. Defiant, she clutches her baby, who, sleeping, is blissfully oblivious to the proceedings.

Opposite is the jury: a small panel consisting of four bürgers and two representatives of the higher council, all sympathetic and well rehearsed by Detlef. Next to them sits the magistrate flanked by his two sheriffs. The magistrate, Heinrich's puppet and a grossly overweight bantam of a man, is infamous for the amount of ale he can consume at one sitting. An insufferable pedant when sober, his colleagues try to keep him constantly intoxicated to avoid lengthy legal proceedings. Now, squeezed into the austere Gothic judge's chair, his feet encased in ridiculously ornate embroidered Turkish slippers dangling a good four inches above the ground, he appears to be entirely drunk.

Below the podium, seated on hard wooden benches, are the onlookers. At the front, with grim faces, sit Elazar ben Saul and Tuvia; behind them the few curious relatives of the jurors, and in the very back row, fully veiled, Birgit Ter Lahn von Lennep.

Determined to discover the source of her lover's recent detachment, Birgit's inquisitiveness has driven her out of her normal Lent retreat and back into the city. From behind her veil she watches the canon take his place before the court, Groot beside him.

Detlef exudes an air of authority. Feeling Birgit's gaze he glances briefly to the back of the room. Her presence irritates him. Does she not trust him, he wonders, finding his mistress's sudden possessiveness less than alluring. Dismissing her, he turns his attention to the rabbi.

Elazar ben Saul stares at Ruth as if trying to will her his strength. The canon cannot help but be affected by the obvious affection between father and daughter. Ruth herself, a diminutive figure in the dock, looks around fearfully. All her previous bravado and determination have vanished, making the manacles on her thin wrists appear an absurdity.

Just then the cathedral minister enters the court, followed by his secretary. What is von Fürstenberg doing here, Detlef thinks. Heinrich had promised no onlookers, no spies. The archbishop himself is not even in attendance. Perturbed, Detlef shuffles the pages of his interrogation notes, hoping that the artifice of the paid jury will proceed smoothly.

Heinrich, determined that the trial should go exactly how he wishes, has removed the Spaniard to take him on the promised tour of the vineyard at Kloster Eberbach further down the Rhine, thus freeing Detlef to conduct the sham tribunal unhindered. But before his departure the archbishop issued strict instructions to both the magistrate and the canon ordering them to arrive at a verdict of innocence within a week. It was his suggestion to hold the trial during Lent, a time when most of the populace were fasting and in prayer, and so distracted would pay little attention.

Von Fürstenberg would be wise not to intervene, Detlef muses, knowing that it will be difficult enough to prove the midwife's innocence without his meddling. As if reading his thoughts the minister nods to Detlef, his portly face grim.

The air in the windowless court is foul. It is the perfect atmosphere for discomfort, which is precisely why Detlef insisted on this particular chamber, knowing the participants will want to conclude the trial as soon as possible, if only to escape their soporific surrounds. He glances over at the jurors. One of them, a middle-aged blacksmith from the powerful metalworkers' guild, is already dozing, head rolled back, his velvet cap slipping down over one eye.

"Good Meister Brassant, is it true that Fräulein Saul delivered your wife of a child on January the thirty-first of the year of our good Lord 1665?" Detlef begins authoritatively.

The merchant glances across at Ruth. Struggling to hide her fear, she looks tentatively back. Abigail Brassant will not meet her gaze but Meister Brassant smiles at the midwife, embarrassed by her humiliation. He motions to the sleeping baby. "It is true. If it were not for her, we wouldn't have little Franz here."

"It were either her or magic," Abigail Brassant interjects, widening her blue eyes dramatically at the word. Her husband snorts derisively.

"I care not a pox whether it were hocus pocus or not. The child lives and is healthy, that's all that matters." He turns to Detlef. "Forgive my wife, she is young and the young see demons in mud. She was my housekeeper's daughter before I married her and she is still new to her station."

A smattering of laughter around the court brings a blush to Abigail Brassant's cheeks. Belittled, she scowls at Ruth. "I know what I saw."

"In that case you should see what you have sleeping in your arms and be thankful," Brassant retorts curtly. "I'm sorry, Canon, but I have lost five children before this one and as far as I am concerned it is good to be thankful for miracles. For miracles are miracles, wherever they come from."

Nervous about estranging his key witness, Detlef adopts a paternal tone which he hopes will calm the jittery wife. "I believe that is what we are here for: to deduce whether it was *scientia nova* or indeed something of a more supernatural nature that saved the child."

"But she used amulets! I saw them!" the young woman shouts out. The court falls silent. As Ruth turns pale, Detlef struggles with his prosecution, mentally fishing for the right angle to continue his questioning.

"Is this true, Fräulein?" he asks Ruth sternly, praying she will not drop her humble demeanor.

"I used everything I thought fit to save both child and mother," Ruth answers in a small voice.

Perfect, Detlef notes, she continues to appear the martyr. From the corner of his eye he can see von Fürstenberg whispering to his secretary who is frantically scribbling notes. The notion of betrayal begins to gnaw at the edge of his focus.

"Did you use witchcraft to harm anyone?"

"I swear I did not." The midwife lowers her burning face.

Elazar, outraged, tries to stand. Tuvia tugs him back into his chair, stroking the old man's hand to calm him.

Detlef nods to Groot who presents a large doll to the court, a makeshift copy of a child in roughly sewn cotton with pieces of the straw stuffing still protruding at the seams, its face crudely drawn features upon the bulge of thin cloth which serves as the head. With a dramatic flourish, Groot holds it up to the magistrate.

"I have had this posy made as a crude model of the baby," Detlef announces.

The magistrate peers blearily at the facsimile then glances at the chubby infant asleep in the merchant wife's arms. "A wonderful likeness, Canon, well done," he declares pompously in a surprisingly deep voice for such a short man.

"Thank you, sire."

Detlef swings back to his audience.

"For the benefit of the jury, Meisterin Brassant, I would like you to describe what you saw Fräulein Saul do to the child after the birth."

"But she cannot. I had administered a draft to stop her pain," Ruth interjects, now worried that she might become victim to the woman's fictions.

"Despite the opiate I saw what happened."

"And what was that?" Detlef gently asks, trying to coax both witnesses into a friendlier discourse.

"My child was born blue and lifeless. I saw with my own eyes the witch holding the poor thing up by its feet. It was dead. It was then that I started screaming."

"The child was born with the umbilical cord wrapped around its neck, Canon. It is not an uncommon occurrence. I had to cut the cord and peg it while the babe was still emerging in order to save both mother and babe. I also knew that if I untangled the cord quickly enough and brought air into its lungs, the child would live."

The jurors, captivated by the sudden flourish of activity, sit up as Ruth gazes pensively at the misshapen parody of a baby lying before her.

"Fräulein Saul, would it be possible to demonstrate just how you brought the child back to life?"

Ruth tentatively picks up the stuffed doll.

"As the baby's head hung from the matrix I manipulated it to free the cord. I pegged it in two places and cut so as to save mother and child from bleeding to death. I then moved the babe so I could free the first shoulder until the rest followed easily, as is the custom in birth. After it was freed, I placed my mouth over the nose and mouth and sucked to clear the passages for breath. I then spat out the birthing fluids and again covered the babe's mouth, this time to breathe air into the tiny creature."

"What happened then?"

"The child finally breathed life into itself."

"There was no witchcraft nor magic used?"

"Canon, I am a midwife. I use only the practices of my art and some medical knowledge I have learned in the Lowlands."

"But I saw something," Abigail Brassant blurts out. "There was a circle of ashes and a talisman, a witch's thing she had hung at the foot of the bed . . ."

Meister Brassant pushes his wife back down in her seat. "Hush, woman, you are full of such fancies!"

"I am not! I saw Lilith, I swear! Satan's dame herself, floating before me, one long leg—the leg of a screech owl—reaching out for me with the shining bell of Hades caught in its claw!"

"She's right, but it was not a leg of Lilith that Meisterin Brassant saw, rather an instrument of *scientia nova* which she mistook while under the influence of the opiate I administered. It is an object I use to listen to the heart beating beneath the flesh, a wondrous device sent to me from Holland. I needed to follow the life force in mother and child."

Detlef watches the jury as Groot hands to the first bürger the device made from a single length of cow gut with a small cap of brass fastened to the end. The merchant, a portly tailor, sniffs the brass cap, sneezes, then places it on his wrist.

"The end is placed in the ear while the small cap goes over the chest," Ruth explains, anxious that the object should not be misinterpreted.

Amused, the tailor puts the end of the tube in his ear and places the cap on the chest of the bürger beside him, a scrawny undertaker. Shocked by the deafening heartbeat which suddenly fills his head, the tailor tears off the listening device.

"'Tis indeed wondrous!" He turns to the undertaker, "Wim, for a cadaverous slip of a man you are thunderously alive."

The instrument is eagerly seized by the other members of the jury who, one by one, listen to each other's heartbeat.

"Gentlemen, gentlemen!" Detlef shouts over the clamor. "As you see, it is definitely *scientia nova* not the black arts that makes Fräulein Saul an eminent and highly successful member of her profession."

"'Tis true," exclaims the third member of the jury, a robust ruddy-faced sailor in his twenties from the influential guild of fishmongers. "She delivered my Maria of twins and both were bonny and very healthy. It would be a crime to wrongfully execute such a valuable midwife. I say we acquit her with no more ado," the young man finishes forcefully, repeating with naive sincerity the line Detlef rehearsed with him barely two hours before.

The other bürgers, thankful for the prospect of liberation from the unbearably stuffy chamber, join in with eager yeas.

Confident of a victory Detlef glances at the judge, who winks back. Lifting the hammer, a veritable mallet in his tiny hands, the magistrate slams it down onto his lectern. "Silence in court!"

Immediately the merchants cease their chattering. The magistrate, immensely pleased now that he has managed to flex his authority, pulls up his shoulders and adopts a fierce visage which fools no one.

"I dismiss all the charges on one proviso: that the midwife Ruth bas Elazar Saul is refused the right ever to practice midwifery again within the walls of this fair city."

Immediately Elazar is on his feet. Tuvia embraces him while the onlookers break into a babble. "Court dismissed!" the judge shouts over the commotion.

Relieved, Detlef swings around to Ruth. Her face is dazed with disbelief as her father hobbles forward to embrace her. Behind them von Fürstenberg hurriedly leaves the chamber; at the same time Birgit slips out unnoticed.

In the sanctuary of her coach, Birgit lifts her veil. She has never seen Detlef so alight with passion, not even in the pulpit. She admires him for it: he is more of a philanthropist than she had realized. She decides to send a message and wait for him that night.

As for the Jewess, she is so plain that Birgit sincerely doubts whether Detlef even perceives her as female. All the midwife represents to him is the key to a spiritual quest, the gentlewoman concludes, the answer to the moral emptiness he has felt of late. And so, excited at the thought of how she intends to reward her lover for his legal victory, she orders the coachman to drive on.

*T*he swaying of the carriage causes the hem of the midwife's full skirt to rustle against the wooden edge of the leather-covered seat. It is a demure black dress made of bombazine, opened in the front with a cream lace petticoat showing. Ruth, unaccustomed to such elegant and feminine costume, wriggles uncomfortably. They are garments purchased by Detlef with the help of Groot's landlady, at his insistence that Ruth cannot attend the prince dressed in her usual simple woolen cloak and plain hessian dress.

She has not worn anything as decorative or as womanly since Aaron's bar mitzvah and she feels painfully conscious of both her physicality and sex. More than that, she is unbearably aware of the fact that she is not wearing the yellow circle that is the compulsory insignia for Jews. Although she lived and traveled in Holland in plainclothes, it was as Felix van Jos—a deceit so profound it was tolerable. But now, traveling through Germania in the guise of an aristocratic Christian woman, Ruth feels a fraud and a betrayer of her race.

At her feet sits her bag of medical equipment. Staring down she wonders whether she really has the training to cure the young prince. From the few facts she has been able to obtain she knows the aristocrat's ailment is of an abdominal nature. She learned much from Dirk Kerckrinck and has studied for herself Galen's definitive text on anatomy, but with her life depending on the outcome she is suddenly besieged by doubt.

The coach jolts violently as the wheels hit a deep rut. The canon's foot slips across the floor and touches her own. Startled, Ruth looks across. Detlef appears undisturbed, his carved profile in repose.

He has changed from his clerical attire into that of the aristocrat. It is the first time she has seen him in such a guise and initially she thought the powdered wig with its ribboned pigtail total foppery. But now as she stares at his heavy eyelids, the sweep of his patrician nose and the full mouth that betrays an innate sensuality, she feels a part of her, long buried, begin to shift. Embarrassed she looks down again, only to be distracted by the sight of Detlef's shapely leg visible up to the thigh in hose. This time, shocked by her carnal thoughts, she closes her eyes and begins to quietly recite in Latin a particularly difficult passage of Ovid. Ovid! She has to concentrate to remember something a little less erotic, settling this time on Virgil, the most cerebral of the ancients. Thankful for the distraction, she relaxes into a stanza.

Feigning sleep, Detlef watches her through the stuttering gates of his eyelashes. Ever since Ruth reluctantly donned the clothes he purchased for her, the canon has been in a state of extraordinary confusion. The midwife has magically metamorphosed into a noblewoman of his own status, an individual he would in normal circumstances happily seduce across the crowded floor of some ballroom or even in the intimacy of a literary parlor. The fusion of these two personas—the visionary who holds the key to knowledge he has until now only dreamed of, and the female—suddenly makes her obtainable. Overwhelmed by desire, Detlef has never been so profoundly disturbed in the presence of a woman.

And this is exactly how he finds himself, having gazed surreptitiously for over an hour at her slender waist, the skirt which blossoms over surprisingly full hips, her narrow ankles, the delicate white bone of her wrist, the lattice of veins beneath the translucent skin, the pulse of her blood that beats mercilessly in the hollow of her slender neck. And most torturous of all, the swelling of her two breasts, the curved milky contours of which he has already fantasized making love to a thousand times over. Even now, in this moment as his foot bumps innocently against her own, he finds himself imagining how it would feel to intertwine his naked toes with hers, to draw her into the curve of his own body, to taste what lies between those thighs.

Another jolt sends the coach swerving. Detlef's long waistcoat, which has been concealing the growing bulge beneath his breeches, is flung up. Swiftly he tucks it back across himself then looks over at Ruth. Thankfully she still has her eyes closed tightly. He crosses his legs and stares out at the passing landscape in an effort to distract himself.

Judging by the short shadows of the passing trees, he estimates that it is midmorning. They left Cologne at dawn, partly to arrive at Das Grüntal as soon as possible, but also to leave before the city awoke.

Maximilian Heinrich, wary of condemnation by the Gaffeln which is still outraged at Voss and Müller's executions, insisted that the departure be made in absolute secrecy. Having dealt with the inquisitor's fury on discovering upon their return from Kloster Eberbach that the trial of the midwife had proceeded without him, Heinrich felt overwhelmed by attacks from all fronts and wanted to avoid infuriating the Dominican further. At a secret meeting he promised Ruth that he would deliver her safely back to her father should her mission prove successful. The same day in a private audience with Detlef, Heinrich ordered the canon to watch the Jewess's every move. If she should make a mistake and hasten the death of the Hapsburg prince it will prove disastrous for both Heinrich and his archbishopric. But if she should cure the prince, Leopold will be beholden to him and an indebted emperor is exactly what Heinrich needs in order to continue his covert relations with the French unhindered by Vienna.

Because she is a Hebrew, Ruth is banned from touching the prince directly. This is the law. With this understanding Detlef has assured Heinrich that he intends to uphold the decree and that while treating the young royal, the midwife's instructions will be executed by the most competent of the count's servants.

The coach rolls past a peat collector. Detlef watches the lone figure in his short smock and hose, his pointed cap pulled down over his freezing ears, slicing the sodden earth into small squares of black. In the near distance a solitary wisp of thin blue-gray smoke rises from the peasant's ramshackle cottage, barely more than three crooked walls challenging the wind. In front a young child in rags plays on the frozen mud while a small pug chases its own tail. It is a scene that has not altered for hundreds of years and probably will not for a hundred more. Detlef thinks. His mind wanders to the peasants' revolt of 1525, a bloody and shameful episode engraved on the German psyche, an event his grandfather used to recount as a victory of birthright over lower animal spirit. Glancing back at the pitiful man struggling against the elements, Detlef wonders whether he himself wouldn't have picked up hoe and pick to rebel against a life of enslavement.

"Are we on your family lands yet?"

Ruth's voice pulls him back to the charged atmosphere of the carriage.

"No, it will be a few more miles until we get to the von Tennen estate. Do you wish to stop and refresh yourself?"

"No, thank you. The bones in my corset have managed to suspend all bodily functions including hunger."

Detlef, unsure whether there is sarcasm in her voice, is at a loss. "Are you uncomfortable?"

"I am not used to such attire. I am unconvinced by the sentiment that women should endure for beauty."

"The dress becomes you regardless of your convictions. I now see that you are first a woman, second a renegade."

"I would rather be a comfortable renegade than a suffering beauty."

"Perhaps one day you shall be both."

"I fear not; not in these times at least. Canon, if I should fail . . ."

"You will not." His answer is direct, determined to curtail any burgeoning anxiety in her mind. "You cannot, for your sake and for mine."

Again they lapse into silence.

Ruth watches the breeze bending the branches of the linden trees, rustling through the budding leaves like water streaming through river weed. What if she does not succeed? What if the prince cannot be cured, what then? One moment of doubt unleashes a multitude of others. Remembering Spinoza's philosophy of applying intellectual discipline to rein in one's passions, she tries to become as detached as possible. She will separate her emotions from her craft. She will approach the prince like any other patient. Images of the anatomy of the midriff float across her mind's eye: the spiraling length of the bowel, the small intestine, the stomach, the spleen. It has to be the bowel, she concludes just as Detlef interrupts.

"You know, in that dress you could be mistaken for a Bavarian princess."

"But why should I wish to be?"

"I just meant—"

"You meant that I no longer resemble a Hebrew?"

Detlef blushes for this is exactly what he meant. "I intend no offense."

"You are right, Canon, in these clothes I could pass for a dark-haired southerner or perhaps an Austrian. But as soon as I walked into a banquet hall or a court my bearing would give me away. I cannot picture what it is to travel and live freely, unencumbered by race. I cannot imagine what it is to be born a count or a lord or a countess, to believe in one's innate superiority. My own father taught me to believe in intelligence, spiritual wisdom and the written word. But he also brought me up in a world where we are unwanted, mistrusted and must learn to become invisible to survive." She smiles ruefully. "I was a bad pupil. So you see even in this dress I could not walk beside you without fear."

Silently Detlef grapples with the reality of her world. Ruth, reading his stillness as acquiescence, continues.

"He also tried to teach me to be a good Jewish wife, to never ask questions, to watch hidden above the men at prayer. Pointlessly he wrestled with me in an attempt to convince me to respect the confines of my sex and finally, when he betrothed me, I fled."

"You are an unusual creature. I have not yet met a woman like you."

"I am surprised that a man of the cloth should have many female acquaintances, unless of course they are also in service."

"Fräulein Saul, my dedication is to the piety of the soul not to the purity of the body."

He stares directly at her with candor, his desire obvious. Suddenly Ruth knows with absolute certainty that he wants her. Trembling, she waits.

Leaning forward Detlef takes her hand, and turning it palm up begins to unbutton the row of seed pearls that fasten the kid glove. The tips of his fingers draw small circles of ecstasy across her skin, stroking the center of her palm so softly it is as if he has guessed the intelligence of her pleasure, every caress sending ripples throughout her whole body while he maintains his steady gaze, a knowing smile playing across his lips.

It is the smile of a connoisseur, of one who delights in his craft, Ruth thinks, shivering at the thought of what those hands so skillfully promise. After an eternity he reaches her naked wrist, where he pauses for permission. Bewildered, she pulls away, struggling to rebutton what he has undone.

"Of the soul I know something." She tries to cover the rawness of her confusion with words. "Of the body nothing, except in the landscape of the medic. Perhaps I shall die this way. I cannot see myself as a wife."

"If there is a man who can fire your imagination, he will deserve your hand."

"Perhaps."

Blushing, she turns away.

The coach begins to climb. Ruth watches as the thick forest thins out to mountainous scrubland with a sparse cover of spruce trees and pine saplings. A herd of rugged-looking goats grazing amid the undergrowth comes into view as the coach continues up the broken muddy track. Finally the land opens out to a windy savannah. Here icy banks lie thawing while spring growth breaks the stained snow with shoots of bright green.

Detlef knocks against the roof of the coach with his cane. The coachman shouts out to the horses in a guttural dialect; their gallop slows to a canter and then pulls to a halt.

"Forgive me. I am, alas, all too human under my breeches." And with that Detlef climbs out.

Ruth gives him a moment then follows. The fresh alpine air sears her lungs and blows away the mustiness of the coach. A few feet away Detlef makes water while Ruth casts her eyes over the panorama.

One side of the road is the mountain climbing upward, while below lies a valley with a broad river snaking a path along the bottom of it. Ruth watches a band of sunlight travel across the sloping tracts of forest, transforming the trees from dark olive to a luminous emerald as the light catches their waving tops.

"See yonder?" Detlef points down. The glistening roofs of a small settlement cradled in a curve of the river are just visible. "That is my brother's land. I grew up riding through the lanes of that village. Das Grüntal, the hunting lodge, is beyond the next valley. The forest is good for boar in winter and pheasant in spring. My brother is uncommonly fond of the hunt. If only he had such a love for his serfs."

"Do you have no jurisdiction?"

"Fräulein, I am the second son. Naturally the only path which promised influence was the church."

"Perhaps it is a blessing. At least you will have the joys of being an uncle."

"The possibility of my brother begetting an heir is remote. His marriage is a childless sham and shall remain so. No, I'm afraid the property will go to my cousin upon the count's death."

"Would you wish it to be otherwise?"

"I should wish it only that I might instigate changes."

Detlef points again and Ruth, squinting against the sun, can see a patchwork of fields, most of which appear fallow.

"The count has neglected his duty as farmer for too long. Not since before the war has this land been run properly. There is much disease and poverty among our peasants yet my brother does little to relieve their misery."

"If I have time, and with the count's permission, I shall visit the women myself. There could be tasks I can do to make their burden easier."

"Be warned: my brother is a creature of politics, he has no sensibility of the needs of others."

Behind them one of the horses snorts impatiently. Ruth glances around; the coachman sits on the box chewing a wad of tobacco. He peers down suspiciously but is unable to meet Ruth's eye. She turns to Detlef.

"You have endangered your position bringing me here. Even the coachman suspects that I have you under a spell."

Detlef laughs and, biding his time, pulls a sprig of mountain sage from a large bush. He buries his nose in it and inhales deeply. He does not want to think about the difficulties that lie ahead. All he desires is for the sense of exhilaration and calmness he feels standing next to her to continue.

Ruth, infected by his boylike abandonment, is confused. She wonders whether he understands how dangerous the situation could be for both of them. Suddenly he thrusts the sprig toward her.

"Sage."

"The herb to render man immortal," she answers, smiling.

The coachman spits out his tobacco and shouts to them, wanting to move on while the horses are still fresh. Detlef tucks another sprig of sage in his coat pocket. As they walk back Ruth suddenly turns to him.

"Canon, I lied . . . about the Birthing of Frau Brassant. There was an amulet . . ."

Detlef, aware of the watchful driver, hurries her toward a stream where he knows the tumbling waters will drown out their voices.

"Was there witchcraft, Ruth? Tell me honestly."

Distracted by the use of her name in a familiar and loving manner, Ruth hesitates. An extraordinary sense of excitement rushes through her. Should she tell him about Lilith, about the circle of protection she drew around the ailing mother? Would he comprehend the way the demon has shadowed her life? Can she trust him with her great secret fear or will he crucify her as others wish to? She does not know him well enough, Ruth reminds herself. He is of another race, another world, he will always be other.

"It is a weakness in me. I cannot let go of the ways of my mother. The amulet was there for protection, of both child and mother. The three angels, Snwy, Snsnwy and Smnglf, and Chesed, the kabbala symbol for mercy, that is all," she answers carefully.

"No incantation, no appeals to the black master?"

"None, I swear."

"Then it is a custom not a spell, a harmless token to ensure safety, and no one need know of this but ourselves."

"Do you think me weak? For all my belief in *scientia nova*, I must appear a primitive."

"Not weak, only human." He hoists her up into the coach. "And that is of great comfort to me as I had begun to doubt otherwise."

Outside, the coachman shakes the reins and the six black stallions arch their muscles into a graceful trot.

Inside, looking away from Detlef, Ruth feels her heart reverberating over and over with the sound of his voice whispering her name.

*T*he heavy drapes are drawn against the cold afternoon. Two Kammerhunde, their large elegant bodies draped over each other in rough affection, lie sleeping in front of the glowing embers of a fire. The air is filled with the scent of burning cloves and camphor: protection against disease and the terrible smell emanating from the ailing royal. A housemaid removes the copper warming pan from the bed and empties out the cooling coals to replace them with red-hot ones.

The count, in a Persian day coat, reads in an armchair. Breaking the silence he laughs out loud. Alphonso, bent over the prostrate figure of Ferdinand, sponging the sweat from his unconscious face, hushes him. The count looks up guiltily then back down at his tome, the satirical wartime account, *The Adventures of Simplicius Simplicissimus*. The tension is shattered only by the clatter of hooves outside the window.

The prince's face shines a mottled gray, the skin papery, flaking off around the nostrils and eyebrows. Ruth leans closer; she needs to take her patient's pulse but it is forbidden.

Behind her the count, Alphonso and Detlef wait anxiously. Alphonso stares at the midwife as if she is the embodiment of hope, which indeed she is. Ruth notes the color of her patient's lips then instructs Alphonso to lift his eyelids. The actor, trembling slightly, peels back the young man's lids; beneath the eyes roll back white.

"Has he been bled?"

"Every day for a week," the count replies dismissively and glances suspiciously at the hide sack the midwife has placed at the base of the curtained bed, expecting her at any minute to produce some ridiculous quackery. Ignoring him, Ruth leans down and pulls out the cow gut and brass cup instrument that was presented in court.

"What is that?" The count alarmed, jumps back.

Detlef, amused by his brother's uncharacteristic loss of control, steadies the count's lace-clad arm. "Fear not, Gerhard, it is an instrument of *scientia nova*."

"Indeed. I believe I might have seen one myself at the French court," the count replies unconvincingly, trying to cover his humiliation.

Ruth, sensing that her best protection is to remain enigmatic, shows Alphonso how to place the brass cup over Ferdinand's heart. While she listens intently the count pulls Detlef to one side.

"You realize that if he dies the von Tennen name will be endangered, not to mention the fact that we shall have to drive the body back to Vienna at our own expense. Leopold will expect a state funeral."

"The prince shall not perish."

The two men watch as Ruth, closing her eyes in concentration, begins to rock backward and forward on her heels. It is not a sight the count finds reassuring.

"Nevertheless, you will oblige me by performing the last rites if necessary?" he whispers to his brother.

"Naturally."

Ruth asks Alphonso to pull up the prince's nightshirt so she may examine his midriff. The sight of the scarred abdomen, now swollen and bloated like that of a pregnant woman, causes both men to turn away as the actor tenderly arranges the linen sheets around Ferdinand.

"What are the scars from?" Ruth asks, wondering at the crusty ridges that crisscross her patient's flesh.

"From an old injury as a boy," Alphonso answers.

"It could be that the current ailment is related to this. Remove the last of the leeches," Ruth instructs, but the count stays Alphonso's hand.

"My medic told us it was an impurity of the blood."

"Sire, with respect, the prince is weak, his heartbeat is faint. He needs to be given nourishment not drained of it."

Reluctantly the count nods his permission and Alphonso removes four bloated leeches from the prince's groin and neck. Ruth looks down the torso, her focus drawn toward the swollen belly. Below the bony ribs, on one side of the extended sac that was once a stomach, there is a visible growth. Gesturing with her hands she shows Alphonso how to massage gently around the area.

"You must tell me exactly what you sense beneath your fingertips. From this I shall be able to deduce the ailment."

Alphonso, almost too frightened to touch his lover for fear of hurting him, softly lies his hands over his sleeping flesh.

"There is a stone, hard to the touch."

"Is there a ridge of muscle that lies above it?"

Alphonso hesitates as Ferdinand groans.

"Please, you must continue if we are to save him."

As Alphonso describes what he feels under his hands, Ruth sketches out an anatomical drawing on parchment, the ink splattering in her jerky haste. Detlef, watching over her shoulder, marvels at her vision and confidence. It is as if she is sensing the prince's body through Alphonso's fingers. The accuracy of the drawing—the stomach walls split open, the rippling coils of the intestines, both greater and minor—indicate that she has been witness to autopsies, a practice punishable by death in archaic Cologne but accepted in Amsterdam.

The count, after glancing at the midwife's frantic sketching, looks at Detlef with disapproval.

"Brother, is it not time we resorted to innovation if we are to advance?" Detlef whispers, distracted by Ruth's powerful strokes with the quill which belie the fragility of her figure.

"But is this knowledge or alchemy?" the count murmurs back, watching Ruth trace in the demonic growth visible in the upper intestine.

"She has had training in Amsterdam with the finest medics of the Netherlands, trust me."

"Just save the youth's life and we all shall live."

Finally Ruth stops her scribbling. A servant places another log on the fire while Ferdinand, unconscious, curls his hands up like a sleeping child. His uneven snore rattles through the warm room as Ruth lays the diagram down beside his torso.

"The ailment is an adhesion made of old scar tissue pressing against the bowel and causing a blockage. It is this that is poisoning the blood."

"Will he perish?"

"If left untreated, yes—it may even be too late now. With your permission I might be able to cut the blockage out, but I shall need to be able to lay both knife and hand upon his highness myself."

The count looks on as Ruth indicates the illustrated growth. Impressed by her draftsmanship he is still hesitant—everyone in the room knows that to allow a Jew to touch royalty is a punishable offense.

"And if I say no?"

"He will be dead by morning."

"And Madame, if you fail you will be dead by the morning after."

"In that case I shall arrive at my natural destiny sooner rather than later and," she adds, smiling gently at her new patient. "I shall have the advantage of company."

"Let us hope you are as skillful with the knife as you are with your tongue."

The count bows slightly, and after giving instructions to his servants to provide everything the midwife should need, is relieved to depart.

Alphonso tenderly pulls a coverlet over the prince while Ruth removes herbs, a scalpel, cleaning tools and a stitching needle from her bag.

"I cannot protect you from my brother."

Detlef, reaching across, clasps her hand for a moment. Alphonso turns away discreetly.

"I don't expect you to." Ruth pulls her hand away. "I shall need clean rags, a cauldron of boiling water and sheets. No one is to be in attendance except the prince's valet."

The authority of her request distances the moment of awkward intimacy. Noticing the tension between the two the actor steps forward.

"As I refuse to leave the room you might as well use me as nursemaid. I am good with small instruments and faint not at the sight of blood—I once played Macbeth for three seasons."

He leans forward, his disheveled hair and week-old beard giving him an air of desperation. "Also, if the prince should perish, God forbid, I would like to be by his side."

Ruth slowly nods. Already she has laid out the operating tools on a square of clean cloth. "I shall come to you when I have finished," she says softly to Detlef.

He nods, secretly thankful to leave the musky room with its nauseating odor of illness.

Outside, the canon pauses at the door. He recites a prayer for the protection of all concerned, then winds his way down the candlelit corridors toward the tiny chapel which the count has dedicated to Saint Hubert and all victims of hunting accidents.

❄

The cotton stitches, long and crossed over, hold the swollen edges of the cut skin neatly together. Ruth, her face flushed from the heat, dark circles under her eyes, blood staining her apron and forearms, inserts the last one, pulling closed the incision like a seamstress.

The room stinks of foul air, mead and gore. The patient, still unconscious, dribbles slightly, his head tilted back drunkenly. Beside the bed lies a bowl in the center of which the putrid growth squats evilly. The brass cauldron bubbles away on the hearth with several stained instruments floating on its surface.

Alphonso, pale with fatigue, dabs at the prince's bloodied stomach with a clean rag. For hours he and Ruth have worked together and an unspoken but evident trust now links them as strongly as a conspiracy.

Ruth, too exhausted to speak, pulls open the drapes then the heavy wooden shutters. The dawn, framed by the window, streaks the sky with pink and mauve hope.

The prince's body, newly illuminated, takes on a porcelain grace. Leaning over him the actor meticulously wipes the last of the blood away from the wound. "I love him," he says softly but definitively.

"I know," Ruth replies, not unaccustomed to this kind of affection between man and man.

But Alphonso persists, looking for some form of absolution from the woman who to him now appears as luminous as a miracle worker. Risking everything he steps toward her.

"Fear not, Fräulein, yours are not the first Jewish hands to touch the prince."

Surprised, Ruth looks up, then without a word leans across and cradles him in her arms.

*M*aximilian Heinrich wakes to the pealing of bells for early morning mass. For a moment he thinks he is still in Cologne, then remembers the hurried ride to Bonn the evening before. Five peals—five a.m. The midwife will have treated the prince by now. The sleepy archbishop shifts his weight around on the lumpy feather pallet, not wanting to open his eyes and face the bureaucratic quagmire that threatens to swallow him up.

In the distance a cock crows and the smell of fresh horse manure drifts in through the half-open shutters. The midwife. Heinrich, eyes squeezed shut, his massive double chin sagging against the feather pillows above his cotton nightshirt, is already struggling with the machinations of his political survival. What is Detlef's interest in the plain little Hebrew? Knowing the canon's susceptibility for the weaker sex, he nevertheless cannot believe that his cousin's interest could be romantic. The midwife is so far removed in station that the archbishop can barely think of her as female, never mind desirable. No, it has to be some latent surge of faith in the man.

Pleased with this hypothesis, Heinrich, eyes still shut, smiles. His valet, having stepped silently into the bedroom, notices the archbishop's expression of pleasure and thinking that he might be disturbing an early morning moment of erotic delight steps back out. Meanwhile the archbishop, continuing his musing, finds himself feeling almost paternal toward the young canon. In his later years Heinrich has started to cherish in others the youthful passions which were once his own inspiration. The idea of reinforcing a moral world in which everything, even the most mundane tragedies, has meaning, has always appealed to him. It was the experience of watching his father being stripped of land and wealth until all that remained was his title which initially led the young Heinrich to yearn for power to reestablish the old ways of the aristocracy.

The strict hierarchy of the church with its pomp and glory seemed to provide a stability he craved in the chaotic aftermath of the Reformation. By the time he realized that the theological order was just as corrupt as any other, it was too late for the idealistic young Heinrich. It delights him now to think that, unlike himself, Detlef still retains his passion, perhaps even a small vestige of faith.

The archbishop opens one eye. From a small side table the timepiece he inherited from his father stares back at him. It chimes again; this time gilded doors fling open and Death, a hooded skeleton, wrestling with Love, a buxom bare-breasted maiden, pop out. It suddenly feels like a bad omen to Heinrich. In an attempt to stem his fears he decides to ignore the chiming timepiece and resume his meditation.

If the midwife saves the prince, Detlef will have pulled off a coup that will serve Heinrich, Cologne and most importantly the emperor, with the added advantage of being an act of both spiritual and ethical grace. The man is a born strategist; *he* is his natural heir, not that buffoon Wilhelm Egon von Fürstenberg. Unless the canon has failed, in which case Heinrich will have to banish him to some remote abbey in Bavaria until the name von Tennen has completely disappeared from the mind of that ridiculous puppy Leopold.

Having swung from a gentle daydream into a full-blown nightmare, and gripped by the ghastly possibility that Ferdinand might actually die and with him all hope of appeasing the emperor, Heinrich sits up and reaches for his quill.

A few minutes later, dressed in riding boots with a long velvet robe flung over his nightshirt, clutching a scribbled appeal to the count asking him to conceal any connection between the cathedral and Ruth bas Elazar Saul should the prince die, the archbishop strides across the muddy courtyard of his country palace toward the dovecote. His falconer, still pulling on his trousers, runs after him, stumbling his way through a flock of geese.

The dovecote, an iron and wooden structure built in the style of a mock Oriental palace, stands over a stable containing some unhappy goats, next to the archbishop's falconry. Several sleepy hooded hawks and kestrels blindly twist their cloaked heads in Heinrich's direction as he arrives puffing in the chilly morning air. Planting both feet squarely in the mud and straw he stares up at the cooing doves and pigeons.

The falconer catches up and stands panting beside the archbishop, wondering what terrible mistake he has made to bring the archbishop out so early. Finally Heinrich turns to the trembling bird handler.

"Count von Tennen has a dove here, does he not?"

"Yes, your majesty."

"Bring it here."

The falconer, donning his cap, climbs up the narrow wooden ladder precariously balanced against the side of the cote and unfastens the small woven door. Below Heinrich plucks two feathers from the air and watches as the falconer crouches in a corner and begins cooing softly. Within seconds the birds have settled. Carefully the peasant makes his way to one small gray dove.

"She's a good bird, swift too."

"How fast?"

"Two hours by daylight to the count, by my reckoning."

Heinrich holds out his cupped hands and with a tenderness that belies their paw-like size wraps his fingers around the bird. Fearlessly the dove cocks her head, her curious beady eye fastening on the archbishop's round, reddish nose which she has mistaken for a juicy caterpillar.

The maidservant throws the sheet over the balustrade and shakes it vigorously. Below she can see the midwife making her way toward the family chapel, her black hair streaming down her back. Unaccustomed to the heavy skirt she is clumsy in her gait. Such an ugly woman, the maid thinks, wondering whether the Jewess is truly a witch, maybe even half-goat under the long skirts. Could it be possible that such a hag has saved the prince's life?

The young wench has already heard from the cook that the midwife and the Italian actor locked themselves in the prince's quarters overnight and were seen through the keyhole conducting a black mass. How can such a puny insignificant woman wield such power? It has to be sorcery. Crossing herself the girl makes a quick prayer for protection to Saint Zita, the Italian patron saint of house servants. Her entreaty is interrupted by the appearance of a single dove flying in from the east. The bird, a small defiant ball of gray feathers, lands beside her and ruffles its wings. Frightened that it might shit on her clean sheets the maidservant immediately shoos it away.

Swooping down to the courtyard, the dove swings in a wide arc toward the enclosure where the count keeps his winged messengers.

Ruth barely notices the bird passing above her. She stands at the doorway of the small chapel, not daring to enter. Oblivious to her presence Detlef kneels in a pew, his head bowed in front of the altar. The statue is of the Virgin Mary, hands outspread, bestowing grace. The painted yellow hair, the rose of her cheeks, the ornate blue robe all look completely foreign to Ruth, but the intensity of the canon's physiognomy—the way his hands clutch the iron railings, his head bowed in desperate supplication, the vulnerability of his curved shoulders—all of these gestures reverberate in her.

This is a man at prayer. A man in direct appeal to his God, she thinks. It is not important to her that he is worshipping a deity different from her own, for it is his spiritual ambition, his drive to surrender his will to a higher power, that attracts her. To her, the humility of his absorption is wondrous.

Sensing her presence, Detlef swings around. "How long have you been waiting there?"

"Not long," she replies, embarrassed to be caught in her reverie.

Detlef gets up, dusts his knees then walks toward her. "You may enter. It is not a sin to let the unchristian into a place of worship."

"If you please, I would rather not."

He joins her at the stone archway, shivering in the dawn chill.

"So, Fräulein, does the prince live?"

"For the moment."

Ruth, unwilling to give any reason to hope, watches carefully as the strain begins to lift from the canon's face.

"Thank the Good Lord himself."

"You were praying?"

"All night."

"Then pray some more for I shall not know if he has fully recovered until tomorrow's sunrise."

Exhaustion drains her voice of any inflection. Weary to within an inch of her life she stumbles in the direction of her sleeping quarters.

———

The count, not knowing how to house the midwife and fearing scandal, has placed Ruth in the room of his mother's favorite maid, an old woman who died only a month before. The tiny chamber, little more than a sparse box dominated by a roof beam, sits off a top hallway which leads into a maze of corridors with peeling plaster and sloping walls that houses the rest of the servants. At night this labyrinth transforms into a treacherous forest of whispered endearments, of shadows that crisscross the wooden ceilings, a lattice of sexual intrigue.

Tucked neatly in the corner of the room is a straw pallet covered with an ancient quilt which, Ruth surmises correctly, the poor woman must have inherited from her mother before being given up to service as a small child. The coverlet, lovingly embroidered by a woman who no doubt feared for the safety of her first-born, depicts the fourteen Stations of the Cross. Above the bed hangs a small icon of the Virgin Mary. Against the opposite wall stands a pewter washing jug and wooden bucket, the hallmarks of a good and clean Christian woman. Ruth's journeybox, an embossed Spanish leather case she inherited from her own mother, sits against the chalky partition.

Ruth is grateful for the sudden tranquillity of the chamber. Although windowless it has the feeling of being securely embedded in the body of the hunting lodge, with life rustling above and below it. She pulls off the damp tippet and drapes it carefully over the beam. Leaning over she takes the icon off its hook. Pinned to the back is a small portrait of a young aristocratic woman who resembles Detlef in her fair coloring and the line of her proud mouth. Attached to the miniature is a faded lock of blonde hair. Ruth, realizing that this is Detlef's mother, is surprised by the sudden rush of intimacy she feels staring at the crudely painted likeness. Holding the picture under the spluttering taper, she can clearly see an earnestness tempered by a look of humor in the eyes, a characteristic she has glimpsed only momentarily in the son.

The maid must have loved the mistress, she thinks, and carefully leans the icon against the leather chest. She opens the journeybox and pulls out a small pebble. Etched onto it, the crevasses of the letters filled with gold leaf, are three kabbalistic words: Chochma, Binah and Netzach—revelation, reason and lasting endurance. Ruth mutters a blessing, kisses the amulet then places it under her pillow.

Outside she can hear the distant village bells pealing for midday. Too fatigued to think, she pulls off her overskirt then struggles to wriggle out of the tight corset. Now clad only in a simple cotton petticoat, she pours water from the jug into the bucket and washes herself with a small cake of salt. Throwing herself onto the pallet she falls instantly into a dreamless sleep.

"Pray tell me, are we in need of an undertaker yet?"

The count sits at the center of the long wooden table in the reception hall of the hunting lodge. Beside him is his land manager, a puny man whose self-effacing manner ill conceals his ruthlessness.

The canon, still in his clothes from the night before, paces restlessly in front of the huge granite fireplace. The count's tone reminds Detlef of the dismissive manner of their dictatorial father. Knowing that his brother is deliberately humiliating him in front of his servants, Detlef is momentarily gripped by anger.

"I received one of Maximilian Heinrich's birds only an hour ago. The good archbishop panics. Along with myself, he fears the emperor's wrath should his nephew perish. The count sounds peevish with impatience.

"You will have to wait until tomorrow morning. The prince lives, but I am told we shall not know for how long until then."

"The incision was successful?"

"I told you, he still breathes . . . I have made prayer for him."

"In that case we have no choice but to wait on God's will. But of course, with a canon's personal supplication I assume we are slightly advantaged, are we not?" The count's sardonic smile further enrages Detlef.

A knock on the door interrupts them. A page ushers in a tall emaciated man, weathered beyond his years by poverty and toil. The peasant, limping badly and dressed in his best but heavily stained clothes, shuffles in behind the page, clutching a cloth cap. His wooden clogs rattle against the stone floor. He stands before the count and stares at his feet in abject terror.

Knowing that his brother is critical of the way he oversees Das Grüntal, Gerhard deliberately postpones dismissing him. Let him see for himself the difficulties I face every day in dealing with these plebeians, the count thinks, ignoring Detlef's obvious exhaustion. At least next time he launches into a diatribe of advice it will be more informed.

His land manager hands him a scroll.

"Herr Braun, you have failed to pay rent for the last three moons for both field and hearth. Do you realize the penalty?"

The count looks up from the report.

"Sire, I have a war injury and the winter's been bad on it."

"Is that your only excuse?"

"That and the frost—it got two crops of turnips and the barley will be nothing to speak of come summer. But fear not, I'll pay the rent, just as soon as I have something to sell at market . . ."

The farmer shifts nervously, glancing apprehensively at both Detlef and the count. His eyes wander around the room, staring at the splendor of the candelabra, the silver ornaments, the bronze lion's feet of the table. The farmer has never been inside Das Grüntal before and he is astounded at the opulence. Like Heaven it is; if he loses everything at least he will have seen this. Gazing up at a portrait of Katerina von Tennen, he reminds himself to tell his wife how like an angel the lady looks.

"From midday tomorrow you and your family shall be cast out and your land and house repossessed," the count announces smoothly.

The farmer's jaw drops open, revealing a row of blackened stumps. For a moment he is too shocked to speak, then, indignant, he bursts into broad dialect. "But sire, I have five children! We will all starve! I can pay you back, I can!"

Clutching at Detlef's robes he drops to his knees, begging. Immediately two lackeys grab him and begin to drag him toward the door.

"Stop!" Detlef cries out.

Confused, the manservants pause, waiting for instruction. The canon turns to his brother.

"Surely it is fitting that we celebrate the prince's recovery? If Ferdinand lives, grant a reprieve of three months to Herr Braun: that should give him enough time to pay back the rent and the gesture will only enhance your reputation as a humane and generous master."

"And if the prince dies?"

"Naturally Herr Braun shall be without a roof," Detlef answers, calculating on the addiction of the gambler, one of his brother's foibles.

Amused by Detlef's stratagem, the count consults with his land manager who scribbles out financial calculations with a quill made from a long
black raven's feather. Angrily the manager explains the sums to his overlord who, smiling at the official's indignation, turns back to the farmer still
kneeling on the floor, his eyes wide in panic.

"So be it."

"Oh, thank you, your highness. You are indeed a kind man, thank
you."

Irritated by his obsequiousness, the count waves him off. As the land
manager continues to splutter in outrage, Gerhard calmly tears up the
eviction notice and with a regal flourish throws the pieces over the trembling serf. Too terrified to move, the peasant stays kneeling.

"But Herr Braun, it would be prudent of you to pack your belongings
anyhow," the count adds before the servants hoist the farmer to his feet
and haul him out.

Yawning, Gerhard turns back to Detlef.

"The inferiority of these people astounds me! He will be running
around the village boasting about the kind heart of his good lord before
cock crow. 'Tis almost a pity we shall be evicting him tomorrow."

"You shall not keep your word?"

"Naturally. But brother, you and I both know the prince will die."

*T*he handsome young musician pauses dramatically at his harpsichord. A periwig in the latest style, imported from the Italian court, balances precariously on his head. His slender muscled figure is clearly apparent under his short-sleeved tunic made of philoselle, bound at the shoulder with an obscenely abundant knot of scarlet ribbon. Before sitting he flicks up the long velvet tails of his waistcoat, revealing for an instant his taut satin-clad buttocks. An audible sigh of desire ripples through the assembled women. Thrilled with the effect, the musician tosses back his locks and stretches his long elegant fingers suggestively over the keyboard. Smiling mischievously he scans the front row of his audience, knowing that his heated stare leaves every woman there convinced of a liaison later that evening. Only then does he begin to play.

Seated in two curved rows, the wealthy wives of the bürgers, desperate for an opportunity to show off their imported finery, preen and fidget like excited canaries. Birgit, her tight-fitted bodice tapering to an elegant point, her embroidered blue underskirt flaring out from beneath a silk skirt of black taffeta, her bosom, neck and shoulders covered by a fine lace gorget fastened at the front with a diamond and emerald brooch her husband has just brought back from a trip to the West Indies, is the most restless of them all. Not even the lascivious glances of the young instrumentalist—a dusky Italian who has threatened to tutor all the ladies and daughters of Cologne—can soothe her irritation.

It has been over a month since she last saw Detlef. Only half an hour ago she suffered the indignity of sending her page to Groot's seedy chamber, wanting to establish whether the rumor that the canon is at Das Grüntal attending the sick prince is true. Groot's diplomatic but highly ambiguous answer has only added to her anxiety. In the sedan chair on the way to the recital she actually wept with frustration. And now, despite the powdered white lead she has applied, conscious of her swollen eyes she affects a shrill air of gaiety—which fools none of the women around her.

"Nice trinket." Meisterin Schmidt, wife of Klaus Schmidt, head of the guild of kegmakers, stares at the brooch at Birgit's bosom. "You must be pleasing the husband then?"

For the millionth time Birgit curses the fact that she married a mere bürger and not one of her own.

"What pleases me pleases him."

But Meisterin Schmidt, winking at another woman who is wearing a ridiculously high cornet headdress, persists. "In that case, Merchant Ter Lahn von Lennep must be more pious than I thought, although I have heard rumor that you have not attended confession for several weeks. Why not visit another priest? Confession is confession. Although, of course, the canon's enthusiasm is legendary and he is much loved."

"There is no need. I have it on good authority that the canon is attending to family business and will be with us by the summer solstice."

"I am much relieved to hear it, Meisterin Ter Lahn von Lennep, as you yourself must be."

They are interrupted by the first notes of a madrigal, a decorative tune ill suited to Birgit's mood. As she sits there a sudden panic sweeps through her. For the first time in their five-year love affair she senses that the bond that has always connected her to her lover—a sensibility that allowed her to intuit Detlef's movements, to visit him in spirit at night, to kneel beside him at prayer, her warm breath on his shoulder, to watch him saying a mass—has been brutally and inexplicably severed.

Terrified by the notion, she starts to tremble despite the heat of the auditorium. Craving reassurance like an opiate, she clenches her gloved hands and summons all her willpower to stop herself running out to look for him, wanting Detlef to tell her that her terror is misplaced, that his affection for her is as strong as ever.

Instead she drops her veil and forces her features into a rigid mask of control. Beneath the lace her jaw tightens as she tries to listen to the music which her distraught ear has reduced to a series of discordant notes.

Ruth's hand is lying palm up on the pillow beside her sleeping head. Her nails are bitten and chewed. A tendril of black hair winds its way across the yellowed hessian, creeping under the petite hand, the fingers of which Detlef now realizes are surprisingly long for such a small palm. They are working hands. Reddened by the cold. Scratched by labor. The skin visible on the fingertips is callused and coarse. They would be rough to touch, abrasive on his body. Distracted by the thought he becomes aware of his breath quickening.

He is standing in the room where Ruth lies sleeping. To him it seems as if this place has a twilight of its own, a half-light between reality and dream. He cannot remember how he got here, only that instinct drove him up the narrow wooden stairs beyond the level where his brother sleeps, up higher to the servants' quarters, knowing that here, somewhere, she would be. Like the kernel that lies at the heart of a rosebud, like the glimmer of pearl fluttering up through green water. And without calling out her name, without knowing which door to push open, but guided by a certainty of sensation, he has found her. As if, for the first time in his memory, he did not have to apply thought or strategy but an inherent knowledge summoned up from his very soul.

He had found her room directly, just as he had known she would be sleeping, her hand in exactly this position, before he even pushed the door open. And now he stands paralyzed, his head bent under the low ceiling, the candle burning in his hand, not daring to breathe, to move a muscle.

Will he ever have this pleasure again? Of seeing the shadows of this woman's life run across her face like quicksilver: one moment a small girl, the next a woman with pain twitching beneath the eyelids, the flesh of which he would swallow like honey. She does not know that he is there. She does not realize that the pulp of his heart pulses only while hers does, that the ambition of her spirit has reawakened his. He would burn for her. He would sacrifice church, power and state, but now, before her, he is too frightened even to utter her name. Such a simpleton, such a stunned idiot is he.

The torrent of jagged emotion and fragmented imagery fills him until he finds his knees shaking. Longing to lie down next to her, to take those fingers into his mouth, he leaves as silently as he entered.

The silver and ruby bead of a rosary looms like a glittering boulder on a vast plain of snow. For an instant Ferdinand speculates that he might actually have made it to heaven. Then, as his eyesight pulls into focus and a dull pain starts to throb in his midriff, he realizes with a curious mixture of faint regret and exhilaration that he is still alive. As sensation rushes back into his numbed limbs he swallows and discovers that his mouth is too dry to speak. Rolling over he finds himself wedged against the side of Alphonso's sleeping figure. The prince lifts an arm that feels as heavy as iron and throws it across the actor.

"Water," he manages to croak. "Water."

תפארת

TIPHERET

Equilibrium

DEUTZ, JUNE 1665

*D*ear Benedict,

It is now the month of June and I am back at Deutz, thank the good Lord. I am released after successfully treating Prince Ferdinand of Hapsburg for a cancer. In the dead of night and in utmost secrecy I was then transported back here. For all this I have to thank Canon Detlef von Tennen, the man I have written of before: a cleric who is a maze of paradoxes and whom I have not seen since the events at Das Grüntal, the country estate of his brother, a good four weeks ago. I may never see him again, which would be a great pity for it is not often one meets a man who can share in the pleasures of the mind as well as the spirit. But I digress. Tell me, are you well? Here there is much talk about the Black Death in Leiden. I fear for you; Rijnsburg is so close to that great city, would it not be prudent to embark for a safer harbor? A great philosopher is not impervious to the perils of a mortal man, Benedict, and in this I beg you to act responsibly.

Your loving friend and colleague,

"Felix van Jos"

The journeyman from Mülheim, a Dutch boy of about sixteen, rides up to the cottage, a leather sack of mail slung over his shoulder. Flicking the flies away with her tail, his old mare rolls her steaming flanks as she throws one hoof in front of the other. It is hot. The forest beyond is vibrant with birdsong, its canopy in full bloom. As the boy approaches, apple blossoms shower down on him, carried by a breeze from the orchard the midwife has cultivated next to her barn.

Ruth, her face and body swathed in the fine net of the beekeeper, bends over a woven cane hive positioned at the end of her herb garden. Upon hearing the journeyman's cry she carefully replaces the tray of honeycomb swarming with indefatigable furry bees in the dome. Pulling the net hood from her brow she runs down to greet him, passing Miriam who stands between the rows of cabbages, hoe in hand. The young girl smiles shyly at the journeyman who waves brazenly back.

"Is she talking yet?" the youth asks Ruth, still staring at Miriam.

"Not yet. But the terror is leaving her eyes."

"She's a good woman, someone ought to marry her—someone of her own people, that is," he adds hastily.

"They should but they won't now. This is for Holland."

Ruth hands him her letter then presses two Reichstaler into his hand.

"Piet, travel safely." She reaches into her skirt and pulls out a small pomander stuffed with rosemary, frankincense and cloves. "And wear this for the plague."

"Don't worry about me. Father says I have horse's blood. The scourge won't get me." The youth shrugs with awkward adolescent bravado but tucks the pomander into his breast anyway.

"Looks like you have a visitor, Fräulein."

Further down the lane a tall thin man has come into view. Tuvia. Carrying a basket, sweating under his heavy wide-brimmed hat and black gown that sweeps the dusty path, he strides with a blind but determined purpose. Sensing that he has been seen, the young rabbi's awkward bearing becomes even more extreme.

"That's the strangest swain I've ever seen, but eager, eh miss?"

With a wink and a smirk the youth gets back onto his horse and trots off.

Ruth watches Tuvia draw nearer. She should go to greet him but finds that obstinacy has pinned her to the ground.

The young rabbi, his olive skin burgundy with the heat, finally reaches her. Now Ruth can see the ridiculous poppy he has slipped into the band of his hat, the bunch of violets hanging out of the straw basket he carries defiantly in front of him, the flush of courtship playing across his tortured features.

"Good morrow, sister."

"Good morrow, Reb Tuvia. You are a long way from home."

"Indeed."

Still she does not invite him in, determined not to encourage him. Tuvia stands in the dust, shifting his weight restlessly from one leg to the other, sweat staining the front of his plain cream jerkin.

"I bring greetings from your father. He is well."

"So he seemed yesterday when I saw him at the synagogue. He did not tell me I would be receiving a visitor."

Tuvia glances at the shadowy doorway of the cottage, it looks enticingly cool. "Will you not invite me in? I am in need of refreshment."

"Would that be proper?"

Momentarily outwitted, Tuvia looks around and sees Miriam hoeing suspiciously vigorously. "But we have an escort," he points out, trying to keep his nerves from showing in his voice.

"If you insist."

"I do."

The three of them sit around the small wooden table beside the kitchen window. Miriam, as chaperone, between Ruth and Tuvia as is the custom. A jug of milk and a bowl of eggs lie before them next to a loaf of bread while a lump of oozing honeycomb sits on a plate Ruth has placed in front of the young rabbi.

Tuvia looks around the room. Even in the shadows he can see the row of books placed on the mantelpiece above the hearth. Surreptitiously he scans them for blasphemous titles. To his relief he finds none.

"For a philosopher you keep a clean house." He smiles, attempting to ease the tension with humor.

Ruth pours the rabbi a glass of milk. "You walked two miles to tell me this?"

"Please, Fräulein, you know your hand has been promised. Why make this even more difficult?"

"Because there is the small issue of my desire."

"Desire will come with time. Besides, with your dubious history you should be honored; there are many mothers in the village who would seek me as a son-in-law."

"In that case there is even less reason for you to be sitting here."

"Ruth, your father gave his word. He wants to protect you, as do I."

"I am able to protect myself."

"That I have not noticed."

Tuvia looks at Miriam who is staring politely down at a struggling bee trapped in the sticky honeycomb. Ruth, noticing his glance, leans forward.

"She is to be trusted. She has ears but as yet has not got her tongue back."

"The archbishop's men should answer for such an outrage."

"But they never will."

"Ruth," Tuvia leans closer, "I have heard from a reliable source that the inquisitor returns to Cologne and is determined to pursue your prosecution again."

"But I have a royal pardon."

"Royal pardons have a habit of bending with the winds . . . Marry me, we shall sell your father's house and together with the good reb we shall join with Messiah Zevi in the Holy Land. It will be like a dream . . ."

"It is a dream."

Tuvia looks at her obstinate profile. It is a face he would love to conquer, to see that stubborn soul broken and submissive. He is convinced that this is his mission: to make a wife and a mother out of the old rabbi's willful daughter. He owes it to the father, the one person he regards as his intellectual superior. He will be Elazar ben Saul's son. Ruth and he shall bear children for Messiah Zevi to populate the new Holy Land. It is his spiritual duty to make her a full Jew, he thinks, remembering the burning shame of the revelation of her baptism. Her own sentiments are nothing more than a mild hindrance.

"I have more patience than you, Fräulein. And you should be careful, you still have many enemies. I'm sure it would be a relief for the archbishop to hear that you have stopped all meddling and become an honorable married woman destined for the Holy Land."

Ruth contemplates his threat. Mindful of the warning Detlef gave her to remain invisible, she has delivered only two babies since her return and those at a great distance from Deutz and Cologne. Now she wonders whether Tuvia has heard that she is still practicing.

"I will give you an answer by Rosh Hashana."

"But that is three months away!"

"It will give you an opportunity to display your famous tenacity, Reb Tuvia."

She stands and opens the door. "Good afternoon."

Reluctantly he rises to his feet, leaving Miriam still sitting shyly at the table.

"Your father wants you back under his roof. It is not safe for you to be living alone, nor is it honorable. Now that you have been accepted back into the community it is your duty to reassure the other women that you are capable of being a good Jewish woman. At least move back into your father's house."

"I cannot shed my skin that quickly, Tuvia. But I will visit for sabbat. That much I can promise."

As the two women watch Tuvia walk sullenly back toward the town Ruth wonders how long she will be able to ward off his advances.

Suddenly a small hawk swoops down and plucks a hare from the bank of a hedgerow. As the animal kicks its legs helplessly midair, Ruth has a sinking sensation of foreboding.

"London, Amsterdam, Leiden . . . it is a Protestant disease, there can be no doubt about it."

"Your grace, the plague discriminates against no man. It is happy to consume Christian, Jew, even Moor in its path."

"But it is not here yet and we can give thanks to the three Magi and the holy virgin Saint Ursula for that. This is a great pilgrim city and is honored by our good Lord."

"Our good Lord has nothing to do with it, it is merely a question of time."

"I have it on good authority: Cologne will be spared."

"Whose good authority?"

"My astrologer's," the archbishop answers, staring Detlef straight in the eye. The canon snorts derisively, unable to hide his frustration.

Maximilian Heinrich, magnificent in his green weekday robes, sits at the head of the oval oak table in a large chamber in the town hall, surrounded by his advisers. To his left are the von Fürstenberg brothers, Wilhelm a place closer than his brother; to his right are Detlef and several sympathetic bürgers. It is the monthly meeting when representatives of the Gaffeln join with the clergy to discuss local policy and tariffs.

Detlef, a new hollowness to his face, senses the growing frustration of the merchant sitting next to him, the head of the bakers' guild. "Your grace, this is a secular matter and the city must take precautions! I suggest we veto all English and Dutch cargo for the summer," he declares.

Heinrich glances thoughtfully at his cousin. Detlef's growing defiance and zeal for social change is not an enthusiasm Heinrich had bargained for. Of more concern is the mounting support Detlef seems to be engendering among the younger tradesmen. The archbishop has even heard a rumor that Detlef is shunning the affections of Birgit Ter Lahn von Lennep; refusing to take her confession, and has given up his luxurious chambers in Cologne and taken a simple room at Saint Pantaleon monastery. It is as if a harder, leaner, more inflexible man has been prised out of the softer, corruptible, but always diplomatic canon. He even has the look of the fanatic, Heinrich thinks, with those sunken cheeks, the dark rings under his eyes. If the archbishop did not know that the canon had been fasting, he would be inclined to think that either politics or a fixation of the cock was the parasite eating at the young man's soul. Nevertheless, the archbishop reminds himself to tread carefully around his cousin's newfound fervor.

"Canon von Tennen, if we were to veto such cargo we'd all starve to death before the plague had a chance to kill us. This is a trade town, we can't afford to lose the business," one of the bürgers ventures.

"I am aware of the implications, but it is better to err on the side of caution. Over ten thousand died last month in Leiden alone and there is a rumor they have started to perish again in London. At least quarantine the ships," Detlef counters.

The table erupts into violent debate. The archbishop has no intention of stopping the pilgrimages to the bones of the three Magi and the eleven hundred martyred virgins of Saint Ursula. Such visits are the cathedral's main source of income. Equally the merchants are determined to keep their exports leaving the city. Finally Heinrich slams his fist down onto the table. Immediate silence ensues.

"There is no argument. The pilgrimages will continue, as will the traders. In the meanwhile we shall be doubly vigilant for any signs of the scourge. This is the cathedral's final word on the issue."

Detlef, disgusted, storms out of the hall. All swing around to Heinrich, whose face remains stiffly impervious to the insult.

After a beat, Wilhelm Egon von Fürstenberg leans toward the archbishop and whispers into his ear in Latin. "Remember, we still have the Spanish card up our sleeve should the naughty child decide to further insult the father."

But inwardly anxious, Heinrich is beyond amusement.

Striding furiously along the bustling Judenstrasse, Detlef heads toward a coffeehouse at the corner of the square. On the way he purchases a news sheet, *Die Flugenden Blätter,* from a war cripple.

The young canon has never offended the archbishop so directly, but at this moment Detlef is concerned not about the consequences of his actions but about the shortsightedness of the city fathers. They will endanger the populace through their greed, he thinks, gazing around at those who might be first to perish: the poor, the half-starved, the orphaned and the aged. Here a beggar woman, her face a web of pain in which her toothless mouth gapes. Pitiful, she rests heavily against a gnarled tree branch, her hand a filthy claw petitioning for alms. There, squatting in the gutter, a child of no more than three years of age, his naked buttocks poking through his ragged smock, too exhausted to beg, too exhausted even to cry as he gazes up at the indifferent world bustling past him.

As a boy Detlef saw the scourge decimate the local village, then witnessed the slow and lingering death of his mother who contracted the disease after attempting to ease the discomfort of her peasants. Is there no one with whom he can share his fears? No one with an enlightened mind? No, not since Das Grüntal. Not since Ruth.

A woman with long black hair turns the corner and Detlef is instantly flooded with memories of the midwife: her gestures, the particular way she speaks with her hands. It is over a month since he last laid eyes on her, the day she left his brother's estate on a cart headed for Deutz. They parted after he had warned her of the temporary nature of her pardon. Knowing that the emperor is fickle and the inquisitor dedicated, Detlef suggested the midwife leave Deutz as soon as she could for a more remote settlement or for the Lowlands itself. But Ruth promised nothing, saying only that she was committed to spending the last of her father's days with him now that they were to be reunited.

The woman with the raven locks passes out of sight and Detlef is reminded that he does not even know whether the midwife is still in Deutz, or if she thinks of him at all. To his shame he realizes that the meditations, the fasting, even the lashing he gave himself with the knotted whip of the flagellant, have not banished Ruth's image but only enhanced it. The picture of her face, her voice, her scent, grows within him like a luminous visitation.

There is not an hour when he does not think of her: the clarity of her logic, the whiteness of her skin, the curve of her cheekbone. She creeps in everywhere, in his prayers, in the faces of the hopeful pilgrims staring up from the pews, in the texts he studies. Ruth, Ruth, Ruth. Desperate to be released, he has taken valerian for slumber and claret to quieten the mind. Groot, smelling wine on the canon's breath before midday mass, has begun to wonder what new fiend possesses his master.

Detlef steps through the low arched doorway of the coffee shop, his nostrils pleasantly assaulted by the fragrance of this novel beverage shipped from the new Americas. The air is thick with tobacco. The scent of ginger and cinnamon rises from the freshly baked pastries that line the marble countertop. Serving maids in white caps and stained aprons carry jugs of the steaming coffee between the crowded tables. Several of the merchants and their clerks look up from their scribbled calculations, then, upon seeing the newcomer is merely a cleric and not one of their own, look down again. Intrigued by the seriousness with which the bürgers carry out their endeavors, Detlef secures a small table to himself by the window then orders a cup of the steaming brown liquid and a pipe. By the dim light filtering into the smoky room through the tiny diagonal glass panes he begins to scan the news sheet's headlines.

MORE PERISH OF DEVILISH SCOURGE IN THE LOWLANDS, THE LATEST TOLL STANDING AT TEN THOUSAND. LEIDEN CLOSES ITS GATES . . .

ITALIAN ASTRONOMER SIGNOR GIOVANNI CASSINI OBSERVES THE HEAVENLY TRACKS OF THE ROYAL PLANET JUPITER AND HIS QUEEN VENUS . . .

The canon reads on, trying to lose himself in the larger world but finding no comfort in the grim reportage.

"Please sire, my good lady is yonder and seeks an audience with you."

A small page wearing a green satin turban and coat and breeches in the colors of the house of Merchant Ter Lahn von Lennep stands before him. Detlef, not having seen the exquisite Moor before, thinks he must be the latest toy from the often absent merchant to his errant wife. He peers out of the cloudy window.

Seated in her carriage Birgit waits across the narrow street. Framed by the window she glances across but does not see him. In a day dress of green satin matching the colors of her page, her hair covered by a demure lace cap, she is a vision of incongruous beauty among the grimy street peddlers that loiter by the coach.

"Tell your good lady that if she wishes to speak to me she may do so herself," Detlef finally replies then looks back down at the news sheet.

The boy, confused, shuffles in his buckled shoes. "Please, sire, a gentlewoman may not enter such an establishment."

"If it is good enough for a canon of the church it is good enough for the wife of a tradesman," Detlef answers curtly.

The page bows and leaves. Detlef surreptitiously watches as he reports back to his mistress. For a second Birgit seems to falter, then she climbs out of the carriage and walks determinedly toward the coffeehouse.

"You have forced me to demean myself. This is not an establishment for a good Christian woman."

She stands over him. The other patrons glance up curiously from their stock figures and bills of exchange. Rising, Detlef offers her a chair.

"Fear not, they will think you are here to plead on behalf of your husband, the good merchant, who must have fallen into some moral disrepute, may God bless his soul."

"You make light of my distress. Why do you refuse to see me, even to take my confession, Detlef?"

Several of the bürgers, surprised by Birgit's use of the familiar, turn their heads again. Feeling the heat of their gaze, the canon leads her out of the coffeehouse and into the shade of the overhanging balcony.

"It is dangerous to be so indiscreet."

"I have no choice. You refuse to answer my messages and I am tired of Groot's diplomacy. Five summers and five winters we have lain together and now it pains you to see my face?"

Detlef wants to look at her but knows he cannot, that if he were to see the agony in her stiff dignity and bewildered eyes his resolve would collapse completely. Instead he looks down and watches her gloved hands worry at her ribboned handkerchief.

"Madame, I cannot persist with the artifice and deceit. I have changed. It would be hypocritical for me to continue to lie with you. That is the reason for my absence."

"You no longer have affection for me?"

Brigit's face twists into a grimace as she struggles to stop her emotions bursting through. Recognizing her fierce pride as a reflection of his own, Detlef reaches across and takes her hand.

"Always."

"Then prove it: take me now."

She lifts Detlef's hand and thrusts it into her bodice. His fingers find themselves fastened around her breast, the nipple erect against his palm. The page boy, embarrassed, looks away.

Reaching up Birgit pulls Detlef's mouth hungrily against her own. Weeks of repressed desire surges uncontrollably through his body, an eon of sexual abstinence heightened by the curious pleasure he felt during his self-flagellation, the hungry mouth of lust that throbbed at the edge of each supplication despite his pleas, the succubi of his dreams that, regardless of his prayers, filled his nights with their twisting naked bodies, many painted with the face of Birgit. He wants her now. He wants nothing but blind release, to purify his body through erotic fury.

"If that is what you desire."

With that he takes her roughly by the hand. She turns to her servant. "Ahmed, take the carriage home. Tell them I am at confession and will return by nightfall."

The small boy, green satin turban bobbing, climbs up beside the coachman, while Detlef ushers Birgit toward The Hunter's Sheath, the one tavern where he knows no questions will be asked.

The room is little more than a closet, still pungent with the aroma of sex. Detlef turns Birgit so her back faces him. She steadies herself by placing her gloved hands flat against the thin partition. On the other side they can hear the cries of a harlot and her Johnnie's quickening gasps and grunts. Without a word Detlef lifts Birgit's skirts over her hips: the full orbs of her arse are perfect pale fruit above the silk tops of her black stockings. Kneeling, he spreads them wide apart. Birgit gasps as he reveals her most private opening.

Running his fingers below and to her front he caresses her as he buries his face between her cheeks, moistening her nether hole with his tongue. Birgit immediately grows wet despite her mounting qualms about the unmentionable blasphemy of his intention. Detlef stands, pulling his hard organ free, then roughly pushes her down so she is bent away from him. Birgit, red from cheek to breast, is doubly humiliated by her own intense excitement. Detlef grabs each cheek of her buttocks firmly, pulling them apart with angry haste, fingers sinking into the soft flesh. For a second he rests his cock against her opening, teases gently before easing himself in. Birgit screams out loudly; to silence her Detlef thrusts his fingers, still fragrant, into her mouth as over and over he plunges. As the pain becomes a growing ecstasy Birgit reaches down and pleasures herself. Until she feels his seed begin to tremble down the length of him and they both come shouting.

In the moment after, Birgit's ecstasy becomes discomfort. Pulling away from him she tries to steady her trembling legs.

"This could have us both executed," Detlef mutters into her hair as a huge wave of guilt and remorse sweeps over him. "I am deeply regretful I have subjected you to this." Ashamed, he covers himself.

Throwing down her skirts Birgit turns, her hair a wild blonde cloud, her cheeks flushed.

"Do you still hold me in respect?"

"Always," he replies, then leans over to kiss her forehead. "But please understand, we can no longer be lovers, only good companions . . . in time."

He takes her arm formally. "Let me escort you home."

Suddenly nauseated by his patronizing tone she pulls away.

"Do you realize how easy it would be to sour the friendship between yourself and Meister Ter Lahn von Lennep? He was most displeased when his good friend Voss was executed. The merchants are watching you and the archbishop very closely. A charge of immoral conduct would be more than useful to their cause."

"Birgit, please, I cannot deceive you or myself. Let us be friends."

"We were never friends."

Unable to contain her fury any longer, she hurries out of the room.

*T*he loaf of golden challah is held above the candles. The gentle voice of the rabbi fills the room.

"Baruch atar adonai
eloheinu melech ha'olum
chamotzi lechem min ha'aretz."

Elazar finishes his blessing, breaks a hunk off the crusty bread and passes it to Tuvia, who in turn hands it over the laden table to Ruth. It is the sabbat and the table is covered with offerings to celebrate the week's end. In the center is a bowl of sauerkraut made with poppyseeds and flavored with sugar, a plate of broiled salted beef, pickled cucumbers. The old rabbi, rubbing his hands with satisfaction, cannot believe that at last his beloved daughter is sitting right here at the family table.

It has taken weeks to persuade the elders of the community that it is safe to allow her among them again. Many still hold her responsible for drawing Cologne's attention back onto the small settlement. Ruth's arrest has given rise to old fears. What if she causes more trouble? Is she really a Jew now they know she has been baptized? Even the women are prepared to forfeit the midwife's skills to avoid the calamity of a pogrom. It was only when Elazar appealed to Isaac Schlam, Deutz's doctor, and asked him and the community spokesperson Hirz Uberrhein to address a public gathering at the synagogue to reassure them that Ruth had denounced the baptism, that she would not be practicing her craft and that she would leave within the year with her betrothed husband Rabbi Tuvia for the Holy Land, that the people had been appeased.

Does Ruth realize she is living on borrowed time, the rabbi wonders.

"Ruth, will you not pour Tuvia his wine? He is in need of the grace of a woman." The old man smiles; the silver of the candlesticks and the best knives and forks kept for the high holidays glisten in the candlelight, reflecting back in his shining eyes.

Reluctantly Ruth stands and leans over the assistant to fill the ceremonial goblet embossed with depictions of the Passover story before him. Tuvia, achingly conscious of her proximity, closes his eyes for a second as he breathes in her scent. Noticing, Ruth feels a flash of sympathy, but fearing that she might accidentally encourage him steps back. Making sure she remains as far away as possible, she takes her place again at the table.

Elazar seizes her hand. "Daughter, I would like to take this opportunity to apologize for my hesitancy in accepting you back into this household. I was wrong and I know it now," the old rabbi announces solemnly, wiping away tears with his sleeve.

"I am here now, abba. That is all that's important." Ruth squeezes her father's dry and wrinkled hand.

"This is true and it gives me immense joy to have you safely under this roof where you belong. Come back, Ruth. You know Tuvia will marry you, and with all that has been revealed it is a generous offer. Make me happy."

"Abba, we agreed not to discuss this."

Rosa bustles out from the kitchen to serve the vegetables, a delicious Sephardic dish she always prepares for Friday night: large aromatic onions stuffed with rice, ground beef and flavored with tomato sauce, cinnamon, pomegranate juice and spice, pepper and salt—her favorite dish which always take her back to her days in Zaragoza as a young serving maid with the Navarros.

"Reb, your daughter has agreed to give an answer by Rosh Hashana, isn't that right, Tuvia?" the old nursemaid interrupts enthusiastically.

"Rosa, you have loose lips," Ruth observes wryly as the rabbi turns to the young man.

"I am blessed with patience, Reb. I can wait for your daughter's answer," Tuvia answers quickly before Rosa can embarrass him further.

"Then you are a better man than I."

Elazar turns to Ruth. "I am not getting any younger. I should like the honor of grandchildren before I die."

"All I ask is three more months," Ruth replies, trying to keep her ambivalence out of her voice.

Elazar raises his glass in a toast. "Then three more months it is."

The other two awkwardly clink glasses while Rosa serves the main courses. Before them lies a feast of dishes, some of them sabbat offerings from the community to the rabbi: a pheasant caught and plucked by the butcher, a roast chicken dressed by the bailiff's wife, beetroots and turnips from the undertaker's garden and, of course, Rosa's famous onions.

"Look at this feast, my children." Elazar smiles broadly. "Are we not blessed? I am reminded of the belief of the ancient Sephardic doctor Israelicus: that food must be really delicious if both disposition and body are to benefit. Is that not right, daughter?"

Ruth cannot help but smile with him. "Indeed, you become what you eat. In which case I am an onion." She picks up one of Rosa's delicacies. "Layered, slightly sour and guaranteed to bring tears to the eyes."

Tuvia, laughing, raises his glass. "I'll drink to that."

Tuvia sits back, satiated. "I am to Maastricht Monday, I have a circumcision to attend."

"Is there not plague in Maastricht?"

"The family lives outside the city walls, I shall be safe." He smiles at Ruth, happy to interpret her concern as an indication of a more intimate emotion.

Ruth watches him: his long white fingers drumming the wooden table, his narrow shoulders hunched over in his black robe, the thin lips and huge mournful eyes seemingly devoid of sensuality. There is nothing about him that moves her. But knowing the obvious affection Tuvia has for her father, she wonders whether she should not surrender the notion of romantic passion and give herself up to a loveless arrangement, if only to grant some last happiness to the dying old man.

Detlef stands in front of the small curved looking glass he normally keeps hidden in a chest. It is testimony to an earlier youthful vanity from his soldiering days. It is late, well after vespers. He can hear the fading rustles of the other monks as one by one they prepare for the short night's rest. The canon does not realize how long he has been standing there. He only knows it has been time enough to feel his resolve solidify into a heart-pounding reality.

The reflection staring back from the surface of the polished metal is unfamiliar. Dressed in a filthy short cloak, torn breeches and a grease-stained waistcoat bought from a journeyman who thought the cleric must be delirious to pay three Reichstaler for the clothes upon his back. Detlef is completely unrecognizable.

The hat, in chevalier style, has a ridiculous battered peacock's feather strung through its band but serves Detlef's purpose well, as he is able to pull it low over his brow. Beneath it sits an old wig he hasn't worn for years, a shoulder-length brown pigtail around which is wrapped an ancient velvet ribbon. His face is smeared with soot in an effort to look unwashed and world-weary like any other journeyman. He has succeeded.

Outside all is quiet as the last of the monks settles down in his austere cell. Detlef touches his heart with his left hand then places the same hand over the reflected heart in the mirror. He cannot pray. He cannot think. The act he is about to commit will bear no scrutiny for it is too primal, too instinctive, to either deny or examine. All he knows is that he will not survive another day without acting.

He opens the heavy wooden door slowly, making sure it does not creak. Along the stone walls of the corridor he sees the last of the reflected candlelight flicker and die. Now is the time to leave.

The ferryman says nothing as Detlef hands him a bribe for crossing the Rhine in the dark. The ancient sailor assumes from the way the man is dressed that he is an impoverished traveler from the north, just another homeless itinerant. The only thing that surprises him is the softness and whiteness of the traveler's hands, they are not the hands of a poor working man. The sailor glances up at the face smudged with dirt, the lanky unwashed strands of hair falling out of the battered hat and believes he is mistaken. But as the stranger settles himself into the corner of the barge and stares back at Cologne, a shadowy skyline punctuated only by the occasional burning torch, the bent crane of the half-built cathedral silhouetted like a witch's long finger with the low moon impaled on its tip, the ferryman wonders about the heaviness of the journeyman's silence. It is not the stillness of an ordinary man but the ponderous silence of the suffering. The horrifying thought that he might be a secret leper crosses the sailor's mind for a moment, but the traveler seems too robust, his limbs intact. No, most likely some nobleman having to flee in disgrace, the old sailor decides, then curses himself for not demanding more money.

They reach the first barge moored a third of the way across the river. As the traveler steps over to the next barge bobbing gently in the water, the ferryman sees that he is wearing good hide boots below the torn breeches.

"I will pay you heavily for your future assistance . . . and your discretion," the traveler, noticing his inquisitiveness, announces in a guttural accent which confuses the man further. Out on the river a swan breaks out in a series of cries that echo back across the water.

"In that case both my service and my silence are yours," the sailor replies, deliberately employing a formal German to indicate that he is conscious of the real station of his passenger. It is then that Detlef realizes he has crossed a boundary he never thought he would have the courage or desire to challenge.

It seems an eternity before he is aware of walking along her streets. The tall narrow houses could belong to any town in the Rhineland, the only thing that marks them as other are the wooden mezuzahs nailed over the front doors. It is now past twelve and the town is sleeping.

A town crier appears at the far end of the road. Detlef ducks into a doorway to avoid being seen. The only other time he has been in these streets was for Ruth's arrest. Then he rode. Then he was indifferent to the fate of this foreign community. Now he is on foot, trying desperately to remember the route the patrol took to reach the small cottage he recalls as being on the bank of a stream at the edge of a field. As he follows the one main road that seems to lead out of the village, the sound of frogs looms up. Water. Stream. Ruth.

Detlef crosses a small bridge and instantly the rattle of the horses' hooves pounding the wooden slats floods his memory. The sweet smell of cut hay and apple blossom drifts across the rushing water. The thatched cottage is there, set against the backdrop of a forest, with its cultivated garden and orchard. A light burns behind the misted window.

Detlef stands transfixed. He is at the border of dream and reality as he stares at the building. Something rushes past at the periphery of his vision. Startled he looks around; a fox gazes back, its rusty head cocked around a tree. The animal appears complicit in its silence. The whole garden seems to be holding its breath as the intruder walks soundlessly toward the door of the dwelling.

To Detlef it feels as if he is gliding over the dew-covered grass. Not even the daisies appear to bend under his weight. He moves compelled by a greater force than rationality, than self-preservation, a force beyond his conscious mind. He is barely aware of his actions but knows that for the first time in his life he is acting out of a greater passion than self-love.

He pushes open the door; the main room is empty. A candle still burns on the table and a fire smolders in the huge fireplace. A half-eaten apple stands on the table. He feels as if he is not here, as if he is an invisible observer, an ethereal spirit that is being swept in with the wind and is able to watch unseen. Everything is vivid. Every detail in the room magnified. He can see the toothmarks left in the apple, he can sense the trail of scent, heat and fine dust Ruth has left swathed across the center of the room. A great desire surges through him, painfully fused with an inherent sense of sorrow, as if he is unable to make one more move toward what he knows undeniably to be his fate.

Ruth is standing in the alcove that houses her bed. On the floor is a wooden bucket filled with water she has boiled on the fire. Naked from the waist up she leans over it, washing herself with a cloth. As she wipes her neck and breasts she finds herself thinking about the canon, how in the silence of that long coach journey she realized there is much that can be communicated without words, that it is possible to have a discourse of the mind with a man she would have expected to share nothing in common. She tries not to remember his beauty. She tries not to think of him as a man. She does not want to be distracted by a passion that cannot afford to exist even in imagination or unspoken longing. An impossible desire. An improbable love. Sighing, Ruth sponges the last of the soap away and in an instant becomes aware of being watched.

The man is standing in the center of the room beyond. He is familiar and yet not familiar. She does not know the face, the hair, the attire or the dirty features beneath the hat, but there is something she recognizes in his physique, in the way he holds his body, that makes her hesitant for one tiny moment. Then, screaming, she covers herself.

Before she can run he is there, holding her, his hands clapped over her mouth. "Ruth! Stop, please! It is me. Detlef," he whispers as he holds her struggling body close, the first words he has uttered in over five hours. Deafened by the panic beating in her ears she does not hear him.

"It's Detlef, it's me, Detlef, Detlef," he continues to murmur, trying to reclaim his action, this intrusion which is so foreign to his nature that suddenly he no longer knows himself. In the same instant Ruth hears him and stops fighting.

They stand suspended: the cloaked man with his arms wrapped around the half-naked woman. Then, to her surprise, the proximity of him, his maleness, his scent, the taste of salt and earth, the bulk of his long fingers against her tongue, awake within her a desire so long denied that she loses control. Her trembling limbs wind themselves around him, she presses herself against his hardening groin, her hands searching for his skin, tearing at the yellowed lace at his neck. Detlef, unable to hold back any longer, finds her mouth and lifting her up onto his hips, draws her facedown to his. Hat and wig fall to the ground, the feather trailing in the bucket of water, as the intelligence of his tongue tames her kisses.

He drops to his knees and traces a path down to one nipple while teasing the other. Her body astounds him. It is not thin as he imagined, but slender with full breasts ripe with large dark areolae. Impatient for the rest of her, he unlaces her skirt and lets it fall to her feet. He is shocked at the smoothness of her skin. Ivory white, the fine down on it jet black. She tastes like cinnamon, the faint scent of lemon across her belly. She is so small that even kneeling his face is breast height. He runs his fingers down, caressing her high buttocks, feeling her quiver beneath his hands, then buries his face into the soft fur between her legs. She smells impossibly sweet. Parting her with his fingers he finds her center between the folds of flesh, a tiny bead between his lips. Above he can hear her moan as her fingers weave through his hair trying to pull him up to his feet.

"Please," she murmurs, "please, I am ashamed."

But he persists, his own excitement growing with hers until he is so hard beneath his breeches that he is frightened his seed will spill. Finally she manages to pull him to his feet. He stands there, breathing hard, rigid against the rough cloth as she reaches down to release him.

"But you are virgin."

He grabs her wrists and holds them for a minute, trying wildly to collect his thoughts. In lieu of a reply she leans forward and buries her face in his chest.

Moaning softly he drops her wrist and allows her to reach down into his breeches and pull him free. For a second she looks at his sex in wonderment. Forgetting who she is or even what she is, she drops to her knees, caressing the velvet head caught so neatly like a pearl in its own case. She touches him, caressing him backward and forward, her touch deceptively deft. Detlef cannot believe that these are her hands encircling him, that these are her eyes staring up at him, watching him lose himself. Now, as his orgasm begins to mount, climbing up gloriously behind his balls, in the pit of his stomach, behind his eyes, he pushes her to the ground, throwing his hand between her legs. Finding her wet he pulls her beneath him and enters her with one hard thrust. She screams, pushing her face deep in the abandoned clothes as, forgetting everything in her tightness, he enters her over and over until they cry out in ecstasy.

She is in his arms, her head cradled between his shoulder and chest. They have been lying like this for hours. She will not sleep for fear that she will wake and find she has been dreaming. She could not believe, while he gently sponged the blood from her thighs, kissed her over and over between her legs until again the pleasure rippled up from her belly, that physical love could be so naturally married with the emotional; how such an act could rid her of all sensible thought and render her future suddenly meaningless without him; how she could ever have considered a life without this utterly human deed which has imbued her suddenly with renewed faith.

"*Shall I be there too, fresh-wounded, your latest Prisoner—displaying your captive mind—/ With Conscience, hands bound behind her, and Modesty, all Love's other enemies, whipped into line,*" she whispers softly in Latin.

"Ovid, from the *Amores*?"

She nods, smiling slightly.

"Where did a woman like you learn Ovid? He is not a poet for chaste women, even philosophising women like yourself."

"Spinoza always said a woman like me should not marry or bear children for I have a man's mind trapped in the body of a female."

"Is sex so separate, Ruth? I for one do not consider your ambitious spirit to be unfeminine."

Ruth, her fingers curled into his hair, her body singing in a way it has never sung before, smiles.

"This shall be the ruin of us," she whispers, hoping that he might not hear her.

But Detlef, savoring her pleasing weight upon him, his loins deliciously emptied, hears everything. He reaches down and tilts her face up to his.

"We are already ruined, for I have ruined you and you I."

"Am I your first woman?" she asks, a sardonic smile playing across her mouth.

"In an unfathomable way."

"To be condemned by our communities, all that we are governed by . . ."

He watches her, trying to read what lies behind her eyes.

"Ruth, if you desire, you can close your eyes and I will depart. It will be as if nothing happened. As if I were a ghost, a specter who has merely slipped through the looking glass."

She leans over him, her breasts soft against his chest.

"No, that shall not be."

"Then let me protect you. For I fear the inquisitor will find a way of avenging himself."

"I cannot leave my father."

"I beg you—"

"Then beg no more. We have the moment, let us not waste it in idle fantasy."

And she pulls him into her arms, as if trying with her slender body to shelter them both from the outside world.

Later, as he watches her sleep, he finds the parameters of his universe have been flung open in a way he could never have imagined, as if a great furnace has finally melted the jail he built so carefully to protect his heart, mind and faith. The mystery of her transfixes him; banal simple things: her bosom as it rises with every breath, the exotic thickness of her pubic bush curling up the curved belly which to his surprise, he longs to fill, the taste of her and the taste of her and the taste of her.

A finger of pale blue light begins to creep across the scrubbed stone floor. The first smoke of the early morning fires lies on the air and he knows that he must leave.

With his hat pulled low Detlef makes his way back across the bridge toward the town. This time he has made sure that his boots are well soiled and that he walks with the limp of the homeless.

The sky is streaked with a red sunrise struggling to shine through the clouds. In the distance a young goatherd prods his reluctant animals with a stick as they bleat their way to the new day's pasture, bells ringing. Detlef walks on into the sleepy town, not daring to lift his eyes to the young wives dressed in the twin-horned cap of the Jewess who shout to each other as they throw their laundry over balconies, the guttural sound of Yiddish floating down. A fetid-smelling cart winds its way slowly along the road as the night-soil man—a dwarf in a makeshift uniform of dark purple breeches and a top coat of black—runs to each household to collect the stinking pails. He hurries past Detlef without noticing him.

Detlef takes comfort in the normalcy of the panorama. This is where Ruth began her life, where she was conceived and nurtured. He finds it impossible to believe that he, a Catholic who has had sexual congress with a Jew, could be at great risk of arrest. Just as he finds it impossible to believe that he is trespassing as he walks along these very streets. The naturalness of his happiness seems to preclude the possibility of danger. And so distracted, he barely notices the intense young rabbi leaving the house by the temple, a bag strung across his back.

But Tuvia, as he climbs into the morning coach bound for Maastricht, spies the tall stranger. Something about his elegance of gait, the nobility of his features, seems odd to the young rabbi, by nature suspicious. The man is obviously not a Jew. In which case, what is he doing in the center of Deutz's Jewish quarter at five a.m.?

Disturbed, Tuvia watches through the window of the coach as the intruder strides toward the Rhine.

My dearest Ruth,

What has happened between us is irreversible as the Dawn which, as I write, threatens to expose us as turncoats of Love. If you will not come under my protection then I shall do my utmost to protect you from Cologne itself. But, my dearest heart, I fear there is only so much I can do. The inquisitor will eventually find a way to prosecute and Maximilian Heinrich will be forced to sacrifice your life. This I believe to be only a matter of time. I beg you to reconsider your decision.

Trust that as I watch you sleep, I leave half my soul here in this cottage. Ours is a union that will suffer no restrictions, no ignorance, no borders. I have no idea how I shall be able to walk back toward the Rhine without you, and I vow that nothing—no law, no army or faith—will keep me from your side.

In love and admiration,
Detlef von Tennen

Ruth lies there, his letter pressed against her face, the urgency of the day filtering in through the thin parchment. She should get up. Open the heavy wooden door. Let the early morning sun warm the cold stone floor. Feed the geese, pump water. Instead she stays sprawled across the bed, reveling in the lingering weight of his body echoing across her skin, in her loins. The taste of him, his sweat, which remains faintly palpable. She rolls over and, curling up, reaches across to the slight indentation in the pallet, still warm. She buries her face into the space where he lay, breathing his scent as deeply as she can.

She cannot believe his visit was real. That, despite geography, social mores, tyranny and huge danger, he came to her. She finds it difficult to fathom how an emotion which she was previously unable to define has become so clear, so overwhelming that it has pushed away all other concerns.

Outside she hears Miriam knocking at the door. She slips Detlef's letter between the bed base and the pallet then, frightened that her young assistant might guess the real reason behind the strewn clothes, she leaps up—only to catch sight of her naked body in the looking glass. To her amazement she appears exactly as the day before. It is as if she had expected the loss of her virginity to transform her, to leave a mark. The absurdity of the thought makes her break into delighted laughter before she covers herself.

Carlos bravely places the morsel of stuffed pig's intestine into his mouth and tries not to gag. Grimacing, he washes it down with a mouthful of wine, thankfully imported from the Mediterranean.

"I see the good priest is having difficulty with our German peculiarities?"

Wilhelm Egon von Fürstenberg smiles. Upon seeing the inquisitor splutter he pours him another glass.

"It is true that we lack the spice and flavor of the south, and we can be a little inflexible in our choice of vegetable. However there are many ways to prepare a cabbage, don't you agree, Monsignor?"

Carlos glances at the portly minister. His obsequious verbosity is irritating. He trusts him even less than the canon, whose views are at least always transparent, but this man, Wilhelm Egon von Fürstenberg, has to be the real manipulator in the shadows. Suspecting him of having great influence over the archbishop, and possibly the prime architect of Heinrich's dealings with the French, the inquisitor wonders why von Fürstenberg has invited him to eat at this palatial dwelling, a luxurious mansion on the outskirts of the city by the river's edge belonging to his mistress, the wealthy widow, Countess von Marck.

Von Fürstenberg must want to strike a deal. But what kind of deal? The internal machinations and politics of this provincial city are beginning to irk him greatly, the Dominican thinks, suppressing a burp. He has been doubly thwarted in his persecution of Ruth bas Elazar Saul by that idiot Emperor Leopold and Maximilian Heinrich. It was a mistake to go to the vineyard, he was seduced by the archbishop's cheap trick when he should have remained in the city to witness that sham of a trial. But he is determined to find the Jewess guilty, even if that means suffering the further indignity of German hospitality. A greater calling is at stake: the annihilation of the unholy, the purging of an evil seed which, unchecked, could infect an entire population.

"A cabbage is a benign plant whereas a swine . . ." Carlos continues von Fürstenberg's allegory, hoping for more clues to the diplomat's opaque proposal.

"A swine can be slaughtered by various means." Von Fürstenberg's tone suddenly becomes very serious. "Wild boar is particularly tasty because it has to be hunted and, being an intelligent animal, is able to conceal itself in many ways. You are naturally discouraged by the turn of events."

Still unsure whether the conversation might turn into an ambush, Carlos hesitates over another glass of wine. The best way for enemies to unite is over another foe, he reflects before replying.

"Naturally."

"I think perhaps we could be of service to one another. The archbishop's cousin has undergone a rather unpleasant transformation, becoming a fanatic since his encounter with the Jewish witch. His newly found enthusiasm for the bürgers and even the serfs is a cause of concern to both the archbishop and myself."

"How much of a concern?"

"The canon and the midwife would not be missed if they should mysteriously disappear. As you may appreciate, the Jews of the Rhineland have some economic value and our communities maintain a delicate relationship which is easily unbalanced. They have no wish to create difficulties any more than we do . . ."

"But what of the royal pardon?"

"Now that the prince is cured and safely back in Vienna I doubt whether the emperor will remember how to pronounce the name Ruth bas Elazar Saul, if he ever did know how to pronounce it. The pardon has all the hallmarks of Samuel Oppenheimer's intervention."

"It is true that the Court Jew is powerful."

"Not powerful enough. And far too fond of his own status to rock the boat for such a small fish."

"The Grand Inquisitional Council would be most grateful to the Holy Keepers of the Magi for such a favor."

"And what pleases Aragon pleases Cologne. But tell me, does the Inquisitional Council really care that much, or is this more of a personal quest, Monsignor?"

Carlos's silence confirms von Fürstenberg's suspicions.

"In that case, Monsignor, you have my sympathy. I understand what it is to be thwarted over generations."

"Of course, we all experience the blindness of familial ties. Even the archbishop in all his wisdom seems to favor blood over talent," Carlos, his face rigid, fires back.

"Heinrich, despite his appearance, is a sentimental man but his affection for his cousin is being tried by the canon's behavior."

"Which in the long term augurs well for other potential heirs—like yourself, perhaps?"

"Indeed."

"I am curious: who really courts King Louis—the archbishop or yourself?"

The stuffed pig's intestines are replaced by a dish of fowl: a goose baked whole with a glaze of black cherries. Von Fürstenberg pushes the dish toward Carlos. "You must try the fowl, it is a French recipe sent direct from Versailles."

Having received an oblique answer to his question, the friar, always frugal in his consumption, leans back, overwhelmed by the extravagance of the meal. He still finds himself questioning the German's motives.

"I believe the midwife has returned to Deutz." Von Fürstenberg bites into a wing, juice dripping down his chin.

"Is she still practicing her devilry?"

"You mean midwifery."

"She is no mere midwife; she is witch, trust me on this."

The steely conviction in the inquisitor's voice sends an involuntary tremble through von Fürstenberg's body, despite his cynicism.

The worst enemy is one whose doctrines are founded in hate and are thus beyond debate, the minister wryly observes to himself. The friar has no heart and a heartless man is the most vicious of all.

Carlos meticulously prises off part of the breast with the traveling fork he carries with him, the practice of sharing food using one's fingers is abhorrent to his fastidious nature.

"She has not been seen since her release, except at her father's house." Von Fürstenberg offers the information cautiously.

"To secure her we shall have to defame her liberator."

"That might be possible. The Countess von Marck is a close friend of

Meisterin Birgit Ter Lahn von Lennep, a woman once much enamored of our colleague von Tennen."

"And now?"

"In his newly found zeal he is refusing to take her confession. Naturally I am happy to console her."

"In the meantime?"

"In the meantime we wait and watch. The patient cat catches the mouse."

"Indeed," Carlos replies carefully, "but be warned, sire, my patience can wear thin."

"Do have the breast, it is the choicest part of the bird, Monsignor."

Von Fürstenberg pulls at the huge glistening carcass with his fingers then thrusts the fatty piece of flesh toward the Spaniard. Carlos, in a heroic gesture of fraternity, takes it between his own fingers and nibbles at it delicately.

Elazar sits before the fire with his breeches rolled up to his knees. The nursemaid stands behind him, her hands covered in a pungent-smelling ointment of chicken fat, almond oil and crushed cloves, massaging the old man's shoulders. Ruth is at the table, grinding a poultice with a pestle and mortar, smiling at her father's groans.

"Woman, I am not a piece of old leather."

"No, you are a gout-ridden piece of old leather with religious ambitions," Rosa retorts as her thick fingers manipulate the swollen tissue.

"Abba, you must stop the rich food."

"It has nothing to do with food. Your grandfather had the gout as did his father. It is in the blood!"

"But the poultice helps?"

"It soothes. You make miracles, daughter, with your magic."

They are interrupted by a pounding at the door. Fearing the worst, they stop still.

"I will go," the old man announces as he struggles to stand.

"No, you won't."

Ruth wipes her hands and walks to the door. Outside a small boy, his reddish prayer locks tumbling down past his ears, waits impatiently.

"Please, Fräulein! My mother needs a midwife. Please, she is in trouble! Please come!"

"No, Ruth." The rabbi, leaning heavily against the doorway, his brow stern, is the figure of immutable authority. "I forbid it."

He turns to the child. "Tell your mother the midwife is not available."

The child, intimidated by the rabbi, is near tears but still he will not budge. "But Rabbi, she will die! She is screaming already . . ."

Without answering Elazar begins to close the door.

Ruth pushes past. "Come" she says to the child and grabbing his hand runs with him down the street.

Elazar, immobile with anger, dares not call out his daughter's name.

My true heart, my beloved.

I sit by the stream that runs past my orchard. It is late, I know not how late. I have broken my father's promise and attended a birthing this very day. The woman was narrow in the hips from rickets and would have died without my attention. The babe was a boy, second child to Herr and Frau Rechtschild. The father is a tailor for my people and I had to make him swear not to tell of my service nor to pay me for it. It is of necessity of the heart that I attend these women. Many have died before their time—my mother among them— through ignorance and unnecessary pain inflicted upon them by clumsy mid- wifery. And if I risk persecution, Detlef, then I risk it joyously.

Venus, the first star, has appeared, another child is born and the stream runs on. Water must be a celestial element for it has neither time nor history stamped upon it and is as constant as the tides of the sea or the rising of the moon. I long for such constancy, be it in life or in comradeship. Memory is a great deceiver: it embroiders until naught is left but the glory and the pleasure. Did we really lie together? Was it really your voice that spoke of great affection? Was it you who dreamed a future that cannot be?

I have a noble spirit, but I want to live. Tell me how to live and who to live for. I fear I shall surrender too much in love and then survive to regret it . . .

She sits with her naked feet tucked under her long stained skirt. It is barely an hour since she left the birthing, smuggled out of the tailor's meager

dwelling, hidden under an old cloak long abandoned by one of his cus-
tomers. Herr Rechtschild, profusely grateful, led her down a narrow alley
stinking with sewage that only the goats and chickens care to frequent. In
lieu of payment he insisted she allow him the pleasure of mending all her
shawls for a month, claiming that if anyone asks why he shall say that he is
preparing her for her engagement to Tuvia. Ruth, too exhausted to argue,
was sickened by his obvious joy at the imagined union. The encroaching
expectations of the small community are already fastening around her like
tentacles. An old but familiar sense of panic begins to ferment within her:
the desire to leave, to break free.

The gutter ended at a sluice-gate, beyond it a field adjacent to her own
property. As the tailor unfastened the gate she had made him swear not to
tell anyone of her service. As soon as she was out of view, she had run
through the long grass toward the cottage, hoping against all reason that
Detlef would be there waiting for her, like some glorious apparition from a
forgotten daydream.

By the time she reached the dwelling the consequences of her actions
had sobered her completely. But the yearning to talk with her lover, to
touch him, to share the day, was overwhelming.

Night creeps across the orchard now as the first swarm of gnats begins
to dance over the water. Ruth looks down at the sheet of parchment, her
handwriting an erratic scrawl, illegible in its jagged eagerness. How is she
to send it? A courier would be too dangerous. She could bribe a journeyman, but discovery would mean death and disgrace for at least one of
them. Can she trust Detlef? Is she able to discern between the pleasure of
the body and the loyalty of the heart?

Uncertain of anything, she tears the parchment into pieces then scatters
them across the rushing water.

Detlef stands over the font. Behind him he can hear the last of the sext
prayers fading. Looking down he sees his fingertips reflected in the water's
surface as he prepares to dip them to mark himself with the holy cross. He
does not think, he dares not.

It is four nights since he lay with the midwife and the potency of their
encounter has rendered his ecclesiastical life with its rigid rituals and anti-

quated traditions meaningless. The prospect of loving her, the sheer audacity of it, has jarred him into a multitude of different futures, as if the
road he had carefully mapped out has branched uncontrollably into endless
possibilities. Suddenly all his work within the cathedral feels futile, worse
than that: hollow.

He wonders how he is to deal with the day-to-day routines of his clerical life: the singing of vespers, the taking of confession, ministering to the
poor. How is he to go on as before, an ambitious young canon manipulat-
ing his way to a bishopric? Will it be possible for his life to continue without her?

He kneels at the ornate altar. The statue of Saint Ursula is a baroque
carving which vividly depicts the young maiden with scarlet cheeks and
huge sad eyes, her gown torn, her body shot through with arrows, while at
her bleeding feet writhe several of her ravished followers. Here a damsel of
Aryan perfection straddled by a huge dark-haired Briton, his face a puffy
parody of arousal; there a pale creature cowers as her gown is torn from her
body by a rusty-haired sailor. The saint herself seems to gaze down at
Detlef. The more he stares at her the more he is convinced there is a chastising look on her painted face.

Closing his eyes he begins to pray but finds that Ruth's naked form
plays before him: tantalizingly, fragments of memory—the tilt of her chin
below a shy smile, cheeks flushed with excitement, an erect nipple—wash
over him, weakening his resolve. Each supplication as it forms in his mind
concludes with one word: Ruth.

A sharp tap on the shoulder rescues him, jolting him back to within the
stone walls of the chapel. Groot pulls at his robe, gesturing that Detlef
should follow him outside to a place where they cannot be heard. Together
they step through a stone archway into a courtyard where the archbishop's
servants grow vegetables for the kitchen. The midday sun hits the back of
their shaved necks, reddening the skin above the rough linen. A page
squats on some stone steps, busy mending his boots with a hammer.
Groot, edging closer, takes advantage of the loud banging.

"Canon, I have news from a small but friendly bird. Von Fürstenberg
has made water with the Spaniard and we both know how bad their piss
must stink. They have made merry and I fear you are to be the cuckold.
Find yourself a dance master, for if you falter but once they shall take advantage."

Detlef, frustrated by Groot's dramatic and incomprehensible allegories and unsure just how much his assistant actually knows, decides to feign ignorance.

"Groot, you know yourself that I dance superbly."

The cleric leans even closer, his pockmarked face looming like a craterous moon. "In plain talk, sire, you are watched and closely."

For a second Detlef's heart misses a beat. Can Groot know about the midwife when he has been so careful?

The assistant, relishing his master's paling face, elaborates. "Von Fürstenberg seeks favor with the archbishop and both are worried about your recent and growing affection."

He is oblivious to the sudden silence as the page pauses in his hammering and cocks his ear at the second mention of von Fürstenberg, wondering if he might be able to make an extra Reichstaler through eavesdropping.

"Affection . . . ?"

"For those who challenge the way the bürgermeisters favor certain individuals. Even some of the Gaffeln are worried, and everyone knows you haven't taken Meisterin Ter Lahn von Lennep's confession for over two full moons." Groot smiles lewdly. "One might even say you are a chaste man."

"Chaste indeed," Detlef replies with a serious demeanor, fear prickling still at the back of his scalp.

A few feet away the watching page wonders why the handsome young canon looks so uncomfortable at his cleric's words.

The infusion of elderflower and ginger root wafts fragrantly from an elegant teapot of Chinese porcelain. Birgit, demurely resplendent in pale mauve damask, pours the tea into two impossibly fragile cups.

"My husband bought these from an Oriental trader by way of a Dutch ship. They are said to be over one hundred years old."

She hands the cup to Wilhelm Egon von Fürstenberg, who takes it between his pudgy fingers and raises it above his large ruffled collar. Birgit watches him sip with a surprising delicacy.

"But you did not visit me to sample tea, Herr von Fürstenberg, did you?"

"No. I am here on a more somber matter."

Birgit studies the corpulent man as he fiddles nervously with the gold chain which hangs over his black robe. Many times she and Detlef have shared witticisms and cruel observations about the ambitious minister, and on numerous occasions Birgit warned the canon of von Fürstenberg's famed treachery. Now here he is in her own parlor, like a huge spider pausing before deciding to which part of her anatomy he wishes to attach his dangerously sticky web.

"The matter of the salvation of your soul, Frau Ter Lahn von Lennep."

"My soul?" Birgit allows a sardonic smile to spread across her full mouth. "I have not noticed that it is in need of saving, but of course I bow to your professional insight."

Angry at his impertinence she covers herself by reaching for her own teacup. It is only the years of decorum that prevent her hand from shaking with rage.

"You have not taken confession for over two months. Naturally I understand why you would wait for the attentions of your . . . favorite canon. But given his recent and sudden preference for attending to secular matters before his religious duties, it is not correct that you should be without the cleansing of regular confession."

"Are you volunteering yourself?"

Birgit, now icily furious, looks him directly in the eye. Von Fürstenberg does not flinch or blush. He is betrayed only by a slight twitch which appears under one eyelid, as if Birgit might have willed it there herself.

"I am afraid that I have other commitments, Madame, otherwise it would be a great honor to serve such a devout Catholic. I know no other lady in your position who has been taking confession with the same priest for so many years. It must be a great loss to find oneself suddenly without one's cleric."

The delicate teacup shatters under the pressure of Birgit's fingers. Immediately the housemaid darts forward from her position in the corner and mops at the spreading liquid with her apron. Struggling to retain her composure, Birgit methodically gathers the pieces of china, pushing them into a tiny heap. Minute beads of blood well up on her thumb.

Von Fürstenberg takes the opportunity to lean closer.

"The canon's actions threaten the unity of the cathedral council. The archbishop is not pleased. A charge of immoral conduct, Madame, would cause Detlef von Tennen to be excommunicated and banished from Cologne."

Birgit stares at his face as it mottles with excitement. Revolted by the minister's obvious pleasure, she wonders how much he knows about her relationship with Detlef. Could it be that they were spied upon that fateful day at The Hunter's Sheath? Surely not. As she hesitates, Birgit thinks she glimpses the shadow of a leaner, more vicious man emerging from von Fürstenberg's rotundity. The vision reminds her of some monstrous insect climbing out of a deceptively sleek cocoon.

"You could destroy him," he whispers seductively, his breath a foul wind. In his excitement his spittle hits her cheek.

Birgit glares at him, shocked by the vitriol of his outburst, his flushed face, his pupils shining pinpricks of hate.

"Nothing immoral has ever happened between myself and the good canon, Herr von Fürstenberg. To insinuate otherwise would be to suggest there was something unholy about our discourse. To love one's fellow man is to love God, is it not?" she finishes coldly.

She stands, stiff with rage. "Good day to you, sir."

Smiling superciliously at her rebuff, the minister bows then reaches for his hat.

"You know, Madame, that if you should change your mind I shall always be of service," he finishes smoothly before leaving.

Birgit goes to the window. Holding herself, she watches as von Fürstenberg climbs into his carriage. After his coach has disappeared she returns to the table and places her bleeding thumb in the cup of half-drunk tea he has left standing. Blood seeps out, staining the pale beverage with crimson tendrils.

R uth and Detlef lie on the straw. Silent. Apart. Through the barn window the low crescent moon hangs below a velvet awning of stars. He has come to her again by the back roads. Standing over a bowl of flour, her hands covered with the dusty powder, Ruth sensed his approach as a fiery certainty. A phenomenon which burned through her, leaving her shaking at the knees until at last she saw her lover appear at the edge of the field.

There was no need for words. This time it was she who simply took his hand and led him to the barn, the shelf above the stables, the most secret place she could think of, and this time they held each other for a long time before the lovemaking.

Ruth reaches down and touches herself, her thighs are still sticky with his seed. With her finger damp she holds it in a beam of moonlight that cuts through the air and transforms the hay into a mysterious nest of grays and whites.

"Poriut . . . fertility," she murmurs and glances across to Detlef's profile, strong and chiseled, as he stares at the outside sky.

"More sorcery?" He smiles in the dark, reaching for her hand to kiss it.

Turning back toward the sky she watches the moon slowly continue its ascent. "Saturn, Jupiter, Mars," she points, "all celestial bodies with their own moons spinning around them."

"Thanks to Galileo, no longer are we the center of the universe."

"No longer, although sometimes it is hard to remember. Benedict once showed me the moons of Jupiter through a wondrous telescope for which he himself had ground the lens. He said 'Look, Felix, God gives us the gift of knowledge to observe his works just as he gave us the intelligence not to be slaves to our own destinies.'"

"Felix?"

"The name I gave myself when I was in the guise of a youth,"

"Did Spinoza not know your true sex?"

"Yes, eventually, but I was a paradox he could not accept."

"For me you can be both Ruth and Felix: a woman who leads and a man who can surrender."

He pulls her toward him, banging their noses together in the dark. Laughing, she searches out his mouth again, this time sweetness overriding passion. But afterward as he lies there. Detlef feels a foreboding. He knows this stolen time will never be enough, that he cannot put away this desire, contain it as he did with Birgit, for he has already begun to feel as if Ruth is a part of himself, privy to his most private ambitions, secret terrors, unspeakable desires.

"Ruth, we must talk. We must face what is before us and not succumb to the pleasures of the moment."

"But why? You know this love cannot be. Not with who we are, what we are," she answers, not allowing herself hope, her fears warning her to surrender nothing despite the warmth of his arms.

"I will not lose you." His words sound out like a vow. "Against all nature I will not lose you."

Tuvia's throat is dry. He has been sitting for six hours in the back of the wagon, hands gripping the sides to stop himself being bounced around like a herring in a fishing net. At his feet is a bag containing his prayer shawl, his Tefillah and the tools of circumcision. The journey was successful, despite the arduous route they had to take to avoid the plague-ridden villages beyond the border. The household Tuvia visited was orthodox, like the one he envisages for Ruth and himself: a happy home with a modest wife, an adoring husband, bread on the table and salted beef hanging in the parlor, a sanctuary from a hostile world. The brith was executed well: the baby was robust and the young father ecstatic to have his firstborn a male. But just after the circumcision a vision came to Tuvia, the Tetragrammaton in the form of fiery letters dancing over the crib. Tuvia, not unaccustomed to the call of the unknown, had attempted to read the future of the newborn boy in the leaping flames, as is the custom, but the scarlet-blue color did not bode well. Lying, he told the father the child had a great life ahead, perhaps as a statesman for his people. But the experience frightened the mohel, tainting the excitement he felt about returning to Deutz.

Exhausted, he sinks back against the cart, mesmerized by the swinging flanks of the huge drafthorses in front. He closes his eyes, lulled by the rocking. The cry of a startled pheasant flying out from a low holly bush jolts him awake. He recognizes the small wooden bridge ahead and immediately the thrill of seeing Ruth sets him trembling despite his immense weariness.

The sound of the horses' hooves turns to a hollow clamor as they cross the small stream. When the cottage comes into full view Tuvia sinks down low. He wants to surprise her. He wants to see the dream he has of her running toward him with delight made real. In his traveling sack is a stomacher embroidered with gold he bought from a seamstress in Maastricht. It is of a deep maroon velvet which he chose to set off her raven hair. She will wear it for him, of this he is as sure as the knowledge that the sun rises in the morning.

It is then that he spies the intruder, the German he saw in the town the morning of his departure. The tall man steps out of the back door of the cottage then moves back into the shadows as if he wishes to hide. But it is too late. Tuvia immediately recognizes the uncovered head and the distinctive gait despite the old cloak and the worn workman's breeches. Detlef von Tennen, the canon from the cathedral. The last time Tuvia saw him was with the soldiers who came to make the arrests: then the man had gleamed arrogantly with power and beauty, sitting high on his bay horse with aristocratic superiority. Now he is a furtive stranger at the door of the woman Tuvia loves. But why? For a moment the young man is paralyzed by the fear of what might have happened to Ruth. Then, as he watches in horror, the midwife appears behind the Christian cleric. Wrapping her arms around him she pulls him back into the doorway. Tuvia, now quivering with nausea, vomits over the side of the cart into the gutter.

Rosa, standing at the window, cries out when she sees the young rabbi, his face flaming red, stumble off the cart clutching his bags. Running out of the house, parsnip peelings scattering from her long apron, the nursemaid barely catches the thin young man as he collapses.

"Tuvia, Tuvia, what is it? You are burning with fever! Mein Gott!"

"What I have seen would make any man blaze! It is unforgivable! She must burn! She must burn!"

Rosa glances around fearfully then claps her hand over his mouth. She hoists Tuvia's skinny arm across her sturdy shoulder.

"Hush with these blasphemies, Master Tuvia! A dybbuk has got your tongue."

She marches him inside and after leaving him resting on a low day bed, runs to the front door and bolts it securely.

Elazar walks painfully from the yeshiva across the road to his house. The lecture he gave the eager-faced young boys—a sermon on the story of Esther who forfeited her life for her people, his favorite metaphor of self-sacrifice—echoes in his mind. Having noticed some restlessness among his pupils, a motley group of sharp-witted boys ranging from five to twelve, he wonders whether he is losing his oratorial skills. There was a time when he could keep a class spellbound with his stories, Biblical parables ornamented with homespun proverbs and little illustrations incorporating local folklore. Thus Joseph became Josef and the bulrushes an inlet on the Rhine, with Elazar using humor to describe the character of each religious pedant in rabbinical debates about the points of the Torah. But recently the rabbi has become painfully aware of his shortness of breath and the glazed looks from his pupils which tell him he has just repeated the very same allegory without realizing.

He must teach Tuvia some of his tricks. Tuvia will make a good teacher, if a little fanatical. I will have to be firm. Tuvia must not use the classroom to promulgate his zealot notions, the old man thinks as he avoids a goat which has stubbornly planted itself in the center of the narrow road.

The rabbi arrives at his house only to find that the door is bolted from within. He knocks at the window with his stick. No answer. Irritated that he will have to make his old legs walk further to enter from the back lane he kicks impatiently at a stone.

"Rosa! Rosa!" he shouts, finally standing in the empty kitchen. On the table is a half-chopped onion and a bowl of whey covered with a muslin cloth. Elazar listens to the rest of the house, his gray head cocked like an ancient bird. It is then that he notices Tuvia's traveling sack in the corner of the room, the prayer shawl spilling out. Dread falls across the elder like a sudden chill.

Tuvia lies on the pallet, his breath a jagged rhythm. His face above his thin beard is the color of a gray mushroom. Incongruously he is clutching an ornately embroidered maroon stomacher against his chest. A jug of cold water and mint leaves sits on the floor beside him. Rosa, her heavy body melted in an exhausted sprawl, snores in a chair in the corner.

As Elazar leans over him. Tuvia begins muttering in a feverish voice, his tone so vicious that for a moment the old rabbi wonders if the young man is possessed. "He was with her, my love, my love . . . they have lain together, she and the German . . . the one from the cathedral. I shall kill him! Kill him!"

As he tosses about, the nightshirt rides up above his chest and Elazar sees the ugly rings of red sores which have begun to blossom. He has seen these marks only once before but they are unmistakable. Cautiously he lifts a lock of Tuvia's curly black hair to reveal a hideous bulbous pustule swelling below his ear.

"He has a fever," Rosa says, startling the old man. Now fully awake she stretches herself wearily. "And is talking nonsense . . . dangerous nonsense."

Elazar pulls down Tuvia's gown before Rosa has a chance to see the lesions. "It will not be the nonsense that kills him."

The rabbi's sharp tone makes Rosa sit up: she has never heard him sound so stern.

"Close the shutters and send a boy for Isaac Schlam and for my daughter immediately!"

"But Elazar, she has done nothing wrong. Tuvia is just voicing his fears—"

"It is not what he is saying that I am frightened of, but what he is dying from."

"Dying? He will be well by morning."

"Rosa, this is not a fever. Go, go!"

After she leaves Tuvia stirs. "Water . . . water . . ."

Carefully Elazar pours out a glass and holds it up to the young man's lips. He drinks feebly then collapses back on the pillow, clutching at Elazar's hand. Elazar, battling horror, lets Tuvia pull him to his skinny sweaty chest.

"I saw them, Reb, together."

"Who, my son?"

"Ruth and the cleric, the German cleric . . . they have lain together . . ."

"These are the illusions of Bileth the devil, Tuvia. You must resist. And you must rest."

As Tuvia slips back into unconsciousness the old man covers his head with his prayer shawl. Binding his Tefillah around his forehead he begins to berate God for his injustice.

The razor-sharp blade cuts into the puffy sore leaving a scarlet path behind it. The green-yellow pus welling out of it immediately fills the room with a foul stink. Working quickly Ruth drains the pustule and wipes down Tuvia's shaking torso; his protruding ribs are a pitiful birdcage of pain.

"Have you told the elders?" She dares not look at her father who sits at the end of the bed rocking in his grief.

"The declaration has been made. The door is bolted, the sign is hung." He in turn is unable to meet her eyes.

"We shall isolate the sick if it spreads." Isaac Schlam, the doctor, his face a map of anxiety, speaks in a resigned voice. "What more can we do?" he continues, handing Ruth a poultice which she places carefully on the incision.

"Pray," Elazar replies.

Suddenly Tuvia's eyes fly open, pale blue coals in a face of gray, his pupils unfocused dancing black beads. He sits bolt upright in the bed and points wildly at the door.

"The Messiah is here! Reb Zevi, I honor you!" he shouts.

Immediately the old rabbi is by his side. "Tuvia, you must stay calm. Rest, my son."

"But Zevi is there, in the burning chariot! He has heard my prayers, he has the angels with him. They are here to take me to the Holy Land!" He twists violently, calling out, "Welcome!"

"Lie still, do not waste your strength."

But Tuvia pays no heed, gazing with absolute certainty into space.

"The burning chariot is so beautiful, Reb Saul, I can feel its glory hot on my skin and the angels are huge with arms that could carry a nation. Adiriron, Zoharariel, Zavodiel and Ta'zash with his long black beard—they are here for all of us! To free us at last! Take me! Take me!"

With one supreme effort he raises himself up toward his vision, his eyes fastened on nothing but the evening's shadows, then falls back against the pillows, dead.

The contraption, made of light wood with black woolen fabric stretched across its frame and leather bindings, lies on the table like the abandoned false limb of an amputee. The strong smell of herbs—rosemary, cloves, aniseed—and the pungent scent of civet fills the whole chamber. Detlef, his morning robes thrown on, stands near the window trying to breathe what little clean air is filtering in. Heinrich enters hurriedly followed by two valets and a somber-looking man Detlef recognizes as a medic.

Heinrich marches straight over to the table. "Is this it?"

The medic lifts the device and now Detlef can see that it is some form of headpiece in the shape of a long beak, the straps of which are to be fastened around the head.

"Yes, your grace, fashioned in the London style. They swear that it renders the wearer completely impervious to both the stench and spore of the scourge."

The archbishop clicks his fingers and the two valets move forward. Together they lift the contraption and fasten it carefully around Heinrich's head. In his long green robe he looks like the mad offspring of a parrot and a demonic rook.

"Heinrich, at what strange pageant do you intend to wear this mask?"

Detlef, amused, steps forward.

Heinrich, swinging around to face his cousin, almost knocks the head off one of his long-suffering valets with the long beak. He makes a muffled comment, realizes that he cannot be heard and pushes the contraption up to his forehead where it sits like a flaccid cockscomb.

"The pageant of death, cousin. Where have you been? You obviously missed the proclamation this morning. It was rung out all over the city."

"What proclamation?"

"The plague! The first house has been barred up and painted with the red cross."

He turns to his cleric. "Make a record of the date: August twenty-ninth of the year of our good Lord 1665."

Shocked, Detlef hurries to the door. "We must make haste—the pesthouse must be opened up, the sick must be collected. We have to issue plague orders, the dogs and cats must be eradicated, everything must be done to stop the infectious vapors spreading—"

"You will go nowhere, Detlef! As a Wittelsbach it is your responsibility to protect yourself and your lineage. Retire to the country immediately, that is my advice. I myself am off to Bonn."

"You think you can escape the disease by leaving?"

"Indeed, with the help of this wondrous device which I shall wear happily in a closed carriage all the way out of the city. In the meantime I have left instructions with Wilhelm Egon von Fürstenberg and the rest of the council as to the running of the cathedral in my absence, as well as the pesthouse—which has already started to stink with the ailing."

"With all due respect, your grace, you must realize that the city needs its greatest shepherd in this its darkest hour . . ."

"And as their shepherd I have every intention of being there afterward, when the disease has left the city and we have the mending of souls and the rebuilding of families to attend to."

"But even the archbishop of London chose to stay with his parishioners—"

"Do I care? The protection of my health so that I may attend the living and the bereaved after the Black Death has left this city is more important. In other words, Detlef, I intend to survive. Now make haste!"

Maximilian Heinrich pushes the mask firmly back down and sweeps out of the room, his attendants following.

September, 1665

Dear Benedict,

The plague is now upon us. Many have fallen in Cologne: it is said that nearly a quarter of the populace has perished. Here in Deutz we have lost some but not in such large numbers. Miriam and I assist the good doctor Schlam, toiling night and day to tend to the dying. These we have isolated and I believe it is this segregation and the custom of our people to wash daily that has saved many. But a death is a death and our burden is increased by the fact that Cologne has closed its gates and the flow of grain and provisions across the Rhine, upon which our town depends, has ceased.

Tuvia ben Ibraham, my father's assistant, was one of the first to perish. His death has left my father much diminished. It is as if the last vestige of my father's hope died with him. The rabbi has not spoken since and spends many hours alone in the temple, not praying but whispering to ghosts. I fear for his sanity but have not the vigor to attend to him like a good daughter. Instead, when I am not administering to the sick, I like many, search the forest for mushroom, wild fowl, dandelion, anything we can place into our starving bellies. My own hunger is twofold, but of that I cannot speak.

If you have any comforting advice or word of wisdom in these dark times, please write. I can feast on one of your philosophies for many days.

In friendship,

"Felix van Jos'

There is nothing to seal the letter with. She cannot send it anyway for all transportation has stopped between the Rhineland and the Netherlands. She touches her neat script in wonder. How can her hand remain so steady after these last four moons? Even unsent the letter comforts her. It is an echo of life before, a ritual which gives inward definition to a frenzied world in which chaos has flown down the chimney and everything is broken. Almost broken.

Ruth picks up a small stone from the table and begins sucking it. It helps ward off the nauseating hunger which gnaws constantly at her belly. The cheap tallow candle, virtually melted, splutters, sending a puff of acrid smoke toward the blackened ceiling. The cottage is nearly unrecognizable in its disorder: bunches of herbs are strewn across the floor, their stems plucked entirely clean and boiled several times over; an eaten carcass of a rabbit hangs from the curing spit, barely a thread of flesh left on it. One muddy tree root, still half-covered with earth, squats like an animal dropping in front of the huge stone hearth, now empty. Scattered across the table where she is sitting are a few dandelions and a bouquet of straggly nettles. The only clean space is the one she has created immediately around her, a small kingdom in which the single page of parchment reigns.

Outside Ruth hears the bell of the Hevra Kadisha cart as they go to collect another corpse. She does not allow herself to wonder who it is. All such thoughts stopped with Tuvia's death; there has not been time, the containment of the disease has absorbed her waking hours and stolen all her dreams.

Until now, twenty deaths and four full moons later. This day she was called to the house of the tailor, the very same father whose son she delivered after her first night with Detlef. The sight of Herr Rechtschild's pallid face creased in agony, the telltale lumps blossoming like poisonous fruit below his neck, jolted her back to the night of the delivery when her body still sang with Detlef's touch. Before this moment, Ruth has not allowed herself to dwell on either memory or hope. Since the gates of the walled city were sealed there is no way of getting news in or out of Cologne. Ruth does not know whether Detlef is still in residence, or even if he lives.

The candle splutters and finally dies. Now only moonlight filtering through the dusty windows illuminates the room. Ruth, her body racked with exhaustion, stands in its rays. Glancing down at her ragged dress stained with soil and sweat, she cannot imagine that once a man loved her, and that the grieving sleepwalkers who now roam the lanes were once human and in their humanity were once also loved.

She pulls the dress over her head and lets it slip to the ground then steps out of her filthy petticoat. She stands naked. Her breasts are ripe, the nipples a dark wine. She cups her swelling womb and closes her eyes, feeling for the growing child beneath.

Condensation drips down the gray-green stone walls of the pesthouse.

Oblivious to the human agony below, a swallow tends to the mud nest she has wedged precariously between two wooden rafters. Beneath the industrious bird lie row after row of the infirm. Thrown on the dirty straw, the sick are contorted and delirious like the victims of some massive shipwreck, their eyes already flooding with the resignation of the drowning. Nuns in the brown habit of their order scurry between their patients, removing pails of diseased slops, many wearing cotton masks packed with herbs in a desperate attempt to ward off the extraordinary stench of disease.

Detlef kneels in the center of this bedlam, a peculiarly tranquil oasis of calm, his face gaunt, a thin yellow beard creeping up the hollow cheeks. His robe is strangely clean as if he has struggled to keep a semblance of dignity amid the carnage. In his hand he clutches a flask of holy oil with which to anoint the poor creature lying before him. The young man whose ravaged beauty still shines beneath the hideous sores is a law student Detlef once knew as a pupil, barely twenty years of age. His bloodshot green eyes burn in the waxen mask that his face has become as he stares at the canon, furious that he is dying.

Secretly dismayed at the uselessness of the sacrament, Detlef is determined to carry out his task with as much grace as possible. Hiding his revulsion he reaches for the ulcer-covered hand.

"My son, may God be with you at this dark time, may he illuminate your path with light and fill your heart with love." Detlef continues to pray, unable to meet the man's ferocious gaze for dread his emotions will betray him.

Another young man wearing the black gown of the university student enters the hall. Overwhelmed by the foul air the youth retches then covers his nose with a sachet filled with herbs, stumbling between the diseased and dying as he makes his way across the room. As he draws near Detlef can see the resemblance between him and the man languishing before him. At the sight of the canon the boy stops in his tracks, his eyes cold: this is the third brother he has seen perish, the last of his siblings.

The student kneels beside the priest as Detlef begins the anointing, indicating that he is performing the last rites. The canon reaches for the brow, smearing the scented oil beneath each puffy eye, then marks the man's nostrils, mouth and ears. He pauses for a moment, wondering whether the youth is still conscious. The flicker of an eyelid indicates some life. Detlef continues.

"May God pardon thee, whatever sins thou hast committed . . ."

But the brother speaks over him, whispering into the dying man's ear. "It is the Jews, Stefan. They have poisoned the wells. It is they who have brought this foul pestilence to our fair city. I shall avenge you, Stefan. I swear on your deathbed that by nightfall these heathens, these infidels, shall be burning in their houses . . ."

Detlef stops. The student, wondering at the priest's sudden silence, looks up.

"What's wrong? Canon, can't you see that he is dying? Finish the last rites for I shall be damned if I don't see my brother die a good Catholic."

"Is there to be a Schülergeleif?"

"What's it to you? Those people are the anti-Christ. They are murdering our people with their poison."

"This pestilence was not brought by the Jews."

"Think what you want—nothing is going to stop us from crossing the Rhine."

"But such an act is against the principles of Christianity."

"Did not the Jews kill our Lord Jesus? Just as they are killing us now! Look around you! I will not let these people die in vain!"

"You speak from pain and grief. There are Jews dying also."

The man lying between them groans as he tries to speak, but his throat and tongue, a blackened lump that sticks to the roof of his mouth, will not work. He clutches at his brother as his eyes start to roll back.

"Enough! Finish the rites, Canon, if you do indeed have a Christian heart." The student stares desperately down at his fading brother.

But Detlef is already standing, his hands shaking with rage as he starts to walk away. The young student runs after him "Finish!"

Several nuns look over. Groot, attending a patient nearby, moves toward the canon. Before the student has a chance to lay his hand on Detlef, Groot is by his side pushing the student away. "Careful, boy."

Detlef steps between them.

"The good Father Groot will administer the last of the service," he announces calmly, then to the student's amazement runs out of the hall.

Disgusted, the youth spits then turns to Groot.

"You clerics are all the same, all you understand is the glint of gold."

The small crowd of young men is already milling by the jetties. The area is eerily empty: the usual mongrels, alley cats and wandering livestock have disappeared entirely. At one end of the wooden docks lies an abandoned fisherman's net, still full of rotting fish. Neither ship nor sailor has passed through since the plague was declared. One desolate vessel flying the Norwegian flag at half-mast sits in the shallows, caught in quarantine, its crew unable to leave and banned from disembarking. The calls of its cargo of starving livestock drift forlornly across the stagnant bay, adding to the sense that here time has stopped.

Detlef, anonymous in plain clothes, pushes through the rabble. At its center the leader, a student, stands on the back of a cart goading the motley throng of scholars, apprentices and the dispossessed into action. Another youth hands out all manner of weapons: hoes, pikes, old swords, even axes.

"Here, comrade." The boy presses a hoe into Detlef's hand. "Take this to strike down the infidel."

Detlef, appalled, hands on the tool as if it were red-hot iron.

From the distance a group of chanting flagellants, stripped to the waist, their backs a seething mass of open sores and scratches, weave their way toward the crowd, whipping themselves with leather straps studded with metal. The wailing devotees—middle-aged women with gray hair wild and unkempt, burning-eyed priests, ruddy farmers driven off their land by disease—are bound by one desire: to take upon themselves the wrath of God who has decided to inflict such grief upon man.

The student leader holds up a cloth effigy of a Jew strapped to a wooden pole.

"Jude verrecke! Jude verrecke!"

Screaming abuse he holds a torch to it. The crowd cheers as the scare-crow erupts into flames.

Horrified, Detlef watches, then slips toward an abandoned rowing boat.

Elazar, wrapped in his kittel, stands in the wooden pulpit in the center of the small synagogue with the carving of the Lion of Judah watching over-head. Empty chairs line the walls and the enclosed women's gallery is de-void of its usual chattering occupants. The temple is deserted but nevertheless the rabbi has opened the gilded gates of the ark to expose the large heavy scrolls of the Torah.

Elazar bows his head to an invisible congregation then holds out his hands. Before him he can see Tuvia welcoming the community with his usual awkward grace. To the right of the young mohel stands Sara, smil-ing mysteriously at Elazar from beneath her bridal veil. And there is his nephew Aaron, at the age Elazar loved him most, just before his bar mitz-vah, his voice trembling on the edge of manhood, the soft down begin-ning to pepper the upper lip. Beside Aaron, his hand proudly on his son's shoulder, stands his father and Elazar's brother Samuel, aged twenty, as he was when Elazar and he first visited the matchmaker to arrange his marriage. Behind Samuel are Elazar's parents, his father's long white beard hanging down over his velvet robe, his mother's face crinkling with pride as she gazes up at the rabbi. It is an assembly of ghosts. But the elder does not care. These are his people, and love and memory run like beads of glistening dew across the floor and up the walls of the temple, making the old man forget that his congregation are no longer living be-ings.

"I shall read from the Torah, the passage recounting Joseph's courage when he faced the Egyptian Pharaoh with his prophecies. 'Behold, I have dreamed and God has spoken through me . . .'"

But as he recites, the old man becomes aware of a fiery light that has be-gun to burn a small hole in the second scroll which still sits within the gates of the opened ark. The radiance deepens, begins to etch out a golden word upon the silky parchment. Below him Elazar senses the rustle of clothes, a faint sigh, as the spirits turn to watch the miraculous light complete its message.

"*A'doni* . . ." Elazar reads out loud as he starts to name the unnameable: the sacred appellation of God. "*A'doni*," he repeats.

Just then a rock comes flying through the window sending shards of stained glass across the floor.

Gravel squeezes up between her toes, clouds of white mud swirl around her naked shins. Determined, Ruth wades deeper into the river, her skirts hitched to her waist. Behind her Miriam follows tentatively, carefully placing one foot in front of the other on the slippery unseen rocks.

Ruth, water to her thighs, throws one end of the homemade net back toward the hesitant girl. Miriam grabs it, almost falling over. Pulling the net taut in the rushing river they move forward in unison. Feeling the mesh tighten Ruth peers down into the white water. But before she can see whether it is a fish or a reed the other end of the trap floats loose. Furious, she looks across to Miriam, only to find the girl staring in the direction of Deutz.

A thick column of smoke billows high above the forest that lies between them and the town. Without a word the two women drop their work and wade as fast as they can back toward the bank. Behind them the net, now a swirling eddy of mesh, twists itself around a pike that, curious, has ventured to the surface.

The sound of the rabble reaches Deutz before the mob itself. Like a foul wind from the east, the banging of drums, boots against cobbles, stick against stick, rumbles up from the docks and sends a collective shudder through all who hear it.

In the yeshiva the startled boys look up from their study, their teacher pauses midsentence. In the bakery, Schmul, alone since his beloved young wife Vida perished of the plague, thinks an army is approaching and in his terror allows the challah to burn. In the small cottages and crowded lodging rooms mothers and daughters drop their spinning and run for their sons and brothers.

"*Hep! Hep!*" they scream, the ancient cry that spans centuries.

By the time the shouting youths pour into the town square, most of the community has fled, except for one infant who crawls lost beside the town pond. Screaming with fear, he stares around wild-eyed until a yeshiva boy darts across the square in front of the marching boots and rescues the bewildered child. With the babe in his arms he rushes toward an open door behind which the terrified mother cowers. The door bangs shut just as the leader of the horde is hoisted high onto the shoulders of a massive blond youth.

"Burn them!" he screams. "Bolt them into their houses and burn them!"

Immediately a dozen students start tearing apart a discarded cart, throwing the planks of wood to their comrades who are armed with hammers and nails.

"Stop! Stop!" A huge voice booms across the square. The leader swings around.

Standing in front of the yeshiva is a group of elders. Hirz Uberrhein, the leader of the community, an imposing man in his fifties, steps forward. "I am the bürgermeister of Deutz. State your grievances."

For a moment the dignity of the man and the stern patriarchal faces of the old men behind him intimidate the rabble. Then someone yells out, "You have poisoned our wells, you have brought the Black Death to our city!"

"We have our own dead too!" Hirz shouts back, then has to duck to avoid the first stone. It is followed by another and then another. One old man falls to the ground bleeding; the others, driven by the rain of missiles, retreat. Panicked, they pour back into the school building. Hirz picks up the fallen man in his arms before running back toward the shelter.

Suddenly a small group of Jewish youths appears from behind carts, from around stone walls, clutching branches torn from trees and fence pickets wrenched from the ground. They walk toward the crowd. "Leave us alone," the oldest, fourteen at the most, shouts.

"Where are your weapons!" one of the rabble yells back, a taunting reference to the ban against Jewish men carrying arms.

"Yes, Jew, show us your sword!" another cries out.

The boy, still beardless with prayer locks tumbling down his cheeks, steps forward and swings a lump of wood blindly. The crowd laughs. Within seconds the boy is knocked to the ground, his arms wrapped over his head as fists and feet rain down. A brawl breaks out as his companions move forward to protect him.

It ends as quickly as it began. While the first youth lies senseless, the others are dragged semiconscious into the yeshiva. As soon as the door is closed one of the mob begins to nail a plank across the frame; others join him in a frenzy. Soon the square rings with hammering as board after board is fastened over entrances while the terrified faces of the occupants stare out from the windows.

Holding a flaming torch high, the leader steps forward and throws it.

Detlef is running down the lane. His hood has fallen off and his face is streaked with dirt and sweat. His legs are pumping beneath him despite the exhaustion which tears at every muscle. In the distance he can hear the screams and shouts of the Schülergeleif.

"Please let her be home, please," he prays to the God he fears has abandoned him, trying desperately to keep hold of his sanity and his faith, his sight blurring as the sweat pours into his stinging eyes. Over the bridge toward the cottage. But there is no smoke coming from the chimney. Detlef's heart starts pounding with dread. He has not allowed himself to fully contemplate the possibility of her death. But now as he runs toward the dwelling, the thought of finding her body contorted by the Black Death, flung across the hearth or sprawled on the stone floor in the graceless posture of disease like so many others he has found, makes him ill to his stomach.

Down the garden path, stumbling over an abandoned milking pail and farming tools scattered across the moss, brambles scratching at his legs. To her door. Which is open. Wide open.

Please, good Lord Jesus, spare her life. Take mine if you have to, but not hers, please, my good Lord Jesus.

He flings himself into the cottage, almost slipping on the muddy floor. "Ruth! Ruth!"

His voice bounces off the bare walls. Pushing open the bedroom door he sees nothing but an empty pallet in the corner and a bowl of water. Relief and disappointment conflict, twisting in his gut.

Through the window he can see the undulating columns of smoke beyond the forest. Outside again, Detlef gasps for breath in the pungent air. He leans for a second against a stone bench before sprinting off in the direction of the burning ghetto.

The woman stands on the balcony. Her shawl, hanging from her twin-horned hat, billows out in the wind. She clutches a baby in swaddling and stares down at the jeering crowd, her face as white as the plumes of smoke behind her. A tongue of fire shoots out, catching at the edge of the veil. Without a word the woman jumps, flames licking the crown of her hat like a halo. When she hits the cobblestones her head smashes like a ripe plum, her limbs thrown askew like a broken doll. The baby rolls out from her body and is kicked between the legs of the roaring youths.

Ruth stands on the other side of the square behind the mass of strangers—young men, students and craftsmen all in the dress of the Christian. She is screaming, a howl that is inaudible in the cacophony of falling timber, roaring fire and the delighted shouting of the horde. A cry which empties her mind, her body, her memory, of everything except the pain and the horror. A second later she is knocked flat.

"Don't move," Miriam whispers, her body pinning her to the ground. "They will see us."

Wide-eyed with excitement the midwife's assistant draws her cloak over both of them, as if by hiding their own eyes they will be concealed from the mob. Ruth lies there for a second, stunned.

"You spoke! Miriam, you spoke!"

"This way," the girl continues, in the voice of a small child. "This way they will never catch us, but if they do they will kill us," she giggles.

She has lost her sanity, Ruth thinks. My life now lies in the hands of a madwoman. Panicking, the midwife scrabbles to lift the cloak.

Suddenly the two women are hauled to their feet. For a moment Ruth lashes out blindly, until she hears Detlef's voice.

"Stop! Ruth, it is me, Detlef!"

The cloak is pulled off to reveal the canon. He pushes both women behind a dairy cart which is lying on its side in a pooling lake of milk.

"We must go before it is too late," Detlef says urgently into Ruth's ear.

"But my father . . ."

Ruth cranes around just in time to see fire leap across the rafters of the rabbi's house toward the synagogue. For an instant Rosa's face appears at the top window, her mouth a silent howl as her fists pound uselessly against the clouding glass before the house explodes into flames.

"Rosa!" Ruth shrieks, fighting Detlef as he claps his hand over her mouth.

Behind them Miriam makes a dash back toward the outskirts of the town.

"Let her go! It is too dangerous to run yet." Clutching the flailing woman to his chest Detlef tries to calm her, holding her tightly. "We must stay silent and still."

Ruth, shaking with anger and fear, stares up into his hollow eyes as the strength of his arms draws her back into the possibility of survival.

"Ruth."

Elazar's voice startles both of them. The old man, his hair a wild storm, his kittel stained green with grass and torn with brambles, stands behind them. Immediately Detlef pulls him down behind the cart.

"Abba! I thought you were in the synagogue," Ruth sobs with relief.

"I was but then it started raining hailstones as big as rocks and the word of fire drew us out to the stream. Your mother is still there, washing her feet, her beautiful feet," Elazar announces solemnly, his eyes glazed over.

"What is that smell? I know that smell." He turns toward the burning houses. "I must go back to the temple, the lanterns are all lit for Yom Kippur, the day of atonement. The congregation will be expecting me."

"But Rabbi, there is a Schülergeleif. Your people are being slaughtered, you cannot go!" Detlef reaches out to stop him.

"Daughter, who is this man? He is not one of us. I do not know him." The old man hits out with his walking stick.

Ruth grabs it. "Abba! They will kill you!"

Standing against a horizon bloody with flame, Elazar smiles calmly. "Nonsense, child. I must be with my people. The burning word is calling me."

Before Detlef can once again attempt to drag him back to safety, a boy at the edge of the rabble turns at the old man's voice.

"Look! It's one of them! One of their devil worshippers!"

Several youths swing around, stunned for a second at the sight of the old rabbi standing erect, slowly lifting his kittel above his head and advancing upon the horde.

"Behold the wrath of Moses, for he shall come among you and strike down all whose hands are awash with the blood of the children of Israel . . ."

"Sure, old man! We'll part for you like the Red Sea itself!" they jeer, moving aside to let the rabbi walk between them toward the burning synagogue.

"Your sons and their sons shall wear the wrath of the Israelites upon their foreheads. It shall be a flaming brand for all to see," Elazar continues as he walks fearlessly down the opened pathway strewn with broken glass, smoking embers, pieces of smoldering cloth.

He reaches the old oak door and pushes against it with one hand. It falls flat, creating a wooden bridge into the temple. The crowd falls silent as the rabbi steps onto the burning door.

Swinging around, he faces them. "Hear O Israel, the Lord our God, the Lord is one! For my children are the children of God, they shall rise from the ashes and sing with the wind. And there shall be a Paradise and in it we shall all be free!"

Several of the young men turn from his fiery gaze. One crosses himself. Another drops to his knees. Elazar spreads his hands wide in the silence, his body a crucifix against the flaming building. He begins to sing Kaddish then turns and walks into the blazing temple.

❋

They shelter in a ditch, the dried-up bed of what was once a creek. Above them an awning of tree branches engraves the black sky. A light wind brings the faint barking of dogs but there are no church bells, no town crier, no night birds, not even the owls. Ruth is lying beside him, her body rigid, her face dirty with soot, staring up at the stars. She has been like this for hours.

"Ruth," Detlef whispers. "Ruth . . ."

Her eyes, in a face crisscrossed by moonlight and shadow, flicker.

"Come back to me."

He glances in the direction she is gazing and wonders whether the woman he knows still lives in this shattered heap of fear and bone. Here, pressed against the twigs and sandy soil, he can feel them dwindling into nothing. Without status, without civilization, just two tiny figures stretched against the surface of a tumbling world. Free-falling through the great velvet chasm.

Her mute face squeezes his heart until, after a century of silence, he wonders whether they will ever speak again. Shivering, he pulls her stiff body closer. Just as he is about to drift into sleep, he feels her reach up, touching his cheeks, his nose, his lips. Like a blind woman. Like a woman who, after a long absence, is spellbound by her lover's features and searches for the memory of him with her fingertips. And it is then that this silent woman, this broken hollowed spirit-creature he barely recognizes, covers his body with hers, runs her tongue over his eyelids as if trying to wash away the image of this terrible day. Daring not to breathe nor to move, Detlef lies like a child. Waiting.

She draws his hands up to her breasts, warm under the rough cloth. Surprised by their heaviness he pushes her robe from her shoulders then touches her again in wonder; the nipples are far darker and larger than he remembers. She guides him down to her belly. His large hands draw the arc down to the hollow of her thighs then back up again. Amazed, he sits up and lays her gently down on her back, his eyes straining in the dark as he peers more closely at her body.

"You are with child?"

She nods.

Astonished, he lays his cheek against the soft downy skin, cool to his burning ear. In all of this destruction, his seed, a new life. It is a miracle to him, a thread of dream against desolation. He presses his lips against the curved flesh, tracing with his hand the fine feathers of black hair growing down from her navel. Her vulva is swollen, the lips swelling beneath his touch, the bead of pleasure growing hard, pushing against his thumb. He parts her legs and lowers his mouth between them, then gazes up in wonder at the arched horizon of her womb above him. Running his fingers slowly across, he plays her until he hears her groan, then takes her into his mouth, caressing her over and over until her hips writhe under his hands. Only then does he lift himself up above her and enter her with the rushing ecstasy again and again until their shouts swallow the stars and the pain and the burning smoke and for a brief moment they forget their mortality and all that has gone before.

נצח

NETZACH

Victory

♀

DAS WOLKENHAUS, LATE WINTER, 1666

uth sits at the virginal feeling the music pulsate through her fingers. Her feet pump in rhythm as the thin sound tries to fill the echoing chamber. Her embroidered shawl is draped over her shoulders and hangs below her womb which is full and round under the black muslin skirt. The piece she is playing is a romantic work from the Parthenia collection. As she searches for the notes she recalls her mother playing this particular passage over and over again, the forlorn prelude bringing back the earlier time so vividly that the image of Sara sitting in the front room in Deutz appears before her, the figure upright and visibly pregnant. It is as if the sensation of the child within the midwife has its own memory that stretches back through time, through the tissues of the body itself, from daughter to mother to mother.

Ruth, fascinated by this notion, turns it over in her mind as she plays on. E, G, C sharp, F. It distracts her, and diversion is the opium she craves during this endless autumn and winter when she has been confined to Detlef's country retreat. He has been gone for one long week, returned to Cologne to attend to his clerical duties. It is these separations that Ruth has begun to find increasingly difficult.

She changes the tune to a vigorous ditty. She cannot bear silence any more than she can tolerate reflection. Reflection means thinking and that means descending into a terrain that is utterly barren: a landscape which was once fecund with hope is now a graveyard, devoid of intellect, belief, humanity.

At night Ruth rocks herself for hours to hold back the deluge of grief that is ever present, and there is nothing Detlef can do or say. Sometimes she feels like an insect trapped in amber, paralyzed, all emotion suspended, looking up through the thick golden crystal while the heartbeat of her un-born baby drums on relentlessly.

She lays her hands over her womb. This child, she thinks, our child, conceived in love, a miracle, all the more so for its ordinariness. You shall be all to me, she tells the child within, the crystalization of her father, a living manifestation of her affection for Detlef. The only future they have.

Then, fearing a draft, she pulls her shawl tighter around herself.

"Jugged hare and stewed cabbage!"

Hannah marches across the parlor and plonks a platter piled high with food onto the small table.

"You haven't eaten since yesterday. It's not right, you should be eating for two."

Ruth, smiling, gets up and puts her arm around the vast waist of the housekeeper. "Hannah, you feed me enough for twins."

"God willing." The housekeeper touches her pocket. "Finish that plate and I'll give you another surprise."

"Is the master due back?"

"That I don't know, but I have other news. From Holland . . ."

Ruth, unable to wait, thrusts her hand into Hannah's pocket and pulls out a letter. As she unrolls the parchment, the housekeeper peers over her shoulder.

"Is it news about the war with the English? I have a cousin on the Dutch fighting ships there."

"No, although he mentions the war."

"He? This isn't a rival for your heart, is it, Fraülein Saul, because if it is and the master finds out I won't be long in this house."

"No, this man is a rival for no one's heart. He is a great prophet and, as you know, prophets live above the weakness of the flesh."

"Does such a man exist? I think not!" Hannah snorts and marches out again in her noisy clogs.

Smiling, Ruth wonders what Spinoza would make of the stoic house-keeper's pragmatic truths. Then she stretches, her back aching from the weight of her womb. Glancing out at the band of sunlight which has just begun to cut through the bluish morning she decides that, better than jugged hare, some fresh air will improve her mood.

———

Sitting on a stone bench with moss creeping over its marble feet, she barely notices the tang of spring just tinting the breeze, the pale green tips of the daffodils and lilies of the valley which have begun to break through the stubborn winter soil.

Rijnsburg, January 1666

Dear "Felix,"

Forgive my long silence. Here too there has been plague and it, and the long English war, have kept me from correspondence.

I am much grieved to hear about your plight. I too know the despair into which you must now be plunged. I have lost many dear friends this season—including Pieter Balling, which is a profound loss indeed—and despite many deaths to the scourge on both sides of the North Sea, the English continue to raid and wage war on our navy. These are unpredictable times and with that uncertainty comes the most insidious passion of all: fear. The Dutch are turning to the certainties of the past; Jan de Witt and his Republican cause lose support daily. It becomes increasingly dangerous for the enlightened philosophers who support my work. Even at the university of Leiden I have heard of several who have been severely reprimanded for quoting my texts. There is a necessity to protect ourselves, my dear earnest little Felix, for it is precisely in these dark days that there is a need for those who can see beyond the starving belly, beyond the plague cross painted on the door, beyond the priest offering penance and a holy wafer.

Stay cautious and be like the wind: invisible but far reaching.

Yours, Benedict Spinoza

His voice seems to speak out from another universe, one so remote that Ruth can see it only as a mirage in which she once lived, gloriously naive, wonderfully hopeful. It is not a being she can relate to now. Smiling sadly she folds up the letter and tucks it deep into her bodice.

Lord, give me strength to battle my doubts and believe in my love, she prays, yearning for Detlef's reassuring presence to dismiss the ghost of her father's burning figure, Rosa's screaming face and the terrible guilt of the survivor.

※

They say they will declare the scourge officially over as soon as next week. A good third of the city has perished but this last week there were only ten new deaths reported. Sadly Birgit Ter Lahn von Lennep's sister was among them. We are blessed, Ruth, to escape all this and more."

Detlef stands naked in a large horse's trough beside an old barn. He pours the icy water over his chest, gasping with the cold, his skin reddening, then scrubs himself down with a wet rag and a cake of salt. Ruth, her arms holding clean clothes for him, a woolen shawl crossed across the breast of her long muslin dress, shivers in sympathy. His horse, still restless from the long ride from Cologne, stands fastened to a post, munching on a bucket of oats.

"The archbishop waits until we have buried our last before he returns. I suspect he has lost his stomach for funerals, but his absence has been to my advantage."

After rinsing himself with the bucket, Detlef steps out.

"I hear you are championing a young man from the ribbon guild, Nikolaus Gülich," Ruth says, handing him a drying cloth of rough hessian. Detlef rubs the towel against his skin until it burns.

"Who told you that?"

"Hannah."

"He is challenging the city council and seeks my support and that of Maximilian Heinrich. It is an old argument but a persuasive one in this dangerous era. Let those who work honestly be rewarded for their labor. The time is over when a family name should be enough to buy one a seat on the council."

"What about your enemies, Detlef? You know you are closely watched."

"Truly, I expect both Heinrich and von Fürstenberg will try to obstruct me."

Ruth holds out a clean pair of breeches made of serge. Detlef pulls them on over a loose cotton undergarment then slips his feet into a pair of clogs.

"But it would be a wondrous thing for a man to be judged on merit alone, would it not? A small step toward a true democracy. Ruth, think of that!"

He caresses her hair. It is two weeks since they last saw each other and even in that short time Detlef observes how her womb has swollen, how the planes of her face have softened despite the grief still trapped in her eyes. If there was only a way of exorcising this specter of horror that still haunts her, of hastening her healing, he thinks to himself. He saw men like this after the war, crippled by appalling memories, and then too he felt the same helplessness. There have been moments since the pogrom when he has despaired of seeing Ruth smile or laugh again. He has tried to talk to her of her family, but found that with remembrance comes agony and so has decided to let time work its own medicine. Still, he is painfully conscious of a mistrust that has risen up in her, an emotion she seems unable to control. Powerless to intervene, he secretly prays that the arrival of their child will return Ruth to him completely. Concealing his anxiety, he kisses her forehead.

"We shall be the architects of change, you and I."

"That sounds dangerous."

Gazing at him she finds that she cannot bring herself to reach toward him, much as she craves to. Noticing, he covers her hesitancy with humor.

"Too late, my love, you have corrupted me with your philosophies and I cannot be what I was before."

He kisses her lightly on the lips and leads her back into the kitchen. He sits her down and ladles out two bowls of the vegetable broth that has been left simmering in a large cauldron over the fire. Ruth watches him eat, waiting for her nausea at the oily smell of the soup to settle before joining him.

Even after three months of living with him she finds herself looking at him with wonder. She is still astounded that they are living as man and wife, albeit in complete secrecy. Yet so much of him remains an engima; on each return he becomes a stranger again and she is compelled to discover him anew.

Ruth consoles herself that this may be the very nature of love, a passion as fickle as the sea, full of certainty when the object of desire is absent, yet dubious when confronted again with the lover's presence. An ambivalence she is able to exorcise when they make love or when Detlef's intellect shakes her mind awake again with a brilliant observation which only the two of them can share. And yet she knows Detlef's devotion to her to be unquestioning and constant. It is the steady foundation against which Ruth sets her own doubts: if he knows it must be so, how can it not be? Perhaps it is just not in her nature to surrender completely, she muses.

"Ruth, you are very quiet."

"What news of the inquisitor?"

Detlef reaches for some bread and pulls off a hunk, allowing the coal-black pumpernickel to sink into the broth before eating it hungrily.

"Detlef, I am full of whispering spirits that speak of peril, I know them to be the chatterings of my fear but I am filled with foreboding."

"You should not think of such things. It is bad for the child."

"How can I not when there is no one here to speak with except Hannah and the barn animals? My mind is growing soft. I fear I lose both my wit and my craft."

"There is rumor that Solitario will return from Vienna when the road is open again. Wilhelm Egon von Fürstenberg has decided the inquisitor is needed for the resurrection of the Catholic spirit which has been much damaged by the scourge. At the same time he is watching me and calculating that my challenge to the nepotism that governs Cologne shall cause disfavor among the nobility. He has even spread word that I have lost my sanity as a result of my attendance on the dying in the pesthouse."

"Detlef, we should leave . . ."

"Not yet. Not until the child is born and it is again safe to travel."

Inwardly angry that he does not seem to feel the same panic she now finds herself wrestling with, Ruth gets up and walks over to the cracked marble bench upon which sits a wedge of Edam, a hock of smoked ham and a jar of pickled beetroot. She slices into the ham with the long hunting knife that hangs from a hook above: three thick slices of the meat and a wedge of cheese for her lover.

Does he not realize we are living on borrowed time, she thinks to herself, frustrated by his lack of urgency. What does he intend for the future? She cannot remain hidden at Das Wolkenhaus forever, less so with a child.

Obeying the kosher rules of her upbringing, she chooses a clean knife to cut her own cheese—the ham she will not touch—then carries the two platters back to the table, determined not to allow her irritation to show. Detlef, seemingly oblivious to her anxiety, pours himself a glass of wine.

"Did you see the good Meisterin Ter Lahn von Lennep on the eve of her bereavement?" she asks, then immediately regrets her provocation.

Detlef, ham in hand, pauses; there is much he has not shared with her and yet there is little his mistress cannot guess. He wonders how much Hannah has confided to Ruth.

"I have not seen her for many months," he answers carefully. "I was her confessor."

"Then surely there is even more reason to visit her now?"

Detlef again speculates on Ruth's intentions. Convinced by her tone that she knows he and Birgit were lovers, he wonders if this is another trial of his affection.

"You are suggesting I should take her confession?" he asks incredulously.

"I am suggesting that we should do everything in our power not to attract suspicion."

"Naturally, but I cannot execute what you suggest, out of respect both to Meisterin Ter Lahn von Lennep and to myself. I am no longer a man governed by his bodily desires alone."

Ruth turns away to hide her dismay at the confirmation of what she had only suspected, questioning the perversity which has forced this revelation. He is a man, naturally he has loved before, she thinks. Again she finds herself trying to apply Spinoza's philosophy, to achieve liberation through reining in her passions.

The philosopher's animated face appears before her. *"If you can free yourself from the dictatorship of the passions then all that occurs will be a result not of your relations with the external but of your own true nature within, which is God himself."*

His words come back to her, a consoling remembrance that anchors her to some semblance of reality. Rebuking herself for depending on Detlef's affection for her contentment, she decides she must rely only on the happiness she can muster from within: the strength of man's inherent state, solitary, at one with nature. But still she loves him. Only God knows how much she loves him.

Detlef watches her, her eyes downcast, staring at a line of ants that are transporting a crumb of cheese down the carved leg of the table. It is this very complexity which causes him both to adore her and suffer for her, but there is a mystery about her that is equally tantalizing and infuriating. He fears she is a *terra incognita* that he will be driven to possess over and over.

"You are unhappy?"

"I am not unhappy, I am asleep and it is taking a long time for my furies and joys to shake themselves awake," she answers softly, hoping he will be assuaged by the plea in her eyes.

Detlef drinks down the last of the wine then reaches for the leather traveling sack slung across the arm of a chair. He takes out a small red silk pouch.

"I purchased a curio for your pleasure. From Adolf Bescher of the watchmakers' guild."

He opens her curled hand and places the soft pouch into it. "I hope it will amuse you."

She pulls open the purse: a ground lens falls out, its curved surface glinting on the wooden table. Crying out with delight she holds it over the trail of ants.

"Now we shall be the giants who decide the fate of others and marvel at the most intricate of God's work."

She places a fork across the insects' path and watches through the lens as one ant, an Atlas dwarfed by its globe of Edam, struggles bravely to climb the massive pewter arm of the utensil.

"Let us be benign giants, in case our actions be judged by less generous giants above us, my Ruth, for tolerance must be the only way."

"Something I have seen little of these past few months."

"Indeed, but faith is an inspiration toward the betterment of the self. We must not allow ourselves to be contaminated by hate."

She suddenly grips his hand. "Promise me you will never travel without bearing arms. Swear that if you are attacked you will fight back to defend yourself."

"You forget that I was a trained soldier before I was a cleric."

But Ruth, instead of being comforted by these words, winds her arms around her womb and rocks gently.

�֎

The heavy scents of rose and benjamin fill the chamber. Crinkling petals cover the small walnut side table where they have fallen from a brass vase in which Ruth has arranged a bouquet of the yellow and burgundy blooms. The window, its diamond panes creating a prism of moonlight, has been pushed open. A heavy tome, its yellowed pages fluttering slightly in the breeze, sits open at a reading stand beside a silver candleholder embossed with the von Tennen shield.

Across the stone floor is a bed whose carved wooden frame is over a hundred years old. Ruth and Detlef lie stretched out half under the embroidered coverlet. Eyes open, his long lean form is curled around her, his arms under and around her belly, a glistening pale sphere. The tautness of her flesh amazes him, her breasts are like veined fruit about to burst. He buries his face in her hair and breathes in her scent. He has never felt more at peace, never closer to God. Suddenly he feels the child beneath kick.

Ruth is woken by the movement. "He will have strong legs like his father," she murmurs, pulling the coverlet across her chilled skin.

"She will be willful like her mother," Detlef answers, smiling in the dark as he feels another ripple in the flesh.

"It is a male child."

"But how do you know?"

"I have seen him in my dreaming and also he is sitting high in the womb."

She pushes herself further into the feather pallet and begins to fall back to sleep. Detlef lies for a time imagining the son he has sired. Will he be healthy? Sharp of mind and vigorous of body? How will they protect him, this hybrid creature, both Jew and Christian?

In the far distance a wolf howls. Detlef, restless, gets up to make water. As he urinates into the chamberpot he notices a letter peeping out from his mistress's abandoned bodice. The Dutch seal is unmistakable.

"Ruth." He gently shakes her awake, holding the letter before her. "Who is this letter from? You know how dangerous it is to receive mail here."

"It is from Benedict Spinoza. I wrote to him for words of comfort and he has replied."

"This was unwise."

"Please, Detlef, I must rest."

"Don't you understand the peril we live in here? It would take just one peasant, someone my brother has wronged, to betray us."

Drowsily she sits up.

"Who was your messenger?"

"Hannah has a brother who is to be trusted."

"I know the man, but no one is to be trusted. There is famine throughout this land, one Reichstaler would buy our lives."

"He does not know what he carries. He thinks it to be news from Hannah to her Dutch cousin."

"It must stop, do you understand? We have to be careful for only a little longer, until the child is born."

"And then what?"

"I have a plan."

"What plan?"

Detlef falls silent. In truth he has not allowed himself to think further than this secret parallel existence, her waiting for him in this simple sanctuary, a paradise away from his other life.

"I suppose I am to continue as your mistress, a plaything you keep stored in your closet to take out at your leisure," she says, unable to hide the bitterness in her voice.

"Ruth, pray let us not argue. Please, trust me."

In the thickening silence an owl hoots in the distance.

"Forgive me the indiscretion, but I needed some consolation, some wisdom to carry me through this dark passage." She reaches over to caress his hand.

Detlef stares down at the page: the distinctive calligraphy speaks to him of a realm that transcends the limitations of orthodoxy, a place where man can dream of democracy, a belief that places God everywhere—in the calling bird outside, in the impenetrability of his loved one—a belief in which the body is the outward form of the soul.

He looks at Ruth: that she is deemed worthy to share discourse with this man who so intrigues him, inspires him immensely. She is the key to a world in which he might rise above all the restrictions his birth and career have placed upon him. Forgiving her, he begins to read the scroll.

*I*s there no end to the decrees, legislations and proclamations I must sign? What have you and the evasive Herr von Fürstenberg been doing these past months? Supervising the miracles of the Magi?"

Maximilian Heinrich, resplendent in a new robe tailored especially for his glorious return, sits at a large wooden desk. Grouped around him are several clerics, the von Fürstenberg brothers, Detlef and Groot. The archbishop, craving the usual hilarity from his entourage, looks expectantly at his audience—far fewer in number due to the pestilence—but the hollow-faced young clerics are silent, some looking at the ground. Ravaged by misery and disease, the archbishop notes not entirely without sympathy.

"If ever there was a time Cologne needed miracles, this was it. I am afraid much of our time was taken up with funerals, your grace. Then of course there was the enormous task of administering the last rites, to a mere ten thousand at last count," Detlef responds, looking up from the open ledger in front of him. Disgusted by his cousin's tardiness in returning to the city after it has been officially declared plague-free, he finds it hard to remain courteous.

Heinrich, pausing to calculate his response, watches the reaction of the clerics, several of whom peek admiringly at the fervent canon. Detlef really is becoming a liability, the archbishop thinks, I shall have to patronize Wilhelm after all.

"Indeed, it has been a grave time. A period of great spiritual reckoning and introspection. Which is precisely why we need a festivity to celebrate all those who have survived." He turns to the corpulent minister, a smooth smile hiding his disgust. "Do you not think so, Wilhelm?"

Von Fürstenberg, who has spent most of the disease-ridden summer at the residence of the Countess of Marck, thirty miles out of the city, nods gravely.

"Precisely. The people need to be reminded how wondrous it is to have an archbishop here in one of the most important cities of the Holy Empire. I suggest a procession, a mass blessing and then a sermon on the theme of the Resurrection—a most suitable allegory."

"An excellent proposal. I shall read the sermon. The nuns of Saint Ursula shall lead the way bearing palms, followed by the choir boys of Saint Severin accompanied by flutes, and then the cathedral guards shall bring up the rear on horseback. It shall take place on Saint Stephen's day—it is fitting that the city's patron saint should represent fair Cologne's survival of the plague. All the ruling families shall attend. We should invite Prince Ferdinand. Is he still in Vienna?"

"I believe so."

"Then make sure he comes as a representative of the Holy Emperor himself. I shall make the decree at the Sunday sermon."

The minister shuffles his papers ostentatiously. "Monsignor Solitario would be delighted to receive an official invitation also. It would serve Cologne well to extend diplomatic courtesy to the Inquisition, particularly after the confusion of the last trial conducted here," von Fürstenberg adds, glancing at Detlef to gauge his response. "I believe the witch perished in the Schülergeleif—is that correct, Canon von Tennen?" the minister continues fearlessly.

Detlef stares back at von Fürstenberg, not a single emotion betraying his smooth features.

"The midwife's whole family including the chief rabbi were burned to death in their own house." Detlef's soft voice is tense with hatred.

Heinrich, fearing an argument, interjects. "Yes, well, the death of the chief rabbi is naturally regrettable. We all know the presence of Jews is irritating but it doesn't pay to exterminate a loyal hound when all the hound wants to do is serve. Do you not agree, Detlef?"

Heinrich winks at his cousin, a genuine attempt at reconciliation. Detlef, his gut churning with revulsion, forces himself to smile back. Satisfied, the archbishop continues.

"It would be of great benefit to appease the Grand Inquisitional Council by inviting their loyal servant back to our fair city. Send a messenger at once. And now I believe it is time for sext and for eating." Heinrich stands, rubbing his hands at the prospect.

The plague caused a shortage of imported goods—spices, cheeses and cured meats—as all the trading routes had to be closed down. Now they have been reopened, the city is inundated with gourmet delicacies and many, including the archbishop, have happily plunged themselves into an orgy of culinary abandon.

Eating helps numb the grief, the archbishop thinks to himself, swept up in gastronomical self-righteousness. It is both a holy celebration and a defiant gesture of abundance and survival, he concludes, salivating at the notion.

"There is something else we need to discuss." Detlef remains seated, an open insult to the archbishop's authority. Heinrich, reluctant to enter into further conflict, rubs his rumbling belly and sits down again, followed by his entourage.

"Klüngel: nepotism," Detlef announces solemnly.

Heinrich stares at him, then realizing the canon is entirely serious bursts into laughter.

"Cousin, in Cologne favoritism is a tradition. And we all know that Cologners are great traditionalists."

"Maybe so, but there are new traditions and new power afoot. To ignore them would be dangerous. The constitution allows only entitled citizens to vote—that is, only one tenth of the population—and they may vote only for others within their privileged group. The Gaffeln, despite its twenty-two subdivisions, has power to choose only four councillors. The system is a breeding ground for favoritism. There are too many without a voice: day laborers, bondsmen, journeymen, clergymen, women and Jews—all live without any influence, yet all contribute to the economy of this city."

"This is not the cathedral's concern and neither is it yours, unless canons have suddenly become politicians. Remember, we are here only because the bürgers have consented to our presence. Do I have to remind you of the events of 1396 when the merchants and bürgers threw all the aristocrats out of Cologne, including your own family, Detlef?"

"But it will be our concern if the bürgers revolt again. It is no longer enough for one's family name to guarantee a position on the city council. There are good working men who are demanding recognition of their true worth."

"Your cousin is an idealist, perhaps even a secret Republican." Wilhelm Egon von Fürstenberg, delighting in Detlef's ill-placed bravado, slams a ledger shut as if to emphasize his point.

"What say you to Wilhelm's accusation?" Heinrich asks archly.

"I say this. These are changing times: a man will not survive if he ignores the rising tide, and neither will Cologne. Tradition has never favored trade."

Frowning, the archbishop twists his ring around his finger, an indication that he is displeased. He knows Detlef is right: there is a growing unrest among the bürgers, which accelerated after the abandonment of the city by many of its privileged during the Black Death. But the discontent existed before the plague, influenced by the growing number of talented craftsmen rising up from the peasant class, all wanting representation on the city council.

"But cousin, what role is the clergy to play in all of this? I am a shepherd of the spiritual not the purse," Heinrich says coyly, still playing to the gallery. Detlef refuses to be swayed.

"A young man came to visit me. He is of a poor family but managed to win himself an apprenticeship and then a business. But because of his lack of good name he is denied the privilege of certain levies, even access to some wharves. He is angry and has gathered much support among his guild, the ribbon merchants."

"Nikolaus Gülich?" von Fürstenberg interjects with a sneer.

"You know the gentleman?"

"Gentleman? He is no gentleman, merely a troublesome upstart who means to manipulate the discontent of the common man for his own profit."

"I beg to differ. Meister Gülich intends to challenge the corruptness of the nepotistic system and I suspect he will succeed."

Heinrich is acutely conscious of the avid attention the younger clergy are paying to the canon. The archbishop knows he must tolerate Detlef's radicalism, worse he must be seen to support him, for Nikolaus Gülich is not the only man to engender enthusiasm among the lower ranks.

"As neutral observers we may act as a diplomatic bridge between the guilds and the city council. Your grace, it is our duty to find a way of appeasement, by appointing a few who have won their influence through their trade not their blood," Detlef continues.

"Cousin, those who have power will not give it up without force."

"Discontent is rising like the North Sea, one day it will burst its dam. Let me go to the mayors, I can be the unofficial spokesperson for Gülich—"

"You shall be no such thing! As a member of the cathedral council you have no right to intervene in civil matters! Enough. We are to sext."

Heinrich stands and sweeps out of the room, followed by the others. Detlef stays sitting, staring down at the ledger as if trying to find within it a meditation to calm his frustration.

As the archbishop strides angrily down the stone corridor past archway after archway, he turns to the panting minister who struggles to keep abreast.

"My dear von Fürstenberg, I think perhaps it is time I abandoned the indulgence of familial love. I shall leave to you the means of disposal."

The small but ornate banquet hall has remnants still of its medieval heyday: the walls are hung with rich tapestries depicting the triumphs of the trading guilds and a variety of more recent military victories from the Great War, and several Oriental statues—Crusades bounty—adorn the corners of the chamber. A small ensemble of musicians, a flautist, lute player and harpsichordist, perform on an upper balcony while below some twenty guests sit around a long ebony table covered with half-eaten dishes. A suckling pig dominates one end of the table while a stuffed swan accompanied by a flotilla of roasted ducks presides at the other.

The banner of the garment makers—a shield divided into four showing a three-tiered tower alternating with an oak tree—dangles from the balustrade. Peter Ter Lahn von Lennep stands at the head of the long table, a wineglass in hand.

"It is my honor as president of the guild to usher in our one hundred and fiftieth anniversary! May the guild reign profitably for many more centuries!"

The merchant takes his chair as the audience, his peers and their wives, bang the table with their goblets in approval. Detlef, his clerical robe a stark contrast to the brightly colored gowns of the women and the rich velvets, embroidered waistcoats and wide ruffled collars of the men, sits on one side of the merchant. Opposite is Birgit, in black taffeta for her dead sister.

Radiating a certain smugness, Peter Ter Lahn von Lennep turns to Detlef.

"Four invitations, Canon, and you refused all of them. Have we fallen out of favor?"

"Forgive me. I have been otherwise occupied."

The merchant glances at his wife. He has noticed a certain remoteness between Birgit and her confessor and speculates on the nature of their argument. Damn Birgit's pique, he has business with the man whether his lady approves or not, the pragmatic merchant concludes. Covering his irritation he turns to the canon.

"In that case we are honored to have such a busy cleric at our banquet. But pray illuminate me, I have heard rumors that your distraction is of a secular nature?"

Startled, Detlef glances at Birgit—could she have guessed? He has experienced such transformation he is convinced it is as obvious as a stigma on his forehead. But Birgit, her eyes fastened on the plate before her, refuses to look up. The merchant again wonders why his wife is being so cold.

"With a certain ribbon merchant?"

Detlef's relief causes him to speak more quickly than he had intended. "Nikolaus Gülich has genuine grievances."

"If he has a grievance he should appeal to the city council, not involve the cathedral. Or are you thinking of giving up the cloth?"

"I have no such intention."

"I spoke in jest. However I am most displeased that you have become involved in Gülich's petty complaints. There are many in this city who have contributed to the young man's success—his father was a mere journeyman, they say he wasn't even a Cologner. His complaint is poor thanks to a system which I personally believe has worked successfully for many centuries."

"What about the weavers' rebellion and then your very own bürgers' revolt in 1482, when they stormed the town hall? The history of this city is built on challenging nepotism."

Several of the merchants turn at the sound of Detlef's raised voice. Ter Lahn von Lennep, embarrassed, signals to the musicians to begin the quadrille as Birgit lifts her eyes for the first time that evening.

"The good canon is a passionate man. It is a weakness you must forgive, husband."

"If he is passionate then he must respect loyalty also. He has too many enemies to afford to make new ones among his friends."

A shadow falls across the merchant's normally placid face. He plays with a ball of dough between his fingers then crushes it.

"Dance with my wife, Canon. She is in mourning but it would be seemly for her to dance with her confessor."

Reluctantly Detlef offers Birgit his arm. Her wrist under the black satin feels frail and he guesses she has lost weight through grieving.

"Madame, I am sorry for the death of your sister."

"It is hard, but there are many who have lost far more. What about you, Detlef, what has been your loss? I would swear there is a change in your demeanor, but not one that suggests pain or bereavement."

They bow and begin the formal steps of the dance.

"I have been sobered by my work in the pesthouse. It is hard to continue to believe in God when one is surrounded by so much suffering of the innocent."

"Indeed. Then explain, pray, why your face and manner seems even more infused with faith. If I did not know that you lacked one, I should say it is a matter of the heart."

He spins her around, the scent of her body drifts up and jolts him suddenly back into the memory of her.

"Birgit, I have great regret for the distress I caused you, but it was a dangerous game, one that went on far too long."

Filled with the agony of rejection, Birgit is thankful that her face is turned away. Struggling, she composes herself then gracefully spins back to him, her face now an adamantine mask.

"We were always equally matched in strategy as we were in lovemaking, Detlef. But be warned: you would be a simpleton to consider the game over yet."

But Detlef, reading her face and seeing her smile, refuses to heed her warning, deluding himself with the thought that they are still allies.

The canon walks hurriedly along, hugging the dark walls of the brick and wooden houses that tower over the lane on either side. It is too late to return to the monastery so he is making his way to Groot's dwelling, an illicit room his assistant rents from a tolerant landlady who is happy enough to accept that a man is a man whether he wears the cloth or not. Lately Groot is the only individual Detlef feels he can trust, but even he has no knowledge of the midwife's existence, least of all the child she carries.

For some time now the canon has been aware of footsteps behind him, which seem to stop every time he halts. Fearing an assault he clutches a dagger close to his chest, hidden under the short cape. He has not felt safe since he left the banquet hall. Perhaps it is the abandoned buildings left empty by the plague, like broken teeth in a gaping mouth. Perhaps it is the sensation that the city is full of ghosts who carry on their business regardless: old men shuffling along the gutters, the homeless begging at corners, the children skipping excitedly as they go off to the puppet show, the demure young women walking to church—oblivious phantoms, unaware they are no longer living beings.

Detlef swings around; a shadow darts back against the ancient Roman wall. Surely an assailant would have attacked by now, he thinks, cursing himself for not taking a carriage. Not trusting the narrowing lane he turns into a wider street which is better lit. Groot's boarding house looms up, jutting out at the corner. Detlef is comforted to see candlelight still flickering in one window on the first floor. He throws a small pebble against the stained glass then waits nervously until Groot's face appears, peering shortsightedly into the dark street below.

"It is me," Detlef whispers hoarsely in Latin.

The assistant disappears behind a drape. A second later Detlef slips into the sanctuary of an opened door.

"It gives me immense pleasure to see you back among us, Monsignor Solitario. I trust you had a safe journey."

Wilhelm Egon von Fürstenberg holds open the heavy curtain which divides a small room from the rest of the coffeehouse, revealing a lit alcove furnished with chairs and a table.

"Safe enough, considering the conflicts which continue to afflict our good emperor."

The inquisitor, just two days from Vienna, already misses the palatial Hapsburg architecture and its eating houses. This coffeehouse, although considered by the locals as the epitome of modernity, is just a glorified beer hall, Carlos notes bitterly. Grimacing he steps into the airless booth and takes his place at the table.

"Do you indulge in this latest opiate?" Von Fürstenberg squeezes his bulk into the seat beside him.

"Coffee has been available in Vienna these last five years. I have sampled it but I believe it to be a blasphemy."

"In that case you shall have tea while I sin."

A man no taller than five feet, his face pockmarked and his demeanor so undistinguished it is hard to place an ethnicity upon him, tips his cap then slips in next to von Fürstenberg.

"This is my good servant, Monsieur Georges. One might call him my invisible right hand. I am happy to report that he has spied for the Spanish and whored for the French. Georges is a master at wall-hugging and is utterly without loyalty except to his pocket. Of late he has been courting our mutual friend, Detlef von Tennen."

The inquisitor does not bother to look up, merely studies the cup of tea a young servant has just placed before him. The spy, an expert at espionage, recognizes the taciturn nature of a fellow misanthrope and stays silent. Sagaciously he awaits a signal from his master before divulging information.

Smiling, von Fürstenberg places his hand over the inquisitor's gloved fist.

"Friar, rest assured we are comrades in this, and we now have the blessing of the archbishop himself. Our dear friend the canon has suddenly become ambitious in the area of secular politics and there is genuine fear from both the aristocrats and the bürgers that he means to upset the status quo. If there was only a legitimate way of arresting him . . ."

At this Carlos slowly raises his head.

"The archbishop has finally come to his senses? That I find hard to believe."

"Believe it. I have written authority."

Von Fürstenberg pulls out a long clay pipe and packs it with tobacco. Reaching across he takes his light from a candle and sucks in deeply. Exhaling, he covers the Spaniard with a cloud of smoke.

"As in French drafts, I have always believed in attacking one's enemy from several angles. I had thought our best tactic to be a charge of immoral conduct."

Carlos looks surprised.

"I have strong evidence that von Tennen has been engaged in an improper liaison for many years with one of his congregation, Birgit Ter Lahn von Lennep. Of late they have argued. Seeking to exploit the anger of a wronged woman I sought her out. Alas, she was most fixed in her opinions. I had all but despaired until my invaluable servant Georges presented me with the following information."

The spy clears his throat then spits into the corner of the room.

"I have been following the good canon for several days now and found nothing of undue concern whatsoever on which to pin any charge of immoral or lewd conduct, sire. So being somewhat at a loss I decided to use my head and look to the recent past, as it were, namely his relationships. Upon hearing about his protection of the Jewess, I thought naturally I should travel over to the right bank and visit the ghetto of Deutz—what's left of it, that is. There, having disguised myself as a Hebrew and claiming I was from Buda and therefore spoke only bad German, I heard a most peculiar story. That at the time of the Schülergeleif several houses, including that of the midwife's father, the rabbi, were burned and the occupants with them. But the midwife's cottage was untouched and although she has not been seen since, her body was never found. Leading me to the conclusion that perhaps our canon could be harboring the witch. Find her with him and you've got yourself a right proper trial and an execution which will be very popular with King Mob."

"Do you think he has lain with her?" Excited by the thought Carlos feels his scar begin its telltale throb.

"Even if he hasn't it would be easy to invent such a notion. Just leave it to me, sire. All we have to do is catch them in the same place at the same time," the spy concludes with a crooked grin.

Von Fürstenberg finishes his clay pipe and knocks the bowl clean. Glowing ash spills onto the marble tabletop.

"The canon has recently been leaving the city far more regularly than before. Initially I had assumed this was because of concern for his brother, the count, during the plague; now I have my doubts."

"I have with me my secretary Juan and an alguacil. I also have ten soldiers of the emperor's army. I am sure Count von Tennen will be most hospitable should we decide to visit." Carlos smiles for the first time that day.

A young serving wench peeps around the curtain and gestures to the minister. With his permission she enters and whispers into his ear.

"Excuse me, gentlemen, but I believe we may have a surprising ally."

A minute later Birgit Ter Lahn von Lennep is ushered in. Dressed like any common bürger's wife, she is wearing the traditional Cologne hat with its distinctive protruding stem and a ribboned bauble on the end. From the brim streams a dark blue veil, covering a ruffled white collar and black bodice. After curtsying she holds out her hand; von Fürstenberg kisses it greedily.

"A surprising honor, Madame. Pray join us."

Flustered, her cape wet from the rain, Birgit sits. Nauseous with misgiving, she can hardly stop herself gagging at the strong smell of the stimulant the wench brings to her.

"The Countess von Marck told me where I might find you but not before some explanation. She is a good friend indeed, Herr von Fürstenberg."

"I would trust her with my life, as indeed on some occasions I have. I assume you have had a change of heart, Madame? The moral path manifests slowly but, thank the good Lord, it always prevails."

Birgit plays with a lace handkerchief tucked into her waist. Now she is actually there, sitting before the enemy of the man she still loves but has also begun to hate, she finds herself caught in an internal struggle as loyalty and affection conflict with fury. Should she betray Detlef? It will mean losing him forever, and there still remains somewhere deep within her a stubborn belief in a future together. Can she be untrue to their ardor, even if for him it no longer exists? These and other darker thoughts swirl through her mind like the cream in her coffee: Detlef's face at the guild dance, closed and indifferent, telling her that their affair had merely been a game to him, seems to stare up from the bowl of pale liquid. The memory of his indescribable cruelty at that moment propels her to speak. But then she hesitates, still reluctant to surrender the hope of reconciliation.

Frustrated by her reticence, the minister leans forward.

"He has wronged you, Madame, both as a man and a confessor. I have reason to believe that he is sheltering the midwife . . ."

The logic of von Fürstenberg's statement hits Birgit like a hammer. Suddenly jigsaw pieces of Detlef's behavior slot into one another to create a complete puzzle picture which horrifies her in its clarity: his first distraction, his morality . . . How could he have risked so much for an insignificant Jewess, Birgit wonders, surmising that the midwife's persecution must have awoken the idealist within him.

"You lie." She tries unsuccessfully to control the anger in her voice.

Von Fürstenberg, sensing that he has secured his prey, takes her arm eagerly.

"Madame, he shelters her at this very moment at the estate of his brother."

"No, it would not be at Das Grüntal, but somewhere nearby. A place I know well . . ."

"Then you will assist us?"

Birgit nods, trying to hide her tears behind a stiff dignity. But already the men have begun to whisper among themselves.

As they continue their strategizing, Birgit gazes into the grains of black coffee at the bottom of her cup, despairing at the thought of what her life holds without Detlef.

❋

The monk and the canon sit side by side in the stone athenaeum. The bibliotheca is empty apart from themselves. The walls are covered with shelves of books, their spines a medley of languages, from Latin to Portuguese, English to Greek, Persian to Hebrew. It is midafternoon and already the spring rains have begun.

Detlef writes in a painstakingly slow hand, his calligraphy elegant but deliberate. He is recording the proceedings of the last month. Each entry is written down, a day's events captured in a succinct statement: *Baptized baby Herman Kuller same day I buried his uncle. The lacemakers' guild protested to the city council over the levy imposed on Belgian lace. Merchant Knoff accuses hopmaker Franz Hausen of watering down his beer.*

As he finishes each page he hands the loose parchment to Groot, who is waiting with his inks and brush. Happily the assistant begins the caricature for that day's observation. Three strokes of black ink and there is the robust baby squalling beside a font of holy water, struggling in the arms of the canon, an elongated figure, his forehead a magnificent bundle of frowns.

It is at these times that the symbiotic relationship between servant and master is at its zenith: each content to be assisting the other, entirely absorbed in the task at hand, politics forgotten. It is at such times that Groot remembers why he chose to apprentice himself to Canon von Tennen rather than another older and more learned cleric: it was Detlef's distinctive humor and irreverence for authority that attracted him. No other priest maintains a day book like Detlef, and although he insists that it is for posterity only, Groot suspects the canon keeps it for his own amusement. 'Tis a great pity, Groot thinks, that his master should be so expert at human observation yet so naive in his strategies.

Secretly devising plans for his own promotion, the assistant places the fresh cartoon to one side to dry then reaches for the next leaf. Their labor is interrupted by a cough.

"Please, Canon."

A young novice steps out from a stone arch. He is followed by a roughly dressed farmer stinking of horse, his feathered hat clutched between two huge hands reddened by labor, the carrot beard and whiskers streaked with mud from riding hard through the rains. The peasant steps forward and reaches out to Detlef. The young priest, fearing an assault, speaks hurriedly.

"Please sire, he insisted he knows you."

"Indeed he does. Joachim."

For a moment the two men grasp hands, the canon's pale soft skin, the mark of the scholar, dwarfed in the farmer's huge paw.

Detlef's heart has leaped at the sudden appearance of Hannah's brother but conscious of Groot's steady gaze the canon portrays nothing but the demeanor of a magnanimous overlord.

The novice, relieved, returns to his chamber, leaving Groot to wonder how Detlef could know such an unlikely figure.

"Joachim, this is my assistant, Father Pieter Groot. Joachim is the brother of my housekeeper in the country."

"Sire, we must hurry back. Hannah made me swear that I would bring you with me directly. There is trouble at the house."

"What kind of trouble?"

"That she would not tell me, but you know Hannah, she would not ask unless it were serious indeed. I have been riding for a day straight, sire, and that through dangerous country."

"I thank you for your loyalty."

"I seek not gratitude, just that you will do what my sister commands."

Groot waits until Detlef has departed then takes up his brush again and in the margin of the sheet for today sketches the portrait of a lascivious she-demon, equipped with breasts and a scaly tail which is wound around the small figure of a priest with a patrician nose remarkably like Detlef's.

Closing the volume, the cleric begins a long and thoughtful walk through the cloisters toward the chambers of Wilhelm Egon von Fürstenberg.

The acrid smell of amber, saltpeter and brimstone taints the air, obscuring all other odors. Ruth, now laboring, has had Hannah smoke both the house and the grounds for fear of pestilence. With the birth imminent she finds herself in the grip of an irrational terror that she will suffer the same fate as her mother and die in childbirth. For two days Hannah has been running around executing Ruth's instructions to protect against any unforeseen circumstances, and most of all to ward off the possible intrusion of the demon herself, Lilith.

Now the housekeeper, with a thin willow stick dipped in henna, traces the last of the Hebrew letters in thick red paste across Ruth's white stretched skin.

"Have you completed the three names?"

Ruth, her nightdress pushed up to her breasts, tries to peer over her huge shiny belly. Hannah sits back on her haunches.

"I've copied them exactly like your drawing but I'm no artist."

"As long as the lettering is correct they will work as protection."

"With this much quackery soon not even the daylight will be able to get through," Hannah says, glancing around the room. Hanging on all four walls of the bedchamber are talismans against Lilith and her demons: here the Shield of David, there the three angels, Snwy, Snsnwy and Smnglf, covered from wing to tail with kabbalistic scrawlings. Pinned above the bed is a Hebrew prayer for safe delivery, while another amulet is wrapped around Ruth's wrist.

"But this amulet is tattooed on my very flesh. Whatever happens Lilith will not be able to penetrate there." Ruth mutters through clenched teeth as a contraction suddenly grips her. Frightened that the young woman might be becoming delirious, Hannah touches her forehead. She is hot but not unnaturally so.

"Why such a fear of the devil's grande dame?" Hannah asks.

Groaning, Ruth props herself up. "She took my own mother when she was birthing with her second child. Both died."

"That will not be your fate, Fräulein. I am sure of it."

Sighing, the housekeeper wipes her hands and returns to a stone bowl she has resting in the corner. She starts to stir, mixing a concoction of pellitory, sanicle, chamomile, melilot, green balm, red balm, white mullein, mallow, betony, marjoram, nipp, march, violet and mugwort with three pints of white wine—which she now splashes in liberally. She sniffs the mixture, grimaces, then pours out a glass of the foul-smelling liquid and holds it to Ruth's lips.

"Not again," Ruth groans.

"It's your own recipe, three times a day you instructed—to bring the child forth."

"And now I feel pity for my poor patients." Ruth manages to smile despite another spasm.

Hannah wipes her brow. "There was a woman in the village who was birthing for four days."

"Did she live?"

"She did, both her and the child. Big baby it was, the length of three hands."

"Who was the midwife?"

"They sent for one from Bonn, but she got here too late. Was Mother Nature in the end—and your Hannah. So, you see, you should not fear."

Ruth reaches out and grasps the sturdy forearm of the housekeeper, the skin greasy from the oil of violets she has been using to massage Ruth's womb.

"I'll try not to, but I am impatient for the child to come."

She rests her head a moment on the bosom of this sturdy countrywoman who has become mother, friend, nursemaid and now midwife to a midwife.

Ruth has been in labor for a day and a night and knows from the opening of her womb that the baby will not be hurried. But still she cannot stop the dread which has been eating into her ever since her waters broke. Narrow like her mother, she knows it will not be an easy birth. The memory of Sara perishing from a hemorrhage after the birth of her stillborn son is deeply engraved within her. Will this be her fate too? Or will all the amulets and prayers ensure that it is not so? Still her trepidation has grown until she had to summon Detlef to be by her side.

"It be almost two days since my brother left, they'll be here before sunset," Hannah remarks as if reading Ruth's thoughts. "Master Detlef's a good man, for all his dangerous ideas. He reminds me of my mistress, his aunt, when he talks like that, filling the air with fanciful notions."

Another contraction begins, rippling from the base of Ruth's spine, sending out waves of intense pain. Immediately she starts breathing deeply.

Hoping to distract her, Hannah wipes her brow. "Mind you, dreams like his could get a man killed—just like his aunt. I used to say 'Master Detlef, 'tis a good thing no one can hear you except the wind else we'd both be hanging.' He was a lovely young boy, handsome as the day, always thought he was wasted in the church."

She waits until Ruth has stopped thrashing then straightens the robe around her sweating torso.

"The child will be beautiful, despite the poor bastard he is."

Ruth, her eyes wide, stares up at the ceiling and tries to breathe some relief into her pain-racked body. Hannah pulls her up so that her back is resting against the wall. She places a goblet of water against Ruth's bitten, swollen lips.

"Drink, you need to keep drinking."

Exhausted, the two horses trot into the overgrown courtyard then invigorated by the scent of their home meadows toss their manes impatiently as Detlef and Joachim slip wearily out of their saddles, thighs and buttocks burning from the long ride. Detlef looks up at the house. Seeing a light glowing in the master bedroom, he fears that he might have arrived too late.

"I'll leave you here, sire, as is Hannah's wishes. If there's anything else you need, I'll be on the farm with the wife . . ."

"Could you take my mare? There is better eating for her over your way and she deserves a good feed."

Joachim nods but Detlef is already running toward the house.

———

He pauses in the corridor, he can hear the soft murmuring of Hannah's voice as she hums an old folk song. The heavy scents of the birthing herbs float under the closed door. For a moment Detlef hesitates, unsure whether he should enter a domain that is forever the realm of women, until he hears Ruth call out his name.

The mounted soldiers wait in the cover of the trees, their green uniforms blending in with the low branches and bushes. Beyond, on the other side of an open meadow, lies the house, a low stone building so ancient and well masked that it takes the eye a few minutes before it is able to focus on the dark thatched roof, the gray walls that merge into the shadows of the forest. It is only with instruction from Birgit Ter Lahn von Lennep that they have been able to approach the estate from this angle. Any other direction would have caused them to completely miss sight of the building.

Carlos slides gingerly from his mount. He has been riding for hours, struggling to keep up with the soldiers who are all experienced horsemen. Doubled over with pain the inquisitor hobbles toward the captain who silently hands him the eyeglass. The friar, mouth dry with anticipation, peers through it. Instantly his backache disappears and all regret for the agony of the journey evaporates as he sees the burning light, almost hidden under the eaves, on the first floor of the low farmhouse.

"The rat is in his hole," he whispers to the captain, who smiles back, his olive face split by the white of his teeth.

"Monsignor, we will catch your rodent. If we surround the house, there will be no escape. The forest is too thick and if he runs across the open meadow he will be like a duck on a shooting range."

"I want them both alive. I will have them tried and make them a public example. They are no good to me dead."

The captain nods then signals to his men. The ten guards slip off their horses with the practiced stealth of the mercenary, as indeed some of them are. After silently tying their horses to trees, they unhitch their heavy chainmail vests and drape them expertly over the saddles. Then armed with short swords, their plumed helmets glinting in the sun, their tunics blazing with the Hapsburg double-headed eagle, its talons arching proudly over scepter and sphere, the men glide noiselessly through the waist-high grasses of the meadow like a huge emerald and silver snake whose twisting mass catches the sunlight only now and then. Moving in short bursts, each soldier is an extension of the captain as they follow his signals with razor-sharp precision. Ten feet into the tall grass the soldiers halt.

Carlos, sweating heavily under his cassock, squats beside a clump of wild wheat. Pollen and seeds sting his eyes as he struggles not to sneeze. Beneath his foot something—probably a toad—squashes down unpleasantly. To console himself the inquisitor holds in his mind the image of the German canon mortified, his head hanging in shame at the great public auto-da-fé Carlos plans to conduct in the city square of Cologne.

Detlef strokes Ruth's damp hair which hangs in ribbons down her back. The nightdress stuck to her sweating flesh barely conceals the heavy breasts, now laced with a filigree of pulsating veins, above the enormous sphere that is her belly. She breathes in short pants, her fingernails digging into Detlef as Hannah probes between her open thighs.

"What do you sense?" Ruth gasps over her pain.

"The crown of the head is at the lip. It won't be long now."

Hannah withdraws her hands and washes them in a basin of water which quickly becomes bloodied. With Detlef's help Ruth pushes herself up so that she squats supported by the birthing stool.

"My love, promise me that if there is any danger you will save the child first," Ruth whispers as she wraps her arms around his neck, drawing him to the rich fecundity of her scent.

Detlef has never seen a woman so naked and so undone. And to his amazement, he still finds beauty in the swollen flesh, the struggle in her body and in her face. But birthing is women's business and the midwife's doubt of her own survival fills him with an ancient dread.

"My love, this is demons speaking, there will be no danger to either you or our child."

But before she can answer him she is swept away by another spasm.

Suddenly there is the sound of heavy banging at the door below. Detlef, his face blanching, stares at Hannah.

"What is that? Do you hear it? Or is it the pounding in my own head?" Ruth murmurs.

Detlef races to the bedroom door but the housekeeper is already standing before it.

"Let me pass!"

"No. 'Tis better I go, but first hide yourselves."

"Where?"

"Follow me, there is a secret passage."

Quickly she bundles up some rags and the birthing stool while Detlef picks up Ruth, now delirious with pain, in his arms. Again there is the sound of fists drumming against the door.

"Open up! This is the emperor's men!"

The captain's voice rings out as a rain of stones hits the side of the house, smashing a window.

Hannah, running, leads them back out into the corridor, past the wide staircase, past two abandoned rooms and then into her own small bedroom tucked into a corner under the rafters. She pulls aside a wooden panel to reveal a small alcove and pushes them into it. Then she slides the wooden panel closed, pulling the tapestry over it so it is as if the alcove does not exist.

As the housekeeper clambers back downstairs she quickly composes herself, adjusting her cap and throwing off the bloodstained apron. Taking a deep breath she strides toward the oak door that is shaking violently with the guards' pounding. Just before she slips the huge bolt open she crosses herself, muttering a quick prayer to Saint Martha, the patron saint of housekeepers, and Katrina von Tennen, her former mistress, to fortify herself with courage and wit.

The housekeeper stands on the threshold, hands on hips, legs apart. The casualness with which she surveys the soldiers with their swords at the ready, their chests heaving in patriotic excitement, confuses Carlos who thinks for a moment that they might have raided the wrong estate.

The captain, also momentarily bewildered by the sight of this motherly figure, glances back at the friar whose hood is pulled low over his sunburned face.

"What do you boys want?" The housekeeper is flippant in her inquiry, as if confronting a group of errant farmhands, not the guard of the emperor.

"Not you, mother!" one cheeky soldier yells out and a few of the others grin sheepishly.

Carlos, sensing a lull in the momentum, steps forward. He pushes back his hood and reaches into his cassock. Speaking in Latin he begins to read out a charge of immoral behavior against Canon von Tennen by the Holy Roman Empire and the Grand Inquisitional Council.

Hannah listens, not allowing one sign of terror to creep from under her irreverent expression.

"Good sir, I don't understand the tongue of priests. Speak plain German."

"In plain German, Madame, we are here to arrest your master Detlef von Tennen on two charges of misconduct: congress with a Jewess and wizardry. Now move aside."

But the housekeeper does not budge.

"I know not this gentleman."

"Then, Madame, you are both a liar and an accomplice."

Carlos nods to the captain, who calmly knocks the housekeeper to the ground. She lies gasping for breath as the soldiers, stepping over her, pour into the house.

❋

The only light seeps in from a tiny crack between the wooden panels. From outside come the sounds of smashing furniture and ripping wall hangings as the soldiers search the rooms.

Detlef reaches for the small dagger he wears at his belt. Slipping it free he tenses, barely able to contain the anger which surges up through his muscles. The soldier within him, long buried, is suddenly alert: he wants to defend his own, to kill the intruders who threaten the life of his woman and unborn baby. He will not squat here in the corner like a coward waiting to be slaughtered: better to perish fighting than to die like a pantry rat run through by a blind sword.

Trembling, he closes his eyes, a picture of himself bursting through the wooden panel and grasping the inquisitor by the throat fills his imagination: the roar of blind satisfaction at plunging his knife in again and again, the blood splattering against the tapestries and coursing down to the wooden floor. Detlef's sinewy fingers curl around the hilt of the blade. Slowly he lifts the dagger, his weight shifting as he readies his body to leap out of the confined space. At his side Ruth squats, her body heaving in labor.

The sound of running footsteps and Hannah's screams pierce the thin paneling. Detlef feels Ruth twitching in fear. Instinctively he reaches out to the wooden partition. But Ruth grabs his wrist as she presses against the back wall for support, a rag between her teeth to prevent her groans being heard. In the dim light he can barely see her terrified eyes but knows they are pleading with him. As she stares at him Detlef suddenly realizes that she has total comprehension of the events outside despite her body arching with each spasm of the birthing, her face a yawning mute cry of agony. Fumbling in the dark he runs his hand up her legs then between her thighs; inserting his fingers he can feel the slippery top of the babe's head. It has almost descended. He glances at Ruth, willing her to push.

Her face clenched and red from exertion, she bears down and with a great gush of blood and pungent meconium the baby whooshes out straight into Detlef's arms.

Swiftly he wipes the muck from its tiny nose and mouth, then wonders what he is to do with the pulsating birth cord still raveling out from the child's belly and back into Ruth. The midwife, feeling blindly, touches the thick slippery cord. Concentrating, she steadies her trembling fingers long enough to tie two pieces of thread around it then reaches for Detlef's knife. Straining his eyes, he watches her as she cuts the throbbing band. Blood spills then ceases.

Exhausted, she relaxes against the wall then smiles at the baby. Outside the soldiers shout to each other as they run down the stairs. Seeing that the babe is about to bawl, Ruth covers his mouth with her hand. The cry is still perceptible.

Two rooms away in the master bedroom, Carlos rips down the mystical amulets from the walls.

"Witchcraft!" he spits, revolted.

He tears up the drawings and throws the pieces into the air where they flutter down like chaotic snow. Spinning around, he stares at the blood-stained pallet. Furious, he pushes it onto its side. Underneath there is nothing, just the dusty wooden floor. But there is a greasy stain beside the pallet.

"Look, look what magic the witch has made with her wizard!"

The inquisitor pulls down the remaining amulet still hanging over the bed.

"Canon! Wherever you are hiding we will find you!"

He is answered only by a barking dog out in the courtyard. Just then the captain, his face covered in scratches beading with blood, enters.

"We have searched the house, there is nothing."

"Have you looked everywhere? The servants' quarters? The barn? The pig sty? I want you to examine every nook, every cranny, everywhere!"

The captain shakes his head slowly and sniffs the air. He starts to back out of the room fearfully. "That smell . . . I know it—they have smoked the place to ward off the plague!"

"It's a decoy, you idiot!"

"How do you know?"

"I am in command here! Search the rest of the property. I order you! Now!"

Reluctantly the captain goes back to the landing and yells for his men to search the upper floor again. Swearing and sniffing the pungent air nervously, the soldiers march up the staircase, their uniforms incongruous in the domestic setting.

Carlos, still standing in the middle of the master bedroom, looks around slowly. There are the witch's combs, the soft hair still wound around the ivory teeth. Here are the canon's boots, fancy French imports. Carlos kicks at them: the idea that a cleric should own such expensive footwear revolts the frugal Spaniard. There is a corruption in the German Catholic soul that must be stamped out, he thinks, but despite himself cannot help marveling at the softness and length of the black hairs caught in the ornate comb. The midwife has hair like her mother's, witch's locks that can twist themselves around a man and milk him dry.

He runs his finger along the straw pallet: here the canon must have lain with the witch, how many times? As many as the days in a year? Carlos, both fascinated and sickened, suddenly has to leave this room of vice.

Out on the landing he retches then leans his burning face against the cool stone wall. It is then that he hears it: a soft wailing, like an animal or a baby, vibrating through the stone beneath the noise of shouting soldiers and crashing furniture.

Alert with renewed hope, the inquisitor stares down the corridor, assessing which room the faint wail might have come from. He walks across the wooden boards and into the first room. Empty now, it was once a library and several of the bookcases are still piled high with ancient manuscripts. A stately woman stares down from above a small desk; she bears a slight resemblance to the canon. Carlos, unable to tolerate the noblewoman's supercilious gaze, jabs his short hunting knife into the canvas which rips loudly. He slashes at the eyes, the arrogant face, over and over. Finally, satisfied that the chamber is concealing nothing, he leaves.

Back in the corridor he falters as confusion overwhelms him. Several doors present themselves like the riddle of a maze: which one are they hiding behind, which one? Bewilderment and nausea rise up in him, piercing his brain alongside the insistent acrid odor of brimstone.

"Lilith," Carlos speaks the demon's name. "Show me the right way.

Help your loyal servant," he continues in Aramaic, knowing the incantation will be incomprehensible if overheard. The smoke from the bonfire the soldiers have lit outside curls up the staircase creating a fog. Carlos, sensing something more, stares into it. At its misty edge the shape of the fiend appears, a curvaceous phantom of vapor; one graceful arm of swirling gray lifts and points. Following its direction, Carlos approaches a door barely visible beneath a low arched beam. Bending his head he turns the handle and enters.

The chamber is deserted. The purifying smoke seems more intense here. Carlos can smell nothing but amber, brimstone and saltpeter. There is a neatly rolled-up pallet in the corner, a washing stand and a rosary hanging over it. The housekeeper's sleeping quarters, he guesses. A small window is framed by a lip of thick slate and glows with the sunset. The inquisitor reaches across and lights a candle. The flame leaps up and illuminates the wood paneling of the walls. Nothing seems amiss but he cannot allay his suspicion.

Inside their hiding place Ruth and Detlef hold themselves statuelike as they listen to Carlos's creeping footsteps and labored breathing. The sleeping baby is on the breast. The bloodstained rags are pressed between Ruth's legs, crusty with afterbirth. Suddenly the child stirs. Detlef reaches for him but Ruth stays his hand; both stare down at the wrinkled crimson face, willing the child to keep his peace. Oblivious, the babe innocently shifts his weight, snuggling closer to Ruth's breast. Again Detlef reaches for his blade.

Outside Carlos is convinced he can hear faint rustlings behind the wall. He freezes, waiting for another sound, a sign that will reveal his prey. On the other side of the panel, inches away, Ruth runs her fingers over the raised hennaed hex on her now slack womb and prays.

In that instant Carlos is distracted by the miaow of a cat. Looking down he sees that a small kitten is rubbing itself against his legs. It miaows again, sounding remarkably like a baby. The friar picks it up and ruefully carries it out of the room.

Inside the alcove Detlef's blind fingers find Ruth's face; her cheeks are wet with tears. He pulls her and the baby into his arms. They lie with her head curled against his chest, the sleeping babe at her breast. To Detlef it seems as if this darkness is beyond fear, beyond time and space, perhaps beyond mortality itself. Feeling the weight of Ruth's slight body against his, and the extraordinarily soft flesh of this tiny mortal which is now his child, he suddenly understands love in a way he has never experienced it before, as if tendrils of his very being have intertwined with this woman to make a new soul. Part of him remains in wonderment at the circumstances that have led him to this moment: this instant of great danger yet great hope.

Aware of a new, raw creature emerging from within him, unfurling like the tentative blossom of a poppy, translucent damp petals reaching out of a spiky bud of cynicism and disbelief, Detlef is both exhilarated and exhausted by the abundance of possibilities his future now holds. Weary beyond terror, he finally closes his eyes and lets his head rest against Ruth's shoulder.

The soldiers crouch beside the roaring fire. A chaotic mountain of broken tables, mirrors, paintings and ornaments waits alongside to feed the blaze. The young guards' faces, stained with grime and dust, are flushed with the wine they have raided from the cellar. One of the chevaliers sings a mournful Basque melody as he throws a leg of the broken virginal into the flames. The bonfire flares up, throwing light onto the façade of the house, silhouetting a sinister shape that rotates at the end of a rope.

The inquisitor and the captain stand some distance away beside the tethered horses.

"Monsignor, with all due respect we have explored both the cottage and the grounds. I fear the accused and his accomplice escaped before our arrival."

" 'Tis strange for I sense that they are still nearby."

"My men have searched everywhere—the barn, the pig sty, the servants' quarters, even the chicken coop. And you won't be getting anything out of the housekeeper now."

Carlos looks over to the raided house, the oak door swinging open, the smashed china, the tapestries scattered on the ground, the wooden shutters banging in the wind. Violated, it is a shattered reflection of its former tranquillity.

"He will be at his brother's estate. I am told it is thirty miles east of here."

"My men will not ride at night."

"They must and they shall."

The captain stares briefly into the determined face of the inquisitor. The officer has taken this commission reluctantly; if he had his way he would be fighting the Ottomans for the glory of the Hapsburg Empire, not chasing an errant canon and his Jewish mistress. But his colonel allowed him no option. If the Spaniard wants to be at Count von Tennen's estate before dawn, so be it. Let the zealot Dominican deal with the disgruntled chevaliers. The captain spits into the mud.

"In that case, my good Monsignor, perhaps it would be more appropriate for you to announce your intentions to the men yourself. They are weary in body and spirit but I am confident your rhetoric shall be pretty enough to inspire them to new spiritual heights and maybe even back into the saddle. And if not your rhetoric then your purse will suffice. Good luck to you, sir."

With a smile he saunters back to his troops.

An hour later the small platoon, exhausted but fortified by thoughts of the extra one hundred Reichstaler the inquisitor has promised them, ride out of the courtyard and down the narrow tree-lined lane.

A huge yellow moon transforms them into a mass of benign silvery phantoms whose pensive silence is broken only by the clinking of their brass stirrups and the whisper of the plumes on their helmets. The only witness to their departure is a solitary bull, made restless by the scent of a cow in heat four miles away. The creature paws at the ground, nostrils flaring at the aroma of horse and man. But even he knows better than to bellow.

*T*he point of light slowly grows to a slim crescent. It travels across the cracked wall grimy with ancient dust, suddenly hitting a glint of gold which, as the light becomes stronger, reveals itself as blond hair. The bar of light continues its path down the creased forehead, over the closed orbs fringed with long dark eyelashes that open and blink for a second as the pupils, swimming in the center of a deep sapphire, dilate and focus.

Detlef stares into the sliver of dawn sunlight. As the feeling slowly needles back into his cramped limbs he remembers where he is. For a moment he panics—is she safe? Where is the babe? Terror fills him until the warm weight of Ruth's body makes itself apparent. He looks down: she is curled up asleep, her head resting against his chest. The baby, wrapped in rags, one arm extended, still stained with blood and mucus, fist clenched resolutely, lies at his mother's naked breast, eyes screwed shut, mouth pursed in concentration. For a moment Detlef fears the child has died in the night, when suddenly his eyes blink open and the perfectly formed baby boy stares up at his father with a wide and fearless gaze, as if challenging him on the very reason for his existence. Detlef, caught between wonder and amusement, stares straight back. He reaches down and caresses the soft furry blond down which covers the small head. To his amazement he can cup the whole skull in one palm.

My child, he thinks, allowing the thought to become a solid truth, my own flesh and blood. A wave of emotion surges through him, leaving him wanting to use all his powers to cast a circle of protection around his new family.

Just then Ruth wakes and immediately the babe nuzzles blindly into her breast.

❋

Detlef harnesses the large drafthorse to the simple wooden buggy. Bandits will be a constant threat, he thinks, trying to gather his thoughts while deeply conscious of the danger of lingering. They cannot afford to look like aristocracy or even wealthy bürgers, especially crossing the border and certainly not on the roads between. The cart is rough but it will suffice, he rationalizes. At least this way they will look like poor farmers not worth robbing. But as a precaution he has sewn several bags of gold coin into his clothing—protection money—while strapped to the back of the cart are the few expensive antiques the soldiers did not destroy: a chest filled with linen, his aunt's fine French walnut desk and a box of family jewels to sell in Amsterdam to secure enough money to rent lodgings.

"Ruth!"

She looks up from where she is kneeling beside a freshly dug mound of earth. A makeshift cross, two pieces of broken wood nailed together, mark it as a grave. Hannah's grave. Carefully Ruth pushes a small scroll covered with Yiddish writing into the soft earth. It is a woman's prayer for finding peace.

"Say your prayers but they won't bring her back."

Joachim, Hannah's brother, full of anger and grief, stands clutching his cap in his hand. His ruddy face is rigid with the struggle to hold back tears.

"Last sister I had. One gone in the Great War, two in the plague, and now this. She died for you, she would have done anything for the master." He spits into the newly turned earth.

"She was a good servant," Ruth says faintly.

She would like to take the laborer's hands, to comfort him in his glowering resentment, but knows this would only fuel his anger. Instead she places a single spray of lilac on the grave.

"Aye. That's one way of putting it. Should have thought about herself and run. But not Hannah—them that serve don't survive."

Donning his hat, he walks sullenly over to Detlef and helps him haul the last box up onto the cart.

They had found her body swinging from the old linden tree in the center of the courtyard. Detlef cut down the battered corpse and tenderly laid the housekeeper on the ground, talking all the while, reassuring her that all would be right, that the meats would be cured, the apples picked, the apricots dried, that he would make sure Brunehilde the sow was taken care of. He even promised to carry a message to her cousin in the Dutch navy until he realized that he was talking to himself. It was then he found himself weeping over the long gray hair which lay like a halo around the bloated blue face, twigs and straw still woven between the strands.

The baby, wrapped in a blanket and lying on the grass beside Ruth, wakes and starts bawling.

"My love, we must leave now!"

Detlef tightens the strap around the horse. He would like to pick Ruth up in his arms and tell her that life will resume its normal shape, that one day it will be safe to love again, but he cannot. The raped and desolate house is testimony to his own horror, a horror he cannot yet articulate nor has the energy to battle, but senses that one day he will. The only thing he can do now is force his body into flight and save his family.

"Please, it is dangerous to tarry."

Finally Ruth hears him. Lifting their son, she walks to him, knowing that beyond lies Amsterdam and freedom.

הוד

HOD

Glory

☿

*T*he midwife, weary from the night's work, stops to catch her breath after climbing down two flights of narrow wooden stairs. The maid, a buxom blonde with the attractive features of a Frisian, carries a small placard covered in red silk and trimmed with lace. She smiles as she leads Ruth through the *voorhuis*. As they step into the large entrance hall with its immaculately scrubbed black and white tiled floor, the morning sun floods in through the large windows. The room is empty apart from two elegant French chairs and a three-legged pedestal table placed against a wall. A large Ming vase sits proudly on top of the table beside a bowl of blooming tulips.

"Where are the rest of the family? The neighbors?" Ruth asks in Dutch, surprised to see the hall devoid of expectant faces.

The maid holds up the red silk notice with the small white card in the center. After four years back in Amsterdam Ruth knows that the white card means the newborn is a girl while the red silk indicates that the baby lives. "They are waiting to see this, then they will visit. It is Madame's third child."

"But this one will survive," Ruth replies, wondering about the skills of the midwife who delivered the first two, both stillborn. An incompetent judging from the scarred labia of her poor patient.

"Praise be to God . . . and your craft." The servant crosses herself.

She then unlatches the heavy oak door that opens onto a tree-lined road running along a canal which forms a luminescent band of dancing light. Smiling proudly the girl hangs the sign over the silver door handle cast in the shape of a dolphin.

"They say that your husband is a great preacher. A Remonstrant who speaks of the Republic and a future that we—even working folk—can shape ourselves."

"He is a great thinker but sometimes he takes unnecessary risks," Ruth answers cautiously.

"So the story about him having to climb out of a church window to escape arrest is true?"

Smiling at the open admiration in the young girl's face, Ruth answers without thinking. "Yes. That was the sermon that suggested Jesus' birth might not have been as virginal as the Bible says; that the divine spirit came through Joseph and Mary's very mortal love for each other."

"A dangerous notion indeed."

The midwife looks sharply at the housemaid. For a minute the thought crosses her mind that this innocent-faced wench might be a spy. Recognizing her accent as northern. Ruth wonders whether she could be a royalist, following the young Prince William of Orange as most in the north do, and not a supporter of Jan de Witt's Republic.

"My husband was pardoned by the authorities."

"As he should have been," the maid answers, reaching into her pocket to pay the midwife.

But Ruth cannot dismiss her distrust. She has become suspicious like the rest of Holland, she realizes. The midwife is still amazed at how Amsterdam's famous tolerance has begun to evaporate as financial insecurity looms. Jan de Witt has come under fire for his naval war with the English and, disapproving, the hidden royalists have begun screaming for Prince William of Orange, barely a man, to be reinstated. The country Ruth has begun to love grows ugly with reactionary sentiment. It is but fear of the French king and his growing greed for the Dutch colonial wealth, she thinks, a dread which infects the bürgers who care only for their own prosperity from the spice islands. These Hollanders forget nothing and forgive even less. Armed with these fears they tear at de Witt's glorious dream of the Republic.

Staring up at the immaculate façade of the mansion, she remembers the arrest of the revolutionary lawyer Adriaan Koerbagh. That event terrified every liberal thinker in the city, for what was the young radical's crime other than being a close supporter of Benedict Spinoza and her old Latin tutor Franciscus van den Enden? Ruth shivers with sudden dread, her fears growing by the minute. Koerbagh was a brave man, a man of the future, who claimed that the Bible is a human work and that Jesus was mortal not divine. Even more revolutionary was his announcement that the real teaching of God is simply knowledge of God and love of one's neighbor. And how did the good man pay for this brave revelation? With his life. A fate that could easily be her husband's if Detlef continues with his dangerous outspokenness. As for de Witt, the leader in support of whom many intellectuals had spoken out and risked all, what did he do for poor Koerbagh? Nothing. Now every thinker and philosopher in the Lowlands fears persecution. Ruth worries for Detlef: his voice is too loud; his views anger as many as they inspire. But how are they to live if not by their beliefs? Was not that the reason they fled to Holland? If Jan de Witt is not willing to stand up for his defenders, what hope is there, Ruth wonders.

The maid, reading her fears, reaches out.

"Be not alarmed. I follow the beliefs of my master and your husband's courage is appreciated here. I wish merely to attend his sermons."

"Thank you. I do believe a notice will be posted soon announcing Pastor Tennen's next lecture," Ruth replies curtly.

As the midwife walks away the maid speculates about what the woman is concealing. Surely she could feel only pride to be married to such a visionary.

The Herengracht is a broad canal flanked by wide affluent streets on either side. Many of the wealthiest trading families of Amsterdam live here and the elegant redbrick houses, packed neatly alongside each other, run the entire length of the canal. The ridged roof of each immaculate residence is decorated with the crest of the guild the owner belongs to. Some houses even have pulleys attached so that heavy goods and furniture can be hoisted up into the building.

Ruth, dressed in a fashionable bonnet and a satinisco blue and yellow overcoat, walks across the cobblestones, hurrying from the shade of one elm tree to another. She hails a boatman and instructs him to take her over to Harlemmerstraat.

The boatman, a tall thickset man bearing a scar across his cheek from the Spanish wars, holds out his palm, a straw held between his fingers. He watches the shadow cast by the makeshift sundial, surmises the correct time then agrees to the journey. His son steadies the midwife's arm as she steps into the barge carefully balancing her bag of instruments.

Ruth glances across the shimmering water toward the sun. With luck she will be home before Detlef begins his morning toilet. She left him dozing heavily, his arm thrown beyond the curtain which separates the sleeping alcove from the rest of their humble room. He had just returned from Rotterdam where he gave sermons in the scattering of Remonstrant institutions across northern Holland.

Once Detlef decided to become a Protestant, he chose to join the Remonstrants over the other Calvinist faiths because he was drawn to the Dutch theologian Arminius, their founder, who had challenged Calvin's doctrine of predestination some sixty years before. The Remonstrants are the most liberal and least dogmatic of their revolutionary brethren: their variations from orthodoxy are conditional rather than absolute, they believe in universal atonement, the necessity of regeneration through the Holy Ghost, the possibility of resistance to divine grace and the possibility of relapse from grace. All this, and more, drew Detlef to them, and within their ranks he has found acceptance of both his marriage and his beliefs.

Although Ruth is proud of him, a gnawing apprehension always grips her when he is away on his travels. Part of her wishes they had stayed anonymous: Herr and Frau Tennen, married by a Protestant preacher in a forest chapel near the German border with Mother Nature the only witness. But after two years as pastor in a small church in the Nieuwendijk, a working-class slum famous for prostitution, Detlef became swept up in the intellectual fury of the times. His sermons spoke increasingly of the importance of the Republic, of a democracy where all should be equal, of the human aspects of the Bible rather than its divinity. But it is only since he has introduced antislavery sentiments and disapproval of the Dutch slave traders into his orations that he has begun to attract real enemies.

Would she have him any other way? It is impossible to imagine. She has watched Detlef transform from an individual with little belief in the notion of the inherent goodness of man to a humanist convinced that, with guidance, man is able to elevate himself above his base nature. Now, free from the machinations and politics of Cologne, Detlef has found a vocation in direct communication with his congregation and it has infused him with purpose. How could she wrest him away from that for the sake of remaining incognito? To do such a thing would be to strip him of a dignity he has finally won through his actions rather than his birthright.

The canal narrows and the streets on either side become visibly poorer, the newer elegant mansions replaced by slender older houses sandwiched together, the upper stories hanging over the cobbled pavements, the frontages noticeably dirtier. A stench rises up from the water, a dead cat floats by forcing Ruth to hold a handkerchief to her face.

The barge approaches the small pier at the bottom of her street. Already at the *musico* on the corner—a bordello thinly disguised as a theater— several sailors and a chevalier are sitting around an oval table smoking clay pipes. Ruth guesses they are revelers from the night before. A stout prostitute, her broad face flushed with beer, straddles the lap of one man while coquettishly snatching the meerschaum of another. The rosy-faced men, drunk, roar with laughter as she blows smoke rings into the haze of morning light.

The barge bumps up against the straw-filled buoy and after handing the boatman his fee of two stuivers, Ruth climbs up onto the wharf and makes her way toward a humble redbrick dwelling with open wooden shutters.

Detlef is sitting at his desk, a heavy day coat of blue serge hanging over his shoulders. There are gray flecks through his blond hair which now hangs down to his shoulders. She watches his hands as he writes, the feathered quill dancing across the page. Youthful in their energy, they are now more worn, the chafed knuckles bonier, vulnerable. She walks up behind him and buries her face in his neck and shoulder, breathing in deeply. Home. The scent of him, and with it trust, security.

He drops his pen and reaches blindly for her behind him.

"How was the birthing?"

"Hard but successful. They now have their first child and she will live."

"My wife, the savior of many."

"In this case your fame preceded my own. The young maidservant was most curious about the infamous Pastor Tennen and his radical teachings."

"You are jealous?"

"I would prefer it if my husband were less of a public figure and more a creature around whom I could wind my domestic security."

"We are safe, Ruth. This I promise you."

Detlef swings around and faces her. The lines in his face have deepened and the last vestiges of youth have vanished. A new maturity has blunted the edges of a severity she once found arrogant. It is as if finally he is comfortable in his own skin.

Mein Mann, my husband, she thinks, marveling again at the intimacy, the unquestioning bond between them, which has blossomed over the past four years. Four years of extraordinary change, and also loss, for after Jacob Ruth failed to hold another pregnancy. She has suffered three miscarriages and suspects that, in the haste of the first birth, her cervix was torn thus destroying the chance of a second child. With each loss she grieved anew, despite Detlef's reassurances that one healthy child was blessing enough.

He pulls her face to his and kisses her, the intelligence between them quickening as their tongues explore, finding that familiar core of desire which shoots through both their bodies and leaves them trembling.

Detlef pushes off her linen cap as Ruth's hands pluck at the laced crotch of his hose. She wants him naked, against her. The sweat of his skin sweetening her mouth. She desires him now. But he makes her wait, his mouth traveling down her neck, biting into her as his hands throw up the back of her skirt and roughly tear down her petticoats. Cupping her buttocks he buries his face between her breasts, searching for the long hard nipples that press against the silk of her undergarment.

Staring for a moment at the darkening areolae which glow beautifully against the pale skin of his wife's breasts, Detlef marvels at how the familiar can remain so inherently unattainable. No matter how many times he makes love to her, how many times he sees her face quicken with ecstasy, there is an aspect of her closed to him, as if somewhere between her own arrest and the murder of her father she lost the ability to trust, and with that the ability to truly surrender herself. It is this impassable landscape which he is always trying to conquer that keeps him in a constant state of burning. And it is this restless state of exclusion that propels him across the countryside, as if he can only know he is truly loved through his impassioned sermons and the fevered eyes of his inspired audience.

Squeezing one nipple he sucks down on the other hard, sharp, feeling her pain quicken to pleasure then back to pain, while his fingers play her, penetrating her roughly, wanting to possess her, reach her, make her moan. Then, when she is tearing at his hair, her legs quivering, he buries his face beneath her skirts and kneeling plays her with his mouth until she bursts in bliss. Only then does he gently place his thick hard organ against her swollen lips, resting for an infinitesimal exquisite moment as he stares into her eyes, the memory of their lives together spiraling back like a delicate seaplant in an ocean of deep emerald. He enters her so slowly that Ruth fears she will scream again, wanting him to fill her, to obliterate all but his pulsating flesh throbbing within her.

He takes the tip of her tongue, sucking gently he mirrors the action of his cock, riding her faster and faster until he has her feet locked behind his neck, the bulk of him encompassing her whole body as he fills her over and over until both of them come in a shuddering wave. The intensity of which, as it ebbs, makes them break into spontaneous laughter.

Lifting her up on his hips, he carries her over to their sleeping cot set high in the wall, enclosed by a curtain. There he lies her down, and after peeling off his jerkin and hose falls beside her, one heavy hand curled across her narrow waist as they both tumble into deep sleep.

"Papa! Papa!"

A small pink hand creeps around the edge of the drape. Detlef opens one eye as the hand finds its way to his big toe and pulls. A shriek of delighted laughter follows as Detlef, smiling, gently shifts Ruth's sleeping head from his shoulder and pulls the curtain across. Jacob, naked except for a smock, a spinning top trailing behind him, stares up at his father with huge eyes, blond curls tumbling to his shoulders.

"Papa!" he demands, stamping his bare foot as he reaches out to be held. Detlef swings him into the cot, tucking the restless child down beside Ruth who sleepily cradles both her husband and son.

Jacob pulls at his father's ears then tries to put a finger up his nose as Detlef allows his son to crawl over his chest. The boy is indulged, that Detlef realizes: his colleagues are always ridiculing him for being such a lenient and attentive father, but he cannot help but adore his only child.

He has never quite recovered from the immeasurable happiness he first felt on staring into that face which reflects so much of himself. A certain pensiveness he has seen flickering in the young boy's eyes; Jacob's joy at small things—ants dragging a beetle, his first snowflakes, the cat yawning. The four-year-old's mouth and nose, a distinctive bent to his forefinger, are of Detlef's family but the green eyes and the determined chin are his mother's, as is the child's quickening to anger.

Through half-opened lashes Ruth watches her husband with their child. He is so calm with him, she thinks, marveling at the way Detlef's face softens immediately when Jacob is in his arms. Instinctively the boy knows his father, recognizes Detlef's quiet but intense curiosity, his sudden flashes of impatience, his gentleness, as character traits of his own. Perhaps this is why so few words pass between them, she observes, as if father and child can read each other's minds without the necessity of speech. She is a lucky woman indeed, to have married for love and intellect and now to have the gift of a child who will carry on both their spirits in time.

"My colleagues wonder why my son is not yet baptized," Detlef remarks upon hearing Ruth sigh.

"'Tis none of their business."

"The Remonstrant brotherhood is most liberal, however for one of their own ministers to have an unbaptized son and a wife who will not attend church . . ."

"By his mother's heritage the child is a Jew, he cannot be baptized. I will not permit it, not after what happened to me."

"So not baptized but circumcised. Ruth, what are we bringing up in the world? A Jewish Protestant? The poor babe is neither fish nor fowl."

Ruth props herself up and stares at her husband; a cheeky smile is playing across his mouth. Just then Jacob triumphantly inserts one of his fingers into Detlef's nostril. Detlef pulls the offending finger out then grabs Jacob and lifts him up in the air. The child squeals with delight, his limbs kicking freely.

"Jacob shall be a citizen of the new world. When he is of age he shall choose for himself which faith, if any, he wishes to pursue. I will not have any doctrine thrust upon an innocent," Ruth replies then playfully bites Detlef's shoulder.

Smiling, he lowers the laughing child. "Until then, to whom, pray, are we to entrust our child's soul?"

"Ourselves. As parents we are guardians of both the physical and the spiritual well-being of our child."

"I think I could persuade the brothers to accept that argument."

"A pox on them all if they don't."

"Wife, you are still the heretic, even in this liberal city."

"Now more a seeker of knowledge than a heretic, in as much as my sex will allow."

"I will not have you adopt male attire again. I suspect that would create a scandal even the Remonstrants might find hard to explain. We shall employ the maid at night also to allow more freedom for your studies."

"Detlef, they will burn you yet," she murmurs, smiling.

"Indeed they may. But my deal is not struck yet. My barter has conditions," he says, tickling her.

She pushes him off. "Which are?"

"That you attend the next collegiate meeting in Rijnsburg which, it is said, a great mind and a great mentor has promised to attend."

"Benedict Spinoza?"

"The renegade Hebrew himself, and with your attendance he should feel most at home."

"And who am I to be, Detlef? Felix van Jos, the earnest apprentice? Ruth bas Elazar Saul, the heretic midwife? Or the good Frau Tennen?"

"It is time you wrote to him as your true self. They say that Spinoza is much troubled over Adriaan Koerbagh's death."

"We all are—it is a warning that should be heeded, Detlef."

"Perhaps. But I refuse to live my life in fear. I will preach what I preach and suffer the consequences."

"What about us, your family?"

"You have my love and protection, always, Ruth. Enough gloom. You must come with me to the meeting. I am sure it will be of great solace to Spinoza to see an old associate."

"Perhaps."

They are interrupted by Jacob demanding that he be told, again, the story about Hanke the mouse and how he was taken by the terrible stork.

Leopold bends over a tall pale pink orchid and sniffs at it tentatively. "Some of these blooms are entirely without scent. One wonders if they are to be pollinated by color alone."

The emperor, dressed in his morning robe, stands in the baroque conservatory where he is dwarfed by a cascade of tropical plants and ferns, all gifts from allied colonies.

"It is a magnificent plant, a veritable feat of creation. A present, your highness?"

The inquisitor, his face etched more deeply with the frustrations of the past four years, sniffs at the offered flower then sneezes vigorously. Leopold, amused by the priest's obvious lack of sensuality, smiles.

"From the Grand Fez of Morocco—he courts me for he fears Sultan Mahomet. So, Inquisitor, what urgent information do you have for me that brings me from my morning repose?"

Carlos steps closer.

"I believe you have been having some trouble with the ambitious Georg Friedrich von Waldeck."

The emperor looks up sharply. As much as he personally dislikes the friar he cannot help but admire his political astuteness. For a second he envies the Dominican his spies.

"The leader of the Wetterau Union, like many of the Wittelsbach princes of the Rhineland, is nervous about the Dutch war. He fears it will spread," Leopold replies cautiously.

"So much so that he has opened his court to his Catholic counterparts . . . unusual for a Protestant." The friar's smile broadens.

"Indeed."

"In fact I hear that our good friend Count von Tennen has started a flirtation with von Waldeck. Von Tennen has supplied you with both troops and money in the past to fight the Turk, has he not?"

"Along with many of the Wittelsbachs," Leopold plunges a hand into a flowerpot and rubs the soil between his fingertips.

"A clan so loyal that even Maximilian Heinrich has been seen in the company of von Waldeck. Perhaps Cologne will join the Wetterau Union." Carlos's voice is rich with sarcasm.

Leopold looks away, trying to control a nervous tic in his eye. This is indeed news to him: after Count Gerhard von Tennen's hospitality toward his nephew, the emperor had thought it safe to count on von Tennen's future loyalty. But Maximilian Heinrich . . . he is a constant anxiety.

"It is only natural that the German leagues should feel insecure. Who wouldn't with that buffoon de Witt in the west and Louis' greedy French fingers spreading out from the southeast?"

"Naturally. And naturally we would not want them getting any ideas about their own independence, would we? Somehow I suspect von Waldeck's ambitions might be secular. Before we know it, the Protestants will be getting into bed with the Mohammedans as well as the Catholics. Frankly, it all seems rather obscene not to mention blasphemous."

Barely controlling his anger Leopold snaps the stem of a pale yellow lily then immediately regrets it.

"What are you proposing, Friar? Our audience is quickly drawing to an end."

"Detlef von Tennen—Gerhard's brother—once a Catholic canon with the Cologne chapter is now a Protestant pastor whose lectures openly question both the divinity of the Bible and the territorial rights of your own dynasty, the exalted Hapsburgs, your highness."

"So I have heard, but what of it? He is in Holland—out of our reach, my good friar. Perhaps it would be wise to resign ourselves to his maledictions . . . after all, they are only words."

"He gathers support, and draws interest from your own territories, including some powerful allies within the Wetterau Union."

"He does?"

Seizing his opportunity the inquisitor leans across.

"Detlef von Tennen might be beyond our grasp but Gerhard von Tennen is not. I have a notion that might appeal, for it serves both of us, your majesty: namely, jolting Archbishop Heinrich into remembering who is his emperor and, at the same time, bringing the heretical canon to his knees."

After glancing over his shoulder for spies, the friar steps forward to whisper into the royal ear.

"I know where Detlef von Tennen is, and I believe there is a way of luring him to Cologne to stand trial."

The emperor, brushing an attentive bee away from his face, sits down heavily on a large upturned flowerpot and steels himself for the friar's conspiratorial strategies.

Maximilian Heinrich stares out at the pouring rain. The half-built spire juts out lonely and abandoned. The archbishop has again failed to inspire the funds to resume construction of the cathedral; he has almost given up his vision of the massive Gothic structure soaring above all else in Cologne. Heinrich has felt the power of the Catholic church ebb away during the past four years. Detlef von Tennen's shameful flight to Holland has not helped, nor his very public conversion to the Protestant church—worse, to one of its radical mutations that the decadent Netherlander liberalism seems to encourage like field mushrooms blossoming out of a pail of horse manure.

How could Detlef have betrayed his cousin so? Heinrich can find nothing comprehensible or forgiveable in the canon's actions, as much as he has tried, examining Detlef's exodus again and again. Rather it is a multitude of treacheries: first of the archbishop himself as his cousin's spiritual guide; second of his role as Detlef's mentor, having personally nurtured the young man's career; and third, of his fellow aristocrats. As a Wittelsbach prince, Heinrich feels Detlef is morally obliged to remain loyal to the notion of birthright.

He has shat soundly on us all, Heinrich thinks, and now the family must bear the responsibility. To convert is one thing, but to marry and breed with a Jewish infidel? Unimaginable. Of course, all could be forgiven if the defector would only stop his sermonizing and melt back into the forgettable marshes of Dordrecht, Delft, Amsterdam or wherever the devil it is the irritating man is currently lecturing.

Outside the window, a large raindrop hits the stained glass and rolls down to join a small pool gathering at the base of Saint Anthony's burning feet, drowning two devils with dog's heads and ridiculously oversized corkscrew penises. Heinrich sighs out loud then turns to face Count Gerhard von Tennen, who stands waiting, an unfathomable smile playing over his thin lips.

Impatient, the count slaps his kid and lace gloves against his catalapha breeches, then finding the incense-laden atmosphere of the seminary a little close, sneezes loudly. In sympathy Heinrich offers him his snuffbox. The count, noting the royal crest and thus surmising that the powder is of top quality, takes a large pinch.

"I must thank you for making such a long and precarious journey, Gerhard."

"Oh come, let us not overdramatize. The road is straight and well patrolled these days. Besides, your messenger was most adamant and not entirely without his charms."

"Indeed. How are things at Das Grüntal?"

"Life there varies only with the seasons and thus is safely ensconced in the predictability of nature, unlike the rest of our world, Heinrich. In my mature years I have finally wearied of both court and politics."

"In that case I must apologize, for I bring you here on a political issue."

A very slight twitch mars the count's impeccable features as his jaw tightens.

"I have had word from Vienna, from the emperor himself . . ." Heinrich leans forward and places his hand on the count's stockinged knee. "Our young renegade, your dear brother, causes them much concern. His outrageous sermons have come to Leopold's attention. Detlef must be silenced, otherwise, my dear old friend, there is talk of discrediting the von Tennen name."

"What? Am I to be penalized for my brother's desecrations?"

"As a family originally titled by a prince of the Holy Roman Empire, your name and lands can be repossessed just as easily should the church choose to . . ."

"You would not dare."

"It is not I but a far more insidious and dangerous element who already has much grievance against our errant cleric and his unfortunate choice of wife. The inquisitor arrives from Vienna in a fortnight. If I can persuade him that you will sway your brother into returning to this fair city and making a full and public confession of the error of his ways, then perhaps together we can thwart the will of Vienna, Rome and the Dominican."

"I have no power over Detlef, you know that."

"If you wish to retain your lands, you will find some influence, no matter what it takes."

The archbishop holds out a letter, the emperor's seal clearly visible. "This contains details of the whereabouts of your brother. It is impossible to completely disappear these days, when even the sky has eyes."

"Indeed."

Reluctantly Gerhard takes the letter; already it weighs heavily on him, like a betrayal.

"Heinrich, you astound me. To think that we are cousins."

"Power demands many sacrifices, and matters of the heart belong in the realm of youthful folly—let us not get nostalgic. Besides, beyond twenty years of age there is no such thing as an innocent kindness."

The count laughs bitterly then stands, collecting his ivory-topped cane.

"Heinrich, you deceive yourself. Unlike Detlef, neither you nor I have ever possessed anything remotely resembling innocence from the moment we were born, nay, even conceived. However, I shall endeavor to liberate my brother from his current delusions and bring him back to this city. Until then I trust you will stay the hand of the inquisitor."

With a curt nod, Gerhard von Tennen leaves the archbishop's chambers, followed by his page.

Heinrich, watching the count's trim figure stride through the courtyard some moments later, finds himself remembering a time, many years before, when his own heart would have quickened at the sight. Saddened, he sits back down at his desk.

*M*y dear Brother,

   It may seem strange to you to receive this missive after so many years, but I have grown sentimental in my maturity. The passing traveler has supplied us with some news of you, mainly of your vocation and spreading support among the Lowlanders. Detlef, please be convinced when I swear that I wish to cast aside all religious differences. I seek a reconciliation and, naturally, the acquaintance of my nephew (I do believe you have a son?). My own marriage has proven barren and my life, as you know, has been bereft of children. I would take great pleasure in his company. Also, my health has been failing in this past year. My gamekeeper and companion Herr Woolf was gored in a hunting accident two years ago and I miss him greatly. There is now a hollow echo at Das Grüntal that I wish to eradicate.

   I am willing to make the journey to the port of Amsterdam and have heard that a trading ship of reputation is due to leave the sixth of next month. Please give your reply to the accompanying messenger, he is to be trusted and is instructed to ride back directly to me only.

   Yours in faith and in blood,
   Your brother, Gerhard von Tennen

The Dutch nursemaid playing with Jacob on a low ottoman sneaks a glance at the handsome German chevalier waiting at the door, a royal crest visible on his short cloak, and wonders how the humble Tennen family knows such a man. Meanwhile, at the table Detlef finishes reading the letter from his brother and without a word hands it to his wife.

A moment later Ruth looks up.

"I cannot help myself, Detlef, I mistrust the honesty of his intentions."

"I have my own misgivings, but he is family. I will agree to his visit."

"No."

"Wife, I want him to visit us here. I want him to see what it is to survive by one's wits and not one's estate. This way he will learn humility and true brotherhood."

"But this is a man who has only ever lived by politics. What makes you think his character might have transformed?"

"The awareness of mortality. When a man confronts the end of his life he is left with nothing but a mirror of his actions. Besides, what harm can he do in Amsterdam? We are much loved and well protected, there is nothing to fear. I shall find him a tavern of status for his lodgings. In the meantime I shall compose my reply and you shall trust in the better will of mankind."

"It seems I have no choice."

"Indeed."

Detlef turns away to instruct the nursemaid to offer a jug of hot spiced wine to the messenger.

Intensely frustrated by what she perceives as Detlef's naivety, Ruth sweeps Jacob into her arms and carries him to the kitchen. Will he ever listen, she thinks furiously as she enters the intimate chamber which has become her retreat. How much longer is he going to give untrustworthy people the benefit of his doubt?

The kitchen, a back room dominated by a large hearth which harbors the firepot with the stewpan and peat box on either side of it, is Ruth's private sanctuary, her heart of their house. Against the white plastered wall opposite is a copper sink fed by a pump attached to a cistern, and next to that Detlef's cherished wedding gift to her, a freestanding walnut cupboard of delicate French design with a sparse collection of English porcelain behind its glass doors. Seeing it she cannot help but feel a wave of affection despite her anger, remembering Detlef's childlike enthusiasm when he presented it to her. It is her favorite piece of furniture: a symbol of their marital fidelity and material wealth, and of the Dutch people's acceptance of their union.

Lentil and pheasant soup bubbles on the firepot. Ruth stirs it with a large ladle while Jacob, slung on her hip, plays with her long hair. Mother and child are caught for a moment in a brass mirror hanging on the wall—the reflection of an elliptical magical world. The smell of the soup drifts around the kitchen as the child struggles in Ruth's arms. She puts him down.

As Jacob runs for his spinning top, Ruth finds herself enveloped by a familiar dread, a sensation she has not experienced for years but recalls with vivid intensity as it claws its way through her body. Without thought she begins to recite a kabbalistic chant for protection, but stops when her son, laughing, pulls at her skirts.

In the silence of the sleeping house, in the recess under the stairs—a space little more than a cupboard which Detlef jokingly refers to as Ruth's laboratorium—the midwife is to be found beside the chest she has set up as a desk. The tassel of her nightcap is twisted around her long black plait as she kneels in her damask nightdress, the floorboards cold and hard beneath her reddened knees.

Squinting in the candlelight, she examines a drop of water through a ground lens set in an iron clamp mounted on a saddle of wood. A small dish of pond water waits beside her, while lying next to that is an open book of illustrations, meticulous etchings of the magnified anatomies of insects: the antenna of a beetle, the thorax of a wasp, Beneath the thick lens she watches the minutiae of life enact all manner of dramas. An amoeba propels itself forward in a series of jerky movements, bumping up against a smaller creature, a mass of swirling dots, while another organism divides above it. Fascinated, Ruth holds her breath, waiting while the two sacs, pause next to one another until, with a violent contraction, the larger organism swallows the smaller and doubles in size.

" 'The omnipotent finger of God is here present in the anatomy of the louse, in which you shall find wonder heaped upon wonder and be amazed by the wisdom of God manifest in the most minute matter.' " Detlef's voice startles her.

Ruth smiles at him as he stops reading aloud from the illustrated book. "Swammerdam was right. Here under this lens all kinds of human follies and foibles are repeated in miniature. If the lens could fill a stage, the study of these tiny creatures would be the end of theater."

"It is certainly the end of your sleep, wife."

"Are you displeased I have left your side?"

"No. Just perplexed. I fear you have anxieties you hold from me."

In lieu of a reply Ruth pushes the primitive microscope toward Detlef. He lowers his head to peer through the lens.

"Behold Spinoza's 'substance.' The divine in nature, in the invisible. Sometimes I like to think this is the equivalent of Ein Sof, the essence and light of God, although of course that is a literal intrepretation."

She loves the fact that she can indulge in such discourse, knowing he can contribute.

Detlef studies the pond water a moment then looks up.

"Ruth, we differ in this: you draw your inspiration from *scientia nova* while I draw it from people, from the wondrous transformation faith brings about in them."

"Some do not, or cannot, transform, Detlef."

"I assume you mean my brother?"

She uncovers another dish of water. Brackish, its strong smell fills the alcove.

"This is stagnant water. If I were to place this beneath the glass there would be no signs of life. Nor could I introduce life."

"Ruth, all through my childhood I sought ways of proving my worth and affection to both my father and my brother. I could not prove it through battle, I could not prove it through my service to the church. Let me prove it now through trust."

Ruth closes the book and covers her instruments. She knows there is no purpose in arguing with Detlef, that there is a point beyond which she can no longer sway his judgment. She learned long ago to surrender to this stubbornness of his.

"Come to bed, woman. For tomorrow we are going to Rijnsburg."

Later, as she lies beside him, she finds herself gazing at the few objects she rescued from her cottage in Deutz. Aaron's sword, glimmering in the moonlight, hangs on the wall. Below it, standing on a chest full of linen, is the menorah that once belonged to her father and at its base a bracelet of coral and pearl that was once her mother's. While hidden in the wall lies the Navarros' Zohar. Where is she now in relation to all of this, Ruth sleepily wonders.

Jacob, in the sleeping drawer built underneath the main bed, laughs softly in his dreaming. Ruth peeps through the darnick curtains at her son, his plump cheek sunk into the feathered cushion. Remembering the old suspicion that when a boy laughs in his sleep he is about to be visited by the demon Lilith, she taps him gently on the nose. The child rolls over.

This is what she lives for, her husband and her child, she reminds herself. But how is she to marry her past with her future, the three separate lives she has lived—Ruth, Felix, Frau Tennen—and with her eventual death, who will be left to carry on the history of her father? One day she must find time to write it down for Jacob, for him to have when he is of age. The comforting thought dispels old ghosts and slowly the chattering voices of insomnia begin to dissolve.

Ruth shifts in the bed to curl herself deeper into the sweet aroma of her husband's body, burying her cheek into the fur of his chest where finally she is carried off by a falling and rising sea of half-images and dreams.

It is a small cottage attached to a mill powered by the stream running alongside it. Ruth can hear outside the constant grinding of the heavy stone wheels kept in motion by the turning cogs. It is early evening and the smell of peat fires and manure drifts in through the open window. There are five of them now; four men and herself, sitting silently around a table. Others are still arriving.

Ruth sits at one end of the long table. Roughly hewn, its age is apparent in the wooden top scarred by a thousand knives and a thousand layers of wax. Detlef sits beside her, holding her hand tightly under the table. He is in riding clothes, a short cape slung across his knee, a smudge of dust still visible on his cheek. They have ridden for four hours along the narrow lanes of the Dutch countryside, across bridges, around dykes edging marshy reclaimed fields overlooked by the white and black windmills that watch over the stolen land like lonely sentries, until they reached Rijnsburg, a hamlet on the bend of a river. Once there the couple were silently directed to the low isolated cottage in which they now sit.

Ruth leans over and wipes the smudge from Detlef's face with the end of her sleeve. She cannot help herself, it is an instinctive gesture of intimacy and protectiveness. A wave of pride sweeps over her: he is remarkable, she thinks, this man who has given up everything and risked all both to love her and to live his life freely. Even more so to display the generosity of spirit to accept her for what she is. Detlef looks back at her, a flicker of excitement in his eyes.

She shyly glances away and her gaze falls on the tall man sitting opposite. Conrad van Beuningen. An impressive figure in his late forties, Ruth knows him by reputation only: once the bürgermeister of Amsterdam, now Jan de Witt's greatest adviser on foreign policy. The fact that such a famous man is present means it is indeed a highly significant gathering. Dressed in a somber-colored tunic of the finest wool, Beuningen nods once at Detlef.

They are interrupted by five men entering in cloaks and hats, bending low to step into the cottage then shaking the rain off their clothes. Standing within the protective circle the four others form around him is a far shorter individual. The atmosphere of the room is immediately galvanized by his presence, as if all are unconsciously deferring to the intensity emanating from this otherwise insignificant creature. Of a pale and delicate complexion, his black hair falls to his shoulders and his large dark eyes smolder beneath a battered wide-brimmed hat.

Benedict Spinoza takes off his hat and Ruth, now on her feet, catches her breath. She had forgotten how beautiful he is with his large expressive face, high cheekbones and delicate Spanish features, his evident indifference to his own physical attributes only enhancing his allure.

The philosopher glances around the room, nodding and gently smiling at those assembled, taking his time to shake the hands of all in attendance. Ruth, paralyzed with anticipation, says nothing for she knows he has not recognized her in her female attire. After an eternity he turns toward her.

"We collegians have not had the pleasure of a woman among us since the visit of the English Quaker, Margaret Fell. Indeed, I have never regarded theology or philosophy to be the domain of the feminine."

"Good sir, you know me not as the feminine but as the masculine."

With that she slips off her head scarf. Spinoza looks perplexed then slowly a gleam of delighted recognition crosses his face.

"Felix van Jos?"

" 'Tis the slow-witted youth himself, Benedict."

The others look on bewildered as, smiling, he takes her hands into his own. "Ruth, the girl has become a woman."

"A wife and mother, sir, but I still practice my craft and retain my curiosity in *scientia nova*."

"I had been wondering what became of you. Your correspondence finished so suddenly during the Great Plague. I feared the worst."

"Fear not, it is really me, solid in flesh and spirit. For the last four years I have been living in Amsterdam, but I had not the courage to face you until now."

"Pray why?"

"I have always been aware that your acceptance of my sex is predicated upon your observation that I am a freak of nature: a man's intellect trapped within the form of a woman."

"Indeed, I still hold the opinion that women have not by nature equal rights with men, and that thus it cannot be that both sexes should rule alike, much less that men should be ruled by women."

The other men in the room break into laughter, amused by the absurdity of such a notion. Only Detlef remains sober-faced.

Glancing at him. Spinoza smiles indulgently before continuing. "Therefore it follows that women should be excluded from government because of their natural weakness."

Unable to control himself, Detlef interrupts.

"With all respect, my wife has all the qualities I would look for in a leader although she has no desire to lead."

"Your wife?"

Spinoza glances from Detlef back to Ruth, who is defiant despite her burning cheeks.

"I believe you know my husband, Detlef von Tennen?"

"Naturally, his reputation as a preacher and theologian precedes him, but I see now he has other recommendations."

"He has. For you see, my most valued mentor, I took your notion to heart and I too regarded myself as an aberration and excluded all possibility of being loved and accepted by a man for my true nature. But as you now observe, Benedict, I believe we may both have been wrong."

The room falls silent as all eyes turn to the philosopher. For a moment a cloud of irritation crosses Spinoza's benign features, then suddenly his face breaks into an expression of amused perplexity as he extends his hand to Detlef.

"I congratulate you on your enlightenment, but you must forgive me if I can only meet you halfway. Women should never be in government, by this I stand."

"Halfway is at least some of the way. In this we can agree to differ. I am honored just to be in the presence of such eminent intellects."

Detlef's reply is firm and not in the least obsequious, Ruth observes. Her husband and she are of one mind, bound by one spirit, she thinks with renewed respect for his courage, although it is this outspoken bravery that makes her nervous for his safety.

Detlef's gaze remains upon the philosopher. If Spinoza's observations about the differences between man and woman are limited, so be it, he thinks. He still has a true comprehension of where man sits in the monumental scale of the universe, and he lives his philosophy. There is no compromise between his beliefs and his actions. His perception makes everything divine. He knows that all that is around him is God. This I respect, he thinks. Inspired, Detlef cannot help but feel immense gratitude toward the woman whose devotion has made the encounter with this luminary possible.

The philosopher takes his place at the head of the table. There is a flurry of chair-scraping and muffled coughs as the other men follow suit. Ruth, beside Detlef again, is reminded of an eccentric Last Supper with the philosopher as a bizarre Christ figure surrounded by his silent yet totally attentive disciples. Who would be Judas? Any man present could notify the ecclesiastical authorities of any philosophizing which might be deemed blasphemous. And these are particularly dangerous times. She shudders, remembering the fate of Adriaan Koerbagh, who, if he were alive, would be sitting among them.

The silence thickens as Spinoza very deliberately packs a clay pipe then places a large bound manuscript on the table before him. Only after balancing a wire-rimmed pair of lenses on his nose does he begin to speak.

"Firstly I wish to thank all those present. In this current climate it is no mean feat to speak out even in the company of trusted and like minds. In many ways it is precisely this that has propelled me to extend my writings to my latest treatise, *Tractatus theologico-politicus*. For within it is illustrated the belief that freedom to philosophize cannot only be granted without injury to piety and the peace of the commonwealth, but that the peace of the commonwealth and piety are endangered by the suppression of this *very* freedom. I have also set out to prove that faith is something separate from philosophy, however there is room for both to coexist in a truly democratic Republic. In fact, I believe this to be a necessity within a Republic.

"These are unpredictable times. There are friends who once sat with us who have already been martyred. I would like to salute the imprisoned, the exiled and those individuals who, despite great personal danger to themselves, have risen above their traditional upbringings to find faith and love through belief born out of the experience of life itself. For to do so is to truly realize the celestial within us," the philosopher concludes, looking directly at Detlef and Ruth.

The coach rolls to a halt outside the narrow redbrick house. The coachman, glancing at the number painted above the brass knocker, snorts derisively and pulls up the horses. What his elegant German passenger wants in such a humble abode one can only imagine; whatever it is it is bound to be sinful, the coachman thinks, winding the reins around the wooden rail of the carriage and wondering at the strangeness of the times in this uncertain Holland.

With a flourish he opens the door. His passenger stares in dismay at the surrounds, a perfumed handkerchief pressed to his patrician nose. Thanking the coachman in bad Dutch, he alights, trying carefully not to soil his kid boots in a gutter awash with mud and swill.

The count gazes up at his brother's house, humiliated that a von Tennen could demean himself thus. There is only one saving grace, he thinks: a beggar is cheaper to buy off than a duke.

As he steps across the cobbled pavement he notices that the front of the house at least is immaculately kept, with a pot holding a rosebush on either side of the oak door. Through the large window on the ground floor he can see the bowed head of his brother illuminated by the dull golden light of a lamp. On Detlef's lap sits a child, a small blond-haired boy who immediately reminds the count of his brother at the same age.

I cannot afford sentimentality, Gerhard thinks, reminding himself that this child, half-Jew, is an abomination, a travesty of the von Tennen lineage. Nevertheless, as he leans on his cane, a distant recollection he thought he had long buried streams through him: Detlef aged six being presented to his father in his first military uniform. The child, fearing the old viscount's disapproval, had stumbled over the miniature sword they had thrust into his sash, then wept at the angry shouts of his father. Gerhard, a youth of eighteen, had done nothing to protect the young Detlef from the irrational fury of the viscount; anger Gerhard had later understood as the embittered frustration of an aristocrat forced to watch his land being carved away section by section.

There was a constant unspoken battle between their mother and her husband. Gerhard had watched the arranged marriage slowly calcify, any façade of happiness disappearing when the old viscount took to keeping a mistress openly in Bonn while his wife retreated into the sanctuary of religion. The viscount, hardened by battle and politics, could not stand the piousness of his Bavarian wife and so when Detlef fell increasingly under his mother's influence, his father penalized him for it, finding the young boy's temperament and physical resemblance to Katrina von Tennen insufferable. As the older brother I was culpable, I should have protected Detlef more, the count thinks regretfully. Tucking his cane beneath his arm he marches up the four stone steps and raps sharply on the door.

Ruth looks up from her sewing but Detlef is already on his feet. "Esther, kindly answer the door," he instructs the maid, determined not to open it himself. The maid puts down her sewing and hurries out.

"Girl, there is no need to stand on ceremony. Let me in, it would be unsafe to loiter on this step any longer," the count commands in German.

The Dutch maid, not understanding a word, steps aside. Behind her the count hears Detlef's distinctive laugh.

"Gerhard, what do you fear? The pickpockets or the whores?"

"Both, you scoundrel."

Stepping out of the shadows Detlef welcomes his brother. Spontaneously the two men embrace with genuine affection. Once released, the count totters for a second, surprised at the passion of the reconciliation. He had forgotten how much he actually misses his brother.

Handing his cape and cane to the maid, Count von Tennen peers into the dimly lit entrance hall which also doubles as the living room. Behind Detlef he can barely make out Ruth standing stiffly, the child in her arms. The count, sensing her disapproval, bows formally. "Fräulein."

"Frau Tennen. We are both officially Protestants and married now."

"So I have heard. Detlef, you should have notified me, I would have sent gifts."

"We managed," Ruth replies, acutely conscious of the circumstances of their last meeting, two lifetimes ago at Das Grüntal when she was called to minister to the young Prince Ferdinand.

His brother has grown old, Detlef observes, there is a sadness about his features, a new humanity . . . or is he merely imagining such things?

"Esther, wine for the count, he needs fortification after such a long journey. I trust that the tavern I recommended suffices?"

"It is very civilized. It is true what they say about the Netherlands, they really are the apex of the New World. Today I saw fruit and spices I have never seen before. For example, a fruit that resembles a love apple yet is hard on the outside, while inside are many sweet red seeds like gemstones. They tell me it is the fruit that Persephone ate in the underworld, to the delight of her husband Hades."

"A pomegranate, that is the name for this fruit," Ruth interjects sharply, still distrusting the count's enthusiasm.

"I see you are as learned as ever, sister-in-law."

The count turns back to Detlef. "You look well, brother, this new life suits you."

"It suits every man to be living honestly and within his own moral skin. But you, sir, there is a sadness I have not seen before . . ."

"I am alone, Detlef. Two winters ago I lost my dear companion, Herr Woolf. My new solitude has left me with little appetite for life or many of the blood sports I did so enjoy."

"There is little that stirs the soul in comparison with the machinations of the court."

"I thought you had abandoned the political life for the elusive pleasure of being a zealot?"

"Zealot? No, I am a Remonstrant."

"One of those newfangled Calvinists," the count remarks wryly.

"I shall resist the temptation to convert you, Gerhard. I fear it would be a waste of a good sermon."

"Indeed!"

"I am merely the servant of my congregation. But tell me, how is our good cousin Maximilian Heinrich?" Detlef asks, smiling.

"Rounded and perhaps a touch more maudlin. Little has changed in Cologne, although we now entertain a good Dutch garrison. As you know, our fair city will always whore herself for the right price. Speaking of which, there is one piece of news that might be of interest: the good lady Birgit Ter Lahn von Lennep is recently a widow, the prettiest and richest in the city. If I remember, you were confessor to the family for many years."

Detlef glances at Ruth, who is twisting a string of seed pearls that hangs low on her dress.

"Gerhard, you must understand that here in Amsterdam we are the Tennens, a plain German immigrant family. Our lives before exist in a world we no longer acknowledge or discuss."

"I am sad to hear that, Detlef. Cologne misses you. There were many who respected you, both aristocrat and bürger. Many still do. But enough of Cologne, let me see my nephew."

Detlef kneels and pushes Jacob, who has been hiding behind a chair, toward his uncle. The boy shyly stands before the count, clutching a toy rabbit.

"Jacob, bow to your uncle."

The four-year-old draws his heels together and bows formally, a gesture which surprises the count. So the Jew-child has some manners, even if they are the mimicked actions of an intelligent monkey, he observes, privately appalled at his brother's obvious love for the illegitimate child. Adopting a fake expression of affection he glances at the boy.

"He is delightful, but sister-in-law, you must allow me to take him to a good Dutch tailor and have him made up some satin breeches and a matching cape."

"Jacob is not lacking in clothes and has no need of charity."

"I should think not. It is just that I have a fancy to commission a portrait of the child and myself. A painter from Delft has been recommended, Pieter de Hooch. I hear he is fair and able to give a reasonable likeness—with your permission of course."

Detlef looks at Jacob who smiles innocently back at him. The idea that his son might be accepted as part of the von Tennen family fills him with a furtive pleasure. Pensive, he looks across at Ruth but is interrupted by Jacob pulling at his sleeve.

"Papa, I would like that."

Relieved that the decision has been made for him. Detlef immediately claps his hands in celebration.

"Excellent. And now we shall eat the good German food Esther and Ruth have prepared for us."

"Thank God, for after a single day I have already tired of herring!"

The tailor measures the child's leg with a piece of string then holds it against a yardstick. Stiflingly hot with the damp air of Amsterdam, the atelier is a small cave filled with bolts of silk, wool, cotton from India and sumptuous pieces of embroidery stretched out on small wooden frames. In the center of the room Jacob stands perfectly still, holding out his arms. Esther, the maid, idly fingers a tassel of silk ribbon.

"He's a good boy," the tailor, a Jew from Lisbon, says to the mother, secretly wondering about her black hair and dark eyes. The exotic-looking woman and the elderly aristocrat make a strange couple. The German, conspicuously moneyed, reclining in the elegant French chair the tailor always presents for his wealthy clients, is obviously a Christian gentleman. But the woman . . . ? Who cares, the tailor reminds himself, as long as their money is good.

"Naturally he is a good boy, he has noble blood," replies the count in an authoritative tone, sensing the tailor's curiosity. Of course it takes one to sniff out another, the aristocrat thinks to himself. Still, he will not have to suffer the indignity much longer.

He points to a bolt of cloth with his walking cane. "The breeches should be in velvet, dark blue of the highest quality to match my own, with an embroidered jerkin ribboned at the waist in the French style," he orders curtly.

"Uncle, am I to have new boots also?"

"You are to have pumps that are buttoned at the side and you shall sit on my right, a hunting dog at your feet."

"A dog! Esther! Mama! I'm to have a dog!"

"Only for the painting, Jacob."

Ruth, watching Jacob's excitement, is anxious that he might be corrupted by his uncle's taste for luxury. She looks at the count, his elegant figure gazing down at the boy. Is it possible that approaching old age and the desire for family have tempered the man? He has been nothing but coolly courteous toward Ruth since his arrival. And what of his distress at his brother's poverty? Is the offer of a stipend out of genuine concern or an attempt to control? Ruth cannot tell. He is either a master of strategy or truly hungry for family. Is Detlef right to refuse? She marvels at his resolve but, more realistically, knows they could use the money. She is growing weary of midwifery and secretly fears the work will make her old before her time. Detlef's stern response floats back into her mind. "*Allow him to spend his money on the child, but not on us. To do so would mean becoming indebted and I will not be beholden to an institution with which I have an ethical disagreement.*"

The moral high ground is not always the most practical position, Ruth finds herself thinking, then, remembering the passions of her youth, wonders what she has become. She is pulled back into the room as the tailor drops his tape and reaches for a bolt of cloth.

"Will the dog eat Punti?" Jacob asks, holding up his toy rabbit.

Swallowing his distaste, the count feigns a laugh and pulls the child onto his lap. "Only if you want him to. Do you want him to tear him up into little pieces?"

Jacob gives his uncle a solemn stare then answers with great seriousness, "No, I don't."

The count laughs. "Then he shan't. I give you the word of a gentle man."

A bell rings at the door and a page enters dressed in the colors of his master's house. He approaches Ruth. "Are you Mevrouw Tennen, the midwife?"

"Is Mevrouw van Voorten in labor?"

"For a good three hours she has been screaming for you," the page replies dramatically.

Smiling at his anxiety, Ruth places a hand on his arm. "When women labor they scream, but there is no need to be afraid, she is a sturdy woman."

"Madame, my mistress needs you now."

She glances at Gerhard and Esther and hesitates, reluctant to leave. The count, seemingly reading her distress, puts a hand on her shoulder.

"Fear not, the child will be safe with me and the maid, I promise."

Ruth looks into his eyes and for the first time believes she sees genuine affection there. The servant tugs at her sleeve,

"We must hurry."

She wraps her cloak around her then pulls her son close, the sweet smell of his hair enveloping her as she lifts him.

"Jacob, Uncle will take you to the painter's this afternoon and then home. You will be a good boy, won't you, and you won't cry for mama?"

Jacob, swallowing, nods.

Ruth turns to the maid. "Esther, make sure he wears his jacket and that he does not go hungry."

The maid nods, her broad face expressionless. The count puts his hand on the boy's tiny shoulder.

"I promise I shall have him safely home before sunset."

Jacob flings his arms around Ruth's neck and clings to her. She kisses him then places his hand firmly into the count's.

"Jacob, you are to be a brave boy and behave for your uncle. I shall see you in the morning when you will have forgotten I was gone at all."

"Kiss Punti."

Jacob holds up the toy rabbit, and after kissing the motley torn face of the one-eyed cloth rabbit, Ruth steps out with the manservant.

The count curls his fingers around the small hand and marvels at the blind trust of both mother and child.

A chill whistling through the crack under the door teases the back of Detlef's neck. He pulls up the collar of his woolen undervest and tries to concentrate on the Dutch pamphlet he is deciphering: a translation of one of his lectures entitled "Must man be a slave to superstition?"

Somewhere in the street a door slams shut. It is past midnight and the house feels profoundly empty without his wife and child.

"*. . . the notion that faith might be a human necessity, a biological need, suggests that perhaps the ability to have faith elevates man above all other animals; but how to transform a belief in witchcraft, goblins, angels and devils to a conviction which embraces the* scientia nova *and the perfect geometry of nature, which, in truth, can only be a manifestation of the substance of God himself . . .*"

Detlef pauses and absentmindedly runs his hand along the underside of the Flemish desk. He is surprised when his fingers bump against a protrusion. He looks underneath, an amulet is nailed to the inside of one of the wooden legs. Detlef pulls it off and gazes at the small stone tablet. Tilting it to the light he can see that it has one Hebrew letter carved into it. Ruth's doing, one of her kabbalistic spells—for what? he marvels, amused. Protection, good study, prosperity? For all her defiant belief in the hard logic of the material world he knows that his wife still clings secretly to the ways of her mother's family. Confronted by her superstition, Detlef has made the conscious decision to see it not as a flaw, but as a strength, and given the Remonstrants' belief that there is no predestination in life, he finds himself wondering whether Ruth's instinctive faith in the written incantations might actually influence the outcome of events.

Ruth. He always aches for her when they are apart although he would never admit to such a weakness. Could it be a sin to love one's wife this much? Possibly, for to love this intensely suggests he cannot accept the inherently transitory nature of both affection and life. He still finds it miraculous that he is able to love at all and that he found love so late in life. It is as if his identity and existence in Cologne now lie under a thick opaque glass, cloudy, out of focus and increasingly immaterial.

The town crier calls one o'clock. Detlef goes to the window and looks out over the narrow canal. A fog has settled on the water, transforming the lit windows of the tavern opposite into an oasis of dull gold in the dirty white. Where is she? And where is the maid? He knows Ruth was called to a birthing but to take the child also . . . ? The notion worries him. Jacob is far too young to be exposed to such female matters. As if to answer his fears the clatter of horses' hooves echoing in the narrow lane draws him from his anxious reverie.

Outside a small coach pulls up. Ruth, her face concealed by a deep hood, climbs down. With one bound Detlef is already running down the steep wooden stairs toward the entrance hall. He hauls open the front door before the midwife has a chance to insert her key.

"Ruth, your face wears the marks of exhaustion. Come, there is broth in the cooking pot. But where is Jacob?"

Ruth, pushing her hood back, wheels around.

"What do you mean? I left him with Esther and your brother. Is the maid not with you?"

"The house is empty."

They stare at each other, horrified. Just then Esther sidles in through the door, stinking of beer, her face flushed and satiated. Ruth grabs the girl and shakes her violently.

"Where is Jacob? I told you to look after him!"

Bewildered, the drunken maid rolls her eyes. "Isn't he in his bed? The gentleman count did say he was going to look after him."

Furious, Detlef pushes Ruth aside. "What do you mean? You should never have let him out of your sight! What do we pay you for?"

The girl's large red face crumples into tears. "He said he would look after him, he said I could go and see my man Joris. I trusted him . . . He's family, Mijnheer Tennen."

Detlef lets her go; immediately the maid runs to her bedroom sobbing.

Panicked, Ruth has already thrown her hood back on.

"Wait, wife, there must be a mistake. Perhaps my brother has taken him to his quarters for the night . . ."

"What have I done? I should never have left my child, I should have stayed!"

"Ruth, you had to attend the birth. It is I who is to be blamed. I should never have trusted Gerhard!"

Ruth throws open the front door, the icy air rushes in.

"What about Jacob? What do you think he wants with our son?" She stares up at him, full of dread.

"We shall go to the tavern immediately and put your fears to rest."

Determined not to let his own misgivings intensify hers, Detlef turns his back to her as he slips a short dagger into his belt.

Staying close to her husband's side, Ruth half-walks, half-runs across the slippery cobblestones. The fog has become a light drizzle yet the tradesmen still have their stalls set up for passing night trade. Flames dance across an alley wall as a fire encased in an iron pot flares up. A crippled man roasts chestnuts over it while a couple of nightwatchmen warm themselves at the glowing coals.

Under one streetlamp a *nagtloper*, a nightwalker, her pox-scarred face lurid with rouge, lurches toward a boatman on his way to work. Grinning toothlessly she reaches for his crotch. Shrugging, the young man pushes her hand away. On the other side of the lane a farmer herds a small flock of pigs toward the slaughterhouse past a herring cart glistening with the day's catch.

Detlef strides along with his hand firmly around Ruth's arm. A multitude of scenarios crowds his mind as he wrestles with his demons. He cannot believe his brother would have taken the child. To what purpose? He is his blood as well as Detlef's, for what reason could he want to hurt Jacob? Surely it is an innocent mistake. Surely he has the boy with him at the tavern, thinking it too late to return him to the house.

The couple cross a narrow stone bridge, making their way from the Harlemmerstraat near the docks at the western edge of the city toward its center. They pass the Achterburgwal. A cart of drunken prostitutes pulls up at the tall iron gates of the Spinhuis. The windows of the grim correctional house are still lit as the pitiful inmates finish their long day of spinning and sewing. Several of the chained whores in the cart break into a mournful rendition of the "Hague Kermis" as the vehicle passes through the forbidding gates.

Ruth peers into the distance, the swinging sign of the count's tavern is just visible through the fog. Shaking off Detlef's arm, she begins to run toward it.

"The smart German gentleman? Might be sleeping, might not."

The nightwatchman wraps his arms over his huge belly which flops over elegant breeches now stained and aged, the weight of the aristocrat's bribe knocking nicely against his thigh.

Detlef reaches into his purse and pulls out five stuivers. "There's more if you tell us exactly where he is."

Ruth pushes forward. "Please, our son is missing. He is only a child."

The nightwatchman weighs the silver; it is exactly the same price the aging aristocrat paid him earlier for his silence. Detlef, taking the hint, adds another coin.

"The count and his nephew left this evening, about three hours ago as the sun falls."

"Left for where?"

"That I do not know, but he has taken his baggage."

"He has gone and he has taken Jacob!"

Ruth, her eyes ringed by exhaustion, lets out an anguished howl. Detlef wraps his cloak around her. She cannot shake the image of the small boy being bundled into a carriage. Will the count have fed him properly? Does he know that Jacob is frightened of the dark and cannot sleep alone? And what of Punti, his favorite toy? Panic confuses her, filling her with irrational anxieties. She clutches at Detlef's jerkin.

"We must do something! Jacob is in danger, I can sense it!"

The nightwatchman, flushed with shame, hurriedly shuts the gate against the couple and his own guilt, his only consolation the heavy purse at his hip. Rain begins to fall as Detlef rocks Ruth while trying to steady his rising fear.

"Sshh, we will try de Hooch and then, if we have to, we shall ride to Cologne this very night. With luck we will catch them at the border."

The hammering at the front door buzzes around the young apprentice's head like a swarm of demented wasps. Half-asleep he swipes at the imaginary creatures then sits bolt upright. Does his new master have debts? The painter swore not when he hired the fourteen-year-old, a talented farmer's son from de Hooch's own town of Delft. A pox on the bailiffs! Perhaps they have the wrong studio.

The apprentice waits for a second then, furious, pulls on an old pair of rough barras breeches. Immediately his crotch starts to itch. Cursing, he runs to the wooden door. Pulling open the top half he is surprised to see a couple, the gentleman obviously a pastor of some Protestant denomination and his young wife who, the apprentice notices immediately, is beautiful, despite her eyes which are swollen from crying.

"Is my master dead then?" the obtuse youth asks, a question which momentarily confuses the couple.

"Is this Pieter de Hooch's studio?"

"What if it is?" the apprentice replies suspiciously, determined to defend his master's privacy at any cost.

"Is the artist here?"

"My master is presently detained in Delft, he is not due back until Shrove Tuesday."

"Were you here throughout the day yesterday?"

"Indeed, sire, never left the place."

"Did a German gentleman visit, with a small boy? My brother has commissioned a portrait, his name is Count Gerhard von Tennen."

"No, Master de Hooch has not taken a portrait as a commission for over three months. Besides, I would know the name."

Ruth pulls at Detlef's sleeve. "They are to Cologne, I know it."

"Is Master de Hooch in trouble?"

"No, good lad. Return to your slumber."

As soon as the bleary-eyed youth closes the half-door, Ruth begins to run through the rain in the direction of their own district.

"Ruth, please, this will require some strategy. We know nothing yet," Detlef shouts, following her.

Swept up by fear, she spins around. "We know that our child has been taken and that he is probably in danger. I was a fool, I should have stayed with him, what have I done?"

"What have we both done?" Detlef answers, desperate with guilt himself.

Ruth clutches at him. "The count will be riding tonight for the

Rhineland. I for one will be following and . . ." she snatches the dagger from his belt, "I shall go armed. I shall wear my cousin's sword if necessary."

He stares at her, seeing the exhaustion drawing a web of lines on her taut face.

"I am sorry, my love, for trusting my brother so blindly. But I hold hope there may yet be a rational explanation. I will ride after them. You are ailing, you will stay in Amsterdam and wait for my word."

She takes his hand firmly. "No. We ride together."

Tucked up in a blanket Jacob sleeps peacefully despite the motion of the coach which bounces over the rough road. His eyelashes are dark against his cheek, the toy rabbit is clutched in one hand while the other lolls over the edge of the seat.

The count sits opposite, snoring slightly, his face pushed up against the darnick upholstery. The carriage lurches over a large pothole, banging his head suddenly against the wood paneling. The aristocrat wakes, irritated. Orientating himself, he stares at the small boy. Thank God the brat is asleep, he thinks, wondering what he will feed him in Cologne. If Detlef had to breed why couldn't he have done it sensibly, with a Christian woman who would at least have provided the family with offspring of a decent lineage? Exasperated, the count pushes open the curtain.

Outside a half moon illuminates the forest beyond. The thick tree trunks stand silent in judgment, staring back at him like a council of magistrates wrapped in their shadowy robes. A broad river runs alongside the muddy track, the moonlight transforming it into a silvery galaxy of sparkling currents. The count guesses it is the Maas. We must still be in Holland, he surmises, wondering how much more of the bumpy ride he must endure before they are in the sanctuary of the Rhineland.

The forest opens up into a field. Already a peasant is out there, harvesting cabbages by the dull light of his lantern, his dog sitting patiently beside him, The count watches, hypnotized by the rhythmic sway of his shovel. A blind serf, little more than a beast, doing the same repetitive work day in day out, he thinks. How can Detlef believe that all men are equal when confronted with the animal stupidity of these people? What mental facilities, do they possess to appreciate the finer things in life—music, literature, a beautiful object? None, as far as the count can see. No, he is correct to take the child, he is rescuing Detlef from himself. This deed, however despicable, is for a higher purpose, to preserve the lineage of the von Tennens, an ancient family, a noble clan who have served kings and princes for four centuries. He cannot sacrifice everything for one deluded sibling, the count thinks. He will not let the church take his land or his title, even if it means using this half-Christian, half-Jewish mongrel as bait.

His task is only to entice Detlef back to the city, after all; he should feel no guilt. They have promised that if Detlef makes a full confession they will reinstate him as canon again. Surely his brother will agree, it is a small price to pay to retain the von Tennen lands. Besides, they would not dare to harm a Wittelsbach. No, the maximum penalty will be but a short prison sentence. Consoling himself with these thoughts, which eventually bleed into the rhythm of the creaking wheels, the troubled aristocrat falls back into sleep.

Jacob jerks open his eyes. The first beams of sunlight stream through the half-covered window and the holes in the coach's ceiling. Confused, he wants to cry, but then remembers Ruth asking him to be brave for his uncle. Mama would be proud, he thinks. He has been courageous all night and hasn't wept once, even when he almost dropped Punti in the gutter. The thought is some consolation for his sudden loneliness.

Comforted by the memory of his mother's expressive eyes, the child sits up. His stomach growls; hungry, he wonders when they will arrive at his papa's cottage and whether the maid will have breakfast ready. Then he remembers that the count has promised him his very own pony and a puppy.

Funny uncle, he thinks, looking at the old man asleep opposite. The count's wig has slipped and his mouth lies open revealing several brown and stained molars. He is not frightening at all. Why was Mama worried?

Suddenly the coach pulls to a halt, causing his uncle to fall off his seat. Jacob, delighted at the spectacle, bursts into peals of laughter.

They have been traveling for three hours straight. Ruth, Aaron's sword strapped to her side, her legs gripping the saddle, is filled with a determination that shapes every muscle toward a sole purpose: to rescue her son. Detlef, racing beside her, has resorted to a galloping motion he mastered while riding with the chevaliers during the war. His flesh now melded with his mount they are one beast, a massive centaur hurtling against wind and time, propelled by a single quest.

The flying hooves consume the narrow track mile by mile as Detlef and Ruth ride on in silence, stopping for nothing. Oblivious to the passing landscape, they ride through worlds that mock them with unblemished sanctuary. Here is a cottage with a light burning, a child safely sleeping within its walls; there is a young son helping his father with the early morning milking.

Detlef is angry. Murderous. Astounded at the audacity with which he has been betrayed. He cannot believe his brother has misled him so deliberately. Shocked by his own naivety, he tries to find a rationale for it as he relives the events over and over in his mind. It is his newfound faith, he thinks as his anxiety poisons everything, his stupid fantasy that the base nature of man is redeemable, that blood is thicker than greed. The very premise of his new life has been shaken. What shall be the legacy of this treachery? Will Ruth ever trust him again? And his son, what of his beloved son?

As the horse's legs pound beneath him, Detlef finds that a part of himself, the idealist, still clings to the hope that somehow there has been a misunderstanding, that his brother has assumed they know about his return to Cologne. But then why take the child?

Gerhard, exasperated, swings around from the window of his Cologne town house. His nephew, sullen and red-faced, sits rigidly at the dining table.

"Come, Jacob, you must eat!"

The count picks up a slice of the meat and holds it under the boy's nose. The child pushes his hand away.

"I want Papa and Mama."

"They will be here tomorrow."

"You said that yesterday."

The young nursemaid the count has hired flinches slightly as the man grabs the child. She has been paid enough not to ask questions but the young boy's obvious distress has her wondering. Where are the parents? Is the child really an orphan as his uncle claims? If so, why does he keep asking for his mother?

"Jacob."

The count leans into the child's face. The small boy, lips pursed, looks downward as his eyes brim with tears.

"Don't you trust your uncle?"

Momentarily confused, Jacob glances up; he doesn't trust him but Detlef has taught him it would be impolite to say so. He wishes his papa was there. He would know exactly what to say, he always knows how to make angry people happy. But Jacob doesn't understand why his uncle is so angry with him. Why didn't Mama say they were going on a trip? Tears well up in the young child's eyes as he remembers his parents and how happy they were the last time they were all together, laughing on Mama's bed. For fear of making a mistake, he decides to say nothing. Instead he closes his eyes, imagining that he is back home, tinkering on the keys of the old clavichord his father has given him.

"Jacob?"

But the child has withdrawn entirely into himself, eyes screwed tightly closed, his chin determinedly lowered to his chest.

The count, losing his temper, shakes him violently but Jacob, fiercely determined to stay out of reach, keeps his eyes shut.

"As you wish, young man."

Curse the brat; if he wasn't the bait in the trap the count would have given him up to the poorhouse by now. Useless ill-bred mongrel, it just isn't in his nature to be helpful, the count concludes, gazing bitterly at the sullen boy. He turns to the nursemaid, a timorous girl little more than a child herself, who has been fighting to keep her hands by her side.

"Take him into the bedchamber and keep him there."

The nursemaid goes to pick up Jacob. Immediately he wraps his legs around her and, eyes still shut, snuggles up against her small bosom. Without a word she carries him out of the elegant dining room.

The count takes a morsel of meat and tears it slowly while staring out the window at the bustling street beyond. Why hasn't Detlef yet come for his son? His brother must be desperate with despair. Could he be in the city already?

Below a street peddler sells a bundle of faggots to a serving maid. His aged wife, her back bent, is beside him. Suddenly the peddler catches the count's gaze. The blue eyes staring up from under the battered felt hat look familiar. Before the count has a chance to flick through his memory, the peddler's woman pulls the man away. The aristocrat turns back to the room. Detlef is here in Cologne, he reassures himself; he can sense it as surely as he can sense a winner in the gambling pit.

Restless, he contemplates the short walk down to the docks. He could buy some distraction among the young sailors if he so desires. Perhaps it is exactly the adventure he needs, he considers, wondering if the violence of a mindlessly sexual embrace would exorcise his agitation. Glancing at the Viennese clock on the wall he reluctantly decides that it would be prudent to keep guard until his brother appears.

Ruth pulls Detlef away from beneath the window of the count's town house. "Are you mad, husband? Do you mean to have us both arrested and our child lost forever?" she whispers, frantically packing the bundle of twigs into one side of the cart which they purchased, along with the old clothes and tattered hats, from an ancient journeyman who was happy to sell his silence and his persona for a handsome sum.

Detlef, trembling with fury, pulls his hat lower over his brow.

"Forgive me, I have lost my wits in anger."

"It will not be anger but strategy that wins our child back. You know that, Detlef."

He nods, smearing the soot deeper into his cheeks, fearing Gerhard might have recognized him.

It is the second time they have journeyed from the tavern in the docklands where they have taken chambers, an area in which no one would suspect they might stay. The inn, infamous for its brawls and bad broth, has the further advantage of being frequented by foreign sailors and members of the Dutch resident garrison, none of whom know or care about a heretic preacher and his wife. The disguise was Ruth's idea. Frightened that they might be recognized on the street, she sees no advantage in confrontation and has insisted they steel themselves against their panic and design a plan of rescue.

It is a strategy that nearly backfired when, on the very, morning they arrived exhausted and wild-eyed with anguish, they spied Jacob in the arms of a nurse at one of the count's windows. It was Ruth then, her heart jabbering in blind urgency, who was prevented by Detlef from pounding on the count's front door.

The archbishop's coach, adorned with trimmings and banners depicting the three Magi, turns into the narrow lane. Immediately Ruth pulls Detlef into a rough embrace, masking his face. The couple crouch inches away from Maximilian Heinrich and Monsignor Solitario as they climb down from the carriage, stepping carefully over the debris in the gutter to make their way toward the elegant portico.

Detlef, seeing the archbishop lace his arm through the inquisitor's, quivers with repressed fury. "We are betrayed," he mutters darkly into Ruth's hair.

Ruth tightens her arms around her husband. "Fight now and all is lost."

"But we cannot cower here like dogs."

"We shall get our revenge, I promise," she whispers back, clutching at his hand which now covers the hilt of his hidden dagger.

While the archbishop's page bangs upon the count's door, Carlos, older and fatter, glances languidly around the street. He sees nothing but a couple of grubby peasants mauling each other passionately beside their broken cart.

"Lust is in the eye of the beholder, evidently," he remarks to Heinrich, who laughs, secretly condemning the priest as a prude.

Inside, the count's reverie is rudely interrupted by a footman. "Sire, the archbishop and the inquisitor wait below for an audience."

The count pulls on his jacket and follows the servant down the elegant wooden stairs.

Outside, Ruth and Detlef quickly pack up their barrow and push it swiftly out of sight.

Maximilian Heinrich and a smaller older man of Mediterranean appearance stand in the elaborately decorated reception room. In the corner a concoction of spikenard and storax burns in an incense holder, sweetening the air. Heinrich is gazing at a painting that depicts the old viscount as Mars, his wife as Venus and their two sons as celestial cherubs, while the inquisitor admires a Venetian vase with a rather violent hunting scene painted on it.

"A Johann Rottenhammer painting, if I'm not mistaken," the archbishop remarks. "A beautiful work. But I don't remember your father ever being quite that heroic."

"A great soldier but not a great connoisseur of culture. Fortunately I seem to display the opposite trait," the count replies smugly as he turns to the inquisitor without waiting for a formal introduction.

"Monsignor Solitario, making your acquaintance is a challenging pleasure."

The inquisitor bows stiffly. "Indeed, and how is your brother? May God protect his soul."

"Ah, but is this God Catholic or Protestant?"

"There is but one God and he is, naturally, Catholic, even in the case of a defector like your brother."

"Naturally. As for my brother, he is alive and hopefully somewhere here in Cologne. Meanwhile, would you partake in some good Rhineland wine? The archbishop tells me he has transformed you into something of an expert on our Rheinwein?"

"He attempted but failed," the Dominican replies coolly.

"We are here on business, Gerhard, but I do believe a little indulgence—more specifically, a bottle of Rudesheimer Klosterberg—would smooth the proceedings. I believe you have a good vintage in your cellar." Heinrich throws his gloves onto a table.

The count gives the order to the footman then leads his guests to his study. A small room dominated by a large map of the Hapsburg Empire and a writing desk, and lined with solid oak paneling, the chamber has the distinct advantage of being almost soundproof and thus spyproof.

"So you have come from Amsterdam. Is our friend willing to recant his chosen religion and return to Westphalia?" Heinrich, impatient, cuts straight to the point.

"My dear archbishop, there are many methods of persuasion. A craft at which I hear Monsignor Solitario is a master."

"Thank you. I shall take that as a compliment." The inquisitor bows his neat shaven head.

"Indeed, Monsignor, your reputation precedes you."

"Enough!" Tired of decorum, the archbishop fills his own glass. "Bluntly, for we have little time, which method of persuasion have you applied? Both Rome and Vienna grow weary of Detlef von Tennen's insults."

"I have the child upstairs."

Surprised, both men look up.

"You have the child? Detlef von Tennen's son?"

Gerhard, noting the hatred in the friar's voice when pronouncing the family name, concludes that he will have to tread with great care to manipulate the inquisitor. Heinrich and Solitario are both experts in treachery and tactics. Will the archbishop keep his promise not to prosecute if Detlef confesses? A sudden doubt stiffens Gerhard's muscles. Covering his discomfort, the count smiles at his guests.

"I am convinced that his presence here will shortly bring the parents. And then, my good sire, you shall have your public confession and my brother shall have his child. I think that is a fair bargain, do you not agree, your grace?"

"Fair indeed. You say Detlef is within the walls of the city?"

"I believe so. I am expecting him at any moment. And when he arrives I shall notify you."

"We shall be watching, Gerhard, of that you may be assured."

"But you will protect his life, will you not?"

"Naturally. Detlef is my protégé, as well as your brother and my cousin."

"He is also a Wittelsbach. I take it I have your word?"

The archbishop holds out his hand; the ring, catching the afternoon light, gleams for a second.

"You have my word."

There has to be a way! I could break in, or bribe my way in through the servants . . ."

"And then what? Appeal to your brother's better nature?"

"I shall regret my naivety until my dying day."

"Enough. What is done is done."

Ruth, dressed in just her petticoat, her face washed of its disguise, sits on a low oak stool beside the fire that burns in the small grate. Detlef paces restlessly in his nightgown, a blue silk sash tied around his waist.

"I will not stand by and watch Jacob be used as barter. This is the coward's way, Ruth, can you not see that?"

"It is a trap your brother has laid for us—for you."

"The worst they could do is force me to repent."

"Detlef, your crime is greater than just conversion, you know it. You have questioned the divinity of the Bible, you have criticized the slave traders. There are other motives to the kidnapping, political ones."

"But what is to become of our son?"

Ruth looks at him, and for the first time in a week sees beyond her own anguish. The strain of little sleep cuts across his face, a new suffering shows behind the eyes. In the loss of her child she has forgotten she has a husband. Reaching up, she pulls him down to her mouth, as if to wipe away the anger, the guilt, and with them all the fear and terror of what could be. Her kisses break down his reserve and, to his amazement, he finds himself weeping in her arms. Covering his face he pushes her away.

"Forgive me, I am not myself."

Instead of answering she wraps her arms around him and rocks his head against her bosom. She takes his mouth again, her lips and tongue tasting salt and tenderness, her cheeks now wet with his tears, as their kisses deepen then quicken suddenly as the urgency of being within each other sweeps through them.

Running her hands under his nightgown she reaches for him. Like an innocent he abandons himself to her caresses as she pushes him back against the wooden floor, laying open his garments, revealing his nakedness and masculinity in all its awkward glory. Lying there, he watches the woman he loves become another as Ruth runs her naked breasts down his torso then tauntingly traces a nipple over the tip of him. Erect flesh against erect flesh, and blind desire pushes all thought, all fear, from her tense mind. His organ arching up to rest between her lips as she teases him with her breath, her tongue, her separateness. Then deep in her mouth she plays the length of him, glorying in his pungent scent of ball and hair, cupping his arse and muscle, feeling his seed beginning to build, to run beneath the skin. In wonder she holds him profound within her mouth, his lust, his love, his trust in her abandonment, and just before she knows he is about to burst in all his sticky glory, she lifts her face and pushes the hard long length of her husband, her man, her lover, deep within her. Already wet without a single touch she rides him, the eye of her love a velvet-tight fist closing with each stroke. His hands reaching for her tumbling breasts, for her flowing hair. Faster, harder. Each knowing the quickening within the other like a map of the cosmos that even the sightless could recognize. Somewhere in the groaning, in the mounting staccato of his lover's cry, Detlef is happy to forget that they are each human and forever separate.

She wakes suddenly, the awareness of someone else in the bedchamber flooding her instantly.

She blindly reaches for Detlef, his warm, sleeping body lies curled around a pillow. Thank God, she thinks, instinct alerting all her senses. Deciding not to wake him, she lights the candle with a flint by the bed.

As the yellow flame flickers the shadow of a woman appears on the wall. Transfixed with horror, Ruth realizes there is no figure standing before it to make the silhouette. Lilith. Terror shrieks through her flesh like a physical convulsion. Quivering, she watches as a faint mist slowly collects in the center of the room. Swirling slightly, it gathers then congeals with mounting speed into the shape of a naked woman, as human and as ordinary as the midwife herself.

Lilith. The stench of the demon, the mockingly seductive demeanor, sweeps Ruth into a torrent of memory. She tries to move, to ward off the apparition, but finds she cannot.

Slowly the creature turns, her long thick black hair falling over her shoulders and drooping breasts. The clarity with which Ruth perceives the demon gives the illusion that time has slowed down, as if the seasons and the skies have stopped turning. An eerie silence fills the room as the howling wind outside fades away. As Lilith moves toward her, Ruth sees that this manifestation is of middle years, some two score or more. The stretchmarks on the creature's womb indicate that she has borne many children. Lilith stares steadily at Ruth. Lifting a large hand, she slowly uncurls the long fingers, offering up the palm. It is covered with thick black curly hair, the hair of the sex. Revolted, Ruth watches as Lilith, lifting her other hand, points to Detlef.

"Who summoned you? Who?" The midwife's voice is a croaking whisper of terror.

"The Spaniard, the musician," the fiend answers, her utterance a baritone pleasure that oozes into Ruth's ears. Slowly Lilith grins at the terrified look of revelation on Ruth's face. The smile is radiant, like sunlight it fills the room and transforms her plain countenance into one of blinding splendor.

The evil spirit rises up into the air and hovering above the ground floats toward the sleeping man. Ruth sees that the obscenely thick growth of black pubic hair also covers the soles of the horny feet. Rotating her hips seductively, Lilith advances until she is beside Detlef. Asleep, he rolls onto his back. Innocent in dream, a half-smile plays across his mouth.

Lilith turns to Ruth who, immobilized by dread, is still lying beside her husband. Grinning triumphantly the she-demon lifts her heavy thigh and begins to mount the dormant cleric. Suddenly a great fury breaks inside Ruth.

"No!"

With a huge burst of energy she pushes Lilith off her man.

"No!"

She wakes, her body drenched in cold sweat, thrashing in Detlef's arms.

"Stop! Stop! You are dreaming!"

Shaking, Ruth comes to her senses then frantically runs her hands over him to assure herself he has not been harmed.

"What was it, my love?"

"Lilith."

"Ruth, I thought you had stopped with all that gibberish."

"She wanted you, she was after you, the inquisitor sent her . . ."

"Hush, this is just fear talking, it is not sane."

"Promise me you will wear an amulet, promise!"

"You know I do not believe in preordained destiny, only in sound judgment and foresight. We shall be safe, I promise you."

"Detlef, please . . ."

Detlef falls back on the pallet. He has not seen Ruth so undone since they left Das Wolkenhaus a lifetime ago.

"If it will make you happy I shall wear the amulet, but only under my garments."

She pulls him into an embrace. "Thank you."

What damage can it do, he thinks. It is not witchcraft, merely a harmless charm to reassure his wife. Surely that cannot be a sin. Taking comfort in the notion he rocks Ruth back to sleep. Watching her, he wonders what they have become, where reason disappears to when man is confronted with his greatest horror.

The coquette, dazzling in a tight-waisted corset, red curls cascading down her back, pulls the young sailor to his feet and begins to jig with him. Throwing her lustring petticoats up she reveals a shapely thigh.

Detlef, having left Ruth to sleep, watches from the corner of the tavern, a long clay pipe between his lips. The boy is so young he barely has a beard. The sailor, roaring drunk, staggers from side to side, his arms clasped with a desperate tenderness around the wench, although in truth it is difficult to tell whether this is for balance or pleasure. The girl, a strong-faced lass with a thick layer of lead over her skin, two circles of rouge plastered on top and a plethora of patches after the English fashion—a virtual galaxy of hearts and stars—seems robust enough, hauling her blade upright every time gravity gets the better of him. Encouraged, the sailor thrusts his hand between her legs, then yells out as if he has been stung by a million bees. "She's got a cock!" he screams in disgust.

Half the tavern double over in laughter while the other half—sailors from Lübeck in the far north, all wearing the same ridiculous striped caps with pom-poms—leap to their comrade's aid as he begins to pummel the exposed transvestite.

Like a crumpled butterfly she falls to the sawdust-covered floor, her skirts collapsing around her as blood bursts streaming from her nose. Instead of protecting herself she offers up her bruised face after each punch like a defiant sacrificial lamb then breaks into convulsions of high-pitched mirth. The dull sound of fist thudding against bone sickens Detlef.

As the red wig slips from the young transvestite's head to reveal a crown of dark cropped hair there is something about the aquiline beauty the cleric recognizes. Dropping his pipe, he dives into the mêlée of flailing arms and flying punches.

"Alphonso!" he screams.

He reaches the bleeding actor and pulls him out of the forest of wrestling men that has suddenly sprouted on the tavern's floor. Together they bolt up the stairs to the sanctuary of Detlef's chamber.

"The fortunes of the actor are as fickle as the sea and invariably involve indignation of one sort or another."

Alphonso, stripped down to undergarments of bloomers and a short petticoat, winces as Ruth stitches a deep gash in his forehead.

"I cannot describe what an odyssey it has been, a great epic of tragic and absurd destiny. I no longer have a heart," he declares dramatically.

"I was grieved to hear of the death of Prince Ferdinand," Detlef tells him solemnly. Alphonso's masquerade of frivolity immediately switches to the raw vulnerability of a grieving youth.

"Sacrificed to his uncle's ambition. Murdered on the battlefield fighting the Ottomans. I begged him not to go—he had about as much soldiercraft as I have—but he was determined to prove himself to that wretched relative of his. It was a plot, I knew it, I had gathered information myself for Leopold's Jew, Oppenheimer. I warned Ferdinand but he would not heed me. Leopold needed a Hapsburg martyr—well, now the bastard has him."

Pushing Ruth's hand away. Alphonso tries to hide his sudden sobs. Detlef, sorry for the actor's loss of the young prince he so obviously loved, puts his hand on the man's heaving shoulders. Alphonso briefly kisses it, then collects himself.

"Thank you for your kindness, Herr von Tennen. I apologize. I have had no will to live since my good prince's slaughter. But perhaps your plight will give me back my purpose. What is your plot?"

Ruth looks at Detlef, then answers for him. "My husband would storm the house and steal back our child, but I fear they plan to arrest him."

"Of that I have no doubt." Alphonso turns to Detlef. "Does anyone know of your presence in Cologne?"

"No one, as far as we know. Although naturally my brother will be expecting me to appear at any minute."

"Then we shall not disappoint him."

"What do you mean?"

"I am not without my resources. I know the count's town house as well as the count himself from accompanying Ferdinand on his visits to Cologne. I also have my troupe with me, my fellow actors are posted around this fair city at various taverns. We are recently returned from an unfortunate season at the spring market at Aachen where we performed a wonderful rendering of Euripides' *Medea*. The artistic sensibility of which, I'm afraid, was lost on the ignorant mob and resulted in an abrupt halt to the performance as well as several of my players being assaulted with a variety of vegetables, most of which were, unfortunately, inedible. However we still have our costumes and paint. I might be able to provide some powerful distraction which will afford you an opportunity to free your son and flee."

"A disguise and an entertainment? My brother is a devious man and knows your face well. This has to be an ingenious plan indeed."

"It is remarkable how men, given the choice, will only see what they want to see. Trust me, in my time I have deceived my own mother."

"I can truly believe it."

"You tell me your brother is recently bereaved?"

"Alas yes, his hunting master was killed in an accident two years ago."

"Herr Woolf?"

"You knew him?"

"From the prince's excursion to Das Grüntal. This tragedy could augur well for our cause. A grieving man is a vulnerable man. The first part of the prologue shall be my acquaintance with the nursemaid . . ." the actor begins thoughtfully, the pulse of inspiration already beating through his veins.

❋

A goblet of fine Venetian crystal containing red wine stands on a table beside the four-poster bed. Draped in a canopy of mauve silk, the roof of the bed is painted with a cavalcade of muscular male angels led by Mars himself. Count Gerhard von Tennen reclines on the feather bed, dressed in a Turkish gown that was a gift from some distant ambassador. This time of night, between the town horn of midnight and two in the morning, is always the loneliest. There is much of the day he would have shared with his companion: humorous observations, ambitions, discourse, the architecture of intimacy that can only be constructed through years of living together. Something one simply cannot buy or replace, the count observes wryly as the now-familiar ache of desire seeps through his body. Two years have passed but Herman's absence has evolved into a longing which seems to increase not decrease with time.

The world-weary aristocrat reaches for the large key hidden under his pillow. It is the key to the lock on the bedroom door behind which his nephew is secured. The shape of it under his fingers reassures him that Jacob is secure and that Detlef's appearance is inevitable.

He glances across the bed. On the other side neatly hangs Herman's nightgown and nightcap, like faithful hounds awaiting their master. The count cannot bring himself to burn them. He likes to bury his nose deep into the fine cotton and find hidden between the woven fibers the lingering scent of his dead lover.

He groans out loud, then reaches for his customary glass of Madeira. Hoping to be transported to some Valhalla where he will no longer be conscious of the loneliness and guilt which infuses his whole being, he drinks the wine swiftly. The culinary pleasures that once delighted him are now rendered bland and tasteless by sorrow.

While his back is turned, a hand reaches up from under the bed and pulls down the dead gamekeeper's clothes, swiftly tugging them out of sight.

Oblivious, the count lies back and stares at the flickering candle that sits on a carved chest beside the French doors which open onto a wooden balcony. Below lies a walled courtyard lined with orange trees imported from Spain; he used to sit there with Herman each day, breaking the morning bread. Smiling, he remembers his lover's laughter, the way it would burst

from a shy placidity, a silence the count used to find truculent until he realized Herman was a man who spoke with his body and hands but would
always struggle with words, as if he found the complexity of language itself an unnecessary hindrance. It was enough for the count when the
gamekeeper used to reach out suddenly in the middle of a half-formed
sentence or a smile and take his lover's finer hand in his own huge bearlike
paw. Language is for scholars and effeminate courtiers who have little else,
the count thinks, turning onto his side as a mysterious drowsiness seeps
through his blood. He stares at the candle flame. It splutters then becomes
a red glow which begins to throb with a strange intensity.

Transfixed, he surrenders to a detachment that makes him feel as if his
body is lifting up from the bed. It is as if Mars himself is reaching down
with his strong muscular arms and gathering the count to his manly
bosom, he could almost stick out his tongue and lick the salt off the
bronzed shining skin of the war god.

"Gerhard . . ."

His lover's voice emerges from the velvet darkness, its seductive timbre
tickling the back of his mind.

"Herman?"

The count struggles to sit but finds that a great weight seems to be pinning him down. He turns his head: a man stands in the doorway of the
balcony, his great broad shoulders and flowing hair silhouetted against the
night sky of Cologne.

"Herman . . . could that possibly be you?"

The ghost says nothing. A cool breeze drifts through the open doors
bringing with it the unmistakeable aroma of worn leather, sweat and the
faint scent of hounds, the smell of the pack the hunting master took with
him always.

"It is you, Herman. Could this be a miracle?"

"No miracle, my knight, but a manifestation to please you, to comfort
you in your grief. But to keep me here you must shut your eyes and silence
your doubts for fear of driving my spirit away. Lie back and allow me to
pleasure you."

How articulate and softly spoken Herman has become now that he is an
angel, the count notes dreamily as he falls back against the pillow. His
heart races as his gown is untied. His lover's hands, the callused palms
achingly familiar, run up his naked legs. The long strong fingers massage

his thighs, the soft skin of his groin, touching him everywhere except his cock, which, now standing, quivers under the warm breath of his lover.

"Herman, Herman," he murmurs, "you were my life, my reason for being."

As his lover's burning mouth finally closes over him, taking him as he always did with unbearably slow strokes, the count, arching in ecstasy, fastens his fingers in Herman's hair. Overcome by pleasure he does not notice that the texture is not even remotely similar to the hair of his dead hunting master.

"Slowly, slowly," the count moans, sitting up, eyes still squeezed tightly shut. Unnoticed, a tiny stunted hand creeps under the pillow and swiftly removes the large key.

The actor, a dwarf affectionately known as La Grande, carefully places the key between his teeth then crawls along the floor to the door. He glances back at the bed where Alphonso, wearing a horsehair wig and Herman's gown with its padded shoulders, crouches over the count performing fellatio. Winking at his colleague, La Grande reaches for the doorknob.

Outside, Ruth and Detlef stand on the landing, immobile like ice sculptures, too afraid to move. Holding their breath they wait at the door of Gerhard's chamber. Ruth's amulet hangs around her husband's neck, hidden under his shirt. Suddenly the door swings open. Detlef, clutching his dagger, lifts it ready to strike. Just before he is about to plunge down, La Grande, his large misshapen face shiny with excitement, pops out like the Punch from a puppet show. The performer gestures lewdly then, grinning, drops the gleaming key into Detlef's free hand.

The three of them creep silently to a door at the far end of the corridor. Detlef slips the key into the lock and turns it. The door pushes open with a sudden creak. They freeze.

Nothing. The household slumbers still.

Jacob lies on a small straw pallet in the corner of the room, clutching his toy rabbit. A china washing bowl and jug stand beside the bed, a bowl of half-eaten whey thrust to one side.

Ruth runs over and wraps her arms around the sleeping child. "Jacob? Jacob!"

She cradles him, resting his tousled head against her bosom, while

Detlef kneels beside them, running his hands over the child to search for any injury.

"Mama?" Jacob opens his eyes sticky with sleep. "You took a long time to come. I have seen four mornings since and yesterday uncle told me he had sent a carrier pigeon. Is that why you're here?"

"No, child, we're here to take you back home to Amsterdam. But you must be a good boy and keep quiet all the while, until we are inside the coach."

"I have been brave. You will be proud of me. But where's Uncle?"

"Uncle is sleeping and we have to be very quiet so as not to wake him, *mein Ayzer*," Ruth whispers, aching with love as the warm smell of Jacob's sleepy body encompasses her.

Detlef wraps his son in the blanket and picks him up. As he does, the leather thread around his neck breaks and Ruth's amulet slips off unnoticed, its fall broken by the soft pallet. The boy curls up against his father's shoulder, his hot arms winding around Detlef's cool neck. Led by La Grande, the three make their way along the wooden landing and down the servants' stairs to the back door.

Alphonso, stripped of his costume but still in the horsehair wig, stands waiting for them.

"The count sleeps but the hemlock will soon wear off. You must hurry, there is a cart beyond the city gates."

The skinny performer arches his body then executes a few sharp dance steps in the vain attempt to warm himself. The straw hat slips rakishly over his head as the empty street echoes with his tapping feet. Suddenly he stops, remembering that he is not meant to be drawing attention to himself and the ramshackle cart beside him. Those were Alphonso's instructions: wait for them at the gates, look like a dumb farmer from south of the Rhine, be prepared to drive as far as the Dutch border and there'd be an extra twenty Reichstaler in it and a better role in the next production. Cheered by the thought of a major part, perhaps even that of a heroine, the ungainly performer—far better suited to comedy—slouches into instant anonymity.

"Hugo!"

He swings around at the sound of his name, a pencil-thin fool spinning like a maypole in the dawn mist.

Alphonso, followed by La Grande then a woman and a man carrying a child, emerges from the shadows. "Anyone see you?" the actor asks anxiously, peering down the Roman wall that leads out of the city toward the west.

"Nothing but the owls and a few drunks who thought I was the rat catcher," Hugo replies, pulling idiot faces at the sleepy child who finally laughs much to the clown's delight.

Detlef examines the simple cart, a mere frame covered by sackcloth. Stinking of pig shit, it resembles the roughest of animal transport. "They are to travel in this?"

Alphonso lifts the sackcloth. Inside is a comfortable pallet; blankets and a basket of fruit and cheese sit in the corner.

"The pig shit is a decoy, to deter the curious. Trust me, you shall be in Holland by nightfall."

"Not I—my wife and child."

Behind Detlef, Ruth moans involuntarily, her deepest fear realized. Horrified, she steps forward. "Husband, you must come with us."

Detlef hands the sleepy child to her. "Take Jacob, I will join you later."

She looks at him blankly, not fully understanding. "That was not the plan." A terrible sensation of déjà vu reverberates through her, the way Detlef is looking at her now, his eyes full of love yet determined.

"Ruth, I have to stay. There is much I must resolve with my brother."

"Have you lost your reason? He took our child! Do not let him take you as well. You must leave with us now, you must."

"If I leave now I will be betraying everything I have fought for, I will be denying the possibility of redemption. He is my brother. I cannot leave without an explanation. It will not take a moment and it will be comfort for a lifetime. I shall be safe, my love. I will join you in less than half a day. Wait for me at the border."

"Detlef, no! I fear . . ."

"Please."

He searches her face for understanding. She has to allow him this, he thinks, for without forgiveness he cannot maintain his faith and that would be a living death. He is at the mercy of her decision and yet there is only one way for her to decide if their union is to survive.

The moment stretches until at last Ruth, reading all in his face, takes his hand and kisses it, then closes his fingers over the kiss.

"We shall wait for you then, just over the border."

Loving her more than he has ever done, he presses his lips to hers.

"Take care of our child. I will join you within the week."

He walks with her toward the cart.

"May love protect you, my husband."

Without glancing back, Ruth climbs up, helped by Alphonso and La Grande.

*T*he spy, Georges, huddles in the doorway of a bakery three doors down and across from the count's town house. Fuck this weather, the winter will be bad if it is this cold in October, he thinks. Shivering, he wonders whether he should send his manservant out for more burning peat in the morning. Deciding that he will, the informant pulls his wide-brimmed hat further over his freezing ears. As an owl hoots in the distance he glances back at the aristocrat's dwelling.

Several shadows move across a pool of moonlight. Georges leans forward, squinting as he tries to penetrate the darkness, muscles tense with expectation. The silhouettes shorten as a pack of stray mongrels emerge silently from the gloom and trot swiftly around a corner.

Disappointed, the spy swings his gaze back to the house. Just then the dull glow of a candle flares in an upstairs bedroom, illuminating the shape of a tall man wearing a hat passing the window. By Georges' calculations he has a quarter of an hour left. Pulling his cap low, he sprints toward the cathedral.

The knife glints as a sliver of moonlight catches its blade. The tip presses into the soft sagging neck of the drugged man, pushing as far as it will go without breaking the skin. The white pores stretch and flood pink at the point where steel meets skin.

Detlef has been crouching over his brother for what seems like hours. His stilled body, motionless like that of the hunter, is deceptive for within him a momentous struggle is taking place.

He could kill him so easily with one swift cut to the throat; it would be almost painless. He wants to, there is an instinct within him screaming with rage, a silent diatribe that roars from his thudding heart to his pounding brain. His brother stole his child from him; he has almost destroyed all that Detlef has fought for. But to murder is a sin, it would reduce his soul to less than an animal. Regardless, anger, revenge and blind fury surge through him like a torrent.

Finally Detlef lifts the knife away and stands, trembling violently. Lifting a jug of water he throws it across his brother's face. Gerhard groans, opens his eyes, then rolls to one side to vomit onto the woven rug next to the bed.

Somewhere in the room the count can hear a voice. His brother's. For a moment he struggles to remember the sequence of events: a memory of Herman . . . the sense of him, his touch, mouth, face come drifting back. How is that possible? The man is dead, you sentimental idiot, long gone, the count chastises himself. Finding that his thoughts still spin, making it difficult to form a cohesive image, he realizes he has been administered an opiate.

"Gerhard!"

Blearily the count turns his head. In the dim light he can just make out his brother's profile as he leans over to light a candle. The flame flares up and, as Detlef crosses the room again, Gerhard can see that he holds a naked blade in his hand. The aristocrat tries to swing his leaden legs off the bed but finds he cannot move.

"Are you to kill me?" His words, slurred, hang in the stale air.

"I tried but found I could not. To do so would reduce me to as lowly a creature as yourself."

The count labors to pull himself upright. "How predictable of you to hide behind that moral superiority of yours. It is all you have ever done your entire life, Detlef. You never had any sense of reality, always hiding behind the skirts of the church, only emerging to play the noble crusader. Well, what real morality lies in your actions? Have you truly examined your soul? You have betrayed both your race and your title."

"I have betrayed nothing. I am guilty of nothing except following the logic of my heart."

"Idealistic fool. You have no idea, have you? They are threatening to take the lodge, our lands, the von Tennen title. Three hundred years of ancestry obliterated, just like that. And all because of your stupidity!"

"You would sacrifice your own brother?"

"There is no sacrifice, all they want is a public repentance. Besides, the family is more important than your paltry ethics. The lineage must go on."

Witnessing the unquestioning conviction of the zealot that makes ugly his brother's face, Detlef has to muster all his strength to stop himself attacking Gerhard there and then. Instead he takes a shuddering breath.

"I forgive you your ignorance and pray that one day you may find enlightenment."

A sudden thud is heard downstairs, then the sound of running footsteps as soldiers burst into the house. Detlef glares at Gerhard with absolute disdain before bolting for the door.

The moth, a stubborn creature with inky-blue wings that are barely distinguishable from the soot that covers the walls of the prison, crawls slowly but with immense determination from the great cold outside through the narrow hole between the granite blocks. It emerges from the tunnel, its furry antennae waving blindly. Delighted to discover a draft of warmer air, it takes off, fluttering around the prison cell until it alights for a moment upon the grimy hand of a man.

Detlef, gazing down, wonders if the fragile creature might live longer than himself, and if, by some wondrous sorcery, it might squirrel him out through the minuscule crack to freedom.

My love,

My foolishness has landed me in this hell. My brother has betrayed me, and with this treachery I fear he has bartered my life.

Forgive me my impetuosity. This trait has led me to tragedy, but also to great joy for without it we would never have come together and I would never have found my soul's work.

My dearest, I pray that you and our child have crossed safely into the sanctuary of the Netherlands and that soon we shall be reunited. I know not what my future holds but I take solace in my belief that they cannot dare to execute a Wittelsbach. The worst I fear is a forced conversion—they will ask me to betray my new faith. Yet there must be some means of escape . . .

"Canon?"

Groot peers through the prison bars. His old master is staring at the wall, mouthing a silent missive.

Detlef whirls around at the voice. Despite the long hair and the peppering of a new beard, Groot recognizes him immediately.

"I am a plain pastor now, Groot. The title canon does not apply."

"So the rumors are true, you are now a follower of Calvin?"

"I am a preacher with the Remonstrants. I travel the Low Countries with a simple sermon."

"You married the witch?"

In a second Detlef's lean form is against the bars, his hand thrusting through grabs Groot's throat. "Respect, my good sir! She is my wife."

Groot's eyes bulge as he chokes under Detlef's steel-like fingers.

"My apologies . . ."

Detlef drops him. Stumbling, Groot claws at the neck of his cassock, loosening it. Detlef pauses then steps back to get a better view of his old assistant.

"You look well, Groot. You have become a substantial man."

The cleric, older and more portly than Detlef remembers him, regains his composure.

"Herr von Fürstenberg treats me with respect. But honor and ease are seldom bedfellows."

"I know the proverb, but of the two I would choose honor."

"Maybe, but it is you who are now on the wrong side of the bars. They will kill you, Detlef."

"I am cousin to the archbishop. They would not dare."

"It would have served you better not to blaspheme so loudly. You have become too noisy a critic to go unheeded."

"Groot, help me . . . for the sake of our friendship."

"You would beg?"

"All pride is false modesty. I am a father as well as a husband. I want to live."

Groot stares at him, noticing a new humility in the aristocrat's eyes.

"I will pray to *my* God for you. Perhaps he will be more forgiving than your jailers."

He turns and walks slowly back down the dim corridor.

"Groot! Groot!"

"Please address me by my new title: Canon Groot," the priest announces to the shadows, too frightened to turn around for fear his old master will see his tears.

❧

Seated with the archbishop in his carriage, Carlos watches as the narrow crowded streets give way to muddy lanes on the outskirts of the city and then to neat cultivated fields, all still within the walls of Cologne: checkerboards of yellow and green, cabbages growing next to wheat. So there is natural beauty here, Carlos concedes reluctantly. A growing excitement fills him despite his inherent misanthropy. They have the renegade preacher incarcerated. A few turns of the screw and the witch shall be his. The notion thrills him to the marrow. He has agreed to the forthcoming encounter only as a courtesy to the archbishop. He has discovered that he has developed a begrudging affection for the drunken buffoon, helped greatly by his delivery of the heretic canon, of course. The meeting is a mere formality, the inquisitor reassures himself. Once over, he will be able to interrogate the criminal preacher and then finally Sara's daughter will be his. By the time the driver pulls up outside a rambling farmhouse built a good few centuries before, Carlos is swept up in a reverie of exhilaration.

The truculent farmer leads the two clerics to an ancient barn, its ivy-covered exterior deceptively innocuous. Inside, beyond a row of stalls filled with restless cattle—a deliberate line of concealment—the floor of the barn lowers dramatically into a gambling pit. To Carlos's amazement, over a hundred men are assembled there, all of them gamblers. It is here that the archbishop has brought him to meet with the count.

Gerhard von Tennen pushes his way through the crowd, watching all the time for the archbishop and the inquisitor. 'Tis a strange place to rendezvous, the count thinks, but knows he is in no position to protest.

In the straw-covered pit a badger squats growling, its long elegant snout twitching with terror. It runs back and forth, unable to escape for its tail is nailed to a heavy plank of wood.

"Ten Reichstaler on the pug!" the pit master shouts, pointing to a small bull terrier snarling at the end of its owner's chain.

Gerhard shakes his head. Turning, he catches sight of Maximilian Heinrich, who in the dress of a merchant is barely noticeable among the spectactors, a motley gang of bürgers, students and journeymen united by one obsession: the love of the wager.

The count sidles up beside the archbishop. "I did not know whether you would meet with me."

"Gerhard, you are my brother in blood and faith. Of course I would grant you an audience."

"In such a strange place of worship?"

"Ah, but I chose the place for you. The joy you take in gambling is legendary, cousin."

The peasant beside the archbishop throws off his hood to reveal the somber visage of the inquisitor.

"Good day, sir. It promises to be a fine competition. The creature with the torn ear, they say, already has three badger pelts to his name."

Gerhard glances over at the small snarling pug whose squashed face is a battlefield of fighting scars. The dog, having caught the scent of the badger, is almost delirious with fury, snapping and growling at all who approach, while the badger, larger but with a disposition that is only vicious when cornered, has edged as far away as it can given the bleeding flesh of its tail.

"I shall back the badger. I have seen these creatures fight, their tenacity is not to be underestimated."

Gerhard throws three gold coins into the badger's corner then turns back to his companions.

"But tell me, how fares Detlef?"

Heinrich reaches into his pocket and holds out a signet ring with the von Tennen crest engraved upon it. The count, with a sharp inhalation, recognizes it as Detlef's.

"He is experiencing the hospitality of the cathedral's dungeon while awaiting trial. But he is in good spirits, so they say," the archbishop tells him, sorry for the obvious dismay that fills his cousin's face.

"But can you guarantee a fair tribunal?"

"The Inquisition is always just for it acts according to the will of God," Carlos answers, pushing between the two men. Ignoring him, the count continues to direct his appeal to the archbishop.

"Heinrich, promise me he shall suffer nothing more than a forced conversion, a signed confession of repentance. Surely that will satisfy Rome, Vienna and the Inquisition?"

Heinrich avoids the count's eyes. "I can speak only for Vienna."

At a nod from the inquisitor the dogkeeper holds up the animal. Carlos reaches over and with an expert hand assesses the muscles in the canine's forelegs.

"Tell me, count, what would you wager for your brother's life?" The inquisitor looks up from the beast.

"Nothing that I have not already gambled."

"Come now, I have heard you are a bigger gamester than that."

The count glances at the badger, it is larger than the pug and on close inspection already bears the marks of previous victories across its striped furry back. For a moment it seems to stare back at the aristocrat, a surprising intelligence gleaming in its bloodshot eyes. Gerhard looks at Heinrich: there is nothing in his face to hint that this might be a game. Is this what Detlef's life has been reduced to, a mere wager? Suddenly the enormity of his treachery tumbles down upon him. He is worse than Judas, he thinks, and a seeping dread begins to sicken him.

"You promised there would be amnesty for a Wittelsbach."

The archbishop turns away.

"Look, the fight is about to begin. Make your wager. Detlef von Tennen's life if the badger wins." Carlos's soft voice cuts under the shouting punters.

The count glares at the inquisitor, every muscle in his body flexed for revenge. Should he accept the wager or simply run the inquisitor through here and now? But what would that achieve? They have Detlef at their mercy.

Despite himself, the rising adrenaline of the gambler surges up, a pounding excitement that battles his logic. Just one win and they will defeat both church and state together, himself and his brother, free to begin a whole new chapter. Should he play? What choice does he have? The badger looks strong and fierce, it will defeat the pug—the creature is half its size. The wager will be easily won.

Gerhard throws ten coins into the pit.

"A further ten on the badger, for my brother's life."

Ten minutes later the dogkeeper holds up the severed head of the badger amid cheering and booing. To the count it is as if he is holding up the head of Detlef himself, the neck still trailing purple arteries. Transfixed, the count sees the eyes suddenly fly open. Snarling, the head turns to gaze upon its brother.

The nightmarish fantasy is broken by a tap on his shoulder. Carlos, grinning, holds out his hand. "You owe me one hundred Reichstaler."

The count looks down at the friar's creased palm then spits into it. Furious, he pushes his way through the celebrating revelers. Heinrich follows.

"Gerhard!"

The count pauses, dizzy with revulsion and anger. Heinrich, breathing heavily, catches up to him.

"I promise you, your brother will keep his life."

"The word of a Wittelsbach?"

"The word of a Wittelsbach."

*D*etlef's body, naked except for a grimy loincloth thrown over him for the sake of decency, is stretched to its absolute length. Each joint shines pale bone through the stretched mottled skin. Leather thongs are lashed around his wrists and ankles where they are fastened to the wooden cogs of the stretching rack, the skin chafed and bleeding. A wide iron band is strapped around his head, a screw bolted at each side of his eye sockets. His face is an ivory mask of anguish but his eyes are defiant.

Carlos, inches away from Detlef's face, gazes along the length of the tortured limbs—as he had envisaged, still beautiful *in extremis*. There is a nobility to flesh under duress that cannot be mimicked, the inquisitor observes silently. It is as if the spirit rises to the very limit of the physical self and shines out before finally departing. This is how our Lord must have looked on the cross. Beauty, spirit and agony incarnate.

The inquisitor puts a finger to Detlef's wrist. The German twitches at his touch.

"Another turn of the screw and this bone will pop out of its socket. Then it will be your knees, then your ankles, then your thigh bones will tear out of the hip sockets. Unless, of course, I decide to destroy your eyesight first."

Detlef licks his lips, trying to find the spittle to form speech.

"What do you want from me, Monsignor Solitario? A confession? Penance?"

"Tell me where the Jewish witch and her bastard are and you shall be freed, maybe even pardoned. Make a public declaration of the error of your ways and you could even be reinstated as canon. One word, Pastor von Tennen, and the pain will vanish magically. Freedom, respectability, how sweet that must sound . . ."

"Never."

Detlef's whisper is barely audible.

Carlos nods and the torturer turns the wooden handle languidly, lovingly. The cogs creak as they rotate slowly. It is a sound Detlef has grown to loathe in the last four hours.

His sinews stretch tauter and tauter until there is a loud popping sound as his left wrist disengages from his hand.

"Ahhh!"

"She is a witch, a succubus, the whore of the devil! I have the evidence. Her mother was the same, as were the whole Hebrew brood that spawned her. She knows the ways of the kabbala, she has used them against the church, used them to bewitch you, my friend. The child is not your child, you have been deceived. He could be any man's. She has lain with many— I know it!"

"She is my wife!"

"She is a child of Lilith!"

The cogs turn again, this time the other wrist cracks and a kneecap shatters. Detlef is close to fainting, he can no longer hear himself screaming. Instead he hears the haunting sound of his son singing a nursery rhyme over and over, his clear young voice sweetly resonating around the stone walls of the dungeon.

The inquisitor's seductive voice is an insidious whisper underneath.

"Repeat after me: I have seen with my own eyes Ruth von Tennen of the Navarro family performing unnatural acts, rites of the black arts . . ."

Detlef shakes his head. The minute movement causes a huge ripple of pain across his bloody brow. Carlos, losing patience, taps the iron band bolted around Detlef's head.

"Canon, you will at least save your sight if you tell me where they are."

Again Detlef refuses. Staring up at the vaulted ceiling which is blackened with smoke, as if the screams of the dying have burned their way into the very stone, he thinks only of Ruth . . . her naked form stepping out of the river the first morning he knew she was pregnant, the sunlight catching her long hair, water gleaming on her pale skin, her womb rounded, and how then he knew she would be his salvation.

Salvation. *Save me, save me, my love.* The words float through his mind like a cooling balm. The image of her appears. Throwing back her black hair, her long white arms reaching out to pull him to her breast. She is smiling. The look in her eyes is so incredibly familiar that it is as if Detlef is looking at a reflection of himself, all his aspirations, dreams, hopes and joys encapsulated in that one glance, as if his soul already resides in her.

My teacher. My lover. My wife.

And then, over the stench of shit and blood and burning tar, comes Ruth herself, the fragrance of her hair, her skin, the music of her laughter scattering like dew over the screaming.

The inquisitor, seeing that Detlef's spirit has begun to withdraw, looses the screw at his temple. Panicking he leans over him, spittle flying.

"Listen to me, you cannot leave now! I am so close to destroying the last of the Navarros, of holding within my grasp Sara herself, that witch! Detlef von Tennen! Are you listening? You cannot die now!"

But Detlef, his cold flesh twisting with the acrid smoke, no longer hears him.

My pain. My lover. My wife. The taste of her, the love of her I fought for, the life within her I gave.

Carlos, watching Detlef's eyes roll back into his head, grabs a bucket of water and throws it over the prostrate figure.

"Wait! You must tell me where she is! For your faith alone!"

But Detlef has already left to be with his family.

There they are in the kitchen, he thinks, seeing them clearly in his mind's eye. *I am standing beside the linen cabinet I can see Jacob, he is on the ground by the stove playing with his tin soldiers. She has her back to me, she has not seen me yet. I gesture to Jacob to be quiet. "We are playing a trick on your mother," I whisper then I step up behind her and put my hands over her eyes.*

At a signal from Carlos, the man in the black hood tightens the iron band. Detlef's eyeballs bulge like reddened hen's eggs then burst out of his head.

"This is your last chance. All you need do is whisper the name of the village, and then freedom!" Carlos, out of his mind with frustration, shouts into the dying man's ear.

I turn her face toward me, she is smiling that mysterious crooked smile of hers. I kiss her, and as she softens in my arms I realize that this is the moment I have been living for. Contentment. In trust. In joy. In peace. For I have come home.

My Lord, I have not failed you in this moment of darkness and you have not failed me. For in love I surrender my life, and in love I am everything and nothing. Forever and ever. Amen.

His body starts to shake violently as it goes into its final throes.

"No! No! You cannot do this to me. Give me the witch! Give me Sara!"

Carlos thuds his fists onto Detlef's shuddering chest over and over until the body stops twitching. Only then does the inquisitor come to his senses, staring at his hands which are covered with the dead man's blood.

He swings around to the guard. "Get a priest! Now! Don't you understand? He needs the last rites!"

"But Monsignor, you are a priest!"

"No. Not me, you idiot! It cannot be me!"

The guard glances at the contorted body on the rack, the prisoner is obviously dead. Confused, he looks back at the inquisitor.

"Go! You fool! Now!"

Carlos pushes the guard toward the door but Heinrich, flanked by two clerics, stands blocking the entrance.

"What have you done? He was cousin to a prince! A Wittelsbach!"

"He was a heretic!"

"Heretic or no, I made a promise. He did not deserve this death!"

"The Grand Inquisitional Council—"

"Out! Out of my sight!"

After the inquisitor has gone, Heinrich tenderly lays the two feet together. Taking Detlef's broken hands into his own, he strokes them, muttering softly as if to a child, and crosses them over the bruised and bloody chest. To the amazement of the guards, the archbishop takes off his own purple cloak and covers the body with it carefully, meticulously tucking the folds around the lifeless flesh. Then and only then, on his knees in his pale undergarments, his face close to Detlef's battered features, does Heinrich perform the last rites, his silent tears falling onto the torn flesh.

Behind the kneeling archbishop there is a sudden splash from the dunking vat. Unable to suppress his curiosity, a guard tiptoes over. He looks in, then jerks his head back in horror as three huge eels writhe up out of the water.

*T*he old woman carefully presses the gold coin into the eye socket. The eyes have gone, but now that she has sponged the blood and broken flesh from the face she can see that this was once a handsome man, grace still visible in the creased flesh. He looks familiar but she knows better than to search her memory, for she is the corpse-dresser brought in to put to rest the secretly murdered, the tortured, those the authorities wish to forget.

She works swiftly, without thought, winding the shroud around the narrow hips, binding the arms against the collapsed rib cage. After stepping back to view her handiwork in its entirety, she pulls the pale cotton cloth low over the dead man's forehead, covering his broken sight. The mouth and the patrician nose jutting out like a sliver of white marble are the only visible remnants of his humanity.

The sound of approaching footsteps makes the old woman pause. She is in an arched vault of a crypt below the cathedral, a hidden place where for centuries the church has brought its renegades to be laid out before the anonymity of a pauper's grave.

A noblewoman in fine lace and a silk veil appears at the door of the chamber, lamp in hand. Without a word she hands the old woman a small purse heavy with gold. The corpse-dresser curtsies and moves to stand discreetly outside the door for a few moments. It is a ritual she has performed many times for many dead men who were once loved.

Birgit Ter Lahn von Lennep pushes back her veil. Her face, now older and fuller, has traces of its former sensuality but a new heaviness born of grief and discontent has worked a web of fine lines across the forehead and around the mouth.

Birgit crosses herself then, trembling, walks up to the corpse laid out on the marble slab. With the lightness of a butterfly descending upon a leaf, she places her fingertips on the cold mouth.

"Once, Detlef. I would have wept to see you thus. Once I would have died for you. Now there are no tears, for there is no time left, my nobleman. Know this: I loved you honestly for all the art between us, but in a moment of weakness it was I who was your betrayer."

In the stillness that follows, a terrible loneliness sweeps through her as she realizes that all that ever mattered in her life were the moments she had loved with this man.

The shovel bites into the icy mud, cutting a sod seven inches deep. Hurled out of the deep hole, the sod lands on a pile of soil beside the grave. The gravedigger, drunk, sings a ditty in guttural Bavarian as he cheerfully continues to work in the rain.

Detlef's body, stiff in its shroud, lies on the grass beside the open grave. Face and hands now entirely covered, the body less than a broken shell. Alphonso, kneeling, pushes back the hood of his short cloak. Allowing the rain to wet his cheeks he looks up at the leaden sky. An ordinary evening like any other, except that he is at the gravesite of a man who is about to be buried with no mourners but himself.

The actor pulls out a short dagger and carefully cuts the sodden fabric away from the corpse's face. The visage is exposed, an ashen death mask of surprising tranquillity. Alphonso, barely pausing, cuts a lock of hair away from the scalp, then makes a rent in the stained cotton through which he takes out the lifeless hand. The silver wedding band is loose on the shrunken white finger. He pulls it off then covers up the corpse again.

He turns to leave, then hesitates. The gravedigger is still singing, a bawdy refrain the actor recognizes from the brothels of Munich. Alphonso tosses a coin into the open grave and, as the gravedigger scrambles for the money, kneels again and in perfect Hebrew begins to recite Kaddish for the dead.

Carlos bangs shut the heavy door of his chamber. Leaning against it, he listens to the sound of his pounding heart.

If only this was all the world he had to deal with, he thinks, weary beyond belief.

A Basque folk song he used to play floats faintly into his mind, as absurd and meaningless as a hummingbird above a battlefield. Is this sorrow or relief, he wonders, suddenly aware that the great construction of his quest has evaporated into nothing but aching regret and the terrible devastation of unrequited love. There is no redemption, he thinks, except death and the peace it will bring.

Feeling every minute of his sixty-four years, he walks slowly over to his traveling chest and, kneeling, painfully brings out the casket that a young girl of twelve once gave him in innocent affection.

Slowly he opens the carved lid and is immediately struck by the absence of scent. There is nothing, no aroma of cedarwood, of oranges, of musk, of the sweet pungency of his youth's passion, nothing but the bitter smell of smoke. He looks closer: the inside of the casket is mysteriously burned, black with charcoal, as if the spirit of Sara's anger has manifested and scorched away the last memory her young music tutor has carried with him all these years.

With great deliberation, Carlos breaks the wooden box against the marble floor. Reaching down to pick up a large splinter, he runs the jagged edge down his unblemished cheek. Bent over the shattered casket, one hand covering the old scar, the other the new wound, he weeps into his own blood.

As the stained tears splash upon the floor, a woman's finger, long and gnarled, the nail resembling the tip of an owl's talon, creeps unnoticed from the broken pieces of the casket. It is followed by a second finger, a third and fourth, then a crooked thumb, until the whole hand, deep purple in skin tone, rests for an instant, still unnoticed, against the priest's heaving chest.

Suddenly the hand springs open like the steel jaws of a hunter's trap, the long nails pierce the gray cassock and punch a hole in the priest's breast. Too shocked to scream, the inquisitor watches in horror as the hand fastens itself around his pumping heart and tears it out of his chest so that he is staring down at his own pulsating organ as the hand squeezes.

The bloody pulp pushes up between the skeletal fingers until the thudding organ shudders to a stop and Carlos falls, his lips still echoing Lilith's name.

I *am waiting, my love, in a small cottage near the border outside the town of Aachen. It is simple but comfortable. The widow here was once a noblewoman who fell onto hard times during the Great War. She is a sincere patron of the arts and has nothing but flattery for our ingenious actor. I have received no word of you yet and it has been four days since our arrival. I write this letter in the small hope that somehow you will receive it, either by messenger or pigeon, or perhaps miraculously through the ether of connectivity. Our child is well and happy. He even has a small playmate, for the widow has a grandson of some three years. Of his stay in Cologne he has nothing to say except that "Uncle promised him a pony!" The simplicity of a child is a blessing indeed.*

Husband, return swiftly for I fear that to dally longer is to tempt the Fates. 'Tis strange, for this morning I thought I heard you calling me. I woke and for a moment you were beside me, your breath upon my cheek. But was just a cruel trick of habit . . .

In Faith, your loving wife, Ruth.

"Mama! Look!"

Jacob opens his hand, in its center squats a tiny pink toad. "He is smaller than my thumb."

"He belongs in the woods, Jacob. You must return him to his home."

"But first he shall go to war with a beetle."

"Jacob, man must not decide these things. You must let the creature go."

They are interrupted by the sound of horses approaching. Before Ruth has a chance to stop the child, he is running to the small iron gate of the sloping cottage garden, his short sturdy legs determined to reach his father before anyone.

"A donkey, Mama! A donkey and a funny little man with a tall man on a horse! But where is Papa?"

Ruth reaches the gate as Alphonso and La Grande ride into view. She waves at the actor but he does not wave back, continuing to ride toward them, face grimly set. Ruth, heart pounding, pulls Jacob off the gate.

"Go inside, Jacob."

"But Mama . . ."

"Go!"

The child, frightened by her tone, runs back toward the cottage and is ushered through the darkened doorway by the widow who waits in a panicky fluster of pale muslin.

Alphonso leaps from his horse and strides toward Ruth, his expression impenetrable. He does not speak and she does not ask. She already knows. Faltering in the bright sunlight she steadies herself against the hot stone wall. All switches into sharp relief. The blades of grass, birdsong, the buzzing of a passing bee.

This is it, she thinks, Paradise before the Fall, the moment of futile hope before knowledge. Detlef, my husband, my love, my life.

Catching her arm as she stumbles, Alphonso presses something into her palm. Ruth stares down, then curls her fingers so tightly around the lock of Detlef's hair that Alphonso fears she will break her hand.

יְסוֹד

YESOD

Truth Speaking

 כ

RAMPJAAR, THE HAGUE, WINTER, 1672

Ruth pours water out of the jug on the washstand in the corner of the bare room and scrubs the grime of the streets from her hands, then splashes her neck with the fragrance of jasmine. The chamber is built into an attic. Sparsely furnished, it contains a three-legged table in another corner, the chest Detlef brought with them from the Rhineland and the glass cabinet he gave her on the eve of their marriage. Over the bare hearth hangs the one possession that has traveled with Ruth throughout her life: Aaron's sword.

Exhausted, the midwife unlaces her long-waisted dark gray serge blouse and unhooks the full black muslin skirt. She hangs the clothes on the back of a chair then throws a woolen shawl around her shoulders. The room is cold, it is January. Outside, a light snow falls from the early morning sky. Ruth pokes at the dying embers of the fire then glances across at Jacob. He lies sleeping in the bed that they share.

Now almost six years of age, his features are those of a boy, the shape of his mouth and jaw so reminiscent of Detlef that it sometimes pains Ruth to look at him. She tiptoes over to the child, treading softly for she knows that her landlady, an older widow with four children of her own, rests lightly and will hear any creaking of the wooden floor above her. Ruth pulls another blanket over Jacob. His blond hair falls across his eyes, his fine features wistful in dreaming.

It is almost two years since Detlef's death. Two summers, two autumns, two winters, during which she has lived a half-life, Ruth thinks, like the water creatures she examines through her lens, swimming slowly, blindly, through thick syrup. The midwife has survived only because of the generosity of friends who have put food in their mouths and the clothes on their backs. If she did not have her son, and if to take one's life was not a mortal sin, she would have put an end to the Hell she has lived beyond Detlef.

Silently conjuring the image of her dead husband, Ruth rocks herself as she watches the child, remembering those first months of constant weeping, of Jacob coming to her each night crying for his papa, of the folding up of Detlef's clothes and papers and laying them carefully in the chest that has become the memory keeper of their lives together. How with every new day she would wake and think for a moment that he was with her, the warm naked length of him stretched out beside her, before the terrible remembering rushed in. Every day for a year.

With no body and no grave to mourn over—for to return to Cologne would have meant certain arrest—Ruth erected her own shrine. A memorial consisting of Detlef's lock of hair, his wedding ring and a small portrait of his likeness she had painted. It was here that Ruth found herself praying, and when the praying stopped the talking started. Whispering, she would tell Detlef about the domestic things, the financial struggles, the failures and triumphs of her midwifery, Jacob's first written words, and sometimes, late at night, of how she longed to touch him, to take his mouth, fingers and hands into her flesh and finally surrender her love in a way she now knew she never had during their time together.

Gradually, reasons for continuing her life crept back: the joy of a successful delivery, a letter from Spinoza urging her to further her work, her mounting research now consolidated into a paper she is trying to find a publisher for, and, most importantly, her son.

Tonight has been long. She has delivered twins, identical boys, but the second babe perished, partly damaged by the birthing hook she had to use to pull him out of the womb. With every inch of her body aching, she stands and goes into the adjoining room.

It is a small chamber with a single window set high, its curved iron casing framing a church spire and a parchment moon plastered onto the indigo night beyond. A wooden desk holding the lens and its mounting stands below the oval porthole.

Ruth pulls out a thick bound notebook and dips a quill into an inkpot. Carefully she sketches the womb with the twins contained, calculating how they must have been sitting for such a disaster to occur. There has to be a gentler way of extracting the baby, there has to be. Ruth sits meditating upon the quandary then, inspired, reaches for her sketchbook.

Later, as she curls up around Jacob, she is gripped by a coughing fit. Pulling the blanket around her, she curses the cold weather.

Benedict Spinoza pushes the shutters open. A warm humid breeze coming off the port enters the room immediately, bringing with it the scent of the city.

"The air is foul in here, Ruth, you must allow the summer in."

"I fear for my lungs."

"We all fear for our lungs. Living is a hazardous profession. And in this current climate more so than ever, especially for Republicans."

He places three oranges on the table. She notices how feminine his hands are, delicate and olive-skinned, unblemished by physical labor.

"They tell me the fruit is good for the body."

"Thank you, Benedict."

The philosopher sits at the table and looks across at the shrunken woman wrapped in a long fur robe.

How old she has become, he thinks, as if her radiance left the flesh with the death of her husband. But still an unstoppable spirit seems to burn beneath the skin, the indomitable will of Felix van Jos, the shy fierce-eyed youth he once taught. Although she is a remarkable individual, she suffers for her abnormality, her fragile feminine form unable to substain the ferocity of her masculine intellect, he notes. It is this will that is making her sick, she is burning up from within. He was right about the physiognomy of the female mind, he reassures himself, yet marvels at the way her husband loved her regardless. Remembering, he reaches across to take her worn hand paternally.

"I am not here just as the Good Samaritan. I have also come to tell you that I think I may have found you a publisher."

Not daring to hope, Ruth looks away. "That I cannot believe. I myself have sent the manuscript at great expense to a dozen or so, even beyond the borders of the Netherlands. Not one will consider it."

"Jan Rieuwertsz will publish. He has published several of my works, including *Theologico-politicus,* he is a man dedicated to the illumination of *scientia nova.* He will publish under your own title, *The dangers of birthing hooks, a treatise on gentler methods of midwifery,* and believes he will receive interest from the medical faculties of both Leiden and Oxford."

Ruth, tears welling up, coughs into a handkerchief and covers her brimming eyes. Spinoza pretends not to notice.

"How shall I be able to thank you?"

"You can thank me by taking better care of yourself, Ruth. Now you have the responsibility of a child and of a burgeoning career as a published medic."

"I am not a child, I am a man."

Jacob stands at the door, playing hoop in hand. He stares at the small dark man who has invaded his home.

"Jacob, it is impolite not to bow. Especially to a great man like Dr. Spinoza who is a friend to both your father and myself."

The young boy cocks his head at the name Spinoza, it is a name he has heard his mother utter in reverent tones to her associates, a name that comes from that mysterious past he can barely remember, the diminishing crystal ball of his childhood and the memory of his father, tall and fair, a flush of excitement transforming his serious demeanor at the mention of this man.

Coughing, Ruth turns back to Spinoza. "Forgive my son, he is quick to defend his mother."

"As he should be. Come here, my boy. Let me look at you in the light."

Dragging his feet, Jacob walks toward the philosopher, who tilts his face up.

"I see that you are both your mother and your father. A beautiful but dangerous collision of two worlds. Do you remember your papa?"

"Of course."

"Then you will recall that he was a brave and courageous man who was not afraid to speak out for his beliefs."

"And I shall be the same."

"An admirable ambition for a six-year-old."

"Are you the same Spinoza that is in our bookcase?"

Spinoza laughs as Ruth blushes. "I suspect so. I should wish to be in many bookcases but there are few who dare to read my words."

"I will when I am bigger! I'm frightened of nothing!"

"Fear has its place, but you will learn that in good time. Now go and play, I must speak with your mother alone."

Ruth stands slowly, coughing again with the effort.

"Obey Dr. Spinoza, but be back before dark."

Jacob takes a last curious look at Spinoza then turns on his heel. The philosopher bursts out laughing.

"He has very well-fashioned attitudes for his age."

"I have tried to teach him the same humane beliefs my husband and I subscribe to, but I fear a child is born with his nature already formed."

"Indeed, but there are graver matters afoot."

Spinoza closes both the shutters and the door. "You know the Orangists have arrested Cornelius de Witt?"

"Even an ailing midwife knows this. It disgusts me, it is a trumped-up charge. Cornelius would never have plotted against the life of Prince William. Suddenly all these so-called Republicans are blaming the de Witts for France invading Utrecht. Have people no loyalty?"

"People have short memories when they are terrified of suddenly finding themselves on the wrong side of a bursting dam. Since the attack against Jan de Witt and the proclamation of William as Stadtholder, I fear the next step will be the assassination of our brave leader and a purging of all who support him. We must be careful, my friend. Hide your books, your pamphlets, your writings. It is more important that we survive to speak out again than die silenced martyrs."

"I shall be discreet."

She breaks into another coughing fit, this time more severe. When she has finished, her handkerchief is bloodstained. Spinoza, rising in alarm, pours her a glass of water.

"You have medication?"

Ruth nods, but her face has a new tautness, the skin beneath her eyes shadowy and blue.

"I must leave you to rest. I shall visit again with Jan Rieuwertsz when this summer storm has passed and it is safe to walk the streets wearing the colors of the Republic."

After he has gone, she collapses on the bed, fever pumping at her temples and in the veins of her wrists.

Published at last, she thinks, as exhilaration tears at her agitated body. Her work is to be recognized, to be of assistance to hundreds of women in the future. It is an impossibility come true. If only she could recover her strength, if not for herself then for her child. Perhaps they will be able to afford a warmer dwelling, a tutor even. Jacob must find a livelihood, a profession that will secure his adulthood. Perhaps she can capitalize on the publication, obtain a small teaching post . . . ? As whom? She laughs at herself—Felix van Jos? She has forgotten her sex again. She must be practical, she must . . .

Fighting delirium, she tries to clarify her waltzing thoughts, new hopes that refuse to stand still but dance like raindrops splashing onto a sundial while the shadows of time turn regardless.

✻

". . . the baby that will not descend should not be forced. A birthing hook that tears open the matrix will result in the death of both mother and child if it should be made of wood and iron. There is a gentler alternative, a loop of cat gut thickened with wax . . ."

"Jacob, will you stop your foolishness!"

Ruth, bent over the small desk, quill in hand, pauses midsentence, her pale face shiny with strain. Jacob, who is pushing a whirligig around the room, looks at her, his hand hovering over the toy.

"You are too old for such childish things," she tells him, unable to keep the irritation out of her voice.

Jacob, sullen, pushes his lip out then kicks the toy into the corner.

"But, Mama, you said I couldn't go out to play."

Ruth lifts herself with difficulty. She is thinner, her skirts hang loose around her hips and beneath her smock her collarbone is a severe arch rising out of a gaunt breast. She looks at her son: the petulant pout she recognizes as her own, but it is Detlef's obstinacy which hangs over the child like a cloud.

"Come here, I will show you something to amuse you."

"No! I am bored! I can't stay here all the time. It is Rutger's birthday, you said I could go!"

"Jacob, you know it is too dangerous."

"Why?"

"Because they have arrested Jan de Witt himself. I explained all this before . . ."

"But what does that mean to us?"

"Jacob, I am weary. I am only trying to protect you. Come here, I will show you something wonderful."

Reluctantly, the boy shuffles over to her. For a week now they have been trapped in the small lodging rooms while outside street brawls rage between the Orangists and the Republicans. Battles which began when the young Prince William of Orange finally rebelled against his protector and ordered the arrest of Jan de Witt, the leader of the Republic.

Ruth pulls the magnifying lens toward her then carefully tips a live aphid from a vial onto a glass slide and places the insect beneath the lens.

Jacob climbs onto his mother's knee. The child is already too big and heavy for her but Ruth smiles into his hair. She has grown to relish moments like this when Jacob, locked in an internal struggle between the restless detachment of boyhood and the need for his mother, reverts to his younger self.

"Look through here."

Jacob gazes through the lens, fascinated. "Mama! It's a dragon! Or at least a large green elephant!"

"It is an insect that feeds on the leaf of the rose. In its world, it is not a carnivore like the dragon."

"But it's green, and hairy! With funny things sticking out of its head!"

"Antennae."

Jacob pauses, then looks up at her. "Did you show Papa these things?"

"This and much more. There were many things I shared with him."

"What was he like?"

"You know what he was like."

The young boy's face changes expression as he searches back into his memory.

"I remember walking by the canal with him. I remember the big black cloak he put on when he was going to church and I remember him reading stories to me at night, but Mama, I begin to forget what he looked like."

"He was fair, like you, with the same shaped eyes and the same mouth, but his eyes were blue. And he had the same temper as you, Jacob."

"Did he kick things too?" the child squeals, delighted.

"In a manner. He kicked at authority and questioned all that others took for granted."

"Sometimes I get frightened because his face has begun to disappear from my dreams. Does this mean he is leaving us?"

"No, Jacob, and I would forgive you if you did forget, for Papa will always be here, inside you, in your nature and in your flesh."

"Is that how we live forever?"

"That is what I believe."

She smiles down at him, marveling at the child's gift for reasoning, which she recognizes as a heritage from both Detlef and herself.

Thank the good Lord for the philosopher, she thinks, pleased that Spinoza has secured the promise of an apprenticeship from the publisher Rieuwertsz for the child should anything happen to her before Jacob reaches his adulthood. She gazes at the long black eyelashes fluttering against the fair skin. She is a fortunate woman to have this bond of flesh, this profound love, which in times of great loneliness jolts her back to a state of grace.

Sleepy, Jacob rests his head on Ruth's bosom, nestling against her like he used to do when he was a small babe, until a tremor of fever forces her to carry him to the bed.

TWENTIETH OF AUGUST, 1672

*M*y love,

I am writing to tell you a wonderful thing. My first paper will be published at the end of this month under the name Frau Ruth Tennen. Is this not an occasion to be joyous? How long have we waited for this moment? Are you not thankful now that you tolerated, nay, cajoled me into all those hours of study?

My husband, when are you to return? It has been two days since I last saw you and my body grows weary of waiting . . ."

"Your body has grown weary because you have been waiting for two years. But now I have come back."

Detlef stands before her, dressed in his old vestments of the canon, his features as young and handsome as they were when Ruth first made love with him in the cottage at Deutz.

"Two years? But that is not possible. And why do you wear the cloth of the church?"

"I wear the cloth for I am here to give you the last rites."

He moves toward her and takes the golden feathered quill from her hand. She looks at the scroll she has been writing on and sees that the calligraphy has begun to fade.

"You are dreaming, my love. You are imagining that you are writing a letter to me and that I am still in the living world."

Startled, she jumps to her feet and for the first time notices that she is wearing her wedding gown. But the plain velveteen dress which she wore when they stood in the small Calvinist forest chapel near Nijmegen, before a minister they knew would not ask questions, is now miraculously embroidered with silver thread and beaded with pearls.

"Am I still in the living world?" she whispers, terrified of the answer.

"Your spirit is at the gateway, but it is time to join with me."

She looks over to the window set high in the wall of her small study. Outside it is brilliant sunlight, yet inside all is shadow.

"Which last rite would you administer, my love? And which afterlife do you promise, as I have faith in neither?"

"But you have faith in me?"

Always. I always did, Detlef, and forgive me if I ever faltered or questioned your love, for I know now that it was merely fear."

"I loved you anyway," he replies with that characteristic shyness she recognizes from the first time he ever uttered those words.

Then she takes his mouth to hers and tastes him. Remembering their lovemaking, desire bolts through both of them, weaving their spirits together again.

"Then this shall be our eternity," he whispers, his voice rippling like heat.

Ruth, her body drenched in sweat, tosses in the filthy bed. The air is rank, the curtains drawn, the window bolted. A bloodstained towel lies tossed on the floor beside a pail filled with soiled bedclothes. In the corner is a bucket of vomit.

Jacob lies sprawled across the foot of the bed, his arms wrapped around Aaron's sword. He has been asleep for hours after keeping vigil for three days, sword in hand, beside his dying mother.

Outside in the streets of the Hague a distant roar rises up from the direction of the castle. It grows louder as the cacophony rolls toward their lodging. Jacob wakes and immediately swings the heavy sword in the air, ready to defend his mother. He glances over at her and reaches out to touch her face. She feels cooler, as if the fever has broken. Momentarily frightened, he places a hand on her chest . . . a heartbeat is faintly perceptible.

Don't die, you can't, not yet. Not before I am grown and can look after us both, Jacob thinks, staring down at her gray face. I shall build a house with a garden, and there shall be an orchard with a river running by it, and a bridge. And we shall live there together, warm and well fed. There shall be geese in the yard and a forest for me to hunt in. You shall never have to work again and shall wear a new dress every week.

The boys ramblings are broken by the noise of a crowd approaching, running, shouting, the banging of drums, all building until the roar beats against the windows and walls.

Jacob pulls open the shutters. A torn flag of the Republic covered with human excrement bobs madly up and down below him.

"Down with the Republic! The de Witts are dead!"

The shout rises up from the street.

The boy leans out to see a mass of people, flushed with excitement, many with blood spattering their clothes, singing and dancing, drunk with power and excitement. Women with their breasts hanging out, disheveled drunken soldiers waving the Orangists' colors, red-faced youths pushing violently through the throng, blowing loudly on horns.

The horde winds into the narrow lane like a demented snake, filling it until there is little room to move. Packed shoulder to shoulder, the crowd becomes as one, waving bloodstained strips of cloth, flowers torn from passing stalls, ripped flags, rocking from side to side, drinking from casks handed from man to man.

An object is lifted high above the crowd, impaled on the end of a pike. Jacob realizes with dismay that it is a body, the stomach split open, its entrails spiraling out like macabre ribbons, the eyes white, the mouth screaming. Just as suddenly a second body appears beside the first. It is a puppet show of dancing horror as the corpses, blood flying from them, bounce absurdly past the window. Despite the blackened cheeks and missing chunks of hair, Jacob recognizes the two men instantly.

"The pensionary and his brother are dead! The de Witts are finished!" someone shouts, only to be drowned out by a huge cheer.

A loud scratching sound causes Jacob to swing back to the room. Crouched in the corner is a gigantic raven, its shimmering purple head crammed up against the ceiling. It turns one glistening black eye to the boy then arches a huge claw toward the feverish woman on the bed.

Jacob slams the window shut and, lifting his sword, moves slowly toward the immense bird of death. A grating rustling fills the bedroom as the raven ruffles its wings, indifferent to the child. Ruth moans very softly. The massive specter cocks its shiny head and slowly a huge gray scaly foot emerges from the blue-black feathers. The claw descends cautiously to the floor, the long yellow nails scratching against the polished wood. With a loud thump the colossal bird hops once toward the bed.

"No!"

Jacob rushes the raven, sword aimed directly at its breast. To his amazement, the blade runs right through as the apparition breaks up with a deafening caw, only to manifest again, this time perched on the end of the bed itself.

"You can't take her! You can't!"

Moaning, Ruth opens her eyes and lifts a feeble arm toward Jacob. As he leans down she pulls him to her.

"My child, promise me you will always remember who your parents were . . . You must fight tyranny always, live for the freedom of belief . . . the freedom of thought. This is our gift to you . . ."

Exhausted, she falls back to the pillow, closing her eyes. Her grip loosens and her hand falls away.

"Mama? Mama!" he cries, shaking her.

The raven squawks, breaking into Jacob's weeping. He looks up. The bird's massive beak opens to reveal a startling pink cavern then it looks back down at him with an almost kindly eye. Lifting a claw, the raven extends it toward Ruth's prostrate figure. Again the boy swipes at the bird, his sword passing uselessly through the phantom as the bird slowly begins to unfurl its long satin wings. A roaring fills Jacob's ears. Sobbing, he throws himself over Ruth to defend her, his arms stretched across her shrunken form.

Ruth can hear Detlef murmuring as he finishes the last rites. She looks up and there he is beside her.

"Come, the others are waiting."

He pulls her into his arms, and as she stares deeper and deeper into his eyes she sees the ghosts of her past, all waiting for her: Sara, Rosa, Hannah, even Aaron with his serious face, and then at last Elazar steps forward to take her hand.

Clutching at her withered arms, his head upon her bosom, Jacob feels the last shuddering breath leave his mother's body, and then the yawning silence as her soul departs the flesh.

מלכות

MALCHUT

Kingdom

❉

THE HAGUE, SPRING, 1683

*T*he scent of poppies fills the chamber. Jacob fingers the silk blindfold. He thinks about cheating by opening his eyes but decides against it. Something luxurious and scented brushes past him. Fabric? Lace? Fur? A perfumed veil of long soft hair falls across his face followed by the touch of a finger against his lips, confusing him further.

"Are you ready for your birthday offering?"

"If it is to be a gift, I am not fully seventeen until after midnight."

"Can you wait until then?"

"Madame, I believe I have waited long enough."

Impatient, Jacob lifts his hands to the knot that has become entangled in his long fair hair, excitement bursting at his loins. As the blindfold falls away she says, "And so begins the corruption of a poet."

She sits before him on a low ottoman. She is naked except for a diaphanous gown, which seems to float above her nudity rather than lie upon it. Her flesh, which he has touched only through clothing, is curvaceous. Her breasts a jutting whiteness crowned by large dark areolae, her stomach a rounded glory with golden curls climbing up her belly. Thus undone she smiles, not with the guarded arrogance he is accustomed to, but with a timorous almost childlike questioning that plays humorously in her huge brown eyes. Jacob's mouth dries, his heart races with anticipation. Fifteen years older, she is the first woman he has seen naked. To him she is beauty itself spread before him.

"Poets are not corruptible for their minds have already been caught and catapulted to the moon by intellect itself," he answers, unable to keep a throaty awe from his voice.

She laughs, surprising herself with her own nervousness.

"But what about their bodies?"

"Their bodies?"

He reaches for her hand and places it on his erection which pushes up against his breeches. "That, Madame, you may judge for yourself."

Kneeling, she begins to unlace him.

"Tomorrow you will no longer be able to call yourself virgin."

In lieu of an answer he runs his hands beneath her gown and clasps the full breasts with their hot, heavy weight. The nipples hardening sends a tremor of excitement through him that is almost impossible to contain. Frightened he might spill before time, he lies back and allows her to undress him slowly. Smiling, she runs her hands down the long-waisted satin coat. Then with excruciating deliberateness begins to unfasten the many pearl buttons, from the bottom to the top one by one. Jacob, trembling, tries to stay completely still. She unties the crimson cravat of lustring then hauls up the silk undershirt to reveal Jacob's smooth muscular chest, a line of fine blond hairs traveling down toward his cock which rests large and hard against his taut stomach.

Surprised by his circumcision she looks up at him. Reading the question in her eyes, he blushes but says nothing. Without a word she takes his organ, holding its thickness firmly between cool fingers. "You are beautiful," she says simply, and in that moment he truly feels it.

Cheeks flushed, his locks of hair snaking across the pillow, he watches her through narrowed eyes, trying to hide his wonder. The maturity of her body touches him, it has a kind of collapsed vulnerability, a ripeness which makes him want to bury his face in the soft folds and bite. The scent of her, a musky aroma of French perfume undercut with the ripeness of her sex, both intoxicates and overwhelms. It is an extension of the complexity of the woman herself and of their relationship, for she is the widowed sister of his employer and guardian, the publisher Rieuwertsz. It is this intricacy, the verbal labyrinths, the subtle flirtations, her open enthusiasm for his ambitions and finally her hard-won respect, that has seduced him. He, who could have had any serving girl or dockland whore before now.

Jacob lifts a languid hand and traces a finger from her chin to her mouth. She wets it between her lips, he pulls it out slowly and after running it across her hip touches her sex, caressing the hardening bud then burying it deep. With a moan she removes his finger and mounts him,

slowly and deliciously sliding down. Engulfed by her tightness, he is fascinated by the beauty of her abandon as she rides him faster and faster, a
mounting ball of intense pleasure gathering at the base of his spine.

If this be the way man obtains immortality, then I for one shall seek it
over and over, Jacob thinks, his hands gripping the luscious buttocks of his
lover. Suddenly he finds himself exploding in a fountain of pure blind
pleasure.

"Master Jacob! Master Jacob!"

Jacob wakes, his body still curled around his mistress. For a moment,
unused to the luxurious softness of the foreign bed, he lies still, confused.

"Master Jacob! I know you're in there!"

The poet, now fully awake, throws a sheet across the sleeping widow
and tiptoes to the door.

Janus, his assistant, a cheeky smile plastered across his face, stands on
the other side.

"You rascal! You'll wake the whole household."

"The whole household is awake. 'Tis morning, master, in case you
hadn't noticed. But there is a more pressing matter. There's a gentleman at
your lodgings, been asking for you. He's a German, ancient as Egypt itself
and dripping with money."

Jacob makes the boy wait outside while he pulls on his clothes.

The arrival of this mysterious visitor makes him nervous. He prefers to
keep his distant past buried, a prism of fleeting memories he has attempted
to erase entirely—and has almost succeeded. Since Ruth's death Jacob has
fought to carve out a new identity for himself. But there is no escaping the
possible link between his German father, aristocratic-born, and the
stranger awaiting him.

He glances down at the sleeping widow. If he were to fall in love, he
would make sure never to abandon his reason, for he has vowed never to
weep at being left alone again. He is his own companion, his own family,
he lacks nothing for he carries his world with him, like a shelled creature
who fears nothing for he feels nothing. His reverie is broken by his lover,
who yawning, stretches her voluptuous body.

"How is the intellect?" she whispers drowsily.

"Hijacked by the heart and cock, as it should be," he answers with a kiss.

"For a seventeen-year-old you know far too much."

"Knowledge is a better weapon than the sword."

"But the pen cuts twice as deep," his lover answers, already grieving the youth's inevitable departure.

With an aching groin he leaves her. Once outside he clouts his grinning assistant.

Out on the street Jacob weaves his way through the traders and merchants hurrying to their places of business. Janus, running alongside to keep up, cannot help but notice a new cockiness to his master's step, a certain glow playing across his high cheekbones, a softening of the arrogance the handsome youth usually wears like armor, particularly when faced with strangers.

"So, is it as good as they say?" The diminutive eleven-year-old tugs on Jacob's lace sleeve.

Jacob stares down at the lad, whose carrot hair is disheveled and ruffled like a parrot's crest, his smock smeared with printing ink, the breeches beneath patched at both knees. For a moment he flushes with anger. The child's query has broken the spell of the lovemaking, he fears that an account of their intimacy will cheapen his experience. But Janus's round face filled with a mischievous but genuine curiosity weakens his resolve. For all his aloofness, Jacob can rarely resist the boy. It was he who found the orphan two years before, sleeping up against the back door of the publishing house one night, and after a solemn declaration from the nine-year-old that he was "good with the written letter" persuaded his employer to take him on for board and lodgings only. Swiftly the two became inseparable, Jacob secretly relishing the role of mentor and protector and—although he would be loathe to admit it—older brother.

"Better," Jacob replies, tugging the boy's hair playfully before marching on.

"Better how? 'Cause I've heard it's better than entering the gates of Heaven itself and that I can't imagine, though I suppose you could," Janus persists, running after the poet eagerly.

"I think perhaps the allegory of the phoenix would suffice—in that one is consumed in the fires of passion only to rise again," Jacob retorts with a wink.

"So how many times did she consume you?"

The youth turns, smiling. He looks like a god, the small assistant notes wistfully, wondering if there is some magic he could use to turn his own lopsided and freckled demeanor into such chiseled beauty.

"Four times."

"Four times to Heaven! 'Tis a wonder your feet still touch the pavement." At which Janus executes a couple of dance steps to illustrate his point.

Laughing, Jacob cuffs him again then, as he remembers the mysterious visitor, falters, his brow darkening.

"Tell me more of the German."

"He's a proper aristocrat, smells like a flower shop and sits like he has a stiff rod up his arse."

Jacob doubles his stride. Could it be who he suspects . . . after all these years? A shadow from the past who will try to draw him back? Having heard about his parents' achievements from his protector Rieuwertsz, how both of them turned their backs on convention and society in pursuit of their beliefs, Jacob is fiercely proud of them, but at the same time furious with resentment at what he regards as their desertion of him. Orphaned at the age of six, he has never forgiven Ruth for dying, blaming her for neglecting her health. Remembering only vague details about the kidnapping, he is convinced that his father's family was ashamed of him, and that somehow he was partly responsible for Detlef's death. Although the publisher took great pains to protect the child, he was unable to fully shield Jacob from bitter remarks by Ruth's less generous associates about the romantic futility of her martyrdom or comments by individuals who had resented both Detlef's politics and position.

Suffering from the innuendo and the overt attacks, but not remembering enough to be able to retaliate articulately, Jacob has become fiercely committed to reinventing himself. He has even changed his name to the plain Dutch Scheems. Jacob Scheems. A talented young poet on the rise, a simple Hollander with no specific race or religion. Damn my mother and my father, what right do they have over my life, he thinks, irritated by the memories and emotions the arrival of the stranger has stirred up in him. He has not shed any tears since Ruth's death, not since he vowed on her deathbed that he would never again feel self-pity or be afraid. He is successful, he reminds himself as he strides past the flower market, breathing in the rolling mist of scent and color. His first volume of poetry is recently published, he has his own lodgings, and now his first mistress. He is complete—what harm can this stranger do to him?

Despite these reassurances he is filled with dread as he hurries up the stairs of his lodgings.

The Gryphon waited, his handsome eagle head laid
Upon a twisted thorny staff cut from Pain,
He shook his lion's mantle wet from morning's dew,
Then roaring, spoke to the Keeper at the Gate:
I am neither Man nor Beast but a noble creature who
In Joy and Terror hath been born from Two
Whose Love cast out a Prince and usurped Nature,
The Empire's Golden Eagle and the Lion of Fair Judah.
And although my changeling form Man doth hate,
Know this: I am a being of my own making, of Living Truth not Doctrine,
As such I shelter the orphaned and courageous beneath my wing,
Stoic and resigned, the lonely path of the Hermit is my Fate,
The prickly quill of Knowledge clasped in my paw,
With Mathematics and Astronomy as my only Law . . .

The sound of the heavy oak door startles the elderly aristocrat. He looks up from the poem he is reading, the pages of which are scattered across the plain wooden table, to see its author enter the room.

The boy is a man now, the count thinks, marveling at the graceful and as yet unscarred beauty of the youth. He stands taller than his father, with the same shaped eyes and brow, yet the full mouth, almost sullen in its pout, is that of the mother, as is the color of the eyes, while the hair is the same gold as Detlef's. The lad is dressed far more expensively than his income allows, the count observes, he has obviously inherited the inclination toward dandyism from somewhere other than his parents. Myself perhaps, Gerhard wonders, amused. In short, the boy is a creature hovering at the apex of his physical beauty, but as yet unconscious of his powers.

"You do not know me, sir, although I now have the distinct advantage of knowing you as a bard." Gerhard speaks formally, a cynical smile playing over his thin lips.

Jacob notes that although his visitor wears the austere uniform of the Lutheran, the dark wool of his tunic is of the highest quality and the white lace at his sleeves and collar appears to be from Bruges.

"Indeed, and how do I rate?"

"You have promise, but the pretense of inexperience taints the verse. However, that is your prerogative."

Jacob steps nearer, then falters as the silver pendant the old man wears around his creased neck comes into view. It is embossed with a family crest, an emblem the young poet recognizes immediately. In an instant he has snatched the pages out of the aristocrat's hand. Gerhard reacts with barely a raised eyebrow, not entirely surprised by the boy's impetuousness.

"I shall not take your criticism to heart for I suspect it lacks objectivity." Jacob stands with the poem clasped to his chest.

"From your actions I assume you know who I am?"

"I do, and now having made your acquaintance, I must ask you to take your leave."

Count von Tennen looks sharply at the seventeen-year-old before him. He guesses the clothes must have been a gift. From the observations of the Dutch spy he hired to find his nephew, he knows the boy has little to no money and is entirely dependent on the patronage of his employer, a publisher of dubious political reputation. It is evident that whatever money the youth makes he spends on books, for the room is lined with them. Volumes on philosophy, poetry, history, *scientia nova*: Descartes, Aristotle, Plato, Grotius, Christian Huygen, Leibniz, Sir Josiah Child, Milton's *Paradise Lost*, and many more.

"Do not be a fool. Judging by the poverty in which you live, you need me as much as I need you."

"I need no man, sir, and certainly no one from my past. I have rewritten myself in a stanza of my own making. And now I want nothing except to be left in peace so I may live out my invention."

Jacob angrily opens the door, but the old man does not budge from his chair. Gripping his cane so tightly that his knuckles show white, he remains steadfast.

"A preposterous notion, young puppy. No one," at this he slams his cane on the table, creating a huge bang that makes Jacob jump, "no one is able to escape his past, not even I, and the good Lord knows there have been many occasions I have wished to."

He leans forward, his face taut with emotion. "We are a composite of our own history and that of our parents; we are all that has lived before us, married together and woven into a tapestry which has been worked and embroidered to become this moment: this room, the face you were born with, you and I staring across at each other. A man who denies his past is a man who truly denies himself a future, for he refuses to know himself, and to deny knowledge of oneself is to stumble through life as handicapped as the blind mute."

"Then let me live blind."

"I shall not! This is the least I owe your parents."

"Sir, I have no parents, none that are worth remembering or forgiving."

At this the old man falters. Staring hard at the youth, whose handsome features have sharpened with his defensiveness, he perceives that the arrogance conceals a deeper vulnerability.

"Oh Jacob, what have we done to you?" His voice drops to a gentle whisper.

"Leave!"

"Not before I hear you utter my name."

"Count Gerhard von Tennen. Are you content now, uncle?" Jacob replies coolly, wishing the specter of the old man would just disappear.

But as he catches sight of the ring adorning the count's hand, a ring he suddenly remembers, a cascade of images return: the coach pelting through the Dutch countryside, being forced to eat as a small boy in the Cologne town house, his uncle's red angry face screaming at him—and an old dread begins to claw its way up from his belly.

"Sir, you have great audacity to appear before me thus, you who caused my family so much injury."

The count stands heavily and turns to the window.

"Jacob Scheems. It is not a pretty choice."

"It is plain, and very different from von Tennen. As I have told you, I wish to disassociate myself from my heritage."

"Your alias has made my search difficult. I have been looking for you for ten long years. Do you know how my spy finally found you?"

The count swings around, searching for a sign to indicate that reconciliation may be possible. With some bitterness Jacob shrugs. Sighing, Gerhard reaches into his waistcoat pocket and pulls out a slim volume which he places carefully on the table between them. The title, *The dangers of birthing hooks, a treatise on the gentler methods of midwifery,* is clearly visible. Jacob immediately recognizes the binding as that of his employer.

"Your mother's text, as published by Rieuwertsz. Her book led me to you. So you see, you can never escape your heritage."

Jacob picks up the volume, trying desperately to hold back a wave of feeling he considers unmanly. How many years, he thinks, and now this? Huge anger grips him as he recalls how he struggled alone after Ruth's death, sleeping at first on a narrow shelf that hung above the printing presses, then, as his literary promise became apparent, his promotion to the publisher's house itself where he shared the servants' chambers, until finally, at fifteen, he was granted a stipend and his own living quarters. It was an excruciatingly lonely existence for the boy, and he learned to survive by dividing his memories into two: the days that had seemed filled with sunlight and happiness before his father's death, then his dark odyssey after Ruth's demise. And now this recreant sits before him . . . for what purpose other than to undo him?

"Why should I listen to your stories? All they do is drag me back into a history I want nothing to do with."

"You must listen, for your mother's sake."

"Isn't it too late for that? Where were you when I was orphaned eleven years ago and would have starved if it were not for the publisher Rieuwertsz and his kind sister?"

"There were complications, first the French invasion and then the battle in Münster. I would not have been welcomed in Holland. But enough; there is much to say and little time, I fear."

"I repeat, sir, I must ask you to leave now."

"I cannot . . . not without your forgiveness."

With these words the last vestige of hauteur crumbles away from the aristocrat and to the youth's astonishment he finds himself confronting an old man whose hands suddenly shake as he clutches at his walking stick. Jacob takes pity. He blows the layer of dust from a flagon of cheap claret and pours his elderly visitor a glass. But after placing it firmly in front of the count he finds he cannot look at him. Agitated, he strides around the room.

"Forgiveness is for our maker to give, not me. Sir, I know you only as the man who betrayed my father and widowed my mother. Your business is with the dead, not the living."

"Jacob, you must believe me, they promised me they would pardon your father, that if he made a full confession he might even be reinstated to his post in the cathedral. You must understand that they were threatening to destroy the von Tennen name, to take our land. I could not allow that to happen. Ours is an ancient family and—"

"You lie, sir!"

"I have lied many times in my life and practiced many deceits, and I have paid penance for them, my boy, both in deed and in spirit. But in this I do not deceive. I have had your father's body exhumed, he now lies in the family chapel where he belongs. Detlef was my kin, my brother, just as you . . ."

The aristocrat's voice cracks with emotion as he realizes how far he has journeyed over the years.

"You are my nephew."

Overwhelmed, Jacob sinks into a chair. The count reaches into the leather satchel lying at his feet and pulls out a bottle of Clos Vougeot, an expensive vintage Jacob has only ever dreamed of tasting. The old man uncorks it vigorously and, after tossing the stale claret onto the floor, pours himself and his nephew a glass.

With an elegant flourish that could only have been taught by a woman of breeding, his mistress perhaps, the count guesses, Jacob lifts the glass to his mouth and allows the delicious liquid to slowly saturate his palate. He is more von Tennen than he realizes, the count notes, secretly delighted.

It has taken Gerhard years of examining his own behavior—his intense remorse over Detlef's death, his subsequent immersion in his duties as overseer of the von Tennen estates, his gradual comprehension of the struggles of his serfs—to attain the realization that all men begin and end equal, in birth, love and death. He is content to have finally found acceptance in his heart. And now he is rewarded, for despite the boy's mixed heritage and his anger toward his parents, Gerhard is pleased to see that he still displays the virtues and, more importantly, the fortitude of his father's class.

"Your father died refusing to betray your mother and you. I believe that at the very end he found solace in both his faith and his love for his family."

"My father was murdered."

"And it gives me great pleasure to inform you that his murderer, the inquisitor Carlos Vicente Solitario, perished a day later—an act of divine intervention, I am sure."

For the first time since the nobleman's arrival the young poet smiles. The count, encouraged, leans closer.

"Nephew, there are many changes in the Rhineland. I myself have converted to Luther and taken to the plain ways and cloth of the Protestant. The Holy Free City has opened up and many non-Catholics, both Jew and Protestant, now trade freely. Even the nepotism that blighted the city council is being challenged. Nikolaus Gülich, a man your father supported, is at the vanguard of the revolt and his power grows daily. Detlef once urged me to take to heart the plight of my peasants and this I have done. My serfs know neither plague nor starvation. All this I have undertaken in the name and spirit of my dear brother. This has been my penance. But I am old, and finally, and most thankfully, I am dying."

Stunned, Jacob looks up. The count suddenly seems to radiate a new frailty.

"I was married once, a loveless arranged affair that proved barren in every way. For all the grief and disaffection between us, you are my heir, Jacob, the only one I have."

"I, to go to Germania? To inherit the von Tennen estate, the title?"

The young poet stares at him astonished.

The count nods, anticipation molten in his veins. To his shock, Jacob leaps up and strides to the door.

"Do not insult me, sir!"

Startled, the count knocks over his glass of wine.

"I am half Hebrew, this you know well. As such I cannot own German land. Good day to you, sir."

With a curt bow Jacob waits at the open door.

Furious, the count draws himself up stiffly in the chair.

"You are a von Tennen! You will always be a von Tennen, whoever and whatever your mother was! I know it will not be easy, I know there will be hostility and resistance to you as my heir. But I intend to defy all authority that stands between me and my decision."

There is a silence; neither man moves. Then Jacob closes the door.

"You must understand that I mean to do well, but entirely on my own talents."

"But I can help you, just as you can help me. We are family, Jacob. Whatever state, crown and church think. You are my blood."

For a moment Jacob seems to waver. His eyes wander down to his mother's slim volume and to his surprise he finds himself contemplating what his parents would have wanted. Ruth's dying words float back into his mind: *"You must fight tyranny always, live for the freedom of belief, freedom of thought—this is our gift to you."* Is this what he has done with his life so far? How much change can he achieve through his sonnets—which are, he thinks ruefully, merely imaginative allegories in the style of his hero, the English poet Milton.

He reaches for a chair and sits again. After some moments of intense contemplation he looks up.

"I shall return with you on the following conditions. Firstly, I must be free to pursue my philosophical pursuits and poetic ambitions. Secondly, each peasant on the estate is to be offered a portion of the land he farms."

He pauses then pulls Ruth's book protectively toward him. "Thirdly, you agree to have a midwife trained in my mother's techniques to service the women of the region."

"You drive a hard bargain."

"Refuse me and you return to your estate without an heir."

Again the count is pleased by the uncompromising astuteness of the boy. He shows more ruthlessness than both his mother and father, the aristocrat notes, he is a survivor. After a long sigh, he places a withered hand upon Jacob's to seal the agreement.

The youth kneels in a wooden pew of the church, once a Catholic chapel, now stripped back to Lutheran simplicity. The dull afternoon light struggles to breach a large hexagonal window set in the wall behind the altar, its stained glass depicting the crucifixion. Jacob, his knees aching, is looking at the figure of a Teutonic knight in the armor of a medieval nobleman standing at the foot of the cross gazing up into the face of the Savior. Which of Father's ancestors is that? he wonders.

The touch of his uncle's hand on his shoulder pulls him sharply back to the present. He stands and turns to where the pastor waits at the tomb of Detlef von Tennen, and hears the small choir begin a hymn in plain German.

Jacob stares at the unadorned marble tomb, its lid pushed to one side, and marvels at how such a vital being could be reduced to dust and bones. Is this all life leads to, the banality of matter? He is young enough to think so, yet staring at the hollowed skull of his father he cannot help but remember being lifted in the air by Detlef's huge hands, laughing down at the smiling face he recalls as alight with warmth. *My father. The mysterious figure whose death has shaped my life.*

For the first time since Jacob was four, he sees before him a physical manifestation of a figure who, after his passing, became myth. So why does the sight not move me? he thinks, wondering at the numbness that seems to paralyze his heart. Is it because, in some ways, the scene is so ordinary? His legs hurt, the back of his neck is cold, he can see a beetle crawling up the side of Detlef's tomb indifferent to all around it.

His musings are interrupted by a nudge from his uncle. Jacob picks up the urn that contains his mother's remains. Surprised at its lightness, he finds himself having to suppress the unexpected desire to laugh: suddenly the somberness and formality of the occasion seems ridiculous to him. Who are these mourners? None of them, except his uncle, knew his parents, and certainly none of them were party to their marriage. He was the only witness of that great love, but what is the point of such a strong union when this is where it ends? Ashes to ashes, dust to dust. What remains of the impassioned flesh, the soaring spirit?

Jacob slowly approaches the tomb and begins to scatter Ruth's remains over the broken skeleton that was once Detlef von Tennen. As he does so, the faint scent of jasmine floats through the chapel.

The pastor moves forward. "Our Father who art in Heaven, bless and grant rest to these two souls who, parted in life, are now finally united in death."

He makes the sign of the cross and the assembled—the count and several servants of the household—follow suit.

As two sturdy peasants push the heavy lid back into place, Jacob notices that two new lines have been etched into the marble above his father's name. *Ruth bas Elazar Saul* he reads, engraved in perfect Hebrew, and below, *die Frau von Detlef von Tennen.*

Reaching out, he traces the letters with his fingers, and finds himself whispering them aloud in the language his mother taught him. It is then, finally, that the grief bursts through and the boy falls to his knees with a wail of sorrow, pain and deep sadness.

The priest glances at Gerhard, mortified at the sight of the weeping youth kneeling with his arms around his father's tomb, but the count ignores him. He walks over to Jacob and, laying his cane upon the ground, lowers himself down beside him, then places one hand on his nephew's heaving shoulders and the other, on his brother's tomb. For a moment the church is silent but for the sound of the boy's muffled crying and Gerhard's voice, direct and clear, asking Detlef for absolution.

A dove who has made her nest at the back of the shrine joins in with her cooing. After peeping curiously down at the figures clustered around the marble tomb, she flies across the rafters and out into the bright sunlight beyond.

Historical Backdrop

GERMANIA

After the Thirty Years' War between the Lutherans and the Catholics ended in 1648, Germania was a confusing quilt of many small princedoms with religious allegiances split between Catholic and Protestant. However, by 1665 Germania had evolved into the fulcrum upon which an international balance of power turned. There were two main forces: in the north, Prussia was controlled by the Lutheran royal, the Great Elector Frederick William (1640–88); in the south, the Catholic Hapsburg emperor, Leopold I, ruled out of Vienna, and had final jurisdiction over Cologne. Each was the nucleus of an international struggle and each exploited the struggle of its rival.

At the same time other tensions existed: in the north, there was a push for new territory prompted by Charles X of Sweden; and in the south, by Louis XIV of France and Mahomet IV, Sultan of Turkey.

The outcome of these struggles was a new European state system, brought into existence by 1715. The German states' involvement in creating the new political Europe deflected their interest away from attempts to strengthen or alter the German structure of state rights as embodied by the Catholic Holy Roman Empire, of which Cologne was a part.

HAPSBURG EMPIRE

By 1665 the Hapsburg Empire was a shadow of its former tyrannical self. Weakened by the Thirty Years' War, the young Emperor Leopold was under attack from the Sultan of the aggressive Ottoman Empire, Mahomet IV, and threatened by the ambitions of the French King Louis XIV who was battling the Hapsburgs for territories in the Spanish Netherlands.

As the Wittelsbach electors of Bavaria (of which Maximilian Heinrich was one) were traditionally allied with France, Leopold had to remain constantly vigilant to ensure that his power over those territories of the Holy Roman Empire was not undermined.

THE NETHERLANDS

Jan de Witt was the councillor pensionary of Holland from 1653–72, and led the Dutch Republic after the end of its war of independence. A remarkable intellectual in his own right, he was the champion of many resident philosophers and scientists who had taken refuge in the tolerant (and comparatively secular) Netherlands. In 1665 Holland was embroiled in an expensive and bloody sea war with the English, primarily over trading rights and ownership of the spice islands. As a result, de Witt came under increased pressure from the royalists within his own country.

Holland was allied with France, but Louis XIV persuaded England and Sweden to betray their alliance with Holland, and England united with France to invade the Dutch Republic in April 1672. During this period the young Prince William of Orange was increasingly gaining support and when de Witt's older brother, Cornelius, was arrested in July 1672, de Witt resigned as political leader of Holland. When de Witt visited his brother in prison, both men were attacked and killed by a large crowd. Holland reverted back to a royalist state.

Glossary

abba: Hebrew for "father."

alguacil: the sheriff of a Spanish municipality, executive officer of the courts and responsible for maintaining the security of the prison.

anusim: Hebrew term for Jews forced to convert to Catholicism. (Anus: singular masculine; anusa: singular feminine.)

Ashkenazim: Jews of Eastern Europe and Germany.

auto-da-fé: The public declaration of the judgment passed on persons tried in the courts of the Spanish Inquisition, followed by the execution of the sentences imposed, including burning of heretics at the stake.

Ba'al Shem: An expert at calling up demons.

barras: A coarse linen fabric, sackcloth.

barvell: A thick leather apron worn by workmen and fishermen.

Beth Din: A rabbinical court with authority over communal ecclesiastical matters.

boarhound: Predecessor to the Great Dane, originally known as the English hound, a cross between a mastiff and an Irish grayhound. Bred specifically for boar hunting and popular in the fifteenth and sixteenth centuries. The last record of the breed was 1860.

bombazine: A twilled fabric woven from silk and wool.

brith: The Jewish ritual of circumcision.

bruja: Spanish for "witch."

bürgermeister: Mayor.

catalpha: A silk textile.

cheder: Jewish primary school.

cornet: Headdress in the shape of a coif, fitted at the back of the head with long flaps on either side of the face.

damassin: Brocade or damask fabric with gold or silver patterns woven into it.

dornex: A fabric with a linen warp and wool weft, used for furnishings.

ducape: A heavy corded silk.

dybbuk: An evil spirit which has not been laid to rest.

ferrandine: A fabric made of silk and wool.

Gaffeln: Board of councillors particular to Cologne, made up of merchants from the city's various guilds.

gehenna: A place where the wicked are punished after death (Hell).

golem: A giant man made from mud brought to life by supernatural means.

hep: Ancient cry from the Latin meaning "Jerusalem has fallen." Still heard in pogroms in the seventeenth century.

Hevra Kadisha: Jewish society which looks after the burial of the dead.

hongreline: Thigh-length overcoat with flared skirt.

kammerhund: Chamber dog. An early breed of Great Dane favored by the aristocracy.

kittel: A white garment worn on important religious occasions. Sometimes used as a burial shroud.

Lilith: The first wife of Adam. After being cast out of Eden she became queen of demons, seducer of men (conceiving her demon children through their nocturnal emissions) and killer of newborn babies by strangling them. Snwy, Snsnwy and Smnglf were the three angels sent by God to negotiate with Lilith when she was cast out of Eden. They threatened to kill a hundred of her sons every day unless she stopped strangling newborns. Lilith's argument was that she had been created solely for this purpose but promised she would not harm a newborn if she should see the images of the three angels at the birthing, hence the use of the Three Angels amulet.

limpieza de sangre: Literally, "purity of blood"; a term used to signify freedom from Semitic blood.

lustring: A glossy silk cloth often used for petticoats.

Magen David/Shield of David: A six-pointed star formed by two equilateral triangles of equal size imposed upon one another. An amulet for protection in popular usage from thirteenth century onward.

mezuzah: Case containing parchment inscribed with religious texts and nailed above the front door of a house.

mikvah: Ritual bathhouse for women.

mohel: An expert in Jewish laws pertaining to circumcision and trained to carry out the procedure.

musico: Bordello disguised as a theater.

paduasoy: A rich strong silk fabric used for vestments.

paragon: Strong watered silk.

patches: Adornments in the shape of hearts, diamonds, triangles and stars stuck onto the face.

Philip and Cheney: A soft woolen fabric.

philoselle: A wrought silk.

poplin: A plain weave usually of cotton with a fine ribbing.

poriut: Hebrew for "fertility."

Rosh Hoshana: Jewish New Year, usually in September.

Schülergelief: A pogrom carried out by university students.

scientia nova: Literally, "new science" (Latin); a term used before the words "science" and "scientific" were adopted.

Sephardim: Jews of Spanish, Portuguese or North African descent.

Shabbetai Zevi: A real historical figure born in Smyrna, Zevi claimed to be the new Messiah and attracted a huge following among the disenchanted European Jewry. He was eventually captured and forced to convert to Islam by the Turkish Grand Vizier Ahmed Köprülü.

talith: Fringed shawl worn by men over the head and shoulders while praying.

tefillah: Phylactery: a small black box containing writings from the Torah bound by leather thongs to the forehead and left arm and worn by Jewish men during prayers.

the Three Angels: An amulet used during childbirth depicting the angels Snwy, Snsnwy and Smnglf and engraved with kabbalistic writings. Used to protect against the demon Lilith.

yarmulke: A skullcap worn by Orthodox Jewish men at all times and others when praying.

yeshiva: Traditional religious school for boys.

the Zohar: Key kabbalistic text, written in Aramaic and sometimes referred to as the "Bible" of the kabbalists. The title means "the sacred light."

Bibliography

These are some of the reference books used during the writing of *The Witch of Cologne*.

Abrahams, Beth-Zion, translator and editor, *Glückel of Hameln, The Life of Glückel of Hameln 1646–1724*, Horovitz Publishing Co., 1962.

Feuer, Lewis Samuel, *Spinoza and the Rise of Liberalism*, Transaction Publishers, 1997.

Israel, Jonathan I., *European Jewry in the Age of Mercantilism 1550–1750*, Littman Library of Jewish Civilization, 1997.

Israel, Jonathan I., *The Dutch Republic, Its Rise, Greatness, and Fall 1477–1806*, Oxford University Press, 1998.

Kamen, Henry, *The Spanish Inquisition: A Historical Revision*, Yale University Press, 1998.

Nadler, Steven, *Spinoza: A Life*, Cambridge University Press, 2001.

Schama, Simon, *The Embarrassment of Riches: An Interpretation of Dutch Culture in the Golden Age*, Vintage, 1997.

Scholem, Gershom, *Kabbalah*, Meridian, 1978.

Seward, Desmond, *Monks and Wine*, Crown Publishers, 1979.

Acknowledgments

Thanks go to the following individuals for their generosity with their time, knowledge and input: Professor Bernard Rechter and Professor Walter Veit of Monash University; Herr Henning Bochert; Herr Volkmar Schultz MdB of the Bundestag; Mr. Eugene DuBow of the American Jewish Committee; Dr. Dieckhoff and Dr. Joachim Deeters of the Historical Archives of Cologne; Herr Carsten Schliwaki and Dr. Klaus Pabst of the University of Cologne; Sister Monika-Clare Ghosh of Ballykileen, Ireland; Gerald Asher, *Ordre du mérite agricole* and wine editor of *Gourmet* magazine; Dr. Christopher and Catherine Tuckfield; Simon Palomares; Ed Campion; Michelle Frankel; Lillian Klein; Fred and Annie Seligmann; Christelle Davis; Leo Raftos; Simon Duffy; Eva Learner; my Australian agent Rachel Skinner for her ego management and astrological insights; Nicola O'Shea for her brave copy editing; and lastly to my publisher Linda Funnell for her tenacity, wisdom and stamina.

Acknowledgments also go to the libraries of UCLA, Los Angeles; University of Judaism, Los Angeles; State Library of New South Wales, Sydney; Cologne Public Library; and the Goethe Institute, Los Angeles.

For the wonderful cover photograph I thank Moshe Rosenzveig, Kristen Anderson and Belinda Balding.

Finally, on a more personal note, my eternal gratitude goes to those friends and family who helped restore my faith, hope and belief during the adverse personal circumstances surrounding the gestation of this book: Rosslynd Piggott; Tushka Bergen; Geoffrey Wright; Paul Schütze; Loris Alexander; Jeremy Asher; Karyn Lovegrove; Siobhan Ryan; Poppy King; Lisa Dethridge; Eva, Adam, Ruth and Danielle Learner—thank you all for being there when suddenly there was no one.

FORGE BOOKS

Reading Group Guide

for

The Witch of Cologne

by Tobsha Learner

Questions for Discussion

1. Ruth bas Elazar Saul has been described as "a woman before her time" and "a potent mix of the old and the new." How does the author use the character of Ruth to illustrate and explore these ideas?

2. What kind of power was available to women in the seventeenth century? Discuss how Ruth uses power both within and outside the system of her time and faith.

3. *The Witch of Cologne* is set during the early years of what came to be known as the Age of Enlightenment; however, this was also a time of hypocrisy and superstition. How does this tension play out in the novel?

4. Many people believe ancient superstitions—"touching wood" wards off evil or spilling salt is unlucky. Some use talismans or light candles to protect themselves or their families. How do we reconcile these beliefs with a more rational view of the universe? Are there similarities between belief in superstitions and religious faith, or are these very different things?

5. How does telling a story almost entirely in the present tense affect the reader?

6. What parallels can be drawn between the restrictions imposed on the Jewish community in Germany in the 1660s and the 1930s? In 2004, France banned the wearing of religious symbols such as headscarves,

yarmulkes, and large crosses in public schools. Is this similar in any way to past constraints on religious communities?

7. Tobsha Learner is a playwright as well as a novelist. In what ways do you think the theatrical is important in *The Witch of Cologne*?